THE BIG BOOK OF TELL ME WHY

BY ARKADY LEOKUM

ILLUSTRATIONS BY HOWARD BENDER

BARNES
& NOBLE
BOOKS
NEW YORK

Contents—Volume #1

Chapter 1
Our World

Chapter 2
How Things Began

Chapter 3

The Human Body

Chapter 4

How Other Creatures Live

Chapter 5

How Things Are Made

CHAPTER 1
OUR WORLD

HOW BIG IS THE UNIVERSE?

It is impossible for the human mind to conceive a true picture of the size of the universe. We not only don't know how big it is, but it is hard for us even to imagine how big it might be.

If we start from the earth and move out, we'll see why this is so. The earth is part of the solar system, but a very tiny part of it. The solar system consists of the sun, the planets that revolve around it, the asteroids, which are tiny planets, and the meteors.

Now, this whole solar system of ours is only a tiny part of another, much bigger system called "a galaxy." A galaxy is made up of many millions of stars, many of which may be much larger than our sun, and they may have solar systems of their own.

So the stars we see in our galaxy, which we call "the Milky Way," are all suns. They are all so far away that distances are measured in light years instead of in miles. Light travels about 6,000,000,000,000 miles in a year. The bright star nearest to the earth is Alpha Centauri. Do you know how far away it is? 25,000,000,000,000 miles!

But we're still talking only about our own galaxy. This is believed to be about 100,000 light years in width. This means 100,000 times 6,000,000,000,000 miles! And our galaxy is only a tiny part of a still larger system.

There are probably millions of galaxies out beyond the Milky Way.

And perhaps all these galaxies put together are still only a part of some larger system!

So you see why it is impossible for us to have an idea of the size of the universe. Incidentally, it is believed by scientists that the universe is expanding. This means that every few billion years two galaxies will find themselves twice as far apart as they were before!

WHY IS THE SOLAR SYSTEM THE WAY IT IS?

As far as we know, there is no reason why the solar system is arranged exactly as it is. It might have been arranged differently, just as there are other solar systems in the universe arranged differently. This has to do with the way it originated. But man has discovered certain laws of nature that seem to keep the solar system in its present pattern.

Earth, like the other planets, follows its path, or orbit, around the sun. The period of time that the earth takes to go around the sun is called a year. The other planets have orbits larger or smaller than the earth's.

How this solar system came to be and how the planets came to have the size, location, and orbits they have, astronomers cannot fully explain. But they have two main types of theories. One type of theory suggests that the formation of the planets was a part of the gradual change of the sun from a whirling mass of hot gas to its present size and brilliance. The planets formed as small whirling masses in the giant gas and dust cloud as it turned.

Another group of theories is based on the idea that at some time there was a near-collision between the sun and another star passing nearby. Large pieces of the sun were pulled away and began to revolve around the sun at different distances. These are now planets.

No matter which theory is right, the solar system came to be as it now is more or less by chance. Why does it stay this way? Kepler's Laws of Planetary Motion state that all planets travel about the sun in an elliptical (oval) path; that a planet moves faster in its orbit as it nears the sun; and that there is a relation between its distance from the sun and the time it takes to make an orbit. Newton's Law of Gravitation, of which Kepler's three laws were an indispensable part, explained how two objects attract each other. So the solar system remains as it is because certain laws of nature maintain the relationship of the sun and the planets.

7

WHAT KEEPS THE SUN SHINING?

It may be hard for you to believe, but when you look at the stars that shine at night and the sun that shines by day, you are looking at the same kinds of objects!

The sun is really a star. In fact, it's the nearest star to the earth. Life as we know it depends on the sun. Without the sun's heat, life could not have started on earth. Without sunlight, there would be no green plants, no animals, no human beings.

The sun is 93,000,000 miles from the earth. The volume, or bulk, of the sun is about 1,300,000 times that of the earth! Yet an interesting thing about the sun is that it is not a solid body like the earth.

Here is how we know this: The temperature on the surface of the sun is about 11,000 degrees Fahrenheit. This is hot enough to change any metal or rock into a gas, so the sun must be a globe of gas!

Years ago, scientists believed that the reason the sun shone, or gave off light and heat, was that it was burning. But the sun has been hot for hundreds of millions of years, and nothing could remain burning for that long.

Today scientists believe that the heat of the sun is the result of a process similar to what takes place in an atom bomb. The sun changes matter into energy.

This is different from burning. Burning changes matter from one form to another. But when matter is changed into energy, very little matter is needed to produce a tremendous amount of energy. One ounce of matter could produce enough energy to melt more than a million tons of rock!

So if science is right, the sun keeps shining because it is constantly changing matter into energy. And just one per cent of the sun's mass would provide enough energy to keep it hot for 150 billion years!

WHAT IS THE EARTH MADE OF?

A sort of rough answer to this question would be: The earth is a big ball, or sphere, made mostly of rock. Inside the earth the rock is melted, but the outside cover is hard rock. Less than one-third of the earth's surface is land and more than two-thirds are water.

Now let's consider this in a little more detail. The outside of the earth is a crust of rock about 10 to 30 miles thick. This crust is sometimes called "the lithosphere." The high parts of this crust are the continents, and the low parts of it hold the waters of the oceans and the great inland seas and lakes. All the water on the surface, including the oceans, lakes, rivers, and all the smaller streams, is called "the hydrosphere."

Men have been able to examine only the outermost part of the crust of rock that forms the outside of the earth, which is why it's so hard to know what the earth is like on the inside. In drilling wells and digging mines, it has been found that the deeper the hole is made, the higher the temperature becomes. At two miles below the surface of the earth, the temperature is high enough to boil water.

But scientists have also been able to find out about the inside of the earth from studies of earthquakes. They believe that the temperature does not increase as rapidly deep down as it does in the crust. So they think that at the core or center of the earth the temperature may not be more than 10,000 degrees Fahrenheit. Of course, that's plenty hot—since a temperature of 2,200 degrees would melt rocks!

The crust of the earth has two layers. The upper layer, which makes the continents, is of granite. Under the layer of granite is a thick layer of very hard rock called "basalt." Scientists believe that at the center of the earth is a huge ball of molten iron, with a diameter of about 4,000 miles. Between the central ball and the rocky crust is a shell about 2,000 miles thick called "the mantle." The mantle is probably made of a kind of rock called "olivine."

WHAT IS A CONSTELLATION?

Have you ever looked at the stars and traced out squares, letters, and other familiar figures? In nearly all parts of the world, people of long ago did this and gave names to the group of stars they observed. Such a group is called "a constellation," from the Latin terms meaning "star" *(stella)* and "together."

The names of the constellations in use today have come down to us from the times of the Romans and from the even more ancient Greeks. What the Greeks knew about the stars came partly from the Babylonians.

The Babylonians named some of their star figures after animals and others after kings, queens, and heroes of their myths. Later, the Greeks

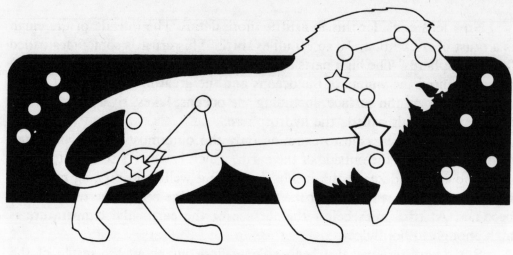

The Constellation Leo

changed many of these Babylonian names to the names of their own heroes such as Hercules, Orion, and Perseus. The Romans made further changes. The same ancient names are still used, but it is not always easy to make out in the sky the figures that suggested them. For example, Aquila is the eagle, Canis Major and Canis Minor are big and little dogs, and Libra is the scales, but the constellations don't look much like these figures to us.

About the year A.D. 150, the famous astronomer Ptolemy listed 48 constellations that were known to him. This list did not cover the entire sky; there were many blank spots. So, in later times, astronomers added constellations to Ptolemy's list. Some of these later constellations are named for scientific instruments, such as the Sextant, the Compasses, and the Microscope. Today, astronomers recognize 88 constellations in the sky.

A constellation is really an area in the sky. This means that every star lies in one constellation or another, just as any city in the United States is in some one state. The boundaries of the constellations used to be very irregular. Many of them had curved lines. But in 1928, astronomers decided to straighten them out so that the outline of any constellation includes only straight lines.

WHAT IS THE MILKY WAY?

There is probably nothing more mysterious and wonderful-looking in the sky than the Milky Way, stretching like a band of jewels from one end of the sky to the other. In ancient times, when people gazed at this spectacle, they were filled with the wonder and beauty of it just as you are. But since they didn't really know what it was, they made up all sorts of strange and beautiful explanations of the Milky Way.

For example, in early Christian times, people thought it was a pathway for the angels, so they could go up to heaven on it. Or they imagined it was an opening in the heavens, so that we here on earth could have a glimpse of the glory that existed beyond.

Knowing the facts about the Milky Way, as we do today, doesn't remove any of the wonder of it. The facts are just as amazing as any "made-up" idea!

Our galaxy is shaped roughly like a watch, round and flat. If you could get above it and look down on it, it would look like an immense watch. But we are inside the galaxy, and when we look up we are looking towards the edge from inside the "watch." So we see that edge curving around us. And since there are millions of stars in it, we see it as the Milky Way.

Did you know that there are at least 3,000,000,000 stars in the galaxy? And here is an idea of its size. It takes eight minutes for light from the sun to reach the earth. For light from the center of the galaxy to reach the sun, it takes about 27,000 years!

The galaxy rotates about its center like a wheel. From our position in it, it takes about 200,000,000 years just to make one revolution!

WHAT IS THE BRIGHTEST STAR?

Have you ever looked up at the sky and tried to find the brightest star?

You may imagine that the number of stars you can see is countless. But the most that can be seen without a telescope are about 6,000 stars, and one-quarter of them are too far south to be seen in North America.

Ever since the days of the Greek astronomers, 2,000 years ago, the stars have been divided into classes according to their magnitude or brightness. Until the invention of the telescope, only six magnitudes, or degrees of brightness, were recognized. Stars of the first magnitude are the brightest, and stars of the sixth magnitude the faintest. Stars fainter than the sixth magnitude cannot be seen without a telescope. Today, stars can be photographed with modern telescopes down to the 21st magnitude.

A star of any given magnitude is about two and a half times fainter than a star of the magnitude above it. There are 22 stars of the first magnitude, the brightest stars, and the brightest star of all is Sirius, which has a magnitude of −1.6. This makes Sirius over 1,000 times brighter than the faintest star that can be seen with the naked eye.

The lower we go down in magnitude, the more stars there are in that class. Thus, there are 22 stars of the 1st magnitude and about 1,000,000,000 stars of the 20th magnitude.

WHAT ARE FALLING STARS?

For thousands of years men have looked up at "falling stars" and wondered what they were and where they come from. At one time it was believed that they came from other worlds.

Today we know that they are not "stars" at all. We call them "meteors." They are small, solid bodies which travel through space, and which may also pass through the earth's atmosphere.

When meteors come within our atmosphere, we can see them because they leave a fiery train of light. This is caused by the heat made by the friction, or rubbing, of air upon their surfaces.

Strangely enough, most individual meteor particles are quite small, about the size of a pinhead. Occasional meteors weigh many tons. Most meteors are destroyed entirely by heat as they pass through the earth's atmosphere. Only the larger meteor fragments ever reach the earth. Scientists believe that thousands of meteors fall to earth each day and night, but since most of the earth's surface is covered by water, they usually fall into oceans and lakes.

Meteors may appear in the sky singly and travel in practically any direction. But meteors usually occur in swarms of thousands. As the earth travels in its path around the sun, it may come close to such swarms of of meteors, they become fiery hot upon contact with the upper layers of the atmosphere, and we see a "meteoric shower."

Where do meteors come from? Astronomers now believe that the periodic swarms of meteors are the broken fragments of comets. When comets break up, the millions of fragments continue to move through space as a meteor swarm or stream. The swarms move in regular orbits, or paths, through space. One such swarm crosses the earth's path every 33 years.

When a piece of meteor reaches the earth, it is called "a meteorite." It has fallen to the earth because gravity has pulled it down. Far back in

Roman times, in 467 B.C., a meteorite fell to the earth and its fall was considered such an important event that it was recorded by Roman historians!

WHAT IS A COMET?

At one time, the appearance of a comet caused people to tremble with fear. They believed that comets were evil omens foretelling plagues, wars, and death.

Today, we have a pretty good idea of what comets are, though we still don't have all the answers about them. When a comet first appears, it is seen as a tiny point of light, though it may be thousands of miles in diameter.

This point of light is "the head," or nucleus, of the comet. Scientists think it is probably made of a great swarm of bits of solid matter, combined with gases. Where this matter originally came from is what is still a mystery.

As the comet approaches the sun, a tail usually appears behind it. The tail consists of very thin gases and fine particles of matter that are shot off from the comet's nucleus when it comes under the influence of the sun. Surrounding the nucleus of the comet is a third portion, known as "the coma." It is a glowing cloud of matter that sometimes reaches a diameter of 150,000 miles, or even more.

Comet tails are very different in shape and size. Some are short and stubby. Others are long and slender. They are usually at least 5,000,000 miles in length. Sometimes they are almost 100,000,000 miles long! Some comets have no tails at all.

As the tail grows, the comet gains in speed because it is nearing the sun, moving toward it head first. Then a curious thing happens. When the comet goes away from the sun, it goes tail first with the head following. This is because the pressure of light from the sun drives off the very small particles from the comet's head to form its tail, always in a direction away from the sun.

As a result, when the comet goes away from the sun, its tail must go first. During its journey away from the sun, the comet gradually slows down and then disappears from sight. Comets may remain out of sight for many years, but most of them reappear eventually. Comets make trip after trip around the sun, but they may require a long time to make a single revolution. Halley's Comet, for example, takes about 75 years to make its trip around the sun.

At present, astronomers have listed almost 1,000 comets, but there must be several hundred thousand comets in our solar system which remain unseen!

WHY IS THE OCEAN SALTY?

Every now and then, we come across a fact about our earth which mystifies us and for which no answer has yet been found. Such a fact is the existence of salt in the oceans. How did it get there?

The answer is we simply don't know how the salt got into the ocean! We do know, of course, that salt is water-soluble, and so passes into the oceans with rain water. The salt of the earth's surface is constantly being dissolved and is passing into the ocean.

But we don't know whether this can account for the huge quantity of salt that is found in oceans. If all the oceans were dried up, enough salt would be left to build a wall 180 miles high and a mile thick. Such a wall would reach once around the world at the Equator! Or put another way, the rock salt obtained if all the oceans dried up would have a bulk about 15 times as much as the entire continent of Europe!

The common salt which we all use is produced from sea water or the water of salt lakes, from salt springs, and from deposits of rock salt. The concentration of salt in sea water ranges from about three per cent to three-and-one-half per cent. Enclosed seas, such as the Mediterranean and the

Red Sea, contain more salt in the water than open seas. The Dead Sea, which covers an area of about 340 square miles, contains about 11,600,000,000 tons of salt!

On the average, a gallon of sea water contains about a quarter of a pound of salt. The beds of rock salt that are formed in various parts of the world were all originally formed by the evaporation of sea water millions of years ago. Since it is necessary for about nine-tenths of the volume of sea water to evaporate for rock salt to be formed, it is believed that the thick rock-salt beds that are found were deposited in what used to be partly enclosed seas. These evaporated faster than fresh water entered them, and the rock-salt deposits were thus formed.

Most commercial salt is obtained from rock salt. The usual method is to drill wells down to the salt beds. Pure water is pumped down through a pipe. The water dissolves the salt and it is forced through another pipe up to the surface.

WHICH OCEAN IS THE DEEPEST?

In many ways, the oceans still remain a great mystery to us. We don't even know how old the oceans are. It seems certain that in the first stages of the earth's growth no oceans existed.

Today, man is exploring the bottoms of the oceans to learn more about them. Covering the floor of the ocean to a depth of 12,000 feet is a soft, oozy mud. It is made up of the limy skeltons of tiny sea animals. The floor of the deep, dark regions of the sea, where the water is more than four miles deep, is covered by a fine, rusty-colored ooze called "red clay." It is made up of tiny parts of skeltons of animals, the coverings of tiny plants, and volcanic ash.

The way the depth of oceans is measured today is by sending down sound waves which are reflected back from the bottom. The depth is found by measuring the time it takes for the sound wave to make the round trip and dividing this time in half.

Based on these measurements, we have a pretty good idea of the average depth of various oceans, and also the deepest point in each one. The ocean which has the greatest average depth is the Pacific Ocean. This is 14,048 feet. Next in average depth is the Indian Ocean which has an average of

13,002. The Atlantic is third with an average depth of 12,880 feet. The Baltic Sea is at the other extreme, with an average depth of only 180 feet!

The single deepest spot so far known is in the Pacific near Guam, with a depth of 35,400 feet. The next deepest spot is in the Atlantic off Puerto Rico where it measures 30,246. Hudson Bay, which is larger than many seas, has its deepest point at only 600 feet!

WHAT CAUSES WAVES IN THE WATER?

If you've ever spent some time near a body of water, then you noticed that on a calm day there are very few waves in the water, and on a windy or stormy day there are many waves.

This, of course, explains what causes waves in the water. It is the wind. A wave is a way in which some form of energy is moved from one place to another. Some sort of force or energy must start a wave, and the wind provides that energy in the water.

When you watch the waves move, one after the other, the water seems to move forward. But if there is a piece of floating wood in the water, it will not move forward as the waves seem to do. It will only bob up and down with the waves. It moves only when the wind or tide moves it.

Then what kind of motion is taking place in a wave? A water wave is mostly the up-and-down movement of water particles. The movement passes on toward the shore, but not the particles of water. For example, if you have a rope you can send a kind of wave along the rope. The up-and-down movement passes along the rope, but not the particles of the rope.

As the bottom of a water wave strikes the ground a short distance from the beach, it slows up because of friction. The top keeps going, and then topples over, and thus forms a "breaker."

The energy that formed the waves loses itself against the shoreline. All you have to do is stand among the waves along a beach and you'll soon find out that they have energy!

In a water wave, the water particles move in a circular path, up and forward, as they are pushed by the wind. Then they move down and back as gravity draws the heaped-up water back to a common level. These up-and-down movements carry the wave along.

The distance from crest to crest of a wave is the wave length, and the low point is called "the trough."

WHAT IS THE GULF STREAM?

The Gulf Stream is an ocean current, the most famous ocean current of all. It is like a river that flows through the sea instead of on land. But the Gulf Stream is so vast that it is larger than all the rivers in the world put together!

The Gulf Stream moves northward along the coast of Eastern United States, across the North Atlantic Ocean, and then to northwest Europe. The Gulf Stream has a clear indigo-blue color and it can be seen clearly where it contrasts with the green and gray waters that it flows through.

The water of the Gulf Stream comes from the movement of the surface waters near the Equator in the Atlantic. This movement or "drift" is westward. So the Gulf Stream starts by moving north of South America and into the Caribbean Sea. It actually becomes what we call the Gulf Stream when it starts moving northward along the east coast of the United States.

Since the Gulf Stream starts in the warm part of the world, it is a current of warm water. And the presence of this huge current of warm water makes amazing differences in the climate of many places!

Here are some curious examples of this: Winds passing over this current in northern Europe (where it is called "the North Atlantic Drift") carry warm air to parts of Norway, Sweden, Denmark, The Netherlands, and Belgium. Result—they get milder winter temperatures than other places just as far north! It also means that ports along the Norwegian coast are ice-free the year round.

Thanks to the Gulf Stream, London and Paris enjoy mild winter climates, though they lie just as far north as southern Labrador, for example, which has bitterly cold winters. The winds that pass over the Gulf Stream are made warm and moist. When these winds become chilled, as they do near Newfoundland, dense fog results. And so we have the famous dangerous fogs of the Grand Banks of Newfoundland.

The Gulf Stream doesn't have as great an effect on the winter climate of North America as on Europe, because the winter winds don't blow over it and then inland, as they do in Europe.

HOW WERE THE MOUNTAINS FORMED?

Because mountains are so big and grand, man thinks of them as unchanging and everlasting. But geologists, the scientists who study mountains, can prove that mountains do change, and that they are not everlasting.

Certain changes in the earth's surface produced the mountains, and they are constantly being destroyed and changed. Boulders are broken from mountainsides by freezing water; soil and rock particles are carried away by rainwash and streams. In time, even the highest mountains are changed to rolling hills or plains.

Geologists divide mountains into four classifications, according to how they were formed. All mountains, however, are the result of violent changes in the earth's surface, most of which happened millions of years ago.

Folded mountains were made of rock layers, squeezed by great pressure into large folds. In many places in such mountains, you can see the rock layers curving up and down in arches and dips, caused by the squeezing and pressure on the earth's surface. The Appalachian Mountains and the Alps of Europe are examples of folded mountains.

In dome mountains, the rock layers were forced up to make great blister-like domes. In many cases, molten lava, coming with great pressure from below the earth's surface, lifted these rock layers. The Black Hills of South Dakota are examples of dome mountains.

Block mountains are the result of breaks, or faults, in the earth's crust. Huge parts of the earth's surface, entire "blocks" of rock, were raised up or tilted at one time. The Sierra Nevada Range of California is a block that is 400 miles long and 80 miles wide!

Volcanic mountains are built of lava, ash, and cinders poured out from within the earth. The usual volcano is cone-shaped with a large hole, or crater, at the top. Among the famous volcanic mountains are Mounts Ranier, Shasta, and Hood in the United States, Fujiyama in Japan, and Vesuvius in Italy.

Many mountain ranges have been formed by more than one of the ways described. In the Rockies are mountains made by folding, faulting, doming, and even erosion of lava!

HOW ARE CAVES FORMED?

Caves have long been linked with the history of man in many interesting ways. We know that late in the Old Stone Age, caves were the winter dwelling place of people who had no other shelter.

But long after man stopped using caves as homes, ancient people

believed many strange things about caves. The Greeks believed caves were the temples of their gods, Zeus, Pan, Dionysus, and Pluto. The Romans thought that caves were the homes of nymphs and sibyls. The ancient Persians and others associated caves with the worship of Mithras, chief of the earth spirits.

Today, huge and beautiful caves all over the world are tourist attractions. Caves are deep hollow places in the rocky sides of hills or cliffs. Large caves are called "caverns."

Caves are formed in many different ways. Many caves have been hollowed out by the constant beating of the sea waves against the rocks. Some caves appear under the surface of the earth. These are usually the old courses of underground streams which have worn away layers of soft rock such as limestone. Others are formed by the volcanic shifting of surface rocks, or by the eruption of hot lava.

The most common type of cave in the United States is that made by the wearing away of thick layers of limestone. This is done by the action of water containing carbon dioxide. In Indiana, Kentucky, and Tennessee, where there are great beds of limestone with an average thickness of 175 feet, such caves are numerous.

Some caves have openings through their roofs, called "sink holes." These formed where the surface water first gathered and seeped down. Some caves have galleries in tiers or rows, one above another. Underground streams wind through some caves, though in many cases after a cave has been formed, the streams that once flowed through it may find a lower level and leave the cave dry.

In many cases, each drop of water that drips from a cave roof contains a bit of lime or other mineral matter. As part of the water evaporates, some of this matter is left behind. It gradually forms a stalactite, shaped like an icicle hanging from the roof. Water dripping from the stalactite to the floor builds up a column called "a stalagmite."

WHAT ARE FOSSILS?

The study of fossils is so important in helping man learn about his own past and that of animals who lived millions of years ago that it has developed into a separate science called "paleontology."

Fossils are not, as some people think, the remains of bodies buried ages ago. Actually, there are three different kinds of fossils. The first is part of the actual body of the organism, which has been preserved from decay, and which appears just as it was originally. But fossils may also be just the cast or mold of the shape of the body, which remains after the body of the plant or animal has been removed. And fossils may merely be the footprints or trails that animals have left as they moved over the soft muds or clays.

When a fossil is found that consists of part of the organism itself, it is usually only the hard parts, such as shells or skeletons, that are preserved. The softer parts are destroyed by decay. Yet, in some cases, even such soft-bodied animals as jellyfish, which are 99 per cent water, have left perfect fossils of themselves in rocks! And certain fossils found encased in ice not only have the skeleton preserved but also the flesh and skin on the bones.

Fossils have nothing to do with size. For instance, the fossils of tiny ants which lived millions of years ago can be found perfectly preserved in amber. The chances for animals being preserved as fossils depend mostly on where they lived. The most numerous of all fossils are water animals because when they die their bodies are quickly covered over by mud and so kept from decaying. Land animals and plants are exposed to the destroying action of the air and weather.

It is chiefly through the study of fossils that we know about animal life as it existed millions and hundreds of millions of years ago. For example, fossils taken from certain rocks tell us that millions of years ago there was an Age of Reptiles, with monsters so huge that they were 80 feet long and weighed 40 tons. These were the dinosaurs. And our entire knowledge about the earliest bird, called "the archaeopteryx," is based on just two fossils of it that have been found!

WHEN DID THE ICE AGE END?

Most people think of the Ice Age as something that happened so long ago that not a sign of it remains. But did you know that geologists say we are just now reaching the end of the Ice Age? And people who live in Greenland are actually still in the Ice Age as far as they're concerned.

About 25,000 years ago, any people who may have been living in central North America saw ice and snow the year round. There was a great wall of ice that stretched from coast to coast, and the ice extended northward without an end. This was the latest Ice Age, and all of Canada, much of the United States, and most of northwestern Europe were covered by a sheet of ice thousands of feet thick.

This didn't mean that it was always icy cold. The temperature was only about 10 degrees lower than it is now in Northern United States. What caused the Ice Age was that the summers were very cool. So there wasn't enough heat during the summer months to melt away the winter's ice and snow. It just continued to pile up until it covered all the northern area.

But the Ice Age really consisted of four periods. During each period the ice formed and advanced, then melted back toward the North Pole. It is believed this happened four times. The cold periods are called "glaciations," and the warm periods are called "interglacial" periods.

It is believed that in North America the first period of ice came about 2,000,000 years ago, the second about 1,250,000 years ago, the third about 500,000 years ago, and the last about 100,000 years ago.

The last Ice Age didn't melt at the same rate everywhere. For example, ice that reached what is now Wisconsin began to melt about 40,000 years ago. But ice that had covered New England melted about 28,000 years ago. And there was ice covering what is now Minnesota until about 15,000 years ago!

In Europe, Germany got from under the ice 17,000 years ago and Sweden remained covered with ice until about 13,000 years ago!

WHY DO WE STILL HAVE GLACIERS TODAY?

The great ice mass that began the Ice Age in North America has been called "a continental glacier; it may have been about 15,000 feet thick in its center. This great glacier probably formed and then melted away at least four times during the Ice Age.

The Ice Age or glacial period that took place in other parts of the world still has not had a chance to melt away! For instance, the big island of Greenland is still covered with a continental glacier, except for a narrow fringe around its edge. In the interior, this glacier often reaches heights of more than 10,000 feet. Antarctica is also covered by a vast continental glacier which is 10,000 to 12,000 feet high in places!

So the reason we still have glaciers in certain parts of the world is that they have not had a chance to melt away since the Ice Age. But most of the glaciers that exist today have been formed in recent times. These glaciers are usually the valley type of glacier.

It starts in a broad, steep-walled valley shaped like a great amphitheatre. Snow is blown into this area or slides in from avalanches from the slopes above. This snow doesn't melt during the summer but gets deeper year by year. Eventually, the increasing pressure from above, together with some melting and refreezing, forces the air out of the lower part of the mass and changes it into solid ice. Further pressure from the weight of ice and snow above eventually squeezes this mass of ice until it begins to creep slowly down the valley. This moving tongue of ice is the valley glacier.

There are more than 1,200 such glaciers in the Alps of Europe! Glaciers are also found in the Pyrenees, Carpathian, and Caucasus Mountains of Europe, and in southern Asia. In southern Alaska, there are tens of thousands of such glaciers, some from 25 to 50 miles long!

WHY DO WE HAVE DIFFERENT SEASONS?

Since earliest times, man has been curious about the changing of the seasons. Why is it warm in summer and cold in winter? Why do the days gradually grow longer in the spring? Why are the nights so long in winter?

We all know the earth revolves around the sun, and at the same time it revolves on its own axis. As it moves around the sun, it's also spinning like a top. Now if the axis of the earth (the line from the North Pole through the South Pole) were at right angles to the path of the earth around the sun, we would have no such thing as different seasons, and all the days of the year would be of equal length.

But the axis of the earth is tilted. The reason for this is that a combination of forces is at work on the earth. One is the pull of the sun, the other is the pull of the moon, the third is the spinning action of the earth itself. The result is that the earth goes around the sun in a tilted position. It keeps that same position all year, so that the earth's axis always points in the same direction, toward the North Star.

This means that during part of the year the North Pole tilts toward the sun and part of the year away from it. Because of this tilt, the direct rays of the sun sometimes fall on the earth north of the Equator, sometimes directly on the Equator, and sometimes south of the Equator. These differences in the way the direct rays of the sun strike the earth cause the different seasons in different parts of the world.

When the Northern Hemisphere is turned toward the sun, the countries north of the Equator have their summer season, and the countries south of the Equator have their winter season. When the direct rays of the sun fall on the Southern Hemisphere, it is their summer and it is winter in the Northern Hemisphere. The longest and shortest days of each year are called "the summer solstice" and "winter solstice."

There are two days in the year when night and day are equal all over the world. They come in the spring and fall, just halfway between the solstices. One is the autumnal equinox, which occurs about September 23, and the other is the spring equinox, which occurs about March 21.

WHAT IS HUMIDITY?

If you put a pitcher of ice water on a table and let it stand a while, what happens? Moisture gathers on the outside of the pitcher. Where does this moisture come from? It comes from the air.

The fact is there is always moisture in the air in the form of water vapor. In the case of the ice pitcher, the vapor condensed on the cold surface of the pitcher and thus became visible. But water vapor in the air is invisible. And the word "humidity" simply means the presence of water vapor in the air. It is found everywhere, even over great deserts.

This means, of course, that we always have humidity, but the humidity is not always the same. We have several ways of expressing the humidity, and two of them are "absolute humidity" and "relative humidity." Let's see what each means.

"Absolute humidity" is the quantity of water vapor in each unit volume of air. There are so many grains per cubic foot of air. But for most practical purposes, this doesn't tell us very much. If you want to know whether you'll feel comfortable or not, the answer "four grains per cubic foot" won't tell you whether the air will feel dry or humid. The more easily moisture from your body can evaporate into the air, the more comfortable you'll be. The evaporative power of the air depends on the temperature, and absolute humidity doesn't indicate anything about the evaporative power of the air.

Relative humidity is expressed as a percentage. "One hundred per cent" stands for air which is saturated or completely filled with water vapor. The higher the temperature, the greater the quantity of water vapor air can hold. Thus, on a hot day, a "90 per cent relative humidity" means an awful lot of moisture in the air—a day that will make you mighty uncomfortable.

WHAT IS FOG?

A fog is a cloud in contact with the ground. There is no basic difference between a fog and a cloud floating high in the atmosphere. When a cloud is near or on the surface of the earth or sea, it is simply called "fog."

The commonest fogs are those seen at night and in the early morning over the lowlands and small bodies of water. They usually are caused by a cold current of air from above striking down upon the warmer surface of the land or water.

In the autumn they are very common, because the air is cooling faster day by day than the land or the water. On still nights after dark, thin layers of fog often form close to the ground in low places. As the earth cools at night, the lower air gets cooler. Where this cooler air meets the moist warmer air just above, fog forms.

As a general rule, city fogs are much thicker than country fogs. City air is full of dust and soot that mingle with tiny particles of water to form a thicker blanket.

Off the coast of Newfoundland, which is one of the foggiest parts of the world, fogs are formed by the passage of damp, warm air over the cold water flowing south from the Arctic Circle. The chill of the water condenses the moisture of the air into tiny drops of water. These drops are not big enough to fall as rain. They remain in the air as fog.

San Francisco fogs are formed in the opposite way. There a cool morning breeze blows over warm sand dunes, and if rain has moistened the sand the night before, a thick fog bank of evaporated moisture forms.

The reason fogs often seem denser than clouds is that the droplets are smaller in a fog. A large number of small drops absorb more light than a smaller number of large drops (as found in clouds), and thus it seems denser to us.

WHAT IS DEW?

You would imagine that dew is a very simple phenomenon of nature, easily understood and explained. Yet strangely enough, exactly what dew is has long been misunderstood, and whole books have been written on the subject!

Since the days of Aristotle until about 200 years ago, it was believed that dew "fell," somewhat like rain. But dew doesn't fall at all! The most familiar form of dew, seen on the leaves of plants, is now known not to be all dew! So you see, there have been many wrong ideas about dew.

In order to understand what dew is, we have to understand something about the air around us. All air holds a certain amount of moisture. Warm air can hold much more water vapor than cold air. When the air comes in contact with a cool surface, some of that air becomes condensed and the moisture in it is deposited on the surface in tiny drops. This is dew.

The temperature of the cool surface, however, has to drop below a certain point before dew will form. That point is called "the dew point." For example, if you place water in a glass or a polished metal container, dew may not collect on the surface. If you place some ice in the water, dew may still not collect until the surface of the glass or container is brought down to a certain point.

How does dew form in nature? First, there has to be moisture-laden warm air. This air must come into contact with a cool surface. Dew doesn't form on the ground or sidewalk, because it still remains warm after having been heated by the sun. But it may form on grasses or plants which have become cool.

Then why did we say that the dew seen on plants is really not dew? The reason is that while a small part of the moisture seen on plants in the morning is dew, most of it—and in some cases all of it— has really come from the plant itself! The moisture comes out through the pores of the leaves. It is a continuation of the plant's irrigation process for supplying the leaves with water from the soil. The action starts in the daytime, so that the surface of the leaf should be able to withstand the hot sun, and it simply continues into the night.

In some places in the world, enough dew is deposited every night for it to be collected in dew ponds and used as a water supply for cattle!

WHY DOES THUNDER FOLLOW LIGHTNING?

Lightning and thunder must have been among the first things about nature that mystified and frightened primitive man. When he saw the jagged tones of lightning in the sky and heard the claps and rumbles of thunder, he believed the gods were angry and that the lightning and thunder were a way of punishing man.

To understand what lightning and thunder actually are, we must recall a fact we know about electricity. We know that things become electrically charged—either positively or negatively. A positive charge has a great attraction for a negative one.

As the charges become greater, this attraction becomes stronger. A point is finally reached where the strain of being kept apart becomes too great for the charges Whatever resistance holds them apart, such as air, glass, or other insulating substance, is overcome or "broken down." A discharge takes place to relieve the strain and make the two bodies electrically equal.

This is just what happens in the case of lightning. A cloud containing countless drops of moisture may become oppositely charged with respect to another cloud or the earth. When the electrical pressure between the two becomes great enough to break down the insulation of air between them, a lightning flash occurs. The discharge follows the path which offers the least resistance. That's why lightning often zigzags.

The ability of air to conduct electricity varies with its temperature, density, and moisture. Dry air is a pretty good insulator, but very moist air is a fair conductor of electricity. That's why lightning often stops when the rain begins falling. The moist air forms a conductor along which a charge of electricity may travel quietly and unseen.

What about thunder? When there is a discharge of electricity, it causes the air around it to expand rapidly and then to contract. Currents of air rush about as this expansion and contraction take place. The violent collisions of these currents of air are what we hear as thunder. The reason thunder rolls and rumbles when it is far away is that the sound waves are reflected back and forth from cloud to cloud.

Since light travels at about 186,284 miles per second and sound at about 1,100 feet per second through air, we always see the flash first and then hear the thunder later.

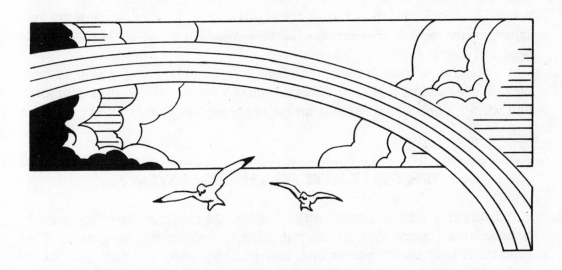

WHAT IS A RAINBOW?

A rainbow is one of the most beautiful sights in nature, and man has long wondered what makes it happen. Even Aristotle, the great Greek philosopher, tried to explain the rainbow. He thought it was a reflection of the sun's rays by the rain, and he was wrong!

Sunlight, or ordinary white light, is really a mixture of all the colors. You've probably seen what happens when light strikes the beveled edge of a mirror, or a soap bubble. The white light is broken up into different colors. We see red, orange, yellow, green, blue, and violet.

An object that can break up light in this way is called "a prism." The colors that emerge form a band of stripes, each color grading into the one next to it. This band is called "a spectrum."

A rainbow is simply a great curved spectrum, or band of colors, caused by the breaking-up of light which has passed through raindrops. The raindrops act as prisms.

A rainbow is seen only during showers, when rain is falling and the sun is shining at the same time. You have to be in the middle, the sun behind you, the rain in front of you, or you can't see a rainbow! The sun shines over your shoulder into the raindrops, which break up the light into a spectrum, or band of colors. The sun, your eyes, and the center of the arc of the rainbow must all be in a straight line!

If the sun is too high in the sky, it's impossible to make such a straight line. That's why rainbows are seen only in the early morning or late afternoons. A morning rainbow means the sun is shining in the east, showers are falling in the west. An afternoon rainbow means the sun is shining in the west and rain is falling in the east.

Superstitious people used to believe that a rainbow was a sign of bad luck. They thought that souls went to heaven on the bridge of a rainbow, and when a rainbow appeared it meant someone was going to die!

WHY IS IT HOT AT THE EQUATOR?

Every time you look at a map or a globe, the Equator shows up as such a prominent feature that it's almost hard to believe it's imaginary. The Equator is only an imaginary line, and you could cross it back and forth without knowing you've passed it.

This may explain why sailors like to remind themselves that they're "crossing the line," as they call it, by making quite a ceremony of it. The word "Equator" comes from a Latin word meaning "to equalize." And this is what the Equator does. It divides the earth into the Northern and Southern Hemispheres. It is the imaginary line that encircles the earth midway beween the North and South Poles.

Imaginary lines, encircling the earth parallel to the Equator are called "parallels." The Equator is the zero line, and lines above and below it measure latitude for locating points on the earth's surface.

The earth, as you know, is also divided on maps into regions. Starting at the top or north, we have the Arctic Region, the North Temperate Region, the Tropical Region, the South Temperate Region, and the Antarctic Region.

The Tropical Region, or the Equatorial Region, extends beyond the Equator to 23½ degrees north latitude and to 23½ degrees south latitude. Within this region, the rays of the sun come down vertically, and therefore it is always hot here.

Let's see why this is so: The earth, as you know, has its axis tilted to its path around the sun. The Equator, therefore, is tilted to this path, too, and that tilt is exactly 23½ degrees. Because of this tilt, as the earth goes around the sun, the direct rays from it sometimes fall on the earth north of the Equator, sometimes directly on the Equator, and sometimes south of the Equator. The sun, however, cannot be directly overhead more than 23½ degrees from the Equator.

This explains why the Equatorial Region is the only place on earth where the sun's rays come down vertically. You can understand why, since this happens the year round, it's always pretty hot near the Equator!

WHAT IS SMOKE?

Smoke is the result of incomplete combustion of certain fuels. This means that if most of our common fuels were able to burn completely, we would have no smoke!

Most fuels consist of carbon, hydrogen, oxygen, nitrogen, a little sulphur, and perhaps some mineral ash. Now, if these fuels would burn completely, the final product would be carbon dioxide, water vapor, and free nitrogen, all of which are harmless. If sulphur is present, small quantities of sulphur dioxide are also given off, and when this comes in contact with air and moisture, it becomes a corrosive acid.

For complete combustion, a fuel must have enough air for full oxidation at a high temperature. These conditions are difficult to obtain, especially with solid fuels, and the result is smoke. Anthracite and coke can be burned without producing smoke because they have no volatile matter.

But bituminous coals decompose at rather low temperatures so that gases and tarry matter are freed; they combine with dust and ash and produce smoke.

The air in any city is full of suspended solid particles, but not all of this is smoke. It may contain dust, vegetable matter, and other materials. All of these gradually settle under the force of gravity. In small towns or suburbs, probably about 75 to 100 tons of these deposits settle down per square mile during a year. In a big industrial city, the deposits may be 10 times as great!

Smoke can do a great deal of harm. It damages health, property, and vegetation. In big industrial towns, it lowers the intensity of the sunshine, especially the ultraviolet rays which are essential to health.

If the wind didn't spread the smoke, big industrial towns would probably have fog every day. In fact, where smoky fog occurs, it often happens that the death rate goes up from lung and heart diseases.

The effect of smoke on vegetation is especially harmful. It interferes with the "breathing" of plants and screens off needed sunlight. Quite often, the acid in the smoke destroys plants directly!

Today, many cities are waging active campaigns to cut down on smoke or to prevent it from doing damage.

WHAT IS SMOG?

Between December 4th and 9th, 1952, in the City of London, about 4,000 people died as a result of exposure to smog! What is smog and why is it so dangerous?

In some cities the combination of different industrial gases released into the air makes up a kind of fog we call "smog." It makes people cough when they breathe it. If certain fumes and fine particles are present in the smog, it can become poisonous.

Now, dust is present in the air at all times. Dust is tiny particles of solid matter that can be carried in suspension by air. Dust may come from soil blowing, ocean spray, volcanic activity, forest fires, the exhaust from automobiles, and from industrial combustion processes. The latter is what you see pouring out of factory chimneys.

The amount of dust in the air is almost unbelievable. It is estimated that over the United States about 43,000,000 tons of dust settle every year!

Of this amount, about 31,000,000 tons are from natural sources. That leaves about 12,000,000 tons of dust that are the result of human activities!

Naturally, the amount of dust is greatest in big industrial cities. For example, here is roughly how much dust falls per square mile each month in some of our big cities: Detroit—72 tons; New York—69 tons; Chicago—61 tons; Pittsburgh—46 tons; and Los Angeles—33 tons. In a section of the city where there are many industrial buildings, it might be as much as 200 tons per square mile each month.

This is such an important health problem that many cities are carrying on intensive campaigns to reduce the amount of industrial dust in the air. Dust-producing machinery is built with hoods to keep the dust down. Ventilation systems, blower fans, and electrical devices that cause the dust to settle are also used. In some cases, wet drilling is done and water sprays are used, too. But the problem of dangerous dust in the air—or "smog"—has not yet been licked.

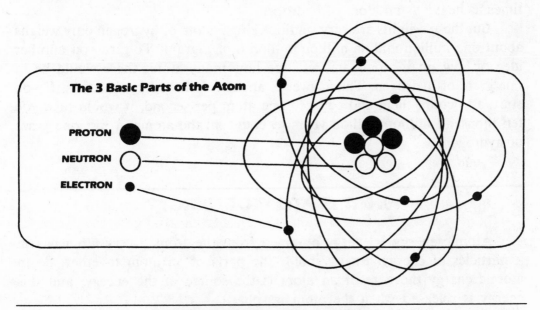

The 3 Basic Parts of the Atom

PROTON

NEUTRON

ELECTRON

HOW BIG IS AN ATOM?

Let us begin by saying that anything we know about the atom today might be changed tomorrow. Science is constantly learning new things about the atom as atom-smashing machines are built.

Oddly enough, the word "atom" comes from the Greek and means "not divisible'." The ancient Greeks thought an atom to be the smallest possible particle of any substance.

Yet today we have found more than 20 different particles in the core of the atom! Scientists believe the atom is made of electrons, protons, neutrons, positrons, neutrinos, mesons, and hyperons. Electrons are particles that carry a tiny negative charge of electricity. The proton, about 1,836 times as heavy as the electron, carries a positive charge of electricity. The neutron, still heavier, carries no electric charge at all. The positron, about the size of the electron, carries a positive charge. The neutrino, about one two-thousandth the size of the electron, has no charge. Mesons may be either positively or negatively charged. Hyperons are larger than protons.

How all these particles or charges are held together to make up the atom is still not known to us. But these atoms make up the elements and they differ from each other. One way they differ is by weight, and thus elements are classified according to atomic weights. For example, hydrogen is "1" on this table and iron is "55." This means that an atom of iron is 55 times as heavy as an atom of hydrogen.

But these weights are very small. A single atom of hydrogen only weighs about one million-million-million-millionth of a gram! To give you another idea of how small atoms are, let's see how many atoms there would be in one gram of hydrogen. The answer is about 6 followed by 23 zeros. If you started to count them and counted one atom per second, it would take you ten thousand million million years to count all the atoms in just one gram of hydrogen!

WHAT IS ATOMIC ENERGY?

Atomic energy is energy obtained from the atom. Every atom has in it particles of energy. Energy holds the parts of an atom together. So in atomic energy the core of an atom is the source of the energy, and this energy is released when the atom is split.

But there are actually two ways of obtaining energy with atoms. One is called "fusion" and one is called "fission." When fusion takes place, two atoms are made to form one single atom. The fusion of atoms results in the release of a tremendous amount of energy in the form of heat. Most of the energy given off from the sun comes from fusion taking place in the sun. This is one form of atomic energy.

Another form of atomic energy comes from the fission process. Fission happens when one atom splits into two. This is done by bombarding or hitting atoms with atomic particles such as neutrons (one of the particles that make up the atom).

An atom doesn't split every time it is bombarded by neutrons. In fact, most atoms cannot be made to split. But uranium and plutonium atoms will split under proper conditions.

One form of uranium called "U-235" (it is known as an "isotope" of uranium), breaks into two fragments when it is struck with neutrons. And do you know how much energy this gives off? One pound of U-235 gives much more than 1,000,000 times as much energy as could be obtained by burning one pound of coal! A tiny pebble of uranium could run an ocean liner or an airplane or even a generator.

WHAT IS RADIUM?

Radium is a radioactive element. Let us see what "radioactive" means.

Elements are made up of atoms. Most atoms are stable, which means they do not change from year to year. But a few of the heaviest atoms break down and change into other kinds. This breakdown or decay is called "radioactivity."

Each radioactive element decays or disintegrates by giving off rays at a certain rate. This rate cannot be hurried or slowed by any known method. Some change rapidly, others slowly, but in all cases the action cannot be controlled by man.

In the case of radium, this decay would go on and on until the radium would be finally changed into lead. For example, half a gram of radium would change to atoms of lower atomic weight in 1,590 years. After another 1,590 years, half of the remaining radium would change; and so on until it all became lead.

Radium was discovered by Madame Curie and her husband, Pierre Curie. They were refining a ton of pitchblende, which is an ore that contains uranium. They knew the uranium was giving off invisible rays, but they felt there must be some other substance there, too, much more powerful. First they found polonium, another radioactive element, and finally they succeeded in isolating a tiny speck of radium.

Radium gives off three kinds of rays, called *alpha, beta,* and *gamma* rays. *Alpha* rays are fast-moving particles of the gas helium. *Beta* rays are fast-moving electrons. And *gamma* rays are like X-rays but usually more penetrating. Whenever one of these rays is ejected, the parent atom from which it comes changes from one element to another. This change is called "atomic transmutation."

WHAT IS RADIOACTIVITY?

Hardly anyone can grow up in the world today without hearing about—and worrying about—radioactivity. We know that testing of atom bombs creates radioactivity, which is why it is one of the greatest problems facing mankind today. But just what is radioactivity—and why is it harmful to man?

Let's start with the atom. Every kind of atom is constructed somewhat like our solar system. Instead of the sun there is a nucleus, and instead of planets there are electrons revolving around it. The nucleus is made up of one or more positively charged particles.

Radioactivity occurs when something happens to cause the atom to send off one or more particles from its nucleus. At the same time, the atom may send out energy in the form of rays (gamma rays).

Now some elements are naturally radioactive. This means the atoms are constantly discharging particles. When this happens, we say it is "disintegrating." When particles are sent off, the element undergoes a change. In this way, radium—which is naturally radioactive—sends off particles and disintegrates into other elements until it becomes lead.

Scientists have now learned how to produce artificial radioactivity. By bombarding the atoms of certain elements with particles, they could make those atoms begin to disintegrate and thus become radioactive. The bombarded atoms would thus send off energy. That's why these machines are called "atom smashers."

Why is radioactivity dangerous to man? Well, just picture these flying particles coming from the smashed atoms. When these particles strike other atoms, they can cause them to break up, too, and change their chemical character. Now, if these particles strike living cells in the body, they certainly can cause changes there! They can burn and destroy the skin, destroy red blood cells, and cause changes in other cells.

So while radioactivity can be useful to man in many ways, it can also be dangerous and destructive.

WHAT ARE X-RAYS?

X-rays were discovered in Germany in 1895 by Wilhelm Roentgen, and thus are sometimes called "Roentgen rays."

They are penetrating rays similar to light rays. They differ from light rays in the length of their waves and in their energy. The shortest wave length from an X-ray tube may be one fifteen-thousandth to one-millionth of the wave length of green light. X-rays can pass through materials which light will not pass through because of their very short wave length. The shorter the wave length, the more penetrating the waves become.

X-rays are produced in an X-ray tube. The air is pumped from this tube until less than one hundred-millionth of the original amount is left. In the tube, which is usually made of glass, there are two electrodes. One of these is called "the cathode." This has a negative charge. In it is a coil of tungsten wire which can be heated by an electric current so that electrons are given off. The other electrode is "the target," or "anode."

The electrons travel from the cathode to the target at very great speeds because of the difference between the cathode and the target. They strike

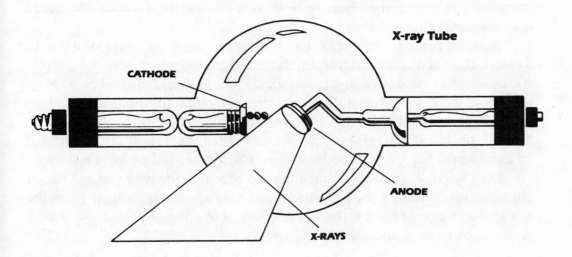

X-ray Tube

CATHODE

ANODE

X-RAYS

the target at speeds that may vary from 60,000 to 175,000 miles per second.

The target is either a block of tungsten or a tungsten wheel, and it stops the electrons suddenly. Most of the energy of these electrons is changed into heat, but some of it becomes X-radiation, and emerges from a window at the bottom as X-rays.

Have you ever wondered how X-ray pictures are taken of bones in your body? The X-ray "picture" is a shadowgraph or shadow picture. X-rays pass through the part of the body being X-rayed and cast shadows on the film. The film is coated with a sensitive emulsion on both sides. After it is exposed, it is developed like ordinary photographic film. The bones and other objects the X-rays do not pass through easily cast denser shadows and so show up as light areas on the film.

Today, X-rays play an important part in medicine, science, and industry, and are one of man's most helpful tools.

WHAT CAUSES A MIRAGE?

Imagine a wanderer in the desert, dying of thirst. He looks off into the distance and sees a vision of a lake of clear water surrounded by trees. He stumbles forward until the vision fades and there is nothing but the hot sand all around him.

The lake he saw in the distance was a mirage. What caused it? A mirage is a trick Nature plays on our eyes because of certain conditions in the atmosphere. First we must understand that we are able to see an object because rays of light are reflected from it to our eyes. Usually, these rays reach our eye in a straight line. So if we look off into the distance, we should only see things that are above our horizon.

Now we come to the tricks the atmosphere plays with rays of light. In a desert, there is a layer of dense air above the ground which acts as a mirror. An object may be out of sight, way below the horizon. But when rays of light from it hit this layer of dense air, they are reflected to our eyes and we see the object as if it were above the horizon and in our sight. We are really "seeing" objects which our eyes cannot see! When the distant sky is reflected by this "mirror" of air, it sometimes looks like a lake, and we have a mirage.

On a hot day, as you approach the top of a hill, you may think the road ahead is wet. This is a mirage, too! What you are seeing is light from the sky that has been bent by the hot air just above the pavement so that it seems to come from the road itself.

Mirages occur at sea, too, with visions of ships sailing across the sky! In these cases, there is cold air near the water and warm air over it. Distant ships, that are beyond the horizon, can be seen because the light waves coming from them are reflected by the layer of warm air and we see the ship in the sky!

One of the most famous mirages in the world takes place in Sicily, across the Strait of Messina. The city of Messina is reflected in the sky, and fairy castles seem to float in the air. The Italian people call it *Fata Morgana,* after Morgan Le Fay, who was supposed to be an evil fairy who caused this mirage.

HOW FAST DOES SOUND TRAVEL?

Every time a sound is made, there is some vibrating object somewhere. Something is moving back and forth rapidly. Sound starts with a vibrating object.

But sound must travel in something. It requires something to carry the sound from its source to the hearer. This is called "a medium." A medium can be practically anything—air, water, objects, even the earth. The Indians used to put their ears to the ground to hear a distant noise!

No medium—no sound. If you create a vacuum, space containing no air or any other substance, sound cannot travel through it. The reason for this is that sound travels in waves. The vibrating objects cause the molecules or particles in the substance next to them to vibrate. Each particle passes on the motion to the particle next to it, and the result is sound waves.

Since the mediums in which sound travels can range from wood to air to water, obviously the sound waves will travel at different speeds. So when we ask how fast does sound travel, we have to ask: In what?

The speed of sound in air is about 1,100 feet per second (750 miles per hour). But this is when the temperature is 32 degrees Fahrenheit. As the temperature rises, the speed of sound rises.

Sound travels much faster in water than in air. When water is at a temperature of 46 degrees Fahrenheit, sound travels through it at about 4,708 feet per second, or 3,210 miles per hour. And in steel, sound travels at about 11,160 miles per hour!

You might imagine that a loud sound would travel faster than a weak sound, but this isn't so. Nor is the speed of sound affected by its pitch (high or low). The speed depends on the medium through which it is traveling.

If you want to try an interesting experiment with sound, clap two stones together when you are standing in the water. Now go under water and clap those two stones together again. You'll be amazed how much better sound travels through water than through air!

WHAT IS THE SOUND BARRIER?

The name "sound barrier" is actually a wrong way to describe a condition that exists when planes travel at certain speeds. A kind of "barrier" was expected when planes reached the speed of sound — but no such barrier developed!

In order to understand this, let's start with a plane traveling at ordinary low-speed flight. As the plane moves forward, the front parts of the plane send out a pressure wave. The pressure wave is caused by the building-up of particles of air as the plane moves forward.

Now this pressure wave goes out ahead of the plane at the speed of sound. It is, therefore, moving faster than the plane itself, which, as we said, is moving at ordinary speed. As this pressure wave rushes ahead of the plane, it causes the air to move smoothly over the wing surfaces of the approaching plane.

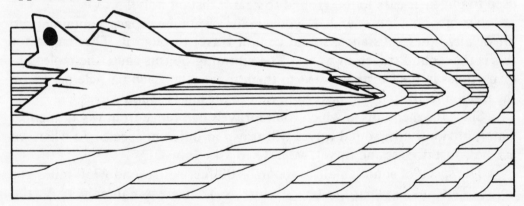

Now let's say the plane is traveling at the speed of sound. The air ahead receives no pressure wave in advance of the plane, since both the plane and the pressure wave are moving forward at the same speed. So the pressure wave builds up in front of the wing.

The result is a shock wave, and this creates great stresses in the wing of the plane. Before planes actually flew at the speed of sound and faster, it was expected that these shock waves and stresses would create a kind of "barrier" for the plane -- a "sound barrier." But no such barrier developed, since aeronautical engineers were able to design planes to overcome it.

Incidentally, the loud 'boom" that is heard when a plane passes through the "sound barrier" is caused by the shock wave described above — when the speed of the pressure wave and the speed of the plane are the same.

WHAT IS FIRE?

The scientific name for burning is "combustion." There are many different kinds of combustion, but in most cases a very simple thing has to take place. Oxygen from the air has to combine with some material that can burn.

This reaction produces heat. If the process takes place rapidly, we may see flames or an intense glow or actually feel the combustion, as in an explosion. When wood or paper combine with oxygen, we usually have flames. But we also have combustion in the engines of our automobiles. The gasoline burns with oxygen taken from the air.

In the automobile engine the combustion proceeds so rapidly that we call it an explosion. At the opposite end, we have a kind of combustion that goes on so slowly that we may not notice it for years. For instance, when iron rusts, a slow burning process is actually taking place!

When slow combustion takes place and the heat that results cannot escape into the air, the temperature may reach a point where active burning begins. This is called "spontaneous combustion." Spontaneous combustion might occur in a heap of oily rags left in some closed place. The oil will undergo slow oxidation or burning which results in heat. Since the heat cannot escape, it accumulates. Eventually there will be enough heat to cause the cloth to burst into flames.

Oxygen, which is necessary in combustion, is one of the most common elements in nature. The air which surrounds us contains approximately 21 per cent of oxygen. This oxygen is always ready to enter the combustion process.

However, materials which are "combustible" are as necessary as oxygen for combustion to take place. We call these materials "inflammable." Inflammable materials which are planned to be used for combustion are known as "fuels." For instance, wood, coal, coke, fuel oil, kerosene, and certain gases are common fuels.

During combustion, two atoms of oxygen from the air combine with one atom of carbon from the fuel to form a molecule of a new substance called "carbon dioxide." Did you know that the combustion process which goes on in our body to generate heat and energy creates carbon dioxide which we breathe out?

WHAT IS OXYGEN?

Every now and then you read about something that man "couldn't live without." Well, one thing you can be sure is absolutely necessary to life is oxygen. Without oxygen, a human being cannot live more than a few minutes.

Oxygen is an element, the most plentiful element in the universe. It makes up nearly half of the earth's crust and more than one-fifth of the air. Breathed into the lungs, it is carried by the red blood corpuscles in a constant stream to the body cells. There it burns the food, making the heat needed to keep the human engine going.

Oxygen combines very easily with most elements. When this takes place, we call the process "oxidation." When this oxidation takes place very quickly, we have "combustion." In almost all oxidations, heat is given off. In combustion, the heat is given off so fast that it has no time to be carried away, the temperature rises extremely high, and a flame appears.

So at one end we have combustion, the fast oxidation that produces fire and at the other end we have the kind of oxidation that burns the food in our body and keeps the life process going. But slow oxidations, by the oxygen of the air, are found everywhere. When iron rusts, paint dries, alcohol is changed into vinegar, oxidation is going on.

The air we breathe is a mixture chiefly of nitrogen and oxygen. So we can prepare pure oxygen from the air. It is done by cooling the air to very low temperatures until it becomes liquid. This temperature is more than 300 degrees below zero Fahrenheit. As soon as the liquid air warms up a little above that temperature, it boils. The nitrogen boils off first and oxygen remains. Many a life has been saved by giving people oxygen to make breathing easier when their lungs were weak.

WHAT IS WATER?

When scientists wonder whether there is life on other planets, they often ask this question: "Is there water there?" Life as we know it would be impossible without water.

Water is a tasteless, odorless, colorless compound that makes up a large proportion of all living things. It occurs everywhere in the soil, and exists in varying amounts in the air.

Living things can digest and absorb foods only when these foods are dissolved in water. Living tissue consists chiefly of water. What is water made of? It is a simple compound of two gases: hydrogen, a very light gas; and oxygen, a heavier, active gas.

When hydrogen is burned in oxygen, water is formed. But water does not resemble either of the elements which compose it. It has a set of properties all its own.

Water, like most other matter, exists in three states: a liquid state, which is the common form; a solid, called "ice"; and a gas, called "water vapor." In which one of these forms water shall exist depends ordinarily on the temperature.

At 0 degrees centigrade, or 32 degrees Fahrenheit, water changes from the liquid to the solid state, or freezes. At 100 degrees centigrade, or 212 degrees Fahrenheit, it changes from the liquid to the gaseous state. This change from liquid, visible water to the invisible water gas is called "evaporation."

Thus, if a piece of ice is brought into a warm room, it starts to become liquid or melt. If the room is warm enough, the little puddle of water formed from the melting ice finally disappears. The liquid is changed into water vapor. When water is cooled, it expands just before it reaches the freezing point.

Water as it occurs in nature is never pure in the true sense. It contains dissolved mineral material, dissolved gases, and living organisms.

HOW IS SOIL FORMED?

If the surface of our earth were not covered with soil, man would perish. Without soil, plants could not grow and human beings and other animals would have no food.

Soil is the loose, powdery earth in which plants grow. It is made up of very small pieces of rock and decayed plant and animal materials. The small pieces or particles of rock were once parts of larger rocks. The plant and animal materials come from plant and animal bodies.

No rock is so hard that it cannot in time be broken into pieces. The crumbling and wearing away of rock, which is called "weathering," goes on all the time and is done in many ways. Glaciers push great piles of rocks ahead of them as they move along and this pushing and grinding help crumble the rocks.

Water with chemicals in it will dissolve and wear away some kinds of rocks. Changes in temperature often help break rocks into small pieces. The heating and cooling of rocks may cause cracks to appear. Water gets into the cracks, freezes, and cracks the rocks even more. Even plant roots may cause rocks to break. Sometimes the seeds of trees fall into cracks in rocks, the seeds sprout, and as the roots of the plant grow, they help split the rock. Wind also helps crumble rocks by hurling sand against the rocks.

But this is only the beginning of soil-making. To make real soil, the sand or fine particles of rock must have "humus" added to it. Humus is an organic material that comes from plants and animal bodies. The bodies of almost all dead land plants and animals become a part of soil, through the work of bacteria.

Bacteria cause the plants and animals to decay and make the soil fertile. Earthworms and many kinds of insects help to make the soil rich. The richest layer of soil is at the top and is called "topsoil." This has much humus in it. The next layer, which is called "subsoil," contains mostly bits of rock. The layer beneath is bedrock, which is under the soil everywhere.

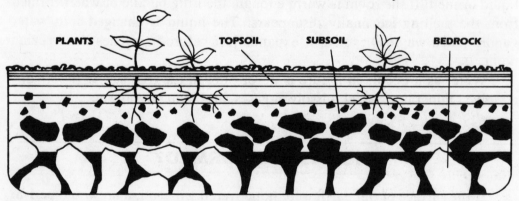

PLANTS   TOPSOIL   SUBSOIL   BEDROCK

WHAT IS SILVER?

The mining of silver has been carried on from ancient times. In Europe, kings depended on it as their source of wealth. In fact, when the Spanish silver mines began to run low, the King of Spain was delighted that the discovery of America led him to obtain the great silver mines of Mexico and Peru. The mines at Potosi in Peru produced $4,000,000 worth of silver every year for 250 years for the kings of Spain!

During the gold rush days in California, people cursed the "black earth" that stuck to their gold dust. It was only by accident that they discovered it was silver ore!

Silver is one of the most widely distributed of all metals. Sometimes it is found in solid pieces, and in Norway a piece of solid silver was once found that weighed three-quarters of a ton! But usually silver comes in ores from which it must be separated.

In this ore, silver is usually combined with sulphur as silver sulphide, or is a part of other sulphides, chiefly those of copper, lead, or arsenic. In the United States, it is found mostly in connection with lead. In fact, silver occurs in so many combinations that there are a great many different methods of separating it from the other elements.

Silver is too soft to be used in its pure state, so it is combined with other metals. Silver coins, for instance, contain 90 per cent silver and 10 per cent copper. The sterling silver of which jewelry and silverware are made contains 92.5 per cent silver and 7.5 per cent copper.

The name "sterling," by the way, has a curious origin. It comes from a North German family called Easterling. The Easterlings were such honest traders that King John of England gave them the job of making the English coins in 1215. They did it so well and truly that their name is still used as a sign of solid worth. All sterling silver is stamped with a hallmark, either the word "sterling" or a symbol, depending on the country.

Pure silver doesn't tarnish in pure air. When it turns black, that's a sign there is sulphur in the air, as from city smoke or oil wells. Next to gold, silver is the easiest metal to work with. One ounce of silver can be drawn into a wire more than 30 miles long! It is also the most perfect known conductor of electricity and heat.

WHY IS GOLD CONSIDERED PRECIOUS?

As far back as man has been known to exist, he has considered gold precious. It was probably the first metal known to man.

One reason primitive man was drawn to gold was that it can be found in the free state, which means gold can be found in small lumps (called "nuggets") uncombined with other metals or rocks. Since it has a bright yellow color and a shiny appearance, even the earliest man liked to possess it and make ornaments out of it.

The value of gold increased when people realized that it is the most easily worked of all metals. A nugget of gold is easily hammered thin and is flexible enough to bend without breaking. This means that early man could fashion gold into any shape he wished. At one time, for instance, it was used for hoops to bind the hair. Out of this came the idea of crowns and coronets made of gold.

The supply of gold that can be obtained easily from the earth is very limited. Soon people who couldn't find their own gold offered to exchange other things in return for some gold. That's how gold came to be a medium of exchange. While other commodities were perishable, gold was not, so it became a means of storing value for the future, and a measure of value, as well.

Centuries later, gold was made into coins as a convenient way of indicating the weight and fineness of the metal, and thus its value.

Later on, bankers would keep the gold itself in their vaults for safety's sake, and give a written pledge to deliver the gold on demand. From this practice, governments began to issue currency, or money, that was also simply a pledge to deliver a certain amount of gold on demand.

HOW HARD IS A DIAMOND?

If you had a piece of putty and wanted to make it hard, what would you do? You'd squeeze it and press it, and the more you squeezed and pressed, the harder it would become.

Diamonds were made in the same way by nature. A hundred million years ago, the earth was in its early cooling stages. At that time, there existed beneath the ground a mass of hot liquid rock. This was subjected to extreme heat and pressure. Carbon which was subjected to this pressure became what we called "diamonds."

Diamonds are the hardest natural substance known to man. But it is not very easy to measure "hardness" exactly. One way it is done is by using the scratch test, scratching it with another hard substance. In 1820, a man called Mohs made up a scale of hardness for minerals based on such a test. On his scale, this is the way the minerals ranked in hardness: 1. Talc. 2. Gypsum. 3. Calcite. 4. Fluorite. 5. Aphatite. 6. Feldspar. 7. Quartz. 8. Topaz. 9. Corundum. 10. Diamond.

But all this measured was how they compared to each other. For example, it has been found that even though corundum is 9 on the scale and diamond is 10, the difference between them in hardness is greater than the difference between 9 and 1 on the scale. So diamonds are the champions for hardness with no competition!

Since diamonds are so hard, how can they be shaped and cut? The only thing that will cut a diamond is another diamond! What diamond cutters use is a saw with an edge made of diamond dust.

In fact, diamond grinding and cutting wheels are used in industry in many ways, such as to grind lenses, to shape all kinds of tools made of copper, brass, and other metals, and to cut glass. Today, more than 80 per cent of all diamonds produced are used in industry!

WHAT IS RUBBER?

Rubber is as old as nature itself. Fossils have been found of rubber-producing plants that go back almost 3,000,000 years! Crude rubber balls have been found in the ruins of Incan and Mayan civilizations in Central and South America that are at least 900 years old.

In fact, when Columbus made his second voyage to the New World, he saw the natives of Haiti playing a game with a ball made from "the gum of a tree." And even before that, the natives of Southeastern Asia knew of rubber prepared from the "juice" of a tree and they used it to coat baskets and jars to make them waterproof!

Rubber has been found in more than 400 different vines, shrubs, and trees. But the amount of rubber found in each varies greatly and it doesn't pay to extract the rubber from such plants as dandelion, milkweed, and sagebrush.

Rubber is a sticky, elastic solid obtained from a milky liquid known as "latex," which is different from sap. The latex appears in the bark, roots, stem, branches, leaves, and fruit of plants and trees. But most of it is found in the inner bark of the branches and trunk of the rubber tree.

Latex consists of tiny particles of liquid, solid, or semi-fluid material which appear in a watery liquor. Only about 33 per cent of the latex is rubber; the rest is mostly water. The rubber particles in the latex are drawn together and a ball of rubber is formed.

Rubber grows best within 10 degrees of the Equator, and the area of about 700 miles on each side of the Equator is known as "the Rubber Belt." The reason for this is that the rubber tree needs a hot, moist climate and deep, rich soil. The best and most rubber comes from a tree called *Hevea brasiliensis*. As the name suggests this tree was first found in Brazil. Today almost 96 per cent of the world's supply of natural rubber comes from this tree, but now this tree is cultivated in many parts of the world within the Rubber Belt.

The first white men to manufacture rubber goods were probably the French, who made elastics for garters and suspenders some time before 1800.

WHAT IS CHALK?

Practically no one can grow up in the world today without coming into contact with chalk at some time in his life. In millions of classrooms around the world, children step up to blackboards to write things with chalk. And, of course, what could teacher do without chalk to help her?

Did you know that chalk was originally an animal? The waters of our oceans are covered with many forms of very tiny plants and animals. One of these is a one-celled animal called "Foraminifera." The shells of these creatures are made of lime.

When these animals die, their tiny shells sink to the floor of the ocean. In time, a thick layer of these shells is built up. Of course, this takes millions of years to accomplish. This layer gradually becomes cemented and compressed into a soft limestone which we call chalk.

As we know, various disturbances in the surface of the earth have often made dry land out of land that was once under water. One of the places where this happened is along the English Channel. The chalk layers at the bottom of the sea were pushed up. Later the soft parts were cut away by water, leaving huge cliffs of chalk. The two most famous ones are the chalk cliffs at Dover on the English side and at Dieppe on the French side of the Channel.

In other parts of the world, chalk deposits appear far inland in areas that were once under water. We have examples of these in our own country in Kansas, Arkansas, and Texas. But the finest natural chalk comes from England which produces more than 5,000,000 tons of it every year!

Chalk in one form or another has been used by man for hundreds of years. The blackboard chalk with which we are all familiar is mixed with some binding substance to prevent it from crumbling. The best blackboard chalk is about 95 per cent chalk. By adding pigments to it, chalk can be made in any color.

When chalk is pulverized, washed, and filtered, it is called "whiting." It can then be used in the making of many useful products such as putty, paints, medicines, paper, and toothpastes and powders!

WHAT IS CHLOROPHYLL?

If you had to pick the one chief thing that sets plants apart from animals, what would it be? The answer is that plants are green. Of course, there are some exceptions, but this is really the one basic law of plants—their greenness.

Now, this greenness of plants is one of the most important things in the entire world. Because the green coloring matter in plants—chlorophyll—enables them to take substances from the soil and the air and to manufacture living food. If plants couldn't do this, men and animals couldn't exist, for they would have no food! Even those creatures which live on meat depend on other creatures who live on plants. In fact, you can trace any food back to its original source and find it was made by a plant!

So you can see that chlorophyll, this miraculous green substance which enables plants to supply man and animals with food, is vital to our life, too! Chlorophyll is contained in the cells of leaves and often in the stem and flowers.

With the help of chlorophyll, the plant's living tissue is able to absorb the energy from sunlight and to use this energy to transform inorganic chemicals into organic or "life-giving" chemicals. This process is called "photosynthesis." The word comes from the Greek words which mean "light" and "put together."

There are some plants which have no green color, no chlorophyll. How do they live? Mushrooms, and a whole group of fungi, which have no chlorophyll, can't make their own food. So they have to get it in some way from something else. If they get their food from other plants or animals, they are called "parasites." If they get it from the decaying remains of plants and animals, they are called "saprophytes."

Chlorophyll can be extracted from plants and used in various ways by man. In such cases, it may help destroy certain bacteria.

WHAT IS A SEED?

One of the ways in which a plant produces another plant of its own kind is the seed. Just as birds lay eggs to reproduce their kind, the plant grows a seed that makes another plant.

The flower or blossom of a plant must be fertilized or the seed it produces will not grow. After the seed is fully grown, or mature, it must rest. The rest period varies among different kinds of seeds. Many of them will not grow until they have rested through the winter.

Seed growth requires moisture, oxygen, and warmth. Light helps some plants start seed growth. If seed growth doesn't start within a certain time, the seed will die. When seeds are stored by man for future use, they must be kept dry and within a certain temperature range.

Seeds vary greatly in size, shape, pattern, and color. The seeds of different plants are made in different ways. There is one kind of seed, for example, that has the tiny new plant in the center. Around this is stored food which will tide the young plant over until it has developed roots and leaves and can make its own food.

If a seed is fertile, has rested, and has received the proper amounts of moisture, oxygen, and warmth, it begins to grow. This is called "sprouting" or "germination." Growth often starts when moisture reaches the seed. As the seed absorbs water, it swells. As chemical changes take place, the cells of the seeds begin to show life again and the tiny young plant within the seed begins to grow. Most parts of the seed go into the growing plant. The seed cover drops off and the new plant grows larger until it matures and makes seeds of its own.

Seeds may be small or large. Begonia seeds are so small they look like dust. Coconuts are seeds which may weigh as much as 40 pounds! Some plants have only a few dozen seeds, while others, such as the maple, have thousands.

There are special ways seeds are made so that they will be spread. Burr-type seeds hitch a ride on the fur of animals. Seeds that stick in mud cling to animals' feet. Seeds contained in fruit are carried by man and animals. Some seeds have "wings" and are blown by the wind, other seeds float on water, and some are even "exploded" away from the parent plant!

HOW DO TREES GROW?

Like all living things, trees need nourishment in order to be able to grow. Where does the tree obtain this?

From the soil, the tree obtains water and minerals. From the air, it takes in carbon dioxide. And the green of the leaves of trees harnesses the energy of the sun's rays to make starches, sugars, and cellulose. So the tree carries on a chemical process of its own in order to be able to live and grow.

Between the wood of a tree and its bark, there is a thin band of living, dividing cells called "the cambium." As new cells are formed here, those that are formed on the wood side of the cambium mature as wood. The cells formed toward the outside mature as bark. In this way, as the tree grows older it increases in diameter.

The diameter of the woody part of the tree continues to grow greater and greater. But this doesn't always happen with the bark. Often the outer bark becomes broken, dies, and falls off.

Trees grow in height as well as in diameter. At the end of each branch or twig there is a group of living cells. During periods of active growth, these cells keep dividing, producing many more cells. These new cells enlarge and form new leaves as well as additional portions of the stem or twig. In this way, the twig grows longer.

After a time, these cells at the tip of the twig become less active and the twig grows longer more slowly. Then the new cells are firm and scale-like and they form a bud. You can easily notice these buds on trees during the winter.

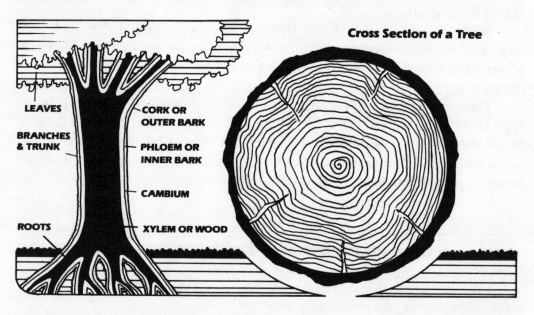

Cross Section of a Tree

LEAVES

BRANCHES
& TRUNK

ROOTS

CORK OR
OUTER BARK

PHLOEM OR
INNER BARK

CAMBIUM

XYLEM OR WOOD

In the spring, the bud scales are spread apart or fall off and the twig starts growing longer again. So you see that by means of the cambium layer in the tree, and by means of the active cells at the tips of twigs, trees may grow both in thickness and in length, year after year.

A cross section of a tree shows alternating bands of light and dark wood. This difference in color is due to differences in size of the cells which make up the wood. The lighter bands have bigger cells which were formed in spring and early summer. The narrow dark bands are made up of smaller cells packed tightly together which were formed in late summer. Together, they show the amount of wood formed during a year, and by counting them, we can tell the age of a tree.

WHAT GIVES FLOWERS THEIR SCENT AND COLOR?

Curiously enough, we often look at a plant and admire its "flowers" when we are actually not looking at the flowers at all! If we think of a flower as something brightly colored which grows on a plant, we may be quite mistaken.

For instance, the "petals of the dogwood "blossoms" that bloom in the spring are not petals at all. Nor is the white sheath on a callas plant a flower. Poinsettia blossoms are another example of colored leaves rather than true flowers.

On the other hand, the bearded tufts at the tips of grasses are really flowers! An unripe ear of corn is actually a flower. According to the botanist, a flower is a group of parts whose function is to produce pollen or seeds or both. Only seed-bearing plants have flowers. And only those parts of a plant which are closely concerned with the formation and production of the seed can be considered as parts of the flower.

What gives flowers their scent? A flower has a fragrance when certain essential oils are found in the petals. These oils are produced by the plant as part of its growing process. These essential oils are very complex substances. Under certain conditions, this complex substance is broken down or decomposed and is formed into a volatile oil, which means it evaporates readily. When this happens, we can smell the fragrance it gives off.

The specific type of fragrance a flower gives off depends on the chemicals in that volatile oil, and various combinations produce different scents. By the way, these same oils are found not only in the flowers of plants but often in leaves, barks, roots, fruit, and seeds. For instance, oranges and lemons have them in the fruit, almonds have them in the seeds, cinnamon has them in the bark, and so on.

What gives flowers their color? "Anthocyanin" is the name for the pigments which give flowers the red, mauve, blue, purple, and violet colors. These pigments are dissolved in the sap of the cells of the flower. Other colors, such as yellow, orange, and green, are due to other pigments. These substances include chlorophyll, carotene, etc. There is no chemical link between them.

So we can attribute the colors in flowers to pigments called "anthocyanins" and to other pigments called "plastids." One group supplies a certain range of colors and the other group supplies the rest of the colors.

WHY DO LEAVES TURN DIFFERENT COLORS IN THE FALL?

When you look at a group of trees in the summertime, you see only one color: green. Of course, there are various shades of green, but it's as if it were all painted by one brush. Yet in the fall, these same leaves take on a whole variety of colors. Where do all these colors come from?

Well, to begin with, as most of us know, the green color of leaves is due to chlorophyll. Chlorophyll is the complete food factory that is found in each leaf. Two-thirds of the color of the leaves (their pigmentation) are due to this chlorophyll. There are other colors present in the leaf, too, but there is so much chlorophyll that we usually can't see them.

What are some of these other colors? A substance called "xanthophyll," which consists of carbon, hydrogen and oxygen, is yellow. It makes up about 23 per cent of the pigmentation of the leaf. Carotin, the substance which makes carrots the color they are, is also present in the leaf and makes up about 10 per cent of the pigment. Another pigment present is anthocyanin, which gives the sugar maple and the scarlet oak their bright red colors.

During the summer, we see none of these other pigments; we only see the green chlorophyll. When it becomes cold, the food that has been stored away in the leaf by the trees begins to flow out to the branches and trunks. Since no more food will be produced in the winter, the chlorophyll food factory closes down and the chlorophyll disintegrates. And as the chlorophyll disappears, the other pigments that have been present all the time become visible. The leaves take on all those beautiful colors which we enjoy seeing!

Before the leaves fall, a compact layer of cells is formed at the base of each leaf; then when the wind blows, the leaves are dislodged. On the twig there is a scar that marks the former position of each leaf.

Most evergreen trees do not shed all their leaves at the approach of winter, but lose them gradually through the year; thus they are always green.

HOW CAN YOU RECOGNIZE POISONOUS MUSHROOMS?

The best rule to follow about telling safe mushrooms from poisonous mushrooms is not to try! Despite what anyone may tell you, despite any "methods" you may know for telling them apart, you should never eat or even taste any mushroom that you find growing anywhere. The only safe mushrooms are those you buy in a food store!

There are a great many false ideas that people have about mushrooms. For example, some think that when poisonous mushrooms are cooked they will blacken a silver spoon if they are stirred with it. This "test" is wrong!

It is also untrue that certain mushrooms can harm you if you simply touch them. And there is no difference between a mushroom and a toadstool. They are simply two names for one thing!

Another false idea about mushrooms is that those with pink gills are safe to eat. This is based on the fact that the two best-known kinds which are safe to eat happen to have pink gills, and that the *Amanitas,* which are poisonous, have white gills. But the truth is that this difference between the two kinds can't always be detected. Besides, many safe mushrooms have gills that are not pink at all.

WHAT IS AN ACID?

Now and then, we read a newspaper story about someone being terribly burned by an acid. In fact, most of us think of acids as dangerous liquids which can burn the skin and eat holes in clothing.

This is only true of a very small number of acids. There are many acids in foods, and they are necessary for good health. Other acids are used to make drugs, paints, cosmetics, and industrial products.

There are many kinds of acids but they all may be divided into two classes, inorganic acids and organic acids. Here is a brief description of some of the more important acids in each group.

Sulphuric acid is an important industrial acid. It can cause severe damage to the eyes and serious burns on the skin. Hydrochloric acid is another very strong acid. It can be made from sulphuric acid and common table salt. It is used to make other chemicals and is very good for cleaning metals. The human body makes a small amount of weak hydrochloric acid, which helps in digestion.

Nitric acid is another powerful acid which can harm the skin and eyes. Boric acid, on the other hand, is a very weak acid. It occurs naturally in Italy. It is used to make ceramics, cements, pigments, and cosmetics. It is sometimes used as a germ-killer, but is not very good for this purpose. Carbonic acid comes from carbon dioxide gas, and there is some of it in the soda pop we drink. Arsenic acid is used to make insect-killing products.

Organic acids are not as strong as inorganic acids. Acetic acid is found in vinegar, and can be made by fermenting apple cider. When sugar ferments in milk, lactic acid is formed. It turns the milk sour, but it is also used in making cheese.

Amino acids are needed to keep the body in good health, and they come from protein foods. Oranges, lemons, and grapefruit contain ascorbic acid, which is the chemical name for Vitamin C. Liver, poultry, and beef contain nicotinic acid, which helps prevent skin diseases.

So you see that the story of acids is a long and complicated one. Some are dangerous to human beings, but useful in industry. Some are necessary for human life and are supplied by various foods. Some are made by the body itself to keep it functioning.

WHAT IS ASBESTOS?

Many people think asbestos is a modern invention, but it has actually been known and used for thousands of years! In ancient temples, it was used for torch wicks and to protect fires lit on the altars. The Romans used asbestos 2,000 years ago for winding sheets to preserve the ashes of the dead when bodies were cremated. There is even a legend that Charlemagne had an asbestos tablecloth. He laundered it by putting it in the fire to burn off stains.

Asbestos is a Greek word that means "inextinguishable" or "unquenchable." Today we apply it to a group of fibrous minerals which have the property of resisting fire. The minerals that make up asbestos differ widely in composition, and each has a different strength, flexibility, and usefulness. From the chemical point of view, asbestos usually consists of silicates of lime and magnesia and sometimes contains iron.

Because it is made up of fibers, asbestos is similar to cotton and wool, but asbestos has the added advantage of being heat- and fire-resistant. This makes it very valuable for many uses in industry, and science has not yet been able to find a substitute for it.

No other mineral we know can be spun into yarn or thread, woven into cloth, or made into sheets. Workers in plants who are exposed to risks of fire sometimes wear complete outfits made of asbestos, including helmets, gloves, suits, and boots. Asbestos can withstand temperatures of 2,000 to 3,000 degrees Fahrenheit, and there are some kinds of asbestos that can even resist temperatures as high as 5,000 degrees!

Asbestos is found in veins in certain types of rocks, and sometimes it's necessary to mine and treat as much as 50 tons of rock to produce one ton of asbestos fiber!

WHAT CAUSES THE TOWER OF PISA TO LEAN?

When something captures the imagination of the world, it is remembered by people far more than things that may be more important. Everybody knows that in the city of Pisa in Italy, there is a tower that "leans." Very few people know that this town has a great and glorious history.

Of course, the tower itself is quite a marvel, too. It is built entirely of white marble. The walls are 13 feet thick at its base. It has eight storeys and is 179 feet high, which in our country would be about the height of a 15-storey building.

There is a stairway built into the walls consisting of 300 steps, which leads to the top. And by the way, those people who climb these stairs to the top get a magnificent view of the city and of the sea, which is six miles away.

At the top, the tower is 16½ feet out of the perpendicular. In other words, it "leans" over by 16½ feet. If you were to stand at the top and drop a stone to the ground, it would hit 16½ feet away from the wall at the bottom of the tower!

What makes it lean? Nobody really knows the answer. Of course, it wasn't supposed to lean when it was built; it was supposed to stand straight. It was intended as a bell-tower for the cathedral which is nearby and was begun in 1174 and finished in 1350.

The foundations of the tower were laid in sand, and this may explain why it leans. But it didn't suddenly begin to lean—this began to happen when only three of its storeys, or "galleries," had been built. So the plans were changed slightly and construction went right on! In the last hundred years, the tower has leaned another foot. According to some engineers, it should be called "the falling tower," because they believe that it will eventually topple over.

Did you know that Galileo, who was born in Pisa, is said to have performed some of his experiments concerning the speed of falling bodies at this tower?

DO THE NORTHERN LIGHTS APPEAR IN THE SOUTH?

The northern lights, or the aurora borealis, is one of nature's most dazzling spectacles.

When it appears, there is often a crackling sound coming from the sky. A huge, luminous arc lights up the night, and this arc is constantly in motion. Sometimes, the brilliant rays of light spread upward in the shape of a fan. At other times, they flash here and there like giant searchlights, or move up and down so suddenly that they have been called "the merry dancers."

Farther north, the aurora frequently looks like vast, fiery draperies which hang from the sky and sway to and fro while flames of red, orange, green, and blue play up and down the moving folds.

According to scientific measurements, this discharge of light takes place from 50 to 100 miles above the earth. But it doesn't reach its greatest brilliance at the North Pole. It is seen at its best around the Hudson Bay region in Canada, in northern Scotland, and in southern Norway and Sweden. It may sometimes be seen even in the United States as it flashes across the northern sky.

We call this "the northern lights," or "aurora borealis." But such lights occur in the Southern Hemisphere, too! They are known as "the aurora australis." In fact, sometimes both lights are called "aurora polaris."

Science is still not certain regarding exactly what these lights are and what causes them. But it is believed that the rays are due to discharges of electricity in the rare upper atmosphere.

The displays seem to center about the earth's magnetic poles, and electrical and magnetic disturbances often occur when the lights are especially brilliant. They also seem to be related to sunspots in some unknown way.

If nearly all the air is pumped out of a glass tube, and a current of electricity is then passed through the rarefied gases, there will be a display of lights inside the tube. The aurora displays seen high above the earth may be caused by the same phenomenon, electrical discharges from the sun passing through rarefied gases.

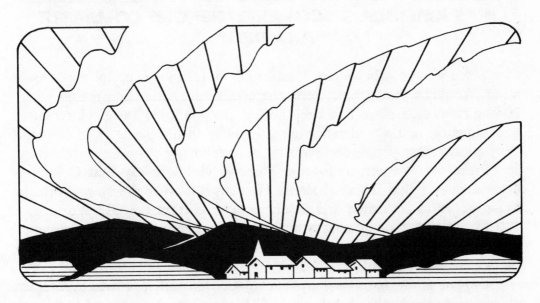

CHAPTER 2
HOW THINGS BEGAN

WAS AMERICA DISCOVERED BEFORE COLUMBUS ARRIVED?

When we say "discovered," we usually have a very special meaning in mind. We mean that people from one civilization came to a region where no one from their place had been before. As you know, an explorer often finds a people and a civilization already living in the place he "discovers." Why not say these people discovered it before him?

From our Western-civilization point of view, we say that Columbus discovered America. This is because after his discovery the New World he found began to be visited and finally populated from the Old World. But 500 years before Columbus was born, the Norsemen did a bit of "discovering," too. They sailed west to discover Iceland, then Greenland, and later the American mainland.

Did you know that the Chinese tell of an even earlier voyage by Chinese sailors to discover what has become California? And people of the South Sea Islands still sing of the great men of their distant past who sailed to South America long before the white man reached either South America or the South Sea Islands.

For all we know, there may have been many ages of exploration thousands of years ago. There were certainly ages of exploration before the time of Columbus. Perhaps we might say that neither Columbus, nor the Norsemen before him, "discovered" America. Weren't the Indians already living here for many centuries before the white man arrived?

And who can say that they didn't set out on a voyage of discovery? It is believed that they came from Asia, though we don't know when or how they made the trip. Probably they reached America over a period of centuries and by different routes. They also probably sent their scouts ahead to seek out routes by land or sea. These scouts were their explorers, and perhaps it was really they who discovered America!

WHAT IS EVOLUTION?

In trying to explain the existence of the complicated body structures we see in living things around us, a theory of evolution has been developed. While most scientists accept this theory, many people do not. They feel it goes against what is written in the Bible.

This theory is that all the plants and animals in the world today have developed in a natural way from earlier forms that were simpler. These earlier forms developed from still simpler ancestors, and so on back through millions of years to the very beginning when life was in its simplest form, merely a tiny mass of jellylike protoplasm.

According to this theory, man, too, developed from some simpler form, just as the modern one-hoofed horse is the descendant of a small five-toed ancestor.

In trying to prove that evolution did take place, scientists depend on three chief "signs." One of these is the study of fossil remains of animals and plants of past ages. Some of these fossils seem to trace the steps of evolution at work. Fossil remains of primitive men have been found that go back to a time 1,000,000 years ago. Fossils of certain crablike animals go back nearly 500,000,000 years. These fossils show that fish developed in the waters of the earth before amphibians, amphibians before reptiles, reptiles before birds, and so on. Scientists believe this proves life has progressed from one form to another.

Another "sign" of evolution comes from the study of embryology, the growth of a new living thing from an egg. In studying the development of the chick from the hen's egg, there is a time when this embryo is like a fish, later it's like an amphibian, then it passes through the reptile stage, and finally develops into its bird form. The unborn young of all animals go through the same kind of process, repeating their history of development.

The third "sign" is the bodies of living animals. For example, the bone and muscle structure in the paddles of a turtle, the wings of a bird, the flippers of a whale, the front legs of a horse, and the arms of a man are similar in structure. And man has many organs in his body which seem of no use. They are thought to be relics handed down from his earlier ancestors. These are some of the "signs" that led to a theory of evolution.

HOW LONG HAVE PEOPLE BEEN USING LAST NAMES?

"Hey, Shorty!" "Hi, Skinny." "There's Fatso." "Here comes Blondie." Sound familiar to you? It's a perfectly natural way to call people—give them a name that describes them in some way.

And you know, that's exactly the way first names were given originally! A girl born during a famine might be called Una (Celtic for "famine"), a golden haired blonde might be called Blanche (French for "white"). A boy might be called David because it means "beloved."

A first name was all anybody had for thousands of years. Then, about the time the Normans conquered England in 1066, last names, or surnames, were added to identify people better. The first name wasn't enough to set one person apart from another. For example, there might be two Davids in town, and one of them was quite lazy. So people began to call this one "David, who is also lazy," or "David do little." And this became David Doolittle.

The last names were originally called "ekenames." The word "eke" meant "also." And by the way, we get our word "nickname" from this word!

Once people got into the habit of giving a person two names, they thought of many ways of creating this second name. For example, one way was to mention the father's name. If John had a father called William, he might be called John Williamson, or John Williams, or John Wilson (Will's son), or John Wills.

Another good way to identify people with second names was to mention the place where they lived or came from. A person who lived near the woods might be called Wood, or if he lived near the village green he might be called John Green.

And then, of course, the work that a person did was a good way to identify him. So we have last names like Smith, Taylor, and Wright. ("Wright" means someone who does mechanical work.)

60

The nearest thing to last names in ancient times existed among the Romans. A second name was sometimes added to indicate the family or clan to which a child belonged. Later, they even added a third name, which was a kind of descriptive nickname.

HOW DID THE CUSTOM OF KISSING START?

We know the kiss as a form of expressing affection. But long before it became this, it was the custom in many parts of the world to use the kiss as an expression of homage.

In many African tribes the natives kiss the ground over which a chief has walked. Kissing the hand and foot has been a mark of respect and homage from the earliest times. The early Romans kissed the mouth or eyes as a form of dignified greeting. One Roman emperor allowed his important nobles to kiss his lips, but the less important ones had to his kiss his hands, and the least important ones were only allowed to kiss his feet!

It is quite probable that the kiss as a form of affection can be traced back to primitive times when a mother would fondle her child, just as a mother does today. It only remained for society to accept this as a custom for expressing affection between adults.

We have evidence that this was already the case by the time of the sixth century, but we can only assume it was practiced long before that. The first country where the kiss became accepted in courtship and love was in France. When dancing became popular, almost every dance figure ended with a kiss.

From France the kiss spread rapidly all over Europe. Russia, which loved to copy the customs of France, adopted the kiss and it spread there through all the upper classes. A kiss from the Tsar became one of the highest form of recognition from the Crown.

In time, the kiss became a part of courtship. As marriage customs developed, the kiss became a part of the wedding ceremony. Today, of course, we regard the kiss an an expression of love and tenderness. But there are still many places in the world where the kiss is part of formal ceremonies and is intended to convey respect and homage.

WHY DO WE HAVE DAYLIGHT SAVING TIME?

Let's say a person gets up at 7:00 in the morning and goes to bed at 11:00 at night. He comes home from work about 6:30, and by the time he's finished with dinner it's after 8:00. He steps outside in the summer to relax—but it's already getting dark! Not much time to enjoy the summer day.

Now suppose you set the clock ahead one hour. This person still does everything at the same hour—but this time, when he steps out at 8:00 o'clock there's still plenty of light to enjoy. An hour of daylight has been "saved" for him!

Daylight saving time doesn't, of course, add any hours to a day. That's impossible. All it does is increase the number of useful hours of daylight during the seasons when the sun rises early.

Daylight saving is most popular in cities. It permits the closing of offices, shops, and factories at the end of the working day while the sun is still high. Farmers, who do their work by sun time, usually do not observe daylight saving time. They cannot work in the field before the morning dew has dried or after it appears in the evening.

Did you know who first thought of daylight saving time? It was Benjamin Franklin! When he was living in France in the 18th century, he suggested the idea to the people in Paris. But it was not adopted then.

Daylight saving laws were first passed during World War I. At this time, fuel for generating electricity was scarce, and so it was necessary to save on artificial light. With daylight saving, the bedtime of many people comes soon after it gets dark, while without it, if they stay up until the same hour they may have to use artificial light.

The first country to adopt daylight saving time was Germany in 1915. Then England used it in 1916, and the United States adopted it in 1918.

During World War II, the United States put it in force again on a national basis, and this ended at the close of the war.

HOW DID THE CALENDAR BEGIN?

When men first began to plant seeds and harvest crops, they noticed that the time for planting came at a regular time each year. Then they tried to count how many days came between one planting time and the next. This was man's first attempt to find out how long a year was!

The ancient Egyptians were the first to measure a year with any exactness. They knew that the best time to plant was right after the Nile River overflowed each year. Their priests noticed that between each overflowing the moon rose 12 times. So they counted 12 *moonths* or months, and figured out when the Nile would rise again.

But it still wasn't exact enough. At last the Egyptian priests noticed that each year, about the time of the flood, a certain bright star would rise just before the sun rose. They counted the days that passed before this happened again and found that it added up to 365 days. This was 6000 years ago, and before that no one had ever known that there were 365 days in a year! The Egyptians divided this year into 12 months of 30 days each, with 5 extra days at the end of the year. Thus they invented the first calendar.

Eventually, the calendar was based not on the moon (lunar calendar) but on the number of days (365¼) it takes the earth to go around the sun (solar calendar). The extra quarter of day began to cause more and more confusion. Finally, Julius Caesar decided to straighten it all out. He ordered that the year 46 B.C. should have 445 days to "catch up," and that every year from then on was to have 365 days, except every fourth year. This fourth year would have a leap year of 366 days to use up the fraction left over in each ordinary year.

But as time went on it was discovered that Easter and other holy days were not coming where they belonged in the seasons. Too many "extra" days had piled up. In the year 1582, Pope Gregory XIII decided to do something about it. He ordered that ten days should be dropped from the year 1582. And to keep the calendar accurate for all future time, he ordered that leap year should be skipped in the last year of every century unless that year could be divided by 400. Thus 1700, 1800, and 1900 were not leap years, but the year 2000 will be a leap year!

This system is called the Gregorian calendar and is now used all over the world for everyday purposes, though various religions still use their own calendar for religious purposes!

HOW DID THE DAYS OF THE WEEK GET THEIR NAMES?

There was a time in the early history of man when the days had no names! The reason was quite simple. Men had not invented the week.

In those days, the only division of times was the month, and there were too many days in the month for each of them to have a separate name. But when men began to build cities, they wanted to have a special day on which to trade, a market day. Sometimes these market days were fixed at every tenth day, sometimes every seventh or every fifth day. The Babylonians decided that it should be every seventh day. On this day they didn't work, but met for trade and religious festivals.

The Jews followed their example, but kept every seventh day for religious purposes. In this way the week came into existence. It was the space between market days. The Jews gave each of the seven days a name, but it was really a number after the Sabbath day (which was Saturday). For example, Wednesday was called the fourth day (four days after Saturday).

When the Egyptians adopted the seven-day week, they named the days after five planets, the sun, and the moon. The Romans used the Egyptian names for their days of the week: the day of the sun, of the moon, of the planet Mars, of Mercury, of Jupiter, of Venus, and of Saturn.

We get our names for the days not from the Romans but from the Anglo-Saxons, who called most of the days after their own gods, which were roughly the same as the gods of the Romans. The day of the sun became *Sunnandaeg,* or Sunday. The day of the moon was called *Monandaeg,* or Monday. The day of Mars became the day of Tiw, who was their god of war. This became *Tiwesdaeg,* or Tuesday. Instead of Mercury's name, that of the god Woden was given to Wednesday. The Roman day of Jupiter, the thunderer, became the day of the thunder god Thor, and this became Thursday. The next day was named for Frigg, the wife of their god Odin, and so we have Friday. The day of Saturn became *Saeternsdaeg,* a translation from the Roman, and then Saturday.

A day, by the way, used to be counted as the space between sunrise and sunset. The Romans counted it as from midnight to midnight, and most modern nations use this method.

WHY ARE EGGS AND RABBITS ASSOCIATED WITH EASTER?

Easter is the most joyous of Christian holidays. It is celebrated in commemoration of the Resurrection of Jesus Christ.

The exact day on which Easter falls may vary from year to year, but it always comes, of course, in the spring of the year. Thus, as Christianity spread, the celebration of Easter included many customs that were linked with the celebration of spring's arrival. This explains why many Easter customs go back to traditions that existed before Christianity itself.

Both Easter and the coming of spring are symbols of new life. The ancient Egyptians and Persians celebrated their spring festivals by coloring and eating eggs. This is because they considered the egg a symbol of fertility and new life. The Christians adopted the egg as symbolic of new life, the symbol of the Resurrection.

There is another reason why we observe the practice of eating eggs on Easter Sunday and of giving them as gifts to friends or children. In the early days of the Church, eggs were forbidden food during Lent. With the ending of Lent, people were so glad to see and eat eggs again that they made it a tradition to eat them on Easter Sunday.

The Easter hare also was part of the spring celebrations long before Christianity. In the legends of ancient Egypt, the hare is associated with the moon. The hare is linked with the night because it comes out only then to feed. By being associated with the moon, the hare became a symbol of a new period of life. Thus the hare stood for the renewal of life and for fertility. The early Christians therefore took it over and linked it with Easter, the holiday that symbolizes new life!

By the way, the tradition of wearing new clothes on Easter Sunday is also symbolic of casting off the old and the beginning of the new!

65

HOW DID HALLOWEEN ORIGINATE?

The name Halloween means "hallowed, or holy, evening." Yet, for some reason this holiday has become one of the most popular and best liked holidays of the entire year and is celebrated with great enthusiasm in many countries.

Halloween, which takes place on October 31st, is really a festival to celebrate autumn, just as May Day is a festival to celebrate spring. The ancient Druids (the Druids were the religious priests in ancient Gaul, Britain, and Ireland) had a great festival to celebrate autumn which began at midnight on October 31st and lasted through the next day, November 1st.

They believed that on this night their great god of death, called Saman, called together all the wicked souls who had died during the year and whose punishment had been to take up life in the bodies of animals. Of course, the very idea of such a gathering was enough to frighten the simple-minded people of that time. So they lit huge bonfires and kept a sharp watch for these evil spirits. This is actually where the idea that witches and ghosts are about on Halloween began. And there are still people in certain isolated parts of Europe who believe this to be true!

The Romans also had a holiday about the 1st of November which was in honour of their goddess Pomona. Nuts and apples were roasted before great bonfires. Our own Halloween seems to be a combination of the Roman and Druid festivals.

Originally, the Halloween festival was quite simple and was celebrated mostly in church. But all over Europe, people looked upon this occasion as an opportunity to have fun and excitement, to tell spooky tales, and to scare each other. So instead of being devoted to the celebration of autumn, it became a holiday devoted to the supernatural, to witches, and to ghosts.

Here are some of the curious customs which sprang up in connection with Halloween: Young girls who "ducked" for apples on this night could see their future husbands if they slept with the apple under their pillow. Stealing gates, furniture, signs, and so on, is done to make people think they were stolen by the evil spirits. And, of course, no one goes near a cemetery on Halloween because spirits rise up on that night! Today we use these superstitions as a way of having fun on Halloween.

WHO FIRST THOUGHT OF THE ALPHABET?

The letters of an alphabet are really sound signs. Those of the English alphabet are based on the Roman alphabet, which is about 2,500 years old. The capital letters are almost exactly like those used in Roman inscriptions of the third century B.C.

Before alphabets were invented men used pictures to record events or communicate ideas. A picture of several antelopes might mean "Here are good hunting grounds," so this was really a form of writing. Such "picture writing" was highly developed by the ancient Babylonians, Egyptians, and Chinese.

In time, picture writing underwent a change. The picture, instead of just standing for the object that was drawn, came to represent an idea connected with the object drawn. For example, the picture of a foot might indicate the verb "to walk." This stage of writing is called "ideographic," or "idea writing."

The trouble with this kind of writing was that the messages might be interpreted by different people in different ways. So little by little this method was changed. The symbols came to represent combinations of sounds. For example, if the word for "arm" were "id," the picture of an arm would stand for the sound of "id." So the picture of an arm was used every time they wanted to convey the sound "id." This stage of writing might be called "syllabic writing."

The Babylonians and Chinese and the Egyptians never passed beyond this stage of writing. The Egyptians did make up a kind of alphabet by including among their pictures 24 signs which stood for separate letters or words of one consonant each. But they didn't realize the value of their invention.

About 3,500 years ago, people living near the eastern shore of the Mediterranean made the great step leading to our alphabet. They realized that the same sign could be used for the same sound in all cases, so they used a limited number of signs in this manner and these signs made up an alphabet.

A development of their alphabet was used by the Hebrews and later the Phoenicians. The Phoenicians carried their alphabet to the Greeks. The Romans adopted the Greek alphabet with certain changes and additions and handed it down to the people of Western Europe in the Latin alphabet. From this came the alphabet we use today.

WHY DON'T WE ALL SPEAK THE SAME LANGUAGE?

At one time, at the beginning of history, what there was of mankind then probably spoke one language. As time went on, this parent language, or perhaps there were several parent languages, spread and changed.

At first, the parent languages were spoken by small numbers of persons or by scattered small groups. Gradually, some groups increased in numbers and there wasn't enough food for all of them. So some people would form a band to move to a new location.

When these people arrived at a new location and settled down, they would speak almost the same as the people from whom they had parted. Gradually, though, new pronunciations would creep in. The people would begin to say things a little differently and there would be changes in the sounds of words.

Some words that were needed in the old home were no longer needed in the new place and would be dropped. New experiences would require new words to describe them. Ways of making sentences would change. And suppose the people had settled in a place where others were already living? The two languages would blend, and thus both of the old languages would change.

At first, when the speech of the new people had changed only slightly from the original language, it would be called "a dialect." After a longer time, when there were many changes in words, sounds, and grammar, it would be considered a new language.

In just these ways, Spanish, French, and Portuguese developed from Latin; and English, Norwegian, Swedish, Danish, and Dutch grew from an early form of the German language.

The ancestor language, together with all the languages which developed from it, is called "a family" of languages.

HOW DID THE ENGLISH LANGUAGE BEGIN?

Practically all languages spoken on earth today can be traced by scholars back to some common source, that is, an ancestor language which has many descendants. The ancestor language—together with all the languages which have developed from it—is called a "family" of languages.

English is considered a member of the Indo-European family of languages. Other languages belonging to the same family are French, Italian, German, Norwegian, and Greek.

In this Indo-European family of languages there are various branches and English is a member of the "West Teutonic" branch. Actually, English dates from about the middle of the fifth century, when invaders from across the North Sea conquered the native Celts and settled on the island now known as England.

For the sake of convenience, the history of the English language is divided into three great periods: the old English (or Anglo-Saxon), from about 400 to 1100; Middle English, from 1100 to 1500; and Modern English, from 1500 to the present day.

So the original language spoken in English was Celtic. But the Anglo-Saxons (the Angles, the Jutes, and the Saxons) conquered the island so thoroughly that very few Celtic words were kept in the new language.

The Anglo-Saxons themselves spoke several dialects. Later on, the Norsemen invaded England and they introduced a Scandinavian element into the language. This influence, which was a Germanic language, became a part of the language.

In 1066, William the Conqueror brought over still another influence to the language. He made Norman French the language of his Court. At first, this "Norman" language was spoken only by the upper classes. But gradually its influence spread and a language quite different from the Anglo-Saxon developed. This language became the chief source of modern English.

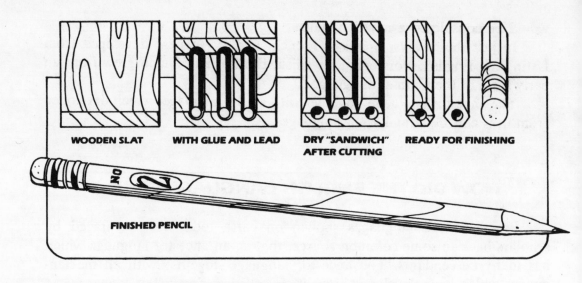

WOODEN SLAT   WITH GLUE AND LEAD   DRY "SANDWICH" AFTER CUTTING   READY FOR FINISHING

FINISHED PENCIL

WHO INVENTED THE PENCIL?

There is a Latin word, *penicillus,* which means "little tail." This word was used to indicate a fine brush, and the word "pencil" originally meant a small, fine pointed brush.

Today, of course, a pencil means something altogether different. Pencils as we know them are less than 200 years old. About 500 years ago, graphite was discovered in a mine in Cumberland, England, and it is believed that some sort of crude pencils may have been made then.

In Nuremberg, Germany, the famous Faber family established its business in 1760 and used pulverized graphite to make a kind of pencil, but they were not very successful. Finally in 1795, a man called N. J. Conte produced pencils made of graphite which had been ground with certain clays, pressed into sticks, and fired in a kiln. This method is the basis for the manufacture of all modern pencils.

As you might have guessed by now, a "lead" pencil doesn't contain lead but a mineral substance called graphite. Graphite, like lead, leaves a mark when drawn across paper. Because of this it is called "black lead," and that's where we get the name "lead pencil."

In manufacturing pencils, dried ground graphite is mixed with clay and water. The more clay, the harder the pencil will be; the more graphite, the softer the pencil. After the mixture reaches a doughy consistency, it passes through a forming press and comes out as a thin, sleek rope. This is straightened out, cut into lengths, dried, and put into huge ovens to bake.

Meanwhile, the pencil case has been prepared. The wood, either red cedar or pine, is shaped in halves and grooved to hold the lead. After the finished leads are inserted in the grooves, the halves of the pencil are glued together. A saw cuts the slats into individual pencils, and a shaping machine gives the surface a smooth finish.

Today, more than 350 different kinds of pencils are made, each for a special use. You can buy black lead pencils in 19 degrees of hardness and intensity, or get them in 72 different colors! There are pencils that write on glass, cloth, cellophane, plastics, and movie film. There are even pencils, used by engineers and in outdoor construction work, that leave a mark that won't fade after years of exposure to any weather!

WHO DISCOVERED HOW TO MAKE PAPER?

Take a piece of paper and tear it in both directions. You will notice two things. It tore more easily in one direction than in the other, and hairlike fibers stick out from the edges of the tear.

The first shows that the paper was made by machine; otherwise it would tear the same way in all directions. The second shows that paper is a mat of tiny fibers, felted together. These fibers are the small particles of cellulose that help form the framework of plants.

Man had created a writing material before he invented paper. The ancient Egyptians, about 4000 years ago, took the stems of the papyrus plant and peeled them apart and flattened them. Then they laid them crosswise and pressed them down to stick them together. When dry, this made a sheet of papyrus and could be written on.

But it wasn't paper. This was invented in China about the year 105, by a man called Ts'ai Lun. He found a way to make paper from the stringy inner bark of the mulberry tree.

The Chinese pounded the bark in water to separate the fibers, then poured the soup mixture onto a tray with a bottom of thin bamboo strips. The water drained away and the soft mat was laid on a smooth surface to dry. Bamboo and old rags were also used. Later on, somebody thought how to improve the paper by brushing starch on it.

Chinese traders traveled far to the west and came to the city of Samarkand in Russia. There they met Arabs who learned their secret and took it to Spain. From there the art of papermaking spread over Europe and to England.

In time, all kinds of improved methods and machines for making paper were discovered. One of the most important, for example, was a machine developed in France in 1798 that could make a continuous sheet or web of paper.

WHEN WERE BOOKS FIRST MADE?

Books as we know them didn't appear until the Middle Ages. The nearest thing to them were rolls of papyrus. Sheets of papyrus were glued together to form long rolls. The Romans called them *volumen,* from which we get our word "volume."

About the middle of the fifth century, parchment and vellum had replaced papyrus. Parchment is made from the skins of sheep and goats and vellum is made from calfskin. Sheets of this material, with writing on one side, were cut to uniform size and bound together at one side with leather tongs. So they were "books" in a way.

But it was in the Middle Ages that books were first made that resemble our printed books of today. Four pieces of vellum were folded in such a way so that each piece formed two leaves. These pieces were then placed inside one another so that there was a group of eight leaves, which is called "a section."

These sections were sent to a scribe to write the book. He took them apart and wrote a single page at a time. Vellum was thick enough so there could be writing on both sides.

The next step was to send the finished sections that made up the book to the binder. He sewed the sections through the back fold with cords. Wooden covers were made and the ends were laced through holes in the boards to bind together the sections and the covers. Then a large piece of leather was glued over the back of the sections and the wooden sides. Other steps were taken to decorate and preserve these books, but these were the first books that resemble those we have today.

Most of the medieval books were Bibles, sermons, and other religious books. Next came books of law, medicine, natural history, and later came a few chronicles and romances. Most books of the Middle Ages are in Latin.

WHO INVENTED CARTOONS?

You know that between the way something started years ago, and the way it is today, there may be quite a difference! There is no better example of this than the cartoon.

The word "cartoon" was originally used by painters during the period of the Italian Renaissance. And in fact, it is still used today by artists. What they are referring to, however, is the first sketch in actual size of any work of art which covers a large area, such as a mural, a tapestry, or a stained-glass window.

When newspapers and magazines began to use drawings to illustrate news and editorial opinion and to provide amusement, these drawings also came to be called "cartoons"!

In the days before newspapers, famous caricaturists like Hogarth, Goya, Daumier, and Rowlandson made series of drawings on a single theme. These drawings often pictured the adventures of one character. They were the ancestors of present-day cartoons and comic strips.

In the 19th and early 20th century there were a number of magazines which specialized in cartoons—*Charivari* in Paris, *Punch* in London, and *Life* and *Judge* in the United States. When most newspapers and magazines in the United States began to include cartoons as regular features, the humorous magazines lost their appeal and many of them stopped appearing.

The first comic strips appeared in the early 1900's. Richard Outcault, the artist who created *Buster Brown,* published this comic strip in 1902. It was so popular that children all over the country wanted to dress in "Buster Brown" clothes.

Another of the early comic strips was *Bringing Up Father*. This came out in 1912. It has since been translated into 27 different languages, and published in 71 countries!

HOW DID OUR SYSTEM OF COUNTING BEGIN?

It seems very natural to you that if you have two pennies and you add two pennies to them, you have four pennies. But did you know it may have taken man millions of years to be able to think this way? In fact, one of the most difficult things to teach children is the concept of numbers.

In ancient times, when a man wanted to tell how many animals he owned, he had no system of numbers to use. What he did was put a stone or pebble into a bag for each animal. The more animals, the more stones he had. Which may explain why our word "calculate" comes from the Latin word *calculus* which means "stone"!

Later on, man used tally marks to count. He would just scratch a line or tally mark for each object he wanted to count, but he had no word to tell the number.

The next step in the development of the number system was probably the use of fingers. And again we have a word that goes back to this. The word "digit" comes from the Latin word *digitus,* which means "finger"! And since we have 10 fingers, this led to the general use of "10" in systems of numbers.

But in ancient times there was no single number system used all over the world. Some number systems were based on 12, others were based on 60, others on 20, and still others on 2, 5, and 8. The system invented by the Romans about 2,000 years ago was widely used by the people of Europe until about the 16th century. In fact, we still use it on clocks and to show chapters in books. But it was a very complicated system.

The number system we use today was invented by the Hindus in India thousands of years ago and was brought to Europe about the year 900 by Arab traders. In this system all numbers are written with the nine digits 1, 2, 3, 4, 5, 6, 7, 8, 9 to show how many, and the zero. It is a decimal system, that is, it is built on the base 10.

WHAT MAKES MONEY VALUABLE?

The idea of having such a thing as money is one of the most fascinating ever developed by man. But many people don't know where this idea came from, or why money is valuable.

Thousands of years ago, money was not used. Instead, man had the "barter" system. This meant that if a man wanted something he didn't happen to make or raise himself, he had to find someone who had this article. Then he had to offer him something in exchange. And if the man didn't like what he offered in exchange, he couldn't get his article!

In time, certain things came to be used as money because practically everyone would take these things in exchange. For example, cows, tobacco,

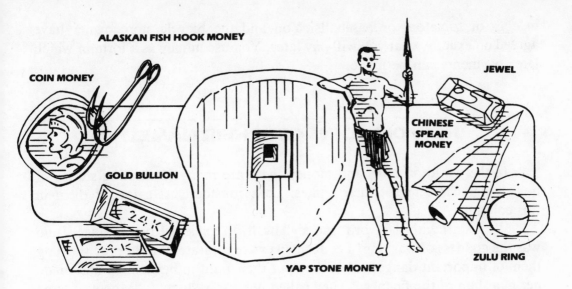

COIN MONEY

ALASKAN FISH HOOK MONEY

JEWEL

CHINESE SPEAR MONEY

GOLD BULLION

YAP STONE MONEY

ZULU RING

grains, skins, salt, and beads were all used as money among people who were always ready to accept them.

Eventually, all these varieties of money were replaced by pieces of metal, especially gold and silver. Later on, coins were made of a certain purity and weight, and these represented certain amounts of various objects. So many coins represented a cow, or 50 pounds of tobacco, and so on.

Today, of course, we have bills and coins issued by the Government, and everybody accepts and uses this money. What makes the money valuable, what use does it have for us? There are four chief things that money does for you.

First, it makes possible exchange and trade. Suppose you want a bicycle. You're willing to work for it by mowing lawns. But the person for whom you mow the lawn has no bicycles. He pays you with money and you take this to the bicycle shop and buy your bicycle. Money made it possible to exchange your work for something you wanted.

Second, money is a "yardstick of value." This means money may be used to measure and compare the values of various things. You're willing to mow the lawn for an hour for 50 cents. A bicycle costs $25. You now have an idea of the value of a bicycle in terms of your work.

Third, money is a "storehouse of value." You can't store up your crop of tomatoes, because they're perishable. But if you sell them you can store up the money for future use.

Fourth, money serves as a "standard for future payments." You pay $5 down on the bicycle and promise to pay the rest later. You will not pay in eggs or tomatoes or baseballs. You and the bicycle store owner have agreed on exactly what you will pay later. You use money as a form in which later payments can be made.

HOW DID COINS GET THEIR NAMES?

In the world of coins and money there are many fascinating stories of how things came to get their names. Let's consider just a few of them in this column.

We'll start with the word "money" itself. In ancient Roman times, Juno was the goddess of warning. The Romans were so grateful to her for warning them of important dangers, that they put their mint in her temple and made her guardian of the finances. They called her Juno Moneta. "Moneta" came from the Latin word *moneo,* meaning "to warn." Our word "money" is derived from this.

The word "coin" comes from the Latin *cuneus,* which means "wedge." This is because the dies that made pieces of money looked like wedges.

Our "dollar" goes back to the days when money was being coined in Bohemia, where there were silver mines. The mint was located in a place called Joachimsthal, so the coins were called *Joachimsthaler.* In time this became *thaler* and finally "dollar."

Our "dime" comes originally from the Latin word *decimus,* which means "tenth." The "cent" comes directly from the French word *cent,* which means "one hundred," and the Latin *centum.* The idea was that one hundred cents make a dollar.

Our "nickel" is so called because it was made of that metal. The coins of other countries also have interesting histories regarding their names. The English "pound" comes from the Latin *pondo,* which means "pound" as a weight. Originally the full expression was *libra pondo,* or "a pound by weight." By the way, that's where we get our abbreviation for a pound— lb. The Spanish *peso* and Italian *lira* also refer to certain weights.

The French *franc* came from the Latin words *Francorum Rex,* for "King of the Franks," which appeared on their first coins. Peru has a coin called the *sol.* This is the Spanish name for the sun. As you know, the Incas of Peru worshipped the sun long ago!

The words crown, sovereign, *krone, kroon, krona,* and *corona,* all used as names of coins in different countries, show that some crown authority first gave permission to make them. In Panama, the *balboa* is named in honor of the great explorer, and Venezuela has the *bolivar* after its national hero.

HOW DID WE GET OUR SYSTEM OF MEASUREMENT?

Every country in the world has some way of measuring weight, volume, and quantity. This is necessary in order to carry on trade or any form of exchange. But the system of weight and measurement in one country is not always the same as that in another.

Most of the measures we use in the United States came from England and are called "the English system of measures." England and the United States are practically the only countries that use this system today.

The units of measurement in this system have come down to us from ancient times. Most of them grew out of simple, practical ways of measuring. For instance, when people in ancient Rome wanted to measure length, they used the length of a man's foot as a standard. The width of a finger, or the length of the index finger to the first joint, was the origin of the inch!

To measure a yard, people used to take the length of a man's arm. In Rome the length of a thousand paces (a pace was a double step) was used for long distances and became our mile. Of course, this was not a very exact way of measuring. In fact, at one time in the Roman Empire there were 200 different lengths for the foot! And in our own country in Colonial times, the units of measurement were different from colony to colony.

In modern times, it is very important that units of measurement be the same everywhere. So Congress was given the right to fix the standards of weights and measures, and in Washington, D. C., the Bureau of Standards keeps the standard units of measure. For instance, there is a platinum bar, very carefully guarded, which is the standard for measuring length. The correctness of all other measuring units can be checked by comparing them with the standard units in Washington.

If a single international system of weights and measures were to be adopted, it would probably be the metric system. This was worked out in France in 1789, and is used by most countries today. The metric system is based on the meter, which is 39.37 inches. The metric system is based on 10, so each unit of length is 10 times as large as the next smaller unit.

WHEN WERE THE FIRST POLICE ORGANIZED?

The "cop" you see in your town is a rather unique individual in this world! He belongs to a "local" police force. In almost all other countries of the world, the police force is a national organization and is part of the national government. But the United States has the most decentralized (independent) police system in the world. There are town police, city police, county police, and state police!

Police date back to the very earliest history of man. The leader or ruler of a tribe or clan in primitive times depended upon his warriors to keep peace among the people and enforce rules of conduct. The pharaohs of ancient Egypt did the same thing—used their soldiers as police.

About the time of the birth of Christ, Caesar Augustus formed a special police force for the city of Rome, and this lasted for about 350 years. But the job of this police force was still to carry out the imperial orders.

Sometime between the years A.D. 700 and 800, a new idea arose regarding a police force. Instead of carrying out the king's orders against the people, it was felt a police force should enforce the law and protect the people! It was this idea which influenced the development of the police force in England, and later in the United States.

The English developed a system of "watch" and "ward." The watch was a night guard and the ward a day guard for the local area. The colonists brought this system to the United States. They had the night watch under constables, with all able-bodied men over 16 serving without pay. Most cities and towns used this system well into the 1800's.

The use of daytime police started in Boston in 1838 with a force of six men. Then two states passed laws—New York in 1845 and Pennsylvania in 1856—that became the basis for setting up the modern police forces in the United States. The early policemen often didn't wear uniforms or badges! But finally, in 1856, New York City police adopted full police uniforms, and soon other cities followed this idea.

WHAT IS THE F.B.I.?

The F.B.I. is one of the best-known and most "glamorous" departments of the Federal Government. Its full name is the Federal Bureau of Investigation, and it was founded in 1908 as a bureau within the United States Department of Justice.

The F.B.I. has authority to investigate violations of Federal laws and matters in which the United States is, or may be, a party in interest. In 1924, the Identification Division of the F.B.I. was created. It started with a library of 810,188 fingerprint records. Today, the F.B.I. has the fingerprint cards of more than 100,000,000 people!

The headquarters of the F.B.I. are in Washington, D.C. Along with its own responsibilities, the F.B.I. is a service organization for local law enforcement agencies. Its facilities are available for the assistance of municipal, county, and state police departments.

The Identification Division serves as the central clearing house for fingerprints and criminal data. When a person is arrested and his fingerprints are sent to the F.B.I., it can be determined in less than five minutes whether he has a previous criminal record. A copy of this record is sent to the interested law enforcement agency within 36 hours after the card is received in Washington.

The facilities of the F.B.I. laboratory are likewise available to all law enforcement agencies. Provided with the most modern equipment, its scientists are daily making examinations of documents, blood, hair, soil, and other types of matter. When evidence in a local case has been examined, F.B.I. experts will testify concerning their findings in the state court.

In June, 1939, the President of the United States selected the F.B.I. as the agency responsible for the investigation of espionage, sabotage, and other national defense matters.

HOW DID FINGERPRINTING START?

Man has known for a long time that the ridges of his fingertips formed certain patterns. In fact, the Chinese have used fingerprints for hundreds of years in various forms and for various purposes.

But the value of fingerprints in detecting criminals was realized by science only in quite recent years. The first man to suggest that fingerprints be used to identify criminals was Dr. Henry Faulds of England in 1880. In 1892, Sir Francis Galton, a noted English scientist, scientifically established the fact that no two fingerprints were alike. He was the first one to set up a collection of fingerprint records.

The British Government became interested in his theories and ordered a commission to study the idea of using a fingerprint system in the identification of criminals. One of the members of this commission, Sir Edward Henry, later became head of Scotland Yard.

Sir Henry devised a system of classifying and filing fingerprints. You can understand that without such a system it would take very long to match up two sets of fingerprints, and in crime detection, speed is often very important.

According to Sir Henry's system, all finger impressions are divided into the following types of patterns: loops, central pocket loops, double loops, arches, tented arches, whorls, and accidentals. By counting the ridges between the fixed points in the pattern, it is possible to classify each of the 10 fingers into a definite group. The 10 fingers are then considered as a unit to obtain the complete classification. With this system, fingerprints are filed in a sequence, without reference to name, description, or crime speciality of the individual. An office can contain millions of prints, and yet identification can be established in a few minutes!

The FBI file of more than 100,000,000 fingerprint cards include fingerprints from many persons who want some means of identification in case of sickness. It also includes fingerprints of those in the Armed Services and Government employees.

Today, all aliens have to be fingerprinted, and many industries vital to the national defense require fingerprinting of their employees.

HOW DID MEDICINE BEGIN?

Medicine is the treating of disease. Now, you yourself know that there are many ways to treat disease. If someone in your family gets sick, you could call a doctor and he would apply all his knowledge and skill. He would treat the disease scientifically. But you might instead depend on some "remedy" your grandmother knew, or try to cure the person by saying some "magic" words. You would then be treating the disease unscientifically.

The history of medicine includes the prescientific stage, before it was a science, and the time when it became a science. The medicine of primitive peoples had all kinds of strange explanations of disease. And in treating disease, primitive medicine depended on magic or on anything that seemed to work. But surprisingly enough, medicine among primitive people included application of heat and cold, bloodletting, massage, the use of herbs.

Ancient Egyptian medicine, which was the best-known medicine before the scientific, depended chiefly on magic. It used all kinds of ointments and potions. Among the "drugs" it used were honey, salt, cedar oil, the brain, liver, heart, and blood of various animals. Sometimes this prescientific medicine seemed to work, sometimes it didn't.

But it wasn't until the time of the Greeks that scientific medicine began. More than two thousand years ago, a man called Hippocrates put together a collection of medical books, "The Hippocratic Collection." It was the beginning of scientific medicine because it depended on close observation of patients for learning about diseases.

In these books there were records of actual cases and what had happened to the patients. For the first time, instead of depending on some magic formula, treatment was given as the result of studying the patient and the disease and applying past experience. In this way modern medicine was born.

WHEN DID PEOPLE START CUTTING THEIR HAIR?

The hair is actually a development of the horn layer of the skin. Like our nails, it doesn't hurt us to cut it because these horn cells contain no nerves. Because the hair is such an important part of our appearance and because it is so easy to cut and arrange in almost any fashion, men and women have been "doing things" with their hair since the beginning of time.

No one can say who first thought of cutting the hair or arranging it in a special way. We know that women have had combs from the very earliest times, thousands of years ago! Men and women have also curled their hair since ancient times.

But the custom of long hair for women and short hair for men is more modern. During the Middle Ages men wore their hair long, curled it, even wore it with ribbons! If the hair wasn't long enough, they wore false hair bought from country people.

Henry VIII of England began the style of short hair for men. He ordered all men to wear their hair short but allowed them to grow beards and curl their moustaches. When James I became King, long hair for men reappeared, including wigs.

About the middle of the 17th century, there were two camps in England when it came to hair: those who believed in short hair and long beards for men, and those who believed in short beards and long hair. For the next hundred years the custom changed back and forth. Finally, about 1800, the custom became definitely established for men to wear their hair short.

Women have always tended to wear long hair, but bobbing the hair was a fad at the Court of Louis XIV! Today, of course, women wear their hair short not only because it is fashionable, but because it is simpler than having to bother with pins and combs and elaborate coifs.

Barbers and barber shops are a fairly recent development, too. In England, barbers were first incorporated as a craft in 1461, and in France, during the reign of Louis XIV.

WHEN WAS SOAP FIRST MADE?

You might think that something as useful and necessary as soap had been one of the first inventions of man. But soap is quite a modern thing in man's history. It only goes back about 2,000 years.

What ancient peoples used to do was to anoint their bodies with olive oil. They also used the juices and ashes of various plants to clean themselves. But by the time of Pliny (a Roman writer of the first century A.D.) we already have a reference to two kinds of soap, soft and hard. He describes it as an invention for brightening up the hair and gives the Gauls credit for inventing it.

By the way, in the ruins of Pompeii, there was found buried an establishment for turning out soap that very much resembles the soap of today! And yet, just one hundred years ago, nearly all the soap used in the United States was made at home!

Soap is made by boiling fats and oils with an alkali. In the great soap factories, the fats and alkalis are first boiled in huge kettles. This process is called "saponification." When it is nearly completed, salt is added. This causes the soap to rise to the top of the kettle. The brine or salt solution containing glycerine, dirt, and some excess alkali sinks to the bottom and is drawn off. This process may be repeated as many as five or six times. More water and alkali are added each time until the last bit of fat is saponified, or converted from a fat into soap.

The next step is to churn the soap into a smooth mass while adding various ingredients, such as perfumes, coloring matter, water softeners, and preservatives. After this, the hot melted soap is ready to be fashioned into bars or cakes, or granules, flakes, or globules. Toilet soaps go through a process called "milling," which shreds and dries them, then rolls them into sheets.

WHO INVENTED SHOES?

When primitive man had to make his way over rocks, he discovered the need for covering his feet to protect them. So the first shoes, which were probably sandals, were mats of grass, strips of hide, or even flat pieces of wood.

These were fastened to the soles of the feet by thongs that were then bound around the ankles. Of course, in colder regions, these sandals didn't protect the feet sufficiently, so more material was added and gradually the sandals developed into shoes.

Among the first civilized people to make shoes were the Egyptians. They used pads of leather or papyrus, which were bound to the foot by two straps. In order to protect the toes, the front of the sandal was sometimes turned up.

The Romans went a step further and developed a kind of shoe called the *calceus*. This had slits at the side and straps knotted in front. There were different forms of the *calceus*, to be worn by the different classes of society.

In some of the cold regions of the earth, people developed a kind of shoe independently. For example, they sometimes wore bags padded with grass and tied around the feet. In time, these first foot coverings developed into the moccasins of the Eskimo and the Indian.

As far as our modern shoes are concerned, their beginnings can be traced to the Crusades. The Crusaders went on long pilgrimages, and they needed protection for their feet, so it became necessary to create shoes that would last a long time. In time, leather shoes of great beauty began to appear in Italy, France, and England.

Shoes have always been subject to whims of fashion. For example, at the time of King James I of England, high heels and very soft leathers were fashionable in society. It made for difficult walking, but people insisted on wearing them. At one time, before the appearance of the high heel, long-toed shoes were considered fashionable. The shoes were very narrow, and the toes were five and six inches long, coming to a point. Shoemaking was introduced into the United States in 1629, when Thomas Beard arrived under contract to make shoes for the Pilgrim colony.

WHO MADE THE FIRST FALSE TEETH?

Nobody looks good when he has some teeth missing. Besides, it sometimes interferes very seriously with eating and chewing. So man decided long ago that when he lost his natural teeth for one reason or another, they should be replaced. Substituting artificial replacements for natural parts in teeth is called "prosthetics."

When the natural teeth are gone, they are replaced either by bridgework or by dentures. In bridgework, the "load" of false teeth is borne by our natural teeth on either side of the gap. The bridge fits on these natural teeth. In a denture, the false teeth are held in place by resting on the gum and other parts of the mouth under the gum.

It may amaze you to learn that bridges with false teeth were made

3,000 years ago by the Etruscans, who worked with gold! Dentures, including "complete" dentures for people who had no teeth left, have been made for about 300 years.

The first problems to be solved in making both bridges and dentures was how to make them stay in the mouth in the right position, and how to make the "baseplate material," the material that held the false teeth. Modern dentistry has solved both these problems so well that people with false teeth can eat and chew as well as anyone, and the false teeth feel light and natural in the mouth.

But what about the teeth themselves? In early times, false teeth were made from bone, ivory, and hippopotamus tooth! Sometimes the entire bridge or denture was carved from the same material, and it was all one piece that fitted into the mouth. Later on, individual human teeth, or the teeth of various animals, especially the sheep, were used. These were mounted on a gold or ivory base.

At the end of the 18th century, teeth were made of porcelain, and soon individual porcelain teeth were mounted on gold or platinum bases. The materials in making teeth are the same as those used in making other fine porcelain. They have a fine texture, are somewhat translucent, and have great strength.

About 100 years ago false teeth began to be designed to harmonize with the shape of the face. Today, false teeth are matched to natural teeth so closely in color and shape that it is hard to tell them apart!

HOW DID FORKS ORIGINATE?

The first man to use a crude kind of fork for eating probably lived thousands of years ago. But the everyday use of forks in dining is a very recent development in the history of man.

The primitive savage used a small pronged twig as a kind of natural fork to pick up his meat. Some authorities believe that the fork really originated with the arrow, and that at first it was a kind of toothpick used to remove food from between the teeth.

Actual forks as we know them were first used only for cooking and for holding the meat while it was being carved. These first forks were long, and two-pronged, and were made of iron, bone, and hard wood.

It took a very long time for forks to be accepted in general use in dining.

Only 300 years ago, forks were great curiosities in Europe. In fact, in France everyone ate with his fingers until the 17th century. We all know about the magnificent Court of Louis XIV and the great banquets at his palaces. Did you know that no one used a fork at this very elegant Court!

When people first began to use forks for eating, other people used to ridicule them as being too dainty. When a rich woman in Venice in the 11th century had a small golden fork made, it was written about her: "Instead of eating like other people, she had her food cut up into little pieces, and ate the pieces by means of a two-pronged fork."

Five hundred years later, in the 16th century, people who used forks in Venice were still being described as somewhat peculiar: "At Venice each person is served, besides his knife and spoon, with a fork to hold the meat while he cuts it, for they deem it ill manners that one should touch it with his hand."

From the 17th century on, table manners developed along modern lines. Silver forks began to appear all over Italy. And by the end of the 18th century, the fork was accepted as a necessity in the homes of most cultivated people.

WHEN DID MAN BEGIN TO DRINK MILK?

Today, when we say "milk" we usually mean cows' milk, since most milk consumed by human beings is from the cow. But milk from other animals is consumed by people all over the world. Half the milk consumed in India is from the buffalo. Goats' milk is widely used in countries along the Mediterranean, and the milk of reindeer is used as food in Northern Europe.

When did man first begin to drink the milk of animals, and use milk products such as butter and cheese? No one can ever know, since it was before recorded history. Soured milks, butterlike products, and cheese were probably common foods of the people roaming the grasslands of Asia with their sheep and cattle thousands of years ago.

The Bible has many references to milk. Abel, son of Adam, was a "keeper of sheep" and probably consumed milk. The earliest mention of milk in the Bible is Jacob's prediction in 1700 B.C. that Judah's teeth shall be "white with milk." Canaan was "a land of milk and honey" in 1500 B.C. Job also refers to cheese. But in all these cases the mention of milk implies that it was used much earlier.

We may think that the idea of making concentrated and dry milk is a modern one. Actually, the Tatars prepared concentrated milks in paste, and probably in dry form as early as the year 1200 and used them as food during the raids under Genghis Khan.

The original patent for evaporated milk was granted in 1856, and this type of milk was widely used by soldiers in the Civil War.

About 87 per cent of the milk from the cow is water, but the remainder supplies man with a high percentage of his daily requirements in calcium, protein, and vitamins A and B.

WHERE DID ICE CREAM ORIGINATE?

The way we eat ice cream in this country—more than 2,000,000,000 quarts of it each year!—you'd imagine that it originated in the United States.

But the fact is the ice cream was first created in the Orient. The great Venetian explorer Marco Polo saw people eating it there and brought back the idea to Italy. From Italy the idea was carried to France. It became very popular in France with the nobility and an effort was made to keep the recipes for ice cream a secret from the common people. But, of course, they soon learned how delicious this new food was and ice cream became popular with everyone. Soon it spread all over the world, including the United States.

The first wholesale factory for the manufacture of ice cream was started in Baltimore, Maryland, in 1851. The real development of ice cream and the ice cream business didn't take place until after 1900 with new developments in refrigeration.

The basis of all ice cream is cream, milk or milk solids, sugar, and sometimes eggs. Vanilla, chocolate, berries, fruit ingredients, and nuts are added as flavors. This is the usual proportion of ingredients in ice cream: about 80 to 85 per cent cream and milk products, 15 per cent sugar, one-half to four and one-half per cent flavoring, and three-tenths of one per cent stabilizer.

The small amount of stabilizer is used in order to retain the smoothness of the ice cream by preventing the formation of coarse ice crystals. Pure food gelatine is usually used for this purpose.

When you eat one-third of a pint of vanilla ice cream you are getting about as much calcium, protein, and the B vitamins as are in one-half cup of whole milk, and as much vitamin A and calories as in one cup of milk.

HOW DID CANDY ORIGINATE?

In almost every country in ancient times people ate something that was like candy. In excavations in Egypt, pictures and written records have been found that showed candy and how candy in Egypt was made!

In those days, of course, the refining of sugar was unknown, so honey was used as a sweetener. The chief ingredient of the candy in Egypt was dates.

In parts of the East, each tribe had its official candy-maker and secret recipes. In these regions, almonds, honey, and figs have long been used in making candy. There is an ancient Roman recipe that directs nut meats and cooked poppy be boiled with honey, then peppered and sprinkled with ground sesame softened with honey. The result would probably be a sort of nougat.

In Europe, they had sweet sirup in early times, but it was used to hide the taste of medicines. No one thought of making candy for its own sake. But when large quantities of sugar from the Colonies began to appear in Europe in the 17th century, candy-making began to be a separate art.

The French candied fruits and developed other recipes. One of these, a nut- and sugar-sirup sweetmeat called "prawlings," may have been the ancestor of the famous New Orleans pralines.

In Colonial days and later, maple sugar, molasses, and honey were used in homemade sweetmeats. Our great-grandmothers candied iris root and ginger "varnished" apples, and made rock candy.

The main ingredients used for the manufacturing of candy are cane and beet sugars combined with corn sirup, corn sugar, corn starch, honey, molasses, and maple sugar. To this sweet base are added chocolate, fruits, nuts, eggs, milk, a variety of milk products, and, of course, flavors and colors. Some flavors are from natural sources, such as vanilla, peppermint, lemon, and so on, and others are imitations of true flavors.

There are more than 2,000 different kinds of candy being made today. In the United States more than 2,500,000,000 pounds are produced every year!

HOW WAS FIRE DISCOVERED?

Fire has been known to man since the very earliest times. In certain caves in Europe in which men lived hundreds of thousands of years ago, charcoal and charred bits of bone have been found among stones that were evidently used as fireplaces.

But how did men learn the trick of making a fire? We can only guess. Early man probably knew how to use fire before he knew how to start it. For example, lightning might strike a rotten tree and the trunk would smolder. From this he would light a fire and keep it going for years.

We can take a pretty good guess as to how the cave men learned to start a fire. In trampling among the loose stones in the dark, the first men must have noticed sparks when one stone struck another. But it may have taken many generations before anyone among these early men had the idea of purposely striking two stones together to produce a fire!

Another way we have of knowing how early men discovered fire is to observe the primitive people of today. Some of them are in a stage of development that our forefathers reached thousands of years ago.

Let's look at some of these primitive methods. In Alaska, Indians of certain tribes rub sulphur over two stones and strike them together. When the sulphur ignites, they drop the burning stone among some dried grass or other material.

In China and India, a piece of broken pottery is struck against a bamboo stick. The outer coating of the bamboo is very hard and seems to have the qualities of flint. The Eskimos strike a common piece of quartz against a piece of iron pyrites, which is very common where they live. Among the North American Indians, rubbing two sticks together to produce fire was a common method.

The ancient Greeks and Romans had still another method. They used a kind of lens, called "a burning glass," to focus the rays of the sun. When the heat rays were concentrated in this way, they were hot enough to set fire to dry wood.

An interesting thing about fire in early days, is that many ancient peoples kept "perpetual" fires going. The Mayas and Aztecs in Mexico kept a fire perpetually burning, and the Greeks, Egyptians, and Romans kept fires burning in their temples.

WHO INVENTED MATCHES?

Man's desire to be able to start a fire to warm himself and cook food has caused him to invent a variety of "matches." The cave man struck a spark from a flint and hoped it would ignite some dry leaves. The Romans, thousands of years later, were not much further advanced. They struck two flinty stones together and caught the spark on a split of wood covered with sulphur.

During the Middle Ages, sparks struck by flint and steel were caught on charred rags, dried moss, or fungus. Such material that catches fire easily is called "tinder."

Modern matches were made possible by the discovery of phosphorus, a substance which catches fire at a very low temperature. In 1681, an Englishman called Robert Boyle dipped a sliver of wood which had been treated with sulphur into a mixture of sulphur and phosphorus. But the matches took fire so easily that his invention wasn't practical.

The first practical matches were made in England by a druggist named John Walker. In order to light them, they were drawn between folds of paper covered with ground glass. By 1833, phosphorus-tipped matches that could be ignited by friction were being made in Austria and Germany. But there was one problem. White or yellow phosphorus was so dangerous to the match-workers that it had to be forbidden by an international treaty in 1906.

Finally, a non-poisonous red phosphorus was introduced, and this led to the invention of safety matches. The first safety matches, which light only on a prepared surface, were made in Sweden in 1844. Instead of putting all the necessary chemicals in the match-head, the red phosphorus was painted into the striking surface on the container. The match was thus "safe" unless it was rubbed on the striking area.

During World War II our troops were fighting in the Pacific tropics where long rainy periods made ordinary matches ineffective. A man called Raymond Cady invented a coating for matches which kept them efficient even after eight hours under water!

WHO DISCOVERED ELECTRICITY?

The curious thing about electricity is that it has been studied for thousands of years—and we still don't know exactly what it is! Today, all matter is thought to consist of tiny charged particles. Electricity, according to this theory, is simply a moving stream of electrons or other charged particles.

The word "electricity" comes from the Greek word *electron*. And do you know what this word meant? It was the Greek word for "amber"! You see, as far back as 600 B.C. the Greeks knew that when amber was rubbed, it became capable of attracting to it light bits of cork or paper.

Not much progress was made in the study of electricity until 1672. In that year, a man called Otto von Guericke produced a more powerful charge of electricity by holding his hand against a ball of spinning sulphur. In 1729, Stephen Gray found that some substances, such as metals, carried electricity from one location to another. These came to be called "conductors." He found that others, such as glass, sulphur, amber, and wax, did not carry electricity. These were called "insulators."

The next important step took place in 1733 when a Frenchman called du Fay discovered positive and negative charges of electricity, although he thought these were two different kinds of electricity.

But it was Benjamin Franklin who tried to give an explanation of what electricity was. His idea was that all substances in nature contain "electrical fluid." Friction between certain substances removed some of this "fluid" from one and placed an extra amount in the other. Today, we would say that this "fluid" is composed of electrons which are negatively charged.

Probably the most important developments in the science of electricity started with the invention of the first battery in 1800 by Alessandro Volta. This battery gave the world its first continuous, reliable source of electric current, and led to all the important discoveries of the use of electricity.

WHEN WERE ROCKETS FIRST USED?

Have you ever watched a lawn sprinkler work—the kind that spins around and around and sprays water in a circle? Well, you were actually watching the principle of the rocket at work!

The water in the sprinkler was escaping in one direction. This force pushed the sprinkler in the opposite direction. In a rocket, a fast-burning fuel or explosive exerts force in one direction, and this pushes the rocket forward in the opposite direction.

We think of ourselves as living in the age of rockets, and of rockets as being a rather modern invention. But rockets are a very old idea. The Chinese invented them and used them as fireworks more than 800 years ago! They then became known in Indian and Arabian countries. The first record of them in Western Europe was in A.D. 1256.

The first use of rockets in war was very similar to the way burning arrows had been used. They were aimed at homes to set them on fire. Soldiers and sailors continued to use rockets as signals, but they were no longer used for war for a long time.

In 1802, a British Army captain read how British troops in India had been attacked with rockets. This gave him the idea of trying them out with the British Army. The experiment was so successful that very soon most European armies as well as the Army of the United States began to use war rockets.

In Europe, rockets were used in the Battle of Leipzig, in which Napoleon was defeated. In the United States, the English used war rockets in the bombardment of Fort McHenry in Baltimore Harbor. This is why in the national anthem of the United States there is the phrase, "the rocket's red glare!"

During the 19th century, as artillery became more powerful and more accurate, it began to replace rockets, and they were not important in war again until World War II and the famous German V-2 rocket.

HOW WAS GLASS DISCOVERED?

For thousands of years glass was thought of as something to look at. It was valued for decoration and for making precious objects. Glass really became useful when it was thought of as something to look through.

No one really knows when or where the secret of making glass was first learned, though we know it has been used since very early days. The chief ingredients for making glass are sand, soda ash, or potash and lime, melted together at a high temperature. Since these materials are found in abundance in many parts of the world, the secret of glassmaking could have been discovered in many countries.

According to one story, the ancient Phoenicians deserve the credit for this discovery. A crew of a ship landed at the mouth of a river in Syria. When they were ready to cook their dinner, they could find no stones on which to support their kettle. So they used lumps of niter (a sodium compound) from the ship's cargo. The heat of the fire melted the niter, which mixed with the surrounding sand and flowed out as a stream of liquid glass!

This story may or may not be true, but Syria was one of the original homes of glassmaking. And ancient Phoenician traders sold glassware all through the Mediterranean countries.

Egypt was another country in which glassmaking was known at an early time. Glass beads and charms have been found in tombs which date back as far as 7000 B.C., but these glass objects may have come from Syria. We know that about 1500 B.C. the Egyptians were making their own glass.

The Egyptians mixed crushed quartz pebbles with the sand to change the color of the glass. They learned, too, that by adding cobalt, copper, or manganese to the mixture, they could produce glass with rich blue, green, or purple color.

After 1200 B.C. the Egyptians learned to press glass into molds. But the blowpipe for blowing glass did not come into use until shortly before the beginning of the Christian Era. It was a Phoenician invention.

The Romans were great glassmakers, and even used glass in thin panes as a coating for walls. By the time of the Christian Era, glass was already being used for windowpanes!

WHO INVENTED THE THERMOMETER?

Do you ever find yourself asking: I wonder how hot it is? Or: I wonder how cold this is? If you are interested in heat, just imagine all the questions about heat that scientists want to know! But the first step in developing the science of heat is to have some way of measuring it. And that's why the thermometer was invented. "Thermo" means "heat," and "meter" means "measure," so a thermometer measures heat.

The first condition about having a thermometer must be that it will always give the same indication at the same temperature. With this in mind, an Italian scientist called Galileo began certain experiments around 1592 (100 years after Columbus discovered America). He made a kind of thermometer which is really called "an air thermoscope." He had a glass tube with a hollow bulb at one end. In this tube there was air. The tube and bulb were heated to expand the air inside, and then the open end was placed in a fluid, such as water.

As the air in the tube cooled, its volume contracted or shrank, and the liquid rose in the tube to take its place. Changes in temperature could then be noted by the rising or falling level of the liquid in the tube. So here we have the first "thermometer" because it measures heat. But remember, it measures heat by measuring the expansion and contraction of air in a tube. So it was discovered that one of the problems with this thermometer was that it was affected by variations of atmospheric pressure, and therefore, wasn't completely accurate.

The type of thermometer we use today uses the expansion and contraction of a liquid to measure temperature. This liquid is hermetically sealed in a glass bulb with a fine tube attached. Higher temperature makes the liquid expand and go up the tube, lower temperature makes the liquid contract and drop in the tube. A scale on the tube tells us the temperature.

This kind of thermometer was first used about 1654 by the Grand Duke Ferdinand II of Tuscany.

WHO INVENTED THE MICROSCOPE?

The word microscope is a combination of two Greek words, *mikros,* or "small," and *skopos,* or "watcher." So a microscope is a "watcher of the small"! It is an instrument used to see tiny things which are invisible to the naked eye.

Normally an object appears larger the closer it is brought to the human eye. But when it is nearer than 10 inches, it is no longer clear. It is said to be out of focus. Now if a simple convex lens is placed between the eye and the object, the object can be brought nearer than 10 inches and still remain in focus.

Today we describe this simply as "using a magnifying glass." But ordinary magnifying glasses are really "simple microscopes," and as such they have been known since remote times. So when we speak of the invention of the microscope, we really mean "the compound microscope." In fact, today when we say "microscope," that's the only kind we mean.

What is a compound microscope? In this kind of microscope, magnification takes place in two stages. There is a lens called "the objective" which produces a primary magnified image. Then there is another lens called "the eyepiece" or "ocular," which magnifies that first image. In actual practice, there are several lenses used for both the objective and ocular, but the principle is that of two-stage magnification.

The compound microscope was invented some time between 1590 and 1610. While no one is quite sure who actually did it, the credit is usually given to Galileo. A Dutch scientist called Leeuwenhoek is sometimes called "the father of the microscope," but that's because of the many discoveries he made with the microscope.

Leeuwenhoek showed that weevils, fleas, and other minute creatures come from eggs and are not "spontaneously generated." He was the first to see such microscopic forms of life as the protozoa and bacteria. With his own microscope he was the first to see the whole circulation of the blood.

Today the microscope is important to man in almost every form of science and industry.

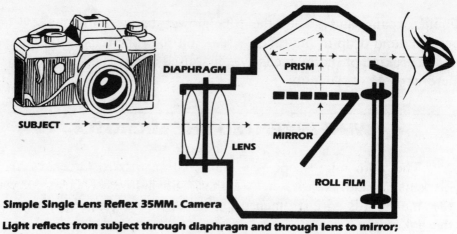

Simple Single Lens Reflex 35MM. Camera

Light reflects from subject through diaphragm and through lens to mirror; then to prism in reflex housing to viewer's eye. When shutter release is pressed, mirror lifts out of way so that light will expose the film.

WHO INVENTED THE CAMERA?

Today, when you snap a picture and have it developed so easily, it's hard to believe that hundreds of years of experimenting were needed before this became possible. Photography was not invented by any single person. Just to give you an idea of what went into bringing it to its present stage of perfection, here is a quick outline of the history of photography.

Between the 11th and 16th centuries, man had "the camera obscura." This enabled him to show on paper an image which could be traced by hand to give accurate drawings of natural scenes. It didn't really "take" a picture.

In 1568, Daniello Barbaro fitted the camera obscura with a lens and a changeable opening to sharpen the image. In 1802, Thomas Wedgwood and Sir Humphrey Davy recorded silhouettes and images of paintings on coated paper by contact printing, but they couldn't make the prints permanent.

In 1816, Joseph Niepce made a crude photographic camera from a jewel box and a lens taken from a microscope. He was able to make a negative image. In 1835, William Talbot was the first to make positives from negatives, the first to make permanent images.

In 1839, Louis Daguerre announced the daguerreotype process, which recorded the image on a silver plate. More and more developments were contributed by individuals all over the world as time went on. Many of them are too technical to discuss here, but as you can see, it was a long slow process of growth.

Finally, in 1888, a box camera was put on the market, developed by the Eastman Dry Plate and Film Company, using the Kodak system. The camera was sold already loaded with enough film for 100 exposures. The pictures were 2½-inch-diameter size. After exposure, camera and film were returned to Rochester, where the film was removed and processed and the camera reloaded and returned to the customer.

This box camera was probably the beginning of popular photography as we know it today when billions of pictures are taken every year by people all over the world.

WHO INVENTED THE AUTOMOBILE?

Unlike so many other great developments, no one man can claim credit for inventing the automobile. It has reached its present state of perfection as the result of a great many ideas contributed through the years.

For all practical purposes, the first land vehicle that was self-propelled with an engine was built in 1769 by a Frenchman named Nicholas Cugnot. It was a cumbersome three-wheeled cart with a steam engine and an enormous boiler. It could travel 3 miles an hour and had to be refueled every 15 miles!

In 1789, an American called Oliver Evans received the first United States patent for a self-propelled carriage. It was a four-wheeled wagon and had a paddle wheel at the rear so that it could operate either on land or in the water. It weighed 21 tons!

For nearly 80 years afterward, other men continued to experiment with powered carriages for use on roads. Most of them were steam, although a few were electrically driven and had to carry large batteries. Then, in the 1880's came two inventions that were to result in the automobile as we know it today. One was the development of the gasoline engine. The other was the invention of the pneumatic, or air-filled, tire.

The first gasoline-powered car was put on the road in 1887 by Gottlieb Daimler, a German. In the United States, two brothers, Frank and Charles Duryea, built the first successful American gasoline automobile in 1892 or 1893. Their machine was described as "a horseless buggy." As a matter of fact, all the early American automobiles that were to follow were really buggies! Nobody attempted to design a completely different kind of vehicle. All they did was add a gasoline engine to the buggies and a connecting belt or chain to drive the rear wheels.

It was only after automobiles began to run successfully that attention was turned to making them comfortable and stronger. Car-makers soon found that the flimsy construction of buggies was not suitable for use in automobiles. Gradually, the familiar form of the automobile as we know it today began to emerge. Engines were removed from under the seats and placed in front. Stronger wheels replaced the spindly bicycle and carriage wheels. Steering wheels replaced "tillers." Finally, steel was used instead of wood to make stronger frames and our modern automobile became a reality.

WHO INVENTED THE AIRPLANE?

Sometimes an invention starts with having the "idea." A man has the idea that people might want a certain kind of machine or product, and then he proceeds to "invent" it.

But when it comes to the airplane, the "idea" has been one of man's oldest dreams. The idea of flying has fascinated men since ancient days. In fact, one of our most famous legends tells of Icarus, who fastened wings to his body with wax and flew off! As he soared toward the sun, however, the wax melted and he fell to his death. Icarus is a symbol of man's striving to new heights.

Leonardo da Vinci, who was also quite an inventor, made sketches of a flying machine that used manpower, and other artists and "dreamers" had the idea of an airplane hundreds of years ago.

The earliest flying machines that were made had no power. They were actually huge kites or gliders, and during the 19th century many experiments with these were carried on.

But nobody had yet made a heavier-than-air machine that was equipped with its own power. In fact, there was some question that such a machine could actually be built. The first man to demonstrate that it could be done was Professor Samuel Langley, who was secretary of the Smithsonian Institution of Washington, D.C. He built two machines, each about 12 feet wide and 15 feet long, driven by 1½-horsepower steam engines. In 1896, these two models made successful flights. In 1903, when Langley's full-sized flying machine was tested, it was wrecked. This was on October 7, 1903.

On December 17, Orville and Wilbur Wright succeeded in making man's first flight in a heavier-than-air machine with its own power. At Kitty

Hawk, North Carolina, they made one flight of 120 feet in 12 seconds, and a second flight of 852 feet in 59 seconds. The airplane was born!

HOW WAS THE TELEPHONE INVENTED?

The story of the invention of the telephone is a very dramatic one. (No wonder they were able to make a movie about it!) But first let's make sure we understand the principle of how a telephone works.

When you speak, the air makes your vocal cords vibrate. These vibrations are passed on to the air molecules so that sound waves come out of your mouth, that is, vibrations in the air. These sound waves strike an aluminum disk or diaphragm in the transmitter of your telephone. And the disk vibrates back and forth in just the same way the molecules of air are vibrating.

These vibrations send a varying, or undulating, current over the telephone line. The weaker and stronger currents cause a disk in the receiver at the other end of the line to vibrate exactly as the diaphragm in the transmitter is vibrating. This sets up waves in the air exactly like those which you sent into the mouthpiece. When these sound waves reach the ear of the person at the other end, they have the same effect as they would have if they came directly from your mouth!

Now to the story of Alexander Graham Bell and how he invented the telephone. On June 2, 1875, he was experimenting in Boston with the idea of sending several telegraph messages over the same wire at the same time. He was using a set of spring-steel reeds. He was working with the receiving set in one room, while his assistant, Thomas Watson, operated the sending set in the other room.

Watson plucked a steel reed to make it vibrate, and it produced a twanging sound. Suddenly Bell came rushing in, crying to Watson: "Don't change anything. What did you do then? Let me see." He found that the steel rod, while vibrating over the magnet, had caused a current of varying strength to flow through the wire. This made the reed in Bell's room vibrate and produce a twanging sound.

The next day the first telephone was made and voice sounds could be recognized over the first telephone line, which was from the top of the building down two flights. Then, on March 10 of next year, the first sentence was heard: "Mr. Watson, come here, I want you."

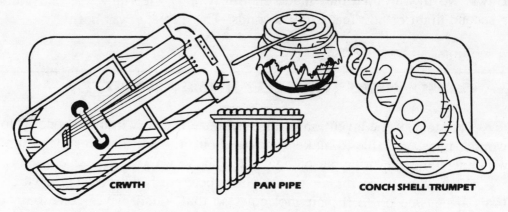

WATER DRUM AND BEATER

CRWTH   PAN PIPE   CONCH SHELL TRUMPET

WHAT WAS THE FIRST MUSICAL INSTRUMENT?

There is a legend about this, but it is pure fancy. According to a Greek myth, Pan invented the first musical instrument—the shepherd's pipe. One day he sighed through the reeds on a river bank and heard his breath produce a mournful wail as it passed through them. He broke them off in unequal lengths, bound them together, and had the first musical instrument!

The fact is we can never trace the first musical instrument because all primitive people all over the world seem to have made music of some sort. It was usually music that had some religious significance and it was shared in by the spectators who would dance, drum, or clap hands and sing with the music. It was done more than for pleasure alone. This primitive music had a meaning as part of the lives of the people.

The legend of Pan and the reeds suggests, however, how man first had the idea for making various musical instruments. He may have imitated the sounds of nature, or used articles of nature all about him to create his music.

The first instruments were of the drum type. Later, man invented wind instruments, made from the horns of animals. From these crude wind instruments developed modern brass instruments. As man trained his musical sense, he began to use reeds and thus produced more natural tones of greater delicacy.

Last of all, man discovered the use of strings and invented the simple lyre and harp from which developed the instruments played with a bow.

In the Middle Ages, the Crusaders brought back many curious oriental instruments. These, combined with the folk instruments that already existed in Europe, developed into many of the instruments now in use.

HOW DID BASKETBALL GET ITS NAME?

If you had to name the game that is watched by more spectators in the United States than any other, which would it be? Surprisingly enough, it is basketball.

Basketball is often called "the international game" because it is played in every civilized nation of the world. Yet basketball did not develop slowly over the centuries, as some of our other games have. It was invented by one man, James A. Naismith, in 1891.

Naismith wanted to provide a game to interest students of physical education at the Springfield Training School, Springfield, Massachusetts. Naismith was a Canadian and he combined the Indian game of lacrosse and the British game of soccer to make a suitable indoor game.

Instead of using a stick as in lacrosse, or kicking a ball with the foot as in soccer, Naismith devised a game by which the ball is passed from player to player, or bounced (the dribble) by a single player and shot into a goal. When he first created the game, the only thing he had to use for a goal was a wooden peach basket, so he called the game "basketball"!

In basketball, as in many other games, the special talent of a player determines what position he is chosen to play. Those who are good at scoring goals by throwing the ball through the hoop are usually stationed at forward, where they lead the team's attack on the opponents' goal.

The center is usually tall. He should be able to tip the ball to a teammate during the center jump. His height should also give his team "control of the backboard," which means being able to regain control of the ball when a shot fails to go through the hoop. The guards have to keep the opposing forwards from scoring, so they have to be agile, tricky, and able to take their part in offensive passing and shooting.

WHEN DID BOXING BEGIN?

Many people say that boxing should be outlawed. In the history of boxing this has happened many times. People have felt boxing was too cruel or barbaric, and have wanted it stopped.

Imagine how they would feel if they could see the first boxing bouts that were held! These were in ancient Greece, and the boxers performed at Olympic games and other public games. Some of the rules they observed were very much like the ones we have today. But there was one big differ-ence: Instead of gloves, the fighters wore the *cestus*. This was a wrapping of leather studded with lead or bronze plates. A blow from a *cestus,* as you can see, could be quite damaging!

After the fall of the Roman Empire, boxing disappeared, not to reappear until it was revived in England at the beginning of the 18th century. It soon became quite a fashionable sport, and it remained so for more than 100 years.

The fights were decided with bare fists, and many of them lasted for several hours. Wrestling and throwing were allowed. A round ended only when a man was knocked down, and the time between rounds varied. This tough fight went on and on until one of the fighters was unable to walk up to a chalk mark at the center of the ring when a round began!

Naturally, this kind of brutal boxing eventually turned public opinion against prize fighting. Something had to be done to save the sport, so padded gloves began to be used. Then little by little, the old rules were made more humane. Finally, in 1867, came the big step that brought boxing back into favor. The Marquis of Queensberry introduced a set of rules that made many improvements. For example, the rounds were limited to three minutes each. The interval between rounds was one minute. These rules were adopted all over the world, and the rules governing boxing today in the United States are based on them.

Until the 20th century, there was very little boxing in countries outside of England and the United States—but it has since spread all over the world.

DID BASEBALL REALLY ORIGINATE IN AMERICA?

For us even to consider this question must seem shocking to many people. After all, isn't baseball our "national game?"

And in fact, almost every book on the subject gives Abner Doubleday the credit for inventing baseball. He is said to have laid out the first baseball diamond in Cooperstown, New York, in 1839, and set up the rules which baseball still follows today.

In 1907, a commission was appointed to investigate the origins of baseball and to settle the controversy about it once and for all. This com-mission published its report in 1908 in which it said that baseball was a distinctly American game, that Doubleday had invented it, and that baseball had nothing to do with any foreign games.

Some people, however, claim that this commission didn't really try to investigate the origin of baseball; its purpose was to prove that it was an American game. A great deal of information has since been published to support this point of view.

Let's consider some of it. The name "baseball" itself was used to designate a popular English game that goes back to the 18th century! A book printed in England in 1744 and reprinted in the United States in 1762 and 1787 describes a game of "baseball" which shows a player at the plate with a bat, a catcher behind him, a pitcher, and two bases. In fact, there are many references in books published before 1830 regarding baseball and even baseball clubs!

But the chief document that ties up the first forms of our baseball with an English game called "rounders" is a book published in London in 1828. It describes a game with a diamond, four bases, in which there are fouls, strike-outs, home runs, and so on. The runner, however, was put out by being hit by the ball. And it is claimed that Doubleday taught the game of baseball also with a runner being put out by being hit by the ball!

So perhaps baseball wasn't really invented in America, after all! There's no question, however, that we developed it into the game it is today.

WHAT WAS THE FIRST MOTION PICTURE?

A curious thing about the development of motion pictures is that the first people who made it possible weren't interested in movies at all! The first inventions were by men who wanted to study the movements of animals.

Even Thomas Edison, who perfected a device called "a kinetoscope" in 1893, thought of it only as a curiosity. But there were many other people who saw great possibilities for entertainment in these inventions and they began to make movies.

At first they were only scenes of something that moved. There were waves on the beach, horses running, children swinging, and trains arriving at stations. The first film which really told a story was produced in the Edison Laboratories in 1903. It was *The Great Train Robbery,* and it caused a nation-wide sensation.

The first permanent motion-picture theatre in the United States opened in November, 1905, in Pittsburgh, Pennsylvania. This theatre was luxuriously decorated and the owners called it "the Nickelodeon." Soon, all over the country, other Nickelodeons were opened.

D. W. Griffith, a former actor, was among the most famous of the early directors and producers. He was the first man to move a camera during a scene and he perfected modern editing technique. He invented the closeup and many other parts of motion picture art. In 1914, he produced *The Birth of a Nation,* one of the most spectacular pictures of all time. This picture about the Civil War cost more than $750,000 and was the most expensive film made up to that time.

Hollywood became the movie capital of the world after Cecil B. de Mille and Jesse Lasky began making a movie there called *The Squaw Man.* Soon other companies came to Hollywood and modern movies were on their way.

WHO INVENTED TELEVISION?

Television, as you know, is a rather complicated process. Whenever such a process is developed, you can be sure a great many people had a hand in it and it goes far back for its beginnings. So television was not "invented" by one man alone.

The chain of events leading to television began in 1817, when a Swedish chemist named Jons Berzelius discovered the chemical element "selenium."

Later it was found that the amount of electrical current selenium would carry depended on the amount of light which struck it. This property is called "photoelectricity."

In 1875, this discovery led a United States inventor, G. R. Carey, to make the first crude television system, using photoelectric cells. As a scene or object was focused through a lens onto a bank of photoelectric cells, each cell would control the amount of electricity it would pass on to a light bulb. Crude outlines of the object that was projected on the photoelectric cells would then show in the lights on the bank of bulbs.

The next step was the invention of "the scanning disk" in 1884 by Paul Nipkow. It was a disk with holes in it which revolved in front of the photoelectric cells, and another disk which revolved in front of the person watching. But the principle was the same as Carey's.

In 1923 came the first practical transmission of pictures over wires, and this was accomplished by Baird in England and Jenkins in the United States. Then came great improvements in the development of television cameras. Vladimir Zworykin and Philo Farnsworth each developed a type of camera, one known as "the inconoscope" and the other as "the image dissector."

By 1945, both of these camera pickup tubes had been replaced by "the image orthicon." And today, modern television sets use a picture tube known as "a kinescope." In this tube is an electric gun which scans the screen in exactly the way the beam does in the camera tube to enable us to see the picture.

Of course, this doesn't explain in any detail exactly how television works, but it gives you an idea of how many different developments and ideas had to be perfected by different people to make modern television possible.

CHAPTER 3
THE HUMAN BODY

HOW DO WE GROW?

All living things grow. They grow in structure (shape, size, and how they are made), and in function (what they can do).

The most important forces that cause growth lie inside a living thing from its beginning. These forces are called its heridity. Animals, including human beings, have stages of growth. These are: embryo and fetus (not yet born), infant, child, youth, mature adult, and old age.

Some creatures have hardly any infancy. Some birds can fly as soon as they hatch. The guinea pig can take care of itself three days after birth. The human being is not an adult until he is about 20 years old.

At birth an infant already has all the nerve cells he will ever have—the cells in his brain, in his spinal cord, and those that reach out into every part of his body. The growth of the connections between these nerve cells will enable him to control his movements, to learn, and to behave like the people in his society.

So all human beings are much alike in their growth. But there are important differences. Boys and girls all follow the same general pathway of growth, but each one follows it in his own particular way and at his own speed.

People's bodies grow faster in the early weeks of life than at any other time. Even before the end of the first year, they are growing less rapidly. Through the whole period of childhood, they grow at a moderate rate. Then growth starts to speed up again.

For girls, this usually begins between ages 11 and 13, and for boys, between 12 and 14. For a while, they grow faster until they reach a top speed. Then they slow down again and grow more slowly until growth in height stops altogether. They have reached full size.

Growth in height and growth in weight often takes turns in a person. First he grows upward for a while, then sideways. For many people, there is a "chubby" period that happens somewhere around 11 or 12 years. But then their height begins to catch up in the next years and the chubbiness is gone.

WHY DO WE STOP GROWING?

The average baby is about one foot, eight inches long at birth. In the next 20 years, man triples the length of the body he was born with and reaches an average height of about five feet, eight inches.

Why doesn't he just keep on growing and growing? What makes the body stop getting bigger? In the body, there is a system of glands called the endocrine glands which controls our growth.

The endocrine glands are: the thyroid in the neck, the pituitary attached to the brain, the thymus which is in the chest, and the sex glands. The pituitary gland is the one that stimulates our bones to grow. If this gland works too much, our arms and legs grow too long and our hands and feet become too big. If the gland doesn't work hard enough, we might end up as midgets.

A child is born with a large thymus gland and it continues to get bigger during childhood. When a child reaches the age of 13 or 14, the thymus gland begins to shrink. The thymus gland and the sex glands may have a certain relationship. As long as the thymus gland is working, the sex glands are small. As the sex glands develop, the thymus gland stops working. This is why, when a person has become sexually mature at about the age of 22, he stops growing!

Sometimes the sex glands develop too soon and slow up the thymus gland too early. This often makes a person below average in height. Since our legs grow later and grow more than other parts of the body, this early development makes the legs short. That's why people who develop too early are often thickset. Napoleon was an example of this kind of person.

If the sex glands develop too late, the thymus continues working and the person becomes taller than the average. Actually, we continue growing slightly even after the age of 25, and we reach our maximum height at about the age of 35 or 40. After that, we shrink about half an inch every 10 years! The reason for this is the drying-up of the cartilages in our joints and in the spinal column as we get older.

WHAT MAKES US HUNGRY?

When we need food, our body begins to crave for it. But how do we know that we are feeling "hunger"? How does our mind get the message and make us feel "hungry"?

Hunger has nothing to do with an empty stomach, as most people believe. A baby is born with an empty stomach, yet it doesn't feel hungry for several days. People who are sick or feverish often have empty stomachs without feeling hungry.

Hunger begins when certain nutritive materials are missing in the blood. When the blood vessels lack these materials, a message is sent to a part of the brain that is called the "hunger center." This hunger center works like a brake on the stomach and the intestine. As long as the blood has sufficient food, the hunger center slows up the action of the stomach and the intestine. When the food is missing from the blood, the hunger center makes the stomach and intestine more active. That's why a hungry person often hears his stomach "rumbling."

When we are hungry, our body doesn't crave any special kind of food, it just wants nourishment. But our appetite sees to it that we don't satisfy our hunger with just one food, which would be unhealthy. For instance, it would be hard for us to take in a certain amount of nourishment all in the form of potatoes. But if we eat soup until we've had enough, then meat and vegetables until we've had enough, then dessert until we've had enough, we can take in the same quantity of food and enjoy it!

How long can we live without food? That depends on the individual. A very calm person can live longer without food than an excitable one because the protein stored up in his body is used up more slowly.

HOW DO WE DIGEST FOOD?

Taking food into our bodies is not enough to keep us alive and growing. The food must be changed so that it can be used by the body, and this process is called "digestion."

Digestion starts when food is put in the mouth, chewed, and swallowed, and it continues in the alimentary canal, which is a long, partly coiled tube going through the body. All parts of the alimentary canal are joined together, but they are different in the way they work. The mouth opens into a wide "pharynx" in the throat, which is a passage used for both food and air. The "esophagus" passes through the chest and connects the pharynx and stomach. The stomach leads into the coiled "small intestine." The last part of the alimentary canal is the "colon" or "large intestine."

Here is a quick picture of what happens to food during digestion. In the mouth, the saliva helps to break down starches (such as in corn or potatoes). When food has been moistened and crushed in the mouth, it goes down through the pharynx and along the esophagus, and finally enters the stomach.

It is in the stomach that most of the process of digestion takes place. Here, juices from the stomach wall are mixed with the food. Hydrochloric acid is one of these juices. Pepsin, another secretion, helps to break down proteins into simpler forms to aid digestion. The starches continue to break down until the material in the stomach becomes too acid. Then digestion of starches almost stops.

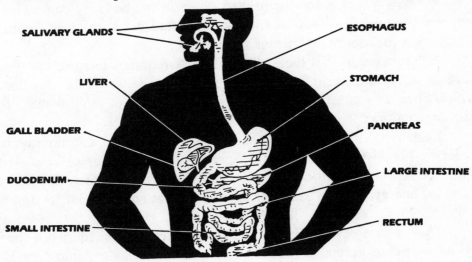

Food stays in the stomach until it is liquid. The materials in the stomach are churned about to mix digestive juices well throughout the foods. When the food is liquid it is called "chyme." The chyme moves out from the stomach into the small intestine through a valve at the lower end of the stomach, the "pylorus."

The small intestine is a tube from 22 to 25 feet long, which lies in coils. In the first part of the small intestine, the "duodenum," digestion continues. Juices from the pancreas and liver help break down the foods. The breakdown of proteins is finished here, fats are split into finer parts, and starch digestion is completed here. Digested food is absorbed here into the blood and lymph. In the large intestine, water is absorbed and the contents become more solid, so they can leave the body as waste material.

WHAT IS A CALORIE?

Nowadays, it seems, everybody is "watching their calories." There are even restaurants which print the number of calories each dish contains right on the menu! To understand what a calorie is and the part it plays in the body, let's start with the subject of nutrition in general.

Today, science is still not able to explain exactly how a cell transforms food into energy. We just know it happens. And we also can't explain why the cell in the body needs certain foods, and not others, in order to function properly.

We do know that food is broken down in the body by combining with oxygen. We might say it is "burned" up like fuel. Now, the way we measure the work a fuel does is by means of calories.

A "gram calorie" is the amount of heat required to raise the temperature of one gram of water one degree centigrade. The "large calorie" is 1,000 times as great. In measuring the energy value of food, we usually use the large calorie.

Each type of food, as it "burns up," furnishes a certain number of calories. For instance, one gram of protein furnishes four calories, but one gram of fat furnishes nine calories. The body doesn't care which "fuel" is used for energy, as long as it gets enough of that energy from food to maintain life.

The amount of calories the body needs depends on the work the body is doing. For example, a man who weighs about 150 pounds needs only

1,680 calories per day if he is in a state of absolute rest. If he does moderate work such as desk work, this jumps to 3,360 calories per day. And if he does heavy work, he may need as much as 6,720 calories a day to keep the body functioning properly.

Children need more calories than adults, since older people can't burn up the fuel as quickly. Interestingly enough, we use up more calories in winter than in summer. The normal fuels of the body are carbohydrates, starch, and sugar. Suppose, however, we take in more fuels than we need? The body uses up what it needs and stores some of it away for future use. The body can store away about one-third of the amount it needs each day. The rest becomes fat! And that's why we "watch our calories."

WHY DO WE PERSPIRE?

The body could be considered a permanent furnace. The food we take in is "fuel," which the body "burns up." In this process, about 2,500 calories are being used every day in the body.

Now this is quite a bit of heat. It's enough heat to bring 25 quarts of water to the boiling point! What happens to all this heat in the body? If there were no temperature controls in the body, we could certainly think of ourselves as "hot stuff." But we all know that the heat of the body doesn't go up (unless we're sick). We know that our body heat remains at an average temperature of 98.6 degrees Fahrenheit.

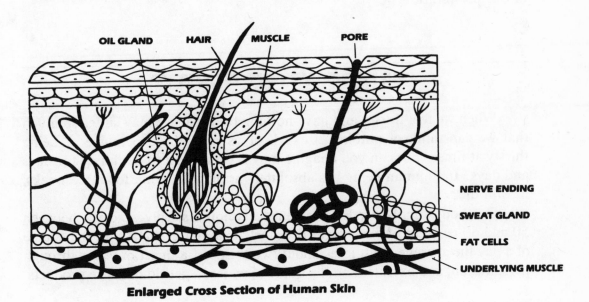

Enlarged Cross Section of Human Skin

Perspiration is one of the ways we keep our body "furnace" at a nice normal temperature. Actually, our body temperature is controlled by a center in the brain known as the temperature center. It consists of three parts: a control center, a heating center, and a cooling center.

Suppose the temperature of the blood drops for some reason. The heating center goes to work and certain things begin to happen. Special glands give out more chemical substances to burn, the muscles and the liver use up more "fuel," and soon our internal temperature rises.

Now suppose the temperature of the blood rises for some reason. The cooling center goes to work. The process of oxidation, or burning up of fuel, is slowed up. And another important thing happens. The vessels in the skin are dilated, or opened, so that the extra heat can radiate away, and also to help our perspiration to evaporate.

When a liquid evaporates, it takes away heat. For example, we feel cold after a bath because the water which remains in contact with our warm skin is evaporating rapidly and cooling us off. So perspiration is part of the process of cooling the body.

Perspiration is like a shower which washes the body from within. The fluid flows out through millions of tiny openings in the skin in the form of miscroscopic drops. And these tiny drops can evaporate quickly and cool the body quickly when necessary.

On humid days, we suffer because the water on our skin can't evaporate easily. So we use fans to carry away the moist air and to help the evaporation of our perspiration.

WHY DO WE GET THIRSTY?

When we feel thirsty and have nothing to drink, we may suffer so much that we can think of nothing else. All of us have the experience of being thirsty at times—but can you imagine how it would feel to be thirsty for days and days? If a human being has absolutely nothing to drink for three weeks, he will die.

Our body simply needs to replenish its liquid supply—and yet between 50 and 60 per cent of our weight is water! As a matter of fact, in the course of a day the average adult loses about two-thirds of a quart of water through perspiration, and excretes about a quart of water to get rid of waste products.

On the other hand, whether we drink or not, we also take in water. When the body digests food, it obtains almost a third of a quart of liquid from this food per day. But this process of losing water and gaining it isn't enough to keep the balance of water our body needs. Thirst is the signal our body gives us that it needs more water.

Dryness in the mouth or throat is not what causes thirst, as many people believe. That dryness may be caused by many things such as nervousness, exercise, or just a slowing-up of the flow of saliva. It is possible to make the saliva flow again (for example, with a little lemon juice), but this will not take care of our thirst.

In fact, your saliva can be flowing freely, your stomach and blood stream and bladder may be full of water—and you can still be thirsty! For example, people who drink whiskey at a bar may have taken several drinks and still feel thirsty—if they happen to have munched on salty peanuts or pretzels between drinks!

The reason for this is that thirst is caused by a change in the salt content of our blood. There is a certain normal amount of salt and water in our blood. When this changes by having more salt in relation to water in our blood, thirst results.

In our brain, there is a "thirst center." It responds to the amount of salt in our blood. When there is a change, it sends messages to the back of the throat. From there, messages go back to the brain, and it is this combination of feelings that makes us say we're thirsty.

WHY DO WE GET TIRED?

Fatigue can actually be considered a kind of poisoning! When a muscle in the body works, it produces lactic acid. If we remove the lactic acid from a tired muscle, it's able to start working again at once!

In the course of a day, we "poison ourselves" with lactic acid. There are other substances the body produces in the course of muscular activity, which are known as "fatigue toxins." The blood carries these through the body, so that not only the muscle itself feels tired, but the entire body, especially the brain.

Scientists have made an interesting experiment about fatigue. If a dog is made to work until it is exhausted and falls asleep, and its blood is then transfused into the body of another dog, the second dog will instantly become "tired" and fall asleep! If the blood of a wide-awake dog is transfused into a tired, sleeping dog, the latter will wake up at once, no longer tired!

But fatigue is not just a chemical process; it is also a biological process. We can't just "remove" fatigue; we must allow the cells of the body to rest. Damages must be repaired, nerve cells of the brain must be "recharged," the joints of the body must replace used-up lubricants. Sleep will always be necessary as a way of restoring the body's energy after fatigue.

However, there is an interesting thing to remember about the process of resting. For example, a person who has been working hard at his desk for hours may not want to lie down at all when he's tired. He'd rather take a walk! Or when children come home from school they want to run out to play . . . not to lie down and rest.

The reason is that if only a certain part of the body is tired—say, the brain, the eyes, the hands, or the legs—the best way to make that part feel fresh again is to make other parts of the body active! We can actually rest by means of activity. Activity increases the respiration, the blood circulates faster, the glands are more active, and the waste products are eliminated from the tired part of the body. But if you are totally exhausted, the best thing to do is to go to sleep!

WHAT CAUSES OUR DREAMS?

Let us begin by saying what does not cause our dreams. Our dreams do not come from "another world." They are not messages from some outside source. They are not a look into the future, nor do they prophesy anything.

All our dreams have something to do with our emotions, fears, longings, wishes, needs, memories. But something on the "outside" may influence what we dream. If a person is hungry, or tired, or cold, his dreams may include this feeling. If the covers have slipped off your bed, you may dream you are on an iceberg. The material for the dream you have tonight is likely to come from the experiences you will have today.

So the "content" of your dream comes from something that affects you while you are sleeping (you are cold, a noise, a discomfort, etc.) and it may also use your past experiences and the urges and interests you have now. This is why very young children are likely to dream of wizards and fairies, older children of school exams, hungry people of food, homesick soldiers of their families, and prisoners of freedom.

To show you how what is happening while you are asleep and your wishes or needs can all be combined in a dream, here is the story of an experiment. A man was asleep and the back of his hand was rubbed with a piece of absorbent cotton. He dreamed that he was in a hospital and his sweetheart was visiting him, sitting on the bed and stroking his hand!

There are people called psychoanalysts who have made a special study of why we dream what we dream and what those dreams mean. Their interpretation of dreams is not accepted by everyone, but it offers an interesting approach to the problem. They believe that dreams are expressions of wishes that didn't come true, of frustrated yearnings. In other words, a dream is a way of having your wish fulfilled.

During sleep, according to this theory, our inhibitions are also asleep. We can express or feel what we really want to. So we do this in a dream and thus provide an outlet for our wishes, and they may be wishes we didn't even know we had!

HOW DOES OUR BLOOD CIRCULATE?

In very simple terms, the blood circulates because the heart "pumps" it and the veins and arteries act as "pipes" to carry it. The blood circulates to carry oxygen from the lungs and food materials from the organs of digestion to the rest of the body, and to remove waste products from the tissues.

The "pipes" are two systems of hollow tubes, one large and one small. Both are connected to the heart, the "pump," but do not connect with each other. The smaller system of blood vessels goes from the heart to the lungs and back. The larger goes from the heart to the various parts of the body. These tubes are called "arteries," "veins," and "capillaries." Arteries move blood away from the heart; the veins carry blood back to the heart. The capillaries are tiny vessels for carrying blood from arteries to veins.

Now a word about the "pump"—the heart. It is like a double two-story house, each with a room upstairs, called the right and left "auricles." The downstairs rooms are the right and left "ventricles."

If we were to trace a drop of blood as it circulated through the entire body, this is the course it would follow. The blood with oxygen from the lungs goes to the left auricle (upstairs room), then to the left ventricle

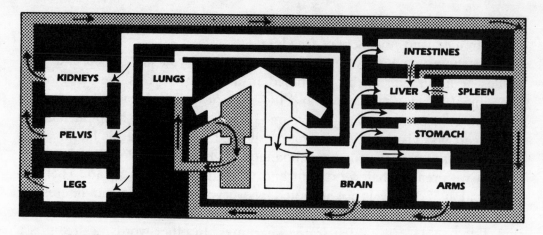

KIDNEYS	LUNGS	INTESTINES
PELVIS		LIVER — SPLEEN
LEGS		STOMACH
	BRAIN	ARMS

(downstairs room), and then to the "aorta." This is the great artery, and it and its branches carry the blood to all parts of the body.

Through the capillaries it goes from the smallest arteries into the smallest veins. It flows through the veins which become larger. Finally, it reaches the right auricle of the heart. Then into the right ventricle, and from there into arteries which carry it into the lungs. Here it gives up carbon dioxide and some water and takes up oxygen. Now it's ready to come back to the left auricle of the heart and start off on its journey again!

The heart squeezes and relaxes about 100,000 times each day and pumps about 3,600 gallons of blood in 24 hours in an adult male!

WHAT IS SKIN?

When we think of the human body, it is easy for us to think of the heart, or the liver, or the brain as "organs." They have certain jobs to do and they do them. But did you know that the skin is an organ, too?

Where other organs take up as little space as possible, the skin is spread out as thinly as possible to form a thin coat. In fact, this coat covers an area of 3,100 square inches. The number of complicated structures that appear in each one of these square inches is fantastic, ranging from sweat glands to nerves.

The skin consists of two layers of tissue. One is a thicker deep layer called the "corium," and on top of it is the delicate tissue called the "epi-

116

dermis." These are joined together in a remarkable way. The bottom layer has "pegs" that project into the upper layer, and this is moulded over them to bind them closely together. Because these "pegs" are arranged in ridges, they form a kind of pattern which we can see in certain places on our skin. In fact, your fingerprints are made by these ridges.

The top layer of your skin, the epidermis, doesn't contain any blood vessels. It actually consists of cells that have died and been changed into "horn." We might say that the human body is covered with horn shingles. This is very useful to us, because horn helps protect us. It is insensitive, so it protects us from pain. Water has no effect on it, and it is even a good electrical insulator.

The very bottom layers of the epidermis are very much alive, however. In fact, it is their job to produce new cells. The new cells are pushed upward by the mother cells. In time, they are separated from their source of food and die to become horn.

Billions of the upper dead horn cells are removed every day in the natural course of our activities. But luckily, just as many billions of new cells are manufactured every day. This is what keeps our skin always young.

There are 30 layers of horn cells in our skin. Every time a top layer is removed by washing or rubbing, a new one is ready underneath it. We can never use up all the layers, because a new layer is always pushing up from the bottom. In this way, we are able to remove stains and dirt from our skins and keep it clean.

WHY DO PEOPLE HAVE DIFFERENT-COLORED SKIN?

People with the whitest skin are found in northern Europe and are called Nordics. People with the blackest skin live in western Africa. People in Southeast Asia have a yellowish tan to their skin. The majority of men, however, are not white, black, or yellow, but represent hundreds of shades of light, swarthy, and brown men.

What is the reason for these differences of color in the skin of people? The explanation really lies in a whole series of chemical processes that take place in the body and the skin. In the tissues of the skin there are certain color bases called "chromogens," which are colorless in themselves. When certain ferments or enzymes act on these color bases, a definite skin color results.

Suppose an individual either does not have these color bases, or his enzymes don't work properly on these bases? Then the person is an "albino" with no pigmentation at all. This can happen to people anywhere in the world. There are albinos in Africa, "whiter" than any white man!

Human skin itself, without the presence of any coloring substance, is creamy white. But to this is added a tinge of yellow, which is due to the presence of a yellow pigment in the skin. Another color ingredient found in skin is black, which is due to the presence of tiny granules of a substance called "melanin." This substance is sepia in color, but when it appears in large masses it seems black.

Another tone is added to the skin by the red color of the blood circulating in the tiny vessels of the skin.

The color of an individual's skin depends on the proportions in which these four colors—white, yellow, black, and red—are combined. All the skin colors of the human race can be obtained by different combinations of these color ingredients which we all have.

Sunlight has the ability to create melanin, the black pigment, in the skin. So people living in tropical areas have more of this pigment and have darker skin. But when you spend a few days in the sun, the ultra-violet light of the sun creates more melanin in your skin, too, and this results in the "sun tan"!

WHAT ARE FRECKLES?

To understand what freckles are and how they appear, we have to understand what gives skin its color in the first place.

The most important pigment in deciding the color of the skin is melanin. You might say that the different skin color of various races depends entirely on the difference in the amount of melanin.

In lower forms of life, by the way, it is the melanin which enables certain fish and lizards to change their colors. In the human being, its most important function, apart from controlling the color, is to protect us against the harmful effects of too much exposure to sunshine.

Melanin is produced by a whole network of special cells that are scattered through the lower layer of the epidermis, which is the thin, outer part of our skin. These cells are called "melanocytes." Now we come to the question: What are freckles? Well, freckles are simply a bunching-up of these melanocytes in spots. That's why freckles have that brownish color, the color of the pigment melanin. Why do some people have freckles and others don't? The reason is heredity. Our parents decide whether we'll have freckles!

The color of freckles (really the color of the melanin in them) can vary from light tan to dark brown, depending on exposure to sun and heat. Sunshine not only can darken them, but can cause new melanin to form.

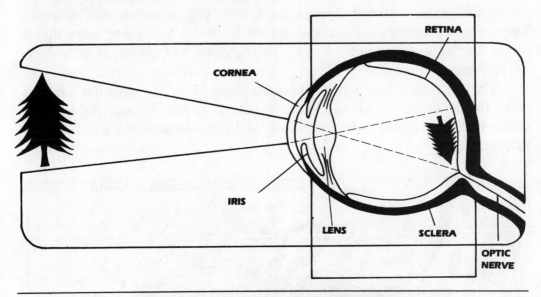

WHAT IS THE EYE MADE OF?

The human eye is like a camera. It has an adjustable opening to let in light (the pupil); a lens which focuses the light waves to form an image; and a sensitive film (the retina) on which the image is recorded.

Inside each human eye are about 130,000,000 light-sensitive cells. When light falls on one of these cells, it causes a quick chemical change within the cell. This change starts an impulse in a nerve fiber. This impulse is a message that travels through the optic nerve to the "seeing" part of the brain. The brain has learned what this message means so we know we are seeing.

The eye is shaped like a ball, with a slight bulge at the front. At the center of this bulge is a hole called the "pupil." It looks black because it opens into the dark inside of the eye. Light passes through the pupil to the lens. The lens focuses the light, forming a picture at the back of the eyeball. Here, instead of film as in a camera, is a screen of light-sensitive cells, called the "retina."

Around the pupil is the iris. It is a doughnut-shaped ring colored blue or green or brown. The iris can change in size like the diaphragm of a camera. In bright light, tiny muscles expand the iris, so that the opening of the pupil is smaller and less light passes into the eyeball. In dim light, the pupil is opened wider and more light is let in.

The entire eyeball is surrounded by a strong membrane called the "sclera." The whites of the eyes are part of the sclera. The sclera is transparent where the eyeball bulges in front. This part is called the "cornea." The space between the cornea and the iris is filled with a clear, salty liquid called the "aqueous humor." The space is shaped like a lens. It is, in fact, a liquid lens.

The eye's other lens is just behind the pupil. You can see what happens when this lens changes shape. When you look at near things, the lens becomes thicker in shape. When you look at distant objects, the lens becomes thinner.

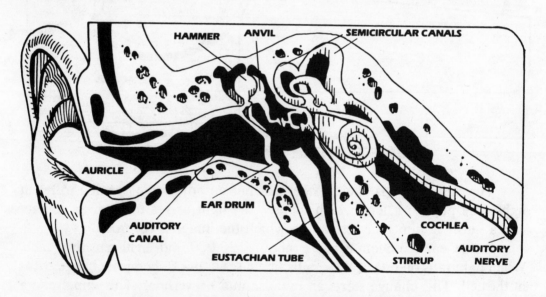

HOW DOES THE EAR WORK?

The ear is one of the most wonderful instruments in our body. Without our having to do any "tuning," it can pick up the tiny tick of a watch one moment and the roar of an explosion the next.

The ear, however, is not the only thing we need to be able to hear. The process of hearings begins with sound. Waves of air, which we call "sound

120

waves," strike on the eardrum. We can neither see nor feel these waves, but the ear is so delicate that the slightest vibration is caught and passed on to the brain. Only when such waves reach the brain do we actually hear.

The ear is made up of three main parts: an outer ear, a middle ear, and an inner ear. Certain animals can move their outer ear forward to catch sounds more easily. But since we cannot move our outer ear, it doesn't really help us much in hearing.

When sound waves enter the outer ear, they travel down a canal. At the end of this canal is a thin skin, stretched tightly across a tube. This skin separates the outer from the middle ear, and it acts as a drum membrane. From the inner side of this drum a short tube, called the "Eustachian tube," leads to the throat. Enough air enters this tube by way of the throat to equalize the pressure caused by the vibrations on the other side of the drum membrane. Otherwise the membrane might be broken by loud sounds.

Directly behind the drum membrane in the middle ear are strung three curious little bones called the "hammer," the "anvil," and the "stirrup." They touch both the drum membrane and the inner ear. When sound waves strike the membrane, they start the three bones vibrating.

These bones, in turn, set up a series of vibrations in the fluid of the shell-shaped inner ear. In this shell, called the "cochlea," tiny cells transfer the sound to certain nerves. These nerves send them to the brain, which recognizes them, and that recognition we call "hearing."

In the inner ear there are also three semicircular canals which have nothing to do with hearing. They are also filled with a fluid, and they give us our sense of balance. If they are out of order, we become dizzy and cannot walk straight.

WHY ARE THERE DIFFERENT TYPES OF HAIR?

The kind of hair you have is a matter of inheritance. But the question is: Why are there so many different types of hair that might be inherited?

The general structure of the hair varies very little among human beings. But its form, its color, its general consistency, and the way a section of it looks under a microscope vary quite a bit. And because these differences occur in certain patterns, the hair is one of the best ways known to determine the race of a person. In other words, the hair you have inherited bears the stamp of your race.

There are three main classifications of hair by the way it's constructed. The first is short and crisp, the kind we call "woolly." A cross section of this hair shows it is elliptical or kidney-shaped. The color is almost always jet black, and it is the hair of all the black races with two exceptions.

The second type of hair is straight, lank, long, and coarse. A cross section of it look round. The color is almost without exception black. This is the hair of the Chinese, the Mongols, and the Indians of the Americas.

The third type of hair is wavy and curly, or smooth and silky. A section of it is oval in shape. This is the hair of Europeans. It is mainly fair with black, brown, red, or towy varieties.

There is also a fourth type, known as "frizzy," which is the hair of the Australian natives. Curly hair is generally hair that is quite flat in structure. The rounder the hair, the stiffer it is.

When it comes to color, some types have a range of colors, some do not. Wavy types of hair vary most in color. That's why, among Europeans, you can find the deepest black hair side by side with flaxen hair. But fair hair is more common in northern Europe and much rarer in the south. Among the races with straight hair, fair hair color is very rare. Races with frizzy hair have red hair almost as often as those with wavy hair. But red hair is related to the individual only—there are no races with red hair!

WHAT ARE FINGERNAILS MADE OF?

If every time you bit your nails you suffered pain, you'd probably never bite them. Or for that matter, if it hurt us to cut our nails there would be a great many people with very long nails!

But cutting, biting, filing our nails don't hurt us because the nails are made up of dead cells. The nails are special structures that grow from the skin. Most of the nail is made up of a substance called "keratin." This is a tough, dead form of protein, and a horn-like material.

At the base of the nail, and part of the way along its sides, the nail is embedded in the skin. The skin beneath the nail is just like any other skin except that it contains elastic fibers. These are connected to the nail to hold it firmly.

Most of the nail is quite thick, but at the point near the roots beneath the skin it is very thin. This part is white in appearance and has the shape of a semicircle or half-moon. It is called the "lunule." The fingernails grow about two inches a year.

Women, of course, have made the fingernails an object of beauty with nail colors and polishes. But to a great many people, the nails present all sorts of problems. One reason for many nail disorders is that the nails become injured. A burn or frostbite, for example, may injure nails so that they'll never grow again.

Nails that are very brittle, or hard, or that tend to split may be the result of many things: infections, a disturbance of the nutritional system, poor circulation of the blood, or even glandular disturbances.

Women who complain of peeling off of the nails at the tips may in many cases only have themselves to blame. They simply let their nails grow too long. Long nails are subject to shocks and this can result in damage to the nails.

HOW DO WE TALK?

The ability of man to speak is due a great deal to the way in which the larynx is made. This is a hollow organ, shaped something like a box. It is really an enlarged part of the windpipe. The walls of this "box" are made of cartilage and they are lined inside with mucous membrane.

At one place on each side, the mucous membrane becomes thicker and projects from the wall into the center of the box. These projections are the "vocal cords." Each cord is moved by many small muscles. When air goes from the lungs into the mouth, it passes between the two vocal cords and makes them vibrate. This produces a sound.

What kind of sound? It depends on the position and tension of these vocal cords. The muscle system that controls them is the most delicate muscle system in the entire body to make possible all the kinds of sounds we produce. Actually, the vocal cords can assume about 170 different positions!

When the vocal cords vibrate, the column of air that is in the respiratory passage is made to vibrate. What we really hear is the vibration of this column of air. If the vocal cords are not too tensed, long waves are produced and we hear deep tones. If the vocal cords are tensed, they vibrate rapidly, so short waves are produced and we hear high tones. When boys reach the age of about 14, the cords and the larynx become thicker and this makes the pitch of the voice lower. This change in pitch is called "change of voice."

So we see that the pitch of the sound we make is controlled by the tension of the vocal cords. Now how about the tone? This is determined by the resonating spaces, just as the tone of a violin is determined by the vibrations of the entire instrument. In speaking or singing, the resonating spaces involved include the windpipe, the lungs, the thorax, and even the spaces in our mouth and nose. The vibration of air in all of them helps decide the tone.

But that isn't all. Our abdomen, chest, diaphragm, tongue, palate, lips, teeth also get into the picture! All of them are involved in producing sounds and letters. So you see that the process of speaking is like playing on a very complicated and difficult musical instrument. It is only because we learned it early in childhood and practice it continuously that we are able to do it so well!

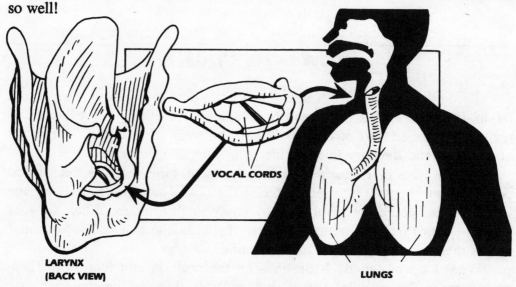

VOCAL CORDS

LARYNX
(BACK VIEW)

LUNGS

WHY ARE SOME PEOPLE LEFT-HANDED?

Many parents of left-handed children worry about this condition and wonder if they shouldn't try to correct it. The answer given by most authorities is: No! If there is a strong preference for the left hand, and the person is able to perform well with it, there should be no interference.

About four per cent of the population is left-handed. In the course of history, many of the greatest geniuses have been left-handed! Leonardo da Vinci and Michelangelo, the greatest sculptors of all times, were both left-handed.

Of course, we live in a "right-handed society"—that is, most of the things we use are made for right-handed people. Our doorknobs, locks, screwdrivers, automobiles, musical instruments—even the buttons on our clothes—are arranged for right-handed people. This may cause a certain amount of adjustment to be made by left-handed people, but most of them can manage quite well.

There is no single accepted explanation of what makes most people right-handed and a small minority left-handed. Here is one theory: The body is not "symmetrical," that is, it is not exactly the same on both sides. The right side of our face is a little different from the left. Our legs differ in strength. Our feet may differ a tiny bit in size. And this "asymmetry" goes through our whole body.

Now when we come to the brain, we discover that while it has a right half and a left half, these two halves don't function the same way. It is believed that the left half of the brain is "predominant" over the right half.

The nerves from the brain cross over at the level of the neck and go to the opposite side of the body. The right half of the brain supplies the left half of the body, and vice versa.

Now since the left half of the brain predominates, the right half of the body is more skilled, better able to do things. We read, write, speak, and work with the left half of the brain. And this, of course, makes most of us right-handed, too. But in the case of left-handed people, there is an "inversion." The right half of the brain is predominant, and such a person works best with the left side of his body!

WHAT CAUSES HICCOUGHS?

In England, there's an old superstition about how to get rid of hiccoughs. It goes like this: "To cure the hiccoughs, wet the forefinger of the right hand with spittle, and cross the front of the left shoe three times, saying the Lord's Prayer backwards."

You've probably heard of dozens of other "prescriptions" for getting rid of hiccoughs, most of them just about as effective as this old superstition! Hiccoughs really have nothing mysterious about them. They are the result of an action the body takes to protect itself. Let's see how this is so.

The body, as you know, has many reflexes. A reflex is a response on the part of the body to some sort of specific stimulation. This response is always the same, and seems to take place because certain nerve connections have been built up in our nervous system. We don't "decide" what action to take; the nerve connections spring into action without our control when there is a reflex action.

Now there are whole series of reflexes that have to do with getting solid and liquid food into our system and with getting rid of these or other foreign objects from air passages into which they sometimes go. For example, there are a whole series of reflexes connected with swallowing food. When food goes "the wrong way," the gagging and choking are reflex actions trying to expel the food.

Sneezing and coughing are actually normal reflexes in which a blast of air is used to help the body get rid of material it doesn't want. Vomiting is a very strong reflex action of this same type. And hiccoughing can be considered a sort of half-hearted and ineffective effort to vomit!

Hiccoughs can start because hot food has irritated some passage inside, or when gas in the stomach presses upward against the diaphragm. The diaphragm separates the chest from the stomach. The diaphragm tightens and pulls air into the lungs. But air can't get through and we feel a "bump" at the moment the air is stopped. So hiccoughs are a reflex action of the body trying to get food or gas out of the stomach, thereby irritating the diaphragm, which in turn affects the passage of air in and out of the lungs. We feel this as a "bump" and say we have the hiccoughs!

WHAT MAKES PEOPLE SNEEZE?

For some strange reason, the act of sneezing has long been considered more than just a physical action. All kinds of ideas and legends have grown up about sneezing, as if it had special significance.

Actually sneezing is the act of sending out air from the nose and mouth. It is a reflex act, and happens without our control. Sneezing occurs when the nerve-endings of the mucous membrane of the nose are irritated. It can also happen, curiously enough, when our optic nerve is stimulated by a bright light!

The irritation that causes sneezing may be due to a swelling of the mucous membrane of the nose, as happens when we have a cold; it may be due to foreign bodies that somehow get into the nose; or it may be due to an allergy. The act of sneezing is an attempt by the body to expel air to get rid of the irritating bodies.

126

From earliest times, however, people have wondered about sneezing, and it has universally been regarded as an omen of some kind. The Greeks, Romans, and Egyptians regarded the sneeze as a warning in times of danger, and as a way of foretelling the future. If you sneezed to the right, it was considered lucky; to the left, unlucky.

The reason we say "God bless you" after someone sneezes cannot be traced to any single origin, but seems to be connected with ancient beliefs. The Romans thought a person expelled evil spirits when he sneezed, so everyone present would say "Good luck to you" after a sneeze, hoping the effort to expel the spirits would succeed.

Primitive people believed that sneezing was a sign of approaching death. When anyone sneezed, therefore, people said "God help you!" because the person sneezing was in danger.

There is a legend that before the days of Jacob, a person died after sneezing. Jacob interceded with God, according to this tale, so that people could sneeze without dying—provided a benediction followed every sneeze!

During the sixth century there was a plague in Italy, and Pope Gregory the Great ordered that prayers be said against sneezing. It was at this time that the custom of saying "God bless you!" to persons who sneezed became established.

WHAT IS HAY FEVER?

If you don't suffer from hay fever, watching someone who does presents quite a mystery. Here you are living side by side, breathing the same air, and you go about feeling perfectly fit, while the other person sneezes constantly and suffers a great deal!

Hay fever is a form of allergy. It belongs to a group of maladies, including hives, asthma, and certain skin problems, that are caused by something called "protein sensitization."

Let us examine what this means. Protein, as we know, is found in foods. But it so happens that the pollens of plants are also protein. At a certain time of the year, many kinds of grasses, such as ragweed, send their pollens into the air in great amounts.

They reach human beings through the nose, mouth, and eyes. If the person whom they reach is not protein-sensitive, nothing happens. But when a person is abnormally sensitive to these proteins, they act upon certain

RAGWEED

GOLDENROD

muscles and tissues and cause those reactions that make them feel miserable.

A person may be sensitive to several different pollens, which is why the treatment of hay fever is a bit complicated. All the causes of the attack of hay fever have to be identified. Some patients are helped by injections of pollen or protein extracts which seem to build up an immunity. Other patients simply try to live in some other section of the country where the troublesome pollens don't exist.

WHAT CAUSES HEADACHES?

The answer to this question might be: anything and everything! A headache can start for any one of hundreds of reasons. You see, a headache is not a sickness or a disease. It is a symptom. It simply is a way of knowing that there is some disorder somewhere—in some part of the body or the nervous system.

Of course we know something about the "mechanism" of a headache, that is, what happens in the body or nervous system to produce the pain of a headache. The pain itself comes from certain structures in the skull. The large veins and others in the brain that drain the surface of the brain are sensitive to pain. It is not the brain substance itself but the coverings of the brain and the veins and arteries that are sensitive. When they "hurt," you have a headache. Also, when your sinuses, teeth, ears, and muscles hurt, the pain may spread to the brain area and produce a headache. If the muscles that are over the neck and near the head are contracted, this can also produce headaches.

When you listen to people talk about their headache problems, you hear them give personal reasons. But most of these are conditions that apply to many people. For example, some people get a headache when they're hungry, others say going without their "morning coffee" produces a headache, or it may be from a "hangover." What is really happening in all these cases is that the arteries in the skull are being dilated (or enlarged)—and this produces a headache in practically anybody. It's known as a "vascular headache."

Or suppose somebody suddenly had a vigorous jolt or twisted his head and began to complain of a headache. There's nothing special about such cases. What happened was that certain pain-sensitive structures in the brain were pulled or tightened and pain resulted. A person may be undergoing great emotional tension and this will cause muscles to contract or tighten over the back, lower part of the head, and neck. Result? A headache!

"Migraine" headaches are a special kind of headache and quite different from these. But as you can see, the symptom of disorder we call a "headache" has many, many causes!

WHAT IS A "COLD"?

Almost everybody knows the joke about the doctor who tells the patient who has a cold: "If you only had pneumonia, I could cure you." The cold is not only one of the most annoying afflictions man has to bear, but one of the most mysterious, as well.

More than 90 per cent of the people in the United States get a cold every year, and more than half of them get several colds during the year. You probably know the symptoms of a cold as well as your doctor does. There's a "running" nose, you sneeze a lot, you might have a sore or tickling throat, and sometimes a headache. Later on, a cough or fever may develop.

In an adult, a cold is seldom serious. But in children, the cold symptoms may actually be the early symptoms of more serious childhood diseases, such as measles or diptheria. That's why colds in children should have prompt medical attention.

A cold takes from one to three days to develop. There are three stages of the common cold. The first is the "dry" stage, which doesn't last long.

Your nose feels dry and swollen, your throat may have a tickle, and your eyes may water a bit. In the second stage, you get the "running" nose. And **finally**, that nose is really "running" and you may have fever and be coughing.

Now as to the great mystery. What is the common cold? What causes it? We can describe it as an acute inflammation of the upper respiratory tract—but that doesn't help much. Medical science simply doesn't know the specific cause of the common cold!

It is generally believed, however, that the infection is caused by a virus of some kind. But here's the strange thing: That virus is probably in your throat most of the time. It simply doesn't attack until your body resistance is lowered. There may also be other bacteria present and they don't attack either until your resistance is low. So it seems that the cold virus weakens the tissues so that other germs can infect them.

The best way to avoid a cold, therefore, is to keep your resistance high with a good diet, plenty of rest and sleep, proper dress, and avoiding contact with people who have colds.

WHY DO WE GET FEVER?

The first thing your doctor, or even your mother, will do when you don't feel well is take your temperature with a thermometer. They are trying to find out whether you have "fever."

Your body has an average temperature of 98.6 degrees Fahrenheit when it is healthy. Disease makes this temperature rise, and we call this higher temperature "fever." While every disease doesn't cause fever, so many of them do that fever is almost always a sign that your body is sick in some way.

Your doctor or nurse usually takes your temperature at least twice a day and puts it on a chart, showing how your fever goes up and down. This chart can often tell the doctor exactly which disease you have. A fever chart for pneumonia, for instance, goes up and down in a certain way. Other diseases have other patterns or "temperature curves" on the chart.

The strange thing is that we still don't know what fever really is. But we do know that fever actually helps us fight off sickness. Here's why: Fever makes the vital processes and organs in the body work faster. The body produces more hormones, enzymes, and blood cells. The hormones and enzymes, which are useful chemicals in our body, work harder. Our blood cells destroy harmful germs better. Our blood circulates faster, we breathe faster, and we thus get rid of wastes and poisons in our system better.

But the body can't afford to have a fever too long or too often. When you have a fever for 24 hours, you destroy protein that is stored in your body. And since protein is mighty necessary for life, fever is an "expensive" way to fight off disease!

WHAT IS CANCER?

As you probably know from the appeals being made for funds to fight cancer, and from all the research that is being done on this subject—cancer is a great menace to the health and life of mankind. We will only discuss cancer in general terms, so you can have an idea of what happens in a body that has cancer.

A cancer is a continuous growth in the body which doesn't follow the normal growth pattern. The cells forming the cancer spread through the body to parts which may be far from the spot where the cancer began. Unless it is removed or destroyed, the cancer can lead to the death of the person.

Cells in the body are growing all the time. As they wear out and disappear, their places are taken by new cells of exactly the same kind. But cancer cells look and act differently from normal body cells. They look like the young cell of the part of the body where they started—but different enough to be recognized as cancer when seen through a microscope.

When these cancer cells divide and increase in number, they don't change into the fully grown form and then stop reproducing. Instead, they remain young cells and continue to increase in number until they are harmful.

As the cancer cells grow, they do not remain in one spot, but separate and move in among the normal cells. They may become so numerous that the normal cells in this part of the body cannot continue to work or even remain alive. When the cancer gets into the blood, it is carried to distant parts of the body. There it may grow to form large masses which interfere with the activities of the normal cells.

Unless the growth and spread of the cancer is stopped, the patient will die. That's why it's important to have periodic examinations to detect and treat cancer before it has spread too far.

Cancers are not spread from man to man by contact. No drug has been found that cures completely and is useful for all kinds of cancer. One of medicine's greatest goals is to understand fully the nature and cause of cancer, and to find a way to prevent and cure it.

CHAPTER 4
HOW OTHER CREATURES LIVE

CAN ANIMALS UNDERSTAND EACH OTHER?

If we mean can animals communicate with each other, that is, pass on certain messages by signs and sounds, the answer is yes. If we mean can they talk to each other as we do, the answer is no.

Even among human beings, all communication is not by means of words. We have expressions to indicate anger, a shrug of the shoulder to indicate indifference, nodding and shaking the head, gestures with hands, and so on. Many animals make noises and signs to do the same thing.

When a mother hen makes a loud noise or crouches down, all her chicks understand this as a warning of danger. When a horse neighs or paws the ground, the other horses "get the message." Some animals can follow very slight signs or signals given by other animals. When a bird merely flies up to a branch to look around, the other birds don't move. But if a bird flies up in a certain way, they can tell it's about to fly off and they may follow.

Dogs communicate in many ways. They not only bark, but they howl, growl, snarl, and whine. They lift a paw, or bare their teeth. Other dogs can understand what these sounds and actions mean.

Animals communicate with each other not only with sounds and movements, but with smell. Most animals that live in herds depend on smell to keep together. And, of course, we know how dogs recognize each other by smell.

Apes are supposed to be among the most intelligent of animals, yet they really have no better "language" than other animals. They make many sounds and expressions of the face to communicate their feelings of anger or hunger or joy, but they have nothing like the words of human speech.

By the way, unlike human beings who have to learn how to talk, apes and other animals know their "language" by instinct. They will make the right kind of cries and sounds and expressions even if they have never seen another animal like themselves before.

Birds, however, learn their way of singing, at least in part. That's why a sparrow brought up among canaries will try to sing like one. It has been learning the wrong "language"!

DO ANIMALS LAUGH OR CRY?

If you have a pet, such as a cat or a dog, you may become so attached to it that in time you almost feel it's "human." That is, you begin to think it can express the way it feels in terms of human emotions, such as crying, or perhaps even laughing.

But this isn't really so. Crying and laughing are human ways of expressing emotions and no animals have this way. Of course, we know that animals can whimper and whine when they are hurt, but crying involves the production of tears with this emotion, and animals cannot do this.

This doesn't mean that animals don't have the tear fluid in their eyes. But it is used to irrigate the cornea of the eye. A creature must be a thinking and emotionally sensitive person to cry. Even children begin to cry only when they learn to think and feel. An infant yells, but he is not crying.

Crying is a substitute for speaking. When we cannot say what we feel, we cry. It is a reflex that happens despite ourselves and that helps us "get out" what we feel.

Laughter is also a human phenomenon. Some animals may give the impression that they laugh, but it is not at all like human laughter. The reason is that man always laughs at something, and this means that a certain mental process or emotion is involved. Animals are incapable of having such a mental process or emotion.

For example, when we laugh at a joke, or at a "funny" sight, our minds or our emotions make it seem laughable. In fact, there are many kinds of laughter and many reasons why we laugh. We may laugh at the ridiculous (a big, fat man with a tiny umbrella), or at the comic (a clown, for example), or at the humorous (a joke), and so on. We may even laugh in scorn.

Psychologists also believe that laughter is a social phenomenon. We laugh when we are part of a group that finds something amusing. Animals, of course, cannot resort to laughter for any of these reasons.

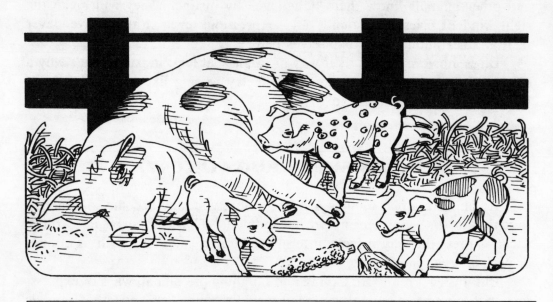

CAN ANIMALS TASTE?

Our sense of taste is a source of great pleasure to us. It makes the enjoyment of food possible. But we have a sense of taste not just to give us pleasure, but to protect us, too. It often prevents us from eating things that might harm us.

What is the process of tasting? It is the ability to perceive the impact of molecules. These moving molecules stimulate the taste nerves and we identify the message we receive as having a certain taste. Only substances that are in solution, where the atoms move about freely, can be tasted. A piece of glass, for example, has no taste. Everything that makes the molecules move about more intensifies the taste. That's why hot things have more taste than cold things.

The sensation of taste is first received by taste buds, which are really nerves constructed like buds. They have the special ability to pick up certain sensations which we call taste.

These taste buds are located, in man and the higher animals, on the tongue. The number of taste buds varies greatly, depending on the taste needs of the particular species of animal. Man, for example, is only a moderate taster. We have about 3,000 taste buds. A whale, which swallows whole schools of fish without even chewing, has few or no taste buds.

A pig, oddly enough, is more particular in its tastes than man, and has 5,500 taste buds. A cow has 35,000 taste buds, and an antelope has as many as 50,000 taste buds! So you see that not only can animals taste, but many of them are more sensitive tasters than man.

Animals that live in the sea often have taste buds all over their body. Fish, for example, taste with the whole surface of the body, right down to their tails! Flies and butterflies can actually taste with their feet. When the last joint of a butterfly's leg touches something sweet, its snout stretches out immediately so it can suck it up.

Snakes and lizards use their tongues for tasting, but not as we do. The tip of the tongue flickers out and picks up particles. It brings them to a special organ in the roof of the mouth which smells or tastes them!

CAN ANIMALS SEE IN COLOR?

The world is so bright with color everywhere we turn that it's hard to imagine that other creatures don't see it as we do. But how can we find out whether animals can see color when they can't tell us?

Scientists have made many experiments to get the answer. The bee has been the subject of hundreds of these tests, because we have been curious to know whether the bee tells flowers apart by their color. In one experiment, a bit of sirup was put in front of a blue card, and no sirup in front of a red card. After a while, the bees would come to the blue card, no matter where it was placed, and even if it had no sirup in front of it. This proved they could tell colors apart.

Two strange things were found out about the bee's ability to see in color. The first is that a bee cannot see red as a color. For a bee, it's only dark grey or black. The second is that bees can see ultraviolet as a color, while for human beings, it is just darkness!

Male birds have bright colors. Can female birds see those colors? In experiments done with hens, it was proven that they can see all the colors of the rainbow! But now comes a surprise. The animal that is probably closest of all to man as a friend, the dog, is color-blind! So far all experiments that have been made prove that the dog can't tell one color from another. Many times when we think the dog is responding to a color, he is really responding to some other clue or sign—smell, size, shape. Dog lovers should not be too disappointed by this because the dog's sense of smell is so great that it probably compensates for the inability to see in color. Cats, by the way, seem to be color-blind, too!

Monkeys and apes have a very good sense of color, but most other mammals are color-blind, including bulls!

The reason for color-blindness in mammals is connected with the fact that most of them hunt by night and don't depend on color, and also that they themselves are usually dull in color, so it isn't important in their lives.

WHY DO ANIMALS HIBERNATE?

Let's look at the woodchuck as a typical hibernating animal. Unlike the squirrel, it doesn't store up a food supply for the winter. It depends on plant food, and when winter comes its food supply is gone. But the woodchuck has stored up a reserve supply of fat on its own body. So when it can no longer find food, it crawls deep into its burrow and goes to sleep. It sleeps through the cold winter and lives on the fat which it has stored up. The word "hibernate" comes from the Latin and means "winter sleep."

Many mammals, like the bear, do not really hibernate. They do sleep more in the winter than in summer, but it is not the deep sleep of hibernation. On warm and pleasant days in the winter, the bear, the squirrel, the chipmunk will wake up and come out into the open.

136

But the sleep of a true hibernator is almost like death and is quite unlike ordinary sleep. While an animal is hibernating, all its life activities nearly stop. The temperature of its body decreases until it is only a little warmer than the air of its den.

Because of this, the animals burn the food stored in their bodies very, very slowly. Since they burn less fuel, they need less oxygen, and as a result, their breathing is slower and their hearts beat only faintly. If the temperature in the den becomes very low, the hibernating animal wakes up, digs itself in a little deeper, and goes to sleep once more.

When spring comes, the animals are awakened by the change in temperature, moisture, and by hunger. They crawl out of their dens.

Did you know that many cold-blooded animals hibernate, also? Earthworms crawl down into the earth below the frost line; frogs bury themselves in the mud at the bottom of ponds; snakes crawl into cracks in the rocks or holes in the ground; and a few fish, such as the carp, bury themselves in the muddy bottom. Even some insects hibernate by hiding under rocks or logs!

WHY DOES A COW CHEW ITS CUD?

Many thousands of years ago, there were certain animals who couldn't protect themselves too well against their stronger, fiercer enemies. In order to survive, these animals developed a special way of eating. They would snatch some food hastily whenever they could, swallow it quickly without chewing, and run away to hide. Then when they were in their hiding place, sitting calmly, they would chew the food at their leisure!

Our "cud-chewing" animals are descended from these and are called "Ruminantia." It so happens that nearly all the mammals that are most useful to man are Ruminantia. These include cows, sheep, goats, camels, llamas, deer, and antelopes.

Here is what makes it possible for a ruminant like a cow to chew its cud. A ruminant has a complicated stomach with five compartments. These compartments are: the paunch or rumen, the honeycomb bag or reticulum, the manyplies or omasum, the true stomach or abomasum, and the intestine.

Each of these compartments of the stomach does something different to the food. When the food is swallowed, it is made into a coarse pellet and goes into the paunch, the largest of the five compartments. There it is moistened and softened and then passes into the honeycomb or reticulum.

Here it is made into balls, or "cuds" of a convenient size.

After a ruminant has eaten, it usually lies down or rests quietly somewhere. At this time it regurgitates the food from the reticulum back into the mouth. Now the ruminant chews the cud for the first time. After chewing, it swallows the food again and it goes into the manyplies, or third stomach. From here the food goes into the true stomach where the process of digestion takes place. Camels, by the way, differ from other ruminants in not having a third stomach.

Cows have no teeth in the upper jaw. Instead, the gum is in the form of a tough pad. This pad holds the grass down across the edges of the lower front teeth. When a cow grazes, it uses a sideways motion of the head to cut off the grass in this manner.

HOW LONG HAVE DOGS BEEN DOMESTICATED?

Hundreds of thousands of years ago, giant mammoths still roamed the earth and the world was covered with dense forests. Men lived in caves and dressed themselves in the skins of wild beasts. It was then that the dog first became man's friend.

At first the dog followed men on their hunting expeditions, to get whatever share he could of the kill. Then the instinct for companionship made him adopt man as his leader. Soon the men trained the dogs to help them in the hunt, to carry their burdens, and to guard their firesides. All this happened long before there was any recorded history. Actually, we can only guess at the story from finding the bones of primitive dogs with the bones of men in the caves of Stone Age.

Since the history of the dog goes back many hundreds of thousands of years, it is impossible to trace it clearly. Some scientists believe that dogs are the result of the mating of wolves and jackals. Other scientists say that some dogs are descended from wolves, other dogs from jackals, others from coyotes, and some from foxes. A widely held theory is that our modern dogs and the wolves are descended from a very remote common ancestor.

This theory helps to explain the differences in size and appearance of the various breeds of dogs and also explains their habits. When a dog turns around three times before he settles down to sleep, it may be because his remote ancestors had to beat down a nest among the forest leaves or jungle grasses. Other evidence of the wild ancestry of dogs is the build of their bodies, which is naturally adapted for speed and strength. This, together with their keen scent and quick hearing, were qualities they needed when they were wild hunters.

From the time there have been any permanent records of man's history, the dog has been mentioned. There are pictures of dogs on Egyptian tombs that are 5,000 years old. The Egyptians even considered the dog sacred, and when a dog died in an Egyptian home, the whole family went into mourning.

Though the dog has been loved and respected by most peoples of the world, there are some exceptions. The Hindus still consider the dog unclean and the Mohammedans despise dogs.

WHEN WERE CATS DOMESTICATED?

The cat has been around for a long, long time. Fossils of cats have been found which are millions of years old!

The domesticated cat we know today is the descendant of the wildcat, but just which wildcat we don't know, because it happened so long ago. Probably our varieties, or breeds, of domesticated cats all came from two or three of the small wildcats that existed in Europe, North Africa, and Asia thousands of years ago.

The best guess we have is that about 5,000 years ago these wildcats were domesticated for the first time. We know that 4,000 years ago the Egyptians had tame cats. In fact, the Egyptians worshipped the cat as a god. Their goddess Bast, or Pacht, was shown in pictures with a cat's head, and sacrifices were offered to cats.

The cat represented their chief god and goddess, Ra and Isis. When a house cat died, the Egyptian family and servants shaved their eyebrows and went into mourning. The death of a temple cat was mourned by the whole city. Many mummies of cats have been found, prepared in the same way as the mummies of kings and nobles. The penalty for killing a cat was death!

In Europe, however, there were probably no tame cats until after A.D 1000. In ancient times, the Europeans had quite a different attitude toward the cat than the Egyptians did. They thought of it as an evil spirit rather than a god. The devil was often pictured as a black cat, and witches were supposed to take the shape of cats.

The various breeds of domestic cats and individual cats vary from each other as much as the different breeds and individual dogs do. Probably the most easily recognized groups are the short-haired cats and the long-haired cats. The Angora and the Persian are the best-known long-haired cats.

WHY IS THE LION CALLED "KING OF BEASTS"?

Throughout the history of man, the lion has been considered the symbol of strength. We say "strong as a lion" or "lion-hearted." In courts throughout the world, the lion was used on shields and crests and banners to indicate power.

Probably this was not because anybody could prove that a lion could defeat all other animals in combat, but because lions strike such terror in man and in other beasts.

The ancient Egyptians believed the lion was sacred, and during the time when Christ was born, lions lived in many parts of Europe. By the year 500, however, they had all been killed. Today, the only places where lions are plentiful are in Africa and in one region of India.

Lions are members of the cat family. The average length of a grown-up lion is about nine feet and they weigh between 400 and 500 pounds. The males are larger than the females. People who hunt lions can always tell whether they are tracking a male or female by the size of the tracks. The male has larger front feet than the female.

The lion's voice is a roar or a growl. Unlike other cats, it doesn't purr, and rarely climbs trees. Unlike other cats, too, it takes readily to deep water. Lions feed on grazing animals, so they live in more or less open country and not in forests. And because they drink once a day, they always live near some supply of water.

Lions rest by day and do their hunting by night. Lions may live singly, or in pairs, or in groups of four to a dozen which are known as "prides." The main food supply of lions comes from zebras, gazelles, and antelopes. Sometimes a lion will attack a giraffe, but it won't attack an elephant, rhinoceros, or hippopotamus. When a lion isn't hungry, he pays no attention to other animals.

When hunting, a lion may lay hidden until an animal passes close by, or it may crawl and wiggle up to its victim and then make a sudden rush. When it makes that rush, it can go as fast as 40 miles an hour!

WHY DOES A MALE BIRD HAVE BRIGHTER COLORS THAN THE FEMALE?

To understand why this is so, we must first understand why birds have colors at all!

Many explanations have been given for the coloring of birds, but science still doesn't understand this subject fully. You see, the reason it's hard to explain is that some birds are brilliantly colored, others dully. Some birds stand out like bright banners; others are difficult to see.

All we can do is try to find a few rules that hold true for most birds. One rule is that birds with brighter colors spend most of their time in tree-tops, in the air, or on the water. Birds with duller colors live mostly on or near the ground.

Another rule—with many exceptions!—is that the upperparts of birds are darker in color than the underparts.

Facts like these make science believe that the reason birds have colors is for protection, so that they can't easily be seen by their enemies. This is called "protective coloration." A snipe's colors, for instance, blend perfectly with the grasses of marshes where it lives. A woodcock's colors look exactly like fallen leaves.

Now if the colors are meant to protect birds, which bird needs the most protection, the male or the female? The female, because she has to sit on the nest and hatch the eggs. So nature gives her duller colors to keep her better hidden from enemies!

Another reason for the brighter colors of the male bird is that they help attract the female during the breeding season. This is usually the time when the male bird's colors are brightest of all. Even among birds, you see, there can be love at first sight!

WHY DO BIRDS SING?

The song of birds is one of the loveliest sounds in nature. Sometimes when we are out in the country and we hear birds singing, it seems to us they are calling back and forth, that they are telling one another something.

The fact is that birds do communicate with one another, just as many other animals do. Of course, at times the sounds birds make are mere expressions of joy, just as we may make cries of "Oh!" and "Ah!" But for the most part, the sounds that birds make are attempts at communication.

A mother hen makes sounds that warn her chicks of danger and causes them to crouch down motionless. Then she gives another call which collects them together. When wild birds migrate at night, they cry out. These cries may keep the birds together and help lost ones return to the flock.

But the language of birds is different from language as we use it. We use words to express ideas, and these words have to be learned. Birds don't learn their language. It is an inborn instinct with them. In one experiment, for example, chicks were kept away from cocks and hens so they couldn't hear the sounds they made. Yet when they grew up they were able to make those sounds just as well as chicks that had grown up with cocks and hens!

This doesn't mean that birds can't learn how to sing. In fact, some birds can learn the songs of other birds. This is how our mockingbird gets its name. If a sparrow is brought up with canaries, it will make great efforts to sing like a canary. If a canary is brought up with a nightingale, it can give quite a good imitation of the nightingale's song. And we all know how a parrot can imitate the sounds it hears. So we must say that while birds are born with the instinct to sing, some learning takes place, too.

Did you know that birds have dialects? The song of the same kind of bird sounds different in different parts of the world. This shows that in addition to their instinct, birds do quite a bit of learning in their lifetime when it comes to singing.

WHAT KEEPS A DUCK AFLOAT?

When we use the word "duck," we are really referring to a very wide variety of birds. It ranges from the familiar barnyard type to the wild traveler in the skies. In fact, the duck family includes swans, geese, the mergansers or fishing ducks, the tree ducks, the dabbling ducks, the diving ducks, and the ruddy ducks.

Most of the wild ducks breed from the Canadian border states to the limit of trees in the Far North. It is only in the winter that they travel to the Central and Southern States. But they stay in the South for only a short time. As soon as the ice breaks up in the North, they head for home, the ponds, streams, marshes, lake shores, and seacoast where they like to live.

Ducks have no problem living in icy waters. The reason they are able to stay afloat is that their outer coat of closely packed feathers is actually waterproof. A gland near the duck's tail gives off an oil which spreads over the feathers. Underneath this coat, a layer of thick down protects them further. Even the webfeet of a duck are designed to protect them from the cold water. There are no nerves or blood in the webfeet, so they don't feel the cold.

The ducks' feet and legs are set far back on the body, which helps them greatly in swimming. It also gives them that peculiar waddle when they walk. A duck can move through the air pretty rapidly, too, and in short flights ducks have been known to go as fast as 70 miles an hour!

Most ducks build their nests on the ground near water. They line the nest with delicate plants and with down from the duck's own breasts. This warm down covers the eggs when the female is away from the nest. A duck lays about six to fourteen eggs, and only the female sits on the eggs.

Ducks molt, or shed their feathers, after the breeding season. Since their wing quills are gone at this time, ducks cannot fly during their molting period. To protect themselves from their enemies, they stay very quiet so as not to attract attention.

There are about 160 different types of species of ducks in the world, and they are found on every continent except Antarctica. In North America, we have about 40 species.

HOW DO FISH BREATHE?

Hundreds of thousands of years ago, long before man appeared on the earth, there were already fish swimming about in the oceans. At that time, fish were the most highly developed form of life in existence. In fact, fish were the first backboned animals to appear.

Since that time, fish have developed in a variety of ways, so that today only a very few even faintly resemble the first primitive fish of the oceans.

As a general rule, fish are long and tapering in shape. Man has copied this shape in his construction of ships and submarines because it's the best shape for cutting through water quickly.

Most fish use their tails as a power engine and guide themselves with tail and fins. Except for a kind of fish called "lungfish," all fish breathe by means of their gills. A fish takes in water through its mouth. The water flows over the gills and out through the opening behind the covers of the gills. This water contains oxygen which the fish thus obtains to purify its blood, just as human beings take oxygen out of the air to purify their blood.

When the water is contaminated in some way, fish will sometimes attempt to come to the top and breathe in air, but their gills are not suited for using the oxygen in the air.

The blood of fish is cold, but they have nervous systems like other animals and suffer pain. Their sense of touch is very keen, and they taste, as well as feel, with their skin.

Fish are able to smell, too. They have two small organs of smell, which are located in nostrils on the head. Fish have ears, but they are inside the head and are called "internal ears."

The reason fish are usually dark on top and light underneath is that this helps protect them from enemies. Seen from above, they look dark like the ocean or river bed. Seen from below, they seem light, like the light surface water. There are more than 20,000 different kinds of fish, so you can imagine in how many different ways they live!

HOW DO FLYING FISH FLY?

If there were fish which actually "flew" through the air the way birds do, they would obviously do it by flapping their "wings," or fins. There are no fish which fly that way.

But flying fish do manage to get about in the air and this is how they do it. The "wings" of the flying fish are the front fins, but greatly enlarged. When the fish in in "flight," it spreads out these fins and holds them at an angle to the body. In some cases, the fish also spread the rear fins.

The fish gets into the air by swimming rapidly through the water with part of its body breaking the surface. It goes along this way for some distance, gathering speed by moving its tail vigorously. Then it spreads the fins and holds them stiffly, and the speed of its motion lifts it into the air!

A flying fish may sail or glide for a distance of several hundred yards in this way before it drops back into the water. Sometimes it strikes the crests of the waves and moves its tail in order to pick up additional power while it is in flight. By the way, the flying fish doesn't just skim over the water. It can fly high enough to land on the decks of large ocean liners.

WHY DO SALMON GO UPSTREAM TO SPAWN?

There are many things that creatures do to produce and protect their young that seem quite miraculous to us. After all, isn't it rather amazing the way birds build nests, or the way certain animals will fight to save their young from enemies?

The instinct that takes the salmon on the long trip upstream must be there because this is the best way new salmon can be born and grow. Not all salmon go to the headquarters of a stream to spawn. Some stay quite close to lower stretches of rivers. The pink salmon is an example of this. It spawns only a few miles above salt water. But in contrast there is the king salmon. It may travel as much as 3,000 miles up a river from the sea!

When the salmon enter fresh water, they are in fine condition, healthy and strong and fat. But as soon as they reach fresh water, they stop feeding. Sometimes they wear themselves out trying to reach the exact place they want to go deposit their eggs.

Since many of the rivers they have to ascend have rapids and falls and jagged rocks, the salmon are often very thin and straggly looking by the time they have spawned. But whether they are worn-out or still in fair condition, the Pacific salmon die after spawning.

When the fish reach the spawning spot (which is usually the very same spot where they were hatched!), the female digs a sort of hole in the gravel or sand with her body, tail, and fins. The eggs are deposited in this "nest" and are fertilized by the male. Then the female covers the eggs.

Now their job is finished and the salmon seem to lose all interest in life. They drift downstream more or less with the current, and then they soon die. Then life begins for the newly hatched fish, which may be about 60 days later.

The young salmon remain in fresh water for a few months or a year, then descend the streams and enter salt water. And so the cycle begins all over again!

146

RATTLESNAKE

WHICH SNAKES ARE POISONOUS?

Man seems to have always had a fear and horror of snakes. Their appearance, the way they move about, and the fact that many people have died of snakebite, is responsible for this fear.

There are more than 2,000 species or kinds of snakes. They live on land, in the earth, in water, and in trees. And they can be found in practically all parts of the world except the polar regions and some islands.

The poisonous snakes possess poison fangs, which are hollow teeth, with an opening at the tip. These poison-conducting teeth, or fangs, are in the upper jaw and connect with poison glands in the head. A poison-snake cannot be made permanently harmless by the removal of its fangs, because new fangs will be grown.

Snakes with poison fangs usually inject the poison into their prey to kill it or make it unconscious before it is eaten.

There are about 120 species of non-poisonous snakes in the United States. Poisonous snakes of the United States consist of only four types. One is the coral snake, of the cobra family. It occurs only in the South.

The other three types belong to the pit viper family, of which the rattlesnake, the copperhead, and the water moccasin are members. There are about a dozen kinds of rattlesnakes. All rattlesnakes may be considered as a type, and are easily recognized by the rattle on the end of the tail.

Rattlesnakes are found in practically all the states. The copperhead is found in the Eastern States from Massachusetts to Florida. The water moccasin lives in the Southeast.

This leaves quite a number of non-poisonous snakes in the United States. These are not only harmless, but are useful in destroying vermin. Among them are the blacksnake, milk snake, king snake, garter snake, green snake, and hissing "adder."

DO RATTLESNAKES RATTLE BEFORE THEY STRIKE?

A rattlesnake is certainly something to be afraid of. And because people are afraid of it, they have developed an idea that makes it seem a little less dangerous—that a rattlesnake will warn you before it strikes by rattling its tail.

Unfortunately, this isn't completely true. When a rattlesnake does rattle, it's usually because it has become frightened. This makes it vibrate its tail rapidly which causes the rattles to strike together. But studies of the rattlesnake have shown that about 95 per cent of the time this snake gives no warning at all before it strikes!

By the way, this idea of rattlesnakes and other poisonous snakes "striking" rather than biting isn't quite true, either. The fact is poisonous snakes both strike and bite, but some snakes bite more than others.

A snake with long fangs, like the rattlesnake, has its long, hollow, movable fangs folded inward against the roof of the mouth when the mouth is closed. When the snake is about to strike, it opens its mouth, the fangs fall into biting position, and the snake lunges forward. As the fangs penetrate the skin, the snake bites.

This biting movement presses the poison glands so that the poison flows out, then goes through the hollow teeth and into the wound. Other snakes, such as the cobra, which has shorter fangs, hold on for a time when they bite, and chew. This chewing motion forces the poison into the wound.

As a matter of fact, the cobra is a much more dangerous snake than the rattlesnake. The cobra is more aggressive, more likely to attack. And while a rattlesnake has more poison, the venom of the cobra is more deadly. People have been known to die from the bite of a cobra in less than an hour!

WHAT IS THE LARGEST SNAKE IN THE WORLD?

There are more than 2,000 different kinds of snakes. Snakes are such fascinating and frightening creatures that people have developed all kinds

148

of wrong ideas about them. One of these is that there are huge, terrifying snakes 60 and 70 feet long!

The truth is that snakes never grow to quite that length, though some are certainly big enough. The largest known snake is the anaconda, which lives in tropical South America. A specimen shot on the upper Orinoco River in eastern Colombia was 37½ feet in length. But in such an isolated region, there may be even larger anacondas that have not yet been discovered.

A regal python bearing the name "Colossus" was the longest snake ever kept in a zoo. It was probably more than 29 feet long when it died at the Highland Park Zoological Gardens on April 15, 1963. At a weighing about six years earlier, it weighed 320 pounds. Most regal pythons are found in southeastern Asia and in the Philippine Islands.

The Indian python, found in India and the Malay Peninsula, may grow to a length of from 22 to 25 feet. The Africa rock python is about the same length. The diamond python of Australia and New Guinea often grows to 20 or 21 feet.

Then we come to a snake that, for some reason, is believed by many people to be the world's largest. It's the boa constrictor, and the most it ever measures is about 16 feet. This nasty creature makes its home in Southern Mexico, and Central and South America.

The king cobra, another unpleasant member of the snake family, reaches a maximum length of about 18 feet. Now what about the United States? What are the largest snakes we're ever likely to run into here? The longest of these is the Eastern diamondback rattlesnake, and it only grows to a length of about seven feet. The black chicken snake, bull snake, gopher snake—all found in the United States—also grow only to maximum lengths of about eight feet.

The longest poisonous snake is the king cobra, and the heaviest poisonous snake is the Eastern diamondback rattlesnake.

WHY DOES A WHALE SPOUT?

Whales are not fish but mammals. They are warm-blooded creatures whose young are not hatched from an egg but are born live. And the baby whale is fed on its mother's milk like other little mammals.

But whales, like all water mammals, are descended from ancestors that lived on land. So they had to adapt themselves for life in the water. This means that over millions of years certain changes took place in their bodies so that they could live in the water.

Since whales have no gills but breathe through their lungs, one of the most important changes had to do with their breathing apparatus. Their nostrils used to be up in the forward part of the head. These have moved back to the tops of their heads. They now form one or two blow-holes which make it easier for them to breathe at the surface of the water.

Under water these nostrils are closed by little valves, and the air passages are shut off from the mouth so that they are in no danger of taking water into the lungs.

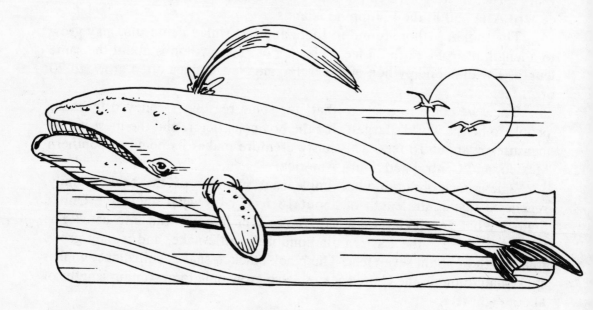

Whales usually rise to breathe every five or ten minutes, but they may remain under water for three-quarters of an hour! On reaching the surface, they first "blow," or exhale the used air from their lungs. As they do this, they make a loud noise which may be heard for some distance. What does this spout consist of? It is not water, but merely worn-out air, loaded with water vapor.

They blow several times until they have completely changed the air in their lungs, and then they dive deeply, or "sound." Some whales have been known to dive 2,000 feet deep! Sometimes big whales, in sounding, throw their tails up into the air or even jump completely out of the water!

FROG

TOAD

WHAT'S THE DIFFERENCE BETWEEN FROGS AND TOADS?

Many people wonder if there is a different between frogs and toads. While there are certain differences, in most important things, they are very much alike. They both belong to that group of cold-blooded creatures that live both in water and on land.

Most frogs and toads resemble each other very closely, and it's often hard to tell them apart. Frogs, however, are smooth and slippery, long and graceful. Most toads are dry, warty, and squat. Also, most frogs have teeth while most toads have none.

Almost all Amphibia lay eggs, so in this, the frogs and toads are alike. The eggs of both frogs and toads look like specks of dust floating on top of the water in a jellylike substance. The eggs hatch into little tadpoles, which look more like fishes than frogs or toads.

The tadpoles breathe through gills and have a long swimming tail, but no legs. The eggs develop into this tadpole stage in from three to 25 days. In about three or four months, the tadpoles lose their gills and their tails and develop legs and lungs. But it still takes about a year for the tadpole to become a frog or toad. Frogs and toads often live to a good old age, sometimes even as long as 30 or 40 years!

A toad lays fewer eggs than a frog, which means anywhere from 4,000 to 12,000 eggs every year, while a female bullfrog may lay from 18,000 to 20,000 eggs in one season! There are certain kinds of toads in which the male plays an important part in hatching the eggs. One kind of male toad found in Europe, for example, wraps the long string of eggs about his feet and sits in a hole in the ground with them until they are ready to hatch. He then carries them back to the pond.

A weird-looking toad which lives in South America hatches out its eggs in holes in its back! These holes are covered with skin, and are filled with a liquid. The young remain in these holes while they pass through the tadpole stage.

Toads which live in temperate regions are usually brown and olive, while those in the tropics are often bright-colored. It is not harmful to handle toads.

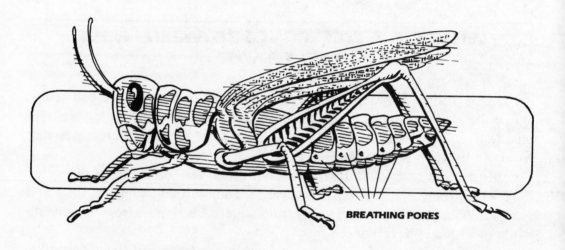
BREATHING PORES

HOW DO INSECTS BREATHE?

All living creatures must breathe in order to sustain life. Breathing is simply the taking-in of air in order to get oxygen, and the exhaling of a changed kind of air. The air we breathe out has had oxygen taken out of it and it has increased amounts of carbon dioxide and water.

The oxygen taken in is needed to "burn" certain food products so the body can use them. Waste products, including water and carbon dioxide, are eliminated by the body in part by being breathed out.

The simplest form of breathing is probably carried on by jellyfish and many worms. They have no breathing organs at all. Dissolved oxygen soaks

152

through their skins from the water in which they live. Dissolved carbon dioxide soaks out. That's all there is to their "breathing."

An earthworm, which is more complicated, has a special fluid, the blood, to carry oxygen from the skin to the internal organs and bring carbon dioxide out. The frog sometimes breathes this way, too, using its skin as a breathing organ. But it has lungs for use when its body needs greater amounts of oxygen.

In insects, breathing takes place in a most unusual and interesting manner. If we examine an insect closely on the abdomen or belly, we see a large number of little openings or pores. Each of these pores is the entrance to a tube called a "trachea." This trachea works in the same way as man's breathing tube or windpipe! So an insect breathes the way we do, except that it may have hundreds of windpipes in its belly to take in air. In a creature as small as an insect, these tubes don't take up too much space. But can you imagine what would happen if man's breathing system were like the insect's? There would hardly be room for any other organs!

By the way, the rate of breathing (how often air is taken in) depends a great deal on the size of the creature. The larger it is, the slower the breathing rate. An elephant breathes about 10 times a minute, but a mouse breathes about 200 times a minute!

WHAT IS THE PURPOSE OF A FIREFLY'S LIGHT?

Is there anyone who hasn't been mystified by the light of the firefly? Children love to catch them and put them in bottles, or hold them in their hands while the little creatures flash on and off. Now, one thing that may surprise you is that scientists, too, have been mystified by the firefly's light. And they are still mystified—because there are many things about it they can't explain.

The light of the firefly is very much like other kinds of light—except that it is produced without heat. This kind of light is called "luminescence." In the firefly, luminescence is produced by a substance called "luciferin." This combines with oxygen to produce light.

But this reaction won't take place unless another substance, called "luciferase," is present. Luciferase acts as a catalyst; that is, it helps the chemical reaction take place but is not a part of it. To put it another way: fireflies have luciferin and luciferase in their bodies. The luciferase enables the luciferin to burn up and produce light.

Now, scientists can produce this same kind of light in the laboratory. But in order to do so, they must obtain the ingredients from the firefly! Chemists cannot produce them synthetically. It remains a secret of nature!

What is the purpose of this light in the firefly? Well, there are some explanations for it, of course. One is that perhaps this helps the fireflies find their mates. Another purpose might be to serve as a warning to night-feeding birds so that they will avoid the fireflies.

But scientists still feel that they don't really know why these lights are necessary to the firefly, since the above reasons don't seem important enough. They think the light may just be a byproduct of some other chemical process that goes on in the firefly's body. A light happens to be produced, but it's not a vital process. Well, whatever the reason for the light, I'm sure most of us are glad it's there—because of the pleasure of seeing these little insects as they move about at night.

HOW DO BEES MAKE HONEY?

The reason bees make honey is that it serves them as food. So the whole process of making honey is a way of storing up food for the bee colony.

The first thing a bee does is visit flowers and drink the nectar. Then it carries the nectar home in the honey sac. This is a baglike enlargement of the digestive tract just in front of the bee's stomach. There is a valve that separates this section from the stomach.

The first step in the making of the honey takes place while the nectar is in the bee's honey sac. The sugars found in the nectar undergo a chemical change. The next step is to remove a large part of the water from the nectar. This is done by evaporation, which takes place because of the heat of the hive, and by ventilation.

Honey stored in the honeycombs by honeybees has so much water removed from the original nectar that it will keep almost forever! The honey is put into the honeycombs to ripen, and to serve as the future food supply.

By the way, when bees cannot obtain nectar, they sometimes collect sweet liquids excreted by various bugs, or secretions from plants other than nectar.

Honey is removed from the hive by various methods. It may be squeezed from the comb by presses, or it may be sold in the combs cut from the hive. Most honey, however, is removed from the combs by a machine known as "a honey extractor." This uses centrifugal force to make the honey leave the comb.

Honeys vary greatly, depending on the flowers from which the nectar came and the environment where the hive is situated. Honey contains an amazing number of substances. The chief ingredients are two sugars known as levulose and dextrose. It also contains the following: small amounts of sucrose (cane sugar), maltose, dextrins, minerals, numerous enzymes, numerous vitamins in small amounts, and tiny amounts of proteins and acids.

Honeys differ in flavor and color, depending on the source of the nectar. In those areas where honey is produced, there are usually only a few plants that produce enough nectar to be a source of supply. Thus, in the Northeast United States, most honey comes from clover; in the West, it may come from alfalfa; in Europe, from heather; and so on.

HOW DOES A CATERPILLAR BECOME A BUTTERFLY?

Have you ever heard people say that a butterfly never eats? This happens to be true of some butterflies—and the reason lies in the story of how a caterpillar changes into a butterfly.

During her life, a female butterfly lays from 100 to several thousand eggs. She is very careful to lay these eggs near the kind of plant that will be useful to her offspring later. If there is only one such plant in a certain area—that's where she'll lay the eggs!

From these eggs hatch out tiny, wormlike grubs, called "caterpillar larvae." They begin at once to feed and grow, and as they grow they shed their skins several times. All the caterpillars do during this time is eat and eat—because the food they store away now may have to last them for the rest of their lives when they become butterflies! The food is stored as fat, and is used to build up wings, legs, sucking tubes, and so on, when the caterpillar becomes a butterfly.

At a certain time the caterpillar feels it's time for a change, so it spins a little button of silk, to which it clings. It hangs head down, sheds its caterpillar skin, and then appears as a pupa or chrysalis. The chrysalis clings to the button of silk by a sharp spine at the end of its body.

The pupa or chrysalis may sleep for some weeks or months. During this time, however, it is undergoing a change, so that when it comes out it is a full-grown insect. When it emerges from its chrysalid skin, it is a butterfly—but it doesn't do any flying at first. It sits still for hours to let its wings spread out and become dry and firm. It waves them back and forth slowly until it feels they are ready to use for flying—then off it goes on its first flight in search of nectar!

By the way, the life history of the moth is almost exactly the same as that of the butterfly. And did you know that there are many more different kinds of moths than there are butterflies? In North America, there are about 8,000 types of moths—and only about 700 kinds of butterflies.

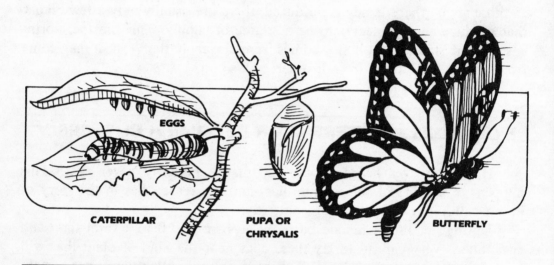

EGGS

CATERPILLAR

PUPA OR
CHRYSALIS

BUTTERFLY

HOW DO SILKWORMS MAKE SILK?

Thousands of years ago China had learned the secret of making silk cloth from the fine web spun by a certain caterpillar in making its cocoon. This secret was jealously guarded, and anyone who carried silkworms or their eggs out of China was punishable by death!

Today, of course, silkworms are raised in China, Japan, India, France, Spain, and Italy. The best silk is produced by the caterpillar of a small grayish-white moth which feeds on the leaves of the white mulberry.

In the early summer, each female moth lays 500 or more eggs. These eggs are carefully kept on strips of paper or cloth until the next spring when the mulberries open their leaves. Then the eggs are placed in incubators where they hatch out tiny black worms. The worms are placed in trays filled with finely chopped mulberry leaves and are fed constantly for about six weeks.

When the worms begin to move their heads slowly back and forth, they are ready to spin their cocoons. Little twigs are put in the trays to support them. The worms loop about themselves an almost invisible thread which they pour out through little holes in their jaws. The cocoon, which may contain as much as 500 to 1,200 yards of thread, is finished in about 72 hours.

Inside the cocoon is a shrunken chrysalis, which may develop into a moth in about 12 days. So the cocoons are exposed to heat to kill the chrysalises. The cocoons are placed in troughs of warm water to soften the silk gum which holds the filaments of the thread together.

Filaments from several cocoons are brought together into a single thread as they are unwound from the cocoons and wound on a reel. The threads from the reel are twisted into a skein of raw silk. This thread of 10 or 12 filaments is called a "single" thread of silk.

When you buy silk stockings marked "two-thread" or "three-thread," the markings are based on this thread of silk. Today, nylon has become so popular and so cheap that it has replaced silk in many uses. But silk will always be appreciated for its beauty, richness, and softness.

WHY AREN'T SPIDERS CAUGHT IN THEIR OWN WEBS?

"Won't you come into my parlor?" said the spider to the fly. The tricky spider is pretty clever, isn't he? He knows the fly will be caught and he'll be able to scamper along and have himself a nice meal!

But if the sticky web clings to the fly and traps him, why doesn't it cling to the spider? The answer to this will surprise you. It does! A spider can be caught just as easily in his own web as a fly is.

The reason this doesn't happen is that the spider is "at home" in his own web. He knows his way around. And when the web was spun originally, the spider made sure that there would be "safe" threads to use, threads he could touch without sticking to them.

There are many kinds of silk that a spider produces. The sticky kind is used in the web to catch prey. But there is also a non-sticky kind, and this is used to make the strong, supporting spokes of the web. The spider knows which is which, and he simply avoids the sticky ones! He can do this because he has a remarkable sense of touch.

WHAT DO ANTS EAT?

About the only place in the world where you won't find any ants is on the summits of the very highest mountains. So as you might imagine, there are thousands of different kinds of ants and how they live and what they eat depend on the species you are considering.

Let us see what are some of the unusual eating habits of certain ants. The harvester ant gathers seed from some grass common to the region and carries them into the nest. Here the seeds are sorted and stored away as the food supply.

Other ants are dairy farmers. They keep herds of plant lice, or "aphids," as they are called. They milk them by stroking their sides until the sweet liquid which they secrete oozes out. The ants relish this honeydew, or milk, so much that they take excellent care of their "cows."

Other ants grow fungi and live on nothing else. The fungus which they eat must have something to grow on. So the ants make a paste on which to raise the fungus, or mold.

Some ants are millers. One variety of ant has a special kind of worker with a huge head. The head holds powerful muscles to work its jaws and do the grinding. This worker ant is really the miller of the colony. It grinds up the grain that is brought in by the ordinary workers. After the harvest season is over, the millers are killed and their heads are bitten off. The reason this is done is the ants want no extra mouths to feed.

One kind of ant maintains living storehouses of food. As the worker ants bring in the nectar from the flowers, special ants in the colony take it and swallow it. During the winter, the other ants come to them and receive from their mouths enough nectar to feed themselves and the colony until the next season.

HOW DO EARTHWORMS EAT?

Earthworms have been called the most important animals in the world! Important, of course, from the point of view of human beings, because the activity of the earthworms prepares the soil for vegetation, upon which life depends.

Earthworms turn the soil over and break it up by eating it. In a single acre of garden, the worms in it will pass about 18 tons of soil through their

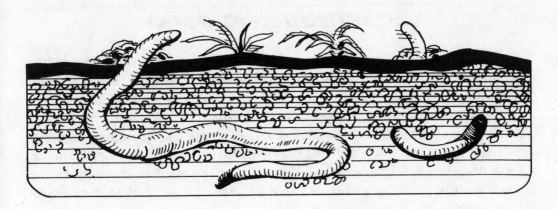

bodies in one year! Worms let air and water get to the plant roots. They turn under decayed plant and animal matter, and they even plant seeds. This is done when they drag leaves into their burrows and thus pull fine seeds from trees and plants below the surface, too.

The manure of earthworms, which is called "worm casts," contains lime which makes the soil rich. The importance of this can be seen when we consider what scientists discovered about the Nile Valley, one of the earth's most fertile regions. They estimated that about 120 tons of earthworm castings are deposited on each acre in the Nile Valley, and this is the real reason why this region has been fertile for hundreds of years!

There are so many earthworms in the soil of the United States that if all of them were weighed it would equal more than 10 times the weight of the human population!

The earthworm's body is made of two tubes, one inside another. The inner tube is the digestive system. When the worm wants to eat, it turns its throat inside out and pushes it forward to grip a piece of dirt. Then it draws the dirt back into the tube with its throat muscles. The dirt first goes into a storeroom called "the crop," and then into the gizzard. Grains of sand help the worm grind up the soil. Then it is digested, and the dirt is pushed from the body as "casting."

An earthworm has no eyes, but it has "sense-cells" on the outside of its body. This enables the worm to tell light from darkness and to feel the lightest touch. The earthworm breathes through its skin.

Earthworms live in fine, moist soil; they cannot live in sand. They come up only at night. During the winter they curl up into a ball and sleep. When you see a worm on the surface, it is because it is looking for a new home or a better feeding ground. Worms cannot live in the sunlight.

WHY DO MOTHS EAT WOOL?

There is a moth known as "the clothes moth," and most people blame it for making the moth holes in our clothes, furs, and rugs. But the moth doesn't do this damage at all!

The moth never eats. It lives only to produce its eggs and then dies. It is when the young moth is in the caterpillar stage that all the damage is done.

The eggs of the moth are laid on wool, furs, rugs, and so on. In about a week, the eggs hatch into caterpillars. What happens then depends on the kind of moth it is, since there are three different kinds of clothes moths in North America.

One is the case-making moth, which is most common in the Northern United States and Canada; the second is the webbing moth, which is usually found in the Southern States; and the third is the tapestry moth, which might appear in all sections.

The caterpillar of the case-making moth makes a little tubular case out of the wool it eats, and lines this case with silk. There it lives as a caterpillar. The caterpillar of the webbing moth always leaves a cobwebby trail of its silk and spins a silk cocoon. As the caterpillar of the tapestry moth eats into wool, it makes a series of tunnels which it lines with silk. When full-grown, it goes into one of these tunnels and stays there until it is ready to come out as a moth.

So you see that the problem of protecting clothes against moths is to make sure that no eggs are laid on the clothes. Before clothes are put away for the summer, they should be aired and brushed to make sure that there are no eggs or moths on them. It's a good idea to wrap them in heavy paper or in a tightly sealed cardboard box, for the clothes moths cannot eat through paper. Moth balls keep the moths away, but do not kill the eggs or larvae which may already be present.

WHY DO MOSQUITO BITES ITCH?

Have you ever heard the expression, "The female of the species is deadlier than the male"? Well, it certainly applies to mosquitoes. Only female mosquitoes suck blood. The bill of the female has some sharp piercing organs, arranged around a sucking tube. When the mosquito bites, it injects a poisonous liquid into the blood. This poison causes the pain and itching and produces the swelling.

Next to its bite, the hum of the mosquito is probably most annoying. This hum is very important to the mosquito, however, for it is a sort of mating call. The males make a deep, low hum by vibrating their wings rapidly, while the females have a shriller note.

Mosquitoes are found all over the world. But wherever they may live, all species begin their lives somewhere in the water. The females deposit their eggs on the surface of ponds, in pools, in rain barrels, in the oases of deserts, even in tin cans. Each female lays from 40 to 400 eggs. These may be laid singly or in compact raftlike masses.

Within a week, small footless larvae hatch out. These larvae wriggle through the water so actively that they are usually called "wrigglers." Since they cannot breathe under water, they spend most of the time on the surface. There they take in air through the breathing tubes on their tails, and weave bits of animal and plant matter into their mouths with the feathery brushes on their heads.

As the wrigglers grow, they molt, or shed their skins. The fourth time they molt, they change into pupae. The pupae spend most of the time near the surface breathing through hornlike tubes on their backs. The pupae do not eat, but after a few days their skins split and the full-grown mosquitoes crawl out.

Adult mosquitoes usually live only a few weeks. In some species, there are 12 generations of mosquitoes during one year!

HOW DID DINOSAURS EVOLVE?

Scientists believe that dinosaurs came into being about 180,000,000 years ago and died out about 60,000,000 years ago. Since dinosaurs were reptiles, they must have developed from reptiles that lived before them. Reptiles, by the way, are a separate class of animals with these characteristics: They are cold-blooded; they can live on land; they have a distinctive type of heart; and most of them have scales.

The first reptiles appeared long before the dinosaurs. They looked like Amphibia (able to live in water and on land), but their eggs could be hatched on land. The young ones had legs and lungs, could breathe air, and probably ate insects.

Then the reptiles became larger and stronger. Some looked like big lizards and others like turtles. They had short tails, thick legs, and big heads. They ate plants.

The first dinosaurs to develop resembled their reptile ancestors, who were like lizards, and who could walk on their hindlegs. The first dinosaurs were slender, about as large as a turkey, and could also walk on their hindlegs. Some kinds remained small, but others grew heavier and longer. In time, many of them were six to eight feet long. There were even a few 20 feet long and weighing as much as an elephant. They had small heads and short, blunt teeth, which were only good for eating plants. They lived in low, swampy places.

Then came the next period in the Age of Reptiles. Some of the plant-eating dinosaurs became so large that even four legs couldn't support them on land. They had to spend most of their lives in rivers and swamps. One of these giants was Brontosaurus, 70 to 80 feet long and weighing about 38 tons!

At the same time, other dinosaurs were able to walk about on land. One of these, Allosaurus, was 34 feet long, had sharp teeth and claws, and fed on Brontosaurus and other plant-eaters! So dinosaurs were a stage in the development of the reptiles. They may have disappeared because of changes in the climate of the earth, which robbed them of places to wade and feed.

WHAT IS A VAMPIRE BAT?

When you think for what a short time man has existed on this earth, it is hard to believe that bats have existed for 60,000,000 years! There are fossil remains of bats going back to that time. There are even pictures of bats that are 4,000 years old, found in an Egyptian tomb.

Today there are several hundred different kinds of bats, and they live everywhere in the world except near the polar regions. Bats are the only mammals that can fly. They range in size from a six-inch wingspread to some that have almost a six-foot wingspread!

Most bats eat insects. Many bats of the warm tropics eat fruit or the pollen from flowers. Other bats eat fish or smaller bats. Some eat blood.

The blood-eating bats are called "vampire bats," and it is because of them that many people are so frightened of all bats. At one time, in Eastern Europe, there were many legends about vampires. A vampire was the soul of a dead person, which assumed the form of some animal at night, and roved the countryside looking for victims from which to suck blood. During

the early 18th century, explorers who traveled to South and Central America found bats that fed on blood. They came back with exaggerated stories, and soon, all the old vampire legends became associated with bats. Since that time, vampires have been thought of mostly as bats.

Vampire bats are found only in Central and South America. They have a wingspread of about 12 inches and a body length of about four inches. The vampire bat has needle-sharp front teeth with which it makes small cuts in the skin of its victim. At one time, it was thought a vampire bat sucked up the blood, but it actually laps it up with its tongue. In fact, a vampire bat can be feeding on its victim while the person remains sound asleep!

It is thought the saliva of the vampire bat contains some substance that deadens the pain of the wound, as well as something that prevents it from clotting. Vampire bats do not prefer to feed on human beings. They are just as happy to feed on horses, cows, goats, and chickens. In some places, vampire bats transmit a disease that is sometimes fatal to the victim.

HOW DOES A CHAMELEON CHANGE ITS COLORS?

How does the chameleon change its colors from a bright green to a grey-black or to yellow spots? Did nature give the chameleon an automatic color changer for its skin, so that it could resemble its background wherever it goes?

The strange fact about the chameleon's ability to change its colors is that it is not caused by the color of its surroundings! The chameleon pays no attention to its surroundings.

The skin of the chameleon is transparent. Underneath this skin, there are layers of cells which contain yellow, black, and red coloring matter. When these cells contract or expand, we see a change in the color of the chameleon.

But what makes those cells go to work? When the chameleon becomes angry or frightened, its nervous system sends a message to those cells. Anger cause the colors to darken; excitement and fright bring paler shades and yellow spots.

Sunlight also affects the chameleon's colors. Hot sunlight will make those cells turn dark, or almost black. High temperatures without sunlight usually produce green colors, low temperatures produce green colors. And darkness makes the chameleon fade to a cream color with yellow spots.

So we see that various things like emotion, temperature, and light cause the nervous system of the chameleon to make its color cells perform their tricks, and not the color of its surroundings.

It so happens, of course, that these changes in color help the chameleon become almost invisible to its enemies like snakes or birds. And because the chameleon is such a slow-moving animal, it needs this kind of protection to save its life.

WHY DOES A BULL CHARGE AT A RED CLOTH?

As you know, bullfighting is the greatest sport in Spain, and a very important one in many other countries. And people are quite excited about this sport. They believe certain things about it and nothing can change their minds.

One of the things most bullfight fans (and others) believe is that anything red makes a bull angry and causes him to attack. Therefore, the bullfighter has to have a bright red cape and he has to be able to use this with great skill.

Well, the sad truth is that if the same bullfighter had a white cloth, or a yellow cloth, or a green cloth, or a black cloth—he would be able to accomplish the same things with the bull! Bulls are color-blind!

Many bullfighters will privately admit they know this. In fact, some matadors conducted experiments in which they used white cloths—and they got the bulls to behave in the same way as with red cloths!

What makes the bull charge then? It is the movement of the cape, and not the color of it. Anything that you would wave in front of a bull would excite him. In fact, since the bull is color-blind, if you waved a white cape or cloth you would probably get a better reaction, since he can see it better!

DOES AN OSTRICH REALLY HIDE ITS HEAD IN THE SAND?

The ostrich is a rather strange bird, and there are many interesting and peculiar things about it, but it does not hide its head in the sand!

According to popular belief, when an ostrich is frightened it feels that it is safely hidden when it has its head in the sand. At such times, according to these stories, a person can walk up to the ostrich and capture it easily.

However, the truth is that no one has actually observed this happening! The ostrich simply does not hide its head in the sand. What may have given people the idea is that when an ostrich is frightened, it will sometimes drop to the ground, stretch out its neck parallel with it, and lie still and watch intently. But when the danger comes closer, the ostrich does just what other animals do—it takes off and runs!

The ostrich, of course, is one of the birds that cannot fly. But it makes up for this in its ability to run with considerable speed. The ostrich is the fastest-running bird in the world. It can go as fast as 50 miles an hour and is able to maintain this speed for at least a half-mile!

You sort of expect the ostrich to do everything on a large scale. The African ostrich, for example, is the largest living bird. No other bird even comes near it. This ostrich has been found to measure eight feet in height and to weigh more than 300 pounds. It would be some job carrying that weight around on a pair of wings, wouldn't it?

When it comes to eggs, the ostrich is champ again. It lays the largest eggs of any living bird. Ostrich eggs measure six to seven inches in length and five to six inches in diameter. It takes more than 40 minutes to boil an ostrich egg, if you happen to be thinking of having one for breakfast!

WHAT CAUSES THE SKUNK'S BAD SMELL?

If there is one animal in the world which you wouldn't want to be—it's probably a skunk. Yet the skunk is a friendly creature and makes a good pet. What makes him so unpopular, of course, is that famous smell of his.

What makes a skunk smell? The skunk has very powerful scent glands which contain a bad-smelling fluid. The skunk can send this fluid out with great accuracy.

The two glands are under the tail. A skunk aims at its enemy and shoots the liquid out in a spray. The spray can travel nine feet or more. The skunk may decide to send out spray from one gland or the other, or both, and each gland holds enough for five or six shots.

The spray is so strong that it has a suffocating effect, which means it makes it hard to breathe when you're near it. And if the spray gets into the eyes, it can cause temporary blindness!

But the skunk doesn't "strike" without warning. It raises its tail first or stamps its feet, so that you should have plenty of time to run away. Since skunks have been used for fur coats and are raised on fur farms, the scent glands, for obvious reasons, sometimes are removed from the young skunk.

There are actually three types of skunks, the striped, the hog-nosed, and the spotted. They live in North, Central, and South America. The striped skunk has a white line on the head from the nose to a point between the short ears, and another that starts on the neck, divides into two stripes on the back, and continues to the tail. Striped skunks live from Canada to Mexico. The largest are 2½ feet long, including the nine-inch tail, and weigh as much as 30 pounds.

The fore (front) feet of skunks are armed with long claws, which are used to dig grubs and insects out of the ground. When you see many shallow holes in the ground, it probably means a skunk has been feeding there.

Skunks are really a great help to man, since their food is mainly beetles, grasshoppers, crickets, wasps, rodents, and snakes.

CAN GROUNDHOGS PREDICT THE WEATHER?

Sometimes an idea is built up, or kept up, by newspapers because it "makes a good story." This seems to be the case with the groundhog and its ability to predict the weather.

The belief that the groundhog is a weather prophet is an old one. The groundhog, or woodchuck, or marmot, is a hibernating animal. It lives in a burrow during the winter months. According to an old tradition it comes out on the second day of February, which has come to be called "Groundhog Day."

Once the groundhog gets out of its burrow, it is supposed to look over the landscape. If the day is cloudy so that it can't see its shadow, it stays out. This is supposed to be a good sign. It means the weather will be mild for the rest of the winter. But if the groundhog sees its shadow because the day is clear, it goes back into its burrow to get some more sleep. According to tradition, this means there will be six more weeks of cold weather.

The reason I say that newspapers seem to try to keep up the tradition is that it always makes a good story, and this despite the fact that most people don't really believe it. To begin with, there is absolutely no reason why the groundhog should be able to predict the weather. It has no special ability of any kind.

Another reason is that the groundhog doesn't really come out of its burrow on the second of February every year. Sometimes it comes out earlier, sometimes later. Occasionally a newspaperman will force the poor groundhog out on the right day in order to take pictures. But obviously, if the weather is still very cold, the groundhog has no desire at all to emerge from its warm burrow.

The tradition is said to have originated in Europe concerning the hedgehog. But the Pilgrims transferred it to the groundhog when they came to this country.

WHY DOES THE KANGAROO HAVE A POUCH?

Animals that have a pouch (and the kangaroo is only one of several animals like this) are called "marsupials."

The pouch that the kangaroo has, which is between her hindlegs, is about as snug and comfortable a little home as a new-born baby can have. It is fur-lined, keeps the baby warm, protects it, enables the baby to nurse, and provides transportation for the helpless infant.

The reason a pouch is provided by nature for kangaroos and other marsupials is that their young are born in a very helpless state. In fact, at birth the kangaroo is a tiny, pink, naked mass, not much over an inch long and as thick as a lead pencil! Can you imagine what would happen if such a helpless thing didn't immediately have a place to keep it warm, snug, and protected?

The mother places the new-born baby in the pouch and for six months this is "home." In six months, the young kangaroo is as large as a puppy. But life is too good in the pouch to leave home. So "the joey," as it is called in Australia, rides around inside the pouch with its head sticking out far enough for it to pull off leaves when its mother stops to feed on tree branches, In fact, even after the mother has taught it how to walk and run, the joey still lives in the pouch. In case of danger, the mother hops over to it, picks it up in her mouth without stopping, and drops it safely into her pouch.

There are more than 120 different kinds of kangaroos. The wallaby, which is the smallest, is only two feet high. The biggest is the great red or gray kangaroo, which is about six feet tall!

Kangaroos have short front legs with small paws, and very long hind-legs with one large sharp toe in the middle of the foot. With the help of its powerful hindlegs, a kangaroo takes jumps of 10 to 15 feet or more. When the kangaroo is resting, it rests on its big, long tail. Kangaroos can travel very fast, and their sense of hearing is so good they can hear an enemy at a great distance.

WHY DOES THE GIRAFFE HAVE A LONG NECK?

Giraffes have aroused the curiosity of man since earliest times. The ancient Egyptians and Greeks had a theory that giraffes were a mixture of the leopard and the camel, and they called the giraffe "a camelopard."

The giraffe is the tallest of all living animals, but scientists are unable to explain how it got its long neck. A famous French zoologist, Jean Baptiste de Lamarck, had a theory that at one time the giraffe's neck was much shorter than it now is. He thought that the neck grew to its present length because of the animal's habit of reaching for the tender leaves in the upper branches of trees. But scientists in general don't accept de Lamarck's theory.

Strangely enough, the body of a giraffe is no larger than that of the average horse. Its tremendous height, which may reach 20 feet, comes mostly from its legs and neck. The neck of a giraffe has only seven vertebrae, which is what the human neck has. But each vertebra is extremely long. Because of this, a giraffe always has a stiff neck. If it wants to take a drink from the ground, it has to spread its legs far apart in order to be able to reach down!

The strange shape and build of the giraffe is perfectly suited to enable it to obtain its food. A giraffe eats only plants, so its great height enables it to reach the leaves on trees which grow in tropical lands where there is little grass.

A giraffe's tongue is often a foot and a half long, and it can use it so skillfully that it can pick the smallest leaves off thorny plants without being pricked. It also has a long upper lip which helps it wrench off many leaves at a time.

The giraffe is able to protect itself from danger in many ways. First of all, the coloring of its hide makes it practically invisible when it is feeding in the shadows of trees. It has well-developed ears which are sensitive to the faintest sounds, and it has keen senses of smell and sight. Finally, a giraffe can gallop at more than 30 miles an hour when pursued and can outrun the fastest horse!

When attacked, a giraffe can put up a good fight by kicking out with its hindlegs or using its head like a sledge hammer. Even a lion is careful in attacking a giraffe, always approaching it from behind!

CHAPTER 5
HOW THINGS ARE MADE

WHAT IS A MAGNET?

There is an old legend that a shepherd called Magnes, tending his flocks along the slopes of Mount Ida, discovered that his iron crook and the iron nails of his sandals were clinging to a large black stone. The fact that certain stones could attract iron was the discovery of magnetism. These mysterious stones were also found near a place called Magnesia in Asia Minor. The name "magnet" may have been created for either of these reasons.

As time went by, a further discovery was made about magnetism. It was found that when pieces of iron were rubbed against the magnetic stones, they also became magnets. Thousands of years ago it was also discovered that a suspended magnet would point approximately to the north. This, of course, was the creation of the compass. The magnetic stones were called "lodestone." The name comes from "leading stone," because they helped guide the wanderer.

In Queen Elizabeth's time it was first discovered that every magnet has two definite poles, which are opposite in nature. Like poles repel each other, and unlike poles attract.

Nothing much was done about magnetism until the beginning of the 19th century. In 1820, Oersted, a Danish scientist, discovered that a wire carrying an electric current also created a magnetic field. This led to the discovery that by putting soft-iron core inside wires that were connected to a battery, the iron core became magnetized. It was the first creation of the electromagnet, much more powerful than any magnets ever known before.

The creation of the electromagnet made possible many of the most important and useful instruments we now have. Not only do electromagnets lift great weights, but they play a part in bells and buzzers, dynamos and motors, in fact, in anything that uses an electrical circuit.

Although it had long been known that the force of a magnet reaches out some distance from the magnet, Michael Faraday was the first one to define and show "the fields of force" and "lines of force." The understanding of this made possible such developments as the telephone, the electric light, the radio, and so on.

HOW DOES A SEISMOGRAPH RECORD EARTHQUAKES?

Sometimes there is a big news story about an earthquake that happened in some distant part of the world, perhaps in South America or Japan. You read and hear about cities being destroyed, hundreds of people being killed. Yet you, in your home, felt nothing! If the earth "shook," why didn't you feel it where you live?

Well, maybe you didn't feel it—but not far from you, in a big city or university, scientists probably made a complete and exact record of that earthquake! They felt it on their instruments.

Such an instrument is called "a seismograph." In fact, the study of earthquakes is known as "seismology." Now let's see why you didn't feel it and the scientists were able to make a record of it.

An earthquake is a trembling or vibration of the earth's surface. Notice the word "surface." That means just the crust of the earth. An earthquake is usually caused by a "fault" in the rocks of the earth's crust—a break along which one rock mass has rubbed on another with very great force and friction. The energy of this rubbing is changed to vibration in the rocks. And this vibration may travel thousands of miles.

Now these earthquake vibrations are a kind of wave motion which travels at different speeds through the earth's rocky crust. Because they have such a long distance to go, and are traveling through rock, by the time they reach your town you can't even notice them. But the seismograph can. This is how it works.

Imagine a block or slab of concrete. Sticking out of this slab is a chart that is fixed to it. It is parallel to the ground, like a sheet of paper. Above it, a rod sticks out from which is hung a weight. At the bottom of the weight is a pen, which touches the chart. Now comes an earthquake wave. The concrete block moves and the chart with it. But the weight, which is suspended, doesn't move. So the pen makes markings on the chart as it moves and we get a record of the earthquakes. Of course, this instrument is arranged very delicately so the slightest motion will be recorded.

WHAT IS PENICILLIN?

Few weapons against disease created as much excitement and became well-known as quickly as penicillin. It was as if suddenly the whole world became aware of a "miracle" happening before its eyes.

Yet penicillin is not one of man's miracles, created by a genius in a laboratory. It is one of nature's own miracles. Penicillin is the name we give to a powerful substance which fights bacteria and which is developed by certain moulds. It is an "antibiotic," which means a substance produced by a living organism and which acts upon other harmful organisms or bacteria.

Oddly enough, the whole idea of antibiotics is not a new one. As far back as 1877, antibiotic action was discovered by Louis Pasteur, and various antibiotic substances were used to treat infections. In fact, moulds and fungi themselves were used to treat infections, and it is quite probable that even a penicillin-producing mould was used against infection many years ago, but no one knew what it was!

In 1928, Sir Alexander Fleming was the first to describe and name this strange substance "penicillin." It was discovered almost by accident, but it soon became the subject of intensive study. It was found that certain moulds produced this substance which had a powerful and destructive effect on many of the common bacteria which infect man, while it had no effect on many others.

Something else very important was discovered about penicillin. While it could act so powerfully against bacteria, it did not have a harmful effect on human cells. This was important because all the other antiseptics in common use had a greater effect on human cells than they did on harmful bacteria!

Penicillin is very selective in its action. This means that it has a powerful effect on some bacteria and little or none on others. It is not an all-around drug used to kill any kind of bacteria, as some people believe.

Penicillin has three different kinds of effect on bacteria. It is "bacteriostatic," which means it stops the growth of bacteria. It is "bactericidal," which means it kills bacteria. And in some cases it even dissolves away the bacteria altogether!

HOW DOES A BATTERY PRODUCE ELECTRICITY?

There are two ways of producing electric current for power. It can be produced by machines called "dynamos," or "generators"—and by battery cells.

A battery cell produces electricity by changing chemical energy into electrical energy. Part of the chemical energy is changed into heat and part of it into an electric current.

There are two kinds of battery cells. One, called "a primary cell," cannot be renewed when it's used except by replenishing its chemicals. The ordinary dry cell (such as in your flashlight) is a primary cell. The other type, called "a secondary cell," can be recharged by sending an electric current through it. The storage cells used to start automobiles are secondary cells.

A battery is a group of two or more primary or secondary cells. A single cell is often called "a battery," but this isn't correct.

Various chemicals are used in primary cells, but the principle is always the same. In every primary cell there are electrodes and an electrolyte. The electrodes, or "cell elements" as they are called, have two different metals or one metal and carbon. The electrolyte is a liquid.

One of the elements, called "the cathode," is usually zinc. The other is called "the anode," and is usually carbon. Chemical action causes the cathode to dissolve slowly in the electrolyte. This sets electrons free. Now if a path, or circuit, is provided through which these free electrons can move, they provide an electric current. When you connect the elements by a wire or other electrical conductor, the current flows through it and you have "electricity."

A storage battery does not really store electricity. It obtains its power from chemical changes, just as all other kinds do. One set of plates in a storage battery is made of metallic lead and the other of lead peroxide. Both sets are immersed in sulphuric acid, and both gradually change to lead sulphate. It is this chemical process which produces the electric current in a storage battery.

HOW DOES AN ELECTRIC BULB GIVE LIGHT?

In 1800, an Englishman called Humphry Davy was conducting certain experiments with electricity. He had what we now call an electric battery, but it was quite weak. He connected wires to the ends of the battery and attached a piece of carbon to each of the free ends of the wires. By touching the two pieces of carbon together and drawing them slightly apart, he produced a sizzling light.

This was called "an electric arc," but it was the first evidence that electric light is possible. Davy also replaced the two pieces of carbon by a thin platinum wire connecting the two ends of the wires leading to the battery. When the electric current passed through it, the wire was heated and began to glow and gave light!

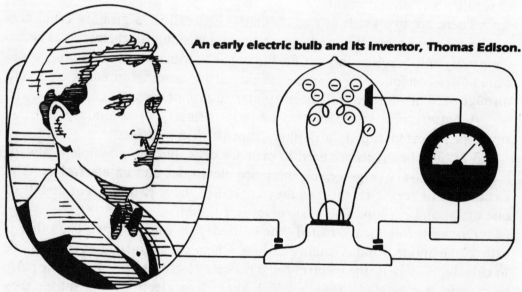

An early electric bulb and its inventor, Thomas Edison.

The trouble with these simple electric lights was that the source of electricity wasn't strong enough. So a pupil of Davy's, Michael Faraday, conducted experiments that led to the development of electric generators. By using steam engines to drive the generators, better sources of electricity were found.

Meanwhile, in the United States, Thomas Edison was experimenting with thin threads of carbon. When the carbon thread, or filament, was heated by passing electric current through it, it glowed. If this was done in air, the carbon itself would burn. So Edison placed it in a glass bulb and pumped out the air. Because there was no oxygen in the bulb, the carbon couldn't burn. It glowed brightly and only wasted away very slowly. Now we had an electric bulb that gave pretty good light.

But scientists knew that the more a filament is heated, the more light it gives. So they looked for materials that could be heated to high temperatures without melting. One of these is tantalum, a metal that melts at a temperature of 5,160 degrees Fahrenheit. It was drawn into fine wires and used for lamp filaments in 1905.

An even better metal for the filament is tungsten, because it melts at 6,100 degrees Fahrenheit. At first no one could draw tungsten into wire, and it took years to develop this process. Today, tungsten-filament lamps are the ones most widely used of all, and about 1,000,000,000 of them are made in the United States each year!

WHAT MAKES FLUORESCENT LIGHTS WORK?

Most things that can be made to glow will do so only when they are hot. In the ordinary light bulbs, for example, there is a filament that must be heated to high temperature in order to give off light.

But there are also many materials which can glow in different colors without being hot. They give off this glow when invisible ultraviolet rays fall upon them. These invisible rays "excite" the materials, and the giving-off of light that results is called "fluorescence."

The word "fluorescence" comes from the name of the mineral "fluorspar," which can fluoresce in different colors. Some materials will fluoresce only when they are a gas, others when a liquid, and still others as a solid material. The most important ones are solid crystal powders which are called "phosphors."

How does fluorescence come about? The first thing that must happen is that the "exciting" rays which fall on the fluorescent material must be absorbed by it. Now, these rays are really a form of energy. So certain atoms within the materials take in some of this energy and become "excited." After a very short time in this excited state, they return again to their natural, original state. During this return, they give off the extra energy they have absorbed in the form of light. This is called "fluorescence."

How do fluorescent lamps work? Mercury vapor is put into a long glass tube. Then an electric current is passed through this tube. This produces

175

ultraviolet rays. The inside wall of the lamp is coated with a phosphor, and this phosphor absorbs all the ultraviolet rays. It becomes "excited," as we have just described. It thus gives off light!

By means of fluorescence, about four times as much white light can be produced as by ordinary incandescent lamps. Fluorescent lamps last ten times as long as ordinary incandescent lamps. They can also be made in various shapes. Because of these advantages, fluorescent lighting is being used more and more in homes, schools, stores, and factories.

WHAT IS GASOLINE?

Why is gasoline a perfect fuel? It's a liquid, it is light, it easily changes into vapor, and it is easily ignited.

Gasoline is a mixture of hydrocarbons, which means it is a compound made up of carbon and hydrogen. The name "gasoline" comes from "gas." It is used because the liquid gasoline is so easily changed into a gas in the cylinder. Once gasoline is ignited, it burns almost completely and leaves very little waste. In burning, it gives more heat than the same amount of any other liquid fuel.

Where does gasoline come from? There are several sources, but the most important is natural crude oil, or petroleum, which is found in deposits under the ground. Gasoline is separated from petroleum by a process called "distillation." The liquid oil is placed in large containers, called "stills," and heated to about 400 degrees Fahrenheit. This is just enough to change into vapor about one quarter of the petroleum containing the hydrocarbons that boil lowest.

The vapor is led through pipes cooled from the outside so that it becomes a liquid again (is condensed). The distillation is repeated, and the gasoline is purified, or refined.

The value of a gasoline depends on its performance; that is, how many miles a gallon will drive a car or fly a plane at high speed. With simple, refined gasoline we hear knocking sounds in the motor. When a gasoline knocks, its performance is poor, because it is igniting poorly. So certain "anti-knock" ingredients are added which make it perform better. We call this "high-octane" gasoline. Today, better and better grades of high-octane gasoline are being produced to give our cars better performance.

HOW DOES GASOLINE MAKE AN AUTOMOBILE RUN?

Today cars are built so efficiently that people can drive all their life without really knowing what makes them run! We just pull up to a gasoline station, fill up the tank, and away we go. If anything goes wrong, a service man fixes it for us.

Now, all of us know that the power to drive the automobile motor comes from the gasoline, but just how does this happen? It isn't very complicated, so let's trace it step by step.

The gasoline is delivered from the fuel tank in the car to the engine by means of a small pump driven by the engine. The gasoline first goes into the carburetor on top of the engine. Here it is thoroughly mixed with exactly the right amount of air.

We now have a gasoline-air vapor which is highly explosive. It next passes through a system of pipes (called "a manifold") on its way into the cylinder. In the cylinder there is a piston and as it moves down in the cylinder it sucks the gasoline-air vapor into the engine. This is the first stroke of what is known as "the four-stroke cycle."

As soon as the piston reaches the bottom of its stroke, a valve closes so that none of the vapor can escape. When the piston moves upward on its second stroke, it squeezes the trapped vapor, making it even more explosive. At just the right moment, when the piston reaches the top of its second stroke, an electric spark is created by the spark plug and this sets off the vapor.

The pressure caused by the explosion forces the piston down again on the third stroke. When the piston reaches the bottom of its third stroke, another valve opens to let the burned gases escape, and they are pushed out as the piston rises on its fourth and final stroke.

The power for the car comes from the third, or power, stroke. The forces pressing downward on the top of the piston are transmitted to the crankshaft to make it turn, and the turning driveshaft drives the rear wheels.

HOW DOES A JET ENGINE WORK?

Although jet engines power the newest, most powerful aircraft we have today, the principle behind them was discovered about 2,000 years ago! That principle is jet propulsion, and it was first shown by a Greek mathematician, Hero of Alexander, in about 120 B.C. He used the force of steam escaping from a heated metal ball to spin the ball like a wheel.

To show how jet propulsion works, let's consider an ordinary blown-up balloon. When the balloon's mouth is closed, the air inside pushes in all directions with the same force. When the mouth is opened, the air pressure is lessened at that place as the air rushes out. However, at the top of the balloon, the point opposite the mouth, the air pushes with greater pressure. The balloon then moves in the direction of the greatest pressure, which is forward. So it is not the exhaust (air rushing out) but the forward push which causes the balloon to move.

This is because there is a law of motion as follows: To every action there is an equal and opposite reaction. In a jet engine, the "action" is the exhaust's backward push, while the equal and opposite "reaction" is the forward thrust.

There are two basic types of jet engines: ramjets and turbojets. The ramjet is like a flying stovepipe. It has no moving parts. Air is forced into the front opening, called "the intake," by its own forward motion. The air is then mixed with fuel and burned, increasing the gas about five times in volume. It is then exhausted through the smaller tail end. The fire in a ramjet creates no push when standing still, but the faster it moves, the more power it produces.

In a turbojet, air is sucked in by a compressor. It is then compressed and forced into the combustion chamber where it is mixed with fuel and burned. The hot, expanded gases go through a turbine and then escape through the exhaust nozzle, producing jet thrust. If the energy is delivered to the turbine, and the turbine shaft is made to turn the propeller of the airplane, we have a jet engine that is called "a turboprop."

HOW DOES A SUBMARINE STAY UNDER WATER?

The basic principle that enables a submarine to submerge or to surface is a very simple one. Most modern submarines have two hulls, or bodies. Water ballast is stowed between the inner and outer hulls, which might be considered similar to "shells."

When a submarine is ready to submerge, large valves known as "kingstons," located at the bottom of the ballast tanks, are opened to let in the sea. The air in the tanks escapes through valves at the top, known as "vents." The submarine goes under water!

When a submarine is ready to surface, the vents are closed and air pressure is forced into the tanks. This blows the water back out through the kingstons, and the submarine rises.

To guide the submarine in diving and rising, there are horizontal rudders fitted to the hull. To steer the submarine when it is moving forward. there is a rudder just like on surface-type ships.

A submarine is divided by crosswise bulkheads, or walls, into compartments. To go from one compartment into another, one has to pass through watertight, quick-closing doors. Submarines have escape hatches and safety lungs for emergency use.

How does a submarine know where it's going? Observation is done by means of a periscope, which consists of a long tube that can be pushed up from inside the vessel. By use of a combination of prisms, someone who is at the lower end of the periscope can see objects on the surface. By revolving the periscope tube, he can sweep the entire ocean horizon.

Submarines also have listening devices which can pick up and locate the sound of distant ships, and radar which enables them to find objects when they are on the surface.

In 1951, the world's first atomic submarine was ordered built, and it was launched on July 21, 1955.

HOW IS CHEWING GUM MADE?

Chewing gum is made of a gum base, sugar, corn sirup, and flavoring. The gum base is what keeps it chewy for hours. Bubble gum is made with a more rubbery gum base so that it will stretch without tearing.

Each manufacturer has his own recipe which is very secret, but the method of manufacturing the gum is more or less the same for all. At the factory, the gum base is prepared. The materials are melted and sterilized in a steam cooker and pumped through a centrifuge. This machine spins at high speed and throws out dirt and bits of bark found in the raw gums.

The clean, melted gum base is mixed with sugar, corn sirup, and flavoring. The usual mixture is 20 per cent gum base, 63 per cent sugar,

16 per cent corn sirup, and about 1 per cent flavoring oils. Some of the more popular flavors are spearmint, peppermint, clove, and cinnamon.

While this mass is still warm, it is run between pairs of rollers. These thin it down into a long ribbon. Powdered sugar on both sides prevents the gum from sticking. The last pair of rollers is fitted with knives which cut the ribbon into sticks. Machines wrap the sticks separately and then into packages.

Most of the gum base that is now used is manufactured, that is, it's a product of industry. But some of it, like chicle, comes from trees. Chicle comes from the wild sapodilla tree of Guatemala and Mexico.

The milky white sap of this tree is collected in buckets. Then it is boiled down and molded into 25-pound blocks to be shipped to chewing gum factories.

People in Central America chew chicle right from the tree. In the same way, early New England settlers chewed spruce gum, after seeing the Indians do it. This was the first gum sold in the United States in the early 1800's. Chicle was first imported in the 1860's as a substitute for rubber. Then, about 1890, it began to be used in making chewing gum, and from then on our modern chewing gum industry became established.

WHAT MAKES CORN POP?

As far as most children are concerned, the most amazing thing about corn is its ability to "pop." The explanation is very simple. Popcorn kernels are small and very hard. When they are heated, the moisture within the hard shells turns to steam and explodes!

But that's only the beginning of all the wonders of corn. It is really one of the most remarkable plants known to man. Here is just a rough idea of the ways in which corn products can be used. Corn starch is used on stamps and envelopes; corn oil is used in food, and in making paints, rubber substitutes, and soap. Alcohol is made from corn; smokeless powder and gun-cotton are made from the corn stalk and so is paper. Even cloth and ink can be made from the corn cob!

This amazing plant, which belongs to the grass family, grows in six general types. Dent corn is distinguished by the fact that when dried, the upper part of the kernel becomes indented. Flint corn has very hard kernels and long, slender ears. Soft corn grows in the Southern United States and has very soft kernels. Sweet corn is the type used for canning or eating directly from the cob. Popcorn is the kind that explodes when heated, and pod corn has each kernel enclosed in a tiny husk of its own.

Originally, the word "corn" meant a small, hard particle of something. It usually referred to the hard seed of a plant. In Europe, the word "corn" is still applied to different grains. In Scotland it means oats, in northern Europe rye, and in other countries wheat and barley. Europeans call our corn "maize," which was its original Indian name.

Three-quarters of all the corn grown in the world is grown in the United States, and that amounts to about 2,500,000,000 bushels a year! In fact, if we could load our annual crop of corn into wagons of average size, a procession of them would reach around the world almost six times. It is by far America's most important farm crop.

Today, of course, the cultivation of corn is carried on along scientific lines and the development of new and better types of corn is going on all the time. Yet even before Columbus discovered America, the Indians were cultivating corn with their simple methods and it was the main source of food for many of the tribes!

WHAT IS DRY ICE?

If liquid carbon dioxide is cooled to a certain temperature and subjected to pressure, it forms a white solid that looks like snow. This is called "Dry Ice." More than a hundred years ago, scientists had succeeded in making solid carbon dioxide. In this form it was like snow, and it produced temperatures as low as 109 degrees below zero Fahrenheit. It was then seen that solid carbon dioxide could be very useful for refrigerating purposes, but chemists weren't able to control it because when it melted it turned into a liquid.

When solid carbon dioxide was mixed with liquids like alcohol, which have very low freezing temperatures, the problem was solved. The trademark name "Dry Ice" is used because the solid material doesn't melt into a liquid but turns into gas. This is very convenient because the gas escapes into the air. Solid carbon dioxide, or Dry Ice, gives more refrigeration than the same amount of water ice.

The first important use for solid carbon dioxide was for packing ice cream. Now fish, meat, and other perishable products are shipped thousands of miles and kept in perfect condition with this material. Eggs refrigerated with solid carbon dioxide remain fresh almost indefinitely. This is because eggs grow stale when carbon dioxide escapes through the pores of the shell. When they are refrigerated with carbon dioxide, a vapor of the gas surrounds the eggs, and they remain fresh! Florists can keep rosebuds from opening for three days when they are kept in an atmosphere of carbon dioxide!

HOW IS SUGAR MADE?

Sugar is one of the oldest products man has been able to make from nature. Thousands of years ago, the people of India learned how to make sugar from sugar cane. But Europe didn't even know such a thing existed until the Arabs introduced it at the time of the Crusades. At first sugar was considered a rarity and was even used as a medicine.

Today, sugar is a relatively cheap food. In the United States, the average person consumes about 100 pounds of sugar every year! By the word "sugar" today, we may be describing any of over 100 sweet-tasting substances, but each has the same chemical composition. It consists of three elements, carbon, hydrogen, and oxygen. While the amount of carbon may vary, there is always twice as much hydrogen as oxygen, which makes sugar a carbohydrate.

Sugar is made by plants for their own use. This sugar is stored away in the plant until it is needed to make seeds and fiber or material for growth. As a food for man, sugar supplies heat and energy and helps to form fat.

The various kinds of sugar come from widely different sources. Milk sugar, or lactose, which is used for babies, comes from milk. From fruit we get a sugar called "fructose." From vegetables, grain, potatoes, we get glucose. The most common sugar, sucrose, comes chiefly from beets and sugar cane.

Sugar cane is a member of the grass family. It grows in the warm, moist climate of the tropics and subtropics, and sometimes reaches a height of 20 feet. When the stalks of the sugar cane have been cut, they are trimmed and taken to the cane mill or sugar factory. There they are washed and cut into short lengths or shredded. The rough pulpy mass is then crushed between heavy rollers.

The liquid pressed out of the cane is a dark grayish or greenish color and is acid. Since this contains impurities, it is necessary to use chemicals to clear it up. The clear juice is then run into vacuum pans and evaporated into a thick sirup, which is a mixture of sugar crystals and molasses. This is revolved in hollow cylinders to force out the molasses sirup, leaving the raw, brown sugar inside. This brown sugar then goes to a refinery, where it is dissolved, treated with chemicals, filtered, and finally it is crystallized again. Now we have pure white sugar, which is then made into granulated, lump, or powdered form.

WHERE DOES STARCH COME FROM?

More food for the human race is furnished by starch than is gained from any other single substance! This alone would make starch one of the most important substances in the world. But, of course, starch has many other uses, too, ranging from adhesives and laundering to use as a basis in many toilet preparations.

Starch is produced by plants and in the plants it is found in the form of tiny grains. With the help of sunshine and chlorophyll (the green matter in their leaves), plants combine water from the soil and the carbon dioxide from the air into sugar.

This sugar is changed by the plants into starch. The starch is stored away as small granules in large quantities in their stems, roots, leaves, fruits, and seeds. The white potato, for example, contains large amounts of starch. Such cereals as corn, rice, and wheat also contain large quantities.

Why do the plants store away starch? It serves as food for the development of seedlings or the new shoots until they can manufacture their own food materials.

For men and animals, starch supplies an energy-producing food. Like sugar, it is made up of carbon, hydrogen, and oxygen. It is not sweet; generally, it is tasteless.

Starch is obtained from a plant by crushing the plant tissue which contains the starch. The starch is washed out with water and allowed to settle to the bottom of large vats. The water is then squeezed out of the wet starch and the mass is dried and ground to a powder.

Some of the most common sources of starch are white potatoes, sweet potatoes, the grain crops, arrowroot, the sago palm, and the cassava plant of tropical America.

HOW DOES YEAST MAKE BREAD RISE?

Thousands of years ago, the Egyptians discovered that it was the yeast which made bread rise and so they were the first people to produce a "yeast-raised" bread. What is yeast, and how is it able to produce those light loaves of bread we enjoy today?

Yeast is a one-celled plant, so small that it cannot be seen without a microscope. But we can see yeast because it grows in colonies, made up of many yeast plants growing together. A yeast colony is almost colorless. It is not green because it has no chlorophyll. This is why yeast is called a "fungus." It cannot produce food for itself.

As yeast plants grow and reproduce, they form two substances called "enzymes," invertase and zymase. These enzymes help to convert (change) starch to sugar and sugar to alcohol, carbon dioxide, and energy.

This energy-producing process is called "fermentation." The carbon dioxide formed is a gas which man may use in a number of ways; one of them in making bread rise.

Years ago breadmakers found that bread would rise, or become light and fluffy, if allowed to stand for a time before baking. This happened because yeast plants from the air entered the dough and began to grow.

Today breadmakers add yeast and sugar to the dough as they make it. The starch and sugar in the bread dough serve as food for the yeast. Carbon dioxide is given off and forms bubbles inside the loaf. Heat from the oven causes the gas to expand. This makes the bread rise even more. Finally the heat drives off the carbon dioxide, and it leaves a light, dry loaf.

Yeast is grown in large vats, strained, mixed with starch, and pressed into cakes. It is then ready to be sold.

If yeast grows in a sugar solution, the carbon dioxide escapes but the alcohol stays in the solution. Whiskey, beer, ale, wine, and other alcoholic beverages are made in this way from fruit juices or grain mashes, such as rye, wheat, or corn.

WHAT IS CAFFEINE?

Today there is hardly a home in the Western world where coffee isn't found. So the effects of coffee and caffeine are of interest to a great many people. But did you know that coffee wasn't introduced into Europe until the latter part of the 17th century? Coffee was first known to the Abyssinians in eastern Africa, and for a period of 200 years all the world's coffee came from Yemen in southern Arabia.

The roasted coffee bean contains many substances, and the best known of these is caffeine. It is a substance chemically related to uric acid. Caffeine is not found in a free state, but combined with acids. A coffee bean contains about one per cent caffeine.

The effects produced by drinking coffee are not due only to the caffeine, but caffeine is the strongest of the substances in coffee. By the way, tea also contains caffeine, but the same amount of caffeine in tea has a different effect than when in coffee. The reason is that in each case the caffeine is combined with different substances. Also, if you add milk or cream to coffee, the caffeine combines with the protein of the milk, and its action is weakened.

What is the effect of coffee on the body? Surprisingly enough, it has not one effect but many. Coffee dilates the vessels in the brain and improves circulation there. It stimulates the nerve cells. It also increases the work done by the heart. (You can see how for some people this would not be desirable.) Coffee works on the movement of the intestine, and so has a mild laxative action.

Coffee also makes the gastric glands secrete more juices, and for some people this produces "heartburn," while for others it helps digestion. Altogether, coffee acts as a stimulant to the body and nerves. This is why some people complain that it "keeps them up" at night.

Generally speaking, drinking coffee is a matter of individual decision. People who are used to it, find it helps them feel better. Nervous people are apt to be injured by it. And, of course, people who drink it to excess may find it quite upsetting. But isn't that true of anything we eat or drink?

WHY IS MILK PASTEURIZED?

Since milk is such an important food, it has to be kept clean, sweet, and free from harmful bacteria. Pasteurization is only one of the many steps that are taken to provide you with safe, healthful milk. Let's see what happens to milk as it goes from the cow to your kitchen.

To begin with, the farmer sees that his cows receive several tests at regular intervals to make sure they are healthy. He also takes care to hire only healthy people to help him in handling milk.

Milking machines and milk pails are kept perfectly clean. As soon as each cow is milked, the milk is carried to the milkhouse where it is weighed, filtered, and cooled to the right temperature in preparation for shipment. Most farmers put their milk into 10-gallon steel cans which are smooth inside and have been well-tinned to prevent corrosion.

When milk has to be shipped to a city milk plant, it travels in milk tanks that are made of steel and highly insulated. A milk tank is like a huge thermos bottle. Even if the shipment is a long one, the insulation is so good that the temperature of the milk changes only one or two degrees!

When the milk arrives at the city milk plant, it is pumped into large holding tanks. Here the temperature is checked again and so is the odor. Other tests are made to assure the quality and sanitary condition of the milk.

Then the milk is pasteurized. This means that the milk is heated to a temperature at which any harmful bacteria which may be in the milk are killed. The process is named after the famous French scientist, Louis Pasteur, who developed it.

There are two methods of pasteurization. In one method, the milk is heated to a temperature of at least 143 degrees Fahrenheit for not less than 30 minutes. This is called the long-time, holding method. In the other method, the milk is heated to at least 160 degrees Fahrenheit and is held at that temperature for not less than 15 seconds. This is the short-time method. After pasteurization, the milk is cooled very rapidly.

Every step involved in the handling of milk is done with great care to make sure that the milk you drink is as clean and healthy as can be!

WHAT IS ALUMINUM?

Aluminum is one of the most abundant metals found in nature. It makes up nearly 8 per cent of the earth's crust. The trouble is that aluminum is never found free in nature, but in combination with various substances, it forms part of many rocks and soils.

The problem that science tackled, therefore, was how to make this metal cheaply and in large quantities. On February 23, 1886, a 22-year-old chemist called Charles Martin Hall solved the problem and a new metal age was born—the age of aluminum.

What he did was to melt cryolite, an aluminum compound, mix it with aluminum oxide, and then pass a direct electric current through the mixture. After a while, little "buttons" of metallic aluminum appeared, the first process ever discovered for producing the metal!

Metallic aluminum is a silvery-white, lustrous metal that is only about one-third as heavy as iron. It can be drawn out into wires that are finer than the finest hairs, and hammered out into sheets many times thinner than the paper in this book.

While certain acids will affect it, under ordinary conditions aluminum does not corrode. And when certain other metals are mixed with it, the resulting combinations, called "alloys," are stronger, harder, or tougher than aluminum itself!

Aluminum got its big start in the kitchen only because one of the first articles cast in this metal was a teapot! Of course it's an almost perfect material for cooking utensils because it conducts heat so well and is so easy to keep clean and bright. But its light weight makes it useful for things that range from electric cables to automobile engines. One of aluminum's greatest contributions to modern life has been its use in bodies, wings, and propellers of airplanes. Today, even railway engines use aluminum alloys!

Every year new uses for this metal are discovered. Ground up into a fine powder, it is mixed with oils and used as paint. It is used as a wrapper in the form of foil for soaps, cheese, cigarettes. Many of the tubes used for tooth paste, shaving creams, and so on, are made from aluminum. And now aluminum has found its way into furniture, buildings, toasters, radios, washing machines—into practically every part of our life!

HOW IS STAINLESS STEEL MADE?

Of all the alloys made, steel is one of the most important. Millions of tons are produced every year and it is used in a tremendous variety of products, from tools to rails.

Now, when other elements in addition to carbon are added to iron, the steel that results is called "an alloy steel." One of the most important alloy steels is stainless steel.

It was discovered that when in addition to the carbon and iron combination, about 10 to 20 per cent of chromium and some nickel was included, the result was a steel that resists rust, oxidation, and the attack of many acids.

Stainless steel then is steel with the addition of chromium and possibly some nickel. The use of stainless steel now extends to hundreds of products we come in contact with every day. It is used for table and kitchen knives, golf-club heads, door knobs, light fixtures, fishing gear—the list could go on and on.

Because stainless steel can take a high polish, it is often used for mirrors and reflectors where glass would be too brittle.

HOW DOES A CAMERA TAKE PICTURES?

The human eye is actually a form of camera. When you look around, your eyes "take pictures" of the things you see. The lens in your eye acts just like the lens in a camera. The retina of your eye acts like the film in your camera.

In your eye, the light acts on the sensitive surface of the retina. In a camera, light acts on a specially prepared sensitive surface of the film. If light didn't have an affect on certain chemically prepared substances, photography would be impossible.

What is this action? It is simply the fact that light makes the chemical silver nitrate turn black. Most photographic processes depend on this reaction, as we will now see.

The first problem is to focus the light on the sensitive material of the film. This is done by the lens of the camera, which collects and bends the light to form the picture. A lens is like "a light funnel" through which the light is directed onto the film.

When we open and close the shutter of the camera quickly, light comes in and strikes the film. When this happens, a chemical reaction takes place on the film. Certain tiny grains of silver bromide undergo a change. When this film is taken out of the camera and treated with various liquids, these grains, which have been affected by the light, turn up as the dark part of the film.

The more intense the light, the darker or denser is the patch it makes on the film. This film is called "a negative" because it has the opposite values of the picture. Dark parts of the scene you photographed look light, light parts look dark.

When the negative is ready, the next step is to make a "positive" print. The negative is placed against a special printing paper, which also is affected by light. So it is exposed to a bright light through the negative. The dark parts of the negative let less light go through to the printing paper, so those parts of the print will look light. In this way, we get again the values of the original subject we photographed. The picture that comes out on the printing paper thus has gone through a negative stage and then through a positive stage, and you have exactly what you photographed with your camera.

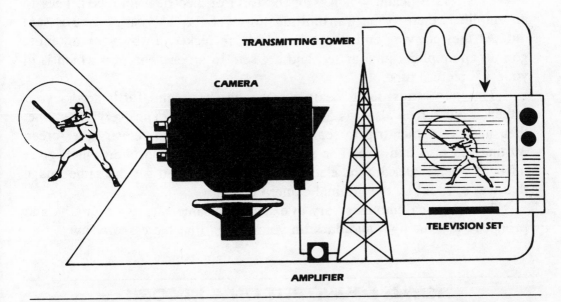

HOW ARE TELEVISION PICTURES SENT AND RECEIVED?

"Television" really means "seeing at a distance." It is a method of sending pictures of events as they happen ("live"), or motion pictures from film, or "video tape" recordings. At the same time the pictures are broadcast, the sound is sent along by radio.

First we must understand that "pictures" are not sent through the air. What is transmitted are electrical impulses. This means that a picture has to be changed into electrical impulses at one end those electrical impulses

189

changed back into a picture at the other end. Let's see, in basic terms, how this is done.

A camera lens focuses a picture on a light-sensitive plate of glass. This plate throws off electrons. In the bright areas of the picture, it throws off many electrons, and in the dark areas, few electrons. The electrons are collected on a target plate.

Now in this camera tube, at the other end from the target plate, there is an electron gun which throws a beam on the target plate. This beam is a "scanning" beam; it sweeps back and forth in 525 lines across the target plate so that it covers the entire surface 30 times in one second! The beam that bounces back is changed (modulated) according to whether it strikes a bright or dark area. The return beam is sometimes strong, sometimes weak, according to the image on the target plate.

This return beam, which is in the form of electrical impulses, goes to an amplifier, then to the transmitting tower of the TV station and is sent out. At the receiving end, these impulses are picked up by your antenna, go into an amplifier in your set, and are sent to an electron gun which is in your TV picture tube.

This gun sends out a beam which goes back and forth across your screen. Your screen also has 525 lines and the beam scans every other line, then makes another trip to scan the remaining lines. It covers the screen 30 times in a second also. The screen is coated with phosphor which gives off light when struck by the electron beam, and so you get the same image that was sent out by the original camera beam!

The electrical impulses vary in exactly the same way as originally, and produce the same light and dark on your screen that the camera saw.

HOW IS SOUND PUT ON A RECORD?

Today, with hi-fi, stereo, LP, and tape all available to reproduce sound in the home, we are certainly far from the simple phonograph that was invented by Thomas Edison. But the basic principles for capturing sound remain the same.

Sounds, whether speech or instrumental music, are caused by vibrations of air. To reproduce sounds, these vibrations must be "caught." Let us say the air vibrations are caught in the mouthpiece of a tube. At the other end of the tube there is a flexible disk and a cutting tool. As the vibrations come through the tube, the disk flutters, and the cutting tool moves with the disk.

At the same time, a plate of soft, waxy material revolves under the tool. There is a continuous groove on the surface of this plate that goes in a spiral from the outside edge to the center. The point of the tool is in the groove, and as it vibrates it marks the groove from side to side. In this way the vibrations are "caught."

Now suppose the cutting tool is removed and we put a needle in its place. As the record spins, the needle follows the markings in the groove. This makes the disk vibrate. The vibrating disk moves the air in the tube and produces the sounds that were caught!

Naturally, this is only the basic, simple principle of how a phonograph and records work. Modern recording methods are much more complicated. For example, sound waves can be converted to a series of electric currents. The fluctuating sound waves are made to produce a fluctuating electric current. This current is amplified. It then goes to a magnet to which a cutting tool is attached.

In picking up sound from the record, the needle presses on crystals in the pickup arm. The crystals set up an electric current that fluctuates with the vibrations of the needle. This current is amplified and it is made to push and pull the cone in the loudspeaker which sets up vibrations that we hear as sound.

HOW ARE TAPE RECORDINGS MADE?

Since the days back in 1877, when Thomas Edison made the first sound recording, so many great improvements have been made that it's almost impossible to keep up with them. Today especially, the whole science of sound recording and reproduction is moving ahead very rapidly, and all of us are enjoying the benefits of these advances.

Tape recording is one of the greatest developments in this field. What most people don't know is that it plays an important part in the making of records. In making records, the original sound is picked up by one or more microphones. It is recorded on a special kind of tape called "magnetic tape." What happens is that sound is changed into electrical signals which cause particles in the tape to be magnetized in a special way. When the tape is played, those magnetized particles give off the same electrical signals, which are then converted into sound.

Magnetic tape is used in making records because it can be edited. This means it can be cut apart and recombined, so that parts can be left out, new parts can be put in place of old, and so on.

The sound from the tape is fed to a disk cutter, which cuts grooves in a smooth lacquer disk. From this disk, master records are made, and these masters are later used to press records. Pressure and steam heat are used in the process of cutting the grooves in the soft record material.

This is how tape is used in making recordings, but as you know, the tape itself can be used as the final recording. The tape can be played without ever making a record. The development of this kind of tape was a long process. At first, spools of wire were used, and later, tape was made of solid metal. But the results were only fair.

When the Allies invaded Germany during World War II, they found that tape recorders of very good quality were being used in broadcasting stations. The secret was that tape made of plastic was being used. Once we found out how to use plastic for making tape recordings, many advances were quickly made.

Because the sound is put on tape by magnetizing particles on the surface of the tape, it can be played thousands of times without becoming noisy or losing its quality. It can be erased by being demagnetized, and then new sounds can be recorded on the same tape!

HOW ARE MIRRORS MADE?

For thousands of years, the only mirrors used by man were made of polished metal—brass, bronze, silver, or gold.

In about 1300, the craftsmen in Venice discovered a way of making mirrors of glass by backing them with a coating of mercury and tin. Very soon, these glass mirrors took the place of metal ones. But even these glass mirrors were far from perfect. In 1691, in France, a way of making plate glass was discovered. Because plate glass has more weight and brilliance, it is much more suited to mirrors than ordinary glass.

The next great step forward was the use of a thin silver coating on the back of a mirror instead of the tin-mercury mixture. Not only were the mercury fumes dangerous to the workmen, but the new silver coating reflected more rays of light and made better mirrors. It also led to speeding up the process of manufacturing and made mirrors less expensive.

Today, plate glass one-quarter inch in thickness is used in making the best-grade mirrors. The glass is first cut to the desired size with a diamond cutter. In the "roughing mill" the edges are treated with sand and water. It is next smoothed with fine sandstone and polished with rouge-covered felt buffers.

Before silvering, a thorough cleansing takes place to insure clearness. The glass is then placed on a warm, padded table. Over it is poured a mixture of ammonia, tartaric acid, and nitrate of silver. This readily sticks to the glass because of the heat. Then the silver is protected with a coat of shellac, and an application of paint which is free from oils and acids that would injure the silver.

Today, of course, mirrors have many more uses than merely to see one's self. Rear vision mirrors in automobiles are important to safe driving. Long-handled little mirrors are used by dentists to let them look into hard-to-see places. Mirrors are a vital part of the periscopes of submarines. The image striking one mirror in a tube is sent down the tube to the other mirror into which the observer is looking.

Mirrors are also used in telescopes, in flashlights, in searchlights, in headlights of automobiles, and in lamps in lighthouses. In most of these, however, the curved reflector, or mirror, is usually of a highly polished metal that concentrates the light and throws it ahead.

HOW DO EYEGLASSES CORRECT VISION?

Just imagine what life was like for millions of people before eyeglasses were invented! If you were nearsighted and you looked up at night you couldn't see clouds or distant mountains or birds flying through the air.

Today nearsighted people can see as much as people with normal eyes, because eyeglasses can correct their vision. To begin very simply, light enters our eye and falls on the retina in the eye, which is like the sensitized plate of a camera. Obviously, if the light falls in back of the retina or in front of it, we won't be able to see. So the eye has a lens to focus the light and make it fall in the right place.

When normal eyes look at distant objects, the image falls on the retina without any problem. But when the same eye looks at a close object (say less than 18 feet away), the image falls behind the retina. So the lens of the eye "accommodates," which means that a certain muscle contracts and

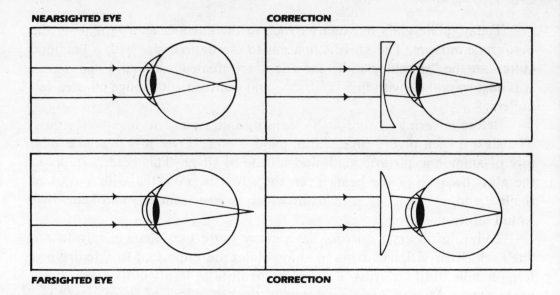

NEARSIGHTED EYE

NEARSIGHTED EYE

CORRECTION

FARSIGHTED EYE

CORRECTION

changes the shape of the lens. This makes the image fall on the retina and the eye sees the object clearly.

Now, two things can happen to make this accommodation impossible naturally. First, as people get older the lenses in the eyes lose their elasticity. They can't change shape to focus images correctly. The second thing is that some people are born with eyes that are too short or too long.

People with too short eyes are farsighted. They can see distant objects well, but they must accommodate very strongly to see near objects. Sometimes it is impossible to do this enough to focus the image on the retina. So they wear glasses. The glasses do the job that their own eye lenses cannot do. They focus the image on the retina and don't have to accommodate at all.

A nearsighted person has eyes that are too long. The image is focused in front of the retina and looks blurred. But the nearsighted person can do nothing about it. If he accommodates (makes the muscle contract the eye), it will only make the image move farther forward. So he wears glasses that focus the image farther back and on the retina, and then he can see clearly.

WHAT IS A CULTURED PEARL?

About 4,000 years ago, a Chinese fisherman who decided that oysters might satisfy his hunger opened a few and was probably the first man to discover pearls!

What are pearls and how are they produced? Pearls are made of the

194

same material as the mother-of-pearl lining in the shell of the oyster. The body of the oyster is very tender, so to protect itself the oyster secretes this mother-of-pearl lining to provide a smooth surface against its body.

When an irritating object, such as a grain of sand, manages to get inside the oyster's shell, the oyster coats it with layer after layer of mother-of-pearl—and this becomes a pearl!

When this happens naturally, the pearl may be perfectly shaped. But man has found a way to help the oyster along in the making of pearls. A bit of sand or a tiny piece of mother-of-pearl is inserted between the shell and the outer skin of the oyster. After two or three years, when these shells are taken from the water and opened, a pearl is found inside. These are called "cultured" pearls, and are usually not perfectly shaped.

In Japan, they have now learned how to make even cultured pearls perfect! The irritating material is put right into the body of the oyster. This is really a surgical operation requiring great care and delicacy, because the oyster must be kept alive. But it's an operation well worth performing!

Pearl divers, almost naked and wearing nose clips, go down by means of a rope about 80 feet and stay under water about a minute at a time. They scoop up all the shells they can and put them into floating tubs. In some parts of the world, of course, pearl divers now have all kinds of modern diving equipment and stay down for hours at a time.

The largest pearl ever found is said to have been two inches long and four inches around! Because real pearls are so expensive, most of us buy artificial pearls. The French make beautiful artificial pearls by taking hollow glass beads and lining them with a substance that comes from the shiny scales of certain fish, then filling the beads with wax. These "pearls" can hardly be told apart from the real thing!

WHAT IS PLASTIC?

The word plastic means "capable of being molded or modeled." When heated, plastics are somewhat like modeling clay. They can be molded into shapes which last when the material is cooled. This is what gives them their name.

There is no need to go into a description of the many uses to which plastics have been put. Probably not a day goes by in our life in which we don't use or touch a plastic product.

But what is a plastic? The starting point in making a plastic is the molecule. It is the smallest division of matter that still acts like the whole material from which it comes.

The chemist causes the molecules of certain materials to form a long chain, the links being the molecules. The new "long-chain" molecule acts differently from the single molecule. It creates materials with new properties. When molecules link into chains we say they "polymerize."

Sometimes two different types of molecules are joined to form materials called "copolymers." A chain of two types of molecules acts differently from long chains made up of either type alone. So you see, the chemist can constantly create new materials, or plastics, to suit his needs.

A "polymer," or material made of long-chain molecules, is the beginning of a plastic. It has to be changed to be suitable for molding. It is ground into fine powder or made into pellets. To this, colors are added, and chemicals are worked in to make it flexible. Sometimes plasticizers are added. These are chemicals which change a plastic that is stiff as a blackboard into a material flexible enough for a raincoat.

Plastics have many special properties which make them very useful for special purposes. They resist the flow of electricity, they insulate against heat, they are light in weight and wear well, and they can be made unbreakable.

Each kind of plastic is derived from different materials. Some may come from coal, some from salt, some from wood or cotton fibers, etc. But in each case the molecules have to be rearranged in the right way and chemicals must be added to produce the desired plastic.

WHAT IS NYLON?

The first fiber ever made entirely by man is nylon, which was announced to the world in 1938.

It was created as the result of some experiments being conducted to find out why certain molecules join together to make "giant" molecules, such as are found in rubber and cotton.

One day, a material was produced that stretched like warm taffy candy. When it cooled, it could be stretched even farther, and as it was stretched it became elastic and stronger. This made the chemists working on the experiment wonder whether this new material could be used to create a textile fiber. They decided to try, and after eight long years of work they announced the new fiber known as nylon.

Nylon is made from four common elements: carbon, hydrogen, nitrogen, and oxygen. These elements are all found in nature. For instance, carbon is found in coal, nitrogen and oxygen in air, and hydrogen in water. Actually, in the making of nylon the basic materials are obtained from natural gas, petroleum, oat hulls, and corn cobs!

Nylon is formed by hooking two different kinds of molecules together to form larger molecules. When these two molecules join together, they form a material called "nylon salt."

When nylon salt is heated in a big pressure cooker, the molecules of the salt hook together and form the long chain of molecules called "a polymer." The polymer becomes a thick liquid when it is heated. This liquid is forced through a disk with tiny holes and it comes out as fibers which become hard as they are cooled. Then these tiny fragments of fibers are gathered together into a single yarn.

After stretching this yarn three or four times its original length, it becomes strong and elastic and we have nylon!

WHAT IS WOOL?

One of the first fibers man ever used for making cloth is wool. The use of wool began so long ago, in fact, that we don't know its beginning. The ancient Greeks spun and wove wool, and they learned how to do it from the Egyptians!

Wool is a kind of hair which grows on sheep and many other animals. The surface of all hair is covered with tiny scales, so small that we can only see them with a powerful microscope. These scales overlap, like the shingles on a roof. In a hair, the scales lie down flat, but in wool the edges stick out, and the natural "crimp" in wool helps make it useful as a fiber for cloth.

There are various grades of wool, depending on the sheep from which it comes. There is an interesting story in connection with this. For hundreds of years, the finest wool was produced in Spain from a kind of sheep called "the merino." When the Spanish Armada was sunk years ago, some of the ships went down off the north coast of Scotland. But a few merino sheep were washed ashore alive. These were bred with the native mountain sheep of Scotland, and from this came the famous Cheviot breed of sheep, which is one of the finest producers of wool in Great Britain.

Wool can be obtained from other animals than sheep. Angora and cashmere goats produce wool, as do the camel, alpaca, llama, and vicuña. A single sheep may yield as much as eight pounds of fleece, which is the name for this hair. But as much as half of this is dirt, grease, and a substance called "the yolk" of the wool. All of this has to be removed by a process called "scouring" before the wool can be used.

After the wool is sorted into various grades, scoured, and dried, it goes through a whole series of steps that includes dyeing, carding, and combing. Then it is spun into yarn and finally it's ready to be woven into cloth.

The first successful woolen mill in the United States was set up at Newberry, Massachusetts, in 1790. But American wool has never really been considered to be of the highest quality, so a third of all the wool used in this country is imported!

HOW ARE BLACKBOARDS MADE?

What would school be like if we didn't have blackboards? Think of the hundreds and hundreds of hours we spend during our school years either writing on the blackboard or reading what the teacher has written on it. What is that blackboard really made of?

Of course, many people know it's made of a substance called "slate." But what is slate? Interestingly enough, slate is a material that is millions and millions of years old. It all began when tiny particles of clay gradually sifted down to the bottoms of lakes and seas millions of years ago.

As they lay there at the bottom of the sea, they slowly formed a soft mud. As time went on, this mud hardened and became a kind of mud-rock called "shale." The earth was still going through violent changes, and at one time the crust heaved upward in that part where the shale was. The layers of shale were folded up into wrinkles. The other rocks squeezed and flattened the shale so hard that it became slate.

Because the original clay particles that made up the slate were deposited in layers at the bottom of the sea, the slate that finally developed has layers, too. This is one of the reasons slate is so useful for so many purposes. It not only makes blackboards, but is also used for roofs of buildings, sinks, drainboards, and a great number of other articles.

Slate is taken from quarries or from underground mines in big blocks, which are divided into smaller blocks, before they are removed to be split.

In making a piece of slate, the splitter takes blocks about 3 inches thick. He holds a chisel in a certain position against the edge of the block, and taps it lightly with a mallet. A crack appears, and by using the chisel the block is split into two pieces with smooth and even surfaces.

The splitter keeps on repeating this process until he has changed the original block into about 16 or 18 separate "slates." In the case of a roofing tile, the slate is split until it's about one-sixth of an inch thick.

Slate comes in many colors—black, blue, purple, red, green, or gray— depending on the presence of various materials in the original clay deposits. Black slate is the result of living materials that turned to carbon in the original muds.

HOW ARE CRAYONS MADE?

On the surface of the ocean there live many forms of very tiny plants and animals. Among these are certain one-celled animals called "Foramini-fera," which have shells of lime.

When these animals die, their tiny shells sink to the ocean floor, and in time they form a thick layer there. This layer becomes cemented and compressed into a soft limestone called "chalk."

Men have used this soft limestone for hundreds of years, and one of these uses has been to make crayon. In fact, one form of this chalk called "red earth" has been used to make crayons since ancient times.

Today, many crayons are also made from artificially prepared mixtures. This consists of a base of certain types of clay, to which a variety of pigments are added. The material is then "cemented" together by the use of an adhesive. By adding varying amounts of coloring matter to a given quantity of the base, any shade of tint can be obtained.

You may think of crayons as something that children use for their drawings. But actually, chalk and crayons have had an important role in the history of art.

At the beginning of the 16th century, the artists used chiefly black chalk on white paper. But later on, they began to use it with other mediums to suggest color First they used black chalk with a little white on a tinted paper. Then they began to use black and red crayon, heightened with white, on various shades of paper.

Finally, the great French artist Watteau began to use red crayon in such marvelous ways that he opened up a whole new field of art.

If you are interested in drawing, and haven't yet begun to use oil paints, you should be encouraged by the examples of some of the world's greatest artists. Holbein, Van Dyck, Titian, and Tintoretto created masterpieces with chalk and crayon. Michelangelo, Raphael, and Leonardo da Vinci also used chalk and crayon to create works of lasting beauty!

WHAT IS GLUE?

The word "glue" comes from Old French and Late Latin verbs meaning "to draw together." The idea of using a substance to hold things together is a very old one. On the walls of an Egyptian tomb more than 3,000 years old, there is a painting showing workmen using glue!

Since the meaning of "glue" is "that which sticks together," many substances are called "glue." For example, there are mineral glues, vegetable glues, marine glues, and many synthetic glues.

But the traditional glue is made from bones, sinews, and the hides of animals. These are properly prepared, heated, and then the solution is dried. In fact, if you've ever taken out a cooked chicken which has been put in the refrigerator, you've seen a jelly on top of the liquid. This is really an impure glue solution.

When glue is prepared commercially, the hot solutions are filtered, clarified, and evaporated. The concentrate is then dried. Another method used in preparing glue is to allow the solutions to chill to a firm jelly. The jelly is then cut into thin slices which are spread on nets. The nets are then dried in currents of warm air in a drying tunnel.

Glue is used in small quantities in hundreds of ways in many industries. For example, wood joints and veneers in furniture, pianos, and toys require glue. It is very important in bookbinding and the making of paper boxes. Gummed paper of all kinds has glue, and so do fireworks, match heads, and dolls' heads!

When you have new paper money and hear it "crackle," it's because the paper has been sized with glue. Sandpaper couldn't be made without glue to hold down the grains.

Glue, being made of natural substances, decays quickly, so preservatives are added. But despite this, if you have a solution of glue standing around, it is likely to mold or rot, and develop a vile odor. That's why glue should be freshly prepared. This means making a solution out of the granulated form, in which form glue is usually sold in bulk.

WHAT MAKES A BASEBALL CURVE?

Everybody who loves and follows baseball knows that a pitcher can make a ball curve. But strangely enough, there have been some attempts to prove that a baseball doesn't really curve! This has been done with a camera, and the idea was that the curve is an optical illusion.

Luckily for all the great pitchers who earn so much money because of their ability to throw a good curve ball, it has been demonstrated that a baseball can be made to curve as much as 6½ inches from its normal path.

The explanation of what makes a baseball curve is tied up with a rather complicated scientific law or "effect." This was discovered by a man called Bernoulli, and is known as "the Bernoulli effect."

Bernoulli pointed out that there are two kinds of pressure in a fluid, such as air or water. One is static, one is dynamic. The dynamic pressure is created when a moving fluid (such as air) comes into contact with an object. Static pressure is the pressure existing within the fluid itself, the pressure of one atom against another. The Bernoulli effect states that the static pressure goes down as the speed goes up.

Now we're ready for the baseball. When the pitcher wants to throw a curve, he makes the ball spin as it leaves his hand. As the ball spins, it carries air around with it by friction. On one side of the spinning ball, this air moves with the current of air caused by the forward motion of the ball. In other words, the air passing the ball and the air spinning around the ball are going in the same direction on one side. On the other side, the air spinning around the ball is going in the opposite direction to the motion of the air past the ball.

The result is, the air speed is greater on one side of the ball than on the other. Now remember, we said greater speed makes the static pressure go down. So the ball moves toward the side where there is lower static pressure and it "curves"!

WHAT MAKES A BOOMERANG RETURN?

One of the oldest and most peculiar weapons ever developed by man is the boomerang. The word "boomerang," by the way, comes from a single tribe in New South Wales, who called it that long ago.

Although the boomerang is hardly more than a curved club, it puzzled science for many years. Nobody seemed able to explain why it behaved as it did in the air. It is used by savage tribes in Australia, northeast Africa, and southern India, and by the Hopi Indians of Arizona.

There are two kinds of boomerangs: the return and the nonreturn. The nonreturn boomerang is the heavier, and nearly straight. It is more deadly as a weapon than the return boomerang. It is said that a native can throw it and cut a small animal almost in two with it.

The return boomerang is better known to the world. But the natives of Australia consider it chiefly a toy, not a serious weapon. It may sometimes be used for killing birds.

It is made of hard wood and is curved at an angle of between 90 degrees and 120 degrees. One side is flat and the other is rounded. The arms are very slightly twisted in opposite directions, so that they are about 2 degrees off a plane drawn through the center of the boomerang. It is the pressure of the air on the bulge of the rounded side, together with the twist given it when thrown, which makes the boomerang circle and return.

The wild bushmen of Australia can make a boomerang curve in an amazing manner. They can throw it so that it will travel straight for 30 yards, describe a circle 50 yards in diameter, and then return to the thrower. Or they can make it hit the ground, circle in the air, and return.

A boomerang is thrown forward with a downward twist of the wrist. Boomerangs have been known to travel as far as 400 feet before returning.

HOW ARE FIREWORKS MADE?

Fireworks are so old that nobody knows who first made them, or when! The credit for inventing "pyrotechny" (the art of making fireworks) is usually given to the Chinese, because they had them hundreds of years before they were known in Europe.

Did you know that the ancient Greeks and Romans had fireworks of some sort? However, fireworks as we know them weren't really made until after gunpowder came into use and the science of chemistry had developed.

The basic materials used in making fireworks are saltpeter, sulphur, and charcoal. These ingredients are ground together into a fine powder. Then, in order to obtain the various spectacular effects that make us say "Oooh!" and "Ahhh!," other things are added, such as nitrates of lead, barium, and aluminum.

The colors in fireworks, which add so much to their beauty and effect, are obtained by adding various salts of metals: strontium for red; barium for green; sodium for yellow; copper for blue. By using iron filings, showers of dazzling sparks can be obtained.

A simple Roman candle is made by stopping the bottom of a cardboard tube with clay or plaster and placing above this a layer of gunpowder. Next comes a hard "ball" of a powder designed to burn but not explode. Around this is a layer of "inflammant," which means a substance that bursts into flame.

Then there is a thicker layer of slow-burning powder called "fuze," another of gunpowder, above this a second "ball" with its inflammant, and so on. When the tube is filled, an igniting fuse sticks out of the paper cup which covers the mouth of the tube.

When this is lighted, it ignites the top layer of slow-burning powder, which gradually burns down to the inflammant surrounding the topmost ball. Then the ball itself catches fire, the gunpowder explodes, and this drives the glowing ball from the tube. This is repeated until all the balls are expelled. So you can see there really is an "art" to making fireworks!

HOW IS CHOCOLATE MADE?

Long before chocolate was made in solid pieces, it was enjoyed as a drink. The Aztecs made it by boiling the crushed beans of the cacao tree with water and serving it cold, highly spiced, and seasoned with pepper!

Spanish explorers, who discovered this drink among the Aztecs, didn't like peppers. So they invented a new recipe by adding an equal amount of sugar to the cacao before boiling it. The Spaniards kept the secret of their new drink for about 100 years! Finally, in the middle of the 17th century, a Frenchman discovered how to make the finely ground cacao beans into cakes of chocolate.

Cacao beans are gathered in this way. Skilled workmen cut ripe pods from the cacao tree. After being cut, the pods are split open and the pulp scooped out. This is allowed to ferment for several days. Then the mass is dried in the sun and the seeds are separated and bagged for shipment to market.

Upon arrival at the chocolate manufacturer's mill, the beans are first cleaned to remove any foreign material, and then roasted. As they roast, their husks are loosened, and in another operation the husks are blown away, and the inner kernel is broken into bits called "nibs."

For chocolate, the nibs are ground under heavy stone mills. The oil within them turns the mass into a thick substance called "chocolate liquor." This, when hard, is the bitter chocolate used in candymaking and baking.

Sweet chocolate is the same product combined with sugar and other substances. In making cocoa, part of the fat is separated after the nibs are ground. This fat, called "cocoa butter," is used for cosmetics and medicines, and forms an ingredient in the manufacture of sweet chocolate. What remains is ground fine to make cocoa.

INDEX

207

TELL ME WHY #2

BY ARKADY LEOKUM

ILLUSTRATIONS BY HOWARD BENDER

CONTENTS

Chapter 5
How Things Are Made

TELL ME WHY #2

CHAPTER 1
OUR WORLD

The moon doesn't look as if it's very far away, but its distance from the earth averages 239,000 miles. The diameter of the moon is 2,160 miles, or less than the distance across the United States. But when the moon is observed with a very large telescope, it looks as if it were only about 200 miles away.

WHY DOES THE MOON FOLLOW US WHEN WE DRIVE?

Because the moon seems so close and big to us, we sometimes forget that 239,000 miles is quite a distance away. It is this great distance that explains why the moon seems to follow us when we drive in an automobile and look up at it.

To begin with, our feeling that this is happening is just that—only a feeling, a psychological reaction. When we speed along a road, we notice that everything moves past us. Trees, houses, fences, the road—all fly past us in the opposite direction.

Now there's the moon, part of what we see as we look out, and we naturally expect it also to be flying past us, or at least to be moving backward as we speed ahead. When this doesn't happen, we have the sensation that it is "following" us.

But why doesn't it happen? Because the distance of the moon from the earth is quite great. Compared to the distance our automobile travels in a few minutes, that distance is enormous. So as our automobile moves along, the angle at which we see the moon hardly changes.

In fact, we could go along a straight path for miles and the angle at which we would see the moon would still be basically the same. And as we notice everything else flying past, we get that feeling of the moon "following" us.

While we can't fully explain light, we can measure it quite accurately. We have a pretty good idea of how fast light travels. Since a light-year is merely the distance that a beam of light will travel in a year, the real discovery had to do with measuring the speed of light.

HOW WAS THE LIGHT-YEAR DISCOVERED?

This was done by a Danish astronomer named Olaus Roemer in 1676. He noticed that the eclipses of one of the moons of Jupiter kept coming later and later as the earth moved in its orbit to the opposite side of the sun from that occupied by Jupiter. Then, as the earth moved back into its former position, the eclipses came on schedule again.

The difference in time added up to nearly 17 minutes. This could mean only that it takes that length of time for light to travel the diameter of the earth's orbit. This distance was known to be very nearly 186,000,000 miles. Since it took light about 1,000 seconds (nearly 17 minutes) to go this distance, it meant that the speed of light is about 186,000 miles per second.

In our own time, Professor Albert Michelson spent years trying to determine the exact speed of light. Using another method, he arrived at a speed of 186,284 miles per second, and this is now considered quite accurate.

If we multiply this speed by the seconds in a year, we find that light travels 5,880,000,000,000 miles in a year — and this is called a light-year.

Thousands of years ago, astronomers probably used the pyramids in Egypt and the towers and temples in Babylonia to help them study the sun, moon, and stars. There were no telescopes then. In time, astronomical instruments were developed, and as they became larger and more numerous, observatories were built to house them. Some observatories were built more than a thousand years ago.

WHAT IS AN OBSERVATORY?

An observatory has to be built in the right place, a place with favorable weather conditions, moderate temperatures, many days of sunshine and nights without clouds, and as little haze, rain, and snow as possible. It must also be away from city lights and neon signs, which make the sky too light for good observation.

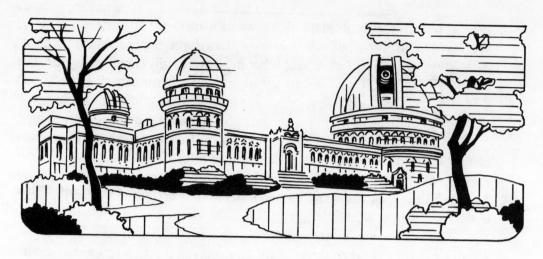

There are buildings which include living quarters in addition to telescopes. The instruments are housed in structures of steel and concrete. The building for the telescope is constructed in two parts. The lower part is stationary, and the upper part, or roof, is in the shape of a dome which can be rotated.

The dome has a "slit" which opens to permit the telescope to look out toward the sky. By rotating the dome on a track, the slit can be opened to any part of the sky. Both the dome and the telescope are moved by electric motors. In a modern observatory the astronomer only has to punch a number of buttons to move the equipment.

Of course, in order to see, the astronomer must always be near the eyepiece of the telescope or the camera attached to it. So, in some observatories the floor can be raised or lowered, or there is an adjustable platform.

Astronomers don't depend on their eyes alone to observe the skies. They have many complicated instruments and attachments to the telescope, such as cameras, spectroscopes, spectrographs, and spectroheliographs, all of which provide them with important information.

The discovery of things in the heavens often comes about much like the solving of a mystery. This is the way the asteroids were discovered.

Two men, Titius and Bode, had at different times figured out that

WHAT IS AN ASTEROID?

there must be a planet between Mars and Jupiter; there was such a large gap in the distance between them. So several astronomers set about searching for this planet.

In 1801, a planet was actually found there. It was named Ceres, but is was a very tiny planet indeed, with a diameter of only 480 miles. So it was believed that it could be only one of a group of small planets and the search went on.

In time, three more tiny planets were found, the brightest of which was only half the size of Ceres. Astronomers decided that a larger planet must have exploded and left these four tiny pieces. But after 15 years of searching, another astronomer found still another tiny planet and this started the hunt again.

By 1890, 300 small planets had been found, and between 1890 and 1927, 2,000 had been discovered! These tiny planets, all rotating around the sun in the area between Mars and Jupiter, are called asteroids.

To indicate how small they are, 195 of them have diameters of more than 61 miles; 502, between 25 and 61 miles; 193, between 10 and 25 miles; and 22 of them have diameters of less than 10 miles!

If the mass of all the asteroids were added together, it would only be 1/3000 of that of the earth. So even if all the asteroids were united, they would form an insignificant planet.

As to how the asteroids were formed, the theory is that a satellite of Jupiter exploded and created these fragments.

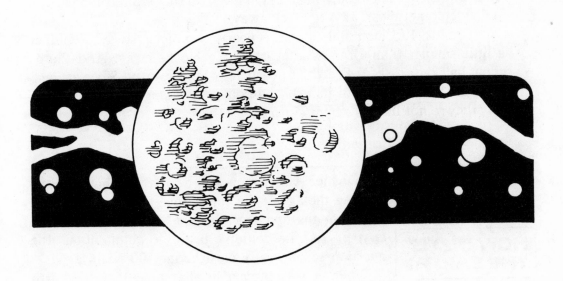

When we look up and see the stars and planets filling the sky, we might wonder if there might not be a collision up there some day. But luckily, this is not likely to happen.

COULD THERE BE A COLLISION OF THE PLANETS?

What we don't realize when we look up is how much farther away certain stars and planets are from the earth than others. To get a better idea of this, let's consider our solar system and its planets. The planets never escape from the pull or attraction of the sun. They keep on moving around it in orbits that are not quite circles. Their speeds depend on their distances from the sun.

So let's start by imagining that your own head is the sun, both in its size and location in the solar system. Your head is then in the center of a number of rings of different sizes. These rings are the orbits which the planets travel around the sun.

With your head as the center, Mercury, revolving in the nearest ring, is 20 feet away from you! It is about as large as the dot at the end of this sentence. (Remember, the size of your head is the size of the sun.) Venus moves around in the second ring 39 feet away, and is about the size of the letter "o." In the third ring is our own planet, earth, a bit larger than Venus. It is 54 feet from your head (actually 93,000,000 miles away from the sun).

In the fourth ring is Mars, smaller than the earth, and 82 feet away. Next we come to Jupiter, the largest of all the planets. In relation to your head (the sun) it looks like a marble, and is as far from your head as the length of a football field! On the sixth ring is Saturn, 1/2 inch in diameter, and nearly a city block away.

Uranus, 1/5 inch in diameter, is nearly two blocks away. Neptune, a little smaller than Uranus, is nearly three blocks away. And Pluto, about half the size of the earth, is nearly four blocks away! Since each of them goes around you in its orbit without ever changing, you can see why they're not likely to bump into each other!

This is a question to which we may never have the exact answer. Man has wondered about the age of the earth since ancient times, and there were all kinds of myths and legends that seemed to have the

HOW OLD IS THE EARTH?

answer. But he couldn't begin to think about the question scientifically until about 400 years ago.

When it was proven at that time that the earth

revolved around the sun (in other words, that the earth was part of our solar system), then scientists knew where to begin. To find the age of the earth, it was necessary to explain how the solar system was born. How did the sun and all the planets come into being?

One theory was called the nebular hypothesis. According to this theory, there was once a great mass of white-hot gas whirling about in space and getting smaller and hotter all the time. As the gas cloud grew smaller, it threw off rings of gas. Each of these rings condensed to form a planet, and the rest of the mass shrank into the center to become the sun.

Another explanation is called the planetesimal theory. According to this, millions and millions of years ago, there was a huge mass made up of small, solid bodies called planetesimals, with the sun at the center. A great star came along and pulled on the sun so that parts of it broke away. These parts picked up the tiny planetesimals the way a rolling snowball picks up snow, and they became planets.

Whichever theory is right, astronomers have figured out that it all probably happened about 5,500,000,000 years ago! But other scientists besides astronomers have tackled this question. They tried to find the answer by studying how long it took for the earth to become the way we know it. They studied the length of time it takes to wear down the oldest mountains, or the time needed for the oceans to collect the salt they now contain.

After all their studies, these scientists agree with the astronomers: The earth is about 5,500,000,000 years old!

Take a look at a map of the world. Now look at the two continents of South America and Africa. Do you notice how South America sticks out to the right where Brazil is, and how Africa is indented on the left

WERE THE CONTINENTS EVER JOINED TOGETHER?

side? Doesn't it seem as if you could fit them together like a puzzle and make them one continent?

Well, 50 years ago a German scientist named Alfred Wegener was doing just that. He wrote: "He who examines the opposite coasts of the South Atlantic Ocean must be somewhat surprised by the similarity of the shapes of the coastlines of Brazil and Africa. Every projection on the Brazilian side corresponds to a similarly shaped indentation on the African side."

Wegener also learned that naturalists had been studying the prehistoric plant and animal life of South America and Africa and had found many similarities. This convinced him that these two continents were once attached and had drifted apart.

He formulated a theory which he called the theory of the displacement of continents. According to this theory, the land masses of the earth were once all joined together in one continuous continent. There were rivers, lakes, and inland seas. Then for some unknown reason, this land mass began to break up. South America split off from Africa and drifted away. North America split off from Western Europe and floated to the west. All of the continents as we now know them were thus formed.

Did this actually happen as Wegener says it did? We don't know. It's only a theory. But as you can see from the map, there is some evidence to support it. And the study of prehistoric plant and animal life makes it seem possible, too. Besides, the earth's crust is still shifting today. So perhaps Wegener was right!

Even if a geyser didn't shoot great streams of water into the air, it would be one of the most interesting marvels of nature. A geyser is really a hot spring, and a hot spring itself is quite amazing. Here is a

WHY IS THE WATER FROM A GEYSER HOT?

hole in the ground filled with hot water. Where does the water come from? Why is it hot? And what makes it shoot up into the air if it's a geyser?

In all geysers, a hole called a tube leads from the surface to underground reservoirs which serve as storage basins for the water. Most of the water comes from rain and snow.

Deeper in the earth, the rock is very hot. This is probably uncooled lava, which is called magma. Gases from these hot rocks, mostly steam, rise through cracks in the rock and reach the underground reservoirs. They heat the water there to boiling and above-boiling temperatures.

This is how a hot spring is created. Now what makes it a geyser? The tube, or passageway from the water to the hot rocks below (where the heat comes from), does not go straight down in a geyser. It is twisted and irregular. This interferes with the natural rise of steam to the surface. If the steam and water can rise freely from below, we have a steadily-boiling hot spring.

The geyser erupts because the water in the irregular, or trapped, section of the underground water system is heated to the boiling point and suddenly turns to steam.

Steam requires more room than the water from which it was formed. So it pushes up the column of water above it. As this steam moves up, it lowers the pressure below, and more water turns into steam. Instead of there just being an overflow at the surface, there is a violent eruption as a result of the steam bursting upward, and we have the spectacle of a geyser!

Have you ever flown through clouds in an airplane, or perhaps been high up on a mountain where the clouds swirled all about you? Then you must have gotten a pretty good idea of what a cloud is: just an accumulation of mist.

WHY DON'T ALL CLOUDS PRODUCE RAIN?

As you know, there is always water vapor in the air. During the summer there is more of this vapor in the air because the temperature is higher. When there is so much water vapor in the air that just a small reduction in temperature will make the vapor condense (form tiny droplets of water), we say the air is saturated.

It takes only a slight drop in temperature to make water vapor condense in saturated air. So when saturated warm air rises to an altitude where the temperature is lower, condensation takes place and we have a cloud. The molecules of water have come together to form countless little droplets.

What happens if all these water droplets in a cloud meet a mass of warm air? They evaporate—and the cloud disappears! This is why clouds are constantly changing shape. The water in them is changing back and forth from vapor to liquid.

The droplets of water in a cloud have weight, so gravity gradually pulls them down and they sink lower and lower. As most of them fall, they reach a warmer layer of air, and this warmer air causes them to evaporate. So here we have clouds that don't produce rain. They evaporate before the drops can reach the earth as rain.

But suppose the air beneath a cloud is not warmer air? Suppose it's very moist air? Naturally, the droplets won't evaporate. Instead, the droplets will get bigger and bigger as more and more condensation takes place.

Pretty soon, each tiny droplet has become a drop and it continues falling downward and we have rain!

Rainfall is now being measured in most parts of the world by means of an instrument called a rain gauge. The gauge of the United States Weather Bureau is shaped like a hollow tube closed at the lower end, with a funnel in the top.

HOW DO THEY MEASURE A RAINFALL?

This gauge is placed in an unsheltered place, and a graduated scale shows exactly how much rain has fallen in it. The Weather Bureau says that there has been an inch of rainfall if enough rain has fallen to make a sheet of water an inch deep over a given area.

A place having less than 10 inches of rainfall during the year is called a desert. Ten to 20 inches supports enough grass for grazing, while more than 20 inches is necessary for agriculture in most regions.

If more than 100 inches fall during the warm season, vegetation becomes so thick that cultivated plants are choked out. This is the case in the jungles of Brazil, in central Africa, and in India. There is a place in India, Cherrapunji, that gets about 450 inches of rainfall a year! By way of contrast, Egypt receives about one and one-half inches. In the United States, the coasts of Washington and Oregon get the most, about 80 to 100 inches. Parts of Arizona get less than three inches a year. Do you know what the average rainfall in your community is?

In an artesian well, the water can leap high into the air like a geyser from its prison far below the surface of the earth. The name comes from the Artois region in northern France where the first European well of

WHAT IS AN ARTESIAN WELL?

this kind was drilled more than 800 years ago.

Artesian wells are possible only under certain conditions. There must be a layer of porous rock or sand that is buried between two layers of solid rock impervious to water. Somewhere this porous layer must be exposed to the surface so that water falling as rain or snow will sink downward until it is trapped between the solid, watertight layers above and below.

There the great pressure on all sides holds it prisoner until man releases it. When an opening only a few inches wide is bored straight down through the solid upper strata to the sandy layer, the freed water gushes to the surface with a mighty force.

The ancient Chinese and Egyptians dug artesian wells. Some of the older European wells required six or eight years to drill. Modern

Artesian Well

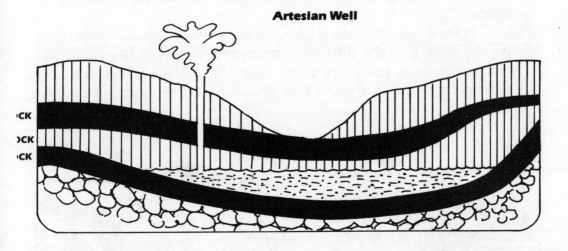

machinery makes drilling today a quick and simple task.

Near Edgemont, South Dakota, two wells drilled nearly 3,000 feet deep supply some 11,000,000 gallons daily. Coming from such a depth, this water registers a temperature of 100 degrees Fahrenheit when it reaches the surface. Another well in this region spouts even hotter water!

Several large cities in the United States, such as Pittsburgh, St. Louis, and Columbus, derive part, or all, of their water supply from artesian wells.

When a stream or river plunges over a wall of rock called a cliff or a precipice, we have a waterfall. If the waterfall is of great size, it is called a cataract. Where the rock wall is steeply slanted rather than

WHAT MAKES A WATERFALL?

vertical, the rushing water is called a cascade. Sometimes in a cascade, the water descends in a whole series of steep slopes.

Niagara Falls is an example of how an overhanging rock ledge can create a waterfall. The upper layers of rock at Niagara are hard beds of dolomite. Below the dolomite is weak shale. The Niagara River plunges over the dolomite cliff into a great pool below, where the swirling water wears away the shale and thus undermines the dolomite above. From time to time, great masses of dolomite fall, keeping the cliff fresh and steep. In other waterfalls of this type, the hard rock may be sandstone, limestone, or lava.

Another type of waterfall is illustrated by Lower Yellowstone Falls. A huge mass of molten rock was squeezed up from below in ancient times. It hardened and later formed a wall in the path of the river's course.

In some cases, ancient glaciers cut deep into mountain valleys, leaving the sides as steep cliffs and precipices from which the waterfalls plunge down. In still other cases, high plateaus have been lifted by movements of the earth's surface and the streams plunge over their edges.

The three most famous cataracts in the world are Niagara Falls, Victoria Falls in the Zambesi River in Africa, and Iguassú Falls between Argentina, Brazil, and Paraguay. Of these three, Niagara Falls has the greatest volume of water.

The world's highest waterfall is Angel Falls in Venezuela, which plunges 3,300 feet down. This waterfall was first seen by Jimmy Angel from a plane in 1935, and was first visited in 1948.

Some waterfalls are very useful to man in providing power. The falls are used to generate the electricity man uses to run factories. About half the world's potential water power is in Africa, but most of it has not yet been developed.

Most of us think of air as being "nothing," but air is definitely "something," if it is matter made up of certain gases. A gas does not have a definite size or shape, but it takes up space.

DOES THE AIR HAVE WEIGHT?
The great ocean of air that surrounds the earth and extends for many miles upward is attracted and held to the earth by gravity. Thus air has weight. And since air is everywhere about us, it adds weight to every object it fills. For example, there is a small amount of air in a volley ball. If you were to weigh two such balls, with the air let out of one of them, you would find it's lighter than the other.

The weight of air exerts pressure. The air presses on your whole body from all directions, just as the water would if you were at the bottom of the sea. The great mass of air pushes down on the earth very hard with a pressure of 14.7 pounds on each square inch, or roughly 15 pounds.

The 15 pounds is the weight of a column of air 1 inch square and as many miles high as the air extends upward. The palm of your hand has about 12 square inches. Imagine 15 x 12, or 180 pounds, all held up on one hand! The reason you don't even know you're doing this is that the air under your hand pushes up with the same force as the air above pushes down. There are about 600 pounds of air pressure on your head. But you're not mashed flat because there's air inside your body, too, which pushes out just as the air outside pushes in.

The higher up you go (to a mountain top, for example), the less air there is above you, so the pressure is less. At 20,000 feet, the pressure is only 6.4 pounds per square inch. At 10,000 feet, it's 10.16 pounds per square inch. If you could get up to 62 miles over the earth, there would be almost no pressure.

Would the world really be so much better off if there were no dust? The answer is: in some ways—yes; in some ways—no. What is dust, anyway? It consists of particles of earth, or other solid matter, which

WHAT WOULD HAPPEN IF THERE WERE NO DUST?

are light enough to be raised and carried by the wind. Where do these particles come from? They might come from dead plant and animal matter, from sea salt, from desert or volcanic sand, and from ashes or soot.

For the most part, dust is not a very desirable or beneficial thing. But in one way, it helps make the world more beautiful! The lovely colors of the dawn and of twilight depend to a great extent on the amount of dust that is present in the air.

Particles of dust in the upper air reflect the sun's rays. This makes its light visible on earth an hour or two after sunset. The different colors which make up the sun's light are bent at different angles as they are reflected by the dust and water vapor particles. Sunsets are red because these particles bend the red rays of the sun in such a way that they are the last rays to disappear from view.

Another useful function of dust has to do with rain. The water vapor in the air would not become a liquid very readily if it did not have the dust particles serving as centers for each drop of water. Therefore, clouds, mist, fog, and rain are largely formed of an infinite number of moisture-laden particles of dust.

Fog, dew, and clouds are all related. In fact, just one change in the conditions—such as the presence or absence of air currents—could make the difference as to whether there will be fog, dew, or clouds. Let's see

WHY IS THERE FOG OVER LAKES?

why this is so, and why fogs appear in certain places.

Fog particles are small, less than 1/25,000 of an inch in diameter. When you have a dense fog and can't see in front of you, it's because there may be as many as 20,000 of these particles in one cubic inch.

In order for fog to form, the moisture must leave the air and condense. This means it must be cooled in some way, because cooler air cannot hold as much moisture as warm air. When the air is cooled below a certain point, called the dew or saturation point, then fog starts to form.

Fog formation also requires that the cool air be mixed into warmer air by an air current. If you have still air, the cooling will take place only near the ground and you will have dew. When there are rapidly rising air currents, the cooling takes place high in the air and you have clouds. So the air currents that mix the cool air into the warmer air must be gentle in order to create fog.

One of the conditions in which this happens is when a mass of warm air passes over a cold land or a cold sea. Or it could be the opposite, with cold air passing over warm water. This last condition is what happens during early morning in the autumn near bodies of water such as lakes and ponds. The cold air and currents of warm air mix gently and you get those familiar fogs which seem to hang in mid-air over a body of water.

Have you ever been at a beach where at low tide you have to walk way out in the water just to get in up to your knees? Yet there are some places where you can hardly tell the difference between high and low tide.

WHY DON'T ALL PLACES HAVE THE SAME TIDES?

The reason for this has nothing to do with the moon. Tides are caused by gravitation. Just as the earth pulls on the moon, so the moon attracts or pulls on the earth, but with much less force. The pull of the moon upon the earth draws the ocean waters nearest to it toward the moon as a broad swell, or wave. This produces high tide.

The water on the opposite side of the earth gets the least pull from the moon since it is farthest away, so it forms a bulge, too. So we have high tide on the side toward the moon and also on the side opposite the moon.

As the moon goes around the earth, these two high "heaps" of water and lower levels of water keep in about the same position on the earth's surface in relation to the moon. In fact, if the earth's surface were entirely covered with water, the rotation of high tides and low tides would be very regular.

But there are many things that interfere with this. One is the great bulk of the continents. They cause tidal currents which follow the shore-lines and pile up in certain places, such as bays.

On coasts that are gently sloping and straight, the incoming tide has room to spread out and may not rise very high. But where the incoming tide enters a narrow bay or channel, it cannot spread out, and the water may pile up to great heights. In the Bay of Fundy, for example, the difference between high and low tide may be more than 70 feet. Yet, in most of the Mediterranean Sea, the water rises only one or two feet at high tide.

Most winds, of course, don't have names. You just say, "It's windy," or "The wind is blowing." Sometimes we might say, "The north wind is blowing." But many of the winds do have special names.

WHY DO WINDS HAVE DIFFERENT NAMES?

Those winds which have special names have acquired them for different reasons. For example, you know how it feels when you have the doldrums. You feel listless and without energy. Well, certain winds are actually called the doldrums! They are found near the equator where there is a great belt of rising air and low pressure. When you are caught in the doldrums in a ship, you are becalmed.

Winds that blow from above and below toward the equator are called the trade winds. Strong and steady, they got their names because in the days of sailing vessels they were a great help to navigation.

There are also some special winds. Monsoon winds, for example, are winds that change their direction with the season. In India, the monsoons blow south as hot, dry winds in the wintertime, and blow north in the summer, bringing heavy rainfall.

In southern France a cold, dry, northerly wind, the mistral, is dreaded by everyone. It blows steadily from the sea for days at a time and makes everybody irritable and uncomfortable!

On a windy day, it may seem to you that the wind is moving at tremendous speed. Then you hear the weather report, and it says, "Winds of 10 to 15 miles per hour." It's easy for us to be fooled about the speed

HOW IS THE SPEED OF WIND MEASURED?

of the wind. But the exact wind speed is important to many people, so there are scientific ways of measuring the wind.

The first instrument for measuring the speed of the wind was invented in 1667 by an Englishman named Robert Hooke. The instrument is called an anemometer. There are many kinds of anemometers, but the most common type now used has a number of aluminum cups on a spindle. They are free to turn with the wind, and the harder the wind blows, the faster the cups will turn. By counting the number of turns made by the cups in a given time, the speed of the wind may be calculated.

When men began to fly, it was necessary to measure the winds at high altitudes. This was done by sending weather balloons up into the atmosphere and watching them with a special kind of telescope called a theodolite. But this wasn't much good when clouds hid the balloon. In 1941, weather radar was invented. And now a radar set can observe the balloon even through clouds and measure the winds in the upper air!

People have long been interested in knowing the direction of the wind. As long ago as A.D. 900, wind vanes were put on church steeples to show the direction of the wind!

Many a student who goes to college complains, "Why do I have to study physics and science, I'll never use these things." Of course, such people are quite wrong about "not using" physics and science. The fact

WHY DOES ICE CRACK PIPES?

is that whether we know it or not, we all use the laws of physics in everyday life many, many times.

Any person who lives in a climate where it gets cold in winter, knows that he must put anti-freeze in the radiator of his car, and close off and empty any pipes that might have water in them. He knows that if he doesn't, the radiator will crack and the pipes might burst. The laws of physics explain why such things happen.

For example, when most substances change from a liquid to a solid state, they shrink. But exactly the opposite happens with water!

Instead of shrinking, it expands. And it doesn't expand by just any amount; it expands by about one ninth of its volume.

This means that if you start with nine quarts of water and this water freezes, you'll have 10 quarts of solid ice! Well, now just picture the water in an automobile radiator, or a pipe, freezing up. Ten quarts of ice need more room than nine quarts of water. But radiator pipes and water pipes can't stretch. There just isn't any more room. So when the water freezes, it makes more room for itself by cracking the pipes.

One of the amazing things about this process of nature, is the tremendous power it has. Pipes are made of pretty strong metals, as you know. In places like Finland, this power is actually put to work.

This is how they do it. In the quarries, they fill the cracks in the rock with water and allow it to freeze. The freezing water acts as a wedge and loosens the rock so that great blocks of rock are broken loose by the freezing power!

Even though ice takes up more space than water, it is lighter than water and floats upon it. This is the reason why large bodies of water never freeze solid. The sheet of ice on top protects the water beneath.

Even though stone and wooden houses have become more popular among the Eskimos, they still construct the igloo for special occasions or while on a journey. It is quickly built and it defies any kind of weather.

WHY DOESN'T AN IGLOO MELT INSIDE?

First a trench is cut about 5 feet long and 20 inches deep in a newly made snowdrift. Then, from the face of the trench, blocks are cut with a knife. These are shaped so that they lean inward when set on edge.

A circle of these snowblocks is laid and then shaved down so that as the Eskimo builds there will be a narrowing spiral. The material is cut from the inside of the house as the man works. Then a keystone, with edges wider above than below, is dropped into the space at the top. Then all the cracks are filled in with soft snow. A small igloo can be built in this way in a couple of hours.

When the house has been built, the woman takes over. She lights her blubber lamp and makes it burn as hot as possible. Then she closes the door with a block of ice and makes everything airtight. Now the snow begins to melt. But because the dome's roof is curved, it doesn't drip. Instead, it soaks gradually into the blocks so that they are nearly wet through.

When the blocks are sufficiently wet, she puts out her lamp and opens the door. The intensely cold air rushes in, and in a few minutes, the house is transformed from a fragile building of snow to a dome of ice! It is now so strong that a polar bear can crawl over the roof without breaking it in. And because it is so solid and hard, it doesn't melt and provides a snug shelter.

Of course, when the winter ends and the temperature rises, the igloo does begin to melt, and it is usually the roof which first caves in.

Coral is one of the most curious and fascinating objects in the world! To begin with, red coral has been prized for jewelry since ancient times. But even more interesting is the amount of supersition that has existed concerning coral.

WHAT IS CORAL?

Romans hung pieces of it around their children's necks to save them from danger. They believed it could prevent or cure diseases. In some parts of Italy, it is still worn to ward off "the evil eye." And most fascinating of all—coral has actually changed the geography of the world!

What is coral? It is the skeleton of the coral polyp, a tiny, jelly-like sea animal with many small tentacles. The polyp secretes a limey sub-

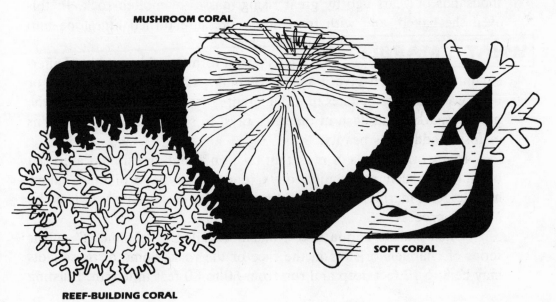

MUSHROOM CORAL

SOFT CORAL

REEF-BUILDING CORAL

23

stance of which the skeleton is composed. It is formed like a cup beneath and around the outside of the polyp.

The polyp first attaches itself to a rock beneath the surface of the water, and young polyp buds grow out from it. When the old polyp dies, the living polyps remain attached to its skeleton, and in their turn produce buds. Thus the process of building goes on as new generations of polyps rise above the skeletons of the old.

As layer upon layer of coral is built up, it actually forms reefs and islands in the ocean! These animals flourish in warm or tropical waters. Coral is found principally in the South Pacific, in the Indian Ocean, in the Mediterranean Sea, and in the waters off the coast of Florida, of Mexico, and of the West Indies.

The most important coral formations are called fringing reefs, barrier reefs, and atolls. Fringing reefs are underwater coral platforms attached to a body of land and extending into the ocean. Barrier reefs are not attached to the mainland but rise from the ocean at some distance from shore. And atolls are coral islands, shaped like a ring.

The Great Barrier Reef, which lies off Queensland, Australia, extends 1,260 miles to sea!

Nature is a master baker. Deep inside the earth is her oven, heated thousands of years ago by great rising masses of molten rock. In this oven she baked, and with tremendous pressure turned limestone into hard marble.

WHAT IS MARBLE?

In its purest form, marble is white. Different impurities often give it shades of pink, red, yellow, or brown, or form wavy lines or patches in it. Different colored crystals caught in the marble sparkle and flash in the sun's rays. In some marble the remains of fossils add to its beauty.

Many other kinds of rock that take on a high polish and are used in building, such as granite, onyx, and porphyry, are often called marble. Real marble, however, is limestone that has been crystallized by nature's process.

When marble is quarried a machine called a "channeler" cuts a series of channels or slots in the face of the rock. Some of these slots may be 8 to 12 feet deep and run from 60 to 80 feet in length. Blasting cannot be used because it would damage or shatter the marble. The blocks are lifted out carefully by large derricks.

A great toothless saw is set to work on the rough stone, while a stream of water containing sand is kept running over it. The friction of the steel blade and the sand soon cuts the marble into the desired sizes. Sometimes a wire saw is used instead of a solid blade.

Pieces of marble are then placed on a circular rubbing bed and held stationary. Sand and water flow over the rotating bed surface, rubbing away the marble to an even level. Then still more grinding is done to give it a smooth surface.

The last fine polishing is done by a mixture of tin oxide and oxalic acid applied to the surface of the marble by means of a buffer wheel.

The first records we have of people deliberately looking for diamonds indicate that this happened in India. Diamond mining as an industry started there more than 2,500 years ago!

WERE DIAMONDS ALWAYS CONSIDERED VALUABLE?

Diamonds were prized from the very beginning. In fact, before the fifteenth century, diamonds were still so rare that only kings and queens owned them.

It was not until 1430 that the custom of wearing a diamond as a personal ornament was introduced. A lady named Agnes Sorel started the fashion in the French Court, and the custom spread throughout Europe. As a result, there was feverish activity in India for more than 300 years to supply diamonds.

Finally, this source became exhausted, and fortunately, diamonds were found on the other side of the world—in Brazil, in 1725. The jungle and tropical climate made conditions very difficult, but for more than 160 years, Brazil was the world's chief source of diamonds.

Today, the capital of the diamond empire is South Africa where, in 1867, important sources of diamonds were discovered by accident. A poor farmer's child found a pretty stone. A shrewd neighbor who recognized it as a gem diamond bought it, and when he sold it, diggers of all ages and nationalities flocked to the scene.

Within a year, three great diamond fields were found and the city of Kimberly, the center of a great diamond empire, was born.

The only difference between an industrial diamond and any other kind of diamond is that the industrial diamond is of an inferior grade. If it were of perfect quality, beautiful in color and without a flaw, the dia-

WHAT IS AN INDUSTRIAL DIAMOND?

mond would, of course, be used in jewelry, where it brings higher prices.

It may seem astonishing to you that something as precious as a diamond is used in industry at all, but the diamond has been called the "emperor of industry!"

Our word "diamond" comes from the Greek word *adamas,* which means "unconquerable." A diamond is truly unconquerable, for nothing in the world can cut it—except another diamond!

So three fourths of all diamonds that are found don't go into jewelry at all. They are used in industry. And they are used because of their extreme hardness. For instance, about 20 per cent of all industrial diamonds are mounted in drills and used by mining companies to drill through rock.

Diamonds are crushed to dust and this diamond dust is used in making diamond-grinding wheels. These wheels sharpen certain tools and also grind lenses. Other diamonds are used in dies. Without diamonds, some of our most important industries would have to shut down.

Man discovered copper before any other metal except gold. Before the dawn of history, it was used by Stone Age men.

Copper is found in a fairly pure state, in lumps and grains of free

WHAT IS COPPER?

metal. Probably men first picked up the lumps because they were pretty. Then they made the great discovery that these strange red stones could be beaten into any shape. This was an easier method of making weapons and knives than chipping away at flints.

Much later, other men discovered that they could melt the red stones and form the softened mass into cups and bowls. Then they started to mine for copper and to make all sorts of implements and utensils out of it.

For thousands of years, copper remained the only workable metal known, for gold was not only too scarce to be considered but also too soft to be practical. Copper tools were probably used in building the great Egyptian pyramids.

When bronze, an alloy of copper and tin, was discovered, still greater quantities of copper were mined. But after the discovery of iron, copper was little used, except among semi-civilized peoples, until the present age of electricity. Because copper is such a good conductor of electricity, it is a very important metal in modern industry.

Few people ever see pure copper or would recognize it if they did. It is a shining, silvery substance delicately tinted with pink that turns a deeper red when exposed to the air. The copper we generally see has a dull reddish-brown surface. This is an oxide formed when the metal combines with the oxygen of the air.

Most of the world's copper exists in combination with other substances from which it must be separated before it can be used. Often it is found combined with sulphur in what we call a sulphide ore. This sulphide ore may be combined with such substances as iron and arsenic and this makes the separation of the copper difficult.

Copper has many other virtues besides that of outlasting most other metals. It is tough, yet soft enough to be pulled and pounded and twisted into any shape. It is an excellent conductor of heat as well as of electricity. It can be carved or etched, but is not easily broken. And it can be combined with other metals to make such alloys as bronze and brass.

Nickel forms many alloys which are used in hundreds of industries in many ways. It is one of the most useful metals known to man. But in early times, when chemists first tried to work with it, it gave

WHAT IS NICKEL?

them a great deal of trouble. In fact, the word nickel is derived from the German word for "imp!"

Nickel is found in meteorites, and it is sometimes found in the free state in small quantities. But the greatest supply of nickel is obtained from certain ores, especially one called pyrrhotite, which is a mineral containing iron, copper, and nickel. Canada is the greatest of all nickel-producing countries.

The ore containing nickel is usually heated in a blast furnace to obtain a rich mixture called a matte. This is then reduced to nickel by mixing it with coke and heating it in a blast furnace.

Nickel is silvery, lustrous, hard, and malleable, which means it can be easily worked and shaped. And nickel is one of the most magnetic materials known, unless heated.

We seldom see pure nickel except when it is used as a coating on other metals. This is then called nickel-plate. It protects other metals from rust or tarnish, and gives them a better wearing surface.

Most of the nickel produced is used in alloys, or in a mixture with other metals. For instance, when alloyed with copper, it is used in coins. Our own five-cent piece is called a nickel for that reason. When it is alloyed with three parts of copper and one of zinc, nickel forms a bright silvery metal known as German silver or nickel silver. This is used for making tableware and as a base for silverplated ware.

But these uses of nickel are relatively minor. Most nickel goes into the making of nickel steel, an alloy which can withstand repeated strains. It is used in structural work, bridges, railroad rails at curves, rivets, locomotive boilers, automobile gears and axles, and the dipper teeth of steam shovels.

Was there a time when there were no plants on earth? According to the theories of science, the answer is yes. Then, hundreds of millions of years ago, tiny specks of protoplasm appeared on earth. Protoplasm

WHERE DID PLANTS COME FROM?

is the name for the living material that is found in both plants and animals. These original specks of protoplasms, according to scientists, were the beginnings of all our plants and animals.

The protoplasm specks that became plants developed thick walls and settled down to staying in one place. They also developed the green coloring matter known as chlorophyll which enabled them to make food from substances in the air, water, and soil.

These early green plants had only one cell, but later they formed groups of cells. Since they had no protection against drying out, they had to stay in the water. Today, some descendants of these original plants still survive, though they have changed quite a bit, of course. We call them algae. Seaweeds are an example of these plants.

One group of plants developed that obtained its food without the use of chloropyhll. These non-green plants are called the fungi, and they include bacteria, yeasts, molds, and mushrooms.

Most of the plants on earth today evolved from the algae. Certain of these came out of the sea and developed rootlets that could anchor

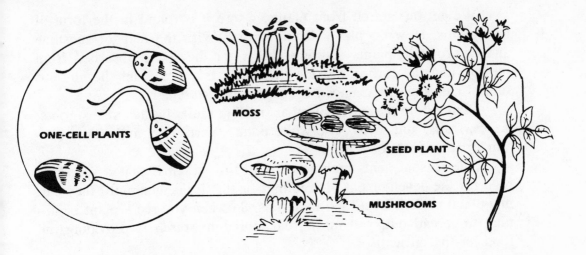

ONE-CELL PLANTS
MOSS
SEED PLANT
MUSHROOMS

them in the soil. They also developed little leaves with an outer skin covering as protection against drying. These plants became mosses and ferns.

All of the earliest plants reproduced either by simple cell division (as in the case of bacteria and yeast) or by means of spores. Spores are little dustlike cells something like seeds, but they contain no stored food in them as seeds do. As time went on, some of these plants developed flowers that produced true seeds.

Now we are pretty far advanced in the development of plants. Two different types of plants with seeds appeared; those with naked seeds and those with protected seeds. Each of these two types later developed along many different lines. In this way, we have traced the plants existing on the earth today back to an original speck of protoplasm that appeared long, long ago. At least, this is the theory of modern botanical science.

Is there anybody in your family on a diet? Then you've probably heard them say as they turned down a certain dish, "Not for me! Too much starch!" Of course, if there are growing children in a house, they are

WHY DO PLANTS MAKE STARCH?

usually fed plenty of starch to "build them up."

Starch—whether people try to cut down on it or to get all they can—is one of the most important substances in the world. The human race gets more food from starch than from any other single substance!

We get our starch from plants, where it is found in the form of tiny grains. How do plants make starch? With the help of sunshine and chlorophyll, plants combine the water they have absorbed from the soil and the carbon dioxide they have taken in from the air into sugar. This sugar is changed by plants into starch.

Plants store the starch away as small granules in their stems, roots, leaves, fruits, and seeds. The white potato, corn, rice, and wheat contain large amounts of starch.

The reason plants manufacture all this starch is that it serves as food for the development of seedlings or the new shoots until they can manufacture their own food materials. So when you see a plant beginning to spread out, you know that stored-up starch is providing the food for that growth.

For people and animals, starch supplies an energy-producing food. Like sugar, it is made up of carbon, hydrogen, and oxygen. It is not sweet; generally, it is tasteless. Certain chemical substances in the mouth, stomach, and intestines change the starchy food to grape sugar, which the body can use easily.

The way we get starch from the plant is to crush those parts of the plant where the starch is stored. The starch is washed out with water and allowed to settle to the bottom of large vats. The water is then squeezed out of the wet starch and the mass is dried and ground to a powder, which is the form in which starch is usually manufactured.

Starch has many unusual uses. It is used in laundering, as an adhesive, in the manufacture of cloth, and as the basis for many toilet preparations.

If a weak sugar solution is exposed to the air, in several days a light, frothy scum appears on the surface and the liquid begins to smell of alcohol. This change takes place because tiny plant cells called yeast

WHAT IS YEAST?

have settled from the air into the liquid. They have found conditions favorable to their growth.

Man has long known that this process takes place and he has used it for thousands of years to make alcoholic beverages of all kinds. Sugar solutions made from molasses, potatoes, rye, corn, malt and hops, apples, and grapes have been exposed to the air to make alcohol, whiskey, beer, ale, cider, wine, and other beverages.

Probably through accident, it was also discovered that if bread dough were allowed to stand for some time before baking, very often a peculiar change took place. The flat lump of dough began mysteriously to swell and rise. It developed a strange but pleasant odor. When this dough was baked, instead of making a flat, heavy slab, it made a light, porous, soft bread!

In 1857, Louis Pasteur announced that he had discovered the explanation for these changes. He said they were due to the presence of tiny, one-celled plants called yeast. Yeasts belong to the fungi family, and are tiny, rounded, colorless bodies. They are larger than most bacteria, but still so small that it would take from 3,000 to 4,000 of them laid side by side to make an inch!

Yeast cells reproduce by budding. This means they send out projections which become cut off from the parent cell by a cell wall. Finally, these projections grow to full size. As they grow, they form substances called zymase and invertase.

These substances are called enzymes, and they have the power to ferment starch to sugar, and sugar to alcohol and carbon dioxide. As fermentation takes place, carbon dioxide is formed and rises to the top. Then it escapes, leaving the alcohol. Beer, ale, wine, and cider are fermented beverages in which yeast has changed some of the sugar to carbon dioxide and alcohol.

In breadmaking, the carbon dioxide collects in bubbles in the dough, which makes it rise. Heat later drives off the carbon dioxide, thus making the bread porous and light.

In millions of homes in Europe and the United States, the mistletoe is hung up at Christmastime. According to a happy custom, when a girl is standing under the mistletoe, a man is allowed to kiss her.

WHAT IS MISTLETOE?

Curiously enough, the use of the mistletoe on holidays and ceremonial occasions goes back to quite ancient times. When the Romans invaded Britain and Gaul (now called France), the people who lived there were called Celts. These Celts were organized under a strong order of priests called Druids.

The Druids taught that the soul of man was immortal. Many of their rites were connected with the worship of trees, and they considered that whatever grew on a tree was a gift from heaven. Among the most sacred of these "gifts" was the mistletoe. They would cut the mistletoe with a golden knife and hang it over their doors to ward off evil spirits. According to them, only happiness could enter under the mistletoe. This was actually the beginning of the tradition of the kiss under the mistletoe!

Among the Scandinavian people, too, the mistletoe was considered lucky. They gathered it up during their winter festivals and each family received a bit of it to hang up over the entrance to their home. This was supposed to protect the family from evil spirits.

One reason the mistletoe came to be considered sacred is that it is a plant that has no roots in the earth. It grows on the branches of other trees. When the mistletoe is very young and just developing from a seed, it produces tiny outgrowths. These pierce the bark of the limb on which the seed fell. After they have grown through the bark to the wood, they spread out and in this way absorb a part of the moisture and the food which the tree contains.

The food and moisture go to nourish the young mistletoe plant, which then grows as most other plants do. So you see it has no direct connection with the soil and it doesn't need any! Sometimes, the mistletoe grows so abundantly it kills the tree that has given it life.

The mistletoe grows on oak and other kinds of trees in the southern and western United States. The berries which the plant produces are loved by birds. When they eat them, the sticky seeds cling to their beaks. In trying to remove them, the birds rub their beaks on other trees and so spread the seeds!

Can one kind of tree produce the fruit of another kind of tree?—Yes! Grafting makes it possible. If a bud from a twig of a pear tree is carefully inserted in a slit made in the bark of a quince bush, a pear twig

WHAT IS GRAFTING?

will grow. The quince bush will bear both pears and quinces!

In the same way, an almond tree can be made to produce both peaches and almonds. Or a crab apple tree can be made to bear a crop of fine cultivated apples. Sometimes grafting is used to produce freak trees and bushes, but it has nevertheless an important place in agriculture.

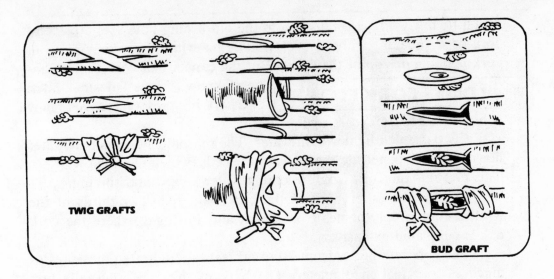

TWIG GRAFTS

BUD GRAFT

The first advantage of grafting is that it makes it possible for a nurseryman or gardener to be sure that his young trees or shrubs will bear the same quality and variety of fruit as the parent tree. A twig taken from a tree and grafted into another tree will produce the same type of fruit borne by the tree from which it was taken.

There are many methods of inserting the budded twigs, or scions, as they are called, into the stock of the other plant, but two rules must always be followed: First, only related species of trees or shrubs can be grafted. This means that apples can be grafted on pear and quince trees, and peaches can be grafted on apricot, almond, plum, or other stone fruit trees. But it is impossible to graft apples on peach trees, for example.

The second rule is that the cambium layer which carries the vital sap of the scion must touch the cambium layer of the stock on which it is grafted. Otherwise, the grafted twig cannot grow.

There are many different kinds of grafting. It can range from inserting a single bud under the bark to grafting long twigs across the wound of a tree in order to heal wide wounds in the bark.

Interestingly enough, grafting is being applied to animals, too. Eyes, for instance, have been replanted in such creatures as frogs, toads, rats, and rabbits. Surgeons have learned from these experiments how to help people who have been injured or disfigured. Bone taken from the ribs has actually been grafted onto the nasal bone to form a new nose, and skin has been grafted onto burnt tissue to remove scars!

The little boy who brings his line to the old fishing hole uses a piece of cork as a "floater" without ever wondering what keeps that piece of cork bobbing on top of the water. But the capacity of cork to float has

WHY DOES CORK FLOAT?

been known since ancient times, and cork life-preservers saved many a life thousands of years ago!

Cork is much lighter than water. The reason it floats is that water does not easily penetrate the walls of the cells, which are filled with air. This prevents the cork from becoming water-logged and sinking.

Cork is the outer bark of the cork oak tree. Two-thirds of the world's cork supply comes from Spain and Portugal, where the cork oak is cultivated extensively.

The cork oak grows from 20 to 40 feet tall and often measures as much as four feet in diameter. The bark of this tree is usually first stripped when the tree is about 20 years old. This doesn't injure or kill the tree; instead, the stripping actually benefits it.

About nine years later, another stripping is taken. The cork obtained from these first two strippings is coarse and rough. Later strippings, which are made about nine years apart for about a hundred years, give cork of a finer quality.

After stripping, the cork is stacked for several weeks to season, and then boiled to soften it and to remove the tannic acid. After boiling, the cork lies in pliable flat sheets, which are dried and then packed for shipping all over the world.

There are two kinds of raw cork: One is known as corkwood. This is the material used to make cork stoppers, floats, and life preservers. The second kind of raw cork is called grinding cork. It is ground up and then baked, some of it with binder materials. This is made into pipe covering, shoe fillers, automobile gaskets, and liners such as you find in the crown of bottle covers.

One of the greatest uses of cork today is for soundproofing rooms, and for insulating warehouses, freezer rooms, and refrigerators.

Bamboo is one of the most phenomenal examples of plant life. It shoots upward at the rate of 16 inches a day. It may reach a height of 120 feet. It spreads so rapidly that if there is a road running through a growth

WHAT IS BAMBOO?

of bamboo, that road may disappear completely in a month if it is not kept open!

There are about five hundred kinds of bamboos. They all have smooth, hollow, jointed stems with a strong, watertight partition at each joint, and all grow very rapidly. While most bamboos flower every year, there are some that bloom only three or four times in a century. The flowers are like those of grains and grasses. The fruit is usually like grain, and in some kinds, like nuts.

The bamboos are tropical and subtropical plants. They grow in Asia, in South America, and a few species grow in Africa. About thirty kinds of tall bamboos from other parts of the world have been successfully introduced into California and Florida.

The uses of bamboo are so numerous it is almost hard to believe. In the United States, bamboo is chiefly used in fishing poles, walking sticks, and phonograph needles. But it is in the Oriental countries that bamboo is really put to use.

People build entire houses with it, using large sections for posts and the split stems for rafters, roofing, and floor planks. They strip off the hard outer layers for mats and lattices to separate the rooms. The joints of the largest kinds are used for buckets and those of smaller ones for bottles.

There are even certain kinds of bamboos so hard that they can be made into crude knives, and beautiful and strong baskets are woven of strips from the outer coverings. In Japan, gardeners use hollowed bamboo stems for water pipes. In China, the inner pulp is made into the finer grades of native paper. The Javanese make bamboos into flutes. And many Oriental people eat the tender shoots of bamboo as a vegetable. So you see how valuable the bamboo is in certain parts of the world.

Amazingly enough, bamboo is a grass. It is the largest member of the family of grasses, though most people think of it as a bush or a tree.

The pomegranate is a fruit with a very interesting background in history. According to a legend of the ancient Greeks, the pomegranate was the fruit which Persephone ate while in Hades. Because she swallowed six of the seeds, she was forced to spend six months of each year in the underworld! To the Greeks, the juicy, many-seeded pomegranate always

WHAT IS A POMEGRANATE?

symbolized the powers of darkness.

35

In China, the pomegranate was a symbol of fertility. King Solomon, according to the Bible, had an orchard of pomegranates. When the children of Israel wandered in the wilderness, they longed for the pomegranates they used to have in Egypt. Mohammed advised his followers, "Eat the pomegranate, for it purges the system of envy and hatred."

So you see the pomegranate was an important fruit in the East in ancient times. It is supposed to have originated in Persia, but from very ancient times, it has been grown in the warm countries of southern Asia, northern Africa, and southern Europe. Now it is common in South and Central America and in the southern United States.

The pomegranate grows as a bushy tree, or shrub. It grows from 5 to 20 feet high. Its leaves are glossy and at the ends of its slender twigs grow its coral-red, waxlike flowers.

The fruit is about the size of an orange. It is leathery-skinned and is colored a deep yellow, tinged with red. Inside this fruit are many small seeds. They are covered with a sweet, red, juicy pulp, which is often made into refreshing drinks. There is something about its taste that makes it especially agreeable to people who live in hot, dry regions.

There are many varieties of the pomegranate. In fact, a Moor who wrote about it 700 years ago described 10 different kinds which were grown in Spain at that time! In the United States, three leading varieties have been cultivated. They are called the Wonderful, the Paper-Shell, and the Spanish Ruby.

There is a difference between the Arctic Region and the Arctic Circle. The Arctic Circle goes around the northern part of the earth in a perfect circle, 66½ degrees north of the equator. At one time, the Arctic Region was considered to be all land and water lying north of this circle.

DOES ANYTHING GROW IN THE ARCTIC REGION?

But today, the Arctic Region is considered to be a geographical unit based on the combination of a number of different elements, especially vegetation and climate. It extends south into Canada and includes all of Greenland.

The climate of the Arctic is not continuously cold, nor is the Arctic an area of heavy snow covered by ice. During the short, hot summer, temperatures may rise to 80 degrees Fahrenheit, and in some places, even reach 100 degrees. What makes the Arctic feel so cold is mainly the frequent, strong wind driving the dry crystals of snow before it.

Over much of the Arctic there are less than 15 inches of precipitation a year, although southern Greenland may have as much as 40 inches. As a result, a great number of plants grow in the Arctic. More than 1,300 different species of plants have been identified there, and more than half of them are of the flowering kind! Large areas are covered with moss and lichens, but in the southern regions of the Arctic, there are fertile valleys and grasslands.

Animals are quite numerous in the Arctic and distributed widely. Land animals include the large herds of caribou or reindeer that perhaps number as many as 5,000,000 to 25,000,000 head. There are also musk oxen, mountain sheep, wolves, foxes, and grizzly bears.

Among the birds found in the Arctic are the eider duck, the goose, the swan, the tern, and the gull. Salmon, cod, flounder, trout and halibut, and, of course, the seal, walrus, and whale live there, too.

CAN AN ECHO TRAVEL THROUGH WATER?

Sound travels outward from its source at a speed of about 1,100 feet per second in the open air. Sound travels in waves much like the ripples made by a pebble thrown into the water. However, sound waves go out in all directions like the light from an electric bulb.

A sound wave may meet an obstacle and bounce back, or be reflected just as light is reflected. When a sound wave is thus reflected, it is heard as an echo. Therefore, an echo is sound repeated by reflection.

Not all obstacles can cause echoes; there are some objects which absorb the sound instead of reflecting it. If a sound is reflected by some obstacle, only one echo is heard. This is called a simple echo. If the sound is reflected by two or more obstacles, the echo may be repeated many times. The echo, however, becomes fainter each time until it dies away altogether. When repeated more than once, it is known as a compound echo, or reverberation.

An echo cannot be heard as a separate sound unless the sound is made some distance away from the reflecting surface. This allows enough time between sound and echo. At a distance of 550 feet from a wall, for example, the echo returns in just one second.

Whether an echo can travel through water depends on whether sound can travel through water—and we know that it can. In fact, sound travels through water at a speed of more than 4,700 feet per second! This ability of sound to produce an echo through water has proven very useful.

Ships are often equipped with devices for sending and receiving sound signals under water. By sending out sharp signals and timing the echoes, a navigator can measure the distance from his vessel to the ocean bottom or to any nearby vessel or obstacle!

CHAPTER 2
HOW OTHER CREATURES LIVE

Do you like to read detective stories or watch them on TV? What makes them exciting for you and me is the suspense. We want to find out who did it, or how, or why. But the world around us is full of mysteries, too.

| WHAT IS BIOLOGY? |

Why do animals behave as they do? What makes plants grow in special ways? How does our body do this or that?

Man has always wanted to solve these mysteries of life. And just the way a detective proceeds on a case, the first thing that had to be done was to gather all the facts. The gathering and the study of these facts was called natural history.

Today we call this science biology. The word comes from two Greek words: *bios,* meaning "life," and *logos,* meaning "a study." So biology is the study of all organisms, plant and animal. What is studied about them is their form, their activities, their functions, and their environment.

But today our biologist-detectives are not satisfied just to collect a lot of facts, helter-skelter. They try to establish some links between the facts, some relationship. For example, they are interested in discovering the relationships that exist between man and the millions of living things that surround him. They want to know what effect these living things have had on man's own development.

Biologists are interested in the greatest mystery of all: how life first started on earth and why it took the forms it did. So they also study all the conditions that are necessary to life. And just as a detective bureau keeps a file, they try to classify every organism which exists on our planet.

In looking for clues that will answer their questions, biologists get a helping hand from nature. They dredge the icy depths of the oceans and scale the peaks of the tallest mountains looking for clues. They hack their way through steaming jungles, and peer for hours into microscopes. Sometimes they perform strange experiments in order to get at the mystery of life.

Biology is a very complex science. It has two main divisions: botany, which deals with plants; and zoology, which deals with animals. And each of these divisions is separated into dozens of subdivisions!

As we move about from place to place, we may feel changes in the temperature around us, but we don't expect the temperature of our body itself to change. And it doesn't. We are classified as "homeothermic,"

WHAT IS THE BODY TEMPERATURE OF ANIMALS?

and in our class are included all warm-blooded animals, all mammals, domestic animals, and birds.

But there are animals whose body temperature does change with the temperature around them. They are called "poikilothermic," and they include insects, snakes, lizards, tortoises, frogs, and fishes. Their temperature tends to be slightly lower than the temperature of their environment. They are cold-blooded animals.

We know that the normal body temperature of man is considered

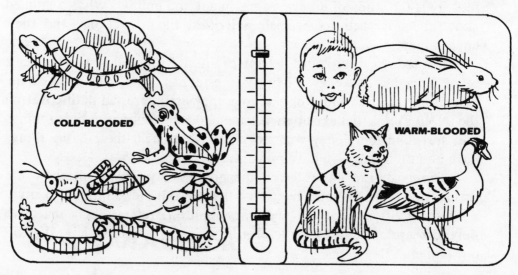

COLD-BLOODED

WARM-BLOODED

to be 98.6 degrees Fahrenheit. But there are many changes in the temperature that occur quite "normally." For example, man's body temperature is lowest about 4:00 A.M.; the skin temperature is lower than the internal temperature; taking in food raises the temperature for an hour or two; muscular work may raise the temperature; alcohol lowers the internal temperature.

The body temperature of animals has quite a range, going from 96 degrees in the elephant to 109 degrees in small birds. Here is how animals may be classified according to their body temperature:

From 96 to 101 degrees — man, monkey, mule, ass, horse, rat, mouse and elephant. From 100 to 103 degrees — cattle, sheep, dog, cat, rabbit, and pig. From 104 to 106 degrees — turkey, goose, duck, owl, pelican, and vulture. From 107 to 109 degrees — fowl, pigeon, and several small common birds.

Animals, like man, have to eliminate excess body heat in order to maintain a constant body temperature. Animals who don't sweat have to do this by panting — which is why your dog often pants on a hot day.

When we use the word "mammoth" today, we mean something that is huge or colossal. But there actually was an animal that lived long ago that is called the "mammoth." It was a kind of elephant that is now

WHAT WAS THE MAMMOTH?

extinct and that lived in many different parts of the world during the Stone Age.

Even though this ancient type of elephant is called the "mammoth," it was about the same size as the Indian elephant that exists today. It had a kind of pointed skull and very unusual tusks curved in a spiral with the tips pointing to each other.

What made this elephant unique and quite different from the elephants we know today is that it was covered with long hair. In fact, the hair was so long that it almost reached the ground. The body was shaped into a great hump at the back of the neck, and the ears were small.

The whole body of this creature was covered with an undercoat of yellowish-brown wooly hair, and the long, black thicker hairs came out through this undercoat. The hair also grew on the ears. The first thing you'd probably say if you saw a mammoth today would be: "Get a haircut!"

Obviously an animal with so much hair on it would be more comfortable in a cold climate. And the mammoth is the only kind of elephant ever to exist that felt at home in a cold or Arctic climate. So it lived in Siberia quite comfortably, and probably survived there until a fairly recent period.

In other parts of the world, such as France and England, it survived only as long as the glacial period, or ice age, lasted. In fact, when things warmed up in England between glacial periods, the mammoth moved up north, following the retreating ice.

There were also mammoths in North America during that age, and some of these reached a height of 14 feet. Mammoths, because of their great weight, often sank into ice-cold mud which later became frozen. That's why frozen mammoths are still sometimes found very well preserved in places like Siberia.

When European explorers visited the New World, they often brought back with them whatever they considered strange and new. Thus the South American opossum was brought back from Brazil in 1500, and

WHAT ARE MARSUPIALS?

Captain Cook in 1770 told about seeing kangaroos in Australia. Nobody in Europe had ever known about such creatures before — they were marsupials.

The marsupials are a separate order of animals. The name comes from the Greek word *marsupion,* which means "pouch." What sets these animals apart is that their young, after they are born, live and are fed in a pouch on their mother's body.

This is necessary because young marsupials are so tiny and helpless when they are born that they cannot take care of themselves. They do not even know how to eat. Even after they have grown to a fair size, young kangaroos and opossums run back to hide in their mother's pouch when they are frightened.

Judging from the fossils found in rocks, marsupials were once common in all parts of the world. Today almost all of them are found in Australia and the nearby islands. The only other true marsupials are the various species of opossums which live in North and South America.

Australian marsupials range in size from tiny molelike creatures only a few inches long to the giant kangaroos. Some of them, such as the bandicoots, look like rabbits. Others, such as the wombats, look like beavers. Still others, such as the thylacines and the Tasmanian wolves, look like wolves.

They may live on the ground or dwell in the trees like monkeys. Some of the phalangers, which are one family of marsupials, can even glide from tree to tree like flying squirrels. The food of marsupials is quite varied. Some eat only vegetables, others are meat-eaters or insect-eaters, and some eat anything they can find.

A bloodhound, of course, is a breed of dog. But how did it develop? Where did it come from?

The history of the dog itself goes back many hundreds of thousands

WHAT IS A BLOODHOUND?

of years. Some scientists believe that dogs are the result of the mating of their cousins, the wolves and the jackals. It is generally believed however that our modern dogs and the wolves are descended from a very remote common ancestor.

During the many years that dogs have been tamed, men have developed more than 200 breeds of dogs. Sometimes they have bred dogs for strength, like that of the mastiff; for speed, like the greyhound; or for keenness of scent, like that of the bloodhound.

The bloodhound is typical of the breed of dog known as the hound. It is probably a descendant of the dog which at one time was called the "St. Hubert." Hounds generally have smooth coats, are heavy, and have drooping ears and upper lips.

Like all hounds, the bloodhounds follow the quarry by scent—keener in them than in any other dog. They are slow put persistent, and if they lose the scent they cast back until they find the trail again. It is these two qualities, their keen scent and their ability to be persistent, that make bloodhounds ideal for tracking down escaped criminals and for other use by police.

There are many other interesting types of hounds. For example, otter hounds, harriers, beagles, and bassets are all smaller than bloodhounds and are used in hunting small game, such as rabbits.

The pointer is a hound that is one of the best bird dogs. It was given its name because it "points" at the game.

Deer live in all parts of the world except Australia, New Zealand, Madagascar, and Southern Africa. There are about 50 different species of deer, but they all have certain things in common.

WHY DO DEER SHED THEIR ANTLERS?

Deer are vegetarians who feed on moss, bark, buds, leaves, or water plants. They are usually very timid animals, and they depend on their speed for safety. They generally feed at night. They have very good eyesight, and their senses of hearing and smell are so sharp that they are able to detect danger easily. Deer vary in size from the little pudu, which is only a foot tall, to the great moose, which may weigh more than 1,000 pounds!

The chief distinguishing marks of the deer are the antlers. Nearly all the males have antlers, and in the case of the caribou and reindeer, females have them too. The antlers are not hollow, like the horns of cattle, but are made of a honeycomb structure. Each spring, the male deer grows a new pair of antlers, and each winter he loses them after the mating season is over. In some varieties of deer, the antlers are single shafts, in others there may be as many as 11 branches to each antler! Since the number of branches varies with age, you can tell how old a deer is from its antlers.

The first year, two knoblike projections appear on the deer's forehead. These are called the "pedicles," and they are never lost. The antlers break off from the pedicle each spring and new antlers are grown during the summer. The second year, a straight shaft grows out of the

pedicle, and in the third year, the first branch appears.

When the antlers are growing, they are covered with a sensitive skin called the "velvet." This is filled with blood vessels which feed the antlers and build up the bone. When the antlers have reached their full size, after a period of two to four months, the blood supply is cut off from the velvet by the formation of a ring around the base of the antlers. This makes the velvet wither and dry up, and it finally falls off. Usually, the deer help by rubbing their antlers against trees.

One of the gentlest of all animals is the hare. When you consider how mild, timid, and defenseless this creature is, you might wonder how it can survive in a world full of enemies. But then you've also probably

WHAT IS THE DIFFERENCE BETWEEN RABBITS AND HARES?

noticed its strong hindlegs. Those legs give it plenty of speed and endurance. And, of course, you know how rapidly hares and rabbits breed.

That's another reason why they manage to survive.

Hares and rabbits are rodents, which means they have long, sharp front teeth. Their hindlegs are longer than their forelegs, so that they actually run faster uphill than downhill! When they are pursued, they resort to some clever tricks. One is to crisscross their tracks, and the other is to take huge leaps in order to break the scent. They can also signal danger to each other by thumping the ground with their hindfeet.

Hares and rabbits are purely vegetarians, but they can live very well on the inner bark of trees. There are many differences between hares and rabbits. Hares are larger, and their feet and ears are longer. Hares do not dig burrows or live in groups, as do rabbits. Hares are born open-eyed and furry, while rabbits are born blind and hairless. Hares and rabbits never mate.

North America is the home of many different types of hares. One of the best known is the jack hare, which is usually mistakenly called "jack rabbit." It is found throughout the West. Jack hares are more than two feet in length and have enormous ears. Jacks are so fast that they can sometimes make a leap of 20 feet. They are a geat nuisance to farmers in the West, and are often rounded up and killed by thousands.

The March hare, whom we know from "Alice in Wonderland," is a common European hare. In March, its mating season, it disregards caution, coming out at all times of the day and performing amusing acrobatic feats.

Rabbits came originally from the western shores of the Mediterranean. They are social animals, living together in burrows, called "warrens." A rabbit may mate when it is six months old. Its young are born within a month. There may be from three to eight in a litter and a female rabbit may bear from four to eight litters in a year. So if the rabbit has no natural enemies, it can become quite a nuisance. In Australia for instance, three pairs of rabbits were introduced many years ago, and today the rabbit is a great national pest!

One of the most interesting animals to be found anywhere is the mole. Moles live in every part of the United States and there are about 30 different species. But they are so seldom seen by people that they have become a kind of mysterious creature.

CAN A MOLE SEE?

You can find a mole by looking for the long ridges of cracked earth it makes across fields. This is the roof of its tunnel, for the mole spends its whole life in darkness under the ground.

A mole grows to about six inches in size. It has a fine, velvety fur, the color of a mouse, and a pink tail about an inch long. It has no neck at all, and its ears are tiny openings hidden in the fur. A mole does have eyes, but they are tiny points covered with fur and skin. This is why it was once believed that moles are blind. A mole can see, but very poorly.

If you picked up a mole and put it down on the ground, it would race about until it found a soft spot and would begin to dig at once. A mole is one of the most efficient diggers in nature. Its forefeet are powerful and shaped like spades. It can dig a burrow and disappear into it in less than one minute! In a single night, it can dig a tunnel 225 feet long.

Moles usually live in a colony in a sort of fortress undergound. From the surface, we see a little hillock of earth called a "molehill." Right under it, there are two circular galleries or passageways, one above the other. Vertical passageways connect them, so the mole can move up and down. The upper gallery has five of these openings which go down to a central chamber where the mole rests.

A whole series of complicated tunnels lead from these galleries and from the central chamber to the feeding grounds, to the nest, and even to an "emergency" exit. These underground tunnels are so well built that field mice and gophers often use them to get roots and plants for food. But it isn't too safe for other animals to venture into a mole's home. It has such sharp front teeth that it can fight viciously and kill mice much bigger than itself. Its chief food, however, consists of insects and earthworms. A mole is so greedy that if it is unable to get food for 12 hours it will die!

The porcupine has always been considered an annoying, disagreeable animal. In fact, even Shakespeare described it that way. In Hamlet, there is the line: "Like quills upon the fretful porcupine."

DO PORCUPINES SHOOT THEIR QUILLS?

Actually, the porcupine is quite a harmless animal, who simply likes to be let alone. During the winter, it curls up in a hollow log or cave and sleeps most of the time. In the summer, it moves slowly through the woods in search of bark, twigs, roots, and leaves of trees and shrubs.

Porcupines can be found in Europe, Africa, India, and South America as well as in our own country and Canada. The American species of porcupine is about three feet long and weighs from 15 to 30 pounds. Its quills are about seven inches long and are yellowish-white, with black tips. The quills grow among the softer hairs of the porcupine, and consist of a shaft with a hard point.

When the porcupine is born, the quills are fine and silky. It takes them several weeks to thicken into hard quills. When a porcupine is attacked, it bristles up its coat of quills and curls into a bristling ball.

These quills are fastened rather loosely into the body of the porcupine. Since the porcupine will sometimes swing its tail into the face of an enemy, the quills come out easily during such an action. This is what has made people think a porcupine "shoots" its quills. It doesn't. They just fly out.

The porcupine usually sleeps during the day and comes out to feed at night. It uses its long, sharp claws to climb trees, and then it sits on a limb to gnaw away at the bark and twigs. It crams bark, twigs, leaves, all into its mouth at once. Because of its liking for bark, the porcupine does much damage to forests. A single porcupine has been known to kill 100 trees in a winter!

Another strong liking the porcupine has is for salt. It will walk boldly into camps and gnaw any article that has been touched by salt or even by perspiring hands!

Some people believe that raccoons wash all their food before eating it. There is some truth to this. Most raccoons do wash their food, and there have been cases where raccoons refused to eat food when they couldn't find any water nearby!

DO RACCOONS WASH THEIR FOOD?

But on the other hand, raccoons have been known to eat food even when they were some distance from water, though perhaps they weren't too happy about it. And some raccoons have been observed to eat without ever washing their food.

Nobody really knows why raccoons wash their food. It isn't because of cleanliness, since they may wash it in water that is actually dirtier than the food! Besides, they will wash food caught in the water, which certainly doesn't need washing. So the reason is probably that the raccoon enjoys feeling the food in water. It seems to make it tastier!

The name "raccoon" comes from the Algonquin Indian word *arak-humen*. The raccoon lives from southern Canada to Panama, except in the high Rockies. Raccoons vary in size from 25 to 35 inches in length. In weight they range from three to twenty-five pounds. The general color of the long fur is grayish or brownish. The 10-inch tail is dark brown with four to six yellowish rings. The eyes are covered with a black mask. The ears are medium-sized, the nose pointed, and the front feet are used like hands.

Raccoons live in places where there is water and trees for dens. Their food, which they hunt at night, is principally crayfish, clams, fish and frogs, which they catch in the muddy water. In season raccoons also feed on nuts, berries, fruit, and paticularly young corn.

The year-round home, or den, where the young are born is usually in the hollow limb or trunk of a tree. Raccoons give birth to young but once a year, with four or five to a litter. By fall, the young raccoons are large enough to start their life alone.

Do you know what the word "armadillo" means? It's a Spanish word meaning "the little armored one." And that's just what an armadillo is, a little mammal with a bony covering that is like armor.

WHAT IS AN ARMADILLO?

There are ten different kinds of armadillos living from southern United States to southern South America. The upper parts of armadillos are covered with bony shells. These include one on the head and two solid pieces on the back. These two pieces are connected by a flexible center section made up of movable bands. This enables the armadillo to twist and turn.

The number of these bands in the center is sometimes used as a name for the armadillo. For example, there is the seven-banded the eight-banded, and the nine-banded armadillo. The nine-banded armadillo is the only one found in the United States. The tail of the armadillo is also completely covered by armor—except in the case of one kind, and naturally it's called the soft-tailed armadillo!

A very curious thing about the armadillo is that its teeth are simple pegs without enamel. It's one of those contradictions that nature seems fond of. A shell of armor on the body—and soft teeth! Most of the animals have just one set of teeth they are born with, and that's all.

As a result of having such teeth, the armadillo has to eat soft food such as ants, termites, larvae, grubs, and bugs. As you know, such food is found in leaves and the soft ground, so to get at it the armadillo has to dig for it. Nature made up for the soft teeth by

giving the armadillo long, strong claws and powerful forearms. An armadillo can dig faster than a dog! And it uses the claws and forearms to dig its burrow or to make itself a hole quickly into which it can escape from its enemies.

The way most armadillos escape from their enemies is by digging or running away. Only one kind, the three-banded armadillo, rolls itself into a ball. Its shell is much heavier than that of the others, so this becomes a good way of protecting itself.

WHERE DID ELEPHANTS ORIGINATE?

Thousands of years ago, many kinds of giant monsters roamed about the great forests then covering the earth. Even though these beasts were immense in size, they were not able to endure the hardships they had to undergo, brought about by changing climate and disappearance of food.

One by one they perished, until of all those huge animals, there are only two species remaining, the African and Asiatic elephants. The ancestors of the elephant were great monsters, known as "mammoths." Their skeletons can be seen in museums, and they are quite awesome sights! Their bones have been dug up in caves and river beds in North America and Europe. In far-off Siberia, the carcass of one was found frozen hard in ice, perfectly preserved even to its eyes!

Although elephants seem to have once inhabited many parts of the earth, they are now found in their wild state only in Africa and tropical Asia.

Elephants are the largest land animals, and in many ways, among the most interesting. They are mild and gentle, and quite intelligent. They are more easily trained than any other beast except the domestic dog.

The shape of the elephant's legs, like four huge pillars, is necessary to support its immense weight. Its ivory tusks are really overgrown teeth. These tusks are used to dig up roots for food and also as weapons for defense. The brain of the elephant is comparatively small, considering the size of the animal.

The most remarkable part of the elephant's body is its trunk. It is an extension of the nose and upper lip, and it serves the elephant as hand, arm, nose, and lips, all in one. There are about 40,000 muscles in the trunk, so it is very strong and flexible. The tip of the trunk ends in a sort of finger which is so sensitive that it can pick up a small pin!

There are few animals that have played as important a role in history as the horse. This is because the horse has been so useful in warfare. Can you imagine what wandering tribes, invading armies, knights,

WHO FIRST TAMED THE HORSE?

and soldiers all over the world would have done without the horse during the last few thousand years?

We can trace the ancestors of the horse back millions of years. But who first tamed the horse, the animal that we know? It is impossible to say. We know that prehistoric man used the horse as one of his chief sources of food. This was probably long before he thought of using the horse for riding.

The earliest pictures and carvings of horses were made by European cave men about 15,000 years ago. The horse in these pictures is very much like today's Mongolian pony. In these pictures and carvings there are marks that suggest a bridle, so perhaps the horse was already tamed!

It is probable however, that the wandering tribes in central Asia were the first to tame the horse, and from there the horse came to Europe and Asia Minor. We know there were horses in Babylonia as long ago as 3,000 B.C.

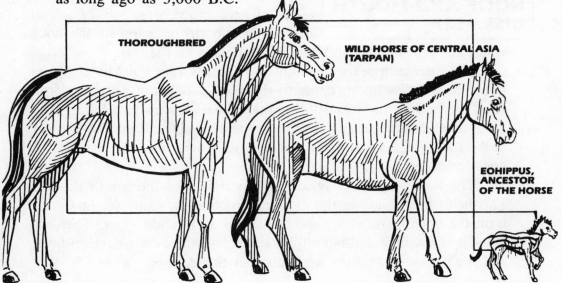

THOROUGHBRED

WILD HORSE OF CENTRAL ASIA (TARPAN)

EOHIPPUS, ANCESTOR OF THE HORSE

Because the horse was tamed before historic records began, it is very difficult to trace the origin of any of the modern breeds. The oldest and purest breed of saddle horse is the Arabian. They have been bred for at least fifteen centuries! They are small horses, their legs are slender, and their feet are small. Their backs are short and strong.

When Julius Caesar invaded England he found horses there. In his time, they were probably small, hardy animals. Later on, during the days of the knights, horses were bred chiefly for size and strength, and used as war horses. Then when gunpowder was invented, speed became more important than strength or size, so faster horses were bred.

As horse racing became more widespread, horses from the Arabs, Turks, and Persians were brought into England. Our modern thorough-bred horse is descended from these combinations.

A thoroughbred, by the way, is any horse eligible to be registered in the General Stud Book. It was begun in England in 1791 and traces the pedigree of horses, going back to about 1690!

WHAT IS HOOF-AND-MOUTH DISEASE?

If you live on a farm or have anything to do with cattle, then you've probably heard people talk about this disease, also called foot-and-mouth disease. It is a highly contagious disease that affects practically all cloven-footed animals.

When an animal gets this disease, it develops blisters on the tongue and lips and around the mouth, on parts of the body where the skin is thin, and between the claws of the feet.

The disease appears suddenly and spreads very quickly. It causes tremendous losses among cattle. If the disease strikes in a serious form, it may kill off as many as 50% of the animals that catch it! And even those animals that do survive are in great trouble. They lose a great deal of weight because they cannot eat. Cows have their milk cut down considerably.

The horse, by the way, does not catch hoof-and-mouth disease. This helps in diagnosing the disease. Suppose, for example, that on a farm the horses, the cows, and the swine all develop fever. Then we know it is not hoof-and-mouth disease. But if the others develop fever and the horses don't, then we know it is this disease.

This disease is caused by a virus that presents quite a problem. For one thing, it is the smallest virus known. The virus that causes smallpox, just to give you an idea, is 10,000 times larger! Another problem is that this virus can resist being destroyed if the conditions are right. It can remain active in hay for 30 days. It can remain active for 76 days at freezing temperature! And it can resist a great many antiseptics.

Still another complication is that there are six types of virus that cause hoof-and-mouth disease. So if an animal develops an immunity to one of these viruses, it may still get the disease from any of the other five!

Because we have all seen trained seals in the circus, and because seals are such fun to watch in the zoo, they have a kind of fascination for us. Yet surprisingly little is known by most people about these creatures.

CAN SEALS LIVE UNDER WATER?

The order of seals includes the fur seals, the sea lions, hair seals, sea elephants, and the walrus. Seals are mammals, and they stand halfway between typical mammals such as cows and dogs, and such sea mammals as whales.

Actually, seals are descended from land mammals, which means that at one time they had to adapt themselves to living in the water. They have not lived in the water for as long as whales have. The result is that seals are not nearly so well adapted to aquatic life as whales are.

Seals cannot live under water all the time. Not only that, but their young must be born on land. In most cases, the babies must be taught to swim by their mothers! So you can see why a seal is halfway between a land mammal and a sea mammal.

As they adapted themselves for life in the water, certain changes took place. They developed webbed hind-limbs and paddlelike fore-limbs to be able to swim fast. They acquired a layer of blubber to keep them warm. They have also either lost or reduced the size of their external, or outside, ears in order to lessen water resistance. And they began to feed on such sea creatures as squid, octopuses, and fish.

Although nature has changed the seal greatly for water life, seals spend a good deal of time on land. They like to sun themselves or sleep on beaches or ice floes. On shore, they move either by wriggling along or by dragging themselves with their fore-flippers.

In the United States, the most familiar seals are the California sea lions. They are active and intelligent. They can be trained easily to do tricks, such as juggling and balancing balls on the ends of their noses.

The habits of seals make them an easy prey for man. This is especially so during their breeding season when they can be approached on the beaches or ice floes. For centuries, the Eskimos have used seals for food, clothing, and their oil for cooking and light.

It is hard to believe that the porpoise is not a fish, but a mammal. Yet it is just as much a mammal as the cow in the fields. Porpoises, dolphins and whales form the order called "Cetacea" of the group of aquatic mammals.

IS THE PORPOISE A MAMMAL?

Actually, dolphins belong to the whale family and porpoises are a variety of dolphins. All these animals may be given the general name of whales, or cetaceans.

There are a great many differences between porpoises and other whales and fish. The baby porpoise is fed on its mother's milk like other little mammals. It is not hatched from an egg, but is born alive. Porpoises have no gills and breathe air through their lungs. Internally, porpoises have a skeleton, circulatory system, brain, and vital organs that are quite unlike those of fish.

Another important difference is the existence of blubber. Mammals are warm-blooded animals, and blubber conserves their animal heat in the cold waters.

The common porpoise is about 5½ feet long. The head is rounded in front, and the underjaw projects slightly. It has a wide mouth with between 80 and 100 teeth. A porpoise is black or grey in color above, and white below, with black flippers.

The porpoise prefers to live in waters near the coast rather than the open sea. It inhabits the North Atlantic but is quite rare in the Mediterranean. Porpoises live in great herds and seem to delight in following ships. There are some species of porpoises that appear in the South Atlantic and the Pacific Oceans.

Porpoise oil, which is obtained from the soft fat of the head and jaw, is used as a lubricant in the manufacture of watches and other delicate instruments because it doesn't gum up and can resist very low temperatures.

When the average person thinks of a reptile, he thinks of a snake. But actually, this class of animals includes many other creeping and crawling creatures.

WHAT IS A REPTILE?

In the animal kingdom, reptiles rank between the amphibians and the birds. Amphibians are animals that can live both on land and in the water. As a matter of fact, scientists believe that birds developed from the reptiles several million years ago. At that time, the reptiles were the the ruling class among animals, and they were often of giant size. But these giant reptiles died out, and the reptiles that are living today are comparatively small. The largest of these are crocodiles and the python snakes.

In many ways, reptiles are much like amphibians. All are cold-blooded, creeping animals with backbones. They are distinguished mainly by their lungs and their skin. Amphibians breathe through gills when they are young, and later many kinds develop lungs. Reptiles, on the other hand, breathe by means of lungs all their lives.

The skin of amphibians is smooth and clammy, being kept moist

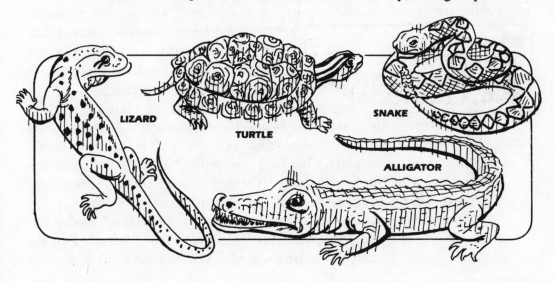

LIZARD

TURTLE

SNAKE

ALLIGATOR

by special slime glands. Water passes easily through this skin; therefore, most amphibians dry out and die if kept out of water for long. Reptiles have no slime glands, and their skin is dry and scaly. Because water cannot pass out through their skin, reptiles are able to live entirely on land.

The reptiles living today are divided into four main groups: the turtles, the crocodilians, the lizards, and snakes, and the strange lizard-like tuatara of New Zealand.

Turtles and tortoises differ from other reptiles in having their bodies surrounded by a bony shell covered with horny shields. All turtles and tortoises lay eggs. Many of the turtles live in or near bodies of fresh water, while tortoises live entirely upon land.

The alligators and crocodiles and their relatives are long, four-limbed animals having scales or plates covering their bodies. Alligators and crocodiles are so much alike that it may take an expert to tell them apart. In the United States, however, the alligators have a shorter and broader snout than the crocodiles.

Lizards and snakes belong to the highest order of reptiles. The main difference between lizards and snakes is in the structure of the jaws. In snakes, both upper and lower jaws have movable halves with sharp recurved teeth.

Turtles, tortoises, and terrapins all belong to a group of four-legged reptiles that have hard outer shells, scaly skins, and horny beaks. Most people use the three words—turtle, tortoise, and terrapin—interchange-

WHAT IS THE DIFFERENCE BETWEEN A TURTLE AND A TORTOISE?

ably. Scientists, however, sometimes make this distinction: a turtle is a sea reptile; a tortoise is a land reptile; and a terrapin is a fresh-water reptile.

It is correct to call all three turtles. They all breathe air through lungs and have shells that are made up of a "bony box" covered with horny plates or with soft skin. These shells are divided into two parts. One part covers the back; the other covers the underpart of the turtle's body. Through the openings between the two parts, the turtle can thrust out its head, neck, tail, and legs.

Turtles have well-developed senses of sight, taste, and touch, but their hearing is quite poor. Most turtles eat all kinds of food. Female turtles are able to make a hissing sound, while the male turtle is able to give a kind of "grunt." Some of the giant land turtles are even able to bellow!

The largest of living turtles is the leatherback, which is a sea turtle. It usually weighs about 1,000 pounds, and the biggest specimen on record is over 8 feet long and weighs 1,500 pounds!

Turtle soup is made from the flesh of the green turtle, which is also a sea turtle. It is usually found in tropical seas, and may weigh as much as 500 pounds. Tortoise shell, which is quite expensive, is obtained from the hawksbill turtle. It is the smallest of the sea turtles and is rarely more than 3 feet long. Its horny shell consists of separate, clear, horny shields of dark brown, richly marbled with yellow.

The biggest North American turtle is the alligator snapping turtle. It weighs up to 150 pounds and lives in the Mississippi region. Snappers, which are fresh-water turtles, have long, large tails and very strong, sharp jaws.

The most common North American land turtle is the wood, which has brick-red skin. It can become quite a friendly pet and will learn to take food from one's fingers. Turtles hibernate during the winter months, hiding either in the bottom of ponds or in holes in the ground. Turtles sometimes live for 200 years or more!

In order for there to be a "queen bee," there must be a colony of bees. But not all bees live in colonies. There are species of bees called "solitary" bees. Among them there are only two kinds of bees, the males and the egg-laying females.

WHAT MAKES A QUEEN BEE A "QUEEN"?

But bees that live in colonies, called "social bees," have a third form of bee known as "workers." The workers are really female bees that ordinarily don't lay eggs. So in a colony of social bees we have the workers, the males, who are called "drones," and the one egg-laying female, the mother of the colony, who is called the "queen."

Here is how a queen bumblebee spends her life. She passes the winter in a hole dug in a sandbank or other suitable place. She is the only member of the colony that lives through the winter! In the spring, she starts a new colony.

She first looks for a home, perhaps a deserted mouse nest. She heaps the soft material of the nest together and hollows out a place under it to serve as a nursery. Then she visits flowers for pollen and nectar and places a lump of beebread in the dry hollow she has prepared. She lays some eggs on this lump, covers them with wax, and sits over them, keeping the cold air away with her body.

Near her she has made a large waxen cell, called a "honeypot," which she has filled with enough honey for food to last until her eggs hatch. As soon as her first brood of young have grown big enough to use their wings, they take over most of mother's work. They prepare wax, make the beebread, and keep the honeypot filled to use in bad weather.

During the early part of the season, the only bees born are the workers. But before the summer is over, young queens and males, or drones, will also grow up in the colony. In the fall, the colony breaks up. All that the queen bee has done all summer long is lay eggs!

Among the honeybees, the queen lays all the eggs, but she cannot care for them. She may lay more than 1,500 eggs per day and about 250,000 in a season! She lays fertilized eggs that develop into workers or queens, depending on the needs of the colony. The unfertilized eggs develop into drones.

Young queens are reared in special queen cells. Before they emerge, the mother queen and about half the workers swarm off to start the new colony. The first young queen to emerge kills her sister queens in their cells and thus becomes the new mother queen!

In the United States alone, termites do about $40,000,000 worth of damage a year! Strangely enough, these creatures which are such a problem to man today, have existed for millions of years. Primitive termites probably lived during the age of dinosaurs!

WHAT ARE TERMITES?

Today, they are found in every state in the United States and in southern Canada. The greatest number are to be found in the rainy tropical regions around the world. There are more than 2,000 kinds of termites, about 50 of which are found in the United States.

Termites are insects that look like ants, but which are quite different from them. They have thick waists, a light color, and evenly curved feelers, or antennae.

Termites live in colonies in wood. They cut out the wood and form rooms for the colony. A colony of termites will consist of a king and

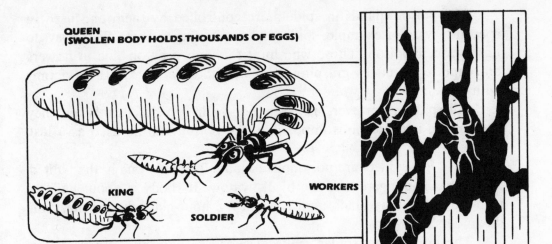

QUEEN
(SWOLLEN BODY HOLDS THOUSANDS OF EGGS)

KING

SOLDIER

WORKERS

queen, soldiers, and workers. The soldiers protect the colony from its enemies. They do not have wings and are blind, but they are the fighters.

The job of the workers is to feed the colony. They eat the wood and then feed this digested wood to all the other termites. In the hind intestine of a worker is a liquid. When this liquid is looked at through a microscope, thousands of single-celled animals, or protozoans, are seen. The protozoans turn the celluose of the wood into sugar. The sugar is digested by the worker and fed to the others.

Wood can be so treated that termites will not attack it. One method is to soak it with coal tar creosote under pressure, so that the creosote reaches the center. When building a house, care should be taken not to let any untreated wood come closer than two feet from the ground. Although moist soil is necessary for the life of most termites, there are dry-wood termites in the South that can live without such soil.

There is hardly a place in the world you can go where you won't find spiders. They can be found at sea level and on Mt. Everest, in forests, meadows, swamps, deserts, and in caves underground.

WHICH SPIDERS ARE POISONOUS?

Many people have a fear of spiders, because some types are known to be poisonous. All spiders, except two species, have poison glands. But this doesn't mean that the spiders with poison glands can harm man.

The poison glands in spiders are controlled by them and used in special ways. For example, spiders who spin nets to catch their prey do not use their poison. Those who hunt for their prey or hide in flowers and capture insects by grasping them with their fangs, kill their victims with poison.

All spiders, however, use their poison in self defense. When they are trapped and escape is impossible, the poison will be used as a last resort.

Very few spiders are poisonous to man. The only one in the United States that is dangerous is the black widow. Its body is about half an inch long and shiny black, and it has a red hour-glass shaped mark on the underside.

The bite of this spider may cause severe pain and illness. Some spiders whose bite is poisonous to man live in Australia. The large so-called "deadly" tarantulas and banana spiders have never actually killed any person. They may cause one's arm or whatever is bitten to swell greatly and to ache for a few days.

The majority of spiders are no more dangerous to man than wasps or hornets. In fact, a great many spiders won't bite even if you hold them in your hand. So unless you know the spider is a black widow, you can feel pretty safe with one.

The most amazing thing about spiders of course, is their ability to spin webs. The silk of spiders is manufactured in certain of their abdominal glands. The silk is forced through many tiny holes from the spinning organs at the tip of the abdomen. It comes out as a liquid which becomes solid on contact with the air.

There are many kinds of silk, depending on the type of spider, and there is a great variety of webs, including one built underwater!

When the presence of the boll weevil within the United States was first discovered, cotton growers refused to believe that this little brown beetle could cause serious damage. The discovery was made about

WHAT IS A BOLL WEEVIL?

1892, in southern Texas. About 30 years later, it was estimated that the boll weevil had decreased the annual cotton crop by more than 6,000,000 bales!

The boll weevil is a native of Central America. It worked northward through Mexico, and crossed the border into Texas at Brownsville. Like most insects, it has a keen sense of smell. Experiments have shown that the boll weevils which have just come forth in the final, or beetle stage of their development can head straight for a cotton field several miles away!

When full-grown, the beetle is about a quarter of an inch long. Its jaws are at the tip of a snout well arranged for boring holes in cotton buds. The beetle sleeps all winter under dry grass and leaves, or in cracks in the ground. In the spring, when the cotton buds are starting to form, it begins its destructive work.

The female insect bores into the buds and lays her eggs in them. Within three or four days, the eggs hatch. and the small grubs feed on the inside of the bud.

The young "squares," as the flower buds are called, are the favorite breeding places; but when squares can no longer be found, the beetles attack the cotton bolls or fiber-filled pods. The worms remain inside the bolls during the period when they are changing into beetles.

There are four or five generations of weevils during a season, so it is easy to understand what a large amount of damage they can cause. The infested buds usually drop off without maturing, and the cotton fibers of infested bolls are useless.

One of the most fascinating and remarkable creatures in the world is the ant. There are more than 3,500 different kinds of ants, and they are found almost everywhere in the world.

WHAT ARE ARMY ANTS?

All ants are very much alike except in size. Ants may be as small as $\frac{1}{16}$ of an inch, or as long as 2 inches. And all ants live in colonies. But there are tremendous differences in their way of life and their habits.

One of the most interesting types of ants, for example, is the "army ant." It eats living things! In Africa, there is a type of army ant called the "driver" ant. These ants go out in armies of many thousands. They kill and eat everything in their way.

Now you might wonder, "How can a little insect like the ant eat and kill everything in its way?" Well, there are thousands and thousands of them. Even the largest animals run away when they are coming. And if a creature cannot run—then good-bye! The army ants will kill and eat it, whether it is a fly or a crocodile or a wounded lion!

Army ants in the Americas eat only small things. They are called "legionary" ants. They may be found in the southern United States, and in Central and South America. Legionary ants travel in lines of thousands of individuals. In Mexico, people move out of their houses when they come. The ants eat all the roaches, rats, mice, and lizards that may be in the houses. Then the people move back to vermin-free houses!

Did you know that there are also ants who own slaves? These are the Amazon ants. The Amazon workers are all soldiers, and so they cannot gather food or tend to the young. So they must raid other ants to get slaves who will do this work.

They raid the nests of certain small, black ants. They kill any ants who try to resist them. Then they take the cocoons and larvae to their own homes. When the black ants come out of the cocoons, they will work in the Amazon colony, just like slaves!

Have you ever turned over a flat stone or a rotting log, and seen a little wormlike creature running quickly away from the light? The chances are it was a centipede.

DOES A CENTIPEDE REALLY HAVE ONE HUNDRED FEET?

Of course you didn't actually have a chance to count all its feet to see if it really had a hundred of them! The name "centipede" means "100-footed," and some species of this creature actually have 100 feet. Some, in fact, even have more legs than that! And some have only 30 legs.

While it seems rather amazing to us that any living thing can have so many feet, such creatures are not as rare in nature as we might think. There is a whole group of animals called "Myriapoda." This means "many-footed," and it includes not only the centipedes, but also the millepedes. Can you guess what "millepedes" means? You're right if you said 1,000-legged! So the centipede is not the champion when it comes to greatest number of legs. Incidentally, this type of creature is one of the oldest in existence. According to scientists, there have been

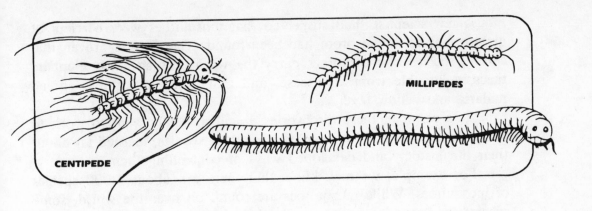

MILLIPEDES

CENTIPEDE

centipedes and millipedes for millions of years!

While some human beings have trouble not stumbling with just two feet—a centipede can manage his hundred or so feet quite easily. The legs are arranged in pairs, and each pair grows out of a segment of the centipede's body, which is flat and has many joints.

On the section next to the head of the centipede, there are two long feelers and two poison-bearing claws. The poison of most centipedes is harmless to man, but in the tropics there are certain species, 8 to 10 inches long, whose bite may be serious. In fact, such centipedes have been known to kill small birds!

Centipedes develop from eggs laid in the open. Some kinds are hatched with their full number of legs. Others start with seven pairs and add a new set each time they shed their skin, until they are full-grown. Centipedes come out at night to hunt their food, and during the day they hide under rocks or in dead wood.

Have you ever been out camping or walking in a beautiful country spot, when suddenly everything was spoiled by a swarm of mosquitoes? These little creatures cannot only ruin our pleasure, they can make

DO ANY AMERICAN MOSQUITOES CARRY DISEASE?

us quite miserable with their stubborn attacks.

For a long time, man considered mosquitoes annoying and troublesome—but that was all. It wasn't until the end of the century that we began to discover they were dangerous, too.

A few scientists had suspected that mosquitoes were carriers of disease, but no actual proof had been found. Then it was proven that certain species of mosquitoes carry the worms which cause elephantiasis, a horrible tropical disease, and that other mosquitoes spread malaria and yellow fever.

As a result of these discoveries, scientists really went to work to study the mosquito. They have studied their species, learned all about their life history, and developed ways of controlling them.

For example, we now know that there are about 1,000 species of mosquitoes. While mosquitoes are found all over the world, some species are found everywhere and other species are found only in certain regions. In the United States, there are about 70 species of mosquitoes.

One of these is the Anopheles mosquito, and several species of this type in the United States are carriers of malaria. An Anopheles has black spots on its wings. It stands, when at rest, with its head down and its bill and body in a straight line.

There is another mosquito in the United States that is quite dangerous, and this is the Aedes mosquito. It carries yellow fever. This mosquito has white stripes around its legs and crosswise on its back. It rests with its bill at an angle to its body.

The best thing to do about mosquitoes is to eliminate them!

It's a natural thing to consider the housefly a nuisance. It makes an irritating buzzing sound; it annoys you when it crawls on your skin; and so on. For ages that's what man considered the fly to be—just a nuisance.

WHY DO FLIES RUB THEIR LEGS TOGETHER?

It wasn't until the twentieth century that we found out that the innocent-looking housefly is one of man's worst enemies. It was discovered that these flies carried disease germs that cause the death of millions of people every year!

When you see a fly rubbing its legs together, it is just cleaning itself, and scraping off some of the material that has gathered there. But how dangerous that material may be! It may be the bacteria of such diseases as typhoid fever, tuberculosis, or dysentery. Flies get such germs from garbage and sewage. Then, if they happen to touch our food, the germs spread to the food, and if we eat it, we may become infected.

How does the fly carry these germs around? If you were to look at a fly under the magnifying glass, you would notice that the fly's body isn't smooth at all. Its whole body, its claws, and its padded feet, are covered with bristling hairs. The fly's tongue is also coated with sticky glue.

This means that practically any place the fly stops for even a moment, it's going to pick up things that stick to its body, its feet, or its tongue. In fact, each foot on its three pairs of legs has claws and two hairy pads—so it can make plenty of "pick-ups!" By the way, a sticky liquid is secreted by the fly's pads, and it is this which enables the fly to walk upside down on the ceiling, or any surface.

Did you know that flies are among the oldest insects known? Fossil remains of flies have been found that are millions of years old. Will we ever get rid of flies altogether? The only way we can bring this about is to prevent them from breeding. And for this to be done, conditions have to be made very sanitary all over the world!

In the Bible, we read of plagues of locusts descending upon a people and causing great suffering. Of course, in those times such a plague was considered a punishment from God, just as floods, droughts, and disease.

WHAT CAUSES PLAGUES OF LOCUSTS?

But plagues of locusts have appeared in other times and in other lands, too. In the western United States, there was such a plague from 1874 to 1876 that did more than $200,000,000 worth of damage!

The word "locust" has been applied to many members of the grasshopper family. A locust is actually any of a group of insects that belong to a family called "Acrididae." The so-called 17-year locust is not really a locust but a cicada.

Many scientists have been studying the question of why these insects descend on a region in great swarms at certain times, and seem to disappear between those times.

It seems that the species of locust that produces the "plague" exists in two phases, or periods. The two phases are solitary and gregarious, or in groups. In these two extreme phases, the locusts are quite different. They differ in color, form, structure, and behavior.

In the solitary phase, the locusts do not congregate and are sluggish in behavior. Their color matches that of their surroundings. In the gregarious phase, the locusts have a black and yellow color, congregate in great groups, are very active and nervous, and they even have a higher temperature. There are other differences as well. The solitary phase is the normal phase for the locusts.

When, for some reason, crowding is forced on the locusts in the solitary phase, they produce locusts of the gregarious type. These locusts are restless and irritable; they begin to wander; they are joined by others; a great swarm develops, and soon millions of them are ready to descend on a region in the form of a plague!

The migration of birds has fascinated man since the very beginning of history. Did you know that Homer wrote about it in 1000 B.C.; it's mentioned in the Bible; and the great Greek philosopher, Aristotle,

HOW DO BIRDS KNOW WHEN TO MIGRATE?

studied the question?

And yet, so many thousands of years later, we still don't have the complete answers to the fascinating phenomenon of the migration of birds. By this migration, we mean the movement of birds south in the fall and north in the spring, or moving from lowlands to highlands, or from the interior to the seacoasts.

We can have a pretty good idea as to why it's good for the birds to migrate. For example, they go to warmer climates because some of them couldn't survive winter conditions. Those birds that feed on certain insects, or small rodents, wouldn't find any food in winter. Oddly enough, temperature alone wouldn't make most birds migrate. Did you know that your canary could probably survive outside in the winter in temperatures 50 degrees below zero, Fahrenheit, if it had enough food?

Whatever the reason for the migration (and there are many), how do birds know when it's time to take off on their long flights? Well, we know that they migrate quite punctually every year when the season is changing. And what is the surest, unmistakable clue to the fact that the season is changing? The length of the day! It is believed that birds can tell when the days get shorter (and longer in the spring), and this is the best "alarm clock" they have to tell them to get along!

Since birds breed in the summer, this is also connected with migration. Only in this case, it's migration northward. Certain glands in the bird begin to secrete chemicals that have to do with breeding. This happens in the spring. The bird feels the need to breed and heads north where it will be summer.

So the change in the length of days and the disappearance of food tell the bird to head to warmer places. And the breeding instinct in the spring tells them to head north. There are many other factors involved, of course, and many things we still don't understand, but these are certainly among the chief clues to bird migration.

HOW DO MIGRATING BIRDS FIND THEIR WAY?

In the late summer, many birds in various parts of the world leave their homes and fly south for the winter. Sometimes they travel to other continents, thousands of miles away. Next spring, these birds return not only to the same country, but often to the very same nest in the same building! How do they find their way?

Various interesting experiments have been made to try to find the answer. In one of these, a group of storks was taken from their nests before the time of the autumn migration and moved to another place. From this new location, they would have to travel in a new direction to reach their winter feeding grounds. But when the time came, they took off in exactly the same direction they would have followed from their old home! It seems as if they have an inborn instinct that tells them to fly off in a certain direction when winter approaches.

The ability of birds to find their way home is equally amazing. Birds have been taken by airplane from their home to places 400 miles away. When they were set free, they flew back to their home!

To say they have an instinct to "go home" doesn't really explain the mystery. How do they find their way? We know that young birds are not taught the road by their parents, because often the parents fly off first on the annual migrations. And birds who fly home often fly by night, so they can't see landmarks to guide them. Other birds fly over water, where there are no landmarks of any kind.

One theory is that birds can sense the magnetic fields that surround the earth. Magnetic lines of force stretch from the north to the south magnetic poles. Perhaps the birds direct themselves by these lines. But this theory has never been proven.

The fact is, science just doesn't have a full explanation of how birds find their way when they migrate or fly home! An interesting bit of history is related to the migration of birds. When Columbus was approaching the American continent, he saw great flocks of birds flying to the southwest. This meant land was near, so he changed his direction to the southwest to follow the direction taken by the birds. And that's why he landed in the Bahamas, instead of on the Florida coast!

Everybody knows that birds migrate. In fact, people use the disappearance and then the re-appearance of certain birds as a sort of way of telling the change of seasons. But no one fully understands why birds make such long journeys.

HOW FAR DO BIRDS MIGRATE?

We cannot explain it by difference of temperature alone. The feathery coats birds have could protect them very well against the cold. Of course, as cold weather comes there is a lack of food for the birds, and this may explain their flight to places where it can be found. But then why do they migrate north again in the spring? Some experts think there is a connection between the change in the climate and the breeding instinct.

For whatever reason they migrate, birds certainly are the champions of all migrating animals. And the champions among the birds are the arctic terns. These amazing birds will travel in the course of a year, going back and forth, as much as 22,000 miles!

The tern nests over a wide range, from the Arctic Circle to as far south as Massachusetts. It takes this bird about 20 weeks to make its trip down to the antarctic region, and it averages about 1,000 miles a week.

Most land birds make rather short hops during their migrations. But one bird, the American golden plover, makes a long nonstop flight over the open ocean. It may fly from Nova Scotia directly to South America, a distance of about 2,400 miles over water without a stop!

Do birds start and end their migrations on exactly the same day each year? A great deal has been written about this and many people believe it happens. But no birds actually begin their migration the same day each year, though there are some who come pretty close to it. The famous swallows of Capistrano, California, are supposed to leave on October 23 and return on March 19. Despite all the publicity about it, their date of departure and arrival has been found to vary from year to year.

No bird has been written about so much by poets as the nightingale. Its song is supposed to be the most beautiful of all and nobody has been quite able to describe it. As a matter of fact, this attempt at describing it goes back to Aristophanes, the ancient Greek writer!

DOES THE NIGHTINGALE SING ONLY AT NIGHT?

According to the poets, the nightingale sings only at night and at almost any season of the year. But this isn't true. The nightingale is a migratory bird and in England, for example, can only be heard between the middle of April and the middle of June. The nightingale does not visit Ireland, Wales, or Scotland. On the continent of Europe it is quite abundant in the south, and even goes as far as Iran, Arabia, Abyssinia, Algeria, and the Gold Coast of Africa.

Only the male nightingale sings. His melody is the song of courtship to his mate, which remains silent in a neighboring bush or tree. He sings during the day as well as at night, but because of other birds, his song is not noticed so much then.

The male keeps singing until the female has hatched out her brood.

Then he remains quiet so as not to attract enemies to the nest. He stays on guard, and his notes are short calls to tell his mate that all is well, or to warn her of some danger.

While the nightingale sings one of the most beautiful songs of all birds, its plumage is very inconspicuous. Male and female are very much alike—a reddish-brown above and dull grayish-white beneath.

The nest the nightingles build is somewhat unusual. It is placed on or near the ground. The outside of the nest consists mostly of dead leaves set up vertically. In the midst of this is a deep cuplike hollow, neatly lined with fibers from roots. It is very loosely constructed and a very slight touch can disturb it. There are from four to six eggs of a deep olive color.

For thousands of years, the owl has been a creature to which people have attached special significance. Primitive people have many superstitions about the owl, chiefly because of the peculiar cries it makes.

HOW CAN AN OWL SEE AT NIGHT?

In many parts of Europe when an owl is heard to hoot, it is considered a sign of death. In ancient Greece, the owl was a symbol of wisdom.

Owls of one species or another are found in all parts of the world. In the frozen arctic districts, owls have snowy-white plumage which blends in with their surroundings and keeps them safe from their enemies. In parts of Texas there are owls so tiny they are no bigger than a sparrow, and they feed on grasshoppers and beetles.

The owl is a bird that really comes to life at night, and its whole body is especially suited to this kind of life. First, let's take the owl's hoot. When the owl utters this cry in the night, creatures who may be nearby are frightened by the sound. If they make any motion or sound, the owl hears them instantly with its sensitive ears.

The ears of an owl have a flap on the outside, unlike most other birds. Some owls have a kind of "trumpet" of feathers near the ears to help them hear better. Once the owl has startled its prey and heard its motion, it can see it even in the dark! There are two reasons for this remarkable ability. The eyeballs of the owl are elastic. It can focus them instantly for any distance. The owl can also open the pupil of its eye very wide. This enables it to make use of all the night light there is.

The owl's eyes are placed so that it has to turn its whole head to change the direction of its glance.

Even the owl's feathers help it to hunt its food. The feathers are so soft that the owl can fly noiselessly and thus swoop right down on the animals it hunts. Some owls are helpful to farmers because they destroy rats, insects, and other enemies of crops. But there are other owls that are fond of chickens and other domestic fowl, and these owls cost the farmer quite a bit of money!

One of the strangest-looking of all birds is the toucan. In fact, it's a kind of freak among birds.

To begin with, the toucan has an enormous bill, actually larger

WHAT IS A TOUCAN?

than its head! In some toucans, the bill is a third of the length of the entire bird. This bill is shaped like a great lobster claw and is marked with bright colors.

If you were to see a toucan, you would wonder how this bird can maintain its balance with such a bill. The answer is that the bill is very light for its size. It is paper-thin on the outside, and it's reinforced on the inside with a honeycomb of bone. At its base, this bill is as large as the head of the bird. It has an irregular toothed or cutting surface along the edge.

The tongue of the toucan is also very unusual. It has side notches and is flat and featherlike. Another peculiar thing about the toucan is the way the tail is joined to the body. It seems to have a ball and socket joint. The toucan can give this tail a jerk and raise it above its back.

The toucan is a tropical American bird that has a family of its own. It is related to such birds as the jacamars, puffbirds, barbets, and distantly to the woodpeckers. There are about 37 different species of toucans, the largest of which are about 24 inches in length.

The toucan's appetite nearly equals its bill. It eats almost anything, and in captivity it has been trained to the most varied diet. At home in the forest it turns with equal greediness to fruits, or to the eggs and young of smaller birds. When feeding, it makes a chattering noise with its great bill. It also has a harsh, unmusical cry.

The toucans live together in small flocks in the depths of the Central and South American forests. Little is known of their life history, but it is believed that they make nests in the hollows of trees. Toucans are easily tamed and thrive in captivity.

One of the most spectacular sights presented by any bird is that of the peacock displaying his feathers. As you might imagine, such a sight has always impressed people. In fact, in ancient times, both the Greeks and

WHY DOES THE PEACOCK RAISE HIS FEATHERS?

the Romans considered the peacock to be a sacred bird. But this didn't prevent the Romans from serving peacocks for dinner!

The peacock is a native of Asia and the East Indies, from which it has been brought to other parts of the world. There are only two species of peacock, and they are related to the pheasant.

Because of the way the peacock displays his feathers and struts around, a common expression has arisen: "Vain as a peacock." Actually, this is quite unfair to the peacock. It is no more vain than many other birds during the mating season.

The male peacock's display of gorgeous plumage is for the sake of the hen and for her alone. Among birds, as you know, it is the male who usually has the brighter colors and more "flashy" appearance. The peacock happens to have more marvelous colors than any other birds.

His head, neck, and breast are a rich purple, splashed with tints of green and gold. His head is also set off with a crest of 24 feathers in paler hues. His back is green, with the wing feathers tipped with copper.

The most remarkable feature of the male peacock of course is the train, or extension of his tail. A peacock is about 7 or 8 feet long, of which the tail takes up between 3 or 4 feet.

The tail is a medley of blue and green and gold. Here and there in the regular pattern are "eyes" which change colors. The train is raised and held up by the stiff quills of the shorter, true tail.

The female peacock, the peahen, is slightly smaller and quieter in tone. She has no train, and only a short crest of dull color. She usually lays ten eggs, of a dirty-brown color. Peacocks are generally kept for ornament and for the sake of their plumage.

Many people imagine that this strange bird lives wherever it is cold, near the North Pole, South Pole, and so on. But the penguin inhabits only the Southern Hemisphere. Penguins live along the Antarctic (not

WHERE DO PENGUINS LIVE?

Arctic!) continent and islands. They are found as far north as Peru or southern Brazil, southwest Africa, New Zealand, and southern Australia.

The penguin is famous, of course, because it is like a comic version of a human being. Penguins stand up straight and flat-footed. Often they arrange themselves in regular files, like soldiers. When they walk, their manner seems so dignified and formal that it looks funny to us. Their plumage covers their entire bodies and is made of small, scalelike feathers. It looks like a man's evening dress of black coat and white shirt front.

The penguin that existed in prehistoric times was six feet tall, and you can imagine the effect that penguin would have on us today! There are 17 species of penguins in existence today, and the largest of these, the emperor penguin, stands about 3½ feet high and weighs about 80 pounds.

Ages ago, the penguin could fly as well as any other bird. But today its wings are short flappers, of no value at all in flying. How did this happen? One of the reasons, strangely enough, is that the penguin had few, if any, enemies. It lived in such remote areas in the Antarctic regions, that there was practically no one around to attack it. So it could safely spend all its time on land or in the water.

As generations of penguins were born and died without ever using their wings, those wings in time became very small and stiff, until today they are useless for flying. But the penguins became wonderful swimmers and divers, and those wings make excellent paddles! Penguins also developed a thick coat of fat to protect them from the icy cold of the regions where they lived.

Penguins are hunted by men today for this fat, and it may be necessary to pass laws to protect them from extinction.

Even though the sea horse is a fish, there is very little about it to suggest a fish. It has a head shaped like a pony. Instead of scales, the body of a sea horse is encased in rigid plates and thorny spikes. And its tail is like a snake's!

WHAT IS A SEA HORSE?

The sea horse doesn't even behave like other fish. It usually curls its tail around a bit of seaweed in the water so that it won't be swept away by the current. When it does swim, it moves about with the help of a single fin which is located on its back, and it moves upright through the water.

The mouth of a sea horse is a pipe-like tube through which it sucks in its food. Unlike other fish, it has a distinct neck and movable horse-like head, which is set at an angle to its body.

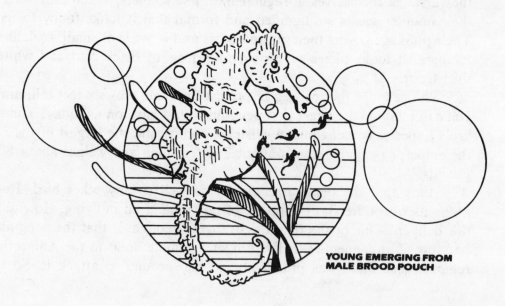

YOUNG EMERGING FROM
MALE BROOD POUCH

Perhaps the most peculiar thing about sea horses is the way they care for their young. The female fish, when she lays her eggs, puts them into the broad pouch beneath the tail of the male. So the father, instead of the mother, carries the eggs about until they hatch. Even after the young hatch out, they remain in the father's pouch for a time until they are able to take care of themselves.

Sea horses can be found in nearly all the warm and temperate seas. They belong to the pipefish family, and their food consists of small sea creatures and the eggs of other fishes. A sea horse never eats a dead thing.

There are about 50 different kinds or species of sea horses. Their size may range from 2 to 12 inches. The sea horse found along the Atlantic Coast of North America is usually about 6 inches long.

Sea horses are seen only in the summer and they are known as summer fishes. Nobody knows what happens to them in the winter!

Even though the sea horse hasn't many ways of defending itself against its enemies, it is quite safe from attack. It seems that other fishes in the sea just don't like to eat or attack sea horses!

The starfish is one of the most curious of sea creatures. Among its queer relatives are the prickly sea-urchins, the sea cucumbers, and the sand dollars. There are more than 6,000 of these relatives and they are called

DOES A STARFISH HAVE EYES?

"echinoderms," which means spiny-skinned. The starfish and its relatives all have well-developed nervous and digestive systems. This system follows the same five-armed arrangement which occurs in all echinoderms. The starfish are sometimes divided into three groups. There are the brittle stars, which break off their long snaky rays if they are caught. Their arms may extend 8 to 10 inches. There are the feather stars, whose waving rays resemble little plumes. And there are the ordinary sea stars which usually measure about 5 inches.

The tough, leathery skin of a starfish is covered with very short spines. In the center of their bodies, on both the upper and undersides, are button-shaped disks. Through these disks they draw in or expel sea water. The disks on the under sides act as mouths. The eyes are at the tips of their arms and are protected by a circle of spines.

Along the underside of their arms are grooves, and along these grooves are arranged little tubelike sucker feet. These are used both for moving about and as organs of smell. Sea stars cannot travel very fast with their little tube feet, but they can do something more remarkable. They can open an oyster! They attach the sucking disks of their feet to either half of the oyster shell and pull at it until the oyster finally opens. Then the starfish turns its stomach inside out, brings it through its mouth, and wraps it about the oyster.

Starfish can also eat by taking food into their mouths in the ordinary way. They can also replace broken arms. They may even grow a whole new body from one arm!

If you have ever been near the sea and walked along the shore where there are piers, rocks, and breakwater walls, then you've almost certainly seen barnacles. In fact, the "crust" you saw that was formed on the piers

WHAT ARE BARNACLES?

and rocks was made up of millions and millions of barnacles!

A barnacle is simply a small shellfish. When barnacles are hatched, they swim about freely. But when they reach adult state, they no longer move about. They attach themselves to any convenient surface and actually lose their power of locomotion.

This habit of attaching to a surface, since it is done by millions of barnacles at a time, is quite a nuisance to man. For example, when barnacles form a crust on the hull of a ship, they can cut down its speed by 50 per cent! In the days of smaller ships, barnacles were a real danger because they made steering very difficult and could delay a ship from reaching its port for quite a while.

The pirates who sailed the Caribbean Sea had to tip over their ships on beaches and scrape off the barnacles. Many an old-time whaler could hardly get home after a two-year cruise because of the masses of barnacles clinging to its hull. Even today, with our modern, powerful ships, barnacles cost the world's shipping industry about a hundred million dollars a year because of the loss of time and wear and tear on machinery.

There are many different varieties of barnacles, among them the rock barnacles, which prefer to live on rocks rather than on wood or iron. As we said, when first hatched they resemble tiny crabs or lobsters and can move around. But once a barnacle attaches itself to a surface, it's for life!

An attached barnacle begins to grow a shell which encloses its body completely. The only thing that moves from then on is tentacles or antennae of the barnacle. There are six pairs of these feathery tentacles and they are able to move about to reach and draw in smaller water creatures for food.

The ancestor of the goldfish is the carp. In the lakes and rivers of China and Japan, the greenish-gray carp is found in great quantities, and this is where the goldfish was first developed.

WHAT IS THE ORIGIN OF THE GOLDFISH?

The Chinese have been breeding goldfish for centuries, and the Japanese have raised goldfish for more than 400 years! Goldfish weren't known to Europe until a few were brought over about 200 years ago. These were given to Madame Pompadour of the court of King Louis XV of France. Because she was the leader of fashion, other people began importing them.

Goldfish vary in size from 1½ inches to about 12 inches. The common goldfish, the fantail, the comet, and the nymph, are the breeds best known to the Western world. The common goldfish has a slender body and rather short, tough fins.

The fantail has a shorter, fatter body with double tail and fins. The American-bred comet is slender, with a long, single, deeply forked and free-flowing tail. The nymph is like the comet but has a short, round body.

All these breeds may be kept in an aquarium, and millions of people have them in their homes. If you would like to keep goldfish, there are certain things you should know about them and their care.

The lowering of the back fin of a fish is a sure sign that it is not in good condition. A fungus disease, caused by plant parasites, is also common. In this, a white scum develops on the fins of the fish and extends over the body. If this scum reaches the gills, it keeps the fish from breathing and kills it.

This disease can be cured by giving the fish a salt-water bath, which will also correct the lowered-fin condition. One tablespoon of salt to a gallon of water the same temperature as that in the aquarium may be used for a daily 30-minute bath. The fish should be placed in a shallow basin containing this solution and set in a dim light.

Then the aquarium and plants should be soaked for four hours in a very weak solution of potassium permanganate, washed, and filled with a fresh supply of clean water. In two, or three days, the fish may be put back into it.

Did you ever eat a dish of fried scallops? As you looked at the little squares of food on your plate, did you wonder why you had never seen them in the water? What kind of creature was this that existed in square chunks of meat?

WHAT IS A SCALLOP?

Actually, what are sold as "scallops" and what you eat as "scallops" are only the large muscles of certain mollusks. These muscles are used to open and close the shells, and they are the only part we eat.

The scallop itself is a curious creature. As you probably know, most bivalves (mollusks with two shells) find a place to live and stay there. They may fasten themselves to rocks or to timbers, or form a bed on the bottom of the ocean as the oysters do. But the scallop is quite different.

The scallop likes to wander about. He is constantly moving from place to place. The way he moves is by sucking water into his shell and then squirting it out suddenly. This gives him enough force to push himself forward in zigzag fashion.

Did you know that the scallop became a symbol for travelers because it is always moving? In the Middle Ages, pilgrims wore a scallop shell in their hats to indicate that they had made a long trip by sea.

Scallops belong to the great group of mollusks which includes snails, clams, and oysters. There are more than two hundred different species of scallops. The kind that are caught in New England waters and which we enjoy eating are chiefly the common scallop and the giant scallop. The common scallop lives in bays close to shore, and measures up to 3 inches across. The giant scallop is a sea scallop. It is found off-shore in deeper waters and measures about 6 inches across.

The octopus belongs to a group of animals called "cephalopods." The name means "head-footed" because the foot is divided into long armlike tentacles that grow out around the head. The octopus has eight such tentacles.

HOW DOES AN OCTOPUS MOVE?

Even though the octopus belongs to that part of the animal kingdom known as mollusks, it is quite different from clams and oysters, which are mollusks, too. It is more closely related to the squids.

None of these has shells. They have only a soft mantle to enclose the body. The tentacles are long and flexible with rows of suckers on the underside. These enable the octopus to grab and hold very tightly to anything it catches.

In the back part of the body of the octopus is a funnel-siphon. Water comes into this siphon and the octopus extracts oxygen from it the way a fish does. The siphon is also the way it manages to move swiftly. The octopus can shoot a stream of water from this siphon with such force that it propels itself backward very rapidly. That is the way it can get away from an enemy that comes too quickly to allow it the chance to crawl over the rocks or into crevices by means of its eight tentacles.

When an octopus lies quietly, the tentacles rest spread out over the floor of the shallow pool. Should an enemy approach, it will either escape or grab the enemy tightly. If things grow too serious, it can throw up a "smoke screen" and escape. From a sac in the lower back

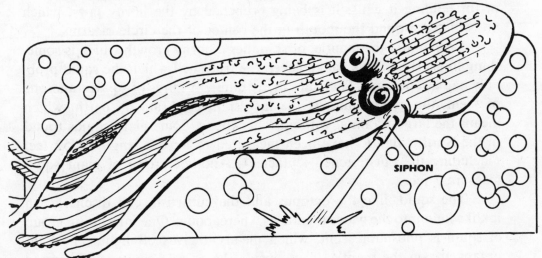

SIPHON

part of its body it can throw out a black inky fluid that clouds the surrounding water.

Also, an octopus can change color to match its surroundings. It can go from red to gray, yellow, brown, or blue-green.

In the days when Columbus sailed the seas there were stories told of long-armed monsters that reached out of the water to scuttle ships and pull the sailors down to the depths of the ocean. Such stories were exag-

WHAT IS A SQUID?

gerations. There never were such monsters, and what the sailors probably saw were giant octopuses or giant squid.

Both of these creatures are mollusks, or shellfish. They belong to the class called "Cephalopoda." This name means "head-footed," because the foot is divided into long armlike tentacles that grow out around the head.

A typical squid has a long, slender body edged by triangular fins, a short square head with well-developed eyes, and ten arms. On the undersurface of the arms or tentacles, are arranged rows of suckers which are strengthened with tough horny rings. Two of these tentacles are longer and more flexible than the others. The suckers are concentrated at the extremity of the tentacles as a sort of "hand."

The two long tentacles are used by the squid to capture its prey. The other eight are used to transfer the food to the mouth of the squid. or for holding it while it is being crunched by the horny jaws, which are situated around the mouth in the center of the circle of arms.

Deep under the mantle, or skin, lies a horny growth which is something like a shell. This has replaced the true shell which the squid probably had at one time. There are many different kinds of squids, and one of them, the giant squid, is the largest invertebrate on earth, which means the largest animal without a backbone. Some giant squids found in the North Atlantic have been measured to have a length of 52 feet (including the outstretched tentacles). Another group of giant squid measure 7 feet.

The squid, like the octopus and the cuttlefish, can discharge an inklike fluid into the water to hide its whereabouts. One interesting group of squid is phosphorescent, which means it gives off light. The light organs are on the mantle, arms, inside the mantle cavity, and around the eyes. When seen at night, they appear quite beautiful. Other squid, called "flying squid," are able to leap across the surface of the water.

A catfish might say to you: "why do you call them 'whiskers?' They're not whiskers at all!" And, of course, it's only because those things on the fish's mouth resemble a cat's whiskers that we call them that. Actu-

WHY DO CATFISH HAVE WHISKERS?

ally they are barbels, or feelers, and help the catfish know what's going on all about him.

There's another way a catfish is supposed to resemble a cat: it makes a buzzing or croaking sound when caught that suggests a cat's purring. It's for these two reasons that this kind of fish got its name, "catfish."

Young boys are especially well acquainted with the catfish because it's one of the easiest fish to catch. It will bite at almost any bait, from a piece of red string to a worm. And because the catfish does such a good job of caring for its young and protecting its nest, there always seems to be a lot of catfish around.

Actually, the catfish family has about 2,000 different species. The European catfish is known to grow to a length of 10 feet and a weight of 400 pounds! Some specimens of the great Mississippi catfish and the Great Lakes catfish have been found to weigh 150 pounds.

The catfishes known as the mud cat, the yellow cat, and the

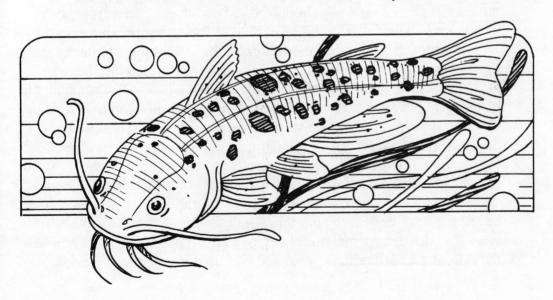

bashaw catfish are found in all large rivers of the West and South. Many catfish are good eating, especially the white cat, found in the waters of the Chesapeake Bay and the Potomac River; the blue cat, found in Southern streams; and the bullheads, bull pouts, or horned pouts.

Some catfish have strange habits. One South American species is said to travel overland from pond to pond, and another builds a nest of blades of grass for its young. There is even an electric catfish in Africa which can give a painful electric shock. In the river Nile is a species which avoids the notice of its enemies by swimming with its black belly up and its white back down!

Anybody who owns a canary probably knows about "cuttlebone," which comes from the cuttlefish. The cuttlebone is given to canaries and other cage birds so they can sharpen their beaks on it.

WHAT IS A CUTTLEFISH?

But, except for this, the cuttlefish is quite unknown to most of us. The cuttlefish is not a fish, but a mollusk. It belongs to the class of mollusks called "cephalopods," which means "head-footed animals." This is because of the arrangement of the arms, or feet, around the mouth. The octopus also belongs to this class of mollusk.

The cuttlefish is a rather remarkable creature. It travels smoothly and silently through the water by moving the row of fins which are fastened to its shield-shaped body. Sometimes when it moves, it erects the first pair of its tentacles, or feelers. When it comes within striking distance of its prey, it suddenly shoots out its two long tentacles from pockets which are located in its broad head behind its staring bulging eyes.

It grasps its victim with the suckers at the ends of these tentacles, and draws it within reach of four shorter pairs of arms, which also have suckers, and are arranged around its head. It also has a parrot-like beak, and if its victim happens to have a hard shell, it simply crushes it in this beak.

If the cuttlefish decides it wants to retreat suddenly from an enemy, it backs away quickly. It does this by forcing out water through a tube called the "siphon." Sometimes, when it wants to discourage the enemy from chasing it, it darkens the water with a cloud of inkline fluid called "sepia."

This inklike sepia is used by man, by the way; it makes a rich brown pigment, or coloring matter. The flesh of the cuttlefish can be eaten after it is dried, and the cuttlebone, which is a bonelike shell beneath the skin of the cuttlefish, is powdered and used in some toothpastes.

CHAPTER 3
THE
HUMAN BODY

Hormones are secreted by the endocrine glands. Endocrine means "the internal secretion of a gland." Another name for them is ductless glands, because they don't send their secretions into ducts but directly into the

| **WHAT IS A HORMONE?** |

bloodstream. Hormones are also produced by some organs such as the liver and the kidney, but most of the hormones in the body come from glands.

Each of the various hormones produces its own special effect in the body. In general, the job of the hormones is to regulate the internal activities of the body, such as growth and nutrition, the storage and use of food materials, and the reproductive processes. If the glands produce too much or not enough, a person may have an abnormal physical appearance.

Here are what some of the chief glands and hormones do in our bodies: The thyroid gland, located in the neck, produces a hormone which helps in the growth, development, and metabolic processes of the body.

The pituitary gland, located at the base of the skull, has two parts. As we know, one hormone produced by one part of this gland has the job of promoting growth.

Another part of the pituitary gland produces two hormones which help control our use of water, fat, our blood pressure, and the way we regulate the heat in our body.

There are two important glands located at the upper end of each kidney. One produces a hormone called adrenalin. This hormone is related to blood pressure and reactions to emotion and emergencies. When you become excited or frightened, you produce more of this hormone.

Other glands in the body produce hormones which have to do with making you act like a boy or a girl. So you see that hormones are responsible for a great deal about you and your health.

In the body of an adult human being, there are about six quarts of blood. Floating about in this liquid there are approximately 25 billion blood cells!

HOW DOES THE BODY MAKE BLOOD CELLS?

It is almost impossible for us to imagine such a tremendous quantity, but this might give you an idea. Each blood cell is so tiny that it can only be seen under a microscope. If you could make a string of these microscopic cells, that string would go four times around the earth!

Where do these cells come from? Obviously, the "factory" that turns out such an enormous quantity of cells must have amazing productive power — especially when you consider that sooner or later every one of these cells disintegrates and is replaced by a new one!

The birthplace of the blood cells is the bone marrow. If you look at an opened bone, you can see the reddish-grey, spongy marrow in the cavity of the bone. If you look at it under a microscope, you can see a whole network of blood vessels and connective-tissue fibers. Between these and blood vessels are countless marrow cells, and the blood cells are born in these marrow cells.

When the blood cell lives in the bone marrow, it is a genuine cell with a nucleus of its own. But before it leaves the bone marrow for the blood stream, it loses the nucleus. As a result, the ripe blood cell is no longer a complete cell. It is not really a living structure any longer, but a kind of mechanical apparatus.

The blood cell is like a balloon made of protoplasm, and filled with the blood pigment hemoglobin, which makes it red. The sole function of the blood cell is to combine with oxygen in the lungs, and to exchange the oxygen for carbon dioxide in the tissues.

The number and size of the blood cells in a living creature depend on its need for oxygen. Worms have no blood cells. Cold-blooded am-

84

phibians have large and relatively few cells in their blood. Animals that are small, warm-blooded, and live in mountainous regions have the most blood cells.

The human bone marrow adapts itself to our needs for oxygen. At high altitudes, it produces more cells; at low altitudes, less. People living on a mountain top may have almost twice as many blood cells as people living along the seacoast!

The blood which flows through the arteries, capillaries, and veins of your body contains many different materials and cells. Each part of the blood has its own special work and importance.

WHY IS OUR BLOOD RED?

There is, first of all, the liquid part of the blood. This is called the plasma, and makes up a little more than half the blood. It is light yellow and a little thicker than water because many substances are dissolved in it.

What are some of these substances? — Proteins, antibodies that fight disease, fibrinogen that helps the blood to clot, carbohydrates, fats, salts, and so on, in addition to the blood cells.

The red cells (also called red blood corpuscles) give the blood its color. There are so many of them in the blood that it all looks red. There are about 35 trillion of these tiny, round, flat discs moving around in your body all at once! And they stay in the blood vessels at all times.

As the young red cell grows and takes on adult form in the marrow, it loses its nucleus and builds up more and more hemoglobin. Hemoglobin is the red pigment, or color. It contains iron combined with protein.

As the blood passes through the lungs, oxygen joins the hemoglobin of the red cells. The red cells carry the oxygen through the arteries and capillaries to all cells of the body. Carbon dioxide from the body cells is returned to the lungs through the veins in the same way, combined mainly with hemoglobin.

Red cells live only about four months and then are broken up, mostly in the spleen. New red cells are always being formed to replace the cells that are worn out and destroyed.

In addition to the red blood cells, there are also several kinds of white blood cells.

You can see that blood, so necessary for life, is not a simple thing. Many different substances have their special work and importance.

Although the red cells are by far more numerous in the blood and

WHAT DO WHITE BLOOD CELLS DO?

give blood its color, the white blood cells have a critical role, too. The white blood cells are called leucocytes.

The most common leucocytes are granular cells. These cells pass in and out of the blood to the spot where germs or injured tissue have collected. Some of these cells, called neutrophiles, take bacteria into themselves and destroy them. They also give off substances which digest and soften dead tissue and form pus.

Other white cells in the blood are called lymphocytes. The lymphocytes often increase in numbers in a part of the body where infection has continued for more than a short time. This is a part of the body's process for fighting infections, so you can see their job is quite important.

Still other white blood cells are the monocytes. These cells, together with other cells in the tissues, have the ability to take up pieces of dead material. They can also surround material such as dirt, and keep it from coming in contact with healthy tissue cells.

By the way, even though white blood cells are so necessary to the body, too many of them are not good either. When too many white blood cells are formed, and they do not grow into the healthy, active cells that are needed, the condition is called leukemia, or cancer of the blood.

So the blood is like a chemical formula in which there has to be just the right amount of each substance — red cells, white cells, proteins, salts, carbohydrates, fats, and so on.

There is no transportation system in any city that can compare in efficiency with the circulatory system of the body.

If you will imagine two systems of pipes, one large and one small,

HOW DO ARTERIES DIFFER FROM VEINS?

both meeting at a central pumping station, you'll have an idea of the circulatory system. The smaller system of pipes goes from the heart to the lungs and back. The larger one goes from the heart to the various other parts of the body.

These pipes are called arteries, veins, and capillaries. Arteries are

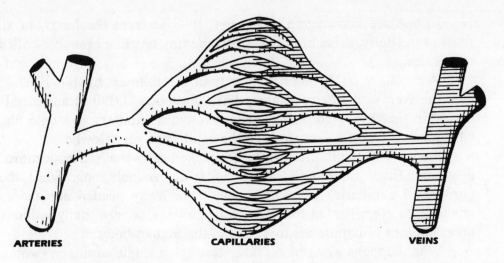

ARTERIES   **CAPILLARIES**   **VEINS**

blood vessels in which blood is going away from the heart. In veins, the blood is coming back to the heart. In general, arteries are carrying pure blood to various parts of the body; and the veins are bringing back blood loaded with waste products. The capillaries are tiny vessels for conducting blood from arteries to veins. The pumping station is the heart.

Arteries lie deep in the tissues, except at the wrist, over the instep, at the temple, and along the sides of the neck. At any of these places, the pulse can be felt, and a doctor can get an idea of the condition of the arteries.

The largest arteries have valves where they leave the heart. These vessels are made of many elastic muscles which can expand and contract. Arterial blood is bright red in color and moves through the arteries in spurts.

Veins lie closer to the surface of the skin; the blood in them is darker and flows more evenly; and they have valves at intervals all along their course.

There are all kinds of big roads and highways connecting big cities so that food and other necessary materials can reach them. But what about the small towns and little villages? They need food and supplies, too.

WHAT ARE CAPILLARIES? The little roads and byways that reach the small towns and villages are like the capillaries in the human body. As we know, blood is pumped out of the heart to all parts of the body and the big vessels through which this blood flows are known as the arteries. But far from the heart, in all parts of the body, these big vessels become tiny hairlike branches called capillaries.

A capillary is 50 times thinner than the thinnest human hair! In fact, the average diameter of a capillary is about 1/3,000 of an inch. It is so thin that blood corpuscles pass through a capillary in single file, which means blood passes through the capillaries very slowly.

About 700 capillaries could be packed into the space occupied by a pin. Each capillary is about 1/50 of an inch long. Since the purpose of capillaries is to bring and take away needed substances to and from every part of the body, you can imagine how many millions upon millions of capillaries there are in the human body.

What happens when blood flows through a single capillary (which takes about a second)? The blood does not leave the capillary. But the wall of the capillary is very thin; it consists of only a single layer of cells. Through this wall, the blood gives up its oxygen to the surrounding tissues. In return, it receives the carbon dioxide which the tissues around the capillary have given up.

At the same time, other substances which supply nourishment to the tissues pass from the blood, and waste products enter the capillary. Eventually, the blood and the materials it has picked up are returned to the heart by way of the veins.

The heart, as we have learned, is a pump that sends the blood circulating through our body. The pumping action takes place when the left ventricle of the heart contracts. This forces the blood out into the arteries,

WHAT IS BLOOD PRESSURE?

which expand to receive the oncoming blood.

But the arteries have a muscular lining which resists this pressure, and thus the blood is squeezed out of them into the smaller vessels of the body. Blood pressure is the amount of pressure on the blood as a result of the heart's pumping and the resistance of the arterial walls.

There are two kinds of pressure: maximum and minimum. The maximum pressure occurs when the left ventricle contracts; it is called the systolic pressure. The minimum pressure occurs just before the heartbeat which follows; it is called the diastolic pressure.

When your doctor measures your blood pressure, he uses an instrument which measures it in terms of a column of mercury, which rises and falls under the pressure. He reads it in millimeters rather than in inches. The average systolic pressure in a young man is about 120 millimeters (about 5 inches) of mercury. The diastolic pressure is about 80 millimeters of mercury. These figures are usually stated as 120/80, or 120 over 80.

When the blood pressure is in this range, it provides the body with a circulating supply of blood without unduly straining the walls of the blood vessels. But there are many variations from this range which may be quite normal.

With age, the blood pressure gradually rises until, at 60 years, it is about 140/87. There are many factors that affect the blood pressure. Overweight people often have a higher blood pressure than people of normal weight. Tension, exercise, and even posture may affect the blood pressure.

You may get a "shock" when you see your mark on a test, or you may say you're "shocked" if you see an accident. But medically speaking, this isn't shock. The word "shock" means a condition in which the

WHAT IS SHOCK?

essential activities of the body are affected. Usually, they are slowed up.

A person in a state of shock may have a sudden or gradual feeling of weakness or faintness. He may become very pale, and the skin may feel cold and clammy. Perspiration is increased, and the pupils of the eyes become enlarged.

Shock is also accompanied by changes in the mental state. It can begin with a feeling of restlessness, and it may develop to a state of unconsciousness.

All of these are symptoms of shock. They are produced because the volume of blood in effective circulation is lowered, along with the blood pressure. As in fainting, blood going to the brain may eventually lead to unconsciousness. This lack of blood in the capillaries also explains why the skin may feel cold.

Of course, if a person has been injured so that he is losing a great deal of blood, this in itself will produce a state of shock. But shock may also be caused by undergoing great stress, by strong emotion, by pain or sudden illness, or by some accident. The important thing is that for one reason or another, the blood doesn't circulate as it should, and as a result, the essential activities of the body are affected.

The best thing to do when a person is in a state of shock is to get a doctor. Do not move the patient, have him sit up, or use a pillow under his head. Lay the person on his back if he is unconscious, and keep him warm until help comes.

There are many things that people sometimes claim they "see" that really aren't there. They may have visions of "ghosts" or strange creatures. Sometimes little children claim they "saw" things that no one else

WHAT ARE HALLUCINATIONS?

did. Sometimes these are fantasies or daydreams; sometimes they are illusions.

There is a difference between an illusion and an hallucination. When a person has an illusion, there is something present that stimulates the eyes or senses. It can be verified, because other people see it, too. A mirage, for example, is a kind of illusion. But the main point is that something is there that causes the person to think he saw what he saw.

When a person has a hallucination, however, nothing is there! There is no outside stimulation to the eyes or the senses. The only stimulation comes from the person himself, from his own fantasy.

Hallucinations can be of various types, relating to the various senses. The most common have to do with hearing. A person imagines he hears voices, mutterings, laughter, cries, bells ringing, music playing or even shots ringing out! The second most common type of hallucination has to do with seeing. People imagine they see certain persons who aren't there, or they may see animals, objects, or whole scenes before them. Sometimes they "see" strange, horrible, and unearthly things that terrify them. And sometimes people even have hallucinations about tastes and smells, or things they feel on their skin!

There are many reasons why people have hallucinations. One of the most common is that a person is very troubled and disturbed by something. If someone has been aroused emotionally to a high pitch, perhaps very angry or frightened, he may have hallucinations.

In other words, persons who are hallucinating are usually in a state of great excitement, fear, ecstasy, or anticipation of something. Certain drugs also cause hallucinations. Cocaine, for example, gives the hallucination of insects crawling on the skin!

Every now and then, you read in the papers about a person who has "forgotten" who he is. He remembers nobody and nothing from his past, not even his name. We say this person is suffering from amnesia.

WHAT IS AMNESIA?

We all get emotionally upset from time to time. We feel hurt, angry, disappointed or frightened for one reason or another. When we feel such emotional pain, we want to do something about it. For example, a simple way of dealing with it is to cry, or blush, or break out in a cold sweat. In fact, these reactions happen without our control. They are considered normal reactions, since practically everyone has them.

But a person may react to emotional stress and pain in another way. Instead of facing the problems that caused him to be upset, he tries to act in such a way that he won't feel the anxiety. He "runs away" from it. He "protects" himself in this way from emotional pain.

One form of this reaction is amnesia. A person simply acts as if all those things which bothered and upset him so much didn't really happen to him but to someone else! He "forgets" his anxiety.

In forgetting this, he also forgets a great many other things that were linked to his anxiety — including who he was! He just can't remember anything about the past. But he may act quite normally about the present. He lives and works as another person, and may not attract any special attention.

Sometimes a person recovers from amnesia suddenly, of his own accord. In many cases, however, a person can be helped to recover by a psychiatrist. A curious thing is that people who recover from amnesia don't remember events which took place while they were suffering from amnesia.

Here's a sure way to win a bet! Challenge anybody you know to walk blindfolded straight down the sidewalk without going off the edge. He is sure to lose because he'll soon start walking in a circle!

WHY DO WE WALK IN CIRCLES WHEN WE ARE LOST?

People who have been lost in a fog or in a snowstorm, have often walked for hours imagining they were heading in a straight direction. After a while, they arrived right back where they started from.

Here's the reason why we can't walk in a straight line without our eyes to guide us. Our body is asymmetrical. This means there is not a perfect balance between our right side and our left side. The heart for instance is on the left side, the liver on the right. The skeleton of our body is asymmetrical too. The spine is not perfectly straight. Our thighs and our feet are different on each side of our body. All of this means that the structure of the muscles in our body is asymmetrical, or not perfectly balanced.

Since our muscles differ from right side to left side, this affects the way we walk, our gait. When we close our eyes, the control of our gait depends on the muscles and structure of our body, and one side forces us to turn in a certain direction. We end up walking in a circle.

By the way, this is true not only of the muscles in our legs, but in our arms, too. Tests were made in which blindfolded people tried to drive a car in a straight line. In about 20 seconds, every person in the test began to drive off the road! It's a good reason for keeping your eyes wide open whether you're walking or driving!

In ancient times, people didn't understand diseases and what caused them. So they often behaved very cruelly to victims of certain diseases. People who had epilepsy in the Middle Ages were thought of as lunatics,

WHAT IS EPILEPSY?

or bewitched! Yet did you know that many great people and many geniuses were epileptic? Among them were the Duke of Wellington, Richard Wagner, Vincent van Gogh, and Louis Hector Berlioz.

Epilepsy is a disease of the nervous system. People with epilepsy have sudden spells during which they have spasms called convulsions, after which they may become unconscious or fall into a coma.

Doctors cannot yet explain exactly what happens and what causes the convulsions. It seems that the normal patterns of activity of the brain become disrupted for a short time. The brain tissue in these people is sensitive to chemical changes, and when some sort of change takes place, the brain responds by sending out discharges that cause the convulsions.

A person has to be predisposed to epilepsy to have such reactions, because other people may undergo the same chemical changes and not have convulsions. There is a possibility that it is hereditary.

An epileptic attack may be caused by a head injury, a high fever, tumors, or scars in the brain substance, disturbances in the blood supply, and so on. Injury to the brain may result in epilepsy.

Epilepsy, however, has nothing to do with mental development. A person who has epilepsy should be considered a normal individual, not an invalid or some sort of outcast. Epileptics can lead normal lives — go to school, work, marry, and raise families.

Medical science has developed drugs to prevent attacks, and to control them when they do occur. These medicines are usually given to people over a period of many years, or even for a lifetime, so that they lead normal, happy lives.

Of all the things that distinguish man from the rest of the animal kingdom, the most important is his brain. Many of the lower animals have no brain at all, or a tiny one, or one that is poorly developed. For

WHAT IS THE BRAIN?

instance, an earthworm has a brain about the size of a pinhead, a rabbit has a thimble-sized brain. The brain of a man weighs, on the average, about 3 pounds.

By the way, the size of the brain is not the most important thing about it. An elephant has a bigger brain than man, but it is not as well developed.

The brain has three main divisions: the cerebrum, the cerebellum, and the medulla oblongata. The cerebrum is considered the most important part. It is from here that all our voluntary actions are controlled.

The cerebrum is also the biggest part of man's brain, filling most of the space in the upper and back part of the skull. The cerebrum is divided into two equal parts or hemispheres, and its surface is covered with wrinkles and folds. This surface is composed of gray matter, made up of cells. The higher the type of animal, the more numerous and deeper are the folds. Under this surface, called the cortex, there is white matter which is made up of nerve fibers. Through this part pass the messages to and from the cortex.

Certain sections of the cortex control certain body functions, so every part of the cortex is different. Science can point to certain parts as the controls over sight, or feeling, or hearing, or movement of certain muscles. That's why an injury to just one part of the brain (for instance, by a blood clot) can impair one's capacity to perform a certain function, such as speech.

The cerebellum is in the back of the skull, beneath the cerebrum. It controls the power of balancing and the co-ordination of the muscles. If it is injured, a man may not be able to walk in a straight line or stand erect.

The medulla oblongata is about the size of the end of the thumb and is found at the end of the spinal cord. It controls breathing, the beating of the heart, digestion, and many other activities that seem to go on by themselves. This is where the nerve fibers that go from the brain to the spinal cord cross. One side of the brain controls the other side of the body. The right half of the cerebrum, for example, controls the left leg, and so on.

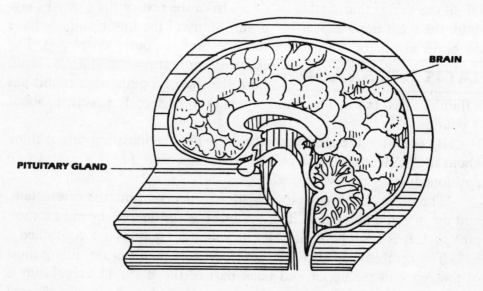

Can you recite the alphabet easily and quickly? Can you write your name easily? Can you play the scale on a musical instrument?

You would probably say that you memorized all this. But what

WHAT IS MEMORY?

you actually did was to learn them. And the way you learned them was by forming a habit! In other words, what was once quite difficult for you, such as reciting the alphabet or playing the scale, became easy and almost automatic when you formed a habit of doing it. So memory can be described as learning by means of forming habits.

A human being has a tremendous number of such habits that enable him to do most of the ordinary things in life, such as fastening a button or washing the hands. But suppose you read a book and someone asked you what the book was about, or to describe the plot. Surely, this cannot be called a habit.

But if you examine the situation carefully, you will see that something very much like habit does play a part. For example, in ordinary habits, you learn how to put certain elements together in the proper order. Now, when you give the plot of a book, or tell what it's about, you are doing the same kind of thing. In fact, some psychologists say that all learning (and this also means memory) is made up of a vast combination of simple habits.

But this doesn't mean that in learning and remembering you simply form habits by mechanically going through the motions of practice, or repeating them. There are several other things that enter into the situation and make it possible for you to learn and remember better.

One of these is the will to learn, or the motive or incentive. Another important thing is understanding what one is learning. For example, you will learn (or memorize) a poem more quickly when you understand it. And you will remember it longer, too.

Still another important help in learning and remembering is the association of new ideas with ideas you have already stored away in your memory.

Most of us think that every action we take is voluntary — that we sit down and stand up because we want to, or shake hands because we want to, and so on.

WHAT IS INSTINCT?

But the actions of people and all living things are really not so easily explained. For example, as you ride a bicycle, you may make dozens of motions without even thinking about them as you do them. These actions are the result of learning and experience.

Now, suppose you touch something hot and instantly draw your finger away. You didn't even think of taking your finger away — you just did it. This action is a reflex action.

Now we come to a third kind of action that takes place without thinking on your part. You are hungry. You don't always tell yourself, "I am hungry, I will look for food." You just go about getting food. This kind of action might be described as an instinct.

Whether or not human beings really have instincts (such as seeking food, caring for one's young, etc.) is something psychologists are still not agreed upon. But we know that other animals act by instinct. An instinct is an action that accomplishes a certain objective without thinking on the part of the doer.

For example, a bird building a nest gathers sticks, grass, fibers, or down. It then arranges them upon a branch or ledge in such a way that the nest has a certain height and stability, and is like the nest of other birds of the same species. The only thing that can explain such behavior is instinct.

An instinctive action is always carried on because there is some natural stimulation inside the creature (such as hunger, fear, the desire to mate). In fact, it is quite probable that the secretions of certain glands in the body cause the bird or animal to perform what we call an instinctive act. Seeking food, mating, maternal care, migration, and hibernation are all related to the actions of the glands in a bird.

Almost all living animals have some instinctive behavior to satisfy some vital need of the body.

When you go to the doctor, does he ask you to cross your legs and then hit your knee with a small rubber hammer?

What the doctor is testing is the reflex action. In this case, it is a

WHAT CAUSES A REFLEX?

special reflex called the patellar reflex, because the hammer struck a ligament called the patellar ligament.

What actually happens when the hammer strikes the ligament? A stimulus passes from a sensory cell in the ligament to the spinal cord. There it is transferred to a motor cell, and this sends an action current to the muscles of the leg. The leg twitches, just as if it were about to kick an enemy in self-defense.

This action is a reflex action. In other words, it is automatic. We have no control over it because it is not an action that is started in the brain. For instance, when you go to bed and close your eyes, you are performing a voluntary act. But if a speck of dust flies into your eye, you close it immediately whether you want to or not. This automatic movement is a reflex.

So we can define a reflex as an automatic response by the body to an external stimulus, without the influence of the will.

How does this happen?—The spinal cord is the transfer point for our reflexes. When sensory cells bring in the stimulus from the skin, they go to the spinal cord and are transferred there to motor cells. These motor cells send out currents to certain muscles and make them act. The nerve impulses do not pass through the brain.

More than 90 per cent of all the actions performed by man's nervous system are reflex actions!

In our bodies there are certain cells which make up connective tissue— tissue that joins the various parts of the body together. All the cells in connective tissue can contract, or tighten up. In some parts of the

HOW DO OUR MUSCLES WORK?

body, these cells can contract to a special degree, so they transform themselves into muscle cells.

At those points in the body where muscle cells are used frequently, they multiply and join together to form a single smooth muscle composed of many fibers. Smooth muscles are found in many parts of the body and help many organs to function. For instance, smooth muscles contract and dilate our eyes, regulate our breathing, make our intestines function.

The fiber of smooth muscles is strong, but it is slow. So whenever rapid motion is necessary, the body has developed the smooth muscles a step further. The fibers of the smooth muscles have developed into a higher form called striated muscle. All the muscles which make our limbs move are striated.

There are 639 muscles in the human body. The muscles are really the flesh of the body, just as the red meat bought at the butcher shop is really muscle. Muscles are all sizes and have many shapes. A medium-sized muscle contains about ten million muscle cells, and the whole body contains about six billion muscle cells!

Each of these six billion muscle cells is like a motor containing ten cylinders arranged in a row. The cylinders are tiny boxes that contain fluid. A muscle contracts when the brain sends a message to these tiny boxes. For a fraction of a second, the fluid in the tiny box congeals; then it becomes a fluid again. It is this action that causes the muscle to move.

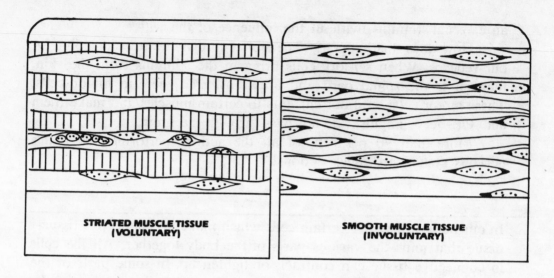

STRIATED MUSCLE TISSUE
(VOLUNTARY)

SMOOTH MUSCLE TISSUE
(INVOLUNTARY)

The only muscles in our bodies that we can move are the striated muscles. The smooth muscles (for instance, those that control digestion) act independently of our will. When a muscle is stimulated into action, it reacts quickly. It may contract in less than one tenth of a second. But before it has time to relax, another message comes along. It contracts again and again. All these contractions take place so quickly that they become fused into one action with the result that the muscle performs a smooth, continuous action!

The strength of normal, healthy human bones is amazing. The saying that our bones are "twice as strong as oak" is not far from wrong.

Bone needs to be strong because it forms the framework, or skeleton, that supports the whole body. Bones vary in shape and size according to the type of animal to which they belong. Fish and small birds have tiny bones. Elephants have bones that weigh several hundred pounds!

WHAT ARE OUR BONES MADE OF?

All bones have similar composition. Bone is a hard, grayish-white substance, of which about two thirds are inorganic, or mineral matter, especially phosphate of lime. This gives the bone hardness, but at the same time, it makes the bone more brittle.

The remaining third of the bone is organic, or animal matter. This gives the bones the toughness which helps them resist breakage. In certain types of bones, there is a fatty substance called marrow, which is organic matter with a very high food value.

There is also a small amount of water in bone, which seems to dry out as the body grows older. As this drying takes place and as the mineral matter in the bone increases, the bones become more breakable and slower to knit and heal.

When you break a bone in your arm, for example, it must be set. This means it must be fastened firmly in its natural place so that the ends cannot move. The bone must knit before you can use your arm again.

The knitting is done by tiny cells known as osteoblasts. They secrete a limey substance that makes the bones hard and firm again. These cells also help in the natural growth of bones. Other cells called osteoclasts tear down old tissue so that growth is possible. This double process of building up and tearing down is going on in the bones all the time.

The average body of a human being contains about three pounds of calcium. Most of this is found in the bones. Calcium is an essential part of the structure of the bone.

WHAT IS CALCIUM?

We might, in fact, compare the structure of a bone to reinforced concrete. The bone has certain fibers called collagen fibers which are like the flexible iron wires often embedded in concrete. Calcium forms the bed in which these bone fibers are fixed.

The calcium content of our bones changes as we grow older. During the first year, a child's bones have little calcium and great flexibility. A child can perform all kinds of contortions without breaking any bones. By the time a man is eighty, his bones may be 80 per cent calcium and break easily.

One of the reasons young children are urged to drink a great deal of milk is that milk is the ideal calcium containing food, and, of course, young bodies need plenty of calcium for their bones. One quart of cow's milk contains almost two grams of calcium. Cheese, buttermilk, and yogurt also supply great quantities of calcium.

In those parts of the country where calcium is hard to obtain, people have trouble with their teeth and often suffer from bone fractures. A frequent cause of calcium deficiency is the practice of making hard water soft by removing the calcium from it.

Hard water interferes with the lathering of soap. The calcium in hard water combines with acids and salts in the soap and produces compounds which don't dissolve.

The practice of removing calcium from hard water also has a bad effect on the foods cooked in the water. If the water has a low calcium content, foods cooked in it actually lose part of their own calcium to the water. But foods will gain in calcium content when cooked in hard water with a high calcium content.

Do you brush your teeth at least twice a day? If you do, and you brush hard, have you ever wondered why you don't wear your teeth down? The fact is that our teeth are pretty tough — about as hard as rocks.

WHAT ARE OUR TEETH MADE OF?

Every tooth is made up of the same two parts: a root, or roots, to anchor it in the jawbone, and a crown, the part that can be seen in the mouth.

Teeth are composed mostly of mineral salts, of which calcium and phosphorus are the most prominent. The enamel is hard and shiny, and covers the crown. The cementum is a bonelike material that covers the root. The dentine is an ivorylike material that forms the bulk or body of the tooth. And the dental pulp is in a hollow space called the pulp chamber inside the tooth. The dental pulp is made up of tissue that contains nerves, arteries, and veins. These enter the tooth through an opening at or near the root end.

As you've probably noticed when you look at your teeth in the mirror, they are different in size, and in shape. In a full set of teeth, there are four types, each having a special duty. The incisors, in the center of the mouth, cut or incise food. The cuspids, which tear food, are on either side of the incisors at the corners of the mouth. They have long, heavy roots and sharp, pointed crowns.

The bicuspids, just back of the cuspids, have two points, or cusps, and one or two roots. They tear and crush food. The molars, in the back of the mouth, have several cusps and two or three roots. They grind food.

When a scientist who has been digging for fossils or other remains of ancient life turns up with some teeth, he is very happy. Teeth are an important clue as to the kind of creature it was that lived there.

ARE OUR TEETH THE SAME AS ANIMAL TEETH?

For example, beasts of prey have tearing teeth, rodents have gnawing teeth, and cattle have grinding teeth. Every animal — whether horse, cow, mouse, cat, or dog — has teeth suitable for its way of life, its food, and even its general nature.

A beaver, for example, has great cutting teeth. The canine teeth of dogs and cats are sharp and long so that it is easy for them to seize and hold their prey. Their sharp back teeth cut up and break the flesh and bones.

A squirrel has teeth that can easily gnaw through the hard shell of a nut. Even fish have teeth that help them with their food. Some sharks have cutting teeth for eating fish, while other sharks have blunt teeth for crushing shellfish. The pike has teeth that lean backward as the prey is swallowed and then straighten up again. The teeth of snakes are set inward at an angle so that their prey cannot escape.

Man has what is known as a "collective" dentition, which means that he has many different kinds of teeth, one alongside another.

According to scientists, the structure of the human teeth is evidence that the human body is adapted to a mixed plant-and-animal diet.

Concentrate right now and imagine that you are about to eat a lemon. Think of yourself biting into this lemon. Do you feel the saliva beginning to flow?

WHAT IS SALIVA?

This is one of the interesting things about our salivary glands. They don't function mechanically, but are subject to the control of the brain. There are three pairs of salivary glands. One is in front of the ear, one under the tongue, and one under the lower jaw.

The salivary glands automatically adapt the amount and nature of the saliva to the immediate task. Animals that eat moist foods have little saliva. Fish have no salivary glands, but in grain-eating birds, they are very developed. When a cow receives fresh feed, its salivary glands secrete about fifty quarts. When it receives dry hay, the quantity of saliva rises to about 200 quarts. The largest human salivary gland

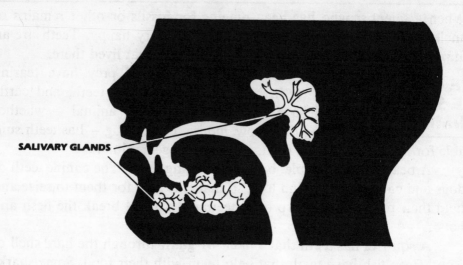

SALIVARY GLANDS

secretes about twenty-five thousand quarts of saliva in a lifetime!

Each of the salivary glands has its own special job. The largest one, the parotid gland in front of the ear, secretes large quantities of watery saliva. The chief purpose of this saliva is to dilute and to moisten the food well.

The glands near the lower jaw secrete a different kind of saliva; it makes the food "slippery."

Which of the salivary glands will produce the most saliva depends on the food we take in. If we bite into a juicy apple that doesn't have to be moistened, the lower glands will function. But if we eat a dry cracker, the parotid gland goes to work and produces large quantities of watery saliva.

Human saliva contains an enzyme known as amylase. This works on starch, splitting the molecules into dextrin and then into malt sugar.

The feeling of hunger is a message sent to your brain by your body. The message is that nutritive materials are missing from the blood. Let's see how this happens.

WHAT MAKES US FEEL HUNGRY?

Our bodies and those of all living things must maintain a state of metabolic equilibrium. This means there has to be a certain balance and control over our intake of fuel and its use. To regulate our body weight we have thirst, hunger, and appetite.

In the brain we have a hunger center. It acts like a brake on the activities of the stomach and intestines. When the blood has sufficient nutritive materials, the hunger center stops the activities of the stomach and intestines. But when there is a lack of nutrition, the intestines and stomach become active. That's why you can hear your stomach rumbling when you're hungry.

But hunger itself has nothing to do with an empty stomach. For example, a person who is feverish may have an empty stomach but not feel hungry. His body uses up its protein supplies and feeds itself from within.

When you feel hungry, your body is crying out for fuel—any kind of fuel. A really hungry person will eat any kind of food. It is your appetite that sees to it that you choose the mixed diet that your body requires. For example, when a man sits down to dinner, one bowl of soup may be all the soup he wants. Then he goes on to meat and vegetables. When he's had enough of these, he may go on to dessert, cake, coffee. But it would be pretty hard for him to eat this same quantity of food if it all consisted of potatoes!

How long a living creature can go without food depends on its metabolism. Warm-blooded animals have a more active metabolism, and so use up their store of fuel more rapidly. The smaller and more active the animal, the more rapidly it uses up its food supplies.

Taste depends on the impact of the atoms given off by a substance on certain specially sensitive organs in our bodies. If the atoms of a substance can't move about freely, we can't taste it. That's why we can only taste things that are in a state of solution.

HOW DO WE TASTE OUR FOOD?

Animals that live in water have taste buds all over their bodies. For instance, fish can taste with their tail fins! Animals that live on land have their taste buds concentrated in their mouths, and in man they exist only on the tongue.

If you examine your tongue in a mirror, you will see that it is covered with tiny, wartlike bumps, which are called papillae. The taste buds are situated in the walls of these papillae.

The number of taste buds found in animals depends on the needs of the particular species. For instance, a whale swallows whole schools of fish without chewing them; it has few taste buds, or none at all. A pig has 5,500 taste buds, a cow has 35,000, and an antelope, 50,000. Man is not by any means the most sensitive taster; he has only 3,000 taste buds!

The taste buds on the human tongue are distributed in different zones, and each zone is sensitive to a different kind of taste. The back of the tongue is more sensitive to bitter, the sides are sensitive to sour and salt, and the tip of the tongue picks up sweet tastes. In the center of the tongue, there is a zone without any taste buds, and it can taste nothing!

Smells are an important part of our tasting process. At least half of what we think of as taste is not taste at all, but really smell! This is true when we "taste" such things as coffee, tea, tobacco, wine, apples, oranges, and lemons. For instance, when we drink coffee, we first sense the warmth, then the bitterness that comes from the acid and the roasting, and then the sweetness, if it has been added. But not until the warm vapor released by the coffee hits our throat and nose and sends its messages to the brain, do we really "taste" the coffee! The proof is that if you close your nose with a clothespin, not only won't you be able to "taste" the coffee, but you'll find you can't tell the difference between two completely different things you are eating or drinking!

The food we take into our bodies supplies us with many important substances such as proteins, fats, carbohydrates, water, and mineral substances. But these alone are not enough. In order to maintain life

WHY DO WE NEED VITAMIN C?

we need still other substances known as vitamins.

Vitamins are substances formed by plants or animals. They must be supplied to the body in minute quantities so that vital processes can continue undisturbed. When there is a lack of vitamins in our body, diseases will occur. For instance, lack of vitamin A affects our vision; lack of vitamin B produces a disease called beriberi, and so on.

Long before man knew about vitamins, it had been observed that when people couldn't get certain types of foods, diseases would develop. Sailors, for instance, who went on long trips and couldn't get fresh vegetables would get a disease called scurvy. In the seventeenth century British sailors were given lemons and limes to prevent this disease.

And this, by the way, is why British sailors got the nickname, "limeys!"

The vitamin that prevents scurvy is vitamin C. It is also called ascorbic acid. Some vitamins are found in the embryos of plants. For example, vitamin B₁ is found in the germ of the wheat. Vitamin C is found in the fresh green leaves, the roots, the stems, the buds and the pods of fully developed plants.

A curious thing about vitamin C is that almost all mammals produce their own vitamin C in the liver and so never suffer from a lack of it. But man, the apes, and guinea pigs are the only mammals which cannot produce their own vitamin C in the liver!

What happens when there is a lack of this vitamin in the body? The blood vessels become fragile and bleed easily. Black-and-blue marks appear on the skin and near the eyes. The gums bleed easily. Our hormones and enzymes don't function well, our resistance to infection by bacteria is lowered, and we may develop inflammations in the throat.

Wouldn't it be wonderful if people who lost an arm or a leg or even a finger in an accident could simply grow another one in its place? Human beings can't do this, but there are living creatures who can! The process

WHAT IS REGENERATION?

by which such organisms can replace structures or organs is called regeneration.

Regeneration varies quite a bit among these creatures. For example, in certain types of worms and in starfish, a tiny part of the body can restore the whole organism. If only a small piece is left, a whole new body will grow!

At the other extreme, we have a kind of regeneration that takes place in our own bodies. The top layer of our skin is constantly being worn off in small bits and replaced by other cells. Our hair and nails are replaced all the time. Even our second set of teeth is a kind of regeneration. And, of course, there is the shedding of feathers and fur and scales among animals, all of which are replaced by a process of regeneration.

The more complicated the organism (and man is a very complicated organism), the less it is able to regenerate. Man, and all mammals, cannot restore an entire organ. But creatures such as salamanders and insects can regenerate a whole limb. What we can regenerate really amounts to repairing damages such as bone fractures, skin and muscle injuries, and some kinds of nerves.

Regeneration takes place in two ways. In one case, new tissue grows from the surface of the wound. In the other, the remaining parts are transformed and reorganized, but new material does not grow.

When new material is grown (such as a limb), it takes place in this way. A regeneration "bud" is formed at the surface of the wound. It is usually cone-shaped and contains an embryonic type of cell, or cells, of the type that were present at the birth of the creature. These cells develop into specialized cells to form the new organ, and as they grow, a new organ is gradually formed!

There are many different kinds of baldness, but in most cases, it's a condition over which a man has absolutely no control and for which there simply is no cure.

WHAT CAUSES BALDNESS?

People say all kinds of things about baldness: It means a man is getting old; or it means he's unusually intelligent; or he's unusually dull. But all baldness really means is that a man is losing his hair!

The kind of baldness we see most often is called pattern baldness. The hair begins to go at the temples, or there's a bald spot at the top of the head, or the baldness appears in some other pattern. This is the most difficult type of baldness to do anything about because it's inherited! The inheritance of pattern baldness is influenced by sex. It appears more in men than in women. Very often the woman carries the gene for this

AGE 19   AGE 32   AGE 42   AGE 50

baldness and passes it on to her children. Once this type of baldness appears, about the best thing a man can do is get used to it!

Premature baldness may appear in men as early as the age of twenty-five or even earlier. One cause of this kind of baldness may be a failure to take proper care of the scalp, keep it clean, etc. Sometimes an imbalance of the sex hormones may bring on premature baldness. If proper scalp care is started at once, it may slow up the progress of this type of baldness.

Symptomatic baldness sometimes appears as a sign of infections or other conditions. When health is restored, the hair may grow back again in such cases. Sudden loss of hair can result from typhoid fever, scarlet fever, pneumonia, influenza, and other serious infections.

When there is a gradual loss or thinning of hair, it may sometimes be due to poor nutrition or a disturbance in the glands, especially the pituitary and thyroid glands. And, of course, baldness may come from disorders in the scalp itself, such as scalp injuries or disease.

Just as feathers are characteristic of birds, so hair is characteristic of mammals. Why do mammals have hair?— There is a variety of reasons. Let's consider some of them.

WHY DON'T WOMEN HAVE BEARDS?

The chief value of hair is that it conserves the heat of the body. In the tropics, it may serve an opposite function. Certain tropical animals are protected from direct sunlight by their hair.

Very long hair on certain parts of the body usually serves some special purpose. For instance, a mane may protect an animal's neck from the teeth of its enemies. Tails may act as flyswatters. Crests may attract the opposite sex. In the case of the porcupine, its stiff quills formed of bunched-up hair help it to attack its enemies. Hair may also serve as organs of touch. The whiskers of cats have special nerves that respond quickly to touch.

So you see that hair can serve a different purpose with different mammals. How about human beings? We know that beautiful hair in a woman can be very attractive to men. But we must assume that hair on human beings formerly played a more practical role than it does now.

When an infant is born, he is covered with a fine down. This is soon replaced by the delicate hair which we notice in all children. Then

107

comes the age of puberty, and this coat of hair is transformed into the final coat of hair which the person will have as an adult.

The development of this adult hair coat is regulated by the sex glands. The male sex hormone works in such a way that the beard and the body hair are developed, while the growth of the hair on the head is inhibited, or slowed down in development.

The action of the female sex hormone is exactly the opposite! The growth of the hair on the head is developed, while the growth of the beard and body hair is inhibited. So women don't have beards because various glands and hormones in their bodies deliberately act to prevent this growth.

To explain why this is so, and why men's glands and hormones act to promote growth of beards, we probably have to go back to the early history of man. At one time, the function of the beard was probably to make it easy to tell men and women apart at a distance. It also probably served to give the male an appearance of power and dignity, and so make him more attractive to the female. Nature was helping man to attract the opposite sex, just as she does with other creatures.

For men who are becoming a little bald, hair doesn't grow fast enough! But in the case of a young boy, the hair seems to grow too fast!

HOW FAST DOES HAIR GROW?

The rate at which hair grows has actually been measured and found to be about half an inch a month. The hair doesn't grow at the same rate throughout the day but seems to follow a kind of rhythm.

At night, the hair grows slowly, but as day begins, this is speeded up. Between 10 and 11 AM, the speed of growth is at its greatest. Then the hair grows slowly again. It picks up speed between 4 and 6 PM, and then the growing slows up again. Of course, these variations in the speed of growth are so tiny that you cannot possibly notice them. So don't expect to stand in front of the mirror at 10 AM and be able to watch your hair sprouting up!

If all the hair that grows on the body were to grow in a sort of hair cable, instead of as individual hairs, you would get some idea of the total amount of hair the body produces. This hair cable would grow at the rate of 1.2 inches per minute, and by the end of the year, the tip would be 37 miles away!

Not all people have the same amount of hair. Blond people have finer hair and more hair than dark persons. Red-haired people have the coarsest and the fewest hairs.

Most of us have a vague idea that somewhere inside of us there are coils and coils of intestines, amazing passageways through which food passes in the process of digestion. But few people have a clear under-

HOW LONG ARE OUR INTESTINES?

standing of just how they work.

The length of the large intestine in animals depends on the kind of food they eat. Meat-eating animals have shorter intestines because there is less digestive work to do. The food they live on has already done part of the job of digestion. People who live on vegetables are supposed to have longer intestines than meat-eating people.

The human intestines are 10 feet long. But when a person dies, the intestines lose their elasticity and stretch to about 28 feet.

Most of the wall of the intestines consists of muscle fibres, so that the intestines can work on the food that goes through them. The intestines mix the food with certain secretions and then pass it along. In order to do this, the small intestine consists of countless loops. Each loop holds a bit of food and works on it, churning it and digesting it for about 30 minutes. Then it passes the food on to the next loop.

To help in this process of digestion, the wall of the small intestine contains about 20,000,000 small glands. These glands send about 5 to 10 quarts of digestive juice into the intestine! This soaks and softens the food so that by the time it goes to the large intestine it's in a semi-liquid state.

If you were to look at the wall of the intestine with a magnifying lens, you would see that it isn't smooth, but resembles velvet. It is covered with millions of tiny tentacle-like villi. The villi tell the glands when to pour out the digestive juice, and also help in the process of digestion themselves.

Food that cannot be digested by juices is digested in the large intestine by bacteria that live there. This is known as putrefaction. Billions of bacteria break down the coarser parts of the food we eat, such as the skins of fruit, and extract valuable materials the body needs.

This is only a rough idea of the way our intestines work. They are among the most amazing organs in our bodies, beautifully organized to do hundreds of things to the food we take in to keep alive.

This certainly isn't a pleasant subject, but many people suffer from tapeworm and so there is great curiosity about it. A kind of flatworm, the tapeworm is an intestinal parasite.

WHAT IS A TAPEWORM?

This means that it lives in the digestive tract of another animal, called the host, and is fed by food which the host has partly digested. The host of the tapeworm is nearly always a backboned animal such as a fish, a dog, or a man. The tapeworm has sucking discs on its head, by means of which it attaches itself to the inside of the intestines. It has no sense organs such as eyes or ears.

The muscles of a tapeworm are almost useless, and its nervous system is primitive. It has no mouth or digestive tract; it absorbs dissolved food through the walls of its body.

There are many species of tapeworms, ranging in length from about 1/25 of an inch to 30 feet! They are of many shapes. They may be unsegmented (undivided), or composed of a chain of segment-like parts. These grow one after the other, always forming behind the head. Each adult is both male and female.

How can a human being get a tapeworm inside his digestive tract? It could happen in the following way: The fertilized eggs of a tapeworm are passed out by the worm. Then a hog eats the eggs. Then the larvae hatch in the hog's intestine.

Inside the hog, these small larvae burrow through the wall of the intestine and go to other parts of the hog's body. When they settle, they form a hard cyst.

Now suppose a human being eats pork that has been improperly cooked. (Proper cooking would kill the larvae in the cyst.) The human digestive juices free the larvae. They then attach themselves to the human intestines and there develop into adults—and a human being finds he has a tapeworm!

The harm a tapeworm does is taking part of the nourishment of the host's food and secreting poisonous substances. Tapeworms do not cause death to man except in rare cases. There are now drugs which can remove a tapeworm from the intestines.

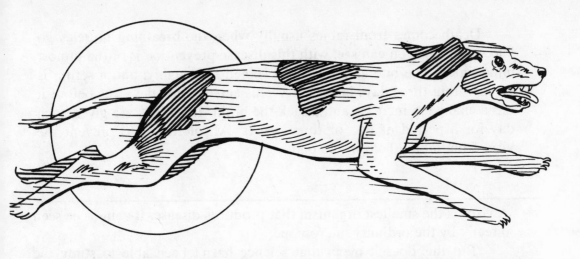

Rabies is one of the oldest diseases known to man. Once the disease appears in man or animals, death is almost certain. There is no cure for it. Just what is this terrible disease?

WHAT IS RABIES?

Rabies is a disease that infects the brain and spinal cord, which is why it is so harmful to the life of the body. The infection is caused by a virus, which means a germ too small to be seen with the ordinary microscope.

The rabies virus can infect all warm-blooded animals, but man receives it most often when bitten by a dog infected with the virus. This is why when a human being is bitten by a dog, an effort is always made to find the dog and examine it to see if it might have rabies. It just doesn't pay to take chances!

It isn't too easy to tell when a dog has been infected with rabies because it takes such a long time for the disease to show up—usually four to six weeks. At first the dog is quiet, has a fever, and isn't interested in food. Then it becomes excited. Saliva froths from the mouth. It growls and barks, and is likely to bite. After these symptoms appear, it's pretty hopeless. The dog will die in about three to five days.

In human beings, the disease begins much as it does in the dog. A man who is infected by rabies will be quiet at first. He will have fever and feel strange. Soon he feels his muscles draw strongly together. When he tries to drink, the muscles of his mouth and throat tighten, as if he were in a spasm. The muscle spasms are due to changes in the nervous system. But it was believed that they were due to an actual fear of the water, so rabies was given another name—"hydrophobia." This means "fear of water," and is not a true description of the disease.

Death comes from rabies usually when the breathing muscles go into spasm. As you can see, with this disease prevention is of the utmost importance. The bite area must be cleaned thoroughly, and a serum is given within three days of the bite. This acts against the virus before it has a chance to increase and attack the brain. Injections are given each day for a period of two or three weeks. All of this is to prevent the virus from taking hold in the body.

A virus is the smallest organism that produces disease. It cannot be seen directly by the ordinary microscope.

But this doesn't mean that science hasn't been able to study the

CAN A VIRUS BE SEEN?

structure of a virus. Today there are ultramicroscopes that enable these tiny organisms to become visible. And science is able to know quite a bit about the sizes and shapes of various types of viruses by means of the electron microscope.

The electron microscope uses beams of electrons instead of rays of light. The electrons pass through the specimen being observed and strike a photographic plate on which a picture is obtained. In this way, it is possible to magnify an object about 100,000 times.

By using the electron microscope, it has been shown that viruses range in size from about 300 millimicrons to 10 millimicrons. What is a millimicron? It is one thousandth of a micron. And a micron is about one twenty-five thousandth of an inch.

Nobody is quite sure yet exactly what viruses are. Some scientists think they are closely related to bacteria. Other investigators believe they are like elementary particles, similar to "genes." Still others believe viruses are possibly midway between living and nonliving matter.

As far as we know, viruses can grow and reproduce only within living tissue. This means it's impossible to cultivate them away from living tissue, and it makes it difficult to study their growth habits. That's why they are classified by their ability to infect living cells and by the reactions they produce in the body of animals or humans.

Does the virus produce a poison or toxin? It is now believed that they do produce toxins, but the toxin and the virus particle cannot be separated. And we still don't know how these toxins produce disease if they do!

Bacteria are the most widespread creatures in the world. Everything we touch, every breath of air contains millions of them. About 80 per cent of all bacteria are harmless. A small percentage is actually useful to

WHAT IS AN ANTIBODY?

us, and a small group of them are harmful to human beings.

Since man is constantly taking in bacteria of all kinds, it is obvious that our body and these bacteria form a kind of "working" relationship. Our body supports colonies of bacteria and in turn these bacteria may perform useful functions, such as helping to decompose food.

But what about harmful bacteria which enter our body? For example, the bacteria that cause diphtheria produce a powerful poison called "diphtheria toxin," which spreads through the blood system. Other bacteria, not so deadly, also produce poisons in our blood.

When this happens, our body produces substances to fight these poisons or toxins. These substances are called antibodies. Certain specific antibodies which are produced to fight bacterial toxins are known as antitoxins.

They have the power to nullify any harmful effect produced by the toxin by combining with it. Each antibody is specific for the substance or toxin which causes it to be produced. It's as if the body had a big police force. As soon as a dangerous stranger enters, a policeman meets him and goes along with him to be sure he'll do no harm.

But the body doesn't produce enough antibodies to handle each kind of harmful bacteria that enters our body. Doctors then inject serum containing antitoxin to combat many diseases.

All around us there are invisible forms of life which we call germs. They are in the air, in the soil, in the water we drink and the food we eat. Many of them are harmless or even beneficial to man, but others may

WHAT IS IMMUNITY?

cause diseases.

The human body has many natural weapons to fight off the attack of the harmful germs. For instance, the digestive juices and the blood itself kill off many kinds of germs. But certain ones enter the body and start an infection. Then the anti-germ "soldiers" in the body spring into action. These are the white corpuscles in the blood. They can pass right through the thin walls of blood vessels and they can wander all over the body. The white blood corpuscles gather at the point of attack and destroy the germs by feeding on them.

But disease isn't always caused by a direct attack of germs. Germs throw off a chemical substance called a "toxin" which acts as a poison in the body. Once again, the body has a built-in defense. The toxin causes certain cells in the body to go to work to produce a substance that destroys the toxin. This is called an "antitoxin." If the antitoxin is produced quickly enough and in enough quantity, the germ poison is neutralized. The body gets well.

This antitoxin is always a very special one that works only against the toxin for which it was produced. It remains in the blood for some time after the toxin has disappeared. Now suppose the same germ attacks the body and produces new toxin. Instead of becoming sick, we show no symptoms of the disease at all! The reason is that our body already has a resistance to the disease; it has the antitoxin all ready. We call this condition "acquired" immunity. It is "acquired" because our resistance came after the original attack of the germs.

Now let us suppose there is an attack of germs upon the body, spreading toxins through our system, and yet we don't get that specific disease. This means our blood had enough antitoxin in it to begin with to prevent the specific poison from doing any harm. We call this a "natural" immunity. It is a quality of our blood that we inherited.

If we introduce a little toxin in our blood so it can produce antitoxin to prevent disease, we call it artificial immunity. This is exactly what happens when we are vaccinated against diphtheria and typhoid.

The next time you step out of the bath tub or shower, notice the tracks made by your wet feet. If the tracks are kidney-shaped, your foot is normal. If the prints your feet make have the shape of a sole, because

WHAT CAUSES FLAT FEET?

the entire sole touches the floor, you have flat feet.

The foot is a tripod, because it stands on three points. One is the heel in back. The other two are the two supporting points in the ball of the foot. Over these three points the foot forms an arch. This arch is not firm, but is elastic and springy. This is due to the arrangement of the bones, cartilage, ligaments, tendons, and muscles of the foot.

Actually, from an "engineering" point of view, a springy arch is the best type of construction for a structure that has to support weight. The space beneath the arch in the foot is filled with fat. Through this fat go the blood-vessels, nerves, and tendons of the toes, without being squeezed during walking.

When man went about barefoot outdoors, he probably never had any trouble with his feet. The reason is that the irregular and "springy" nature of the earth forces the foot to take a new position with every step. In this way, the entire foot, including the delicate muscles and ligaments of the arch, are always active. This gives all parts of the foot plenty of exercise.

When we walk on smooth city streets and hard floors, only a few points of the foot are constantly stimulated. So the foot adapts itself in a special way to this uniform stimulation. It actually remains in a state known as "spastic tension." This spastic state of the foot disurbs the process whereby all parts of the foot are fed and exercised as they should be. Certain tissues, where the blood circulates poorly, become tired, anemic, and weak. Then the arch of the foot becomes unable to bear the weight of the body and it drops down. The result is flat feet!

Of course, some cases of flat feet are due to the fact that certain people are born with naturally weak tissues. They are just born with weak arches.

When we drive an automobile in bad weather, it is very important to have the windshield wiper working efficiently. Yet the best windshield wiper ever made for any automobile can't compare to the "windshield wiper" nature has given us for our eyes!

WHY DO WE BLINK OUR EYES?

The lids of our eyes, which move up and down when we blink, are our built-in windshield wipers. The lids are made up of folds of skin, and they can be raised and lowered by certain muscles. But they move so rapidly that they don't disturb our vision in any way.

A curious thing about our lids is that they work automatically, just as windshield wipers do on an automobile when they're turned on. We blink our eyes every six seconds! This means that in the course of a lifetime, we pull them back and forth about a quarter of a billion times!

Why is blinking important to us? How does it protect our eyes? One reason has to do with our eyelashes. These are the short curved hairs which are attached to each lid. Their job is to catch dust which might go into our eyes. When you walk through rain or a sandstorm, the lids automatically drop down and the eyelashes keep out foreign matter. The eyebrows, by the way, carry off rain or perspiration to a side, so that the drops won't run into the eyes.

But the chief benefit of blinking is that this provides automatic lubrication and irrigation of the eyes. Along the edge of each lid there are twenty or thirty tiny sebaceous glands. These glands have their opening between the lashes. Every time our lids close, these glands go to work and a secretion comes out. This secretion lubricates the edge of the eye lid and the lashes, so that they won't become dry.

Here is how blinking provides "irrigation" for the eye. In each eye we have a tear gland, where the liquid that makes tears is stored. Every time we blink, the eyelid applies suction to the opening of the tear gland and takes out some of the fluid. This prevents the eye from drying out. We might say that we "cry" every time we blink our eyes!

You know what a "cataract" is in nature. It's a great waterfall or down-pouring of water. Now why should a certain kind of eye trouble also be called a "cataract?"

WHAT IS A CATARACT OF THE EYE?

This is because in ancient times it was believed that this particular eye trouble was caused by an opaque film that came down like a cataract over the lens of the eye. A cataract of the eye is simply a cloudy or opaque discoloration within the lens of the eye. It may or may not interfere with vision. In fact, many people may have cataracts without knowing it.

The way people find out they have cataracts is when parts of the field of vision become blurred or cloudy. Another sign is when such a person can see better in the twilight than when the light is good. When there is less light the pupil is larger and this enables more light to enter the eye.

A cataract causes the pupil of the eye to appear gray or white instead of black. Among old people with cataracts, the pupils may become very small or contracted. When a person has total cataract, the entire lens of the eye becomes milky.

A cataract is generally regarded as a disease of old age. But a baby may have a cataract at birth, or in early childhood. Sometimes people get a cataract of the eye as a result of injury or from circulatory diseases.

When children have cataracts, it is possible to restore useful vision to the eyes by means of a surgical operation without removing the lenses of the eye. But usually when a cataract begins to impair the vision so that a person can't carry on his normal activities, an operation is necessary that will remove the lenses. This is done on one eye at a time to avoid a long period of total blindness.

A great many people who must have such an operation naturally worry about it quite a bit. But the fact is that a good eye surgeon can perform such an operation with very little risk of failure. After about six weeks, the eyes are fitted with glasses which enable the patient to see almost as well as he did with the lenses of his eyes.

Sleeping sickness is a very serious disease that attacks men and animals in Africa.

It is an infection caused by parasites called "trypanosomes." These

WHAT IS SLEEPING SICKNESS?

parasites, or germs, are carried by the tsetse fly which is common in many parts of central Africa.

The tsetse fly may pick up the parasites when it bites a sick man or animal. The trypanosomes enter the fly's stomach and begin to multiply.

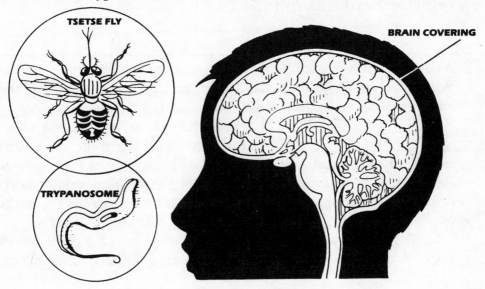

TSETSE FLY

TRYPANOSOME

BRAIN COVERING

They then pass through the salivary glands which supply juice to the fly's mouth. Here they develop into forms which can infect man.

When the fly bites a man, the parasites are injected beneath the skin. A tiny sore spot appears. During the next three weeks trypanosomes begin to circulate in the blood. About this time the infected man begins to have fever that comes and goes. Often, the skin breaks out in a rash. The brain becomes slightly swollen. In some parts of Africa the infection sometimes stops here and the sick man usually recovers.

But in Rhodesia and Nyasaland, the disease takes a more serious form. Within a year, the patient begins to show signs that his brain has become affected. He develops severe headaches. He becomes excited very easily. He begins to act in an uncontrollable way.

Then comes the next stage. He becomes very quiet. And finally, he goes to sleep—and stays asleep. He is in a coma, which means he is unconscious. He still has fever. Finally, he becomes paralyzed, his body wastes away, and he dies.

The reason the person becomes unconscious is that an infection takes place in a very important part of the body—the brain and meninges, which is the covering of the brain. There are many things that may cause an infection, or inflammation, of the brain. Such a condition is called "encephalitis." African sleeping sickness is really a severe form of encephalitis.

By the way, the tsetse fly does not pass on the germ of this disease to its offspring. So sleeping sickness would die out—if there were no sick animals or men for the fly to bite!

Asthma is not a disease itself, but a symptom of some other condition. When a person has asthma, he finds it hard to breathe because there is an obstruction to the flow of air into and out of the lungs.

WHAT IS ASTHMA?

This barrier or obstruction may be caused by a swelling of the mucous membranes, or by a constriction of the tubes leading from the windpipe to the lungs. When a person has an attack of asthma, he develops shortness or breath, wheezing, and coughing. The attack may come on gradually or develop suddenly.

The only way to get rid of asthma is to find out the cause and eliminate it. The cause may be an allergy, an emotional disturbance, or atmospheric conditions. If a person develops asthma before he is 30 years old, it is usually the result of an allergy. He may be sensitive to pollens, dust, animals, or certain foods or medicines.

There are many dusts and pollens which cause asthma. Children, especially, tend to develop asthma from food allergies which may be caused by eggs, milk, or wheat products.

Doctors have also observed that an attack of asthma may be caused by emotional disturbance. For example, if a person has family troubles or financial worries asthma may develop. In many cases the emotional disturbance consists of a feeling of being unwanted or unloved. This produces a state which sets off a chain reaction ending in an attack of asthma.

This is why in cases of asthma the diagnosis by the physician is very important. He will take a complete and careful medical history of the patient. He will ask all kinds of questions about the patient's eating habits, health habits, and environment. If there has been even the slightest change in the person's routine, he will investigate to see if it has anything to do with the attack of asthma. It may have come after a visit to relatives who keep certain animals, or a visit to the beach, or after eating certain new foods. People who have asthma are often put on special diets by the doctor.

Every now and then you meet somebody whose nose seems all stuffed up, or he complains of pains in the eyes and cheeks, and headaches. When you ask him if he has a cold, he may answer: "No, I have sinus trouble."

WHAT ARE THE SINUSES?

What is a sinus, and why do people get "sinus trouble?" Strictly speaking, a sinus is a space filled with blood or with air. But for most people, the expression "sinus trouble" means an infection of one of the cavities connected with the nose.

There are eight or more of these small cavities in the bones of the forehead and face. There are two sinuses in the frontal bones in the forehead. The largest sinuses are in the cheek bones. And there are smaller ones that open into the back and sides of the nose.

All these cavities are lined with mucuous membranes. These membranes are continuations of those in the nose, and the secretions from the sinuses drain through the nose. There are many theories about why we have these sinuses. It may be that they help to warm the nasal passages and to keep them moist. Or, they may give more resonance to the voice, or play some part in the sense of smell. It may be that we have them simply to provide vacant spaces in the skull so it won't be so heavy!

Sinuses may become infected after a severe cold, or influenza, or some other infectious disease. When sinuses are infected, we feel pain in the face, in the forehead, or behind the eyes, which usually comes on about the same time every day. There is sometimes a discharge from the nose.

The pain is caused by the discharge which collects in the sinus and cannot get out because the mucuous membrane which is connected with the nose is swollen. Sometimes the sinus in the cheek bone, called the "antrum," is infected as the result of a dental disease.

An operation for sinus trouble is rarely required. When it is done, the purpose is to enlarge the opening into the nose so that better drainage will take place. The best thing to do about sinus trouble is to prevent it. Great care should be taken to avoid colds. A doctor should be allowed to treat any obstruction in the nose during the early stages, and the dentist should have a chance to treat any dental disease before it becomes serious. Also, it is probably a good idea not to live in hot stuffy rooms, which may help bring on sinus trouble.

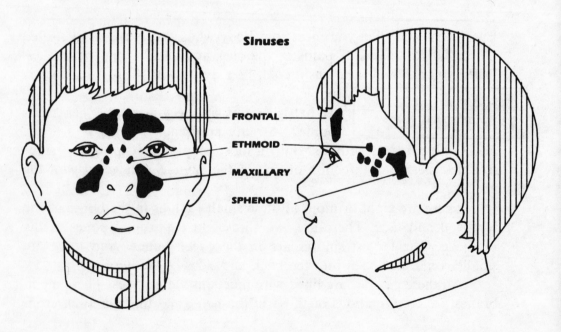

Sinuses

FRONTAL

ETHMOID

MAXILLARY

SPHENOID

120

During the "hay fever season," newspapers in many cities publish the day's pollen count. What is pollen, what does it have to do with hay fever, and what is a pollen count?

WHAT IS A POLLEN COUNT?

A person is said to have hay fever when he is sensitive to pollen and some other substances that are present in the air. Pollen is the reproductive element of plants and is contained in the flowers of most plants. Usually, it occurs as a fine dust or grains.

While insects spread pollen, it is the wind that spreads most of the pollen that causes hay fever. There are three chief groups of plants whose pollen causes hay fever, and each of these groups has a different season. For example, trees produce the pollen that causes hay fever during April and May, various grasses are responsible for hay fever that comes from May to July, and weeds produce the pollen that causes hay fever from August to October.

Since some weeds can produce more than 100,000 pollen grains from a single plant, you can see that at certain times there can be quite a bit of pollen in the air. Naturally, the more pollen there is about, the more the hay fever victims suffer.

This is why a pollen count is taken. People who must leave the area during the heavy pollen season know when to come back. The way a pollen count is taken is quite simple. A glass slide, one side of which is coated with oil, is placed in a horizontal position in the atmosphere to be tested. The slide is usually left for 24 hours. Then the pollen grains collected on it are counted with the aid of a microscope.

Wind and weather have a great deal to do with the amount of pollen in the air. Heavy rains during the summer months cause plants to flourish and produce large quantities of pollen. If the summer months are dry, much smaller amounts of pollen will be produced. Sunshine helps the pollen mature, while damp weather retards it. If it rains in the early part of the day, the spreading of pollen will be held down somewhat.

The reason we call it "hay fever," by the way, is that the symptoms of the disease appeared during the haying season in England. A doctor in 1812 wrote a report on it and called it "hay fever," and the name has remained.

Probably the most complex and difficult musical instrument that can be imagined is the apparatus in human beings that produces speech! In order for sounds and letters to be formed, this entire apparatus must be used. This includes the abdomen, chest, larynx, mouth, nose, diaphragm, various muscles, tongue, palate, lips, and teeth!

WHY DO PEOPLE STAMMER?

The most important ones used in making spoken sounds are the muscles of the mouth, the palate, lips, and tongue. The only reason we can "play" this instrument so well, is that we learned how to do it when we were most adaptable during early childhood, and because we have practiced it ever since!

Obviously, if we can't play this instrument (the vocal apparatus) with perfect coordination, then something happens to our speech. It comes out wrong and we stammer.

Stammering, or stuttering, occurs when there is a spasm in one or more of the organs that are involved in producing speech. Our production of words is suddenly checked; there is a pause, and this is often followed by a repetition in quick succession of the sound at which we stopped originally.

There are many grades of stammering. It can range from a slight inability to pronounce certain letters or syllables easily, to a condition in which muscles of the tongue, throat, and face are caught in a spasm.

Stammering rarely shows itself before the age of four or five. A child may begin to stammer because there is actually something wrong with one of the organs used in producing sounds. Very often, an emotional disturbance will cause stammering.

Usually, when a person stammers, it is the "explosive" consonants that give the most trouble . . . "b, p, d, t, k," and the hard "g." An explosive consonant is produced by checking the air on its way out, pressing the lips together, then suddenly stopping the interruption of the air by opening the lips. Try to see how you make the "b" sound. It's explosive!

Stuttering may often be corrected if a person gets instruction in reading and speaking slowly and deliberately, carefully pronouncing each syllable. Of course, if an emotional disturbance is the cause for stammering, special treatment is necessary.

Nobody ever needs an antidote unless he has been poisoned. An antidote by itself has no meaning. It is a substance which prevents the action of a poison. And a poison is any substance which produces harmful or deadly effects on living tissue.

WHAT IS AN ANTIDOTE?

There are basically four kinds of poisons, divided according to the way they affect the body. Corrosive poisons (like strong acids) destroy tissues locally. Irritant poisons produce congestion of the organ with which they come in contact. The next kind of poison, neurotoxins, affect the nerves within the cell. And finally, the hemotoxins combine with the blood and prevent oxygen from forming hemoglobin. Carbon monoxide (such as comes from the exhaust of an automobile) is a hemotoxin. It causes death because the blood is deprived of oxygen that nourishes the tissues and brain.

In treating cases of poisoning, three things are usually done immediately. The first is to dilute the poison. This is done by having the patient drink as much water as possible. The next step is to empty the stomach, and this is done by inducing vomiting. Then a specific antidote is given against the particular poison.

Antidotes act in several different ways in preventing the action of a poison. One way is by combining chemically with the poisonous substance, thus making it harmless. For example, soda combines with an acid, vinegar combines with lye.

An antidote may also act physically by coating the mucous membranes with a protective layer. Olive oil and milk act as antidotes in this way. A third way antidotes may work is by absorbing the poisonous substances on the surface of finely divided particles. Charcoal acts in this way. Some antidotes actually produce the opposite effect from the original poison in the body, and so they counteract the action of the poison. Of course, one of the chief things a doctor tries to do in a case of poisoning is to eliminate the poison from the body, and there are many ways to accomplish this.

The best rule to follow is prevention. Poisonous substances should be kept where children cannot get at them, and products that contain poison should be clearly marked and carefully stored.

CHAPTER 4
HOW
THINGS BEGAN

What does the word "superstition" mean to you? When you try to define it, don't you find it's quite hard to do so?

Suppose, for example, you said it was a belief in something that

| HOW DID SUPERSTITIONS BEGIN? |

wasn't really so. Well, there are many things all of us believe in that can't be proved. Besides, at certain times in man's history, everyone believed in certain things that we now regard as superstitions. And the people who believed in them at that time weren't superstitious at all!

For example, they believed that the shadow or reflection of a person was a part of the soul. So they considered that you would harm the soul if you broke anything on which this shadow or reflection appeared. Therefore, they considered it harmful or "unlucky" to break a mirror. But remember, at that time this was a belief held by most people.

Today, if someone considers it "unlucky" to break a mirror he is superstitious, because today we no longer believe that a shadow or reflection is part of the soul. So a superstition is actually a belief or practice that people cling to after new knowledge or facts have appeared to disprove them. That's why it's impossible to say when superstition began.

In ancient times man tried to explain events in the world as best he could with the knowledge at hand. He didn't know much about the sun, stars, moon, comets, and so on. So he made up explanations about them and followed certain practices to protect himself from their "influence." That is why astrology was an accepted belief at one time. But with the development of science, the heavenly bodies came to be known and understood. The old beliefs should have died out. When they didn't and when people still believed, for example, that seeing a shooting star brought good luck, then these beliefs became superstitions.

Man has always had superstitions about numbers and about days. Some were supposed to be lucky; some, unlucky. Why the number 13 came to be considered unlucky no one really knows, though there are some theories about it. One explanation has to do with Scandinavian mythology. There were 12 demigods, according to this legend, and then Loki appeared, making the 13th. Since Loki was evil and cruel and caused human misfortunes, and since he was the 13th demigod, the number 13 came to be a sign of bad luck.

WHY IS FRIDAY THE 13TH CONSIDERED UNLUCKY?

Some people think the superstition goes back to the fact that there were 13 persons at the Last Supper, and that Judas was the 13th guest! Whatever its origin, the superstition about the number 13 is found in practically every country in Europe and America.

Superstitions about lucky and unlucky days are just as common as those about numbers, and Friday probably has more than any of them centering about it.

In ancient Rome, the sixth day of the week was dedicated to Venus. When the northern nations adopted the Roman method of designating days, they named the sixth day after Frigg or Freya, which was their nearest equivalent to Venus, and hence the name Friday.

The Norsemen actually considered Friday the luckiest day of the week, but the Christians regarded it as the unluckiest. One reason for this is that Christ was crucified on a Friday.

The Mohammedans say that Adam was created on a Friday, and according to legend, Adam and Eve ate the forbidden fruit on a Friday and they died on a Friday.

Superstitious people feel that when you combine the unlucky number 13 with the unlucky day Friday, you've really got an unlucky day!

It seems almost a shame to learn the true facts about Santa Claus. We almost hate to discover what's really behind some tradition we especially enjoy because that might spoil it for us.

HOW DID THE IDEA OF SANTA CLAUS ORIGINATE?

Well, knowing about Christmas and Santa Claus shouldn't spoil anything for you, but only make it more meaningful. Long before Christ was born, people used to celebrate the winter solstice as the birthday of the sun. This time of year was a holiday in many parts of the world before it became the Christmas celebration. That's why some of the customs and traditions of Christmas go back to pagan times.

The custom of giving presents, for example, goes back to the ancient Romans. In the Bible, as you know, the Wise Men brought gifts to Jesus on the 12th day after his birth. And so in some countries, the children receive their presents not on Christmas, but 12 days later.

In some of the northern countries of Europe, the gifts are exchanged almost three weeks before Christmas. The reason for this is that the gifts are supposed to be brought by Saint Nicholas on the eve of his feast day, December 6th.

Saint Nicholas was a bishop of the fourth century who came to be regarded as a special friend of the children. So, in countries like Holland, Belgium, Switzerland and Austria, and in parts of Germany, Saint Nicholas returns every year with gifts for good children.

When the Dutch came to New York, they brought the traditions of Saint Nicholas with them. They called him *San Nicolaas,* and this soon was changed to *Sankt Klaus,* and then Santa Claus. But in this country, we moved the date of his arrival to Christmas Eve, and gradually his red costume, the reindeer, and his home at the North Pole became part of the tradition.

No matter how much we like our own country, and our way of government, and the people of our country, we know it isn't perfect. In fact, there never has been a place on earth where everyone who lived there felt it to be perfect.

WHAT IS UTOPIA?

But many people have often dreamed of living in a perfect place. What would it be like? Well, no one would be poor. But nobody would be rich either. There would be no need to be rich—since everyone would have all the things he needed. Everyone would be happy all the time. There would be very little need for a government, because the people would be considerate of everyone else.

The trouble with such a place is that no one ever really expects to find it. We know it's "too good to be true." Such a place therefore is "nowhere"—and that's exactly what the word "utopia" means. It's made up of two Greek words meaning "not a place"—or nowhere! But the way we use the word "utopia," we mean a perfect place to live.

The word "utopia" was first used by Sir Thomas More, an English writer who lived in the sixteenth century. He published a book in 1516 called *Utopia* in which he described a perfect island country. His book became very popular.

The idea of utopia, however, goes back long before this book. In fact, More got the idea for his book from the famous ancient Greek philosopher Plato, who wrote a book called "The Republic," in which he described what would be a perfect state.

There were also many legends among such people as the Norse, the Celts, and the Arabs, about a perfect place that was supposed to exist somewhere in the Atlantic Ocean. When the exploration of the Western world actually began, most of these legends were no longer believed. But with More's book, "Utopia," it became common for writers to tell of an imaginary place that was perfect. It existed only in their fantasy.

Today, when people describe certain changes they want to make in government or society, these ideas are sometimes called "utopian." This means they fail to recognize defects in human nature that make a perfect place to live practically impossible.

Marriage, as a custom, goes back to the very earliest history of man. It has passed through three stages. The first was marriage by capture. Primitive man simply stole the woman he wanted for his wife.

HOW DID WEDDINGS START?

Then came marriage by contract or purchase. A bride was bought by a man. Finally came the marriage based on mutual love. But even today we still have traces of the first two stages. "Giving the bride away" is a relic of the time when the bride was really sold. The "best man" at weddings today probably goes back to the strong-armed warrior who helped primitive man carry off his captured bride. And the honeymoon itself symbolizes the period during which the bridegroom was forced to hide his captured bride until her kinsmen grew tired of searching for her!

Today we have "weddings" without realizing that this very word goes back to one of the early stages of marriage. Among the Anglo-Saxons, the "wed" was the money, horses, or cattle which the groom gave as security and as a pledge to prove his purchase of the bride from her father.

Of course, when it comes to wedding customs, most of them can be traced back to ancient meanings which have long been forgotten. For example, the "something blue" which brides wear is borrowed from ancient Israel. In those times brides were told to wear a ribband of blue on the borders of their garments because blue was the color of purity, love, and fidelity.

When we ask, Who giveth this woman to this man? we are going back to the times when a bride was actually purchased. It is believed that the custom of having bridesmaids goes back to Roman times when there had to be ten witnesses at the solemn marriage ceremony.

Why do we tie shoes on the back of newlyweds' cars? It is believed that this goes back to the custom of exchanging or giving away of shoes to indicate that authority had been exchanged. So the shoe suggests that now the husband rather than the father has authority over the bride.

This custom is not only found all over the world, but it goes back to very ancient times.

The marriage ceremony

WHY DO WE THROW RICE AT THE BRIDE AND GROOM?

like so many other important events in life, is full of symbolism. (This means that we perform certain acts as symbols of things we wish to express, instead of expressing them directly.)

The use of rice is one of those symbols. It has played a part in

marriage ceremonies for centuries. In certain primitive tribes, for instance, the act of eating rice together was the way people got married. This was probably because eating together symbolized living together, and rice happened to be the local food.

Among other peoples, the bride and groom first ate rice together to be married, and then rice was sprinkled over them.

In some cases, rice was used at weddings not to bring the bride and groom together, but to protect them from evil spirits. It was believed that these spirits always appeared at a marriage, and by throwing rice after the married couple, these evil spirits were fed and kept from doing harm to the newlyweds.

But for most ancient peoples, rice was a symbol of fruitfulness, and the custom of throwing rice at the bride and groom today goes back to that meaning. It means that we are saying, in symbolic form, "May you have many children and an abundance of good things in your future together!"

The wearing of a wedding ring is one of the oldest and most universal customs of mankind. The tradition goes back so far that no one can really tell how it first began.

WHEN WERE WEDDING RINGS FIRST WORN?

The fact that the ring is a circle may be one reason why it began to be used. The circle is a symbol of completeness. In connection with marriage, it represents the rounding out of the life of a person. We can see how a man without a wife, or a woman without a husband, could have been considered incomplete people. When they are married they make a complete unit, which the circle of the ring symbolizes.

Some people believe the wedding ring really started as a bracelet that was placed on women who were captured in primitive times. Gradually the circular bracelet on the arm or leg, which indicated that she was the property of one man in the tribe, was changed to a ring on the finger.

We know also that primitive man believed in magic. He used to weave a cord and tie it around the waist of the woman he wanted. He believed that with this ceremony her spirit entered his body and she was his forever. The wedding ring may have started this way.

The first people who actually used wedding rings in marriage were the Egyptians. In hieroglyphics, which is Egyptian picture-writing, a circle stands for eternity, and the wedding ring was a symbol of a marriage that would last forever. Christians began to use a ring in marriage around the year 900.

Why is the ring worn on the fourth finger of the left hand? The ancient Greeks believed that a certain vein passed from this finger directly to the heart. But probably the real reason is that we use this finger least of all the fingers, so it's more convenient to wear an ornament on it!

Years ago there used to a great many popular jokes that began: "Confucius say. . . ." It seems as if everybody knows that Confucius said many wise things.

WHO WAS CONFUCIUS?

Confucius was one of the greatest moral teachers of all time. He lived in China about five hundred years before Christ. Confucius studied ancient Chinese writings from which he took ideas that to him seemed important to the development of fine character. Then he taught these ideas to the princes and to the students of all classes who flocked to him for instruction. The rules he laid down 2,400 years ago are still held up as ideals.

Confucius' Chinese name was Kung-Fu-tse. At the age of 22, three years after his marriage, Confucius began to teach men how to live happily. His principle rule for happiness, "What you do not wish done to yourself, do not do to others," was much like the Golden Rule.

Confucius held office under many different princes whom he tried to interest in the right moral conduct, the conduct based on love, justice, reverence, wisdom, and sincerity.

One of his teachings, the reverence for parents, had a tremendous effect on China, because it teaches reverence not only while the parents are living but after they are dead. As a form of ancestor worship, it caused China for a long time to look to the past instead of moving forward.

Confucius did not consider himself a god. In fact, he taught nothing about a supreme being or a hereafter. He believed that man was naturally good and could preserve this goodness by living harmoniously with his fellow men.

Within five hundred years after his death, his teachings became the philosophy of the state. But when Buddhism appeared, the teachings of Confucius were almost forgotten for a period. They were later revived, and even today his teachings influence the lives of millions of people.

We think of our way of life as the only one, and when we learn about other civilizations, we are often shocked, or at least surprised. When we mourn somebody, we naturally wear black. What else could one wear?

WHY IS BLACK WORN FOR MOURNING?

Well, in Japan and China, they wear pure white when mourning! And in some sections of Africa, the natives apply red paint to their bodies as a sign of mourning.

The reason we wear black is simply that, according to our traditions, this is the best way to express grief. When we see people dressed in black mourning clothes they look somber and sad, so it seems natural to us that black is the color of mourning clothes.

But have you ever wondered why we wear mourning clothes at all? Of course, we now do it as a mark of love or respect for someone who has died. But in trying to trace mourning clothes back to their beginnings, scholars have come up with interesting answers.

When we put on mourning clothes, they are usually the reverse of the kind of clothes we wear every day. In other words, it's a kind of disguise. Some people think that ancient peoples put on this disguise because they were afraid that the spirit which had brought death would return and find them!

Now, this might seem pretty far-fetched, if there weren't some peoples who do exactly this even today. Among many primitive tribes in various parts of the world, as soon as someone dies, the widow and other relatives put on all sorts of disguises. Sometimes they cover the body with mud and put on a costume of grass. In other tribes, the women cover their bodies entirely with veils.

So perhaps our black mourning clothes go back to the idea of frightening away spirits or hiding from them! There are other mourning customs that are linked to this fear of spirits. For example, mourning is a period of retirement. We withdraw from normal activities and life.

There are countless examples of primitive and ancient peoples who retired from social life when a relative died. In some cases, the widow spent the rest of her life in a kind of retirement. And it may all have started from the fear of "contaminating" other people with the spirit of death!

The Taj Mahal is a love story, a sad and beautiful one. If it didn't exist, we could easily imagine that the story of its construction was simply a fairy tale.

WHAT IS THE TAJ MAHAL?

Three hundred years ago, there lived in India an emperor called Shah Jahan. His favorite wife was a beautiful and intelligent woman whom he loved greatly and made his counselor and constant companion. Her title was Mumtazi Mahal; its shortened form, Taj Mahal, means "pride of the palace."

In the year 1630 this beloved wife of the emperor died. He was so brokenhearted that he thought of giving up his throne. He decided, out of love for his wife, to build her the most beautiful tomb that had ever been seen.

He summoned the best artists and architects from India, Turkey, Persia, and Arabia, and finally, the design was completed. It took more than twenty thousand men working over a period of 18 years to build the Taj Mahal, one of the most beautiful buildings in the world.

The building itself stands on a marble platform 313 feet square

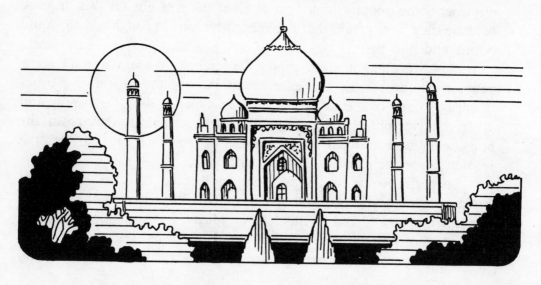

and 22 feet high. Minarets, or towers, rise from each of the four corners. The Taj itself soars another 200 feet into the air. It is an eight-sided building made of white marble, and inlaid with twelve kinds of semi-precious stones in floral designs as well as with black marble inscriptions from the Koran. (The emperor was of the Moslem faith.) The building materials came from many countries, including Arabia, Egypt, Tibet, and various parts of India.

The emperor planned to build an identical tomb of black marble for himself on the other side of the river connected by a silver bridge. But his son imprisoned him in the palace before he could finish, and for the rest of his life, he could only gaze across the river at the shrine of his beloved.

No one knows exactly how old the pyramids are. A thousand years before Christ, they were already old and mysterious. The Great Pyramid at Giza has been attributed to King Cheops of the fourth dynasty (about 2900 B.C.).

HOW WERE THE EGYPTIAN PYRAMIDS BUILT?

The pyramids are tombs. The ancient Egyptian kings believed that their future lives depended upon the perfect preservation of their bodies. The dead were therefore embalmed, and the mummies were hidden below the level of the ground in the interior of these great masses of stone. Even the inner passages were blocked and concealed from possible robbers. Food and other necessities were put in the tombs for the kings to eat in their future lives.

The building of such a tremendous structure was a marvelous engineering feat. It is said that it took 100,000 men working for twenty years to build the Great Pyramid! Each block of stone is 7 feet high. Some are 18 feet across! Let's see if we can trace the story of the building of this particular pyramid.

The blocks of limestone and granite used in building the pyramid were brought by boat from quarries across the Nile and to the south. This could be done for only three months each spring when the Nile was flooded. So it took twenty years and some 500,000 trips to bring all the stone needed!

Boats unloaded at a landing space connected to the site of the pyramid by a stone road. The blocks, weighing about 2 tons each, were then pulled up the road on sledges by gangs of men. Stone blocks pulled up the road were laid out in neat rows and then pulled to the site by other gangs of men. The number of blocks in the Great Pyramid have been estimated at 2,300,000.

As the pyramid rose, a huge ramp was built to get the materials to higher levels. Gangs of men pulled the blocks up the ramp. Each layer of the pyramid was made of blocks of limestone set side by side. Mortar was used to slide the stones, rather than to cement them together. Blocks in the center were rough, but those on the outside were cut more carefully. The final surface was made of very smooth limestone with almost invisible joints. The pyramid has three inside chambers with connecting passages.

WHO INVENTED SIGN LANGUAGE?

The history of man is full of cruelty towards those whose sickness we have been unable to understand. For thousands of years, for example, deaf-mutes were treated as if they were dangerous to society. In many countries they were regarded as idiots and were locked up in asylums. Very often they were killed to get them out of the way.

In the sixteenth century a man came along who wanted to do something to help the deaf-mutes. He was an Italian doctor named Jerome Cardan who believed that deaf-mutes could be taught by using written characters. His work attracted great interest, and by the seventeenth century, a finger alphabet was worked out which was similar to the finger alphabet in use today. It took another hundred years, however, before the first public school for deaf-mutes was established at Leipzig, Germany. Today, every civilized country in the world has institutions for educating its deaf and hard-of-hearing.

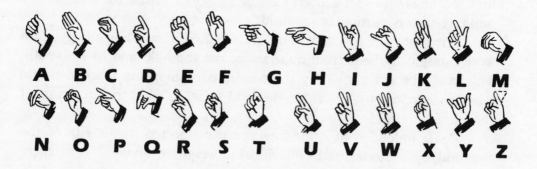

A B C D E F G H I J K L M
N O P Q R S T U V W X Y Z

Most people call a person who has lost any of his sense of hearing deaf. Actually, this term should be used only for those who were born without hearing or who lost their hearing before they learned to talk. Loss of hearing is caused in many ways. It may come about through some disease, or through severe injury to the head, or through something being wrong with the inner ear.

Why can't deaf people talk? Nearly always, it's because the deaf person never heard spoken words! It is a condition that can be remedied. In fact, nearly all deaf children with normal intelligence can learn to talk if they are given special instruction.

Up to about seventy-five years ago, the deaf were taught to communicate ideas almost entirely by means of signs, facial expression, and the finger alphabet. With the hand alphabet, some deaf-mutes can spell out words at the rate of 130 a minute! But they still depend mostly on sign language. For example, the forefinger rubbed across the lips means, "You are not telling me the truth." A tap on the chin with three fingers means, "My uncle."

Today, the deaf are taught to understand what is said to them and even to speak themselves. They learn to speak by watching the lips of the speaker, and by observing and feeling the lips and vocal organs of the teacher and then imitating the motions.

If you were unfortunate enough to be blind, one of the greatest losses you would feel would be not being able to read. Just think how important the ability to read books is to you. Well, people realized this a long time ago and tried to find methods for enabling blind people to read.

WHAT IS THE BRAILLE SYSTEM?

For example, as far back as 1517 there was a system of engraving letters on blocks of wood so blind people could make them out with their fingers. A person's fingertips are very sensitive, and a blind person can "read" with his fingers. A great many other systems were worked out over the years, using raised lines for the letters. But they all presented one big problem: while blind people could learn to read in this way, they couldn't easily write this way because they couldn't see how to form the letters.

In 1829 a man called Louis Braille, who was blind himself and was a teacher of the blind, developed a system that could be read by the

A B C D E F G H I J

K L M N O P Q R S T

blind and written by them too with a simple instrument.

The Braille system consists of dots. Imagine an oblong block. This is called "the Braille cell." On this block are arranged raised dots, from one to six. The cell is 3 dots high and two dots wide. The Braille alphabet consists of different arrangements of the dots. Since 63 combinations are possible, there can be an entire alphabet plus signs for punctuation and contractions and so on. For example, "A" in the Braille system consists of one dot on the upper row at the left. "B" is two dots, in the two upper rows at the left. (Remember, there are three horizontal rows of two dots each.)

The Braille system is one of the most widely used alphabets for the blind, and has helped many blind people to enjoy the pleasures of reading and writing. In fact, today there are about a hundred Braille magazines and newspapers published. Another help for the blind today is the "Talking Book." This is a long-playing record of a book, and there are even special "Talking Books" for blind children.

The word "hieroglyphs" means "sacred carvings." Actually, it is not an accurate name for the ancient writing of the Egyptians. It came about because when the early Greeks first saw these writings, they believed they were made by priests for sacred purposes.

WHAT IS HIEROGLYPHIC WRITING?

But Egyptian hieroglyphics is really one of the oldest known systems of writing. Some of the inscriptions go back to before 3000 B.C., and hieroglyphics continued to be the written language of Egypt for more than 3000 years.

At first the Egyptians used a crude form of picture writing, such as has been used by primitive races throughout the world. The hieroglyphics were simply pictures, each one representing a natural object.

136

The sun was represented by a disk, the moon by a crescent, water by wavy lines, a man by the figure of a man, and so on.

But these "picturegrams" could not represent the things that the eye could not see—such as thoughts, light, and day. So hieroglyphics in time became symbols of ideas rather than pictures of objects. A disk might suggest "day" instead of only the sun; another symbol meant "turn." These idea signs were called "ideograms."

The next step in the development of hieroglyphics was in the use of images to represent sounds instead of the actual objects. For example, the bee might mean, not an insect, but the syllable "bee." A leaf might represent the syllable "leaf." By putting these together, they would make the word "belief." (We are using English words to show how it was done.) Such hieroglyphics used as sound signs, are known as "phonograms."

Now the Egyptians could write down any words they knew, whether the word meant a thing of which they could draw a picture or not. From these phonograms there developed a series of signs, each representing only a letter. In writing, the Egyptians used only consonants. For example, "drink" would be written "drnk" (using Egyptian words, of course). The Egyptians also kept on using old signs in their writing—ideograms, phonograms, and picturegrams all combined. In time, it became so complicated that the common people couldn't understand it!

WHAT IS CRYPTOGRAPHY?

Suppose you and your friends wanted to set up a system of sending secret messages to each other. You might say, "Instead of using letters, let's use numbers." Each number will stand for a certain letter of the alphabet.

You would then have a code. Cryptography is writing using a secret code. Sometimes the word "cipher" is used instead of code. Did you know that Julius Caesar used a cipher to keep his message secret from enemy eyes? In modern times, ciphers and codes are used by both government and business for important and secret messages.

In general, there are two kinds of cipher. One kind is the substitution of a number, letter, or other symbol for each letter in a message. The other kind is the transposition or rearrangement of the order of the letters in a message.

There are endless ways in which these two types can be used. The first type is the simpler system and is the one boys and girls usually use in a homemade cipher. The word "code" is usually used for a message which can be translated by use of a codebook held by both the sender and the receiver of the message.

Codes and ciphers can be "broken," or solved, by direct methods of deciphering and decoding. To do this, the key to a cipher or codebook is necessary. These are sometimes hard to find.

A scientific method of reading cryptograms (secret messages) has been developed and is called crypto-analysis. A person reading cryptograms usually must determine what language the secret message uses. He must decide whether the message is in cipher or code. Tables of the frequency of the use of letters in a language, and many other things, are necessary in breaking ciphers and codes.

The first newspapers were nothing like our papers today. They were more like letters containing news. In the fifth century B.C., there were men in Rome who wrote these newsletters and sent them to people

WHO PUBLISHED THE FIRST NEWSPAPER?

who lived far away from the capital. Something more like our papers was established by Julius Caesar in 60 B.C. He had the government publish a daily bulletin for posting in the Forum. Devoted chiefly to government announcements, it was called *Acta Diurna,* which meant "Daily Happenings."

One of the chief needs for getting news quickly in early days was for business purposes. Businessmen had to know what important things had happened. So one of the first newspapers, or newsletters, was started in the sixteenth century by the Fuggers, a famous German family of international bankers. They actually established a system for gathering the news so that it would be reliable.

In Venice, at about the same time, people paid a fee of one *gazeta* to read notices that were issued by the government every day. These were called *Notizie Scritte* ("Written News").

The first regular newspaper established in London was the *Intelligencer* in 1663. Most early papers that were established could be published only once a week, because both communication and production were slow.

The first American newspaper, *Publick Occurrences,* was started in Boston in 1690, but the governor of the colony quickly stopped it. Benjamin Franklin conducted the *Pennsylvania Gazette* from 1729 to 1765. The people were so eager to have newspapers that by the time of the American Revolution there were 37 of them being published in the Colonies!

One of the most influential newspapers ever published is the *London Times,* which began to be published in 1785 as the *Daily Universal Register.*

Every year, when the Nobel Prizes are announced there is a great deal of publicity about the winners. They are interviewed and articles are written about them. This is because winning the Nobel Prize is consid-

WHAT IS THE NOBEL PRIZE?

ered by most people the highest honor that can be achieved in certain particular fields of work such as chemistry, physics, medicine, and literature. There is also a Nobel Peace Prize, awarded for efforts on behalf of peace.

The curious thing about these prizes is that they were started by a man who did a great deal to help the science of destruction! Alfred Nobel was born in Stockholm and lived from 1833 to 1896. Among the things which he invented and patented were dynamite, blasting gelatin (more powerful than dynamite), and a new kind of detonator for explosives.

It may be that having created such deadly explosives, Nobel felt a need to do something "noble" for the world. He was interested in establishing peace, and had a plan he thought would prevent war. By the way, besides being a brilliant scientist, Nobel was also a poet. He thought that literature and science were the most important factors in human progress.

When he died, Nobel left a fund of $9,000,000. The money was to be used in giving prizes to those who made outstanding contributions in physics, chemistry, medicine, literature, and the advancement of world peace. The prizes averaged about $40,000 each, and were first awarded on December 10, 1901, the anniversary of Nobel's death.

Since Nobel was a Swede, the Nobel Foundation of Sweden distributed the awards. The organizations selected to determine the winners were: for physics and chemistry, the Royal Academy of Science in Stockholm; for medicine, the Caroline Institute of Stockholm; for literature, the Swedish Academy of Literature; for peace, a committee of five persons chosen by the Norwegian Parliament.

Many great people have won Nobel Prizes: among them are Theodore Roosevelt, Albert Einstein, George Bernard Shaw, Marie Curie, Rudyard Kipling, Ernest Hemingway, and Ralph Bunche.

Was there actually a Mother Goose who wrote the delightful fairy tales and nursery jingles that all children love? Three different countries give three different answers as to who Mother Goose was.

WHO WROTE MOTHER GOOSE?

In England, it was believed that Mother Goose was an old woman who sold flowers on the streets of Oxford. In France, there are people who believe that Mother Goose was really Queen Bertha. She married her cousin, Robert the Pious. Because he already had a wife, Queen Bertha was punished by the pope. One of her feet became shaped like that of a goose. From then on, she was called Mother Goose.

In the United States, there are some who say that Mother Goose's name was Elizabeth Fergoose. She was the mother-in-law of a Boston printer who lived in the early part of the eighteenth century.

The first time the tales attributed to Mother Goose were set down was in 1696. For many centuries they had been handed down from

generation to generation by word of mouth. But in that year, a Frenchman called Charles Perrault wrote them down. His collection included *Cinderella* and *Sleeping Beauty*.

Perrault sent the manuscript to a bookseller named Moetjens who lived at The Hague, in Holland. Moetjens published the tales in his magazine in 1696 and 1697. They immediately became popular. In 1697 a printer in Paris published eight of the tales in book form. The volume was called *Histories or Stories of Past Time*. On the cover was a little sign on which was written "Tales of My Mother Goose."

So you see these tales and nursery rhymes have been told and read to children for hundreds of years. The earliest translation of the Mother Goose tales into English was in 1729.

We still don't know who first wrote *Simple Simon, Little Miss Muffet,* and all the others which became part of Mother Goose. But in 1760 a collection of Mother Goose jingles was published in London, and about twenty-five years later it was reprinted and published in Worcester, Massachusetts.

Did you ever walk in a forest and suddenly come upon a little brook bubbling merrily along its path? Didn't it sound like music? When the rain pitter-patters against a roof, or a bird sings heartily—aren't these like music?

HOW DID MUSIC BEGIN?

When man first began to notice his surroundings, there was a kind of music already here. And then when he wanted to express great joy, when he wanted to jump and shout and somehow express what he felt, he felt music in his being, perhaps before he was able to express it.

Eventually, man learned to sing, and this was the first man-made music. What do you think would be the first thing man would want to express in song? Happiness? Yes, the happiness of love. The first songs ever sung were love songs. On the other hand, when man was face to face with death which brought him fear, he expressed this, too, in a different kind of song, a kind of dirge or chant. So love songs and dirges were the first music man ever made!

Another kind of music came with the development of the dance. Man needed some sort of accompaniment while he danced. So he clapped his hands, cracked his fingers, or stamped on the earth—or beat upon a drum!

The drum is probably one of the oldest instruments man invented to produce sound. It's so old that we can never trace its beginnings, but we find it among all ancient peoples everywhere in the world.

The earliest wind instruments created by man were the whistle and the reed pipe. The whistles were made of bone, wood, and clay. From them, the flute was developed. The flute is so ancient that the Egyptians had it more than 6,000 years ago!

Stringed instruments probably came soon afterward. Did you know that the ancient Egyptians had them, too?

Man has always loved to be entertained. From the very beginning of civilization there have been jugglers, acrobats, animal trainers and clowns to entertain people. In ancient Greece there were chariot races,

HOW DID THE CIRCUS BEGIN?

in China there were contortionists, and in Egypt there were trainers of wild animals.

But it was the Romans who first had the idea of combining such acts and other events into a circus. Actually, the word "circus" comes from the Latin pertaining to races rather than to a type of show. So the circus started with races, and the structures built by the Romans for these races were called circuses. The Circus Maximus was the first and largest of these. It was started in the third century B.C. and was enlarged until it could seat more than 150,000 people!

When the Romans came to these circuses, it was much like arriving at a modern circus or fair grounds. There were vendors of pastry, wine (like our soft drink sellers), and various other merchandise. Admission was free, because the government used these circuses as a way of keeping the masses content.

Meanwhile, in Rome there were all sorts of other entertainment going on which eventually became part of what we call the circus. Some theatres had jugglers, acrobats, ropewalkers and animal trainers. Some of them even had boxing bears! And at the race courses, they had people performing such tricks as riding two horses at once, riders jumping from one running horse to another, and riders jumping their teams over chariots, all of which we have in the modern circus.

During the Middle Ages there was no organized circus as such, but troupes of performers would wander about doing various acts. The first circus, as we know it today, was organized by an Englishman,

Philip Astley, in 1768. He set up a building in London with a number of seats and a ring. He did trick riding on horses and had acrobats, clowns, and ropewalkers. After him, a great many other people had the same idea, and the circus became a popular entertainment all over the world.

There are many kinds of puppets, as you know. There are hand puppets, rod puppets, shadow figures, and marionettes. They are little figures operated by strings and wires from above, by rods, or by hands from below.

WHEN DID PUPPET SHOWS START?

Puppets are as old as the theater itself. The first puppets were probably made in India or Egypt. Puppet theaters thousands of years old have been found in both of these countries. Marionettes, which are puppets animated by strings from above, got their name in Italy. During the early Christmas celebrations, small, jointed nativity figures including the Christ Child and the Virgin Mary were made to move by strings. This kind of puppet became known as a marionette, or little Mary.

In China, Japan, and Java puppet showmen have made figures to represent the heroes, gods, and animals of their legends and stories. In Java, Siam, and Greece they developed shadow-plays. They were made by moving cut-out figures against a vertical sheet lighted from behind. Did you know that special operas for puppets have been written by great composers like Mozart, Haydn, and Gluck?

One of the best-loved of all children's stories tells of the adventures of Pinocchio, a puppet who came to life. You will find many of the same puppet characters famous in different lands. Punch, the famous English puppet, is known in Italy as Punchinello and in France as Polichinelle.

Puppet shows are a way to tell a story or express an idea. They are not hampered by the limitations of live actors. For instance, if you want a character to have a very long nose or big hands, or very short legs, or even wings, a puppet can have them without any trouble at all.

Puppets can also be any size needed. There are some marionettes that are only 6 inches tall, and some have been made 30 or 40 feet tall! Also, it is possible to make puppet animals and they can be just as good actors as people!

Probably the greatest honor that could come to an athlete is to win the gold medal at the Olympic Games. But did you know that the idea of having Olympic Games is more than 2,500 years old?

WHEN DID THE OLYMPIC GAMES START?

According to Greek legend, the Olympic Games were started by Hercules, son of Zeus. The first records we have are of games held in 776 B.C. on the plain of Olympia. They were held every four years for more than 1,000 years, until the Romans abolished them in 394 A.D.

The ancient Greeks considered the games so important that they measured time by the interval between them. The four years were called an Olympiad. The games were an example of the Greek ideal that the body, as well as the mind and spirit, should be developed. Nothing was allowed to interfere with holding the games; if a war happened to be going on, the war was stopped!

Fifteen hundred years later a Frenchman named Baron Pierre de Coubertin had the idea of reviving the Olympic Games. In 1894, following his suggestion, an International Congress of fifteen nations was held in Paris. This Congress unanimously agreed to revive the games and to hold them every four years. Two years later, in the rebuilt stadium at Athens, Greece, the first of the modern Olympic Games was held.

The games today include many sports that didn't even exist in ancient times, such as basketball, water polo, soccer, cycling, shooting, and field hockey.

The modern Olympics are governed by an International Olympic Committee, and each nation has its own National Olympic Committee which is responsible for its country's participation in the Olympics.

All kinds of claims have been made about the invention of playing cards. Some people think they originated with the Egyptians, others give the credit to the Arabs, or Hindus, or Chinese.

HOW DID PLAYING CARDS GET THEIR NAMES?

We do know that playing cards were first used for foretelling the future and were linked with religious symbols. Ancient Hindu cards, for example, had ten suits representing the ten incarnations of Vishnu, the Hindu god.

Playing cards were probably introduced into Europe during the thirteenth century. We can trace the playing cards we have today to certain cards that existed in Italy. They were called "tarots," or picture cards, and there were 22 of them. They were used for fortunetelling or simple games.

These 22 picture cards were then combined with 56 number cards to make a deck of 78 cards. One of the tarot cards was called "il matto," the fool, from which we get our joker. There were four suits in this deck,

ENGLISH CARD OF 1656

AMERICAN CARD OF 1800

INDIA DISK CARD

FRENCH CARD, ABOUT 1480

CHINESE DOMINO CARD

145

representing the chalice, the sword, money, and the baton. There were also four "court" cards, the king, queen, knight, and knave.

From these 56 cards of the Italian deck came the 52-card French deck. The French kept the king, queen, knave, and ten numeral cards in each of the four suits, which they gave new names — spade, heart, diamond, and club. The English adopted this deck, which is the deck we now use.

The earliest European cards were hand-painted, and too expensive for general use. With the invention of printing, it became possible for most people to own playing cards.

Early cards were either square, extremely oblong, or even round, but today they are the standard size of 3½ inches by 2½ or 2¼. Many efforts have been made to put the pictures of national heros or current events on cards, but these usually end up as novelties. The figures on American and English cards wear costumes from the time of Henry VII and Henry VIII.

In deciding upon a unit of measurement, it is possible to pick anything. For example, the average height of a man could possibly have been a unit of measurement. In fact, some of the units used today in English-

WHAT IS THE METRIC SYSTEM?

speaking countries are based on such things as the distance from a man's elbow to the tip of his middle finger, or the weight of a grain of wheat.

Because there have been so many differences in weights and measures used in different countries, an international system has been urged. If one system were to be adopted by all countries of the world, it would probably be the metric system.

This is a system worked out by a committee of scientists appointed in France in 1789. The English-speaking countries are almost the only ones that do not use the metric system in their measures. However, it is used in scientific work even in those countries.

The metric system is based on a measure of length called the "meter." This is approximately one ten-millionth of the distance on the earth's surface from pole to equator. It is about 39.37 inches.

The metric system is based on 10 as is our number system, so that each unit of length is 10 times as large as the next smaller unit. There are square and cubic units for measuring area and volume which correspond to the units of length.

The unit of weight is the gram, which is the weight of a cubic centimeter of pure water. The liter is a measure used as the quart is used, but it is a little larger, The hectare, which is 10,000 square meters, is used as the acre is used, but is 2.471 acres. The metric system is more convenient to use than the English system because its plan is the same as that of our number system.

Here are some equivalents for the metric and English systems: one foot equals .305 meter; one inch equals 2.540 centimeters; one mile equals 1.609 kilometers; one quart (liquid) equals .946 liter.

Perhaps you didn't realize that the zero had to be invented! Actually one of man's greatest inventions, it was a concept that has had a tremendous influence on the history of mankind because it made the development of higher mathematics possible.

WHO INVENTED THE ZERO?

Up until about the sixteenth century, the number system used in Europe was the Roman system, invented about two thousand years ago. The Roman system was not a simple one. It is built on a base of 10. Thus the mark "X" means 10. The letter "C" means 100. The letter "M" stands for 1,000. The mark for 1 is "I," for 5 "V," for 50 "L," and for 500 "D." 4 is shown by "IV," or 1 less than 5. To indicate 1,648, you write: "MDCLXLVIII." In the Roman system, to read the number, sometimes you count, sometimes you subtract, sometimes you add.

Long before the birth of Christ, the Hindus in India had invented a far better number system. It was brought to Europe about the year 900 by Arab traders and is called the Hindu-Arabic system.

In the Hindu-Arabic system, all numbers are written with the nine digits — 1, 2, 3, 4, 5, 6, 7, 8, 9 — and the zero, 0. In a number written with this system each figure has a value according to the place in which it is written.

We know the number 10 means 1 ten, because the "1" is written in the 10's place and the zero shows there are no units to be written in the unit place. The number 40 means four 10's and no units, or 40 units. The zero shows that the 4 is written in the 10's place.

The Romans had no zero in their system. To write 205, they wrote

"CCV." They had no plan using place values. In the Hindu-Arabic system we write 205 by putting 2 in the 100's place to show 200, 0 in the 10's place to show that there are no 10's, and the 5 in the 1's place to show that there are 5 units.

In many doctors' offices, you will see a framed document on the wall called the Hippocratic Oath. This is an oath taken by doctors when they graduate from medical school. What is this oath and who was

WHO WAS HIPPOCRATES?

Hippocrates?

Before the age of scientific medicine, which we have today, man had a form of medicine that depended on magicians and witch doctors. Then, in ancient Egypt and India, a more sensible form of medicine developed. The ancient Egyptians, for example, were good observers. They had medical schools, and practiced surgery. But the treatment of disease was still a part of the Egyptian religion, with prayers, charms, and sacrifices as a part of the treatment.

Scientific medicine had its beginning in Greece when a group of men who were not priests became physicians. The most famous of these, Hippocrates, who lived about 400 B.C., is called "the father of medicine."

His approach to medicine was scientific. He put aside all superstition, magic, and charms. He and his pupils made careful records of their cases. Some of their observations are considered to be true even today: Weariness without cause indicates disease. When sleep puts an end to delirium, it is a good sign. If pain is felt in any part of the body, and no cause can be found, there is mental disorder.

Hippocrates also had strong ideas about what a doctor should be and how he should behave. This is incorporated in his Hippocratic Oath, which among many others contains such ideas as the following:

"I will follow that system of regimen which according to my ability and judgment I consider for the benefit of my patients, and abstain from whatever is deleterious and mischievous. I will give no deadly medicine to anyone if asked, nor suggest any such counsel . . . Whatever, in connection with my professional practice or not in connection with it, I see or hear in the life of men which ought not to be spoken of abroad, I will not divulge, as reckoning that all such should be kept secret."

The problem of caring for the weak and sick members of society has existed from the very earliest times. But the idea of hospitals is a new one in the history of man.

HOW DID HOSPITALS BEGIN?

The Greeks, for instance, had no public institutions for the sick. Some of their doctors maintained surgeries where they could carry on their work, but they were very small, and only one patient could be treated at a time. The Romans, in time of war, established infirmaries, which were used to treat sick and injured soldiers. Later on, infirmaries were founded in the larger cities and were supported out of public funds.

In a way, the Roman influence was responsible for the establishment of hospitals. As Christianity grew, the care of the sick became the duty of the Church. During the Middle Ages monasteries and convents provided most of the hospitals. Monks and nuns were the nurses.

The custom of making pilgrimages to religious shrines also helped advance the idea of hospitals. These pilgrimages were often long, and the travelers had to stop overnight at small inns along the road. These inns were called *hospitalia,* or guest houses, from the Latin word *hospes,* meaning "a guest." The inns connected with the monasteries devoted themselves to caring for travelers who were ill or lame or weary. In this way the name "hospital" became connected with caring for the afflicted!

HOSPITAL IN THE MIDDLE AGES—1400

Since living conditions during the Middle Ages were not very comfortable or hygienic, the hospitals of those days were far from being clean or orderly. In fact, many a hospital would put two or more patients in the same bed!

During the seventeenth century, there was a general improvement in living conditions. People began to feel that it was the duty of the state to care for its ailing citizens. But it wasn't until the eighteenth century that public hospitals became general in the larger towns of England. Soon, the idea of public hospitals began to spread, and they appeared all over Europe.

In North America, the first hospital was built by Cortes in Mexico City in 1524. Among the British colonies. the first hospital was established by the East India Company on Manhattan Island in 1663.

We feel very proud in this country about our national cleanliness. Doesn't every home have a bathtub? Well, did you know that at one time there were more homes with radios in this country than with bathtubs?

WHEN DID PEOPLE START USING BATHTUBS?

In spite of all our pride concerning cleanliness, we have never made as big a fuss about bathing and baths as have certain peoples of ancient times! Why right in the heart of Rome, taking up about a square mile, there were the baths of Caracalla that were probably the most luxurious baths man has ever known. There were swimming pools, warm baths, steam baths, and hot-air baths — even libraries, restaurants, and theaters to amuse the people who came to take the baths!

The wealthy classes of Rome took their baths in costly tubs or pools, and they didn't bathe in just plain water. They filled the tubs with the finest wines and perfumes, and even milk!

But long before the Romans, in fact before history was written, man was bathing for pleasure and for health. Swimming in rivers, of course, was always the commonest way to take a bath. But the people of ancient Crete had already advanced to the point where they had baths with running water. In ancient times the Jews took ceremonial baths on special occasions.

By the third century B.C., almost every large Greek city had at least one public bath. By this time, too, the wealthy classes had private baths and pools in their homes.

During the Dark Ages people must have looked rather dark and dirty. They just weren't much concerned about keeping clean. When the Crusaders invaded Palestine they were surprised to find that it was part of the Mohammedan religion to bathe at certain times of the day, before praying.

They tried to introduce regular bathing into Europe when they came back, but they didn't have much success. In fact, it wasn't until about 100 years ago that people began to understand the importance of bathing regularly!

When you see a man with a beard, doesn't he somehow look dignified, or even important? In the history of man, this has been the usual attitude towards beards. It was a sign of manhood.

WHEN DID MEN BEGIN SHAVING THEIR BEARDS?

That's why you will find that in ancient times, when an important person was shown, he was usually shown with a beard. The Greek god, Zeus, was shown with a beard; drawings representing God showed a beard; Abraham, King Arthur, Charlemagne were always pictured with beards!

In our western civilization, there is no general rule about beards. Sometimes they were considered stylish and right for men to have, sometimes no man would want to be seen with a beard!

Long before the conquest of England by the Normans, the beard was considered unfashionable and not worn by men. Then the style changed and beards became popular again! The kings of England, who set the fashions that men followed, varied in their taste for beards. For example, Henry II had no beard, Richard II had a small beard, Henry III had a long beard.

By the middle of the thirteenth century, most men were wearing full and curled beards, and it was common in the fourteenth century. Then beards disappeared again during the fifteenth century, and slowly began to come back into style with the sixteenth century. It was Henry VIII who made the beard fashionable again.

During the time of Queen Elizabeth, lawyers, soldiers, courtiers, and merchants all had beards. But when Anne became queen of England, nobody who was anybody wore either a beard or moustache, or whiskers! In fact, when George III was imprisoned and his beard was allowed to grow, many of his followers felt this was the most insulting thing of all!

So you see that shaving the beard off for a man has not been a question of having a razor. These have existed for thousands of years. To wear a beard or not has been simply a question of style!

Today cooking is quite an art. There are great chefs, famous restaurants, thousands and thousands of cookbooks, and millions of people who pride themselves on being able to cook well.

HOW DID COOKING BEGIN?

Yet there was a time when man didn't even cook his food. The early cave man ate his food raw. Even after fire was discovered, the only kind of cooking that took place was to throw the carcass of an animal on the burning embers.

It was only gradually that man learned to bake in pits with heated stones, and to boil meats and vegetables by dropping red-hot stones into a vessel of water. Primitive peoples used to roast animals whole on a spit over an open fire. In time, people discovered how to bake fish, birds, or small animals in clay. This sealed in the juices and made the food tender. When we come to the ancient Egyptians, we find that they had carried cooking to the point where public bakeries were turning out bread for the people!

Greek civilization advanced cooking to a stage of great luxury. In ancient Athens, they even imported food from distant lands. And the Romans had magnificent banquets in their day!

Then, during the Middle Ages, the art of cooking declined and the only place where fine cooking was found was in the monasteries. When good cooking was revived again, Italy, Spain, and France led the way. These countries prided themselves on having a more refined taste than England and Germany, where the people ate chiefly meat.

A curious thing about cooking is that many primitive peoples knew almost every form of cooking that we practice now. They just did it more crudely. For instance, we cook by broiling, roasting, frying, baking, stewing or boiling, steaming, parching, and drying. Our own American Indians actually knew all these ways of cooking, except frying!

You may think that the chief reason for cooking food is to make it taste better. Actually, the changes cooking produces in food help us to digest it better. Cooking food also guards our health, because the heat destroys parasites and bacteria which might cause us harm.

No matter how good mother's cooking is, we like to go out to a restaurant sometimes (if we can afford it). It's not just because there's different food to eat, but we also enjoy the "going out."

HOW DID RESTAURANTS START?

Long before there were restaurants, there were taverns where people gathered to talk, have something to drink, and perhaps something to eat.

In London, there was another kind of place that was also the forerunner of the restaurant. This was the cookshop. The chief business of these cookshops was the sale of cooked meats which customers carried away with them. But sometimes a cookshop would also serve meals on the premises and was somewhat like a restaurant. There were cookshops in London as long ago as the twelfth century!

The first place where a meal was provided every day at a fixed hour was the tavern in England. They often became "dining clubs," and these existed in the fifteenth century. By the middle of the sixteenth century, many townspeople of all classes had the habit of dining out in the taverns. Most of the taverns offered a good dinner for a shilling or less, with wine and ale as extras. Many of the taverns became meeting places of the leading people of the day. Shakespeare used to be a regular customer of the Mermaid Tavern in London.

About 1650 coffeehouses also sprang up in England. They served coffee, tea, and chocolate, which were all new drinks at that time. Sometimes they served meals, too.

In 1765 a man named Boulanger opened a place in Paris which served meals and light refreshments, and he called his place a "restaurant." This is the first time this word was used. It was a great success and many other places like it soon opened. In a short time, all over France, there were similar eating places called "restaurants." But the word "restaurant" was not used in England until the end of the nineteenth century.

In the United States, the first restaurant of which there are records was the Blue Anchor Tavern in Philadelphia, opened in 1683.

The name of everything we come in contact with has an origin, and sometimes it's quite surprising to discover how certain names began.

Take a name like gooseberry, for example. It has nothing to do

HOW DID FRUITS AND VEGETABLES GET THEIR NAMES?

with geese! It was originally gorseberry. In Saxon, *gorst* from which "gorse" is derived, meant "rough." And this berry has this name because it grows on a rough or thorny shrub! Raspberry comes from the German verb *raspen,* which means to rub together or rub as with a file. The marks on this berry were thought to resemble a file.

Strawberry is really a corruption of "strayberry," which was so named because of the way runners from this plant stray in all directions! Cranberry was once called "craneberry," because the slender stalks resemble the long legs and neck of the crane. Currants were so called because they first came from Corinth. Cherries got their name from the city of Cerasus.

The term grape is our English equivalent of the Italian *grappo,* and the Dutch and French *grappe,* all of which mean a "bunch." Raisin is a French word which comes from the Latin *racenus,* a dried grape.

The greengage plum gets its name from Lord Gage, who introduced it into England, and from its greenish color when ripe. Apricot

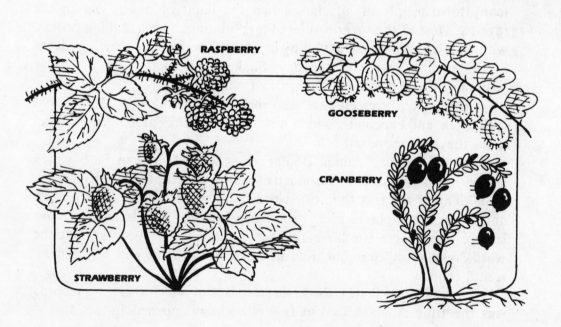

RASPBERRY

GOOSEBERRY

CRANBERRY

STRAWBERRY

comes from the Latin *praecoquus,* which means early ripe. Melon is Greek for apple.

Tomato is the West Indian name for love-apple. The pineapple gets its name naturally from its resemblance to the pine cone. A strange name like pomegranate comes from the Latin *pomum,* a fruit, and *granatus* meaning many seeds.

Chestnuts are so named because they originally came from a city called Castana. Walnut came from the Saxon word *wahl-nut,* meaning foreign nut, since it originally came from Persia. Spinach was *Hispanach,* the Arabic word for a Spanish plant!

All over the world today, wherever big cities have grown up, there are very tall buildings that might be called skyscrapers. There is no special reason for calling a building a skyscraper. It's simply a name we have given to very tall buildings.

WHAT WAS THE FIRST SKYSCRAPER?

In fact, the Bible tells of an attempt to put up a building so tall that it could never be covered by the waters of any flood. This, of course, was the Tower of Babel. During the Middle Ages, the people who lived in the cities of northern Europe began to build great cathedrals. Master builders learned how to fashion stones into pointed arches and flying buttresses to raise ceilings. Tall spires were added to give greater height and majesty to these churches.

For hundreds of years afterwards, these cathedrals stood as the tallest structures in the world. It was simply because no one had discovered materials and methods of construction which could be used to build taller buildings.

In the nineteenth century, as cities grew more crowded, the value of land there rose. In order to make room for more offices on a small plot of land, it was necessary to erect taller buildings. When the hydraulic elevator was invented, it became possible to take passengers and freight as high as 20 stories. But the problem was that to put up a stone building of such height, the walls on the ground floor would have to be more than 7 feet thick to support the weight of the building. So another material was required to make skyscrapers possible.

About this time, three structures were put up that used iron or steel to support great weight with safety. They were the Crystal Palace in London, the Eiffel Tower in Paris, and the Brooklyn Bridge in New York. Architects began to experiment with buildings that had steel frames.

The first skyscraper in the United States was the Home Insurance Building in Chicago, designed in 1883.

We are always hearing about how what happens on Wall Street somehow affects the lives of people all over the world. What is actually meant by "Wall Street," and how can it influence the lives of millions of people?

WHAT IS "WALL STREET"?

Wall Street is literally a street in the lower part of New York City. On it or near it are concentrated the chief financial institutions of the United States. It is, therefore, in a sense, the financial capital of the world. Decisions made here, and activities carried on here influence the economy of our country, and, therefore, touch the lives of all of us in some way.

Wall Street owes its name to Peter Stuyvesant who, in 1652, as Governor of the little Dutch settlement of New Amsterdam, ordered a wall built there to protect the town from attacks by the English. After the Revolutionary War the government offices of the city, of the State of New York, and the United States were located there. President George Washington was inaugurated there in 1789, and the first United States Congress met there.

Today, "Wall Street" indicates the whole financial district, which actually extends several blocks north and south of the street, and also includes an area west of Broadway. In this section are found the headquarters of banks, insurance companies, railway companies, and big industrial corporations. It is also the home of the New York Stock Exchange, which is probably the single most important institution in all of Wall Street.

The securities of about 1,500 different companies producing many kinds of goods and services are traded on the New York Stock Exchange. Within a few minutes after each sale of a stock is made, it is reported to brokerage firms all over the country. These offices receive the information by telegraph on the famous "ticker tape."

If you were stranded on a desert island and you wanted to get something from one place to another, what would you do? You would carry it! In primitive times human muscles were the only means of transporting anything. Man was his own "beast of burden."

WHAT WAS THE FIRST MEANS OF TRANSPORTATION?

In time man tamed certain animals and taught them to carry riders or other loads. The ox, the donkey, the water buffalo, the horse, and the camel were used by early man in various parts of the world for transportation.

This satisfied man for thousands of years, but then he wanted to find some way by which animals could transport more goods. So he developed crude sledges and drags to hitch to his animals.

Flat-bottomed sledges and sleds with runners were fine on snow, but not much good on regular ground. So man developed the rolling drag. This consisted of sections of logs used as rollers under a drag or platform. When the platform was pulled, the logs under it rolled. This made the work easier than pulling the platform along the bare ground. As the platform moved along, it passed completely over the logs at the back. Then these were picked up and put under the front end of the platform.

After a long time, someone thought of cutting a slice from the end of a log and making a hole in its center. This was a wheel, one of man's greatest discoveries. When two wheels were joined by an axle and the axle was fastened to a platform, man had made a crude cart.

Solid wooden wheels were heavy and clumsy, and they wore down quickly. In the course of thousands of years, man improved the wheel. By building wheels with separate hubs and spokes and rims, he made them lighter and more efficient. He made rims and tires of copper or iron so that the wheels would last longer. At last he learned to use rubber tires, and improvements in these are being developed by scientists experimenting with synthetics.

The story of mankind has been divided by historians into three great sections—ancient times, the Middle Ages, and modern times. The Middle Ages span the time between the fall of Rome and the beginning of modern times in the fifteenth century.

WHAT WERE THE MIDDLE AGES?

Of course, when you consider such a great period of time, it's difficult to give exact dates for the beginning and for the end. One age merges gradually into the next. But the date most commonly used as the beginning of the Middle Ages is A.D. 476, when the last of the Roman emperors was dethroned. Its end is usually marked at 1453, when Constantinople, the capital of the Eastern Empire, fell to the Turks.

What was life like during the Middle Ages? What important things happened during this time? This was the epoch during which Christianity triumphed over pagan Europe. In the Middle Ages, the feudal system grew and then decayed in Europe, and the foundations for modern nations were laid.

Although this was the age of chivalry, there was also much cruelty. Lords expressed noble and romantic beliefs in flowery language, but they treated their serfs and slaves with inhumanity.

This was a time when people had unquestioning faith. In no other time did religion play so important a part. The Church and State were not only bound closely together, but often the Church was the State. Towards the end of the Middle Ages, the popes began to lose their power in matters that did not deal with religion.

Modern commerce began in the Middle Ages with the search for new sea routes to India and China.

Science did not make great progress during the Middle Ages, and most of the literature of the time dealt with chivalry and battle. Architecture in the Middle Ages was expressed most fully in the magnificent Gothic cathedrals and their stained-glass windows.

Do you know what the word *renaissance* means? It is the French word for "rebirth." The Renaissance was a period of rebirth that took place in Europe between the fourteenth and sixteenth centuries.

WHAT WAS THE RENAISSANCE?

During the Middle Ages which preceded it, a great many things in life had been neglected. During the Renaissance, learning was revived. Commerce, art, music, literature, and science flourished. The Renaissance changed the whole way of life in Europe.

Before the Renaissance, most people lived on large estates, called manors. There were few towns or cities. All social life centered in the manor, in the nobleman's castle, or in the bishop's palace. Europe was divided into countless small states, each ruled by a prince or a nobleman.

During the Renaissance, this way of living changed completely. Towns and cities grew rapidly as commerce, industry, and trade developed. Wealthy merchants became important. Instead of numerous small states, larger units of government grew up and became nations. People began to use coined money.

People also began to question their old beliefs. They became more interested in the affairs of this world and less concerned about life in the next. This was when the revolt against the practices and ideas of the Roman Catholic Church took place, which resulted in the Reformation and the establishment of the Protestant religion.

The Renaissance didn't begin suddenly, though sometimes the date for its beginning is given as 1453 when Constantinople fell into the hands of the Turks, or 1440, when printing was invented. The forces that brought it about had been at work for many years before.

The Renaissance reached its height first in Italy before spreading to the other countries of Europe. In Italy there was gathered a great group of brilliant artists, among them Leonardo da Vinci, Michelangelo, Raphael, Titian, Botticelli, Cellini, and others whose work we still admire today.

Let us see what we mean by democracy. The word "democracy" comes from the Greek language and means "rule of the people." As we use the word today, we usually mean a government where the people help to direct the work of the government.

HOW DID DEMOCRACY ORIGINATE?

Political democracy has appeared

in two general forms. A government in which all the people meet together to decide the policy and to elect the officials to carry it out is known as direct democracy. When the people elect representatives to carry out their wishes, the government is known as a representative democracy. Because direct democracy is not possible on a large scale with many people involved, almost all forms of democracy practiced today are the representative kind.

No nation can be considered democratic unless it gives protection to various human liberties. Among these liberties are freedom of speech, movement, association, press, religion, and equality before the law.

Political democracy began early in history. In the Greek city-states, especially Athens, there existed direct democracy. In Athens, however, the ruling class of citizens was only a small part of the population. Most of the people were slaves, and these, together with women and foreigners, had no right to vote or hold office. So while a form of direct democracy did exist in ancient Athens, we would today find fault with many of its aspects.

Modern democracy owes a great deal to the Middle Ages. One idea of the time was the contract theory. It was believed that a contract existed between rulers and their subjects by which each was required to perform certain duties. If the ruler failed to perform his duties, then the people had the right to take back the powers they had given him.

Modern representation also began in feudal times because of the needs of kings. The feudal monarchs called representative meetings in order to request grants of money. They felt people wouldn't object to new taxes if their representatives agreed to them beforehand. But this helped establish the idea of representation.

The concept of justice, or law, comes into being as soon as any kind of social relationship is created. For example, Robinson Crusoe, living alone, had no need for laws. There was no one with whose rights he

HOW DID OUR LAWS ORIGINATE?

could interfere by exercising his own freedom of action. But as soon as his man Friday appeared, there was a chance of conflict between his rights and those of his servant. Law then became necessary.

The purpose of law is to set down and to make clear the social relationships among individuals and between the individual and society. It tries to give to each person as much liberty of action as fits in with the liberty of others.

Laws usually develop from the customs of a people. The earliest known system of laws was formed about 1700 B.C. by Hammurabi, King of Babylon. He set down a code, or complete list of laws, that defined personal and property rights, contracts, and so on.

Customs grew into laws because the force of government was put behind them. Later, laws grew from decisions that were made by courts and from books in which lawyers wrote down what had been learned. Still later, laws were set down in statute books, or codes, by kings and legislators.

The Romans were a great law making people and the law books of Emperor Justinian, who lived from 527 to 565, summed up 1,000 years of their working-out of laws. During the Middle Ages, people's actions were largely governed by the church, which developed a body of laws called canon law.

In the twelfth century, the Roman law began to be studied in Italy and gradually spread to the rest of Europe. Thus, a body of laws, based on the Roman law, developed into what is called civil law, as contrasted with the canon law. At the same time, the courts of England were making many decisions about law, and from these grew up a body of laws called the common law.

In 1804, Napoleon put into a book all the civil laws of his time. This Napoleonic Code is the foundation of the law on the continent of Europe and in Central and South America. The common law system, which developed in England, is the basis of the law in the United States, Canada (except Quebec), Australia, and New Zealand.

The supreme law of the United States is written out in the Constitution. It is the one set of laws that everyone — no matter what city or state he lives in — must obey.

WHAT IS THE BILL OF RIGHTS?

When the Constitutional Convention met in 1787 to draw up the Constitution, most of the delegates took for granted that there were various rights people had that didn't have to be written into the Constitution. But Virginia and many other states felt that it would be wiser to protect those individual rights by having them written down, and so they insisted that a Bill of Rights be added to the Constitution.

Ten amendments, known as the Bill of Rights, were added to the Constitution. The Bill of Rights guarantees that:

1. People have the right to say and write what they wish, to meet together peaceably and to complain to the government. Congress cannot set up an official religion or keep people from worshiping as they wish.

2. The states have the right to arm and drill their own citizens in a state militia.

3. In peacetime, people cannot be forced to take soldiers into their homes.

4. An official cannot search a person or his home or seize his property without a warrant. A warrant (a paper signed by a judge) can be issued only if it is necessary to catch a criminal or to prevent a crime.

5. No person can be put on trial unless a grand jury has decided that there is enough evidence for a trial. No person can be tried twice for the same crime. No person can be forced to give testimony against himself. No person can be executed, imprisoned, or fined except after a fair trial. Private property cannot be seized for public use unless the owner is paid a fair price.

6. A person accused of a crime must be tried quickly; the trial must be public; he has a right to have a jury hear his case; he must be told of what he is accused.

7. In a lawsuit for more than $20, a person can demand a jury trial.

8. An accused person has the right to put up bail.

9. The rights listed here are not the only rights that people have.

10. The powers not given to the federal government nor forbidden by it to the States, belong to the states or to the people.

In these times of world tension, we hear a great deal about the United Nations. What is it? Why was it established? What is it supposed to do? We can give only a brief description of the United Nations here, but here

WHAT IS THE UNITED NATIONS?

are some things you should know about it.

The United Nations is an organization of governments. It was set up to prevent war and to build a better world for all by dealing with problems which can best be solved through international action. The UN constitution, known as the Charter, was signed at San Francisco on June 26, 1945, by representatives of 50 nations.

According to the Charter, the UN has four chief purposes. The first is to maintain peace by settling disputes peacefully or by taking steps to stop aggression, that is, armed attack. The second is to develop friendly relations among nations based on the equal rights of peoples and their own choices of government. The third is to achieve international cooperation in solving economic, social, cultural, and humanitarian problems. And the fourth is to serve as a center where the actions of nations can be combined in trying to attain these aims.

The UN is divided into six main working groups. The first is the General Assembly. Made up of all the members, each with one vote, it is the policy-making body of the UN.

The second is the Security Council, which is responsible for the maintenance of peace. China, France, Great Britain, the Soviet Union, and the United States have permanent seats and special voting privileges. The other six members are elected by the General Assembly for terms of two years.

The third is the Economic and Social Council with eighteen members. Its job is to promote the welfare of peoples and to further human rights and fundamental freedoms.

The fourth is the Trusteeship Council which supervises the welfare of dependent peoples under the UN and helps them towards self-government.

The fifth is the International Court of Justice which settles legal disputes.

The sixth is the Secretariat, the administrative and office staff of the UN. Its chief officer is secretary-general of the United Nations.

CHAPTER 5
HOW THINGS ARE MADE

Man has been around on this earth for a long, long time. Yet in all his long history, the biggest change in his daily life has taken place in only the last 200 years! This change in the way man lives and works is based on the development of the machine, and is called the Industrial Revolution.

WHAT WAS THE INDUSTRIAL REVOLUTION?

As far back as history goes, man has been making tools. But only after the year 1750 were real machines invented. A machine is like a tool, except that it does nearly all the work and supplies nearly all the power. This change, from tools to machines, was so important and so great, that it began to affect every phase of our lives. In tracing how one development led to another, you will see how this was so.

Before man could make much use of machines he had to harness new souces of power. Before the Industrial Revolution man used only his own muscles, the muscles of animals, wind power, and water power. To operate the new machines he had invented, man developed a new source of power—steam. This made it possible to build factories, and they were built where raw materials were available and close to markets.

As machines were used more and more, a need arose for more iron and steel. And for this, new methods of mining coal were necessary. Then, as machines were able to turn out more and more goods, it was necessary to improve transportation to get them to the markets. This led to the improvement of roads, the building of canals, the development of the railroads, and also the development of large ships to get some of these products to faraway markets.

As men began to do business with markets all over the world, better communication became important. So the telegraph and telephone were developed. But there was a still greater change to come. As factories developed and large and expensive machines began to be used, people could no longer work at home. So men began to leave their homes and go to work in factories and mills. In time this led to the "division of labor," which meant that in a factory a worker did only one job all day long instead of turning out the entire product as he used to do at home.

And finally, the Industrial Revolution made it possible to produce plentiful and cheap goods which everybody could afford.

If we were to take the value of all the gold, silver, and diamonds that are mined in one year, it would not equal the profits that are obtained from U. S. patent rights in the same year!

WHAT IS A PATENT?

What is a patent? It is an agreement between the government, representing the public, and the inventor. The government agrees that no one but the inventor will be allowed to manufacture, use, or sell his invention for a period of 17 years without the inventor's permission. In return, the inventor files his new discovery in the patent office so that everyone may profit from it when the 17 years are over.

The basic principle for granting patents is based on two questions: "Is the invention useful?" and "Is it new?" This principle is now used all over the word in granting patent rights.

Any person who has invented or discovered a new and useful art, machine, manufacture, or composition of matter may obtain a patent for it. This also includes any new or useful improvement.

Application for the patent must be made by the inventor, who is usually guided by patent lawyers or agents. A written description and drawings of the invention, together with an application fee must be submitted to the Patent Office. There are almost a hundred divisions and subdivisions of the office, each covering a different field of invention.

Government patent examiners decide the patentability of the invention. If the examiner refuses a patent, the inventor may appeal his case all the way to the Supreme Court! Once the patent is granted, it becomes the inventor's own property, and he may sell or assign it. The assignment must be recorded in the Patent Office. If anyone disregards a patent, the inventor can force him to stop using it or sue him for the profits made.

The patented article or the package in which it is sold must be marked with its patent number. If it's marked with the word "Patent" when none has been granted, there is a fine of $100 for each offense!

No one knows where or by whom the windmill was invented. Probably it was suggested by the sails of a boat.

A boat can sail at right angles to the wind by slanting its sail

HOW DOES A WINDMILL WORK?

slightly. In the same way, the "fan" or "sail" of a windmill can be driven around in a circle even when placed at right angles to the wind. The windmill is like a huge propeller, with the source of power that turns it coming from the wind instead of a machine.

The first windmills were used in Holland about 800 years ago to drain the flat fields of water. At one time windmills were common in all the flat countries near Holland. The chief use of a mill as we know it is to grind grain. In most countries mills are placed near running streams, a mill dam is built, and the water turns the mill.

But in the flat countries the streams are too sluggish to be used in this way. So windmills are built to grind the grain. In Germany there are mills in which the whole tower can be turned to face the wind as it changes. But in Holland only the roof of the windmill is revolved.

This is done by a small windmill, which is located on the other side of the roof from the big windmill and at right angles to it. When it begins to work, it turns a mechanism which sets the roof moving on little wheels and soon the big windmill is facing the wind.

The fans of a windmill are usually made of wood over which canvas has been stretched. Ropes are attached to the fans so that they can be adjusted if the wind is too strong. The fans are often 40 feet long!

Windmills of an improved type are still used in the United States and Australia. Windmills in the United States are made almost entirely of galvanized sheet steel. Each has a rudder which swings the wheel around on a pivot to catch the wind from every direction. Windmills are especially common in parts of California and in some dry regions of the West. They serve as a cheap source of power for pumping water from wells to irrigate fields, or to water cattle in pastures.

A few hundred years ago, who would have believed that millions of people would be working and living in buildings so tall that they couldn't walk the distance to their floors? Huge buildings shooting up

HOW DOES AN ELEVATOR WORK?

into the sky in our big cities would be impossible without the elevator.

The elevator is about 100 years old. By 1850 many three and four story buildings in New York were having hydraulic elevators installed. A cage or platform was mounted on top of a long plunger set in a cylinder. To raise the elevator, water was pumped into this cylinder. To lower the elevator, its operator pulled a switch which released the water in the cylinder. The water was tapped into a tank so that it could be used over and over again.

Today there are very few elevators of this type in use. Not only are they slow, but since the rod that lifts the elevator has to go straight into the ground, they cannot be used in very high buildings.

A certain type of hydraulic elevator is still used in moderately high buildings. It has a shaft, or rod, that is pushed up out of the ground; the rod is not under the platform, but is just beside it. It pushes up one end of a set of pulleys, or blocks, the other end of which lifts the elevator.

It was really the electric elevator which made it possible to put up high buildings. The elevator itself is lifted by a cable which turns on a drum set in the top of the shaft. This drum is turned by an electric motor which is stationed at the top of the building. In the newest elevators the drum has been replaced by a single pulley, which is driven directly by the motor. Through this pulley passes the cable, which is attached at one end of the elevator, and at the other end to a weight which balances the elevator.

Modern elevators have many devices built into them to prevent accidents. One of these is the air-cushion box at the bottom of the shaft. As the elevator sinks into it, the platform fits more and more tightly, so that less air escapes. The result is that an air cushion is formed and the fall is broken gradually. Another safety device consists of two steel balls which spread apart as they turn until they press a brake which stops the elevator.

The sun was man's first clock. Long ago men guessed at the time of day by watching the sun as it moved across the sky. It was easy to recognize sunrise and sunset, but harder to know when it was noon, the time when

HOW DOES A SUNDIAL TELL TIME?

the sun is highest above the horizon. In between these times, it was difficult to tell time by the position of the sun.

Then men noticed that the shadow changed in length and moved during the day. They found they could tell time more accurately by watching shadows than by looking at the sun. From this it was an easy step to inventing the sundial, which is really a shadow clock. Instead of

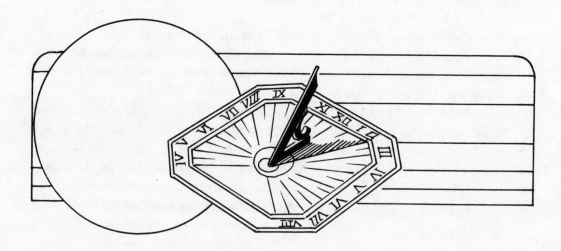

trying to guess the position of the sun and thus the time of day, the shadow gave a more accurate idea of the sun's position.

The first sundials were probably poles stuck into the ground. Stones placed around a pole marked the positions of the shadow as it moved during the day. Thus men could measure the passing of time. Later, huge stone columns were used. Cleopatra's Needle, now in Central Park in New York City, was once part of a sundial. Smaller sundials were used too. One small Egyptian sundial, about 3,500 years old, is shaped like an L. It lays flat on its longer leg, on which marks show six periods of time.

About 300 B.C. a Chaldean astronomer invented a new kind of sundial, shaped like a bowl. A shadow thrown by a pointer moved along and marked 12 hours of the day. This sort of sundial was very accurate and continued to be used for many centuries.

Today sundials are built in gardens for their beauty rather than for their usefulness. However, on the walls and window sills of old houses one sometimes sees crude sundials. They are so arranged that a nail or the edge of the window casing will cast the shadow. In an accurate sundial, the pointer must be slanted at an angle equal to the latitude of the place where it is to be used. A vertical pointer will show the correct time only at one latitude and at one season. If the dial is flat, the hour marks must be spaced unequally on it.

Before man discovered fire, the only heat and light he had was provided by the sun. Since he couldn't control this, he was quite helpless in dealing with cold and darkness.

HOW WERE LAMPS FIRST MADE?

Probably more than 100,000 years ago, he discovered fire. Then he began to notice that some materials burned better than others. Perhaps he observed that fat dripping into the fire from roasting meat burned brightly. As time passed, man began to select materials which, when burned, provided better light. Splinters of certain woods were stuck into the wall and they burned slowly. Pine knots were used as torches. Animal fats were placed in shallow stone dishes and moss and other materials were used as wicks. These were the first oil lamps. Exactly when this happened we cannot know, since it was before recorded history.

The first candles were made by melting animal fats, such as lard and tallow, and pouring the liquid into a mold such as a hollow bamboo. Fibers twisted together were strung through the center so that when it cooled, the solid rod of fat had a wick in the center. Thus, the candle was created at an unknown date long before Christ was born.

Lard was used in lard-oil lamps in New England around 1820. From whale blubber, oil was extracted for whale-oil lamps. In fact, whatever kind of oil was easiest to obtain was used for lamps. Along the Mediterranean there are many olive trees. So olive oil was used for lamps there. The Japanese and Chinese obtained oil for their lamps from various nuts. Peanuts would probably be used for oil for lamps today—if mineral oil in the earth had not been discovered.

Petroleum was discovered in 1859. By heating this oil in a closed vessel, a thin colorless product known as kerosene is obtained. This became the oil most commonly used for lamps. In fact, it was first called "coal oil," because people thought petroleum was associated with coal.

Do you have an oil lamp in your house today? Many homes keep one on hand to use in an emergency if the electricity should fail!

It is a curious thing how boys of all times in all countries seem to get the same idea about games. The game of marbles for instance, which is played in every city in this country, has been played all over the world

HOW WERE MARBLES MADE?

practically since the beginning of history!

Nobody knows just when marbles began, but it probably goes back to the first time somebody discovered that a round stone pebble would roll. And that goes back at least to the Stone Age. Scientists have discovered among Stone Age remains little balls which were too small to be used for anything but games.

Long before the Christian Era, children in ancient Egypt and Rome were playing with marbles. In Europe, marbles were played in the Middle Ages. In England the game of marbles developed from a game called "bowls," very much like bowling.

Today, some form of the game of marbles is played almost everywhere in the world. The South American boy called his marbles "bolitas." In China, boys play a game of marbles that involves kicking them. The Persian peasant boy plays with marbles he has made out of baked mud or he uses small stones. Even the Zulus play a game of marbles!

In our own country, boys usually play with two kinds of marbles. They are called "shooters" and "play marbles." Shooters are also called "taws" in some sections of the country. A shooter or taw can not be larger than 3/4 inch in diameter, and it must not be smaller than 17/32 inch. It may be made of either glass, baked clay, agate, or plastic. It is the player's favorite marble which he uses over and over again to shoot at other marbles.

Play marbles, or "mibs," are the marbles at which the player aims his shooter. They are made of baked clay, glass, stone, onyx, marble, alabaster, or plastic. Sometimes the play marbles are named after the material they are made of, such as glassies, clayies, and agates.

Most of the natural baked clay marbles and those of natural onyx come from Ohio. Glass marbles are usually made by melting the glass and, while it is hot, pressing it between the two halves of polished metal molds.

We may think of glass as being produced by the mixture of some very special chemicals in a very special way, a sort of miracle of chemistry. But actually, glass is made by a rather simple process using quite ordinary materials.

WHAT IS USED IN MAKING GLASS?

Glass is a substance made by "fusing" (melting together) certain materials, and then cooling the mixture so that the atoms arrange themselves in an unorganized pattern. What materials? Well, about 95 per cent of the raw materials in the earth could be used in making glass! The most important materials used in making glass, however, are: sand (silica), soda, limestone, borax, boric acid, magnesium oxide, and lead oxide.

Nature herself produced the first glass. About 450,000,000 years ago molten (melted) rock in the core of the earth forced its way to the surface and broke through the earth's crust in volcanoes. When the hot lava contained silica and cooled rapidly, it formed a glass as hard as a rock. This volcanic glass is called obsidian.

Glass has been made by man since very ancient times. The Egyptians, more than 5,000 years ago, knew how to make a kind of colored glass with which they covered stone and pottery and sometimes made into beads. Perfume and ointment bottles made of glass were used in Egypt more than 3,500 years ago.

The Roman Empire (1st century B.C. to 5th century A.D.) was one of the greatest periods in the history of glass. It was at this time that man learned how to blow glass and thus form hundreds of different shapes and sizes of glass objects.

Today, of course, there are many new ways of making glass that have been developed. But this is the basic process. The raw materials for glass are brought to the glass factory and stored in huge bins. The raw materials are carefully measured and then mixed into a "batch." Then broken glass of the same formula, called "cullet," is added to the batch to speed the melting. The batch is fed automatically into the furnace. The glass then flows out of the furnace at lower temperatures.

Then the glass goes through many processes such as blowing, pressing, rolling, casting and drawing—depending on the type of glass that is being made.

Glass blowing is one of the oldest of skills. But as modern machines have been developed and perfected, and as the use of glass has increased, glass blowing by hand is becoming rarer and rarer.

HOW CAN GLASS BE BLOWN?

When glass is in a melted state, it can be "worked" in many ways. It can be blown, pressed, drawn, or rolled. For hundreds of years, the chief method of working with glass was blowing.

The glassworker gathered a ball of molten glass on the end of his blow-pipe and blew, just the way you would blow a soap bubble. Using his skill, he shaped the glass as he blew, and drew it out to the correct thinness. He kept reheating the glass to keep it workable, and then he would finish it with special tools.

In this way, many kinds of glass objects were made. Glass could also be blown into molds and shaped in that way. Surprisingly enough, window glass used to be made by blowing a long cylinder of glass which was split and flattened to produce a sheet of glass. Of course, the size of these sheets was limited by the lung power of the glassblower!

Today, this method of blowing glass (called "freehand") is still used to produce special scientific apparatus and very expensive and beautiful glass articles. But the demand for glass containers such as bottles became so great that efforts were made to create a glass-blowing machine, and finally in 1903 the first automatic machine for blowing glass was invented.

This machine uses a vacuum to suck in a sufficient amount of glass to form each bottle. First the neck of the bottle is molded. Then compressed air is turned on, and the finished bottle is blown. After that, the bottle is automatically annealed, which means it is cooled gradually to make it tough and strong. This machine can turn out more bottles in one hour than six men doing free-hand blowing can do in a day!

Later, another machine was developed for automatically blowing light bulbs, which made possible the wide use of electric light. Most of the world's bottles, jars, tumblers, and other blown-glass containers are made by machine.

Can you imagine a modern city without neon signs? This form of illumination and advertising has become so popular that it can be seen all over the world. What is neon and how are the signs made?

HOW ARE NEON SIGNS MADE?

Neon is a gas. In every 65,000 parts of air there is one part of neon gas. Even though it occurs in such small amounts, neon is taken from the air and used in electric signs.

In 1898, Sir William Ramsay and M. W. Travers, English chemists, distilled liquid air and found a small residue left. This gas they called "neon," meaning "the new." Neon is a gas that has neither color,

173

taste, nor smell. It is one of the "inert" gases. Like helium and other heavier gases, neon will not unite with any other element, and for that reason is found only in the free state.

A neon lamp contains this gas through which flows a current of electricity. As this current, which consists of moving electrons, moves through the gas, the electrons collide with gas atoms and impart some of their energy to the atoms.

Now electrons normally circulate around the nucleus of the atom. But when the collision takes place, some of them are dislodged from their usual positions. Atoms which contain such disturbed electrons are said to be in the "excited state."

After a brief period, the excited atoms lose their extra energy and snap back into their normal positions. Each time this happens, a bundle of light is produced and emitted.

The light that is given off is a reddish-orange glow. Like any other red rays, these rays can penetrate thick fog and atmosphere more easily than other types of light. By adding very small amounts of mercury, a light blue color can be obtained. By using different combinations of rare gases, such as helium and argon, with neon, signs in all colors are possible.

Rubber is a sticky, elastic solid obtained from a milky liquid in plants known as latex (not sap). The latex appears in the bark, roots, stem, branches, leaves, and fruit of certain plants and trees. Rubber has been

HOW DO WE GET RUBBER?

found in more than 400 different vines, shrubs, and trees—though the amount found differs greatly in each case.

The question then is how long ago did man discover that certain plants and trees contained this substance we call rubber? Rubber itself existed millions of years ago. Men have found fossils of rubber-producing plants which date back almost 3,000,000 years! So we'll probably never know exactly when the first primitive man discovered rubber.

We do know that man knew about rubber at least nine hundred years ago. Archeologists have dug up crude rubber balls in ruins of Inca and Mayan civilizations in Central and South America.

As a matter of fact, we might give Christopher Columbus some credit for discovering rubber. A Spanish subject who was with Columbus on his second voyage to the New World, wrote a report in which he told of natives in Haiti playing a game with a ball made from "the gum of a tree."

In 1520, Emperor Montezuma entertained Cortes and his soldiers in Mexico City with a game played with rubber balls. And it is believed that even earlier the natives of southeastern Asia knew of rubber prepared from the "juice" of a tree. They used it to make torches, and coated baskets and jars with it to make them waterproof.

In 1736 a Frenchman named La Condamine sent a report and samples of rubber to Paris from an expedition to South America. He described how the natives made shoes, battle shields, and bottles from the rubber, and how it was used to waterproof clothing. So rubber seems to have been one of man's early discoveries.

Like so many other things created by man or produced by nature, chlorine can be both harmful and helpful! In wartime, some of the most terrifying poison gases use chlorine as a base. In peacetime, it is one

WHAT IS CHLORINE?

of man's most valuable safeguards of health.

Chlorine forms a part of many germicides and disinfectants (substances which destroy germs). Most city water purification systems use chlorine to kill any bacteria that survive after the water has been treated. Only about 4 or 5 parts of liquid chlorine per 1,000,000 parts of water are used for this. This amount is not harmful to humans although the water may sometimes have a chlorinated taste.

Chlorine combines readily with many other elements so that it is not found free in nature, but in compounds. Common salt (sodium chloride) is the most familiar example of this.

Pure chlorine is a suffocating, greenish-yellow gas. It was first prepared by a Swedish chemist in 1774. In 1810 it was recognized as an element by Sir Humphry Davy. It is now obtained cheaply and in large quantities by passing a current of electricity through a solution of common salt.

Chlorine may be liquefied by refrigeration or compressed to a liquid. In that form, it is shipped in iron cylinders or even in specially designed tank cars.

Chlorine is used for bleaching and in preparing bleaching powder. The largest single use is in beaching in the process of making paper. Chlorine is an important part of modern antiseptics and of the anesthetic, chloroform.

In most of the secretions that animals produce in their body, there are some chlorine salts. For example, the gastric juice in the stomach contains an acid formed of chlorine and hydrogen, known as hydrochloric acid.

You've probably seen pictures of police using tear gas to break up riots, or to make criminals leave some building in which they have barricaded themselves.

WHAT IS TEAR GAS?

Tear gas is only one of many gases which have been developed to produce certain effects on the human body so that the victim is helpless or injured, or even killed. It is not pleasant even to think about these gases and their effect, but they are all part of what is considered "chemical warfare."

Choking gases act on the respiratory system, inflaming the lungs. They cause coughing and make it hard to breathe. Blister gases attack any part of the body which they touch, especially moistened parts. They cause burns and destroy tissue. Mustard gas is one of these.

Sneeze gases cause sneezing, intense pain in the nose, throat and chest, and have other strong effects. Blood gases directly affect the heart action, the nerve reflexes, and may interfere with the breathing in of oxygen. Carbon monoxide is one of these gases.

Nerve gases cause nausea, twitching of the body, and may result in death.

Tear gas irritates the mucous membrane around the eyes, causing intense smarting, a flow of tears, and makes it impossible for a person to see clearly. In its original form, tear gas is a sugarlike solid material. When it is heated it forms a vapor that attacks the eyes. Tear gas is placed in grenades and paper projectiles and fired through the windows into the room where the criminal has taken refuge. The white cloud of tear gas soon blinds him so that he gives up. The effect of tear gas is only temporary. As soon as a person leaves the contaminated area he recovers.

But it isn't only in war or against criminals that poison gases must be considered. Gasoline engines throw off a poison gas called carbon monoxide, which is why automobiles must not be run in closed garages!

Tar seems to be such a simple ordinary thing, yet few products have had a history that can match it in importance or excitement!

When people first began to heat coal to get coke for furnaces, the

WHAT IS TAR?

stiff black liquid that came from it was thought valueless. It was coal tar and it was thrown away. Today, more than 200,000 by-products are made from coal tar—products that we use every single day of our lives!

The first use of coal tar was as a fuel. Later on, it was used as a protective coating on wood and ropes. Finally it was discovered that other useful substances could be made from the tar. When the tar was heated and distilled, different oils were obtained. One of these was used as a substitute for turpentine.

Then in 1856, a 17-year-old chemistry assistant in England, William Henry Perkin, accidentally discovered that certain dyes, called aniline, could be made from coal tar. This opened a whole new world of industry.

How are various products obtained from coal tar? It is done by the process of distillation. The tar is boiled in big ovens that have bent tubes leading from them. The gases and liquids that are given off are collected. Coal tar itself contains a little of everything. As it is distilled again and again, different substances are drawn off. The pitch that remains is the tar we are familiar with in tar shingles, tar-paper roofing, and in asphalt for paving streets.

What are some of the by-products of coal tar? Most of the colors now used for dyes and printing inks are made from coal tar. Carbolic acid, used as antiseptic in hospitals, comes from coal tar. Aspirin comes from coal tar. Saccharin, which is 550 times as sweet as cane sugar, is a coal-tar product. The entire modern plastics industry is based on coal tar. Nylon is a combination of coal, air, and water. Clothing and textile fibers are being made from coal today.

Mothballs, artificial flavors, and soda water are coal tar products. Chemicals made with the help of coal are used in food. So you see that in a lump of coal, and in the tar which comes from it, we have the source of thousands of products we all use every day.

The love of perfume is probably as old as the human race. Vases containing oily pastes that were still fragrant have been found in Egyptian tombs 5,000 years old.

HOW IS PERFUME OBTAINED FROM FLOWERS?

The Arabians were the first to distill rose petals with water to produce rose water. This was 1,200 years ago. Today, there are two chief methods used to extract the perfume from flowers. One that is widely used is called "enfleurage," which means enflowering.

In this method, sheets of glass are set in wooden frames. They are coated with purified lard and covered with flower petals. Then they are stacked one above the other. The flower petals are replaced at intervals until the pomade, as the purified lard is called, has absorbed the desired amount of perfume.

A more modern method is to extract the perfume from the flower petals with a very pure solvent obtained from petroleum. This solvent is repeatedly circulated through fresh petals until it is saturated with perfume. The solvent is then removed by distillation and the perfume purified with alcohol.

Flowers are only one of the sources of perfume essences. There are cedarwood and sandalwood, cinnamon bark, myrrh, and the various aromatic resins and balsams. There are many leaves such as rosemary, lavender, patchouli, peppermint, geranium, and thyme. The rinds of the orange, lemon and lime, as well as the roots of orris and ginger, are also used. Among the great families of flowers especially famous for fragrance are roses, violets, jasmine, orange blossoms, tuberoses, and jonquils.

Very few perfumes on the market today are pure floral essences. Most of them are a blend of small quantities of natural flower essences with animal and synthetic materials. Chemists are now even able to make beautiful floral scents which would be very difficult to obtain in nature.

If you've ever gone out on a picnic or had a barbecue in your back yard, you've probably used charcoal for cooking the food. Charcoal gives a hot fire with very little smoke or flame.

WHAT IS CHARCOAL?

But charcoal has many other important uses too. It has a part in making gas masks, water filters, pencils, polishes, tooth pastes, and medicines. What is charcoal? It is a black, spongelike substance left when animal or vegetable material is partially burned. It is almost pure carbon.

It may be made from wood or from animal bones by heating or burning them in such a way that the water and gases contained in them are driven off and the solid material is left. The charcoal which is made from bones is called "bone black." It is very useful as a filtering agent, because it absorbs impurities, coloring material, and bad odors.

Lamp black and ivory black are used in making printing inks and as a pigment in oil paints. Lamp black is the soot obtained by burning resin, turpentine, tar, oil, or fats with a limited amount of air. Ivory black is made from waste chips of ivory.

Wood charcoal is usually made in one of two ways. The first method consists of covering piles of wood with dirt or sods. Then a fire is built at the bottom of the pile and the wood is allowed to burn slowly, or char. This method has been followed for hundreds of years in the forests of northern Europe. It is wasteful because it makes no use of the gases which keep escaping during the process.

In the second method the wood is piled into iron buggies. These are pulled or pushed into huge ovens, called "retors." When the fire is burning brightly, it is partially smothered by closing the draft. The wood gradually turns to charcoal. The escaping gases are collected in another chamber and valuable substances such as wood alcohol and acetic acid are condensed from them.

Since wood charcoal is a poor conductor of heat, it is also used as an insulator. It is used in gas masks because of its power to absorb gases. And sticks of charcoal made from willow wood, are used by artists and art students for drawing.

Milk is considered to be the nearly perfect food. It supplies the body with proteins, with a form of sugar (lactose), minerals, and vitamins.

Years ago most people used to drink milk just about as it came

HOW DO WE PRESERVE MILK?

from the cow. Today milk is treated in various ways for many reasons. Some of these are health reasons. Some are for convenience.

Milk is evaporated in order to preserve it. Evaporated milk has had about one half of the water in it removed. It is made by heating the milk in a vacuum to evaporate the water without overheating or scorching the milk. The thickened milk is canned, sealed, and sterilized.

The food value of evaporated milk with an equal amount of water added, is about the same as the food value of whole pasteurized milk. When evaporated milk is sealed in the can and sterilized, it can be stored without refrigerating it. You can see what a great convenience this is under certain conditions. Once the can is opened, however, evaporated milk needs the same care as fresh pastuerized milk.

Another form of preserved, or concentrated, milk is sweetened condensed milk. It is milk evaporated to about half its volume to which sugar has been added. Sweetened condensed milk is not sterilized. It depends on the sugar in it for preservation.

One of the most widely used ways to preserve milk is to dehydrate (or powder) it. In dehydration, water is removed from milk and only the dry milk powder is left. The most common method of making dried or powdered milk is the spraying process. The milk is first evaporated. The thickened milk which is left is then forced as a fine spray into a large drying chamber. Blasts of hot air quickly absorb the moisture from the milk spray. The milk powder falls to the bottom of the drying chamber. It is then removed and packaged.

Powdered milk is changed to liquid milk by adding water. Nine pounds of water added to one pound of milk powder make it taste like whole milk.

It would be hard for us to imagine life without soap. Staying clean is such an important need, that most of us would think soap was one of man's first discoveries. Yet soap was absolutely unknown until the

HOW DOES SOAP CLEAN?

beginning of the Christian Era. So man has had soap for less than 2,000 years!

Soap is made by the action of alkali on fats or oils. In simple terms, when these are boiled together, soap is produced. The alkalies used are usually soda and potash. How does soap clean?

There are several ideas as to how this happens. One is that soap breaks the greasy dirt into particles so small that the water can wash them away. They become emulsified, or like a milky liquid, with the water and are easily rinsed away.

Another idea is that the soap lubricates the dirt particles, making it easier for the water to remove them. In other words, the soap makes the dirt so slippery that it can not hang on the surface to which it has been attached. Water has what is called a surface tension; that is, it behaves as if it were covered with a thin, elastic film. This surface tension keeps the water from getting in and under and around small particles of dirt, soot, and dust on the skin and in soiled fabrics. Soap dissolved in water is supposed to lower this surface tension so that the soapy solution can surround the dirt particles and pry them off, making it easy to flush them away.

Soaps and other cleansing agents are often called detergents. This comes from the Latin word detergere, which means to wipe off. Many people think that a detergent is not a soap, but actually, soaps as well as special cleansing agents can be called detergents.

Modern chemistry has created powerful cleansers that are special "wetting agents." These are sometimes called "soapless soaps." The special ability of these to clean is due to the way they break down the surface tension of water. They are thus able to penetrate especially well under all kinds of dirt. Wetting agents are used in shampoos, washing powders and in toothpastes.

There are many kinds of soap made for special uses. Scouring soaps contain abrasive material. Naphtha soaps contain naphtha for cutting heavy grease. Saddle soaps have a little wax which remains on the leather when dried. Castile soap is made with olive oil.

Do you know of any candy that is not sweet? As a matter of fact, people sometimes refer to candy as "sweets." This is because the most important part of all candy is sugar.

WHEN WAS CANDY FIRST EATEN?

Now that we know this, it will not surprise us to learn how the word "candy" came into being. In Persia, about the year 500 A.D., they were able to make sugar in solid form. The Persian name for white sugar was "kandi-sefid." And that's where we got the word "candy!"

In ancient times, most people had something that could be considered a sort of candy, even if they didn't have sugar. The Egyptians, for example, have left written and picture records of candy and candy-making. But since they didn't know how to refine sugar, they used honey as a sweetener. And they used dates as the basis for their sweetmeats. In many parts of the Far East, even today, each tribe has its official candy-maker and secret recipes. They use almonds, honey, and figs to make their candy.

Oddly enough, nobody in Europe had the idea of making something sweet to eat for its own sake until quite recently. They would use sweet syrup to hide the taste of bitter medicines. Then, in the seventeenth century, a great deal of sugar began to be shipped to Europe from the colonies. So candy-making as a separate art began in Europe at that time.

The French were the first to candy fruits and to develop their recipes. One of these, a nut and sugar-syrup sweet called prawlings, may have been the forerunner of the famous New Orleans pralines.

The early American settlers boiled the sap of the maple tree to make maple-sugar candy. Taffy pulls were social events, and sugar crystals were grown and formed on strings to make rock candy. About 1850 small lozenges, many of them heart-shaped, had romantic messages printed on them. Later on, candy shops began to sell peppermint lozenges and chocolate drops, and the candy business was on its way!

Did you know that Napoleon had a great deal to do with the development of canned food? Of course, people had been trying for thousands of years to find better ways to preserve food for a long time. But it was

Napoleon, during his military campaigns, that really gave canning a start.

The French soldiers and sailors who were fighting Napoleon's wars often had to fight on a diet limited to smoked fish, salt meat, and hardtack. Thousands of men died from scurvy and slow starvation. So, in 1795, the French government offered a prize of 12,000 francs for the most practical method of giving French armies and navies fresh and wholesome food. Fifteen years later, the prize was awarded to Nicholas Appert, a chef and confectioner who lived near Paris.

What Appert did was to pack the food into wide-mouth glass bottles. Then he sealed the bottles with cork and wire, and put each bottle into its own cloth sack for protection. He next lowered the bottles into a boiler filled with hot water. A lid was put on, so that the bottles would heat in their boiling water bath.

Appert's method is as effective today for some foods as it was then, although the theory upon which he worked was not correct. He thought it was only necessary to keep out air to preserve cooked food. Later it was learned that preserving canned food depends on absence of invisible bacteria.

The first patent for a "tin canister" for preserving food was granted in England to Peter Durand in 1810. He got the idea from the canisters in which tea was packed. In America, the name was shortened to "tin can," and we call this industry "canning," while in England it is known as "tinning."

The first cannery in the United States was one for fish, and was started by Ezra Dagget in New York City in 1819. The next year, fruit preserves and tomatoes were put up in glass in Boston.

To can a food successfully, it must be heated enough to kill the organisms (molds, yeasts, bacteria) that may cause fresh food to spoil; the tin can or glass jar must be free from germs, and it must be sealed air-tight.

For some reason, Americans have not become as fond of tea as the people of other countries. In the United States, we use only about a pound of tea a year per person, but in England it takes nine pounds to satisfy their needs!

HOW IS TEA PROCESSED?

The Chinese, of course, are the world's original and greatest tea drinkers. They have enjoyed tea for more than 4,000 years! It was only about 300 years ago that Europeans first tasted tea.

The tea bush, or tree, actually doesn't grow wild in China, so it is believed that the Chinese themselves imported the first seeds from India. When the British came to India and discovered tea, they began to establish large plantations there and in Ceylon. In time, more tea was exported from Ceylon than from China!

There are two main varieties of tea plants. The Chinese kind grows only three or four feet high, while the Indian plant can reach heights of 20 feet. Tea leaves, if they are not picked, can grow to the size of a man's hands. But since small, tender leaves make a better grade of tea, the tea plants are usually pruned. It takes a tea bush three years to produce its first crop, and that's only half an ounce of tea!

Next to the tenderness of the leaf, the next most important quality about tea is the altitude at which it is grown. The best tea comes from high mountain plantations. Once the leaves are picked, they are carried to the factory where the curing process has to begin immediately.

The leaves are spread over shelves to wilt. Then they are passed into rolling machines, which free the juices. Black and green tea leaves come from the same plant. When black tea is desired, the rolled green leaves are spread out again and covered with wet cloths. This makes the leaves ferment and change to a blackish color. Afterward the leaves are dried, sorted, and then packed for shipment. The best black tea is orange pekoe, which is made from the youngest and tenderest leaves of the plants.

Oolong tea, which is a favorite in this country, comes from Formosa. It is neither green nor quite black, since it is only partly fermented.

The reason tea is stimulating is that it contains caffeine, just as coffee does. Another substance in tea is tannin, which sometimes makes the tea bitter.

It would be natural to assume that clothing originated because of the desire of man to protect himself from the weather. Yet, actually, this was only one of the reasons.

HOW DID CLOTHING ORIGINATE?

Equally important was the desire of people to make themselves attractive in the eyes of other people. Primitive man spread colored clays over his body for this purpose. Later on, as he invented knife blades of bone, flint, and stone, he slashed his skin and rubbed colored clay into the cuts. This was the beginning of what we call tattooing.

As time went on, primitive man found other methods of gaining attention. He would suspend trophies of battle and hunting from his body, such as strings of teeth and bones. Around his waist he hung the skins of animals, pieces of horn, feathers, scalps, and the like. Later the necklace was replaced by a tunic or shirt and a skirt was added to the waistband.

The next step in the development of clothing was the actual covering of the body with some sort of material. Soon this was worn not only for adornment, but for protection and modesty.

When the glacial periods came, and snow and rain fell, a naked tribesman would seek shelter in the cave of some wild beast, perhaps a bear. If he could find a live animal, he killed it. Then, he made a hole in its body, crawled inside and slept until the carcass was cold. Then he flayed off its skin and wore it by day and slept in it by night.

In this way the furs and skins of wild beasts became the clothing of man. These early hunters invented the art of sewing. They used sharp-edged knives for skinning animals. They made awls of flint for boring holes in which to insert thongs to bind the cloth together. The most important part of their inventions was the needle with an eye.

Needles with eyes, buttons, and clasps have been found in Stone Age caves of central Europe and the Swiss villages of 30,000 to 40,000 years ago! Some needles that are very long were made from the leg bones of large birds. Others were made of ivory and are fine enough to sew almost any garment today! In some parts of the world, grasses and leaves were tied, interwined, and woven together into clothing.

The making of clothing was thus one of the first arts developed by man.

Of all the fibers used in making cloth, cotton is the most important. It is the world's chief material for clothing. There are good reasons for this. Cotton is cheap, it has a natural twist which makes it easy to spin

WHAT IS COTTON?

into thread, it needs no special preparation, it washes well, and it is strong.

Cotton has been used by man for more than 3,000 years! It was known to the people of India and China long before Europe found out about it. In fact, when Europeans first learned of cotton, they described it by comparing it to wool, and for a long time it was even called "cotton wool." At first, cotton was very expensive and only the rich could afford it. When Columbus tried to reach India, one of the treasures he hoped to find was cotton.

Cotton grows on a plant which reaches a height of about 3 or 4 feet. When the flowers first appear they are creamy white, and they turn pink later. Then the pod, or boll, appears and in about 6 to 9 weeks the boll ripens, turns brown, and bursts open to reveal the soft white fibers. The fibers are long hairs which grow out of the seed coats.

Cotton picking means picking the ripe bolls from the plant. This has to be done with great care, in order not to injure the unripe bolls on the plant. After the cotton is picked, it is loaded into wagons and hauled to a nearby gin, where it goes into a ginning machine. A cotton gin (short for "engine") removes the seeds from the cotton fibers. Before Eli Whitney invented the cotton gin, it took a man an entire day to remove the seeds from one pound of cotton! A modern gin can clean several thousand pounds of cotton a day.

After being ginned, the cotton fibers are pressed into bales weighing about 500 pounds each, and shipped to the textile mills, where it is manufactured into cloth. Cotton cloth may be as flimsy as gauze for bandages or as strong as fabrics for making canvas tents and awnings. When it is waterproofed it may be used in making umbrellas and raincoats. Cotton is one of the most versatile fabrics known to man!

There is an old French word *boton*, which means a "bud." And this word probably came from a still older word *bouter*, which means "to push out." Our word button comes from these words, because this is exactly what a button does. It sticks out from whatever it is attached to, ready to be pushed out through a buttonhole or loop to fasten articles together.

WHEN WERE BUTTONS FIRST USED?

Nobody knows by whom buttons were first used, or when. They go back to the beginning of history; some experts say to 30,000 or 40,000 years ago! Yet a funny thing about buttons is that in some parts of the world they have never been used. After all, think of all the ways there are to fasten clothing and keep it in place: pinning, buckling, lacing, belting down, wrapping around and draping, and tying together!

Another thing about buttons is that sometimes they go out of style for clothing and are not used for long periods of time, perhaps hundreds of years. From the time of the ancient Romans until almost the end of the Middle Ages, buttons were not worn by people in Italy, Spain, and France!

In the fourteenth century, buttons became popular in Europe and from that time on they have never gone entirely out of fashion. Buttons have been made from almost any kind of material you can imagine. Metal buttons have been made of gold, silver, steel, copper, tin, aluminum, nickel, brass, pewter, and bronze.

Animal products have been used for making buttons and these include: bone, horn, hoof, hair, leather, ivory, and shells! In addition, buttons have been made from cloth, thread, paper, glass, porcelain, rubber, wood, sawdust, oatmeal, peach pits, and birds' feathers!

At one time, men and boys wore buttons for jewelry. In 1685 King Louis XIV of France ordered many diamond buttons for himself, including one set of 75, each costing more than $200.

Tartan is the name for a woolen cloth woven in a pattern of crossbars. These bars are of a certain width and color for each pattern of tartan, and are the same in both directions. A distinctive pattern for tartan is called a sett.

WHY DO THE SCOTS MAKE VARIOUS TARTANS?

The different setts of tartan get their names from the clans. In ancient days in the Scottish Highlands, life was organized into clans. The people living in a certain district put themselves under the leadership of a chief for protection. The title of chief remained in the same family, and the name of the chief's family became the name of the clan.

The Highlanders made their clothing from the wool of sheep which grazed on the hillsides. This wool was colored with native vegetable dyes and was woven into garments. Gradually the different clans began to adopt certain colors and patterns to set themselves apart. Since these clans frequently waged war on each other, their tartans served as a uniform, and showed membership in a special clan.

In time, other types of tartans developed. A hunting tartan was adopted to have suitable colors for blending with the countryside. District tartans were worn by people who didn't belong to any clan. The clergy developed its own sett.

Before the eighteenth century, a tartan was worn as a garment about five feet wide and six yards long. It was worn with the lower half draped around the waist and held by a belt. The upper half was draped over the belt, brought around to the back, and fastened at the left shoulder with a pin. Later, this garment was cut into two pieces. The lower half became the kilt, and the upper half the plaid. Plaid, by the way, does not mean tartan, it refers to a garment worn like a shawl.

To crush the Scottish national spirit, the English Parliament passed laws in 1746 abolishing the clan system, prohibiting the playing of bagpipes and the wearing of kilts and tartans. These laws were repealed in 1782, and after that the kilt and the wearing of the tartan came back into fashion among the Scots. But now it has become a national costume, and is kept for special occasions.

The making of leather is one of the oldest industries. Even before man began to make rude axes and spears, he must have wrapped himself in the skins of animals to keep off the cold and the rain.

HOW WAS LEATHER FIRST MADE?

Since ancient man usually hung his skins over the fire to dry, he found that smoke preserved the hides. Later he found that the wood and bark of certain trees preserved skins even better than smoke. He also removed the hairs.

When recorded history began, man was making almost as good leather as that which is made today. Pieces of leather made by the Egyptians as early as 3000 B.C. are still in good condition. The Babylonians and the Hebrews knew ways of making leather which are almost the same as present processes.

Sometimes the leather was preserved by tanning it with the bark of trees, sometimes by curing it with salt, and sometimes by rubbing it with oil. The American Indians made especially fine leather by cleaning the hair and flesh from the hides, dressing the hides with oil, and finally smoking them.

Like the people of today, the ancients found leather one of the most useful materials. Much of our knowledge of ancient nations comes from records written on parchment, which was made from the skins of sheep, goats, and calves. Leather was used by soldiers for helmets, shields, and jackets. It served sailors as sails and coverings for ships. Bottles, rugs, shoes, and even coins were made of leather.

Hides of cattle form one of the chief sources of leather, but the skins of many other animals are also used. As a rule, the skins of larger animals, such as cattle, buffaloes, or elephants, are called hides, while those of smaller animals are simply called skins.

Among the animals whose skin is used for leather are calves, pigs, horses, sheep, goats, deer, ostriches, alligators, lizards, snakes, seals, whales, sharks, and walruses.

Early man who lived where sharp rocks hurt his feet, soon began to think of some way of protecting them. So he made a mat of woven grass, or used a strip of hide or a flat piece of wood as a "sandal." He

HOW WERE SHOES FIRST MADE?

fastened these to the bottom of his feet with thongs cut from hide. Sometimes these thongs were brought between the toes and tied around the ankles. In colder parts of the world, man soon felt a need to give the foot even more protection, so he added more material to the top of the sandal, and thus the shoe was born.

Sandals were worn by the ancient Egyptians as long as 5,000 years ago! At first, in fact, the sandals were worn only by the rich Egyptians. They would walk along followed by a servant who carried a pair of sandals, just in case the master would need or want to put them on. Later of course, all the people began wearing them. Sometimes they made the sandals with upturned toes, to give the foot more protection. Egyptians were the first shoemakers in the world.

The Greeks developed the boot by gradually changing the straps which held the sandals to the feet into solid leather. Even today many primitive forms of shoes still survive. We still wear sandals very much like those worn by ancient Romans and Greeks. We have moccasins which are like those worn by the American Indians. And people in Holland still wear wooden shoes!

Modern shoes as we know them began to appear in the Middle Ages about the time the Crusades started. Because the Crusaders went on long journeys they needed good protection for their feet, and so people began to make shoes that would last for a long time.

In time shoes became an object of fashion and all kinds of ridiculous styles appeared. At one time it was the fashion to wear long-toed shoes, with toes six inches long coming to a sharp point! These were so uncomfortable that they had to be abandoned, so another new fashion was invented—the high heel.

In America, a shoemaker named Thomas Beard arrived on the second voyage of the Mayflower in 1629, and his little shop was the start of our great shoe industry.

The reason photography is possible is that light acts a certain way on a chemically prepared substance. This substance is called the emulsion and it coats the film which is used in taking a picture.

HOW IS CAMERA FILM MADE?

When light strikes the chemical silver nitrate it turns black. So the first step in making film is to obtain silver nitrate crystals. The film is prepared somewhat the way a piece of bread is spread with jam. The "jam" is the emulsion on the face of the film, with the "seeds" representing silver particles or grains which are sensitive to light. The "bread" is the flexible, transparent plastic base. The main parts of the emulsion are the silver particles and gelatin.

The first step in making the film itself is to mix gelatin with silver nitrate and potassium bromide in a warm, syrupy form. This must be done in total darkness because the silver crystals are sensitive to light. The nitrate and potassium combine as potassium nitrate, and this is washed away. Silver bromide crystals are left in the gelatin. This is the emulsion.

The film itself is made by first treating cotton fibers or wood pulp with acetic acid. This makes a white flaky product called cellulose acetate. The cellulose acetate is then dissolved and the mixture forms clear, thick fluid known as "dope."

The dope is fed evenly onto chromium-plated wheels. As the wheels turn, heat drives off the solvents, and the dope becomes a thin, flexible, transparent sheet. Next, the film base is coated with the emulsion. The dry film is then slit into proper widths and wound into spools.

When a picture is taken, light strikes this film. When this happens, the tiny silver bromide grains inside the film emulsion are exposed. They become, in the developing process, the dark part of the film negative from which positives, or prints, are made.

One of the most beautiful ways to decorate a church is to fill the windows with designs in stained glass. In addition to providing decoration, the designs usually illustrate the Scriptures.

HOW ARE STAINED GLASS WINDOWS MADE?

No one knows when stained glass was first made. It probably started in the Near East, the home of the glass industry, about the ninth century. Before that time glass wasn't made in a great variety of colors. The first reference that can be found to stained glass as we know it (which means not just colored windows but windows that tell a story) goes back to the year 969, and tells about such windows being installed in the cathedral at Reims, France. The oldest stained-glass windows still in existence are from the eleventh century.

In the design of a stained-glass window, six things play a part in the composition: (1) the glass containing color as a stain; (2) small details such as the features of people, which are painted on the glass with brown pigment; (3) lead strips which hold the pieces of glass together; (4) iron T-bars which support the leaded glass in sections; (5) the tracery of stone or wood which divides the window itself; (6) round iron "saddle" bars, which are fastened across the glass to take the wind pressure. So you see that designing a stained-glass window is not like painting a picture. All these elements have to be considered by the designer in creating his effect.

To make a window, the designer makes full-sized drawings first. This shows each piece of glass and its color, and all the elements listed above. He then cuts pieces of glass to fit the drawing. Then each piece that requires paint is painted, and these are fired in a kiln which turns the paint to an enamel. Then the pieces are leaded together and the whole design is put into place.

The dominant color in stained-glass windows is always a primary one—red, blue, or yellow. In old stained-glass windows it was always a rich red or blue, which made the windows quite dark. Later, more yellow was used to admit more light.

WHAT IS STERLING SILVER?

Silver is one of the most widely distributed of all metals. About 2,000,000 tons of it float about in solution in the sea, but it would not pay to get it out. In the main, silver comes only in ores from which it must be separated.

In this ore, silver is usually combined with sulphur as silver sulphide, or is a part of other sulphides, chiefly those of copper, lead, or arsenic. Silver therefore has to be separated from these sulphides to obtain it in pure form.

But silver is too soft to be used in its pure state. That's why silver coins contain 90 per cent silver and 10 per cent copper. The sterling silver of which jewelry and silverware are made, contains 92.5 per cent silver and 7.5 per cent copper.

The name "sterling" comes from a German family named Easterling. The absolute honesty of the Easterlings as traders persuaded King John of England (in 1215) to give them the job of making the English coins. They did it so well and truly that their name is still used as a sign of solid worth. All sterling silver is stamped with a hallmark—either the word "sterling," or a symbol, varying in different countries. The English symbol is a lion.

Many people in former generations, although they wanted sterling silver, could not afford it and they welcomed the invention of Sheffield plate. To make this, a sheet of copper and one of silver are rolled together so that the silver completely hides the copper. This fine plated ware was made in Sheffield and Birmingham, England, and was not cheap. To reduce the cost still more, a thin layer of silver may be coated on any desired metal object by electroplating. Silverplate is widely used in our country and elsewhere. Silver is also used in many ways in industry.

Hundreds of things we use every day are objects that have been electro-plated. The metal decorations on cars have been chromium-plated. Knives and forks and spoons may be silver-plated. Other things around the house may have been copper-plated.

WHAT IS ELECTROPLATING?

Electroplating is the process of putting a coating of metal on an object through the action of an electric current. The purpose of electroplating is usually to give a metal better appearance, or protect it against corrosion. Sometimes it is for reasons of health, as when the steel for food cans is tin-plated.

In order to electroplate an object, three things are necessary. First, a supply of direct electric current. Second, a piece of pure metal. And third, a liquid which contains some of the metal to be used in plating.

Let's see if we can follow the remarkable process that takes place in electroplating by imagining that we are going to plate a bolt with copper. We take a glass jar or beaker and put in a solution of water and copper sulphate. We thus have a liquid which contains the metal to be used in the plating.

Now we put in a piece of pure copper, and this is attached by a wire to the positive pole of a battery, which is our source of direct current. Now we put in the bolt which is to be plated, after it has been thoroughly cleaned. The bolt is attached by a wire to the negative pole of the battery.

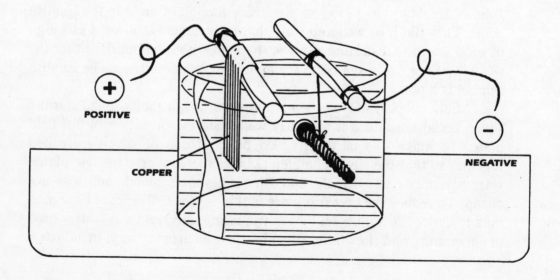

POSITIVE

COPPER

NEGATIVE

When the current flows, an interesting thing happens. The bolt becomes negative, because it is attached to the negative pole of the battery. As you know, electrical opposites attract each other. So the negative bolt attracts the positive part of the copper sulphate and it pulls the copper out of the solution. This copper coats or plates itself on the surface of the metal bolt!

But this is only part of the story! The sulphate which is left in the solution has a negative charge. So it is attracted by the positive charge of the piece of pure copper we put in. When it reaches the copper, it pulls off enough copper to make a molecule of copper sulphate again. So our solution remains as before . . . copper sulphate. In this way, the piece of copper is slowly dissolved and added to the surface of the bolt until it is copper plated. This process, but using different metals and solutions, enables us to beautify or protect metals by electroplating.

There was a time when bows and arrows were the chief weapons man had to defend himself against his enemies. They were also the way he earned his livelihood. With bow and arrow he hunted wild game, which

WHO INVENTED THE BOW AND ARROW?

supplied him with food, shelter, and clothing.

Nobody knows who made the first bows and arrows because they go back so far in history. They were probably first used in the Stone Age. We have found drawings thousands of years old on the walls of caves which show archers drawing their bows. There are also ancient arrowheads made of flint which have been found in many parts of the world.

During the Middle Ages, archery was developed to a high degree in England and France. Many of the most important battles and wars in history were waged with bows and arrows as one of the chief weapons. Willam the Conqueror won the Battle of Hastings by having his archers shoot their arrows high into the air so that they would drop upon his English enemies.

Archery, which is the use of bows and arrows, is associated with many of the romantic tales we all know, such as the adventures of Robin Hood, and the story of William Tell. In fact, most of the stories of old England include some mention of archery contests.

Both bows and arrows have to be made with skill and care, using special woods. Usually the bow is made from yew, which comes from Italy, Spain, and the west coast of America. A really good bow is made of one piece of wood. For men, the bow is from 5 feet 8 inches to 6 feet in length. It has a pull, or draw, of from 36 to 80 pounds, so you see it takes a bit of strength to use it. For women, the bow is smaller, about 5 feet to 5 feet 6 inches in length, and its pull, or draw, is only 18 to 35 pounds.

Arrows are usually made from spruce, Norway pine, or a special kind of cedar wood. They have a tip, usually of steel, at one end, and a "nock" at the other. Just below the nock are three feathers, which help steady the arrow in its flight. For men, the length of the arrow is 28 inches, and for women, 24 to 25 inches.

These modern bows and arrows are used chiefly in the sport of archery, but there are many people who hunt deer, bear, and other large animals in this way today!

If an atom is so tiny that it cannot be seen, how can it be "exploded?" And how can this explosion create bombs so terrible that they are the most powerful weapons known to man?

HOW IS AN ATOM "EXPLODED"?

What we are really talking about when we talk about an atomic explosion—is energy. Energy comes from matter. Energy and matter are the two things that make up everything in the universe and keep everything going.

Matter is made of atoms, and every atom has in it particles of energy. Energy holds the parts of an atom together. This energy is so tremendous, that if it can be set free it supplies enormous force. For example, the energy released by exploding one pound of uranium (uranium-235) is greater than the energy released by burning 2,600,000 pounds of coal!

How do we get the atom to release its energy? We have to get to the core of the atom, which is the source of the energy. We do this by splitting the atom. This process is called "fission."

How is it done? By bombarding the atom with neutrons from other atoms. A neutron is a particle within the atom. But this doesn't happen when you bombard just any atoms. In some cases, only a small amount

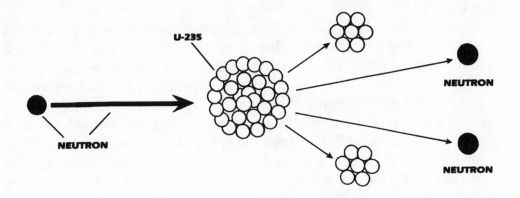

U-235

NEUTRON

NEUTRON

NEUTRON

of energy is released. But when uranium-235 is bombarded by neutrons, a great amount of energy is released.

But that energy is from only one atom. Suppose we could get many atoms to release their energy at one time? This is done by producing what is called a "chain reaction." By having a certain amount of uranium-235 as the target, and bombarding it with neutrons, we would have this happening: as one atom of uranium-235 split and released some of its neutrons, these neutrons would strike the core of another atom. This would release more neutrons which would split more atoms, and so on. In a fraction of a second, a tremendous amount of energy would be released and we would have an "explosion."

This, of course, is a very simplified explanation. But it gives you an idea of how we obtain atomic energy.

Nobody knows who first had the idea for making a vehicle on two wheels on which a person could ride. But some such vehicle did exist as long ago as the days of ancient Egypt! It had two wheels and was set in motion by the feet of the rider.

WHO INVENTED THE BICYCLE?

The bicycle as we know it began to be developed in the nineteenth century. In 1817 Baron Karl von Drais, a German, introduced into England a machine which he named the draisine, after himself. It was a development of an earlier invention by a Frenchman, J. N. Niepce, and was a real forerunner of the modern bicycle. The two wheels of the draisine were connected by a wooden bar.

The rider rested part of his weight on a wooden arm rest in front and propelled himself by kicking on the ground, first with one foot and then with the other. He steered by turning a handle on the front wheel, which was pivoted. The machine was expensive and ordinary people couldn't afford it. Because of this, they nicknamed it the dandy horse.

The craze for the dandy horse spread throughout Europe, but after reaching the United States it soon died out. Then, about 1840, a Scotsman named Kirkpatrick Macmillan took an old dandy horse and put cranks on the axle of the rear wheel. These were connected by driving rods with pedals in front. But little was done with this invention.

The name "bicycle" was first used in 1865. At that time, a Frenchman, Pierre Lallement, attached cranks and pedals to the front wheel of a velocipede, much like the dandy horse. These "bicycles" were called "boneshakers," for they had heavy wooden frames and iron tires and it was quite an experience to ride them. In 1868 light metal wheels with wire spokes and solid rubber tires were introduced.

The modern "safety bicycle" was developed about 1885. It had two wheels of equal size, and the rider's seat was slightly forward of the rear wheel. The pedals were attached to the frame in a convenient position and power was transmitted from them to the rear wheel by sprockets and the chain.

When we think of some of the great tunnels that exist in the world today, we might imagine that the tunnel is a modern invention. But surprisingly enough, tunneling is one of the oldest types of engineering!

HOW IS A TUNNEL BUILT?

Ancient peoples not only built tunnels but were very expert at it. Among those who built tunnels thousands of years ago were the Egyptians, the people of India, the Assyrians, the Greeks, and the Romans.

Of course, building a tunnel today is quite a different kind of operation than it was in ancient times. Modern equipment makes it easier and safer, and more rapid.

Engineers usually divide tunnels into two classes—those through rock, and those through earth. One of the greatest advances in tunnel building was the invention of the tunneling shield by Mark Brunel, an English engineer. This device made under-water tunneling safe.

The modern tunneling shield is a cylinder of steel, which fits into the head of the tunnel being built. At the front edge of the cylinder is a strong cutting edge. The shield is pushed forward through the earth by powerful jacks.

Men dig out the earth within the front part of the cylinder, while other men build up the lining of the tunnel within the rear part of the cylinder. Where necessary, compressed air may be used to withstand pressure at great depths.

The first step in building a tunnel is to make a geological survey to find out the best route. After the size and shape of the tunnel have been decided, the center line for the tunnel is laid out on paper. The beginning and end are marked on the ground. Then the actual work of tunneling begins.

Thousands of years ago, great barriers of earth or stone were built across the Nile River in Egypt and the Tigris River in Babylon. They were built to control the floods of these rivers and to store water for irrigating crops.

HOW ARE DAMS BUILT?

Today dams are built in all countries. They range in size from small embankments to great engineering works which require the labor of thousands of men and heavy machinery.

In modern construction, concrete has taken the place of stone masonry. Dams up to about 300 feet high are built of earth or rock, in addition to concrete. Higher dams are almost always built of concrete.

A safe dam must rest on a sound foundation and against firm abutments at the ends. However, the foundation immediately under the base of the dam is not always solid rock. Sometimes dams have to be built on overlying material which may be gravel, sand or other earth layers. Such layers are made watertight by means of a steel, concrete, or clay wall.

In all dams some sure means must be provided to care for surplus water after the reservoir behind the dam is filled. This may be accomplished by a spillway, or a concrete overflow, or through openings built through the body of the dam.

The stability of a dam depends on sheer weight, so certain types of dams are called "gravity" dams. In their simplest form, gravity dams are roughly triangular in cross section. Earth and rock dams have sloping faces both upstream and downstream, whereas masonry and concrete gravity dams have their upstream face nearly vertical and a sloping face downstream. The triangular face gives a broad base to resist the overturning force of the water against the dam.

The very largest and highest modern dams are always of the solid concrete gravity type. When they are built in a straight line across the river, they are called straight gravity type; when built on a curve, they are called arch gravity type.

One of the most remarkable feats in the history of engineering is the building of the Panama Canal. It has had an effect on the commerce of the whole world. For example, it not only shortens the distance from

WHY DOES THE PANAMA CANAL HAVE LOCKS?

many Atlantic to Pacific ports by 8,000 miles, but it cuts the distance from Great Britain to New Zealand by 1,500 miles.

Originally, the canal was going to be built by the French. The plan called for a canal at sea level, 29½ feet deep, and 72 feet wide at the bottom. But the French plan couldn't be completed for many reasons, and the United States undertook to build the canal in 1904.

The French were going to cut below the level of the sea from ocean to ocean. But this plan had its dangers. If the tide happened to be higher at one end than at the other, a dangerous current might result. It also required much more digging. So a lock canal was decided upon. That

THE GATUN LOCKS

meant that there must be water available at the higher levels to fill the higher parts of the canal. This was obtained by damming the Chagres River.

The locks form a kind of "staircase" for taking ships through the canal. This means the ships are raised at certain points to where the water level is higher, and then lowered to other levels. Nearly half of the canal runs through Gatun Lake. Vessels approaching the lake from the Atlantic side are lifted to the lake level, a distance of 85 feet, by a series of three locks. Near the Pacific side is the Gaillard Cut, about 8 miles long. Vessels are then lowered 31 feet in one lock. A mile farther on two more locks lower them another 54 feet, to sea level. Within the locks, the vessels are hauled by electric locomotives moving along the banks. Locks have now been built which are capable of handling the largest ships afloat.

Today you can pick up the telephone and in a few minutes be speaking to someone on another continent. Or you can give your telegraph office a message and in a short time a person anywhere in the world can be reading it! Without the cables that

HOW WAS A CABLE LAID ACROSS THE OCEAN?

lie at the bottom of the oceans, linking all the continents together, this would be impossible.

The first problem that had to be solved in connection with cables was to insulate wire so that electricity would not escape. After many experiments, various materials were discovered that could be wrapped around the cable to insulate it.

Then men began to lay cables, connecting various points. In 1841-42, a telegraph cable was laid under New York harbor. In 1850 the English Channel was spanned by a submarine telegraph cable. A little later, Scotland and Ireland, Sweden and Denmark, and Italy and Corsica were joined by cable.

Finally, in 1857, Cyrus W. Field and an English scientist, Lord Kelvin, tried to span the Atlantic Ocean from Newfoundland to Ireland with a submarine cable. This was quite an undertaking and there were many disappointments before success was achieved. The United States and British governments loaned two warships for the job. Each ship carried half the cable. It was spliced in midocean and then "paid out" as the ships steamed to opposite shores.

The cable broke several times while being laid. Finally, on Aug. 13, 1858, the first message crossed the ocean by means of this cable. But the cable worked for only three months before it burned out. The electric current was too strong for the insulation. No attempt was made to replace the cable until 1865, by which time Lord Kelvin had invented a telegraph instrument which didn't need such a strong current.

The "Great Eastern," then the world's largest ship, was fitted out to lay the cable. The first cable broke about two thirds of the way across from Ireland. In 1866 another cable was laid which reached Newfoundland safely. Then the broken end of the lost cable was found and spliced to another piece, and so there were two cables working. A new age in communication was born.

The largest of all musical instruments is the pipe organ. Sometimes, in smaller models, you can see the rows of pipes over the keys, but a large pipe organ usually is built as part of the building with the pipes and most

HOW DOES A PIPE ORGAN WORK?

of the machinery hidden away. In the largest organs, there may be as many as 18,000 pipes!

The pipes produce the tones—the big ones the deep heavy tones, the small ones the higher tones. Pipes in a large organ may range from as large as the trunk of a tree to as small as a lead pencil.

The pipes are arranged in groups, and each group is controlled by a stop. When the organist wants to use a particular group of pipes he opens the proper stop. This connects that group with the keyboard.

A large organ may have as many as five rows or banks of keys. Each row is connected with a particular set of pipes. When the organist presses down a key, this moves a valve which lets air into a certain pipe.

These rows of keys, incidentally, are called "manuals" because they are played by the hands (from the Latin word *manus,* meaning "hand"). Since each manual controls a group of pipes, it really controls an organ of its own. The most important manual is called the "great" organ, and the others are called the "choir," "swell," and "solo" organs. The fifth manual, which some organs have, controls the "echo" organ.

The sound produced by the pipes is caused by the air which rushes through them. This air is forced into them from an air chamber into which it has been pumped by a great bellows. This is done today by a blower driven by a motor that may have from 25 to 40 horsepower. But long ago it was necessary to use manpower to operate the bellows. There was an organ in Winchester Cathedral, England, that had a bellows so big it needed 70 men to pump it!

INDEX

TELL ME WHY #3

BY ARKADY LEOKUM

ILLUSTRATIONS BY HOWARD BENDER

CONTENTS

Chapter 1
Our World

Chapter 4

How Things Began

Chapter 5

How Things Are Made

TELL ME WHY #3

CHAPTER 1
OUR WORLD

Because in early times the study of plant life dealt mainly with plants as food, it became known as botany, from a Greek word meaning "herb."

The first people to specialize in the study of botany were primitive

WHAT IS BOTANY?

medicine men and witch doctors. They had to know the plants that could kill or cure people. And botany was closely linked with medicine for hundreds of years.

In the sixteenth century, people began to observe plants and write books about their observations. These writers were the "fathers" of modern botany. In the nineteenth century, the work of an English scientist, Charles Darwin, helped botanists gain a better understanding of how plants as well as animals evolved from simpler ancestors. His work led botanists to set up special branches of botany.

One of these branches is "plant anatomy," which has to do with the structure of plants and how they might be related. Experiments on plant heredity were performed to find out how various species came to be and how they could be improved. This study is called "genetics."

"Ecology," another branch of botany, deals with studies of the distribution of plants throughout the world, to find out why certain species grew in certain places. "Paleobotany," another branch, works out plant evolution from the evidence of fossil remains.

Other branches of botany include "plant physiology," which studies the way plants breathe and make food, and "plant pathology," which is concerned with the study of plant diseases.

According to the theories of science, there was a time when there were no plants on earth. Then, hundreds of millions of years ago, tiny specks of protoplasm appeared on the earth. Protoplasm is the name for the living material that is found in both plants and animals. These original specks of protoplasm, according to this theory, were the beginnings of all our plants and animals.

WHERE DO PLANTS COME FROM?

The protoplasm specks that became plants developed thick walls and settled down to staying in one place. They also developed a kind of green coloring matter known as "chlorophyll." This enabled them to make food from substances in the air, water, and soil.

These early green plants had only one cell, but they later formed groups of cells. Since they had no protection against drying out, they had to stay in the water. Today, some descendants of these original plants still survive, though they have changed quite a bit. We call them "algae."

One group of plants developed that obtained its food without the use of chlorophyll. These non-green plants are "the fungi."

Most of the plants on earth today evolved from the algae. Certain of these came out of the sea and developed rootlets that could anchor them in the soil. They also developed little leaves with an outer skin covering as protection against drying. These plants became mosses and ferns.

All of the earliest plants reproduced either by simple cell division or by means of spores. Spores are little dustlike cells something like seeds, but containing no stored food in them as seeds do. As time went on, some of these plants developed flowers that produced true seeds.

Two different types of plants with seeds appeared. Those with naked seeds and those with protected seeds. Each of these two types later developed along many different lines.

If you were to cut down any tree more than one year old and look at the cross section, you would see alternating bands of light and dark wood. The two bands together are called "the annual ring," and they make up the amount of wood formed by the tree during a single growing season or year.

WHAT MAKES THE RINGS ON A TREE?

Why are the bands lighter and darker? This is because the wood grows in a different way during the different seasons. In spring and early summer, the cells of the wood are bigger and

7

have thinner walls. This makes them look lighter. In late summer, the cells are smaller, have thick walls, and are closely packed together. This makes a darker band.

The age of a tree can be told by counting the annual rings. When you look at the rings of a tree, you will notice that they vary in width and in many other details. These variations are caused by the weather conditions that prevailed during the given season. A difference in the light, the amount of rain, and the minerals in the soil, will produce a difference in the rings of a tree. That is why scientists often use the rings to obtain a clue to the weather conditions that prevailed years ago in certain parts of the world.

When a tree grows, the wood of the tree is not the only thing that increases in size from year to year. Additions are also made to the bark of the tree. This is done by means of a thin band of living, dividing cells between the wood and the bark. This layer is called "the cambium." The new cells which are formed on the wood side of the cambium become wood. The cells formed toward the outside become bark.

The outer portion of a woody stem or root is called "bark." Sometimes it is hard to tell how much of the stem should be called bark. In the palm tree, for example, there is no clear separation between bark and wood.

WHY DO TREES HAVE BARK?

What does bark do for the tree? One of its main functions is to protect the inner, more delicate structures. It not only keeps them from drying out, but also guards against outside injuries of various sorts.

The thick, fibrous barks of some redwood trees show burns and scars as a result of fires near the ground, but the inner portions of the tree escaped injury.

The process by which bark is formed may go on year after year. In the very young branch of a maple, for example, there is at first no rough bark. The surface of the shoot is nearly smooth. As the twig forms more wood and grows in size, the outer portions may split open. The injury caused in this way is healed from the inside.

Some of the outer portions become dry and die. The dead, broken portions give the bark a rough appearance. Some of the dry pieces are shed or broken off as the twig grows larger and older.

8

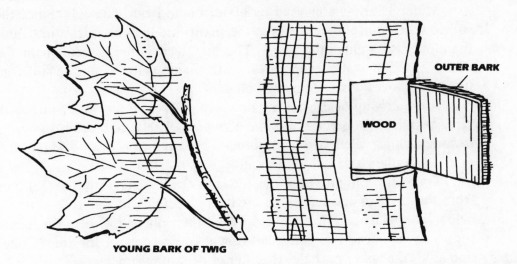

YOUNG BARK OF TWIG

OUTER BARK

WOOD

Man finds the bark of many trees very useful. Commercial cork is obtained almost entirely from the cork oak tree. The bark of the hemlock tree is used in the tanning of leather. The spice we know as cinnamon is the powdered bark of a tree which grows in India and Malaya. Quinine is obtained from the bark of the cinchona tree. Extracts from the bark of other trees are used for flavoring, and the bark of the roots and branches of many trees are used in medicines.

Every single part of the human body receives a constant supply of blood which is pumped by the heart. In plants and trees, every single part receives water and nourishment, which we call sap. But a tree has no pump because it has no heart. Then how does the sap go up a tree?

WHAT MAKES SAP GO UP A TREE?

Science still cannot explain this mystery exactly! Of course there are several theories about it, but no single theory seems to offer the complete answer. Scientists believe that there are several forces at work to make this possible.

One explanation has to do with "osmotic pressure." In living things, liquids and dissolved materials pass through membranes. This is called "osmosis." When there are dissolved chemicals in contact with a membrane, they press against the membrane. This is called "osmotic pressure." If there are many particles in a solution, more particles press against the membrane and seep through than in solutions with fewer particles.

Minerals and water used by plants come from the roots. Since the soil contains more minerals than the plant, the osmotic pressure causes the minerals to enter the plant. The dissolved minerals remain in the plant cells. The water evaporates. In this way, water from the soil continuously moves upward through plants.

Another way of explaining how sap goes up a tree has to do with "transpiration" and the cohesion of water. The evaporation of water from leaves is called "transpiration." The attraction of one water particle for another is called "cohesion."

Transpiration provides the upward "pull." As water evaporates from the cells of the leaves, it creates a vacuum in the cells directly below the surface. So these cells draw on the cells below them for a new supply of sap. And this continues down to the roots of the tree Cohesion holds the water particles together as they move up.

We know that human beings and animals have to find ways to protect themselves against enemies. Plants need protection to survive too. One of the natural protections a plant can have is a poison which makes it dangerous to eat or even touch the plant.

WHAT IS POISON IVY?

One of the most common poisonous plants in North America is poison ivy. Contact with this plant causes an inflammation and itching, though not everyone is affected by it in the same way.

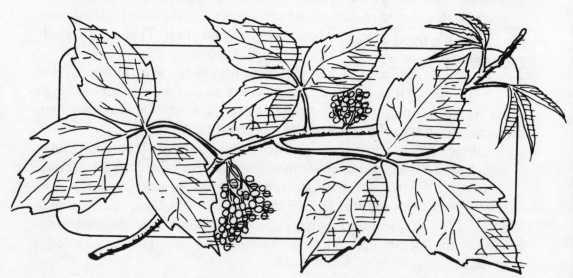

Poison ivy grows in the United States as far west as eastern Texas, eastern Kansas, and Minnesota. It climbs up the tall trunks of trees, grows among bushes along the road, and may even grow in sandy places where most other plants cannot grow.

Usually it is a three-leafed vine, but sometimes it grows in an upright, shrubby way. It stays shining green even in the driest hot days of summer. In the autumn it changes to rich shades of scarlet.

The poison that is in poison ivy is an oil called "toxicodendrol." It is found in all parts of the plant, not just the leaves. This is why cases of poison ivy can develop at all seasons of the year.

About one person in five is not subject to ivy poisoning in any way. Many people believe when the fluid in the blisters which form is spread on other parts of the body, the poisoning will spread. But this is not so. What happens is that the effects of the poisoning appear on various parts of the body to begin with.

There are enough varieties of apples to satisfy everybody's taste. In the United States alone, more than 7,000 varieties of apples have been recorded. And when you consider the whole world, there are probably a few thousand more.

HOW MANY KINDS OF APPLES ARE THERE?

We know that it is one of the earliest fruits raised by man. The apple probably originated in southeastern Europe and southwestern Asia, and was eaten and raised by the very earliest inhabitants there. More than 2,000 years ago, different varieties of apples were already being raised in Europe. In ancient Rome, the natives enjoyed seven different varieties of apples.

How are all these varieties obtained? A great deal of experimenting is always being carried on by apple growers. When you graft a bud or twig of any given variety onto any kind of young apple tree, the mature tree yields apples of the same variety as the graft. So nurserymen always experiment with grafting and by fertilizing the blossoms to cross-breed them.

Sometimes a new variety appears unexpectedly. The Red Delicious appeared in this way. An ordinary tree, producing average good fruit, grew one branch on which appeared apples quite different from the rest. A new variety of apple was born!

Not so long ago in West Virginia, there were some gnarled old apple trees that yielded only a small, bitter, misshapen fruit. The farmer, a patient man, experimented with seedlings for a long time. Then finally one autumn he received his reward. From one of the young trees hung a heavy crop of luscious fruit, now known as Golden Delicious.

The banyan tree is one of the giants among trees. Anything in nature that is a "giant" presents all kinds of problems, and trees are no exception.

For example, a giant tree has the problem of drawing water from the

WHAT IS A BANYAN TREE?

roots to the top. The trunk of the tree must be strong. A tree cannot grow too tall and remain slender, or it would break. So a giant tree must be wider at the base to support the load above it. And if the branches are large and heavy, they could pull down the trunk to one side or another.

The banyan tree is a giant tree that has solved these problems in an interesting way. It is a tree of the mulberry family, and it is found in eastern India and near Malaysia.

The most unusual thing about the banyan tree is the way its branches grow. They spread out in all directions all around the trunk. And even though the trunk is huge, it cannot support these branches. So thick roots grow from the underside of the branches directly to the ground.

When these roots take hold, they provide support and nourishment for the tree. They also develop into new trunks. The result is that the ban-

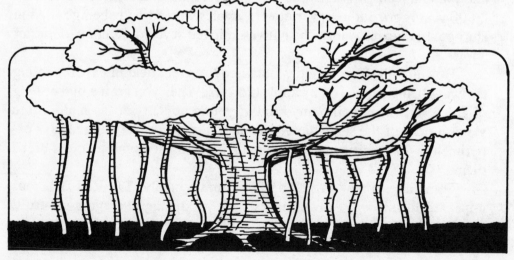

yan tree grows more in circumference than in height. Eventually, "arcades" of these roots are formed, and a banyan tree may have a circumference that reaches 1,500 feet!

These arcades of roots are actually used as marketplaces by people, who find it a perfect sheltered place to gather and do business. If these roots are cut, they are useful for making tent poles and the fiber is used for making rope.

The banyan tree produces tiny figs. When they become ripe they are bright red and are eaten by birds and bats.

The flower is the means by which the plant can reproduce new plants like itself. A botanist defines a flower as a group of parts whose function is to produce pollen or seeds or both.

WHAT IS POLLINATION?

The most important parts of the flower, from this point of view, are "pistils" and "stamens." Many flowers contain both, the pistil or pistils in the center, surrounded by the stamens.

In the enlarged, bottom part of the pistil there are tiny bodies called "ovules." Each ovule may develop into a seed. The most important part of an ovule is a tiny egg cell, so small it can only be seen under a microscope.

The stamens contain a pollen sac at the end of a stalk. When these pollen sacs open, they release the pollen they contain as a fine dust which is usually yellow.

In order to produce new seeds, the pollen grains from the stamens must be transferred to the pistils. This transfer of pollen is called "pollination."

Pollination is brought about in many different ways. Sometimes the pollen simply falls onto the pistil, but usually the wind or insects are needed for pollination.

Among the plants that are pollinated by the wind are the grasses; not just the grasses of the meadows, but wheat, corn, and other grains. The stamens wave in the breeze. The pollen is shaken off and flies through the air and lands on pistils.

Another form of pollination is carried on by insects. This usually happens with flowers that have bright colors or fragrance, and thus attract insects. Insects visit the flower for nectar which they make into honey, and for pollen which they use as food. As an insect collects pollen from a flower, some of it rubs off on the insect's body. Then when the insect visits another flower, some of the pollen rubs onto the stamens.

Sometimes toadstools seem to appear as if by magic on a lawn after a rainy day. But of course no magic is involved. Toadstools grow from spores. And toadstools and mushrooms are exactly the same thing. There is no difference between them.

WHERE DO TOADSTOOLS COME FROM?

A typical mushroom consists of a cylindrical stem, or "stipe," supporting a circular cap, or "pileus." On the stipe is a collar known as a ring, or "annulus." Radiating from the stipe to the margin of the cap on its underside are gills, or "lamellae." This is where the spores are formed.

Spores have a similar purpose to that of seeds, but they should not be confused with seeds. Spores are produced in great quantities. In fact, so many are produced by a mushroom, that there is a good chance the wind will carry some of them to spots favorable for growth.

If a spore falls in a place that is warm and moist and where food is available, the spore, which consists of a single cell, begins to absorb nourishment. It grows by division until long chains of cells resembling threads are formed. Such a chain is called a "hypha." A tangle of them is called a "mycelium." At various points along the mycelium, tiny balls no bigger than pinheads develop and become mushrooms.

So you see that when mushrooms or toadstools seem to appear suddenly, it is really the end of a long process that started with the spores leaving some mushroom that could have been quite a distance away!

"Force" is a push or a pull which changes the motion, or movement, of objects. When you push a chair, you are exerting force on it. When you stop pushing, the chair stops moving. But suppose you roll a ball along the ground. It keeps on rolling after you have stopped pushing it! Why?

WHAT IS CENTRIFUGAL FORCE?

The explanation for this (developed by Sir Isaac Newton, the first scientist to explain the theories of force) is the idea of "inertia." Inertia makes an object keep up whatever motion it has. Every bit of matter has inertia and will keep moving in a straight line at the same speed unless another force changes its motion. For example, if you are riding in a bus and the driver jams on the brakes, your body will hurl forward because of its inertia—it will keep on going forward at the same speed the bus was traveling.

Now let us get to centrifugal force. All of us have experienced this force. We notice it whenever an object travels in a curved path. Let us say you are on that same bus and it suddenly turns a corner. You will probably find yourself falling off the seat into the aisle! The reason is centrifugal force.

Centrifugal force can be explained by using the idea of inertia. When the bus turns, inertia tends to keep your body moving in a straight line. So you tend to move toward the outside of the curve so as to keep your original straight motion. Centrifugal force always seems to push objects to the outside of the curve.

This is why highways are often tilted around a turn; why airplanes bank when they turn; and why, when you are riding a bicycle, you lean inward! This leaning inward, and the banking of roads and airplanes, helps to balance centrifugal force, which would otherwise tend to hurl objects outward. The leaning inward balances the tendency to move outward and you can make the turn properly.

We speak of ordinary light as being "white"; we call it white light, or sunlight. But this light is really a mixture of all colors.

When sunlight strikes the beveled edge of a mirror, or the edge of a glass prism, or the surface of a soap bubble, we see the colors in light. What happens is that the white light is broken up into the

WHY ARE THE COLORS IN A RAINBOW ARRANGED AS THEY ARE?

different wave lengths that are seen by our eyes as red, orange, yellow, green, blue, and violet.

These wave lengths form a band of parallel stripes, each color grading into the one next to it. This band is called a "spectrum." In the spectrum, the red line is always at one end and the blue and violet lines at the other end, and this is decided by their different wave lengths.

When we see a rainbow, it is just as if we were looking at such a spectrum. In fact, a rainbow is simply a great curve spectrum caused by the breaking up of sunlight.

When sunlight enters a droplet of water, it is broken up just as if it had entered a glass prism. So inside the drop of water, we already have the different colors going from one side of the drop to the other. Some of this colored light is then reflected from the far side of the droplet, back and out of the droplet.

The light comes back out of the droplet in different directions, depending on the color. And when you look at these colors in a rainbow, you see them arranged with red at the top and violet at the bottom of the rainbow.

A rainbow is seen only during showers when rain is falling and the sun shining at the same time, but on opposite sides of the observer. You have to be between the sun and the droplets of water with the sun at your back. The sun, your eye, and the center of the arc of the rainbow must all be in a straight line.

One of the great mysteries of the world in which we live is light. We still do not know exactly what it is. It can be described only in terms of what it does.

HOW DOES LIGHT TRAVEL?

We know light is a form of energy. Like some other forms of energy—heat, radio waves, and X-rays—the speed, frequency, and length of its waves can be measured. Its behavior in other ways makes it similar to these other forms of energy, too.

We know the speed of light. It travels at about 186,000 miles per second. This means that in a year, a beam of light travels 5,880,000,000,000 miles. That is the distance which astronomers call a "light year," and it is the unit used to measure distances in outer space.

In trying to understand what light was and how it traveled, many theories have been developed. In the seventeenth century, Sir Isaac Newton said that light must be made up of "corpuscles," somewhat like tiny bullets shot from the light source. But this "corpuscular" theory of light could not explain many of the ways in which light behaved.

At about the same time, a man named Christian Huygens developed a "wave theory" of light. His idea was that a luminous or lighted particle started pulses, or waves, much as a pebble dropped into a pool makes waves.

Whether light was waves or corpuscles was argued for nearly 150 years. Gradually, as certain effects of light became known, the idea of light corpuscles died out.

Scientists now believe that light behaves both as particles and as waves. Experiments can show either idea to be true. So we simply cannot give a complete answer to "What is light?"

A molecule is the smallest bit of a substance that can exist and still keep the properties of the whole. For example, if you broke down a molecule of sugar, the elements would not have the characteristics of sugar—its taste or its color, among other things.

HOW BIG IS A MOLECULE?

Some molecules are very simple, others have thousands of atoms arranged in a complicated pattern. In some gases, such as helium and neon, a molecule consists of only one atom. Some molecules contain two or more atoms of the same kind. A molecule of water, for example, is made up of two atoms of hydrogen and one of oxygen.

In contrast, the molecule of pure natural rubber is thought to contain about 75,000 carbon atoms and about 120,000 hydrogen atoms. So you can see that molecules differ greatly in size.

Simple molecules like that of water are only a few billionths of an inch in length. The rubber molecule is thousands of times larger. Some molecules are shaped like footballs, others are long and threadlike.

It is really impossible for us to imagine how small molecules are. For example, let us take a single cubic inch of air. In this space there are 500 billion billion molecules (5 with 20 zeroes after it). And that cubic inch of air is not packed tightly because it actually contains a great deal of empty space.

The weight of a molecule is measured by scientists on a relative scale. The weight of the molecule depends upon the weight of the atoms that form it. And the weight of the atom, in turn, depends upon the number of protons and neutrons in the nucleus of the atom.

DOES A MOLECULE HAVE WEIGHT?

A molecule of water is made up of two atoms of hydrogen plus one of oxygen. Hydrogen is a simple atom with only one proton in the nucleus. Its atomic weight is 1. The weight of other elements is in multiples of the weight of hydrogen. Oxygen has eight protons and eight neutrons, making an atomic weight of 16. So, water has a molecular weight of 2 x 1 plus 16, which makes its molecular weight 18.

Molecules are held in their places in a solid or a liquid by the forces of attraction between molecules. This attraction is of an electrical nature, and this force is strong enough to account for the strength of most solid materials.

All material things on earth are made up of one or more elements. Elements are substances that have atoms of only one kind.

Any one element may have some of the same properties that other

WHAT ARE THE ELEMENTS?

elements have, but no two elements are exactly alike. For example, hydrogen and helium are both colorless, odorless, and tasteless gases. They are both light, but helium is heavier. Hydrogen burns, but helium will not.

All elements have a certain weight. They can be a solid, a liquid, or a gas. Some will dissolve in water. Others must be heated to a certain temperature before they will change from a solid to a liquid or to a gas. These characteristics are called "the physical properties" of elements.

After scientists studied the physical and chemical properties of elements, they grouped the elements that were alike together. These elements are called "chemical families."

All the families were combined into "the periodic table of elements." They were listed in order of their "atomic number." The atomic number of an element depends on how many protons, particles with a positive charge, the atom of each element contains. A hydrogen atom has one proton and its atomic number is one, so it is first on the periodic table.

Some elements are named after people or places or countries: Einsteinium, Europium, Germanium, Californium, and Scandium. Among the familiar elements are carbon, copper, gold, iron, lead, mercury, nickel, platinum, tin, radium, and silver.

People have been terrified of quicksand for centuries. It is supposed to have the mysterious power of sucking victims into it until they disappear.

The truth is, quicksand has no such power. And the fact is that if you

WHAT IS QUICKSAND?

know what it is and how to deal with it, it cannot hurt you at all.

What is quicksand? It is a light, loose sand which is mixed with water. It does not look different from sands which might be right next to it. But there is a difference: quicksand will not support heavy objects.

Quicksand usually occurs near the mouths of large rivers and on flat shores where there is a layer of stiff clay under it. Water is collected in the sand because the underlying clay keeps the water from draining away. This water may come from many different places, such as river currents or pools.

The grains of quicksand are different from ordinary grains of sand because they are round instead of being angular or sharp. The water gets between the grains and separates and lifts them, so that they tend to flow over one another. This makes them unable to support solid objects.

Some quicksand is not even made of sand. It can be any kind of loose soil, a mixture of sand and mud, or a kind of pebbly mud.

People who step into quicksand do not sink out of sight. Since it contains so much liquid, it will enable them to float. And since quicksand is heavier than water, people can float higher in it than they do in water.

The important thing is to move slowly in quicksand. This is to give it time to flow around the body. Once it does this, it will act like water in which you are swimming.

The dust and other materials that are in the air as the result of a nuclear explosion—that is, from atom bombs—is fallout. It contaminates, or poisons, the air, soil, and water.

WHAT IS FALLOUT?

Fallout contaminates the world around us because it is radioactive. This means that it contains certain kinds of atoms that are breaking down. As they break down, they give off tiny amounts of energy and matter, which are called "radiations."

A nuclear explosion produces a huge blast, a lot of heat, and many radioactive atoms. These radioactive atoms become mixed with particles of soil and dust from the earth. Tons of radioactive dust are blown or sucked into the atmosphere by a nuclear explosion. This returns to earth as radioactive fallout.

The heaviest particles of this debris drops to earth within minutes or a few hours after a nuclear explosion. The lighter particles are carried up and come down more slowly. They may circle the earth for months or even years. Eventually, they fall to the earth, mostly in snow, rain, and mist.

Fallout that falls on the outside of the human body can be washed away. But if fallout radiation gets inside the body, it may stay there for years. Fallout enters the body with the air, water, and food taken in. Mainly it comes from food. Fallout dusts the leaves of plants and their fruits. It falls on the soil and is taken into plants through their roots. Animals eat the plants, then human beings and other animals eat these animals.

Inside the body, radioactive atoms from the fallout send off radiations. When too much radiation passes through living cells, it may damage the cells or weaken the body's defenses against disease.

Platinum is a metal—but what an amazing metal it is! It is grayish white in color, and its names comes from the Spanish *plata* and means "little silver."

WHAT IS PLATINUM?

Platinum is harder than copper and almost as pliable as gold. You could take a single ounce of platinum and stretch it out into a fine wire that would reach from New York City to New Orleans, Louisiana. A cube of platinum measuring a foot each way would have a weight of more than half a ton! Platinum is almost twice as heavy as lead.

Platinum is usually found in ores often mixed with the rare metals palladium, rhodium, iridium, and osmium, which are called "platinum metals." Occasionally, it is found with metals such as gold, copper, silver, iron, chromium, and nickel. It is found in the form of small grains, scales, or nuggets.

Large deposits of platinum were first discovered in South America in the eighteenth century. For a great many years it was considered quite useless, and so it was cheap. Then, when people began to find how useful this metal could be, and since it is quite rare, the price went up to the point where that cube of platinum mentioned above would have been worth $2,500,000.

What makes platinum especially useful is that it resists oxidation, acids, and heat. The melting point of platinum is about 3,190 degrees Fahrenheit! For most purposes, platinum is mixed (alloyed) with one of the other "platinum metals" or with silver, gold, copper, nickel, or tin.

While the chief use of platinum is for jewelry, it is also used for contact points where electrical circuits are opened or closed, in laboratory weights, in instruments for exact measurement of temperatures, and for fuses in delicate electric instruments.

Many people consider milk to be the most nearly perfect food we have. And when you consider all the good things for your body that you obtain when you drink milk, you can see why this is so.

WHAT IS MILK MADE OF?

Proteins used to build and repair muscles are found in milk. Another important part of milk is fat, an energy-giving food. The fat in milk is called "butterfat." When globules (tiny, round pieces of fat) are present in milk, butter can be made.

Milk also has sugar, which is an energy-giving carbohydrate. Lactose, the sugar found in milk, is less sweet than cane sugar, and is more easily used by the body than is any other kind of sugar.

Milk also supplies the body with important minerals. The body uses minerals as bone-building and blood-building foods. Calcium and phosphorous make up a large part of the mineral content of milk. There is more calcium in milk than in any other food.

Other minerals in milk are iron, copper, manganese, magnesium, sodium, potassium, chlorine, iodine, cobalt, and zinc. And we're not finished yet! Milk also provides us with many vitamins. Milk is rich in vitamins B_2, A, B_1. It also contains vitamins C and D. And, of course, milk also contains water. But the amazing thing is that there is about a quarter of a pound of food solids in each quart of milk!

Early man, living thousands of years ago, made caves and rock shelters his home. In fact, some of the earliest cave dwellers did not even look like people living today.

WHO WERE THE CAVE MEN?

These were the Neanderthal people. Their brains were as large as modern man's, but they had rugged faces with heavy ridges over their eyes. They were only a little over five feet in height and could not stand as straight as people do today.

These "cave men" or cave dwellers, were not good housekeepers. Anything they did not want, they left on the floor of the cave. Over thousands of years this mass of rubbish piled up and sometimes filled the caves.

The caves were large, dark, and frightening. The people lived in the mouth of the cave where they were protected from wind, rain, and snow, without going into the darkness deep in the cave.

During the last part of the Ice Age, Cro-Magnon men, people who looked much like people living today, started to move into Europe. Like the Neanderthals before them, they lived in the mouths of caves.

But there were not enough caves for everyone, so some made tents and underground houses to live in. These are the men who made the famous cave paintings found in southern France and northwestern Spain.

These paintings are quite remarkable. They are full of life and power, and show many of the animals these cave dwellers hunted, such as the bison, the bear, the wild boar, the mammoth, and the rhinoceros.

Far back in prehistory, before man could write, was a period of time known as the Stone Age. Man has lived on the earth for at least 500,000 years, but he did not begin to write until about 5,000 years ago. So prehistory covers a very long time.

WHAT WAS THE STONE AGE?

Because man learned to make stone tools during this time, it is called the Stone Age. The early part of it is known as the Old Stone Age.

The first type of stone tool that was made was probably a big stone chipped so that it had a sharp cutting edge all around. Scientists have called it a "hard ax." Chips struck off pieces of stone were also used as tools. The hand ax and the chips, or flakes, were all-purpose tools that man kept making and using for thousands of years.

Later, in the Ice Age, there were people living in Europe who are called Neanderthal by scientists. They had better tools than the people who had lived in the earliest days, and they hunted in groups instead of alone.

After the Neanderthals came the Cro-Magnon men, who were a more advanced people. They had all kinds of tools: spear points, harpoons, scrapers, and knives. They too lived by hunting.

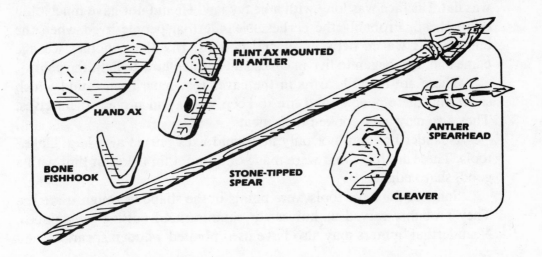

FLINT AX MOUNTED IN ANTLER

HAND AX

BONE FISHHOOK

STONE-TIPPED SPEAR

ANTLER SPEARHEAD

CLEAVER

About 6000 B.C., there came a great change in man's way of life. He learned to grow crops. This marked the beginning of the Neolithic, or New Stone Age.

He used animals as a source for food and the skins for clothing. He kept flocks of animals, built homes, and soon began to make new things that were not found in nature.

Clay could be molded into dishes and bowls. When it was baked it could be used for cooking food. Wool and flax could be spun into yarn. When men worked together, villages and then cities grew. And from these beginnings all that we call civilization came into being.

In trying to learn how man developed, scientists study whatever remains of prehistoric man they can find. These include tools, cooking utensils, skeletons, and parts of the body.

WHO WAS NEANDERTHAL MAN?

In 1856, the remains of men were dug from a limestone cave in the Neander Gorge in Germany. These were the first complete skeletons ever found of prehistoric men, and this was because these people buried their dead.

Neanderthal people probably lived for about 70,000 years in central Asia, the Middle East, and many parts of Europe. This was in a period of about 150,000 to 30,000 years ago.

What was Neanderthal man like? He was heavy and stocky. His skull was flat. His face was long with a heavy jaw. He did not have much chin or forehead. Probably the earliest Neanderthal people lived when the climate was warm, between glacial periods. But then another ice age came and they began to live in caves and learned how to fight the cold.

There are many hearths in the caves that have been found which show that these people used fire to keep warm and protect themselves. They also may have cooked their meat.

Neanderthal man not only had hand axes but he also had "flake" tools. These are tools that were made of broad, thin flakes of flint with a good, sharp edge.

Some of the flake tools were points in the shape of rough triangles. They probably served as knives for skinning and cutting up animals. Neanderthal hunters may also have used pointed wooden spears.

Deserts have come to symbolize for us places of extreme heat. The fact is, most of the famous deserts of the world are places where the thermometer goes bubbling away and where the sun beats down without mercy.

ARE DESERTS ALWAYS HOT?

But this does not mean that a desert must be a place where it is always hot! Let us get a definition of a desert and we will see why this is so. A desert is a region where only special forms of life can exist because there is a shortage of moisture.

In a "hot" desert, there simply is not enough rainfall. So the definition holds true. But suppose there is a region where all water is frozen solid and cannot be used by plants. This satisfies the definition too. Only it would make this a "cold" desert!

Did you know, for example, that much of the Arctic is really a desert? There is less than 15 inches of rainfall a year, and most of the water is frozen. So it is quite properly called a desert. The great Gobi Desert in the middle of Asia is bitterly cold in winter time!

Most of the dry, hot deserts with which we are familiar are found in two belts around the world, just north and south of the Equator. They are caused by high atmospheric pressures that exist in those areas and prevent rain from falling. Other deserts, which are found farther away from the Equator, are the result of being in "the rain shadow." This is the name for an effect that is caused by mountain barriers that catch rainfall on their seaward side and leave the interior region dry.

No great rivers originate in deserts. But a river may rise in moister areas and cross great deserts on their way to the sea. The Nile, for example, flows through the desert region of the Sahara and the Colorado River flows through a desert too.

ARE OCEAN TIDES USEFUL?

If you lived near a coast line, or have ever visited the coast, then you have probably seen the great difference that can exist between high tide and low tide. Boats that float in the water at high tide may be sitting on dry land at low tide, and a big area of beach or land be exposed. In some parts of the world, the height of high tide above low is more than 40 feet!

Obviously, this movement of water is a great source of unused energy. If this energy could be put to work, as it is from waterfalls and rivers, the power would be enormous. For example, if a large bay could be dammed so that it did not empty at low tide, the water could then be turned into electric power by directing it through power plants.

But so far this has been only on a small scale. The ocean tides can be useful to man, but he simply has not been willing, or has not found it necessary, to spend the money and do the work to use this energy.

WHY IS IT HOT INSIDE THE EARTH?

The outside of the earth is a crust of rock which is about 10 to 30 miles thick. When we go down into this crust, we find that it begins to get hotter and hotter.

For about every 60 feet we go down, the temperature grows one degree higher. At two miles below the surface of the earth, the temperature is high enough to boil water! If it were possible to dig down 30 miles, the temperature would be about 2,200 degrees Fahrenheit. This is hot enough to melt rocks. At the center of the earth, scientists believe the temperature to be about 10,000 degrees Fahrenheit.

The crust of the earth has two layers. The upper layer, which makes the continents, is made up of granite. Under the layer of granite is a thick layer of very hard black rock called "basalt." This layer supports the continents and forms the basins that hold the oceans. At the center of the earth, it is believed that there is a huge ball of molten iron, with a diameter of about 4,000 miles.

How did the center of the earth get to be this way? According to most scientific theories, the earth and sun were once related in some way. Most scientists believe that the earth was once a hot, whirling mass of gas, liquid, or solid that began its regular trips around the sun. As years went by, it slowly cooled and the large mass grew smaller. As it whirled, it slowly took a ball-like shape. It was red-hot and held in its path by the attraction of the sun.

As the earth cooled, a hard crust formed on the surface. Nobody knows how long it took for the crust to form. But underneath that crust there remained the hot center core of the earth, and it is still there today.

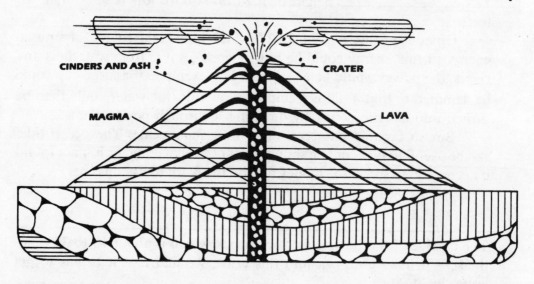

CINDERS AND ASH

CRATER

MAGMA

LAVA

In February, 1943, in the middle of a cornfield in Mexico, people saw a rare and amazing thing taking place. A volcano was being born! In three months it had formed a cone about 1,000 feet high. Two towns were destroyed and a wide area damaged by the falling ash and cinders.

HOW DOES A VOLCANO FORM?

What makes a volcano form? The temperature under the surface of the earth becomes higher and higher the deeper you go down. At a depth of about 20 miles, it is hot enough to melt most rocks.

When rock melts, it expands and needs more space. In certain areas of the world, mountains are being uplifted. The pressure becomes less under these rising mountain ranges, and a reservoir of melted rock (called "magma") may form under them.

This material rises along cracks formed by the uplift. When the pressure in the reservoir is greater than the roof of rock over it, it bursts forth as a volcano.

In the eruption, hot gaseous, liquid, or solid material is blown out. The material piles up around the opening, and a cone-shaped mound is formed. The "crater" is the depression at the top of the cone where the opening reaches the surface. The cone is the result of a volcano.

The material coming out of a volcano is mainly gaseous, but large quantities of "lava" and solid particles that look like cinders and ash are also thrown out.

Actually, lava is magma that has been thrown up by the volcano. When the magma comes near the surface, the temperature and the pressure drop, and a physical and chemical change takes place that changes the magma to lava.

HOW DOES AN EARTHQUAKE START?

You can get a pretty good idea of what causes an earthquake from thinking about what happens during an earthquake. During an earthquake, there is a trembling of the ground. It is this trembling of the earth which may cause buildings to fall.

So an earthquake is a trembling or vibration of the earth's surface. What makes it happen? Well, the rock of the earth's crust may have a "fault," a kind of break in the crust. The earth blocks shift. Sometimes the sides of the fault move up and down against each other. At other times, the sides of the fault shift lengthwise.

But when one rock mass has rubbed on another with great force and friction, we have a lot of energy being used. This vast energy that comes from the rubbing is changed to vibration in the rocks. The vibration is what we feel as an earthquake. And this vibration may travel thousands of miles.

The reason earthquakes take place in certain regions frequently and almost never in other regions, is that the faults in the earth's crust are located in these regions.

There are many things about our own earth that still remain a mystery to us, and one of them is how the oceans were formed.

Actually, we do not even know for sure how old the oceans are.

HOW WERE THE OCEANS FORMED?

It seems certain that oceans did not exist in the first stage of the earth's growth. Perhaps they first came into being as clouds of vapor which turned into water as the earth grew cool. Estimates have been made of the ocean's age based on the amount of mineral salt in the ocean today. These estimates range between 500,000,000 and 1,000,000,000 years.

Scientists are pretty sure that most of the earth's land was covered by the sea at one time in the past. Some areas of the earth have been under water several times. But we do not know if any part of the deep ocean ever was land, or whether any land existing today was once beneath the deep ocean.

There is a great deal of evidence to show that certain parts of the land were once the bottom of shallow seas. For example, most of the limestone, sandstone, and shale found on land were deposited as sediment. The chalk that is found in England, Texas, and Kansas was deposited on the bed of a sea. It is made up of the shells of tiny creatures that sank to the ocean bed to form what we call chalk.

Today, the waters of all the oceans cover nearly three-quarters of the surface of the earth. While there are many great ocean areas where man has not yet explored the bottom or taken soundings, we have a good, rough idea of what the bottom is like. There are sections that are like mountain ranges, and there are plateaus and plains. But the ocean bottom is not as varied as the surface of the continents.

Rain and other water on the earth's surface is constantly being carried off. Rivers are the larger streams that accomplish this task. Streams smaller than rivers are brooks. And still smaller streams are rivulets.

HOW DO RIVERS FORM?

These flow together and join until the growing stream may become a large river.

Many rivers flow into the sea. But some rivers flow into inland lakes, and rivers that enter dry plains may even grow smaller and smaller until they disappear by evaporation or by sinking into the dry soil.

River water comes in part from rain water that flows along the ground into the stream channel. Or the river water may come from melting snow and ice, from springs, and from lakes.

Large rivers have many tributaries, or smaller streams, that flow into the main stream. The Ohio and Missouri—which are giant rivers themselves—are really tributaries of the still greater Mississippi. Each tributary has its own smaller tributaries, so that a great river system like the Mississippi is composed of thousands of rivers, creeks, brooks, and rivulets.

The land drained by a river system is called its "drainage basin," or "watershed." The Missouri-Mississippi, which is about 3,890 miles long, drains about 1,243,700 square miles. The Amazon River, some 3,900 miles long, has a watershed of over 2,722,000 square miles!

Rivers wear away the land and carry it, bit by bit, into the sea. During thousands of years, this can cause great erosion in the land. The Grand Canyon and the Delaware Water Gap show how rivers can cut great valleys into the land.

Meteors, also called "shooting stars," have long been a mystery to man.

Today, astronomers feel they have a pretty good idea of what meteors are. They believe them to be broken fragments of comets. When

WHAT ARE METEORS MADE OF?

comets break up, the millions of fragments continue to move through space as a meteor swarm or stream. The swarms move in regular orbits, or paths, through space. Some of the larger fragments may become detached and travel through space singly.

Most individual meteors are quite small, but occasionally there are some that weigh many tons. They are usually destroyed entirely by heat when they pass through the earth's atmosphere. Only the larger ones reach the earth.

When a piece of meteor reaches the earth it is called a "meteorite." The largest one found so far weighs between 60 and 70 tons and is still in its resting place in Africa.

There are two main kinds of meteorites. There are those composed chiefly of nickel and iron. These are called the "metallic" meteorites. Some are composed of minerals and look like a piece of igneous rock (rock formed by intense heat). These are called the "stony" meteorites or "aerolites." The outer surfaces of either kind usually have black crusts which are the result of the terrific heat experienced in passing through the atmosphere to earth.

A star is a ball of very hot gas which shines by its own light. Planets, as you know, and our moon too, shine only by light reflected from the sun. And planets shine with a steady light while stars appear to twinkle. This

WHAT MAKES THE STARS SHINE?

is caused by substances in the air between the star and the earth. The unsteady air bends the light from the star, and then it seems to twinkle.

Why does our sun shine? Because it is a star! And not a very big or bright star at that. Compared to all the other stars in the sky, it might be considered medium-sized and medium-bright. There are millions of stars that are smaller than our sun. And many stars are several hundred times larger than the sun. They look small only because they are so far away.

Ever since the days of the Greek astronomers, some 2,000 years ago, the stars have been divided into classes according to their "magnitude," or brightness. Another way of grouping stars is according to their spectra, or the kind of light that comes from the stars. By studying the differences in these spectra, the astronomer may learn about the colors, the temperature, and even the chemical composition of the stars!

You've heard the expression: "As sure as the sun will rise tomorrow." The sun is for us a pretty steady and dependable thing. Whether we see it or not, we know it is always there, shining in the same old way.

DOES THE SUN SHINE THE SAME ALL THE TIME?

And for all practical purposes, that is good enough. The sun is a star, and so it shines by its own light. Where does it get this energy? It is now believed that hydrogen atoms in the very hot interior of the sun combine to form helium. When this happens, it sets free energy which flows steadily to its surface. And the sun should be able to continue radiating this energy for many billions of years to come.

But if we examine the sun in a little more detail, we do not get quite the same "steady" picture. First of all, the sun is not a solid body like the earth, at least at its surface. In fact, different parts of the sun rotate at different rates. The sun's rate of rotation increases from 25 days at its equator to 34 days at its poles.

The outer layer of the sun, called "the corona," is composed of light, gaseous matter. The outer part of this corona is white, and it has streamers that extend out millions of miles from the edge of the sun. These may cause small, but definite differences in the way the sun shines.

Another layer of the sun, called "the chromosphere," is about 9,000 miles thick and is made up largely of hydrogen and helium gas. From this there project huge clouds called "prominences," which may rise to heights of 1,000,000 miles. These also are part of the "unsteady" way the sun shines.

Without the sun, life would be impossible on earth. Among other things, the atmosphere would be frozen, no green plants would be living, and there would be no rain. So we think of the sun as some kind of very special thing in the sky.

WHAT IS THE ORIGIN OF THE SUN?

But there is really nothing special about the sun. It is just a star! Not the biggest or the smallest, not the brightest or the dullest—just an ordinary star like billions of others in the universe! It happens to be the nearest star to us, and we are at just the distance from it that makes it possible to enjoy the benefits of its heat and energy.

Since the sun is a star, scientists cannot really know what its origin was—because they still do not know how the stars in the universe came to be. In fact, there are many things about the sun that cannot be explained. What keeps it "burning," for instance? Well, the sun does not really "burn." It is believed that heat and pressure in the sun change matter into energy. So the sun is using up its matter to send out all that energy.

But this energy is produced at such a great rate, that we do not have to worry for quite a while. Just 1 per cent of the huge mass of the sun could maintain the heat of the sun for about 150 billion years!

It is rather hard for us to realize that our sun is merely just another star in the sky. This is probably because we think of the stars as looking so tiny. The sun looks larger than any star because it is only about 93 million miles from the earth. The nearest star is 25 trillion miles away!

HOW HOT IS THE SUN?

What is the temperature on the surface of the sun? Scientists believe that it is about 10,800 degrees Fahrenheit. To give you an idea of how hot this is, white-hot molten iron used in making steel reaches a temperature of about 2,600 degrees. So you see how much hotter the sun's surface is. And as for the interior of the sun, astronomers estimate it may be as hot as 36,000,000 degrees Fahrenheit!

Remember, scientists are only taking a "guess" about this, because we know almost nothing about the interior of the sun. We do know something about the composition of this star. For example, it has been learned that the sun contains more than 60 of the chemical elements present in the earth. But it is hard to study the sun's interior because the sun is surrounded by four layers of gaseous matter.

In 1610, soon after the telescope was invented, Galileo became the first man to see spots on the sun. Through the telescope the sunspots look like dark holes in the sun's white disk.

WHAT ARE SUNSPOTS?

Sunspots may be observed on almost any clear day. They vary greatly in size. Some appear like mere specks on the sun's surface. One very large spot was about 90,000 miles long and 60,000 miles wide. Groups of sunspots are known to measure 200,000 miles in length!

Astronomers are pretty sure that sunspots are electrical in nature because of certain effects they produce. One astronomer has shown that

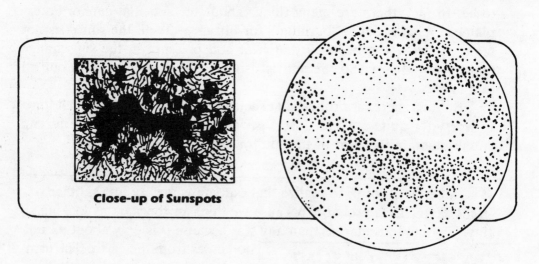

Close-up of Sunspots

they are tremendous whirls of electrified matter that come bursting out from the interior of the sun in pairs like the ends of a U-shaped tunnel.

Sunspots, or their release of electrical energy, send beams of negatively charged electrons shooting into space. Some of these electrons enter the earth's atmosphere and produce certain electrical effects.

One of these effects is the "aurora borealis" (or Northern Lights). Electrical energy from sunspots also disturbs radio transmission. These electrons also seem to increase the amount of ozone in the upper atmosphere. This extra ozone may absorb more of the sun's heat than usual, so sunspots may have a bearing on our weather.

Most sunspots last only a few days, but some last two months or more. They increase in number, then diminish, in a regular cycle which runs about 21 1/5 years. Records of sunspots have now been kept for more than 100 years and we are still learning about what they are and how they affect us.

WHY DOES THE MOON SHINE?

In ancient times, the moon was worshipped as a goddess who ruled the night. Since then, man has learned a great deal about the moon, especially due to space flights by the United States and the Soviet Union, and the *Apollo* moon landings, which enabled astronauts to collect moon soil and rocks for scientific study.

But there is no mystery at all as to why the moon shines. It is a satellite of the earth. That is, it is a small body that revolves around it, just as the earth revolves around the sun.

The only reason we can see the moon from earth, or that it "shines," is because light from the sun strikes its surface and is reflected to us. Strangely enough, we can only see one side of the moon from the earth. This is because the moon rotates on its axis in the same length of time it takes for it to make its journey around the earth. Of course, man has already "seen" the other side in photographs, taken when instruments landed on the other side of the moon.

Since the moon has no atmosphere, or air, that light from the sun which hits it has rather interesting effects. For about 14 days, the surface of the moon is heated by the direct rays of the sun to a temperature above that of boiling water. The other half of the lunar month, it is exposed to the cold of a long, dark night.

There is gravity on or in every single object that exists in the universe. For gravity is simply the force which pulls every object in the universe toward every other object in the universe.

IS THERE GRAVITY ON THE MOON?

But the force of gravity depends on two things: the mass of the objects involved, and their distance from each other. For example, there is a force of attraction between you and the earth. But the earth is so enormous compared to you, that it pulls on you. The force of this pull is what you weigh at the earth's surface. But if you were twice as far from the center of the earth as you are now (or 4,000 miles in the air), you would weigh only one-quarter of what you weigh here on earth.

The moon is a huge object but compared to the earth it is rather small. The moon weighs only 1/81 as much as the earth. So its gravity, or pull, on its surface is much less than that of the earth. In fact, it is only one-sixth as strong as that of the earth.

On the moon, an astronaut's weight is only one-sixth of his weight on earth. When he jumps, while moving about, he can jump six times as high. And, as Alan B. Shepard, Jr. demonstrated during the *Apollo 14* mission, a golf ball can be driven six times as far—because the pull of the moon's surface is so weak.

What is the weather anyway? It is simply what the air or atmosphere is like at any time. No matter what the air is—cold, cool, warm, hot, calm, breezy, windy, dry, moist, or wet—that's weather.

WHAT MAKES THE WEATHER?

Weather may be any combination of different amounts of heat, moisture, and motion in the air. And it changes from hour to hour, day to day, season to season, and even from year to year.

The daily changes are caused by storms and fair weather moving over the earth. The seasonal changes are due to the turning of the earth around the sun. Why weather changes from year to year is still not known, however.

The most important thing to "cause" weather is the heating and cooling of the air. Heat causes the winds as well as the different way in which water vapor appears in the atmosphere.

Humidity, the amount of water vapor in the air, combined with the temperature, causes many weather conditions. Clouds are a kind of weather condition, and they are formed when water vapor condenses high above the ground.

When the cloud droplets grow larger and become too heavy to be held up by the air currents, they fall to the ground and we have the weather known as rain. If the raindrops fall through a layer of air which is below freezing, the drops freeze and our weather is snow.

One of the ways the weather forecaster studies the weather is to look at the "fronts" that exist. Fronts are boundary lines between the cold air moving southward from the north, and the warm air moving from the tropics. Most of the severe storms which cause rain, snow, and other bad weather are in some way related to these fronts.

Sometimes when we are outdoors, a sudden and mysterious thing takes place. A wind begins to blow. We cannot see it, but we feel it, and we have no idea what started it.

WHAT MAKES A WIND?

A wind is simply the motion of air over the earth. What causes the air to move? All winds are caused by one thing—a change in temperature. Whenever air is heated it expands. This makes it lighter, and lighter air rises. As the warm air rises, cooler air flows in to take its place. And this movement of air is wind!

There are two kinds of winds, those that are part of a world-wide system of winds, and local winds. The major wind systems of the world begin at the Equator, where the sun's heat is greatest.

Here the heat rises to high altitudes and is pushed off toward the North and South poles. When it has journeyed about one-third of the distance to the poles, it has cooled and begins to fall back to earth. Some of this air returns to the Equator to be heated again, and some continues on to the poles.

These types of winds, which tend to blow in the same general direction all year round, are called "prevailing winds." But these world-wide winds are often broken up by local winds which blow from different directions.

Local winds may be caused by the coming of cold air masses with high pressure, or warmer air masses with low pressure. Local winds usually do not last long. After a few hours, or at most a few days, the prevailing wind pattern is present again.

Other local winds are caused by the daily heating and cooling·off of the ground. Land and sea breezes are examples of this kind of wind. In the daytime, the cool air over the ocean moves inland as the sea breeze. At night, the ocean is warmer than the ground, so the cooler air moves out to sea as the land breeze.

Of course we are all quite accustomed to thunderstorms. These are usually local storms. But there are certain kinds of storms that may cover thousands of square miles. One such type is called a "cyclonic storm" or

HOW DO TORNADOES START?

"cyclone." In a cyclone, the winds blow toward the center of an area of low pressure.

A curious thing about them is that the winds blow in spiral fashion. In the Northern Hemisphere such storms turn counterclockwise, in the Southern Hemisphere they turn clockwise!

A tornado is simply a special kind of cyclone. A tornado arises when the conditions that cause ordinary thunderstorms are unusually violent. There is an updraft of air. There are winds blowing in opposite directions around this rising air. This starts a whirling effect that is narrow and very violent. When this happens, centrifugal force throws the air away from the center. And this leaves a core of low pressure at the center.

This low-pressure core acts like a powerful vacuum on everything

it passes. This is one of the destructive things about a tornado. It can actually suck the walls of a house outward in such a way that the house will collapse. The other destructive thing about a tornado is the high winds that may blow around the edges of a whirl. These winds can reach 300 miles per hour and blow anything down.

There are many people who actually tremble with fear at the sound of a clap of thunder during a thunderstorm. There is absolutely no reason to have any fear of thunder. By the time the sound of thunder reaches you,

IS THUNDER DANGEROUS?

the bolt of electricity which caused it has already done its work. You hear the thunder after the lightning flash simply because sound travels much more slowly than light.

Should you be afraid of lightning? Well, there is no question that lightning can cause damage, and in some rare cases it has even been known to kill people. But your chances of being struck by lightning are quite small.

Lightning, of course, is a form of electricity, and this is what can make it dangerous. It is a giant spark of electricity that we see as a bright flash of light. It may jump across the space between two clouds, or from cloud to earth, or even from earth to cloud!

During a storm, different electrical charges (positive or negative) are built up by the clouds and the earth. When the difference between the charges becomes great enough, a spark—which is lightning—jumps the space between.

During and after an electrical discharge, currents of air expand and contract. The expanding and contracting currents violently collide, and produce the noise we call "thunder."

One of the most unusual weather conditions we can experience is a hailstorm. It is quite a thing to see and hear hailstones coming down, sometimes with such force that great damage is done. Animals, and even men,

WHAT CAUSES HAIL?

have been killed by hail!

A hailstorm usually occurs during the warm weather and is accompanied in many cases by thunder, lightning, and rain. Hail is formed when raindrops freeze while passing through a belt of cold air on their way to earth.

Single raindrops form very small hailstones. But an interesting thing can happen to such a raindrop. As it falls as a hailstone, it may meet a strong rising current of air. So it is carried up again to the level where raindrops are falling. New drops begin to cling to the hailstone. And as it falls once more through the cold belt, these new drops spread into a layer around it and freeze, and now we have larger hailstones.

This rising and falling of the hailstone may be repeated time after time until it has added so many layers that its weight is heavy enough to overcome the force of the rising current of air. Now it falls to the ground.

In this way hailstones measuring three or four inches in diameter and weighing as much as a pound are sometimes built up. Snow, too, freezes around hailstones when they are carried into regions where it is forming. So the hailstones are frequently made up of layers of ice and snow.

Frozen rain is sometimes called hail, but it is really "sleet"! And soft hail which sometimes falls in winter is only a form of snow.

Snow is really nothing more than frozen water. Then why doesn't it look like ice?

There are a large number of ice crystals in each snowflake, and

WHAT IS SNOW?

the reflection of light from all the surfaces of the crystals makes it look white.

Snow begins to be formed when water vapor in the atmosphere freezes. Tiny crystals are formed that are clear and transparent. Since there are currents in the air, these tiny crystals are carried up and down in the atmosphere. They fall and rise as different air currents move them along.

While this is happening, the crystals begin to gather around a nucleus, so that in time there may be a hundred or more gathered together. When this group of ice crystals is big enough, it floats down toward the ground. We call this collection of ice crystals a "snowflake."

Some crystals are flat and some are like a column of needles. But regardless of the shape, snow crystals always have six sides or angles. The branches of any single snowflake are always identical, but the arrangement of the branches is different in every case. No two snowflakes are ever exactly alike.

Did you know that snow is not always white? In many parts of the world red, green, blue, and even black snow has been seen! The reason for the different colors is that sometimes there are tiny fungi in the air, or dust is floating about, and this is collected by the snow as it falls.

Because snow contains so much air, it is a poor conductor of heat. That is why a "blanket" of snow can protect dormant vegetation in the ground and why igloos and snow huts can be made of blocks of snow and keep people inside quite warm.

Everybody knows that Columbus "discovered America." Then why wasn't it named after him?

The reason for this might be considered an accident of fate. When

WHY IS OUR CONTINENT CALLED "AMERICA"?

Columbus made his first journey, he sighted land early in the morning of October 12, 1492. Columbus went ashore, took possession in the names of King Ferdinand and Queen Isabella of Spain, and named the land San Salvador. That land however, was not the mainland of the continent. It is what we now call Watling Island, in the Bahamas. Columbus actually thought he had reached India (which was his goal), so he called the natives Indians.

Columbus cruised on, looking for Japan. Instead he discovered Cuba and Hispaniola (Haiti and the Dominican Republic today). On March 14, 1493, Columbus returned to Spain.

On his second voyage, which started on September 24, 1493, Columbus discovered several of the Virgin Islands, Puerto Rico, and Jamaica. But he was still determined to find India. On his third voyage, in 1498, he discovered Trinidad and touched South America. But he thought he had found a series of islands.

Another explorer, Amerigo Vespucci, meanwhile was claiming that he had been the first to reach the mainland of South America. This was on June 16, 1497. (Many experts believe that Vespucci did not really make his voyage until 1499.)

On a trip in 1501, Vespucci sailed along the coast of South America and wrote letters saying he had found a new continent. His information was used by a German map maker—and in his maps he used the name "America" (after Amerigo Vespucci) for the new continent. And that name has been used ever since!

Stamp collecting, or philately, has been a hobby of millions of people all over the world for about 100 years. The United States Post Office has even established a special department to help stamp collectors!

WHY DO PEOPLE COLLECT STAMPS?

Of course many people collect stamps to make money. But you have to know a great deal about stamps to make big profits this way. In fact, many "collectors" never make money on stamps because they have mistaken ideas about them. They may think age alone makes a stamp valuable. Or they may see a strange stamp and think it is scarce and valuable.

Stamp collecting can be a very educational hobby. Every picture on a stamp was selected for some particular reason. Each has some bit of knowledge to give concerning the country from which it came.

The most valuable stamps, of course, are the scarcest ones. Usually there is some peculiar circumstance connected with the very scarce and valuable stamps. For instance, in certain United States post offices in 1847, there occurred a shortage of five-cent stamps. The postmasters merely cut ten-cent stamps in half, each part paying five cents postage. Today these halves are worth several hundred dollars each!

Errors occur in printing stamps, and such errors increase the value of stamps. In 1918, the first United States airmail stamps went on sale. A sheet of them sold for 24 cents each. In a certain post office, the clerk sold such a sheet at the regular price. What he did not notice was that on this particular sheet the airplane happened to have been printed upside down. Later, each of those stamps was worth $2,000!

Flags of one sort or another have been used in war since earliest times. But when the design of our flag was approved on June 14, 1777, the idea of a national flag was still very new. Most European nations were fighting

WHAT ARE SOME RULES FOR DISPLAYING OUR FLAG?

under the private flags of their kings. But after the United States had chosen a national flag, many other nations followed our example.

Since the flag is the symbol of our nation, it must be treated with reverence. There are a great many rules regarding the display of our flag, but all of them have this idea of reverence to our national symbol in mind. Here are a few of these rules of "flag etiquette":

The flag must always be flown right side up, unless used as a signal of distress. No flag must ever be flown above the flag of the United States on the same staff. When the flag is carried in procession with other flags, it must always be on the right of the line of march.

The flag should be hoisted briskly at sunrise, and lowered slowly at sunset. It should be saluted as it is being hoisted and lowered. The flag must never be used for coverings or drapery except when it is used to cover a casket.

The flag must never be allowed to touch the ground. It can be flown at half-mast as a sign of mourning. In such a case, it must first be run up to the top of the staff as usual, then slowly lowered.

The flag of the United States may be dipped at sea in a salute to a passing vessel, but it should never be dipped on land to any flag or any person. After the flag has been lowered, it is carefully folded into the shape of a three-cornered hat, to symbolize the hats worn by the soldiers of the American Revolution.

The taking of a census by a government is as old as the custom of collecting taxes and raising armies. In early times, the ruler's only object in taking a census was to discover how many people he could send to the

WHY IS THE CENSUS TAKEN?

wars or how much money he could get. Since the people suffered from the census, they did all in their power to make it incorrect.

In most countries, fairly simple questions are asked in a census—the age of the people living in a house, the relationship of these people, their birthplaces and nationality, their jobs and for whom they work. Some questions ask about date of marriage and number of children. Figures about agriculture may also be included, such as acres of land and kinds of livestock owned.

After all the information is gathered, the figures are totaled and separated according to sections or classes. They then become available and helpful to many agencies. For example, a total of age groups can be useful to governments in figuring out how many schools will be needed at a certain time, or in estimating future costs of pensions.

The census shows whether the population is increasing or decreasing. It shows the movement of population to the city or the country. It reveals whether social conditions are improving or growing worse. It tells which industries are advancing and which are slowing up.

Where office holders are elected on the basis of population, a census helps decide the number of office holders from each section. It helps the government in making laws, and it helps business, social, and economic agencies in conducting their affairs and making their plans.

The Alamo is a building in San Antonio, Texas. It is actually the chapel of the Mission San Antonio de Valero, which was founded by Franciscans in 1718. A popular name for it became "the Alamo mission,"

WHAT WAS THE ALAMO?

because it stood in a grove of cottonwood trees and the Spanish name for this tree is *alamo*.

The mission originally consisted of the chapel, a convent yard, convent and hospital building, and a plaza, all surrounded by a strong wall. When the Indians disappeared from this region, the mission was abandoned, and after 1793, it was sometimes used as a fort.

In 1835, a group of United States settlers in Texas revolted against Mexico. Texas at that time was part of one of the Mexican states. Many Americans from others parts of the United States came to help these men in their fight. Among them was a man called Davy Crockett.

Late in 1835, the Texans captured San Antonio and began to use the Alamo as a fort. The Mexican general, Antonio López de Santa Anna, marched on San Antonio with about 4,000 men. In the Alamo

were about 180 men. They were led by Col. William Travis and Col. James Bowie.

On February 23, 1836, the Mexicans surrounded the fort but were held off for 13 days. On March 6, 1836, they finally blasted a hole in the wall of the Alamo. As Mexican troops poured into the mission, the Texans continued to fight with knives and bayonets.

More than 500 Mexicans were killed, but the battle was soon over. There were not enough Texans to hold the fort. Five men were taken prisoner and later shot. "Remember the Alamo!" became the battle cry of the Texas army. Six weeks after the fall of the Alamo, the Texans, under Sam Houston, defeated Santa Anna's army and captured him in the Battle of San Jacinto.

The way we live in our society is to divide ourselves into families. Our immediate family and our relatives are our "group." But there are many primitive tribes and people who divide themselves differently.

WHAT IS A TOTEM POLE?

Among such people there are "clans," and all members of a clan are considered to be related. This relationship may be real, or they may just decide to call themselves related.

These clans usually have an "ancestor," who may be a kind of mythical human being, and the deeds of this ancestor are glorified through the ages. Or this "ancestor" may be an animal or even a plant or natural object!

Usually, the clan is descended either from an ancestor who had a special relationship with a certain animal, or from the animal itself. In such cases, the clan takes its name from the animal, and some symbol of the animal becomes the badge or "totem" of the group. The animal is called "the totem animal." Such a group is known as a "totemic clan."

Many of these clans have a totem pole. On this pole are carvings in color. They may show the totem animal or ancestor and other beings important in the story of the clan. The totem pole is usually set up in the village to give the clan prestige and to show their pride in their ancestor.

People who live in such totemic clans have different practices in different parts of the world. As a rule, members of the same clan are not allowed to marry. The children belong to the mother's clan, and not the father's.

Ever since the time of ancient Greece, stories have been told about the lost island, or continent, of Atlantis. It was thought to be a very large island in the Atlantic Ocean, just west of the Rock of Gibraltar. It was

WHAT WAS THE LOST CONTINENT OF ATLANTIS?

believed to be a perfect place—a kind of paradise.

According to legends, Atlantis was a powerful kingdom whose people conquered all of southwestern Europe and northwestern Africa. They were finally defeated by the Athenians from Greece.

The people of Atlantis then became wicked. As a punishment, the island was swallowed up by the ocean. This legend is told in the *Timaeus*, written in the 300's B.C. by the Greek philosopher Plato. The island was supposed to have been lost more than 9,000 years before Plato's time.

During the Middle Ages, the stories about Atlantis were believed to be true. In the fourteenth and fifteen centuries, many voyages were made to try to find Atlantis. The stories may have come from some true happenings. Perhaps a voyager brought back tales of his discovery of a new and strange land, and in time these tales became part of the legend of Atlantis.

Even today there are people who firmly believe there was such a place. According to the man who is considered the greatest expert on Atlantis by these believers, Atlantis was a place where man first became civilized. He also believes many of the gods worshipped by ancient peoples were really the kings and queens of Atlantis, and that the Atlanteans were the first to manufacture iron and have an alphabet.

If you ever make a trip to Italy, one of the most fascinating sights to see is Pompeii. For here is a city almost 2,000 years old that you will be able to see and study in greater detail, and better preserved, than almost

WHAT WAS POMPEII?

any other ancient city.

Why is this so? On August 24, in the year A.D. 79, there was a great eruption of Mount Vesuvius, a volcano in southern Italy. The lava, stones, and ashes thrown up by the volcano completely buried two nearby towns.

The town of Herculaneum, about two miles away, was deeply covered by a stream of mud which flowed down the slope of the mountain. Pompeii, farther along the coast, was buried by the rain of ashes

44

and pebbles of light pumice stone. These fell over Pompeii in a dry state, and the mass which covered the city was from 18 to 20 feet thick.

When water came down on top of this, the material became like clay or plaster of Paris. As a result, objects that were caught in it made molds of the material, and the two towns were remarkably preserved underneath!

Survivors of this disaster returned to the towns, and by digging down and tunneling were able to remove most of the valuable objects, including slabs of marble that were on the large buildings.

In the Middle Ages, this place and everything about it was forgotten. In 1594, an underground aqueduct was started here, and the ruins were rediscovered. But it took until 1763 before any real excavating was done, and it has been carried on ever since. But nearly half of Pompeii is still buried!

This is certainly a strange name for a body of water—but no other sea in the world has had such a variety of names!

It was first called "dead sea" by ancient Greek writers. The He-

WHAT IS THE DEAD SEA?

brews called it "the salt sea," among other names. Arab writers called it "the stinking sea."

What is so strange about this sea? It is really a large, narrow salt lake that lies between Jordan and Israel. It lies in a deep trough, or "rift," which is a deep depression in this area.

The Dead Sea is about 48 miles long, and ranges from 3 to 11 miles in width. Now comes the amazing part. The Dead Sea is the lowest body of water in the world. The surface of this sea is about 1,300 feet below sea level. The southern part of the sea is very shallow, but in the north the depth is about 1,300 feet.

There are no streams flowing out of the Dead Sea. But into it drain the Jordan River from the north and many smaller streams from the surrounding slopes. There is only one way the surplus water is carried away—by evaporation. This leaves behind in the water a large concentration of minerals, such as salt, potash, magnesium, chloride, and bromine.

The Dead Sea is the world's saltiest body of water. The water is about six times as salty as that of the ocean! There are so many minerals concentrated in this sea, that a man swimming in it will float with his head and shoulders out of the water at all times! These minerals can be valuable to man. In fact, it is estimated that dissolved in this water are about two million tons of potash, which is used in making artificial fertilizers.

The Dead Sea is one of the strangest bodies of water to be found on the earth. Millions of years ago, the Dead Sea was about 1,400 feet higher than it is today, and so was on a higher level than the Mediterranean Sea.

IS THERE ANY LIFE IN THE DEAD SEA?

At that time, life did exist in it. But then a great dry period came, and so much of it evaporated, that the sea gradually shrank in size to its present state.

One of the most amazing things about the Dead Sea is the amount of salt it contains. Normal ocean water contains about 4 to 6 per cent of salts. The Dead Sea contains 23 to 25 per cent of salts! If you taste this water, it is not only salty, but it may make you nauseous because of the chloride of magnesium in it. The water also has a smooth, oily feeling because of the chloride of calcium in it.

No animal life can exist in the Dead Sea. The Jordan River flows into it, bringing fish along with it. But the fish die, furnishing food for the sea birds.

When we try to learn of the accomplishments of ancient man, we usually have to search or dig for evidence. But there is a case where ancient man has left all the evidence standing in a huge structure, and we still cannot

WHAT IS STONEHENGE?

figure out what it is, what it was used for, and who built it!

This is Stonehenge. It consists of large, standing stones in a circular setting, surrounded by an earthwork, and located near Salisbury, England. As long ago as the year 1136, it was written that the stones were magically transported from Ireland by Merlin. Of course, this was only a legend. More recently, it was believed that Stonehenge was put up by the Druids, who were priests in ancient England. But there is actually no reason to believe this is so.

Stonehenge has a somewhat complicated structure. On the outside is a circular ditch, with an entrance gap. Then there is a bank of earth.

Inside the bank is a ring of 56 pits. Between these and the stones in the center, are two more rings of pits.

The stone setting consists of two circles and two horseshoes of upright stones. Then there are separate stones which have been given names, such as the Altar stone, the Slaughter stone, two Station stones, and the Hele stone.

In most of the holes that have been excavated, cremated human bones have been found. By studying the pottery and objects found, and by making radioactive-carbon tests, it has been estimated that parts of Stonehenge date back to about 1848 B.C., and possibly 275 years earlier or later than this date.

Part of Stonehenge is aligned so that the rising sun in midsummer is seen at a certain point, but nobody is sure if this was intentional.

So this huge and remarkable structure, which may be 4,000 years old, still remains a fascinating mystery!

The proper name of this great and famous statue is "Liberty Enlightening the World," and it stands in New York harbor as a symbol of freedom.

The statue was a gift from the people of France to the people of the

WHEN WAS THE STATUE OF LIBERTY BUILT?

United States, but there were many problems involved with the presentation of this magnificent gift. In 1865, a French historian named Edouard de Laboulaye proposed that his country present a memorial to the United States on the 100th anniversary of the signing of the Declaration of Independence. The Franco-Prussian War intervened, and nothing was done about this idea for some time.

Then in 1874, a sculptor named Frédéric Bartholdi was sent to New York to confer with American authorities about the idea. As he sailed into the harbor, he got the inspiration for a huge "Goddess of Liberty" to stand at the gateway to the New World.

The Franco-American Union was formed to collect the money this would cost. The total cost of the statue itself was contributed by the people of France. The people of the United States contributed about $250,000 for the pedestal on which the statue stands. It was dedicated on October 28, 1886, ten years later than had been originally planned.

The total weight of the Statue of Liberty is 225 tons. It is nearly 152 feet tall and stands on a pedestal 150 feet above the water. The pedestal rests upon a 23,500 ton concrete foundation that reaches down 20 feet to bedrock.

Maybe you did not even know the Nile River had a "riddle." Well, it is something that has puzzled people for thousands of years, and it has to do with a very curious event.

WHAT IS "THE RIDDLE OF THE NILE"?

Every year in Egypt, the Nile River starts to rise in July and continues to rise until October, when its level is about 25 feet above the level in May. During the high-water season, the Nile spills over its banks and deposits fertile silt on the fields along its course.

What makes this rising of the river mysterious is that there is practically no rainfall in Egypt! So for hundreds of years people have wondered what makes the Nile rise so regularly each year. This "riddle of the Nile" was not solved until late in the nineteenth century.

The Nile is the longest river in the world. It flows over 4,000 miles from south to north in the northeastern part of Africa, mainly in Sudan and Egypt. The yearly flooding of the Nile has made its valley a fertile ribbon in a hot, dry, barren wasteland, and people have lived here for thousands of years.

There are two main streams and sources of the Nile River—the White Nile and the Blue Nile. The White Nile has its origin at Lake

Victoria in Uganda. It has a fairly even flow throughout the year, so it cannot cause the annual rise of the Nile River. During April and May, when the water in the lower Nile is at its lowest, 85 per cent of the water is coming from the White Nile.

But what about the Blue Nile? It rises in Ethiopia. In the Ethiopian Mountains there are heavy rains and melting snows. And when these come down every year, they cause the Nile River to rise and overflow. And that is the answer to "the riddle of the Nile"!

It is quite an amazing experience to be in a city where most of the "highways" are canals! But unlike most cities, Venice's roadways, the canals, were there before the city was built!

WHY DOES VENICE HAVE CANALS?

Venice is built on a group of mud banks that formed over 100 small islands at the head of the Adriatic Sea. All buildings are erected on pilings driven into this mud. In between the mud banks are strips of the sea, and these are the famous canals of Venice!

In this city, transportation is either by boat or on foot. There are no cars or carts allowed inside the old town. There are numerous narrow alleys and little bridges which span the canals. And everywhere one sees that small boat known as "the gondola." The gondolier, the driver of the boat, stands on a platform in the rear of the boat and propels it with a long pole.

Venice is a very old city. Long before the Huns swept down through Italy in about the middle of the fifth century, there were people already living on the little islands of the lagoon. After a while, 12 lagoon townships were formed. This was the beginning of the state of Venice, within which developed gradually the city now known as Venice.

In 1450, Venice was the head of a huge colonial empire and was the chief sea power in the world. Beginning with the sixteenth century, new trade routes were discovered and the trade of Venice began to decline.

In the following years, Venice was involved in many wars, lost its empire, and was practically destroyed by its enemies. In 1866, Venice voted to become part of the kingdom of Italy.

Today, Venice is one of the great artistic centers of Europe and is beginning to regain its position as a great port.

On Easter Day in 1722, a Dutch admiral called Jacob Roggeveen landed on a grass-covered island in the South Pacific. He named it Easter Island and discovered it to be a very strange place indeed.

WHAT ARE THE EASTER ISLAND STATUES?

The island was more than 1,000 miles from the nearest inhabited land. There were over 2,000 natives living on the island, and they were a dark Polynesian people. But the most curious thing of all was what this explorer saw on the island.

All along the coast he found large, stone heads. They had long faces and exceptionally long ears. Some of these statues had hands and

some wore hats that were made of red lava. He soon discovered that these statues not only appeared along the coast, but they were at scattered points inland. Many were found partially finished in the quarries where they had been carved.

Primitive peoples all over the world have various art forms, usually connected with their religion, but nothing like these statues had ever been found anywhere else! And the truth is, they still remain a mystery. How could these heavy figures, some of which weigh about 50 tons, be moved from the quarries to their places? What form of transportation could the primitive people have developed?

No one knows! It is believed that the statues were probably connected with primitive religious practices and burial customs of the people. And many of the statues were purposely broken during native wars that took place on the island during and after the eighteenth century. But even the natives living on the island today cannot explain the meaning of the huge statues!

Today the island is governed by Chile. Except for a small section reserved for the natives, the entire island is used for grazing cattle and sheep. The island is only about 13 miles long and 7 miles wide at its broadest point.

Before the year 1700, many different groups of Indians lived who constructed mounds of earth, clay, shell, and stone. A popular name for them is the Mound Builders.

WHO WERE THE MOUND BUILDERS?

The first kind of mounds built by these Indians were burial mounds, built over the graves of the dead. They were made of earth, clay, shells, or stones. These cone-shaped or dome-shaped burial mounds ranged from several feet in height and ten feet in diameter to a size like the Miamisburg mound in Ohio. This was about 68 feet high and 250 feet in diameter. It was the custom of the Mound Builders to bury certain small, personal ornaments or utensils with the body.

After the custom of mound-burial was begun, a different kind of mound began to be constructed—an effigy mound. They were called effigies because they were built in the form of animals: bears, deer, buffalo, birds, and serpents. Most of them were found in Wisconsin and many of these contained burials.

A somewhat different style of effigy mound is found in Ohio. It was associated with the Adena and possibly the Hopewell Indians. The most famous is the Great Serpent Mound in Adams County, Ohio. This mound is four feet high and spreads out in zigzag fashion for more than 1,330 feet. It looks like a great snake with a triangular head. Just in front of the head is an oval mound. This may be a frog or an egg which the snake is about to swallow.

The most recent type of mound built by these Indians was the flat-topped pyramidal type. It had a temple on top and a ramp or stairway led to the temple.

Mounds are found over a wide area between the Great Lakes and the Gulf of Mexico, and between the Atlantic Ocean and the Great Plains of the West. Most of the mounds are in the Mississippi Valley.

At one time, people believed that there lived on this earth with us all kinds of strange beings who had magical powers. Sometimes they were called fairies, and sometimes they had special names, depending on their power

WHAT IS A LEPRECHAUN?

or on the country where they were supposed to live.

Leprechauns were the fairy shoemakers of Ireland. They were little old wrinkled men, not even as big as a new-born child. In Scotland, similar fairies about two feet high were called brownies. A brownie chose some house to serve and, coming at night, scrubbed and cleaned and did all sorts of work. All he would take in payment was a bowl of cream and a bit of white bread.

In England, the very smallest fairies were called pixies. They would wear green jackets and red caps and dance to the music of crickets and grasshoppers. In France, they were called fees and in Scandinavia, white elves. They lived in the woods and fields and a mortal could find his way to their home only on one of the four magical nights of the year—Midsummer Eve, May Eve, Christmas Eve, or Halloween.

Fairies that were bigger in size had different names. For instance, if they were from 18 inches to the size of small children, they were called goblins. In Germany they were called gnomes and dwarfs. And in Scandinavia they were called trolls.

Sometimes there were human-sized fairies, and they were hard to tell from mortals. In Germany, if you met a man with green teeth he was a nix, or water spirit. When nixes ventured on land, some bit of their clothing was always wet.

Of course it was considered very difficult to know the real size of a fairy because they were so seldom seen.

Sometimes a man, or a thing he does, captures the imagination of a country. His deed may not be decisive in his country's history, but he becomes a kind of national hero. Such a man was George Armstrong

WHAT WAS CUSTER'S LAST STAND?

Custer.

Custer graduated from the United States Military Academy in 1861, and joined the Union forces in the Civil War. He became one of the most daring cavalry leaders in the Union Army. When the war ended, Custer was made a lieutenant colonel in the regular army and went to Kansas to fight Indians.

In 1876, Sioux Indians were attacking the Western settlements. A large United States force was sent against them. Custer, with about 600 men, was sent on a scouting expedition. On June 24, 1876, he was told that Indians under the leadership of Sitting Bull were encamped on the Little Big Horn River in Montana. Custer's scouts reported only a few hundred Indians, but the number turned out to be more than 2,500.

Custer then made the mistake of dividing his small force in hopes of surrounding the enemy. One unit attacked and then retreated when it saw the size of the Indian force. A second never got into the fight. With about 225 men, Custer attacked the Indians. In hand-to-hand fighting all of his little band was killed. This desperate fight they made became known as "Custer's Last Stand."

The tragedy stunned the country. Today, a monument and national cemetery mark the site of this battle. Custer himself is buried at West Point.

Usually you hear of Mason and Dixon's Line as a sort of boundary between the North and South in the United States. People say that a certain way of life exists south of the line, and another way of life exists north of it.

WHAT IS MASON'S AND DIXON'S LINE?

Here is how Mason and Dixon's Line came into existence. When the kings of England were giving away land in America, there were no accurate maps of the continent. As a result, the descriptions of the grants were confused and there were many disputes. In one case, some of the same land was given to William Penn of Pennsylvania and to Lord Baltimore of Maryland.

In the grant to Penn, the southern boundary of Pennsylvania was designated as the parallel marking "the beginning of the 40th degree of northern latitude." And the northern boundary of Maryland was defined as a line "which lieth under the 40th degree of northern latitude."

So after much dispute, two astronomers were sent from England to survey the boundary in 1763. They were Charles Mason and Jeremiah Dixon, and they spent four years marking a boundary 244 miles long. They even brought over milestones from England, and set them up on the eastern part of the line. Every fifth stone had the arms of Baltimore on one side and the arms of Penn on the other side. But many of the stones were never set up because it was so hard to transport them.

The British government approved this line in 1769, and Mason and Dixon's Line became the boundary of Maryland and Pennsylvania. North of Mason and Dixon's Line was a land of small farms and growing cities. South of it were fewer cities and many large cotton and tobacco plantations. By 1804, all of the states north of the line had abolished slavery.

So Mason and Dixon's Line became more than a symbol. It actually divided two ways of life in the United States.

The first "Americans" came to America so long ago that we cannot really know as much as we would like to know about their earliest history. But this is what most authorities think happened.

WHERE DID THE AMERICAN INDIANS COME FROM?

About 12,000 years ago, bands of hunters on foot wandered into a strange new land, following herds of elk and caribou. The land these early hunters came from was probably Siberia. They crossed over to Alaska where the continents of Asia and North America are closest together at the narrow strip of water now called Bering Strait.

For thousands of years more hunters came to North America. They did not come all at once, but came in small family groups. Although they came from the same homeland and were originally alike, they came

Eastern   Plains   Northwest Coast

WOODLANDS IROQUOIS   SIOUX   TLINGIT

54

over a period of thousands of years and thus the groups differed in many ways. They differed in language, in appearance, in customs, in ways of making a living, and in the way they adapted themselves to life in the new land.

They all had straight, black hair and high cheekbones. They were all dark-skinned, but their shadings varied. The skins of some had a reddish tinge and so these people were often called "red men."

They used the same sort of weapons and tools, and methods to provide themselves with food, clothing, and shelter. But they used different materials to satisfy these needs.

The biggest differences that developed among these people were a result of where they settled to live. There were five main living centers where these people settled: the Northwest Coast, the California region, the Southwest, the Eastern Woodlands, and the Plains. The tribes that developed in each of these centers were quite different from each other —though they were all what we came to know as "Indians."

Practically everybody has heard of or read stories about King Arthur and his Knights of the Round Table. They are not considered to be true stories, but legends. What are they based on?

DID KING ARTHUR EVER EXIST?

Well, no one knows who King Arthur really was. Most writers of history believe that there was a great chief of one of the tribes in Britain around the year A.D. 500, and the legends have grown up about this man.

King Arthur may have been part Roman and part British, for the Romans had ruled England for nearly 400 years. Arthur probably led a large army against the Saxon invaders.

In both Wales and Brittany, Arthur was remembered and admired. Stories about him were passed from one generation to another. Each story was more wonderful than the last. Finally, Arthur became one of the greatest heroes who ever lived. He killed horrible monsters, had great magical powers, and became a great and good king.

Nobody knows for sure just where Arthur had his castle. There are about six different places in England that claim to be the location of Camelot, his home.

The first writer to mention Arthur was an early Welsh historian who lived about the eighth century. After that first mention of Arthur, nothing was written about him for about 400 years. Then in the twelfth century, stories about King Arthur became quite common. The earliest were written in Latin, and then French and English poets began to write about him.

In the fifteenth century, Sir Thomas Malory wrote down many of the stories about Arthur in a book called *Morte d'Arthur (Death of Arthur)*.

Paul Bunyan is a legendary hero of American folklore. There is probably no other figure in America about whom so many wonderful and fantastic tales have been told, and who is supposed to have done so many remark-able things.

WHO WAS PAUL BUNYAN?

There was a real man called Paul Bunyon, who lived in the early 1800's and who was a French-Canadian. He operated a lumber camp, and the people who worked for him told marvelous tales of his bravery and strength.

The American lumberjacks adopted him as a sort of hero who symbolized their own hearty and exciting life. In their tales, they had him cross the border into the United States, change his name to Bunyan, invent logging, and start on a life of great adventures and deeds. By 1860, Paul Bunyan had become a legendary American hero.

All the stories about Paul Bunyan have an element of exaggeration about them, but they are full of delightful imagination. Paul's voice was like a clap of thunder, and he could carry 20 grindstones weighing a ton apiece. By swinging his axe around him in a circle, he cut down all the trees within reach.

Paul's chief helper was an enormous blue ox named Babe. Paul and Babe together changed the map of the United States. Paul made the Great Lakes as reservoirs for Babe's drinking water. Kansas is flat because Paul hitched Babe to it and turned it over to make good corn land. When Babe lay down and rolled, Lake Superior was formed. Babe made the Mississippi River by upsetting a cart of water. Once when Paul was strolling along the Colorado River, he dragged a pick along the ground; the scratch it made formed the Grand Canyon.

For many years these stories were only spread orally. In 1914, some of them were published, and since then many other books about Paul Bunyan have come out.

If a person has some way in which he can be hurt, or some spot in which he can be wounded, he is said to have an Achilles heel.

This expression goes gack to one of the greatest heroes of Greek legends, the story of Achilles. When

WHO WAS ACHILLES?

Achilles was born, the Fates, the goddesses that controlled man's destiny, foretold that the infant would die young. Achilles' mother, Thetis, wanted to avoid this fate for her son, so she dipped him in the waters of the River Styx. This was supposed to make him invulnerable and protect him from deadly wounds.

Every part of Achilles was thus made safe against injury, except one part—the heel by which his mother held him! And later on, he was to die from a wound in the heel.

Achilles grew to be a handsome young man, swiftest of mortals in the race, and the joy of all who beheld him. Eventually Achilles became famous as the greatest of the Greek warriors during the Trojan War.

In the tenth year of the struggle, he captured a girl named Briseis. But the leader of the Greeks, Agamemnon, took the girl away from him. Achilles was furious and decided not to fight any more. The Greeks were helpless without their great hero. So they persuaded Achilles to lend his armor and his men to his friend, Patroclus.

But Patroclus was slain by the Trojan hero Hector, and the armor was captured. Then Achilles decided to obtain revenge. He became friends again with Agamemnon, and put on armor and a shield. He took the field and killed Hector. And in revenge he dragged Hector's body around the tomb of his slain friend.

Later, Hector's brother, Paris, shot a poisoned arrow at Achilles. It entered his heel, the one part of his body that had not been dipped in the Styx, and Achilles died from the wound.

Socrates has come to stand for the ideal of a wise man, yet one of his principles was that it is wise to know that your wisdom is worth nothing!

He was born in Athens, Greece, about 470 B.C. Little is known of

WHO WAS SOCRATES?

his parents or childhood. He left no writings. His disciple, the great philosopher Plato, wrote down in the form of dialogues Socrates' teachings and ideas, together with many scenes from his life.

According to Plato, Socrates spent his time in the market place of Athens talking to anybody who would listen. He liked especially to find someone with firm ideas on a subject. Socrates would draw him out with leading questions and show him he was ignorant of the subject he had been so sure about. Hence, the method of arguing by asking questions is called Socratic. His one fundamental principle was "Know thyself."

The Athenians disliked him because he upset all their former ideas. Therefore they said of him that he did not believe in the gods, or in truth, or in justice.

In the year 399 B.C., his enemies brought him to trial on the charge of having corrupted the youth of Athens and of neglecting his religious duties. No one believed the accusations and Socrates realized this. The defense he made, known as "the Apology of Socrates," was afterward written out by Plato. It was mocking and courageous. Although Socrates knew that he would be condemned to death, he said he must go on leading the same life, devoting himself to the search for truth.

In prison, Socrates passed his last day discussing with his friends the immortality of the soul. He took the cup of hemlock, the poison which was given him, without trembling and drank it. His friends burst into tears, but he begged them to be silent. He died with a smile on his lips.

It is not often that we make a hero of a robber, but Robin Hood somehow seems to be different. Everybody knows it is wrong to steal, yet Robin Hood is admired. The reason for this, of course, is that he stole from the rich and gave to the poor.

WHO WAS ROBIN HOOD?

Did Robin Hood ever actually exist? We know that he was a favorite figure in the ballads and stories of England in the fourteenth and fifteenth centuries. He was supposed to have lived in the twelfth century. In a Latin history which appeared in the year 1521, this is what was written about Robin Hood:

"About the time of Richard I, Robin Hood and Little John, the most famous of robbers, were lurking in the woods and stealing only from rich men; they killed none except those who resisted them or came to attack them. Robin kept 100 archers on the proceeds of these robberies, well trained for fighting, and not even 400 men dared to come against them.

"All England sings of the deeds of this Robin; he would not allow any woman to be hurt, nor did he ever take the goods from the poor; indeed he kept them richly supplied with the goods he stole from the abbots."

One can see how such a character must have captured the imagination of the English people of that period, because they loved chivalry and archery. Robin pleased them and they built around his name one legend after another. They made him a great sportsman, a wonderful archer, and a lover of the green woods where he lived.

There are many theories about Robin Hood. One of these suggests that he was a Saxon, and among the last of those who held out against the Normans when they conquered England. It seems certain that a Robin Hood really did exist. But it is also pretty certain that many of the stories that existed in other legends came to be told about Robin Hood.

The Incan civilization was at least 400 years old at the time Columbus discovered America.

The land of the Incas included what is now Bolivia, Peru, Ecuador,

WHO WERE THE INCAS?

and part of Argentina and Chile. In the center of the Inca Empire was Cuzco, the capital, the Sacred City of the Sun. It was the center of the only world these people knew, and to this city came caravans from every part of the empire with grain, gold and silver, fine cloth, and fresh, green coca leaves.

The Incas were stern but just rulers. They allowed the people they conquered to follow their own customs. The family was the center of government. Each group of ten families had a leader. He reported to a captain who had 50 families under him, and so on up to the Inca, who ruled the empire.

Everyone in the Inca Empire worked, except the very young and the old. Each family had a certain amount of land to farm. The people wove their own clothing, made their own shoes or sandals, their own dishes of pottery, and objects of gold and silver.

The people had no personal freedom: the Inca decided what clothes they wore, what food they ate, what work they did. The sick, poor, and old were cared for. The Incas were wonderful farmers and grew excellent crops. They built great aqueducts to bring mountain streams down to water their fields.

Many of the buildings which the Incas erected still stand. And they built unusual bridges made of vines and willow branches braided into huge ropes. The people were very skilful at weaving and pottery. They made cotton cloth so fine the Spaniards thought it was silk, and they made fine clothing of wool.

After many centuries of prosperity, the Inca Empire was divided between two half-brothers who began to fight each other. When the Spaniards came, they found it easy to conquer them and destroy the empire.

One of the most important peoples of ancient America were the Aztecs, who lived in the valley which now contains Mexico City. Long before the Europeans came from across the sea, these American Indians were making history.

WHO WERE THE AZTECS?

They had developed a way of life almost the equal of many of the European peoples. They carved their history in stone. They built temples and towers and homes of solid masonry. They were quite skilled in astronomy, law, and government, and were expert in many arts and crafts. They were in some ways a kind and gentle people. They were lovers of nature, especially birds and flowers. They also were fond of music, dancing, plays, and literature.

The Aztecs, however, had also risen to power through military abilities, and warfare was often carried on for the purpose of capturing enemies for sacrifice to their war god. The custom of sacrificing human life was shocking to the Europeans, but this developed naturally among the Aztecs because they combined religion and warfare.

The Aztecs were also called Mexica. From this, or from one of their gods, comes the word for Mexico. In 1325, 167 years before Columbus ever saw an Indian, the Aztecs, according to tradition, started to build their capital which they called Tenochtitlán. This city was later to become the capital of the Spanish and finally of the Mexican republic.

No one knows exactly where the Aztecs came from. The legends about them indicate that they came from the north. They probably arrived in the Valley of Mexico in the twelfth or thirteenth century. In these early times they were known as Tenochcas. The Toltecs, who already lived in the valley and were quite cultured, considered the Aztecs as barbaric newcomers. Because of this the Aztecs had a difficult time settling in the valley. But in time they rose to great power and ruled over the peoples of the Valley of Mexico.

About 1,200 years ago there was a group of people, the Northmen, who came from the coastal regions of Norway, Sweden, and Denmark. Their name "viking" was probably taken from the *viks,* or sounds, of

WHO WERE THE VIKINGS?

their home region. The vikings were great sailors and adventurers.

They were strong and sturdy, often with blue eyes and fair hair. At a time when the rest of Europe was terrified to sail the sea, the vikings were great explorers and traders. They preferred conquest and adventure to a life of quiet safety.

In A.D. 793, the vikings made their first attack on the English coast. From that time and up through the eleventh century, they raided the coasts of western and eastern Europe. They plundered England, Ireland, France, and Spain. They even journeyed as far south as Algiers.

Vikings discovered islands to the west of Greenland and a portion of the North American continent, which they called Vinland. A colony was attempted at Vinland and settlers remained on the continent for three years.

The Northmen had a civilization of their own. Viking ships, carriages, household dishes, and ornaments have been discovered in their graves. There were many iron deposits in viking lands and the Northmen became skilled workers in this metal.

The vikings were originally pagans. Odin and Thor were their chief gods. According to viking beliefs, the gods lived in a place called Valhalla, and heroes who died in battle were welcomed there. They also had a literature of "sagas," or stories, which were about life among the kings, chieftains, and common people.

The Northmen had a good system of law based on fairness and sportsmanship. It is even believed that the jury system we have today can be traced back to the ancient Northmen.

There are actually no such things as weeds. When a farmer plants certain seeds which he hopes will produce a valuable crop, he calls any other plant which grows up in his field and interferes with his crop a weed!

HOW DO WEEDS SPREAD?

Basically, though, weeds are plants that do harm. Some are poisonous to cattle and horses. Others injure crops by robbing them of sunlight, soil, minerals, and water. Others act as parasites, or serve as hosts to insects or plant diseases that cause harm.

Weeds are spread by various means. Some weeds are carried from place to place in fodder, in dust, in rubbish, and in manure. But most weeds that cause so much trouble do not spread because of man's carelessness. They have their own devices for spreading their seeds.

Some weeds, such as pimpernel, knotweed, dodder, and goldenrod, produce their seeds in such great quantities that some of them are likely to survive practically no matter what the conditions.

Other weeds have hairlike or winglike projections on their seeds and fruits. These make it possible for the seeds to be carried by the wind for considerable distances. Such weeds include dock, sorrel, thistle, and dandelion. Still other weeds have little hooks or spines on their seeds. These hooks catch in the fur of animals or in the clothing of man, and in this way the seeds are spread to new territory.

Some of the most successful weeds do not even spread by means of seeds. They have spreading underground stems which send up erect

branches. If the underground stem is cut, these erect branches merely become separate plants.

Because of the harm they can do, weeds are fought and controlled by man. Today there is a whole variety of chemicals that have been developed to destroy weeds or prevent them from appearing.

Air is everywhere about you. Every crack, hole, and space that is not already filled with something else is filled with air. Every time you breathe, your lungs are filled with air.

WHAT IS AIR?

Even though you cannot see air, nor taste it, nor feel it (unless the wind is blowing), air is "something." It is a substance or material which scientists call "matter." Matter may be a solid, a liquid, or a gas. The matter called "air" is almost always a gas.

In fact, air is made up of certain gases. Two of these, nitrogen and oxygen, make up 99 per cent of the air. They are always found in the same proportion of about 78 per cent nitrogen and about 21 per cent oxygen. There is also a small amount of carbon dioxide in the air which is added to it by living things. The remaining part of 1 per cent is made up of what are called rare gases: argon, neon, helium, krypton, and xenon.

The great ocean of air extends for many miles above the surface of the earth. Because air is something, gravity attracts, or holds it, to the earth. Thus air has weight. The weight of the air exerts pressure. The air presses on your whole body from all directions, just as water would if you were at the bottom of the sea.

If you climb a high mountain or go up in an airplane, there is less air above you, so the pressure is less as you go up. About eight miles up, the pressure is only one-eighth that at sea level. At 62 miles, there is almost no pressure.

All over the world, there are people who are waging "conservation" campaigns. Conservation means many things to many people.

WHAT IS CONSERVATION?

To some it means preserving the wilderness in certain sections. To others it means preserving the wildlife. Conservation includes efforts to protect forests as well as the wise use of all natural resources.

The problem of conservation has arisen because mankind is using the world's natural resources in greater quantity and variety than ever before. As the world's population grows, and as more people live at a higher standard, there is a greater demand for resources. These resources must be "conserved" to assure that there will be enough for the future.

What do we mean by "resources"? Well, they can be divided into three basic kinds. One is renewable resources. For example, water, farmland, forests, and grazing land, even while they are being used, can be improved and renewed through good management. This would include protection from erosion, irrigation, and fertilization.

A second group of resources is not renewable. These are mainly minerals. They are used up once they are taken from the earth. These include coal, oil, and natural gas.

There are some natural resources that cannot be used up. For example, solar energy, climate, and oceans cannot be increased, decreased, or damaged by man. Man can also destroy the beauty of scenery, or cause pollution of air.

The only reason a day has 24 hours is that man has decided he would like to figure time that way.

Nothing occurs in nature or in the world that has anything to do

WHY IS THE DAY 24 HOURS?

with hours or minutes or seconds. These divisions of time were made up by man for his convenience. But something does happen that has to do with what we call a "day." And that something is the rotation of the earth on its axis from west to east. Every time it goes around once, a specific amount of time has passed. We call that time a "day."

Scientists can measure that time exactly and they use the stars to do it. Observatories have what is called "sidereal" clocks. A sidereal day begins the instant that a given star crosses a meridian and lasts until the instant that it recrosses the same meridian.

Since man has broken up the day into hours, minutes, and seconds, we can say exactly how long a sidereal day is. It is 23 hours 56 minutes and 4.09 seconds long. But it would be difficult to use a day of sidereal length for ordinary purposes, so we use a 24-hour day, with an extra day added during leap year to correct the difference.

To early people, a day meant simply the space between sunrise and sunset. The hours at night were not counted. The Greeks counted their day from sunset to sunset. For the Romans, it was from midnight to midnight.

Before clocks were invented, day and night were divided into 12 hours each. This division was not practical as the length of the two periods differs with the seasons. Today, most countries have a day which, by law, extends over the 24-hour period from midnight to midnight, following the Roman method.

Capital punishment is the inflicting of the death penalty for a crime. Where capital punishment exists, it is carried out by the government in accordance with its laws regarding crime. In the United States, the matter of capital punishment is subject to the laws of individual states.

WHAT IS CAPITAL PUNISHMENT?

It is possible to say that the death penalty is the most effective form of punishment—since it makes sure that the offender will never commit another crime. It is also considered to be a way of preventing crime, since the threat of capital punishment may frighten people who would otherwise do wrong.

But there are a great many people who believe that capital punishment is wrong. They say that man has no right to take another person's life, and they claim that it does not even help prevent crime. Such people believe that capital punishment will eventually disappear in all civilized lands.

In ancient times, when people had not yet learned how to behave in a disciplined way in society, it was probably to be expected that capital punishment existed. In Egypt and Babylonia, death might be the penalty for any action that the ruler did not like. The ancient Hebrews showed an advance in humanity by limiting the crimes punishable by death to murder, blasphemy, breaking of the Sabbath, and various social crimes.

Both the Greeks and the Romans had well-organized criminal laws which inflicted the death penalty for crimes against the state. In Athens, some of those condemned to death, among them Socrates, were forced to drink a poison made from hemlock. In Rome, criminals who were not citizens were executed by crucifixion.

During the Middle Ages, the death penalty was inflicted for even minor offenses, such as stealing a sheep or cutting down someone else's tree. It wasn't until early in the nineteenth century that civilization had advanced to the point where capital punishment was limited to major crimes of murder and high treason.

When we say "country," we usually mean an independent state that has a distinct territory and its own government.

The world's smallest independent state is Vatican City. It lies in

WHAT IS THE SMALLEST COUNTRY IN THE WORLD?

the midst of Rome, Italy, and has a total area of only 0.17 square miles! It is the place of government of the Catholic Church.

The pope, the head of Vatican City, rules through a civil governor. Vatican City has its own flag, post office, railway station, and money. It also has a telephone system and radio broadcasting station. Support for this tiny state comes chiefly from contributions made by Catholics throughout the world.

Within Vatican City there is the Vatican Palace (the pope's residence), the gardens, and the large St. Peter's Basilica. In the palace are art museums and libraries. The Vatican Library, in a separate wing, is one of the greatest in the world.

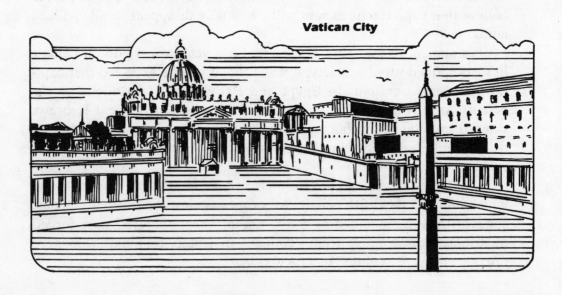

Vatican City

Vatican City has diplomatic relations with other countries and receives representatives from many nations.

Over the years, political control was gained by the popes over a large territory in central Italy. In 1859, this land, called the "Papal States," covered about 16,000 square miles.

In 1870, Rome was made the national capital of Italy. Against the objections of the pope, the Papal States were made part of the kingdom of Italy.

In 1929, an agreement was reached between the pope and the Italian government and the Vatican City was set up.

The eucalyptus is a native tree of Australia, where it is sometimes called "the gum tree" or "string-bark" tree. It now has been introduced into Europe, Algeria, Egypt, India, South America, and southern United

WHAT IS EUCALYPTUS?

States.

The eucalyptus is one of the most striking trees in appearance. Its leaves are leathery and hang down vertically in most cases. The trunk is tall and straight, and grows at a remarkable pace. Saplings of the eucalyptus tree have been known to grow as much as 13 feet in a single year! In height, a eucalyptus can even challenge the giant sequoias of California. There are eucalyptus trees that are taller than 450 feet!

The eucalyptus is an extremely useful tree. It requires a great amount of moisture, so it is often planted in swampy regions. By drawing water out of mosquito infested swamps, it can actually help fight malaria in certain regions of the world.

One of the most remarkable things about this tree is that it actually provides man with a medicine. The leaves are dotted with pores that hold a straw-colored oil, which smells somewhat like camphor oil. This is eucalyptus oil. This oil is sometimes given to patients to be inhaled to clear the nasal passage.

Eucalyptus oil is also used as medicine internally. It has an effect on the kidneys, and it also depresses the nervous system so that it slows up breathing. It has even been used as an antiseptic by surgeons!

The wood of this tree is adaptable and durable. Eucalyptus wood is valuable in building docks and ships, and it is in great demand for the interiors of houses because it can be given an attractive, highly polished finish.

The words "perpetual motion" by themselves just mean motion that goes on forever. But usually when we say perpetual motion we are referring to a very special thing.

WHAT IS PERPETUAL MOTION?

For hundreds of years, men have had the dream of creating a machine that, once it is set in motion, would go on doing useful work without drawing on any external source of energy. Every machine now known has to have a source of energy.

A perpetual motion machine, however, would create its own energy in the form of motion. Every time a complete cycle of its operation was finished, it would give forth more energy than it had absorbed.

Most of the people who tried to create perpetual motion machines had practical purposes in mind. They thought it would be wonderful to have machines that could raise water or grind corn without the need of supplying any energy to the machine.

Is it possible to create a perpetual motion machine? Any scientist will tell you that the answer is no. The reason is based on what is one of the most important laws of science, the principle of the conservation of energy. According to this principle, energy cannot be created and cannot be destroyed in nature. Energy can be transferred from one place to another, energy can be freed or unlocked, but energy cannot be created. This means that any machine that does work must have a source of energy.

In the course of history, thousands of attempts have been made to create perpetual motion machines. The first attempts were made at a time when the law of the conservation of energy was still unknown. A great many others were simply fakes that were later exposed.

The antarctic region is the area around the South Pole. It includes the continent of Antarctica, which is the fifth largest continent. It is almost as large as the United States and Europe combined.

IS THERE ANY KIND OF LIFE IN THE ANTARCTIC?

This region is the coldest and bleakest part of the earth. It is surrounded by the world's roughest seas. It has strong winds, blizzards, little rainfall, and such severe cold that the whole region is almost useless. There is never enough sunlight to warm the land, and there is a year-round covering of snow.

The coldest temperature ever recorded in the world was in Antarctica, more than –100 degrees Fahrenheit. Because of the extreme cold, nothing seems to spoil, for there is no rot, rust, or bacteria.

What is to be found under the icy blanket of Antarctica? Not enough of it has been explored to really know. A few coal layers and small mineral veins have been seen by explorers. Probably other minerals do exist, but it would be so hard and expensive to get at them that they remain untouched.

ANTARCTICA

The only plants that exist there are the simplest forms—a few mosses, lichens, fungi, and algae—which are of no value and furnish no food. Only birds and animals that can find food in the sea live in the region.

The most common birds are skua gulls, snowy petrels, and several species of penguins. The penguins live and nest near the edge of the continent. They have underdeveloped wings and cannot fly on land, but in the water they are good swimmers. There are several kinds of seal in antarctic waters. The only industry in Antarctica is whale hunting. But so many whales have been caught there that there is now an international control to limit whale hunting.

Men have always identified themselves with animals or birds they admire. You have probably noticed how often the lion is used as a symbol by nations or in family crests.

WHY IS THE EAGLE THE NATIONAL EMBLEM OF THE UNITED STATES?

The eagle is such a majestic looking bird and gives such an impression of power in flight, that it has been used by man since ancient times as a symbol of might and courage. Did you know that as long as 5,000 years ago, the Sumerian people used the spread eagle as the emblem of their power?

In ancient Rome, the eagle was such an emblem too. The great emperor Charlemagne used the eagle as a symbol, and many German kingdoms later had it as an emblem. Even Napoleon adopted the eagle as his emblem of power!

So it is quite natural that when the new country, the United States, wanted an emblem, it turned to the eagle. Now it so happens that the eagle it chose, the bald eagle, is a bird found only in the United States and Canada. It is unknown in Europe.

In 1782, Congress chose the bald eagle as the emblem of the United States. On the national seal, the bird is shown with wings outstretched, holding an olive branch in one claw and arrows in he other. When the eagle is used in coins, military insignia and so on, it appears in many different poses.

By the way, it is called the bald eagle for a reason that may surprise you. It has nothing to do with hair. When the early colonists came to this country, this American eagle looked quite different from the gray eagle they had seen in Europe. The word "bald" originally meant "white," so they called this eagle "bald-headed," meaning it had a white head!

Every nation is proud of its Executive Mansion, or the home where its chief of state lives. In the United States, this is called the White House. Every year hundreds of thousands of people come to see it, or take a tour through certain parts of it.

WHO DESIGNED THE WHITE HOUSE?

Like any great building, the White House has a varied history. The cornerstone for it was laid in 1792, and it was completed in 1799. James Hoban, an Irish-born architect, designed the building. He based the design on certain buildings he knew and admired in Ireland.

The first residents of the White House were John and Abigail Adams in 1800, and since the house was quite new, the house was bleak and cold and not very comfortable. On August 24, 1814, during the War of 1812, the British burned the building, and only the walls were left standing. Hoban then rebuilt it, following his original design. The gray sandstone walls were painted white to cover the smoke stains. This, of course, explains the name it has—the White House. While this name was used for

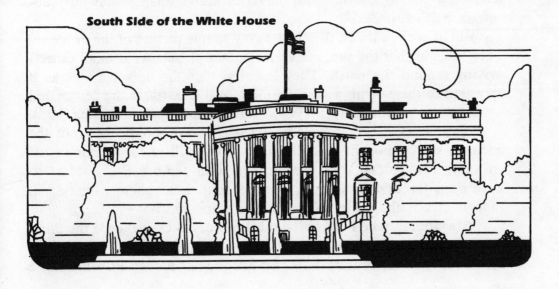

South Side of the White House

the building for some time, it did not become official until the administration of Theodore Roosevelt.

The White House has been remodeled and altered many times, but the basic design remains. The main building is 170 feet wide and about 85 feet deep. Terraces extend from both sides of the main building. At the end of the east terrace is the three-story East Wing. There are offices here and this is where the public enters to tour the White House. Beyond the west terrace is the three-story Executive Office. This is where the president's office staff works.

Many of the upstairs rooms have been used for different purposes by different presidents, and their decoration has changed with the occupants.

It is much harder for us to understand the universe as we know it today, than it was for ancient man to grasp his idea of the universe. Today we consider the universe to include not only the earth and our solar system,

HOW DID ANCIENT ASTRONOMERS PICTURE THE UNIVERSE?

but the galaxy to which this solar system belongs (called "the Milky Way"), and all the other galaxies as well. There are some 200,000,-000,000 stars in just our own galaxy—and there are millions of other galaxies stretching out into the universe. Man's imagination just cannot grasp this vastness!

But in ancient times, they had a very simple picture of the universe. They thought that the sun, moon, stars, and planets were small objects moving around the earth. They believed that the universe was as it appeared to them—with a vast, flat, immovable earth in the center and a great dome overhead, sprinkled with thousands of little shining lights.

The Greeks started the true science of astronomy. Most of the ancient Greeks thought that the earth stood still in the center of the universe. Pythagoras, who lived in the sixth century B.C., seems to have been the first to suggest that the earth is a sphere. But he still thought it was the center of the universe and did not move.

Aristarchus, who lived in the third century B.C., believed the earth was a sphere that rotated on its axis and revolved around a stationary sun. In the second century A.D., an astronomer named Ptolemy wrote a book called the *Almagest*. He thought the earth was the center of the universe, and he tried to show how the planets, the sun, and the moon moved around the earth. His ideas were accepted for 14 centuries!

Copernicus, in 1543, suggested the sun as the center of the universe. Then came the discovery of the telescope and man had a better means of finding out what the universe is really like. As more and more facts were gathered, our modern idea of the universe was gradually developed.

Suppose there were somebody in your town who cheated every time he sold you something. If you and your friends got together and decided not to buy from him anymore, you would be conducting a boycott!

WHAT IS A BOYCOTT?

The word "boycott" had a very interesting origin. In the days when many Irish landlords lived in England, their estates in Ireland were managed by land agents. It was the job of these agents to collect as much money as they could, regardless of whether or not the tenants could afford to pay.

One of these agents was Captain Charles Cunningham Boycott. In 1880, he refused to let the Irish tenant farmers decide how much rent they should pay and evicted them from their homes. As a result, the tenants chased away his servants, tore down his fences, and cut off his mail and his food supplies. Other tenants began to treat other land agents in the same way. When it happened to other land agents, it was said they had been "boycotted." Today it is applied to any organized refusal to trade or associate with a country, a business concern, or an individual.

When labor unions developed in the United States, they often used the boycott against employers. There were two kinds of boycotts. A primary boycott was when a body of workers refused to work for an employer or to buy his products. A secondary boycott was when these workers persuaded or forced other groups not to have any dealings with the employer.

In courts of law, the primary boycott has generally been held legal. But decisions by many courts have held the secondary boycott to be illegal because they affected the rights of third parties.

It is practically impossible to turn anywhere in our modern world and not see a form of art. Your furniture, your rug, the dishes in the kitchen, the car, your watch, even your clothes—all represent art in some form.

WHAT ARE THE FINE ARTS?

The reason is that somebody designed each thing, chose colors, and tried to make it attractive. But there is an important purpose behind this kind of art—and that purpose is to have things used. What we call "the fine arts" have a different purpose—and that is beauty.

The fine arts are considered to be painting, sculpture, literature, drama, music, dancing, and architecture. Of these, the only one which is also involved in "use" is architecture. Architects have to think about the usefulness of their buildings as well as about their beauty.

But in the fine arts, the end result of a lot of hard work by the artist may have absolutely no use at all. It was created to provide certain satisfactions we get from beauty, and that is all. So a statue, a tune, a picture, a play, a book, and a dance are all examples of the product of the fine arts.

Today, many curious experiments are being made in all the fine arts. But the traditional methods and products of the fine arts all have things in common. For one thing they have "design." Design can be with sounds, with stone, with words, with building materials, with lines, and paint. A work of fine art is designed. And within that design, the creator uses "rhythm," "balance," and "harmony."

Rhythm comes from the more or less regular repetition of similar sounds, colors, shapes, and movements. Balance is the arrangement of what the artist works with so that the result seems right to us. And harmony is putting things together that seem to belong together. These, of course, are only rough ideas of what a creator in the fine arts tries to do.

CHAPTER 2
HOW OTHER CREATURES LIVE

In the folklore and legends of countries all over the world, there are tales of great and horrible dragons.

DID DRAGONS EVER EXIST?

They were pictured as huge, snakelike monsters frightful to behold. They had bulging eyes, their nostrils spouted flames, and their roar was so great they caused the earth to tremble.

One of the most famous of these ancient dragons was the Hydra, which had nine heads! It devoured many beautiful young girls before it was slain by Hercules. Another famous dragon was the Chimera, a fire-breathing monster that met its death at the hands of a young warrior, Bellerophon, who was helped by his winged steed, Pegasus.

Many dragons were supposed to be guarding great treasures. The Golden Fleece was guarded by a dragon with a hundred eyes! In other cases, great heroes always fought battles with dragons.

Although the dragon usually represents the spirit of evil, it has also been used as a symbol of protection. The early warriors painted fierce dragons on their shields to frighten away enemies.

People at one time actually did believe that dragons existed. For example, before the time of Columbus, sailors used to be afraid to venture into unknown seas because they believed huge dragons would swallow up the ships and men.

Of course, dragons never existed except in legends, myths, and fairy tales. Then why did the belief in them arise? In prehistoric times, all kinds of huge reptiles roamed the earth. The most terrifying of these beasts, the dinosaur, lived long before man appeared on the earth. But it is possible that during the time of the cavemen some reptiles of great size still survived, and from this came the legends of the dragons.

Scientists believe that dinosaurs first appeared on the earth about 180 million years ago, and died out about 60 million years ago. This is long before human beings appeared on earth, and also before such animals as

HOW DO WE KNOW WHAT DINOSAURS WERE LIKE?

dogs, rabbits, horses, monkeys, or elephants. Then how can we possibly know anything about these giant creatures?

Everything we know about dinosaurs—and everything we will ever know—comes from fossils. These are remains which these creatures left in the earth. But there are many different kinds of fossils.

The most common fossils are petrified remains of what were the hard parts of their bodies—bones, teeth, and claws. Scientists can study these remains and from them reconstruct how the whole body of the dinosaur was built!

Sometimes, petrified tendons and skin are found, and this provides even more clues. Fossils can also be trails or footprints that were made in wet sand or mud that hardened into stone over the ages. From these, it is

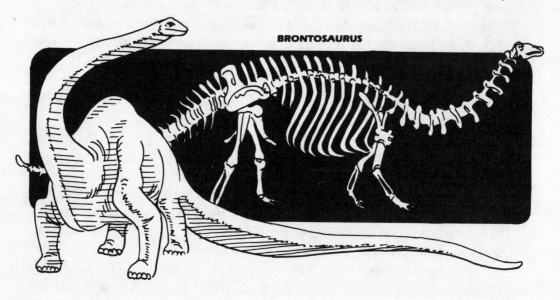

BRONTOSAURUS

possible to tell how the dinosaurs walked and whether it was on two legs or four. And the rarest fossils of all from this time are dinosaur eggs.

In this way we can tell that the Brontosaurus was a monster from 70 to 80 feet long and weighed about 38 tons. We know it lived in swamps and was a plant-eater. And we also know that a dinosaur called Allosaurus had sharp teeth and powerful claws and it fed upon Brontosaurus and other plant-eaters. You see, scientists have found, among the broken and deeply scratched bones of Brontosaurus—fossil teeth of the Allosaurus!

To begin with, there are many kinds of deserts. Some are the familiar deserts of bare rock and shifting sand, upon which the hot sun beats down. But some deserts, such as the Gobi, have bitterly cold winters. So a desert

HOW DO PLANTS AND ANIMALS LIVE IN THE DESERT?

is really a region where only special forms of life can exist. And the form of life is the kind that has adapted itself to the particular conditions of the particular desert.

For example, cacti are well-known desert plants. They have thick, fleshy stems without true leaves. Desert shrubs that have leaves usually have small ones. Little or no leaf surface prevents too much evaporation of water from the plant.

Many desert plants have thorns, spines, or a disagreeable taste or smell. This discourages animals that might eat them and so helps them survive. Desert plants usually lie dormant during the dry or cool season, or drop seeds that can survive such a period.

When the period for growth arrives, the seeds germinate and give rise to plants that rapidly flower and drop more seeds. Within a few weeks or months, the plants are ready again for the long season of dormancy.

When it comes to animals, they must be able to do without water for long periods, or be able to reach water holes at great distances. The camel, for example, is highly adapted to desert life. It has padded feet to walk on sand, a water-storing stomach, humps of fat as a reserve supply of energy, and nostrils that can be closed to keep out sand during windstorms.

Many of the smaller desert creatures need to drink no water at all. They get what liquid they need from the sap of food plants and from night dew on leaves or stones.

Long ago, voyages to distant lands were lengthy and dangerous under-takings. Travelers who dared make these trips brought back strange tales of the wonderful sights they had seen. Often they told of mythical animals,

WHAT WAS A UNICORN?

which were both strange and hor-rible. These tales grew more mar-velous each time they were told.

Sailors told of seeing sea serpents, fearful man-eating creatures which were 200 feet long, 20 feet thick, and had bright blue eyes. Mer-maids with long, green hair and shiny, scaly tails were supposed to haunt the seas and lure sailors to destruction.

Travelers said that in the countries they had visited they had seen unicorns. These were animals with the head and the body of a horse, the hind legs of an antelope, the tail of a lion, and the beard of a goat. Each unicorn had a single long, twisted horn set in the middle of its forehead. The horn was supposed to have the magic power to detect poison and was much sought after for drinking cups.

But the unicorn was a mythical animal that never existed, even though many people believed it did. Other mythical animals that people thought really existed included the griffins, animals that were a cross between a lion and an eagle. The Greeks told stories of centaurs, crea-tures which were half man and half horse. Almost everyone believed in dragons, huge winged serpents that breathed forth fire.

Although modern scientists have tried to explain what some of these mythical creatures really were, no one can explain where people got the idea that unicorns, centaurs, or griffins existed. A unicorn, by the way, is still on the coat of arms of England!

There is a very good reason why animals cannot learn to talk as human beings do, that is, use words to express ideas.

Most of the intelligent things animals do is a result of inheriting

WHY CAN'T ANIMALS LEARN TO TALK?

certain patterns of behavior. This works in special situations, but when you change the situation the animal usually does not know how to deal with it. The other reason animals behave "intelligently" is that they go through a trial-and-error method of learning.

Neither of these two ways of "thinking" can ever lead to talking. Talking means the use of words as symbols. The word stands for an idea or a thing—it is a symbol of it. And animals do not have the ability to deal with symbols. Their minds cannot use combinations of symbols the way human beings do.

The animal that most closely resembles man is the ape. Not only does the ape have a skeleton structure like man's, but he also has an "opposable" thumb. This means the thumb can be made to meet the finger tips,

WHICH ANIMAL RESEMBLES MAN THE MOST?

enabling the ape to use his hands to grasp things and to climb trees. Man's opposable thumb makes it possible for him to use tools.

Some people imagine that the ape is the ancestor of man, but this is not so. The theory of evolution holds that the apes and man may have had a common ancestor long ago, the so-called "missing link." But they evolved along different lines.

There are four kinds of "anthropoid," or "manlike" apes. The biggest and most powerful of these is the gorilla. Next in size is the orangutan. Then comes the chimpanzee. Finally, smallest of all is the gibbon.

The gibbon is the least known of the apes; he also resembles man the least. The gibbon can stand up straight on his hind legs and he can walk like a man instead of half-stooping. But the gibbon does very little walking because he spends most of his life in trees. He swings from branch to branch with his long arms, stopping to pick leaves and fruit.

When a gibbon eats, he is likely to sit erect like a man, even though his diet may include spiders, birds, and eggs. The family life of the gibbon is closely knit. His mate and their children stay with him night and day. And since a young gibbon will stay with the parents until about the age of six, a gibbon family may have as many as eight or nine members. In the wilds of the jungle, a gibbon may live to the ripe old age of thirty!

When an animal sheds its skin or feathers and replaces it, we call that "molting." Amphibians, reptiles, birds, and even insects molt.

Birds grow a whole series of feathers during their lifetime. When

WHAT IS MOLTING?

they reach the adult stage, they have the plumage that is typical of their kind of bird. Then adult birds change this plumage from time to time as old worn feathers molt (drop out) and new ones grow in their place.

If a feather is pulled out, it begins to replace itself at once. In addition, some birds grow bright, new feathers for the breeding season by molting. So most birds molt twice a year, once before and once after the breeding season.

Since most birds do not shed many of their flight feathers at the same time, they are able to fly all through the molting period. Also, flight feathers are often shed in pairs, one from the right and one from the left wing, so the flying balance is not upset. Ducks, swans, and geese are exceptions to this. They lose all their flight feathers when they molt, so they cannot fly. But since they are water birds they do not have to fly to escape from danger. They just take to the water.

During the molting season the brightly colored males often take on a drab-colored set of feathers. This gives them the protection of camouflage and makes it easier for them to hide.

Snakes have an interesting way of shedding their skin. A snake does not shed its entire skin, just the thin outermost part. The snake rubs its snout against something rough to loosen the old skin around the lips. Next it manages to get the loose parts caught on a rock or twig. Then the snake crawls out through the mouth opening of the old skin. It leaves the old skin in a single piece and wrong side out.

The chimpanzee is a monkey, but it is a special kind of monkey. It is the most intelligent one of all!

Monkeys belong to the highest order of mammals called "primates,"

IS THE CHIMPANZEE A MONKEY?

which includes man. All monkeys are covered with hair, usually live in trees, and have nails instead of claws on each of five fingers and toes.

Monkeys may be divided into four general groups: the lemurs; the Old World monkeys, including baboons, leaf monkeys, and others; the

New World monkeys, including the spiders, howlers, and others; and the apes, including the gorilla, orangutan, chimpanzee, and gibbon.

Of the three manlike apes, the orangutan, the chimpanzee, and the gorilla, the one that is most like man is the chimpanzee. This ape is smaller than either the gorilla or the orangutan, and it is more intelligent than either of the others.

The body of the chimpanzee, which has no tail, is similar to that of man, except that the chimpanzee has 13 pairs of ribs and man usually has only 12 pairs. Its flesh-colored skin is covered with coarse, black hair, except on the hands and face. As it grows older, gray hairs appear about the mouth and the skin becomes dusky or black.

Chimpanzees live in small bands in central African forests, from Sierra Leone eastward to Lake Victoria. They are captured quite easily, and live quite well in zoos. Sometimes they become so attached to favorite keepers in zoos that they will cry for them when sick!

Scientists who have studied them say there are at least 20 separate sounds that might be called a "chimpanzee language." On the ground they walk and run on all fours, and use their knuckles to support the weight of their trunk.

A male chimpanzee may weigh as much as 160 pounds and be about five feet tall, though most of them are somewhat smaller.

Dogs have been tamed by man longer than any other domestic animal. Hundreds of thousands of years ago, when giant, woolly mammoths still roamed the earth and men lived in caves, the dog first became man's friend.

WHY DO DOGS BURY BONES?

Despite the long history of being domesticated animals, the habits of dogs today can only be explained by going back to their ancestry before man tamed them. Strangely enough, scientists are not able to trace the origin of the dog as clearly as they can trace the history of the horse, for example. Some believe that dogs are the result of the mating of wolves and jackals a long time ago. Other scientists say that some dogs are descended from wolves, other dogs from jackals, others from coyotes, and some from foxes. The best theory seems to be that the wolf and our modern dog are descended from a very remote, common ancestor.

It so happens that many animals have instinctive habits today that are quite useless, but which their ancestors found necessary to life. These habits or instincts do not die out even though hundreds of thousands of years have passed. So if we recall that our dogs are descended from beasts which lived in a wild state a long time ago, we can explain some of their habits.

When a dog buries a bone today, it may be because his ancestors were not fed regularly by man, and had to store food away for future use. When a dog turns around three times before he settles down to sleep, it may be that he is doing it because his remote ancestors had to beat down a nest among the forest leaves or jungle grasses. When a dog bays, it is probably a reminder of the time when all dogs used to run in packs like wolves.

If you have a dog you love as a pet, you share some of your life with it. The dog lives in your home, keeps you company, and goes on trips with you. So it is hard to believe that the world this same dog sees is quite different from yours. For dogs cannot see any colors.

CAN DOGS SEE COLORS?

Test after test has been made to find out if dogs can be made to respond to different colors in any way. Usually this has been done with food. One color would be a signal for food, the other colors were not. A dog was never able to distinguish colors from one another. Dogs probably rely on their remarkable sense of smell to tell things apart.

What about cats? The same kinds of tests were made. It was impossible to train a cat to come for its food in response to signals of different colors. It seemed that all the colors were like grey to a cat.

Is there any animal that is able to see colors? As far as tests so far have been able to prove, the only animal other than man that is able to distinguish colors is the monkey. Monkeys and apes have been trained to open a door which had a particular color in order to obtain food.

Actually, the color blindness of animals is quite understandable. Most wild animals hunt at night or graze in the evening when colors are dim. Most animals have coats that are rather dull-colored. Being able to see colors is not really that important to them in order to survive.

And most of them have developed their other senses such to the point where they can get along quite well in their own world.

When something tastes good, or you feel pleased about something, you might make a sound like "Mmmm—mm!" When a cat wants to express contentment, it purrs!

DO ALL CATS PURR?

The purring sound is caused by the vibration of the cat's vocal cords. When a cat takes air into its lungs, the air passes through the voice box that contains the vocal cords. If the cat then wants to express its satisfaction about something, it will allow the vocal cords to vibrate as the air passes in and out of the lungs during breathing. When it chooses not to purr, the passing air does not affect the vocal cords—and no purr!

Of course when we think of "cat," we usually mean only the domesticated cat. But there are many other members of the cat family. Did you know that the lion, tiger, leopard, cougar, jaguar, ocelot, and lynx are also members of the cat family?

When it comes to making sounds, our own domesticated cat not only purrs, it can also meow, howl, and scream. The other kinds of cats make different sounds. The lion and tiger can roar. The jaguar and leopard make a sound that is described as a hoarse cough or bark.

But an interesting thing about the lion, tiger, jaguar, and leopard is that because of a difference in the formation of certain bones in the throat, they cannot purr!

But all cats, large or small, have the same general proportions of the body. If you blew up a picture of a cat to a very large size, you would see that it looks very much like a tiger.

Three names for the same animal are: donkey, ass, burro. Then what is a jackass? It is simply the name for a male donkey. A female is called a "jennet."

ARE A DONKEY AND A JACKASS THE SAME?

The donkey is one of the oldest of domesticated animals. It was domesticated more than 5,000 years ago by the Egyptians.

Because it is such a useful animal to man, it has spread around the world, and there are many different kinds of donkeys. For example, the Somali wild ass, which is found in Somalia and other parts of Africa, is a shy animal that lives in groups of from 5 to 20. It eats the dry grass and shrubs of the desert. Some natives do not hunt it, but others hunt it for food, for its hide, or to export it alive. Today it is a rare animal.

There are wild asses that live in Asia. One type, the Syrian ass, once lived in Syria and other parts of the Middle East, but is now probably extinct. The ass is strictly a desert animal, and can go for some time without water. Just before the young are born they gather into great herds, but soon break up into small groups and scatter over the country.

The donkey of today is a descendant of the Nubian wild ass of northeastern Africa, where it once lived from the Nile to the Red Sea. Most of the wild types that existed in various parts of the world have been killed off. Today, man is trying to protect some of the few kinds that are left.

In many parts of Mexico and Central America, the ass, or burro, is a common means of transportation, instead of the horse or automobile.

There are many things about the opossum that make it a strange and interesting animal. To begin with, did you know that opossums belong to a group of animals called "marsupial"? The females of this group have

WHY DOES AN OPOSSUM HANG BY ITS TAIL?

pouches on the underside of the body in which the young develop. The kangaroos of Australia are probably the best known of this group.

Opossums are from 9 to 20 inches long with tails that are 9 to 13 inches long. Their fur is grayish white in color. Their round ears, long, narrow tails, and the palms of their feet are hairless.

The inside toe on the hind foot can be bent like a thumb to meet any of the other toes. The opossum uses his hind feet as hands. They help him climb trees. His long, flexible tail is also used in tree climbing.

Opossums spend a lot of time in trees, hunting and eating. Since they can use their hind feet like hands, they like to hang upside down when they eat. To do this, they wrap their tails around a branch, hang down, and grasp their food by all four feet. If they did not hang by the tail they could not use all four feet.

And what a variety of food they eat! Their diet includes small mammals, insects, small birds, eggs, poultry, lizards, crayfish, snails, fruit of all kinds, corn on the cob, mushrooms, and worms. At night, opossums invade orchards for fruit and hen houses for poultry and eggs.

The camel is called "the ship of the desert," and there is good reason for it. Just as a ship is constructed to deal with all the problems that arise from being in the water, so a camel is "constructed" to live and travel and survive in the desert.

WHY DOES THE CAMEL HAVE A HUMP?

Where other animals would die from lack of food and water, the camel gets along very nicely. It carries its food and water with it! For days before it starts on a journey, a camel does nothing but eat and drink. It eats so much that a hump of fat, maybe weighing as much as 100 pounds, rises on its back. So the camel's hump is a storage place for fat, which the camel's body will use up during the journey.

The camel also has little flask-shaped bags which line the walls of its stomach. This is where it stores water. With such provisions, a camel is able to travel several days between water holes without drinking, and for an even longer time with no nourishment except what it draws from the fat of its hump.

At the end of a long journey, the hump will have lost its firm shape and will flop to one side in flabby folds. The camel will then have to rest for a long time to recover its strength.

Did you know that the camel is one of man's oldest servants and has been used by man in Egypt for more than 3,000 years!

If you have never raised plants or flowers of your own, you probably thought of how delicate and harmless they are.

But there are at least three different plants that feed on insects, and each one seems to be as clever and as cruel as any animal that goes hunting for its food.

CAN PLANTS EAT INSECTS?

The best known of these is the Pitcher plant, which grows in Borneo and tropical Asia. The Pitcher plant gives out a sweet juice that attracts insects. To make doubly sure of luring victims, this plant has a red-colored rim and cover. The insect comes over to take a look and to drink the nectar. It climbs over the rim of the plant, which is shaped like a pitcher. The inside of the pitcher is so smooth that the insect slides down and cannot stop itself. At the bottom, there is a bath of powerful liquid waiting for it. The insect is drowned and the liquid goes to work and digests the insect, thus providing food for the plant.

The Sundew is another tricky insect-eating plant. The upper part of each leaf is covered with little hairlike projections which give out a sticky fluid that attracts insects. This sticky fluid looks like dewdrops, which gives the plant its name. The moment an insect touches one of these hairs, it is stuck. Then all the other hairs start to bend toward the center of the leaf until they have wrapped up the insect in a neat package. The fluid that surrounds the poor victim starts digesting him. After about two days the job is done and the hairlike tentacles open up again.

In certain parts of North and South Carolina, we find a plant called Venus's-flytrap. This plant is the most business-like insect eater of all. It sits there with leaves spread open like hungry jaws. When a fly touches the hairs that grow along the leaf, the plant snaps it shut like a trap. After the fly is digested by juices in the plant, it opens up again.

Imagine yourself sitting or playing outdoors on a pleasant summer day. You hear a humming noise. Soon you feel a sting on your leg or arm. You slap hard. You look down and see a tiny speck of blood.

WHY WAS THE MOSQUITO MAN'S GREAT ENEMY?

You have just been engaged in a battle with one of the great enemies of mankind. To most of us, the mosquito is just an annoying pest. The humming noise about our heads (especially when we try to sleep) irritates us. The mosquito bite and the itching feeling afterward is a nuisance.

But this little insect is much more than a pest. The mosquito, by spreading such diseases as malaria and yellow fever, played a part in the fall of the ancient Greek and Roman civilizations. It killed many of our pioneer ancestors when they were opening our West. It prevented countries along tropical coasts and in hot climates from being settled and developing as they should. Fortunately, we have learned how to deal with the diseases that this "pest" used to spread throughout the world.

The male mosquito feeds only on plant juices, but the female prefers blood! So the female is the only one that bites you. And what equipment she has for doing an expert job of it! The "beak" of the female mosquito holds daggers with sawlike tips, plus a tube for injecting and a tube for sucking. As soon as she settles on your skin, she starts sawing. Into the tiny hole she injects a chemical so that your blood will not coagulate, or form a dry clot. Then she sucks up the blood she has prepared and flies off.

The itching you feel is not caused by the "bite." It is caused by the liquid she has injected. So if you kill her before she can suck back that irritating liquid, your itching will be worse!

Most of us think that spiders use silk only to spin a web. Actually, no other animal uses silk in as many ways as do spiders. They make it into houses, life lines, diving bells, cocoons, "airplanes," lassos, spring traps, and the web we all know.

HOW DO SPIDERS SPIN THEIR WEBS?

Spiders are not insects, but belong to a species called "arachnid." Unlike insects, they have eight legs, eight eyes in most cases, no wings, and only two parts to their bodies.

Spiders are found in practically every kind of climate. They can run on the ground, climb plants, run on water, and even live in water.

The spider manufactures its silk in certain glands found in the abdomen, or belly. At the tip of the abdomen there are spinning organs which contain many tiny holes. The silk is forced through these tiny holes. When the silk comes out it is a liquid. As soon as it comes in contact with the air, it becomes solid.

The spider makes many different kinds of silk. It makes a sticky kind that is used for the web, because this catches insects. For the spokes of the web it makes a stronger silk, which is not sticky. And it makes a still different kind of silk for the cocoon.

Even the webs that spiders spin are of many different kinds. The wheel-like web is the one we see most often. There are also "sheet" webs, which are flat and shaped like funnels or domes. And the trap-door spiders make a burrow out of their web with a lidlike opening at the top to catch and hold their prey. Other spiders build a bell-shaped home of silk which is entirely under water!

Everybody knows that birds migrate. This means that during certain seasons they travel over special routes. But few people realize that many butterflies, and some moths, also migrate.

DO BUTTERFLIES MIGRATE?

One example of this is the painted-lady butterfly. Each spring it travels from Mexico to California. In Europe, the same kind of butterfly crosses the Mediterranean Sea in spring, going from northern Africa to Europe. When there is a butterfly migration, thousands, and even millions, travel together across the sky.

The best known of all migrating butterflies is the monarch. It spends the winter along the Gulf of Mexico and other southern areas. In spring, the young female lays her eggs on the milkweed plants that have begun to grow. The caterpillars that hatch from the eggs feed on the milkweed leaves.

When the adult butterflies develop, they fly some distance north. There they mate and lay eggs on the milkweed that has just begun to grow with the advance of spring.

Now this is an interesting kind of migration. Because it means that within a few months time several generations of monarch butterflies travel farther and farther north in search of milkweed. By the time it is late summer and the monarch butterflies reach Canada, they are not the original ones that started out—but descendants of them!

When autumn approaches and cooler weather appears, those monarchs that have survived fly back in great numbers. They make a huge swarm of butterflies in the sky, and people have seen them spread out in a swarm 20 miles wide!

Such masses of butterflies migrate like this year after year, and they always follow the same routes.

The fly is an amazing and deadly creature. The fly spreads more death and suffering than an invading army. It does harm by spreading disease with its hairy feet and legs from the filth on which it feeds and in which it breeds.

HOW CAN A FLY WALK ON THE CEILING?

This little insect is wonderfully made. The house fly has two big brown eyes and each eye is made up of thousands of lenses. These two big eyes are called "compound eyes." The fly also has on top of the head, looking straight up, three "simple eyes" that can be seen only through a magnifying glass.

The feelers, or antennae, of the house fly are used as organs of smell, not of feeling. These antennae can detect odors at great distances. The mouth is made up of an organ that people call a tongue, but it is really all the mouth parts of an insect combined in one. This tongue is really a long tube through which the fly sucks juices.

The body of the house fly is divided into three parts: the head, the middle section, or thorax, and the abdomen. Behind the two transparent wings are two small knobs that help the fly balance itself in flight. The thorax is striped and has three pairs of legs attached to it. The legs are divided into five parts, of which the last is the foot.

The fly walks tiptoe on two claws that are attached to the underpart of the foot. Sticky pads under the claws allow the fly to walk upside down on the ceiling or anywhere else with the greatest of ease! It is because of these sticky pads and the hairs on the legs that the fly is such a carrier of disease germs.

Did you know that the entire life of a house fly is spent within a few hundred feet of the area where it was born?

There are thousands of different species, or kinds, of bees. So their habits and ways of life differ quite a bit. But probably the two things that we find most interesting about bees is how they produce honey, and how the "social" bees have organized their life.

WHAT HAPPENS TO BEES IN WINTER?

In producing honey, a bee visits flowers, drinks the nectar, and carries it home in its honey sac. This is a baglike enlargement of the digestive tract just in front of, but separate from, the bee's stomach. The sugars found in nectar undergo chemical changes while in the bee's honey sac as the first step in changing nectar into honey. Before nectar becomes honey, the honeybees remove a large part of the water by evaporation processes. Honey stored by bumblebees in cells called "honeypots" is almost as thin as nectar and will sour in a short time. Honey stored in the honeycombs by honeybees has so much water removed from the original nectar that it will keep almost forever.

What about the winter? In temperate regions, the young queen bumblebees pass the winter in holes they dig in well-drained sandbanks or in other suitable places. They are the only members of the colony that live through the winter! In the spring, each surviving queen starts a new colony.

The honeybees are luckier. They can adapt themselves to all extremes of climate. They have a social organization that is so efficient and complicated that it has been compared to that of man.

In the hive where they live, worker bees regulate the temperature with great exactness. They keep it at 93 degrees Fahrenheit where the young bees are being developed. During the winter, they do not let the colony temperature fall below 45 degrees. Honey stored in the hive is used as fuel by the bees. They have an efficient way of preventing the loss of more than a very small part of the heat they produce by consuming honey.

There is no other animal that man has fought with such energy for so long in so many places as the rat! There are many species of animals called rats, and most of them are harmless and interesting animals. But there

ARE RATS OF ANY USE TO MAN?

are two common rats, the black rat and the brown rat, that have caused all rats to be hated by man.

Why does man hate and fight the rat? Each year rats ruin hundreds of millions of dollars worth of grain. They destroy eggs, poultry, song birds, and spoil food in homes and on ships. Fires are caused by rats gnawing matches, gas pipes, and insulated electric wires. Houses may be flooded when they gnaw through water pipes. They damage floors and furnishings. Finally, they spread diseases such as the bubonic plague.

There are probably as many rats as people in the cities of the world. In the country, they actually outnumber human beings by three or four to one! They climb and burrow and live indoors or outdoors, in dry places or wet. Although they like vegetable food best, they will eat almost anything from dead animals and garbage to other rats.

And since they can live almost anywhere and increase so rapidly, they are hard to control. A female rat may have ten litters of young in a year, and the young are ready to produce more young in only four months!

RAT IN SPACE SUIT FOR TESTS IN SPACE CAPSULE

But rats do have one important use to man. Since many of their organs work very much like man's, rats are used in laboratories for many experiments. New knowledge about diet, glands, and nervous reactions has been gained by experimenting on them. White rats, an albino variety of the brown rat, are used most often in tests.

If you have ever watched a snake move, there were probably two things about it that impressed you. The first, of course, was simply the mysterious ways in which a snake moves. You do not see any legs, the body does not seem to have anything to push or pull it, and yet there it is moving! And the second thing is that the body seems to "flow" along the ground. It does not seem to have a bone in its body!

DO SNAKES HAVE BONES?

The fact is, however, that a snake is simply full of bones! A snake has a sectioned backbone, and to this backbone are attached pairs of ribs.

Some snakes have as many as 145 pairs of ribs attached to that very flexible backbone.

Ball-and-socket joints attach the sections of the backbone to one another, and each rib to a section of the backbone. So great freedom of movement of that backbone and the ribs is possible.

The tips of each pair of ribs are attached with muscles to one of the scales that are on the "stomach," or abdomen, of the snake. Because of this, a snake can move each one of these scales independently. When the snake moves one of these scales, that scale acts like a foot.

Snakes also have bones in their heads and jaws. A snake can open his jaws pretty wide when it is swallowing its dinner. This is because all the bones around the mouth and throat are loosely attached so the mouth can be stretched very wide. In fact, most snakes swallow their catch without trying to kill it first. Later on they digest it.

So you see snakes do have bones in their body, even though their slithery bodies look as if there's nothing solid in them!

Just because snakes do not have legs now, does not mean they did not have them at sometime in their development. But how and why they came to lose their legs is not known to science.

WHY DON'T SNAKES HAVE LEGS?

Some experts believe that the ancestors of snakes were certain kinds of burrowing lizards. There are many kinds of such lizards today, and all of them have very small legs or no legs at all. In time, the legs disappeared altogether. And despite this, snakes are able to move and get along very well indeed. One of the most helpful things for them in moving are the belly scales that cover the entire undersurface of most snakes.

There are four ways in which snakes move. One of them is called "lateral undulatory movement." In this method, the snake forms its body into a number of wavy, S-shaped curves. By pressing backward and outward against rough places on the ground, the snake slips forward on those scales.

A second way snakes move is called "rectilinear movement." In this case, small groups of the belly scales are pulled forward on part of the body, while other scales project backward to keep the snake from slipping back. Then the scales that have been holding the body are pulled forward. The scales that moved first hold the body.

A third way is a "concertina" method, which is used for climbing. The snake wraps its tail and rear part of the body around a tree, stretches out the forepart of its body and hooks it on the tree higher up. Then it releases the rear part and pulls the rest of its body upward.

"Sidewinding" is another method by which snakes move. A loop of the forebody is thrown to one side. Then the rear part is shifted to the new position, and another neck loop is thrown out.

All of us have seen pictures of "snake charmers" blowing on some musical instrument, while a snake rises up and seems to "dance" to the music. What is really happening?

CAN A SNAKE REALLY BE CHARMED?

The truth is that the "snake charmer" is not charming the snake at all! He is just putting on a show to make people believe that his music is making the snake perform. To begin with, snakes are deaf, so they cannot even hear the music he is playing! But snakes can pick up vibrations with great sensitivity. Even when they lie in a basket, if there are any vibrations in the ground near them, they notice them and respond.

What the snake charmer does, therefore, is to tap the basket or stamp on the ground, pretending he is merely keeping time to the music. The snake reacts to this vibration. The snake charmer also moves his body constantly, and the snake "dances" because of these movements the man makes. In fact, what the snake is doing is keeping its eyes fixed on the man, and as he moves it moves in order to keep him right before its eyes!

In Capistrano, California, there is a San Juan Mission. There are a great many cliff swallows there. For many years, newspapers have published stories about how these swallows return to Capistrano on March 19th, and not a day early or late.

DO SWALLOWS RETURN TO CAPISTRANO ON THE SAME DAY?

Now there are many birds all over the world that migrate and return each year to the same place. But no birds begin their migration on the same day each year, and no birds return on the same day each time. Many, however, do come fairly close to keeping such an exact schedule, which is why the stories arise.

The swallows of Capistrano leave the mission sometime near the date of October 23rd, but not always exactly on that day. And they return sometime near March 19th, but not necessarily just on that day. It is just a nice legend that people like to believe.

Swallows are interesting birds, even if they do not perform this migrating miracle. There are actually more than 100 species of swallows throughout the world. Cliff swallows are found in wild places and build their nests on the faces of exposed cliffs, or sometimes under the eaves of a house.

There are about 50 different kinds of birds of paradise, but they are all found in the tropical islands of the western Pacific and in northern Australia.

WHAT ARE BIRDS OF PARADISE?

Birds of paradise range in size from that of a crow to that of a sparrow, and each kind has its own special pattern of brilliant colors. It is this display of brilliant colors in their plumage that makes these birds so unusual. But these beautiful birds are actually related to the common crow.

The first Europeans to see these birds were the early Dutch explorers in the fifteenth century. They looked so beautiful that these men believed the birds were fed from the dews of heaven and the nectar of flowers, which explains their name.

Only the males have the brilliant plumage. The reason for this is not yet understood. It may be to attract the females, or it may be to draw natural enemies away from the nests of the mother and the young and so protect them.

Most birds of paradise build flimsy, platform-like nests in the treetops. In these they lay their streaked and spotted eggs. The birds eat almost anything they can find, from fruit to snails and insects.

During the mating season, the male birds gather and show off their fine feathers before the females. While these birds are usually wary, at this time they concentrate so much on showing off that hunters can shoot them at close range. The natives used to shoot them with blunt arrows so as not to injure the plumes.

There are a great many birds which can be taught to say a few words. But the real "talking birds" can be taught to say long sentences! The best talking birds are parrots, mynas, crows, ravens, jackdaws, and certain jays.

WHAT BIRDS CAN TALK BEST?

According to the experts the best bird talkers in the world are the African parrot and the myna bird of India.

Many people believe that the ability of a bird to "talk" depends on the structure of its tongue. A parrot, for instance, has a large, thick tongue. But many other talking birds have small tongues! Splitting a bird's tongue, which is done by some people to help it talk, actually has the opposite effect.

Do birds understand what they are saying? Most biologists believe birds do not understand the words they say, but they can sometimes form an association between certain expressions and actions.

The ability of certain birds to fly great distances and arrive "home," or at their destination, is one of the most remarkable things in nature. Do you know that carrier, or homing, pigeons were used to carry messages as

HOW DO PIGEONS FIND THEIR WAY HOME?

long as 2,000 years ago by the ancient Romans? And even now, when modern armies have all kinds of wonderful equipment for transmitting messages, they still train homing pigeons for use in those situations when other methods of communication fail!

Many scientists have studied this amazing ability of birds, but no one yet has the full answer. One theory, which is better known than the others, is that pigeons use the sun to help them find direction. As you know, there is a different angle toward the sun as the day progresses—it is low in the morning, high at noon, and then low again. But some scientists believe a pigeon can see which path the sun will follow through the sky, and can figure out direction from this. It seems almost impossible to believe—but so far no one has offered a better explanation.

Not all birds or even all pigeons can do this. In fact, there are 289 different kinds of pigeons and doves, and they vary quite a bit. Some kinds of pigeons like to live and travel alone; others are always found in flocks. Some feed and live mainly on the ground. But most kinds live in forested areas and build their nests among the tree branches.

The electric eel is one of a group of electric fish. These fish capture their prey and defend themselves from enemies by discharging electric shocks. They closely resemble and are related to other fish, but they just

WHAT IS AN ELECTRIC EEL?

happen to have this electric power. Scientists still cannot explain the origin and development of the electric power in these fish.

The most dangerous of all the electric fish is the electric eel of South America, sometimes called "the Brazilian electric eel." This thick, blackish creature is an inhabitant of the rivers emptying into the Amazon and Orinoco rivers. It often grows to a length of six feet or more, and by a blow of its tail, in which its electric organs are located, it can stun an animal as large as a horse! Human beings are also said to feel the effects of the shock for several hours.

Another kind of electric fish is the electric catfish. This is sometimes four feet long and may be found in all the larger rivers of tropical Africa.

Third in the group of electric fish is the electric ray, or torpedo ray, found in all warm seas. It lives mostly in deep water near the shore. The member of this family inhabiting the Atlantic Ocean is said to grow to a length of five feet and weighs 200 pounds.

The electric ray is dark above and light below. It is round and flat and has a powerful tail. Its electric organs are situated between the head and gills. Experiments made on this fish have shown that its electric power can be used up and that the power will not return until the creature has rested and eaten.

Many people have had the experience of being at a public beach when the lifeguards ordered everyone out of the water because of the presence of jellyfish. It is hard to believe when you look at a jellyfish that this creature

ARE JELLYFISH DANGEROUS?

can be so dangerous.

Jellyfish are shaped like an overturned bowl. The digestive system is under the bowl. The digestive tract ends in a tube which hangs down from the center and has a mouth at the lower end. Tentacles, hanging from the edge of the bowl, gather food and are sometimes used for swimming. Between the tentacles are nerve centers and sense organs.

The bowl of the jellyfish is made up of two thin layers of tissue with jelly-like material between them. If a jellyfish is removed from the water

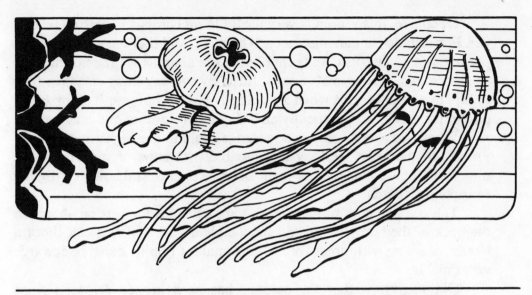

it dries up very quickly because 98 per cent of its body is water.

Of course, if the jellyfish is quite small, being stung by one may not be too dangerous. But when it comes to the big ones, that's a different story. Experts report that there are jellyfish with a bowl of over 12 feet in diameter and with tentacles more than 100 feet long!

When a jellyfish like this "embraces" you, it may make it hard for you to breathe and even partially paralyze you. The Portuguese man-of-war, which is one of the largest jellyfish, can kill and eat a full-sized mackerel. It can cause serious injury to human beings. There is a kind of jellyfish found off the coast of Australia called "the sea wasp," which has been known to cause death in many cases.

What makes the jellyfish dangerous are the tentacles. Some of them are barbed and pierce the body of its prey. The barbed cells are connected to poison glands which kill or paralyze the prey.

If you ever run into an octopus underwater, it might be a good idea to go off in another direction. Octopuses are not as dangerous as they look or are made out to be, but they can be very unpleasant.

WHAT DOES AN OCTOPUS EAT?

This is due to the bite of the octopus, which can be poisonous. An octopus has two very tough jaws that look like the beak of a parrot. Not only can the bite be painful, the octopus can inject venom or poison with its bite.

Of course, this venom is very useful to an octopus in getting its dinner. For instance, it can make a crab helpless, and thus easy for the octopus to eat it. Crabs, fish, and other living sea animals are the normal diet of an octopus. The animals are captured by sucking discs and then torn to bits by the jaws. But when an octopus is very hungry, it stops being particular. It will eat practically anything it can capture and tear apart!

What makes an octopus so strange looking are eight tentacles, or arms. The tentacles are long and flexible with rows of suckers on the underside. These suckers enable the octopus to grab and hold very tightly to anything it catches.

The octopus does not use these long tentacles for getting about. In the back of the body there is a funnel-siphon with which it can shoot a stream of water with great force. This enables him to move backwards very quickly.

Did you know that the octopus has been hunted for food since ancient Greek and Roman times? It was considered a great delicacy by the Romans. And even today, Greeks, Italians, and Chinese enjoy eating pickled or dry octopus.

Perhaps you have sometimes watched a snail moving slowly across the ground and wondered how it was able to move since no "legs" were showing. The fact is that the whole bottom part of a snail's body is

HOW DO SNAILS WALK?

really a "foot"! This foot is flat and smooth and contains muscles which the snail uses to glide along the ground. To help it move more easily, this foot has tiny glands which give out a slimy fluid, so the snail really glides over the surface with a wavelike movement.

Here's an amazing fact about this foot of the snail. It is so tough that a snail can crawl along the edge of the sharpest razor without hurting itself in the slightest! In fact, the snail is a remarkable creature in many ways. For instance, a snail never gets lost. It has an instinct that guides it back to its hiding place no matter how far away it has wandered. And even though a snail may weigh less than half an ounce, it can pull a weight behind it that weighs more than pound!

Snails are chiefly of two types, those with shells and those without. The snail that lives in a shell has a body that fits right into the coil of the shell, and it has strong muscles that enable it to pull its body entirely into

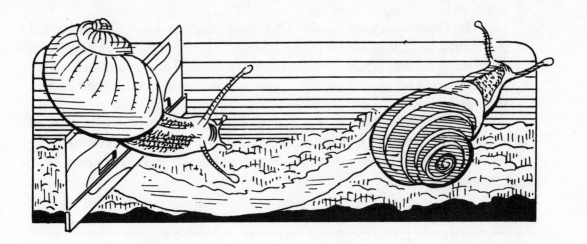

the shell when there is danger. As an added protection when the body is in the shell, a horny disk at the end closes the opening tightly.

Snails live on land or in fresh water. Most snails eat plants of various kinds. The snail has a tongue that is like a file with hundreds of tiny teeth. It uses this to cut and shred its food.

A "fillet" is a thick slice of fish without the bone. So a "fillet of sole" should be a thick slice of a fish called "sole."

But the chances are that when you buy or order "fillet of sole" you

WHAT IS FILLET OF SOLE?

are really getting some other fish. The reason for this is that the sole is considered one of the most delicious fish in the world. In fact, many people consider it the best-tasting of all. But the fish they mean is the European sole—and not the American. The American sole is not a very good fish to eat at all. So when you buy or order "fillet of sole" in the United States, you do not get a "sole" but another kind of flatfish.

Among the more than 500 different kinds of flatfish are sole, flounder, fluke, halibut, and turbot. They have bodies that are flat like a pancake, and they lie and swim on one side with both of their eyes up on top.

But long, long ago, the flatfish did not travel and rest on their sides. They lived and moved in an upright position, and as a result they were being destroyed by their enemies. Then some of them, in order to survive, began to travel and rest entirely on their sides, and after thousands of years all flatfish began to do this.

But there was one problem. This meant that one eye would be buried in the mud and the mouth was at a bad angle for eating. So for thousands of years these fish began trying to twist the buried eye around to where it could see. And gradually this eye developed on the top of the head on the upper side!

The fantastic thing is that today, each flatfish after it is born goes through this process. It repeats the whole process of its evolution during its own lifetime—its eye actually travels across the top of its head and comes out on top!

A manatee looks like a small whale and it is a mammal, not a fish. The American manatee lives in the rivers of Florida, Mexico, Central America, and the West Indies. It measures from 9 to 13 feet in length. The body

WHAT IS A MANATEE?

is somewhat like a fish, but the tail is quite different. It is broad, shovel-like, horizontal, and has rounded edges. It has a thick skin which is hairless, except for "whiskers" on the upper lip.

Manatees live in bays, lagoons, and large rivers, but not in the open sea. As a rule, they prefer to stay in shallow water. When they are not feeding, they lie near the bottom. In deeper water, they often float about with the body arched, the rounded back close to the surface, and the head, limbs, and tail hanging down.

Manatees live on the plants they find in shallow waters. They use their flippers to push food to their mouths, and a manatee may eat 60 to 100 pounds of food a day! But then a grown manatee may weigh as much as 1,500 pounds. Because manatees browse like cows in the shallow waters and often are seen in small herds, they are sometimes called "sea cows."

Manatees usually give birth to one calf, but sometimes there are twins. To nurse the young, the mother rises to the water's surface and, with her head and shoulders out of the water, clasps the youngster to her breast with her flippers.

Manatees move very slowly and are perfectly harmless. But in some places today, manatees are still being hunted because of their flesh, their hide, and the oil which can be obtained from them.

Since a whale lives in the water and has a fish-shaped body, why isn't it considered a fish?

The fact is that the whale is a water mammal, and is descended from ancestors that lived on land. Dur-

WHY ARE WHALES CONSIDERED MAMMALS?

ing the thousands and thousands of years they have been living in the water, whales have grown to resemble fish in their shape and other outside features, but they are built and they live like land animals.

A whale's flippers, for instance, have the bones of a five-fingered hand. Some whales even have the bones of hind legs in their flesh! The most important difference between whales and fish, of course, is that the baby whale is fed on its mother's milk like other little mammals. It is not hatched from an egg but is born alive. And for some time after it is born it stays close to its mother, who takes very good care of it.

Since all mammals have warm blood, and the whale has no fur coat to keep itself warm in the icy water, it has blubber instead. This is a layer of tissue under the skin filled with oil which retains heat and is as good as a fur coat!

Whales breathe differently than fish. Instead of gills, they have lungs and they take in air through two nostrils or "blow holes" on the top of their heads. When they go underwater, these nostrils are closed by little valves, so no water can get in. Every five to ten minutes, a whale rises to the top of the water to breathe. First it blows out the used air from its lungs with a loud noise. This makes the "spout" which we often see in the pictures of whales. Then it takes in fresh air and dives down into the sea to swim about.

The biggest whale also happens to be the largest animal in the world. It is the blue, or sulfur-bottom, whale, which may be more than 100 feet long and weigh 125 tons!

WHAT IS THE BIGGEST WHALE?

It may be found in all waters but is most common in the Pacific Ocean. It belongs to the group of whales known as "the whale-bone whales" (the other is known as "the toothed whales"). So whale-bone whales have no teeth.

It is rather strange to think that the largest animal in the world is able to get along without teeth! How do these whales manage? They have developed a structure in their mouths made up of hundreds of bony plates, known as a "baleen." It grows down from the palate (roof of the mouth) and forms a sort of sieve.

The whale feeds by swimming swiftly through a school of its prey—mostly small mollusks, crustaceans, and fish, with its mouth wide open. When it closes its mouth, the water is forced out between the plates, but the food is caught. The mouth of the whale is like a huge bucket. The head is about one-third the length of its body!

Of the toothed whales, the largest is the sperm whale. They may be 65 feet long and they have huge heads. The grampus, or killer whale (which is really a large dolphin), is the only one that eats other warm-blooded animals. It is about 30 feet long and easily catches seals. Packs of killer whales even attack large whales.

Because whales live in the water and have fish-shaped bodies, we tend to compare them with fish. But the skeleton, circulatory system, brain, and other organs are quite unlike those of fish.

Because the elephant is such a huge creature, it amuses us to think that a little mouse can frighten it. The reason many people believe a mouse can frighten an elephant is the idea that a mouse could get into the end of

ARE ELEPHANTS AFRAID OF MICE?

the elephant's trunk. They imagine this might suffocate the elephant.

The truth is, however, that elephants show absolutely no fear of mice! One can often see little mice running about in an elephant's stall, and the big beast seems to disregard them completely. And since the elephant has a very keen sense of smell, we cannot believe that it does not know the mouse is there.

Even if a mouse did have the courage to crawl into the opening of the elephant's trunk, the elephant could probably take a breath and blow it clear out of the cage!

Remember the trained seal at the circus who could answer questions in arithmetic by blowing on a horn? Or the horse who would tap his foot the right number of times when his trainer asks him to count?

CAN ANIMALS COUNT?

The truth is that these animals were not really counting! What happened was the seal or the horse would notice a sign from the trainer—it might be a movement of the head or lips or eyes—and this sign would tell him when to stop blowing the horn or tapping his foot.

Of course many animals can tell a larger quantity from a smaller quantity. For instance, many animals can pick a pile with six pieces of food instead of a pile with five pieces of food. Children who have not learned how to count yet can do the same thing. But being able to notice differences in quantity is not the same thing as counting.

Scientists now believe that certain birds and animals can actually count. In one experiment, a pigeon was offered one grain at a time. All the grains were good to eat, but the seventh grain was always stuck to the dish. After a while, the pigeon learned to count to six grains, and when the seventh grain was offered it refused to peck at it. This was real counting!

In another experiment, a chimpanzee was taught to pick up one, two, three, four, or five straws and hand over the exact number of straws that was asked for. But this was as far as this chimpanzee could count. It always made mistakes above five.

There are few animals that depend on flying for moving about as much as a bat does. While birds and insects fly too, they can manage to walk about if they have to. But the limbs and feet of a bat are not suited to walking.

WHY DO BATS HANG UPSIDE DOWN?

Which means they also can not stand easily. So when a bat is in its roost, the easiest thing for it to do is to hang on, head down!

The bat does a great many things that are quite remarkable. To begin with, the bat is a mammal—the only mammal that can fly. The young are born alive and feed on milk from the mother. When the young are very small, the mother may carry them with her when she goes hunting!

Bats are nocturnal, which means they are active during the night and sleep during the day. Since they have to hunt for their food, you would imagine that bats would need exceptionally good eyesight. But actually, bats do not depend on their eyes for getting about. When bats fly, they utter a series of very high pitched sounds. These sounds are too high to be heard by the human ear.

The echoes from these sounds are thrown back to the bat when it is in flight. The bat can tell whether the echo came from an obstacle nearby or far away, and can change its course in flight in time to avoid hitting the obstacle!

Most people think all bats behave more or less the same way, but since there are several hundred different kinds of bats, you can see why this is not so. There are bats with a six-*inch* wingspread—and bats with a six-*foot* wingspread!

People seem to think that goats will eat practically anything. And the truth is that's just what they do!

A goat's instincts will prevent it from eating things that will do it

WHAT DO GOATS EAT?

harm, but it will try to eat things most other animals reject. The reason for this seems to be that goats are rarely given the food and care bestowed on other domestic animals. The goat has been called the most optimistic of animals. Since it usually is not fed well, it will try to eat anything in the hope that it may be good.

The goat has always had a rather curious relationship with man. It is one of the most useful of animals. Since ancient times it has supplied man with healthful milk and satisfying meat. Its skin has been made into leather. Its wool has been woven into soft, warm cloth.

In spite of its usefulness, however, the goat has always had a bad reputation. This is probably due to its bad temper and the unpleasant odor of the males.

The goat contributes more to man in comparison to its size than any other animal. Goat's milk, for example, is considered by some to be better and healthier than cow's milk. It is often given to babies and invalids because it is easier to digest than cow's milk.

A few goats are raised for their flesh or are used as beasts of burden. Some are grown for their skins, which are made into goatskin, kidskin, and morocco leather. Other goats, such as the Angora and the Cashmere, are raised for their wool.

Goats were probably domesticated in Persia, but are now raised all over the world. There are about ten breeds of wild goats found in Europe, Africa, and Asia. They are sure-footed, active animals which usually prefer mountainous homes.

SUMMER

WINTER

We think of ermine as a "royal" fur, and there is a reason for it. At one time in England, only members of the royal family were allowed to wear ermine. Later, nobles and government officials were allowed to wear this valuable fur. Their rank was shown by the arrangement of the black tail tips.

HOW DO WE GET ERMINE FROM A WEASEL?

Ermine comes from the weasel. It is the white winter coat that certain species of weasel develop. This happens to weasels only in cold regions, such as Canada, Lapland, and Siberia. Here the fur changes to pure white in winter. In milder climates, the fur changes only slightly from the summer coloring of reddish brown on the back and yellowish white on the underneath.

Weasels are closely related to skunks, minks, and martens. All of the species have slender bodies, short legs, sharp-clawed feet, and quite long necks. In the United States and Canada, the commonest species is the long-tailed weasel. The males are about 16 inches long and the females about 13 inches. Both have tails about four inches long.

The short-tailed weasel is about two inches shorter than the long-tailed species. It is also lighter in coloring, and the tail is only about two inches long. An even smaller weasel is found in Alaska and northern Canada. This is called a "least" weasel. There is a large species in the southern part of the United States that keeps the same coloring all year.

Generally speaking, the weasel can be considered a friend of man. Weasels are tireless hunters and they destroy vermin, rats, mice, rabbits, and certain birds. But many a farmer will tell you the weasel is quite an enemy too, because weasels love to rob poultry houses. A single weasel has been known to kill 40 hens in one night!

The guinea pig is not a pig, and it has nothing to do with Guinea. It is related to the hares and rabbits and its real name is "cavy." In other words, it is really a rodent.

WHAT ARE GUINEA PIGS?

Long before the Spaniards came to the new world, the Incas of Peru, Ecuador, and Colombia had domesticated this rodent. They used it for food, and considered it as a great delicacy. As a matter of fact, soon after the discovery of America the guinea pig was introduced into Europe for the same purpose, and was eaten by people everywhere. Nowadays, the only people who eat guinea pigs are some natives of Peru, but it is still kept as a pet by many people in South America.

A guinea pig is about ten inches long and weighs about two pounds. It has no tail. It has small, naked, rounded ears. The fore feet have four toes, the hind feet only three, and all the toes have broad claws.

They live wholly on vegetable food. While feeding they generally sit on their hind feet. When free they live in burrows and feed at dusk and on dark days. When they get plenty of green vegetation, they can get along without water. In captivity they may be kept on rabbit or rat food, but then they need water.

Guinea pigs have litters of two to eight or more, twice or three times a year. A few hours after they are born they can run about. Because they are gentle, easy to handle, and reproduce fairly quickly, they are very useful in laboratory experiments where live animals are needed. They have been very helpful to man in the development of medicines and medical treatment.

The very mention of the name "scorpion" makes us think of danger and poison. And the fact is that a scorpion can be a rather unpleasant creature to meet.

WHAT IS A SCORPION?

In the United States, scorpions have actually caused deaths in only one place—Arizona. The Arizona scorpion is related to the Durango scorpion that lives in Mexico. The Durango scorpion's bite can kill a man within an hour, and over a period of 35 years it has caused the deaths of about 1,600 people.

Scorpions are related to the spider. A scorpion has four pairs of walking legs and a pair of strong pincers which it uses to grasp its prey. It also has a long, thin, jointed tail which ends in a curved, pointed stinger.

This stinger is connected to poison glands.

When the scorpion walks, it carries its tail arched over its body. When it grasps its prey in its pincers, it bends its stinger over its head and plunges it into the victim. The poison will kill or paralyze the insects, spiders, and other creatures on which the scorpion feeds.

Scorpions are active mainly at night. During the day they hide in dark places, such as beneath a stone, in bark, or in dark corners of buildings. Adult scorpions always live and travel alone.

Young scorpions are born alive and cling to the mother's back. She does not feed them and after several days they go off on their own.

Scorpions are found mainly in warm climates. Of the roughly 500 species, 30 are found in the United States. Scorpions vary in size from half an inch to almost seven inches. The largest are found in the tropics.

Another name for the insects known as "aphids" is "plant lice." They are green or brownish in color, and the largest ones are not more than a quarter of an inch long.

WHAT IS AN APHID?

Aphids reproduce so rapidly that if they were not destroyed by their natural enemies, they would eat up nearly all the vegetation in the world!

Aphids may be found on the leaves, roots, and young stems of many kinds of plants. They often do serious damage to fruit trees, flowers, vegetables, and field crops. They have unusually strong mouths, or beaks, which stick out from their tiny heads. With these beaks they puncture the surface of the leaf and suck out its juices, thus causing the plant to wither and possibly die.

One of the most curious things about the aphids is that they serve as "ants' cows." Ants can actually "milk" them as if they were a sort of cow. What happens is that the aphids produce in their bodies a sweet liquid called "honeydew." Ants love to drink this liquid.

So ants capture these aphids and take care of them, just as a farmer might take care of his cows. The ants carry the aphid to the ant nest, supply it with plenty of green plants on which to feed, and protect it carefully from danger. When an ant wants to milk its cow, it strokes the aphid's sides gently with its long feelers. Then, as the tiny drops of honeydew flow from the rear of the aphid, the ant drinks the liquid!

Man, however, has no interest in protecting these insects, so plants are often sprayed with chemicals to kill them off.

CHAPTER 3
THE
HUMAN BODY

About 60 per cent of the human body is water! If you could squeeze out a human being like a lemon, you would obtain about 11 gallons of water.

This water, which is not like ordinary water because of the sub-

WHY DOES THE BODY NEED WATER?

stances it contains, is necessary to the life of the body. About a gallon of it is in the blood vessels and is kept circulating by the heart. This blood water bathes all the cells of the body in a constant stream. The water also acts as a conductor of heat through the body.

Even if you drink no water during a day, you take in about a quart of water from the solid foods you eat. So when you eat fruit, vegetables, bread, and meat, you are getting water because they are from 30 to 90 per cent water. In addition, the average person takes in about two quarts of water as fluids.

In the course of a day, about ten quarts of water pass back and forth inside the body between the various organs. For example, when you chew something and swallow it, you suck some saliva from the salivary glands and swallow it. In the next few moments, this water is replaced in the glands by water from the blood vessels. The swallowed water later goes from the stomach and intestine to the blood.

The amount of water in the blood always remains the same. Even though you may feel "dried out" after exercising on a hot day, the blood vessels contain the same amount of water. And no matter how much water you drink, it remains the same.

What happens to the extra water? It is stored away in various parts of the body. These include the intestine, the liver, the muscles, and the kidneys.

Most of us feel upset if we skip just one meal, and if we tried to go without food for 12 hours we would really be uncomfortable. But there are some people who seem able to "fast" for very long periods.

HOW LONG CAN MAN GO WITHOUT FOOD?

Various records are claimed for long fasts, but in most cases there is no medical proof and so the records are doubtful. One South African woman claimed that she went for 102 days living on nothing but water and soda water.

There are great differences among living things in the ability to survive without food. For example, a tick, which lives on animals, may survive a whole year. Warm-blooded animals use up their stores of food in the body more quickly.

In fact, the smaller and more active the animal, the more quickly it uses up its reserves. A small bird starves to death in about five days, a dog in about twenty. In general, we can say that a warm-blooded creature will die when it has lost about half its normal weight.

This matter of weight is important. Man and other creatures live in a state of "metabolic equilibrium," which means maintaining the body weight once a certain point has been reached. This regulation of body weight is done by thirst, hunger, and appetite.

When your blood lacks nutritional materials, this registers in the hunger center of the brain and you feel "hungry." The body is crying out for any kind of fuel (food). And it is our appetite that sees to it that we choose a mixed diet, which is the kind the body needs.

In order for the body to carry on its functions, it needs energy. This energy is obtained through the process of combustion. The fuel for the combustion is the food we take in.

WHY IS THE BODY WARM?

The result of this combustion in the body is not, of course, a fire or big heat. It is a mild, exactly regulated warmth. There are substances in the body whose job it is to combine oxygen with the fuel in an orderly, regulated way.

The body maintains an average temperature of 98.6 degrees Fahrenheit. It maintains this temperature regardless of what is going on outside. This is done by a center in the brain known as the temperature center, which really consists of three centers: a control center which regulates the temperature of the blood; one that raises the temperature of the blood when it drops; a third that cools the blood when the temperature is too high.

What happens if the blood temperature drops? Part of the nervous system is stimulated into action. Certain glands send out enzymes to increase oxidation in the muscles and liver, and the internal temperature rises. Also, the blood vessels of the skin contract, so that less heat is lost by radiation. Even the skin glands help by sending out a fatty substance that helps hold body heat in.

Shivering is automatically activated by the temperature of the blood dropping too low. The heating center of the brain makes you shiver in order to produce heat!

If the temperature of the blood rises, the cooling center goes to work. It dilates (opens up) the blood vessels of the skin so that the excessive heat can be eliminated by radiation, and perspiration can evaporate more easily. Perspiration is a quick method of cooling off for the body. When a liquid evaporates it takes heat from wherever it is located.

Every living creature must breathe in some way. All animal life breathes by taking in oxygen. Man gets his oxygen by taking air into the lungs.

It seems a simple thing for us to breathe. We do not even think about

HOW DO WE BREATHE?

it as we do it. But it involves quite a complicated process. When a person breathes in, air passes into the body through a series of tubes called "the upper respiratory tract." This starts with the nose. Here, particles which could be harmful to the lungs are stopped or strained out. The nose also warms the air.

From the nose the air turns down through the "pharynx," or throat. From here, the air goes through two smaller tubes called "bronchi," one of which enters each lung. The lungs are large, soft organs. Around the entire lung is a thin covering called "the pleura."

The lung tissue is like a fine sponge in some ways. But in the lung there are spaces, or air sacs, and it is here that air is received from the bronchi, the proper gases are used, and unwanted gases are forced out. These air spaces are called "alveoli."

The air we take in contains oxygen, nitrogen, carbon dioxide, and water vapor. These same gases are present in the blood but in different amounts. When a fresh breath is drawn in, there is more oxygen in the alveoli than in the blood. So the oxygen passes through the very thin walls of the blood vessels (capillaries) and into the blood. Carbon dioxide goes from the blood into the air sacs of the lung and is exhaled.

While there is much more to the process of breathing, of course, this is the most vital part of it—the exchange of gases that enables all the cells to obtain oxygen and to get rid of carbon dioxide.

An albino is a person without any color, or pigmentation. All races have a certain amount of pigmentation, though some among the white race (especially the Scandinavian) have very little.

WHAT IS AN ALBINO?

What causes color, or pigmentation, in people? It is produced by certain substances in the body acting on each other. The substances are color bases, or chromogens, and certain enzymes. When the enzymes act on the color bases, pigmentation is produced.

If an individual happens to lack either of these substances in his body, there is no pigmentation and he is what we call an "albino." The word comes from the Latin *albus,* meaning "white."

A person who is an albino has pink eyes, and this is because of the red of the blood circulating in the retina of the eye. An albino's eyes are very sensitive to light. So such a person keeps the eyelids partly closed and is constantly blinking.

The hair of an albino is white over his entire body. Even tissues inside the body, such as the brain and the spinal cord, are white.

By the way, albinism is found not only in man, but in plants and among all kinds of animals. It is even found among birds. And there is no race of man that may not have albinos.

It is believed that albinism may be inherited, and many people may not be albinos themselves but pass on the characteristics to their children.

Probably the albinos we are all most familiar with are white mice, rats, and rabbits. But there are people who have seen albino squirrels and even albino giraffes!

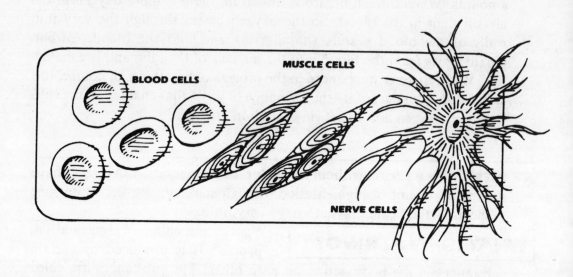

BLOOD CELLS

MUSCLE CELLS

NERVE CELLS

The cell is the building block that makes up living things. Everything that is alive is made of one or more cells. The simplest plants and animals consist of only one cell. Cells in more complicated living things work

WHAT DOES A CELL DO?

together. They are organized in groups, each of which has some special work to do for the plant or animal.

A tissue is a group of cells of a particular kind that does one particular type of work. For example, there is bone tissue, muscle tissue, or bark tissue. When tissues cooperate to perform a special task, such a group of tissues is called an "organ." An example of this is the human hand, which is composed of bone, muscle, nerve, and other tissues.

In the human body there are five important types of cells. Epithelial cells make up the skin and the glands and line the blood vessels. Muscle cells make up the three kinds of muscles. Nerve cells make up the brain, spinal cord, and nerves. Blood cells are found in the blood and lymph. Connective tissue cells make up the framework tissue of the body.

The circulatory system, in higher forms of living, carries food and oxygen to every cell and removes waste products, like carbon dioxide. The individual cells combine the food and oxygen slowly, thus obtaining the heat and energy necessary for their life and work. It is because of this energy that muscles can contract, nerves can conduct messages, and the brain can think.

The pituitary gland is part of the endocrine system of the body, so let us start with that. The endocrine system consists of glands located in various parts of the body. These glands produce active chemical substances called "hormones."

WHAT IS THE PITUITARY GLAND?

These glands send their secretions directly into the blood stream to be distributed throughout the body. The endocrine system as a whole is involved with "regulating" many things that happen in the body. And the pituitary gland, which is part of this system, controls many of the functions of the body. In fact, it is the most important part in the body in regulating growth, the production of milk, and in controlling all other endocrine glands.

A truly amazing thing about this vital gland is that it is about the size of a pea and weights about the same! It is joined to the undersurface of the brain and it is protected by a bony structure.

Even though the pituitary is such a small gland, it is divided into two distinct parts called "lobes"—the anterior lobe and the posterior lobe. And into the posterior lobe, which is the smaller of the two, go more than 50,000 nerve fibers connecting it with various parts of the body!

The pituitary gland controls growth in children by acting on another gland, the thyroid. The pituitary also controls the sexual development of a person. And it regulates the metabolism of the body, which has to do with the transforming of food into various forms of energy. It is also involved with certain muscles, the kidneys, and other organs.

Tumors that may grow on this gland can make it overactive or underactive. And one result of this activity can be to make people grow to giants or develop so poorly that they will be dwarfs.

Man has two sets of teeth: a first (primary), or baby set, and a second, or permanent set. In a full set of teeth there are four types, and each type has a special job.

HOW MANY SETS OF TEETH DO WE GROW?

The "incisors," in the center of the mouth, cut food. The "cuspids," on either side of the incisors, tear food. The "bicuspids," just back of the cuspids, tear and crush food. The "molars," in the back of the mouth, grind food.

There are 20 teeth in the first set, 10 in each jaw. They begin to form about 30 weeks before birth. In most children the first teeth to appear are the lower incisors. They usually appear when a child is about six months old. Between the sixth and thirtieth month, the rest of the primary teeth appear. The primary teeth in each jaw are the four incisors, two cuspids, and four molars.

Of the 32 teeth in the permanent set, 28 usually erupt between the sixth and fourteenth years. The other four, the third molars, or wisdom teeth, erupt between the seventeenth and twenty-first years.

The permanent teeth are four incisors, two cuspids, four bicuspids, and six molars in each jaw. The 12 permanent molars do not replace any of the primary teeth. As the jaws become longer, they grow behind the primary teeth. The bicuspids in the permanent set replace the molars in the first set.

The first molars, which are often called the six-year molars, usually are the first to erupt. They are the largest and among the most important teeth. Their position in the jaw helps determine the shape of the lower part of the face and the position of the other permanent teeth. They come in right behind the primary molars and often are mistakenly thought of as primary teeth.

The human bone is so strong it's a wonder it ever does break! Bone can carry a load 30 times greater than brick can. The strongest bone in the body, the shin bone, can support a load of 3,600 pounds!

HOW DOES A BROKEN BONE HEAL?

Yet as we all know, bone sometimes breaks as a result of violence. Each type of break has a name, depending on how the bone has been broken. If a bone is just cracked with part of the shaft broken and the remainder bent, it is called an "infraction." If there is a complete break it is called a "simple fracture." If the bone is broken into more than two pieces, it is a "comminute fracture." And if the pieces pierce the muscle and the skin, it is a "compound fracture."

Mending a broken bone is somewhat like mending a broken saucer. The fragments have to be brought into as close alignment as possible. But the big difference is that the doctor does not have to apply any glue. This is produced by connective tissue cells of the bone itself.

Bone tissue has an amazing ability to rebuild itself. When bone is broken, bone and soft tissues around the break are torn and injured. Some of the injured tissue dies. The whole area containing the bone ends and the soft tissue is bound together by clotted blood and lymph.

Just a few hours after the break, young connective tissue cells begin to appear in this clot as the first step in repairing the fracture. These cells multiply quickly and become filled with calcium. Within 72 to 96 hours after the break, this mass of cells forms a tissue which unites the ends of the bones!

More calcium is deposited in this newly formed tissue. And this calcium eventually helps form hard bone which develops into normal bone over a period of months.

A plaster cast is usually applied to the broken limb in order not to move the bone and keep the broken edges in perfect alignment.

You probably noticed that when you buy shoes and the man measures your feet, one foot is larger than the other. Since one foot does not do any more work than the other, why should this be so?

WHY IS ONE OF OUR FEET BIGGER THAN THE OTHER?

It is related to the fact that our body is "asymmetrical," that is, it does not consist of two identical halves, right and left. You can see this for yourself in many ways. If you look at your face in the mirror, you will notice that the right half of your face is more developed than the left. The right cheek is more prominent, and the mouth, eye, and ear are moulded with greater precision.

The same applies to the rest of our body. The legs are not equal in strength and dexterity. The heart is on the left side and the liver on the right, so that internally the body is not exactly balanced. The result is that our skeleton develops in a slightly unbalanced way.

Now this slight difference can have a tremendous effect on how we do things. The uneven structure of the body causes us to walk unevenly. The result is that when we cannot see, as in a snowstorm, a fog, or when blindfold, we will walk in a circle. The same is true of animals, whose body structure is also uneven. And if anyone were to drive a car blindfold, he would end up driving in a circle too!

When we come to the question of right-handed and left-handed people, we run into something curious. Ninety-six per cent of all people are right-handed. But this is not due to asymmetry of the body, it is due to asymmetry of the brain. The left half of the brain controls the right side of the body and vice versa. Since the left half of the brain predominates over the right half, this makes the right half of our body more skilled and makes most of us right-handed!

There are two main jobs that the skeleton does—it supports the body, and it protects delicate organs.

The skeleton is the frame that holds man erect. It is made mostly

WHY DO WE HAVE A SKELETON?

of bones. A baby is born with as many as 270 small, rather soft bones in his framework. A fully grown person usually has 206, because some bones become fused, or grow together.

Bones fit together at joints and are held fast by ligaments, which are like tough cords or straps. Some joints can be moved freely. For example, when you run, you move your legs at the hip and knee joints. When you throw a ball, you move your arm at the shoulder and elbow joints.

Some joints cannot be moved at all. At the base of the spine the bones are fused, forming one bony plate that fits into another. Neither moves. The joints in your skull are solid too, except for those in the jaw.

The protection that the skeleton provides includes the hard bony cap of the skull. This protects the brain. The rib cage protects the heart

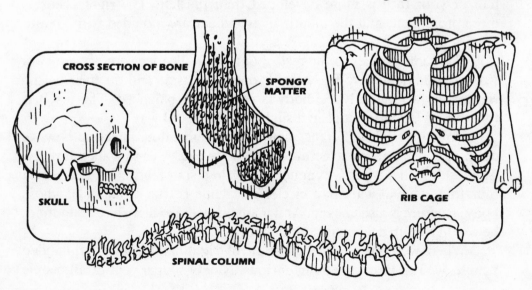

CROSS SECTION OF BONE

SPONGY MATTER

SKULL

RIB CAGE

SPINAL COLUMN

and lungs. And the backbone, or hollow spinal column, protects the spinal cord, the body's trunk line of nerve cables. The backbone is actually a string of small bones.

It is hard for us to think of bone as living tissue, but it is. It grows when a person is young. For example, the thigh bone may triple in length between the time a person is born and the time he is fully grown.

Bones grow in length and thickness as calcium and other minerals are added to them. And since bone is living tissue, it must be fed. The outside of the bone is covered with a thin, tough skin. The skin holds many tiny blood vessels that carry food to the bone cells.

The middle of a bone is spongy and filled with marrow. Some of the marrow is a storehouse for fat, and other marrow makes red blood cells.

Man is a mammal and all mammals have some hair. In the case of other creatures, we can see how having hair is useful. Its chief value is that it holds the heat of the body.

WHY DO HUMANS HAVE HAIR?

Hair protects tropical animals from direct sunlight. A long mane can protect an animal's neck. The hair of a porcupine helps it fight its enemies. But why do human beings have hair?

To begin with, an infant at birth is covered with a fine down. When a child is in the process of becoming an adult, this hair coat is transformed into an adult hair coat. And the development of this adult hair coat is regulated by certain glands containing special hormones.

In the male, these hormones cause hair to grow on the body and face, and hold back the growth of hair on the head. In the female, the hormones act in just the opposite way. There is less hair on the body and face, more hair growing on the head.

These differences in the male and female hair growth are what is called "secondary sex characteristics." That is, they are another way of setting the two sexes apart. The man's beard not only indicates he is a man, but is supposed to give the male an appearance of power and dignity.

Charles Darwin, a famous nineteenth century naturalist, believed that as man developed, he needed the fine hairs of the body to help drain off perspiration and rain water. The hairs that appear in certain parts of the body, such as the eyebrows, lashes, and the hairs in the ears and nose, help guard these body cavities against dust and insects.

The technical name for a birthmark is "nevus" and it refers to a mole which is present at birth or develops shortly after birth.

WHAT ARE BIRTHMARKS?

Medical science still does not know what causes them and no way has been discovered to prevent their appearance. But one thing is known: they are definitely not caused by some frightening experience the mother had before the birth of the child.

Almost everyone has at least one mole somewhere on the body. They can appear on almost any part of the skin, including the scalp. They may vary greatly in appearance since this depends on the layer of skin in which they originate. Most moles develop before or right after birth, but in some cases they do not show up until the child is about fourteen or fifteen.

If left alone, birthmarks rarely cause any serious physical problems. The greatest danger associated with them is the possibility that they may be transformed into a cancerous growth. But this happens very rarely and most people who have moles do not worry about this.

There is a whole variety of other skin disorders that might be considered birthmarks. One of these is a reddish or purplish structure or stain that appears on the skin at birth or shortly after. Sometimes these are strawberry or raspberry in color. They are actually an unusual formation of blood vessels, and usually disappear without treatment. But many doctors believe that strawberry or raspberry marks should be removed early in order to prevent leaving scars.

Medical authorities would even consider freckles to be "skin blemishes." They are caused by exposure to ultra-violet rays usually from the sun. People with blond hair and fair skins are the ones who most often get freckles.

Nobody likes to have pimples and blackheads, and it would be nice if we could say this is what causes them and this is how to avoid having them. But the problem is not so simple.

WHY DO WE GET PIMPLES?

Both pimples and blackheads start most often in the follicles of the hair. Certain glands, called "sebaceous glands," deposit an oily material there. When the hair follicle becomes plugged up and this deposit collects, it forms a blemish we call a blackhead.

Pimples are small raised areas of the skin which often have collections of pus in them. But the cause of pimples is harder to explain than that of blackheads. This is because they may be due to many conditions, including an improper diet, a glandular imbalance, or tiny infections in the skin.

Pimples may also be a sign that a more serious skin disorder is developing, or they may even be a sign of some diseased condition in the body. This is why a person should consult a doctor when he has many pimples on the body. The doctor will try to determine what brought them on. If the pimples are caused by some internal condition, then medication applied to the pimples will not do much good and could even damage the skin permanently. Pimples should not be squeezed. This makes it possible for bacteria to get into the area.

Acne is a condition that occurs in many young people of adolescent age. Acne includes blackheads, pustules, cysts, and nodules, all of which appear together. While the cause of common acne varies from person to person, in some cases it is due to the eating of certain foods, and in others it may be due to improper work by glands. A person with acne should consult a doctor for treatment.

About 10 to 12 per cent of all the people in Europe and America suffer from peptic ulcers at some time in their lives. What is an ulcer and what causes it?

WHAT CAUSES STOMACH ULCERS?

The gastric juice that is manufactured in the stomach contains hydrochloric acid, mucus, and an enzyme called "pepsin." Pepsin breaks down protein in the food into simpler substances.

Sometimes, however, the mixture of pepsin and acid acts on the wall of the digestive tract and the result is a peptic ulcer. These ulcers usually occur in the walls of the stomach.

People who develop such ulcers usually have a higher concentration of hydrochloric acid than is normal. There are other conditions that help in the formation of an ulcer, or hold back the healing process once one is formed. Tense, ambitious, hard-driving people are more likely to develop peptic ulcers than very calm people. Smoking may make an ulcer worse or delay healing of an ulcer. Coarse food also retards healing. But this disease may actually occur in any type of person at any age (though it is rare under the age of ten). Men get it four times as often as women.

How do you know if you have an ulcer? The pain tells you! The pain may occur from 30 to 60 minutes after eating. This pain rarely comes in the morning, but usually follows after lunch and dinner. And it may occur at night, after midnight.

The pain of a stomach ulcer is usually relieved by eating. When a patient has a peptic ulcer, the doctor puts him on a diet of soft foods with a lot of milk and cream, and orders him to rest and avoid fear and worry.

The appendix seems to be a part of the body that we can get along without, and even if it is healthy it does not do anything important for us. The appendix is a hollow tube, about three to six inches long, closed at

WHAT IS THE APPENDIX?

the end. In other words, it is a "blind" tube that does not go any-where. It is found at the beginning of the large intestine in the lower right part of the abdomen.

So it is a kind of off-shoot of the large intestine. The wall of the appendix has the same layers as the wall of the intestine. The inner layer gives off a sticky mucus. Beneath it is a layer of lymphoid tissue. It is in this tissue that trouble may sometimes occur.

This tissue may become swollen when there is infection in the body. The contents of the intestine enter the appendix but are not easily forced out. If the tissue is swollen the contents of the tube may remain

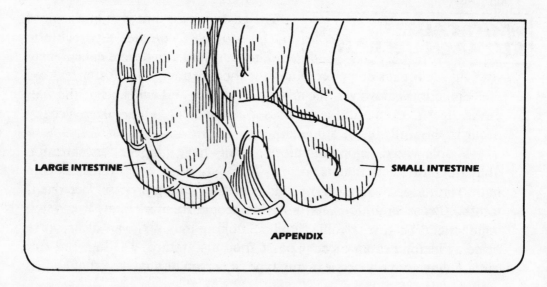

LARGE INTESTINE —   SMALL INTESTINE

APPENDIX

and become hard. The veins of the appendix may be easily squeezed by the hardened material and swollen tissue. This cuts off the blood flow and may cause infection.

Since appendicitis, or inflammation of the appendix, occurs very commonly, many people are constantly on the watch for symptoms. The typical symptoms are pain, tenderness, and spasm in the right side of the abdomen. Sometimes the pain is first felt in the pit of the stomach and then is concentrated on the right side.

In children, the first symptoms of appendicitis may be crying, vomiting, and refusing to eat. Sometimes parents give their children a laxative when this happens, and this is a very dangerous thing to do. A doctor should always be consulted at once when such symptoms appear.

There is only one treatment when a person has acute appendicitis: immediate operation to remove the appendix. It is a simple procedure and can be done quite safely.

You do not have to be an athlete to have athlete's foot. This is basically a fungus infection of the foot, and most persons are liable to catch it to some degree, though some people are especially sensitive to the

WHAT IS ATHLETE'S FOOT?

fungus. The name of this disease comes from the fact that it is often spread among athletes who share a common shower bath.

There are two chief types of athlete's foot. In the more common form, a crack appears in the skin, usually at the base of the fifth toe or between the fourth and fifth toes. There is also some loose dead skin clinging between the toes. When this loose skin is removed, the skin is red and shiny.

The second type of athlete's foot begins with a reddening of the skin between the toes, and it later becomes thick and begins to scale. Both these types may spread to cover part or all of the sole of the foot. And they may appear on both feet, though usually one foot is attacked more than the other.

There are several other diseases that can produce effects similar to athlete's foot. So a person who decides to treat himself with some medicine should be sure it really is athlete's foot. This is why it is safer to have a doctor examine your feet before you start your own treatment.

There are three types of fungi that cause athlete's foot. They are present on the skin at practically all times, so it is possible to get an infection any time. But when the skin becomes warm and remains moist for long periods, the fungi get into the dead outer layer of the skin and begin to grow. The fungi produce certain chemicals in the skin while they grow, and if a person is not allergic or sensitive to these chemicals he may not be bothered by the fungi at all.

Some mild cases of athlete's foot require no treatment and disappear as soon as the weather becomes cooler. But in more serious cases, the feet should be kept dry, socks should be changed frequently, and certain lotions may be helpful.

A stroke is a form of injury to the brain. Another name for it is "apoplexy."

When a stroke occurs, the flow of blood to a part of the brain is

WHAT IS A STROKE?

suddenly cut off. As a result, all the structures connected with that part are injured.

There are several things that can cause this failure of the blood to reach parts of the brain. A blood vessel may be ruptured and cause a hemorrhage. A clot may form within a blood vessel. This is called "thrombosis." There may be spasm of an artery. Or a blood vessel may become closed off because of a small particle, usually a blood clot, floating in the blood stream. This is called an "embolus." An embolus is usually linked up with heart disease, but it may occur in other diseases too.

In terms of damage, it does not matter what cause the stroke. That part of the brain through which pass the nerves that control our voluntary motions, our sensations of pain, our temperature, touch, and vision may be damaged.

The most frequent cause of a stroke is thrombosis. Strangely enough, a person can have this kind of a stroke after a period of inactivity. For example, a person might wake up in the morning to discover that an arm, or a leg, or even a whole side of the body is useless. Or he may find that he can hardly speak or speak not at all. People with this kind of stroke have a pretty good chance for recovery, but there is usually some permanent disability.

In treating a stroke, the doctor has to find out what caused it, so he needs a complete history of the illness of the person. People who become crippled in some way by a stroke can often be rehabilitated, that is, trained to regain the use of the function that was crippled. This includes use of muscles and the ability to speak again.

The human body has 639 muscles, each with its own name! If all the muscles are put together, they make up the flesh of the body.

Most muscles are fastened firmly to the bones of the skeleton. The

WHY DO MUSCLES ACHE AFTER EXERCISE?

skeleton forms the framework, and the muscles move the parts of the body. Without them a person could not live. Not only would it be impossible to eat, breathe, and talk, but the heart would stop because its beating is a muscular action.

All muscle is made up of long, thin cells called "muscle fibers." But muscles differ in what they do and how they do it. They also differ in shape, appearance, size, and in other ways.

When a muscle contracts, it produces an acid known as lactic acid. This acid is like a "poison." The effect of this lactic acid is to make you tired, by making muscles feel tired. If the lactic acid is removed from a tired muscle, it stops feeling tired and can go right to work again!

But, of course, lactic acid is not removed normally when you exercise or work. In addition, various toxins are produced when muscles are active. They are carried by the blood through the body and they cause tiredness—not only in the muscle, but in the entire body, especially the brain.

So feeling tired after muscular exercise is really the result of a kind of internal "poisoning" that goes on in the body. But the body needs the feeling of tiredness so that it will want to rest. Because during rest, waste products are removed, the cells recuperate, nerve cells of the brain recharge their batteries, the joints of the body replace the supplies of lubricant they have used up, and so on. So while exercise is good for the body and the muscles, rest is just as important!

Anemia is a word used to describe many different conditions having to do with disorders of the blood. These conditions exist when the blood does not contain the normal number of red cells, or when the cells do not have the normal amount of hemoglobin.

WHAT IS ANEMIA?

Anemia can be caused by poor blood formation, the destruction of cells, or by too much loss of blood. And these conditions, in turn, may be caused by many different body disorders. So when a doctor treats "anemia," he has to know exactly which type he's dealing with.

One kind of anemia, for example, can be caused by an injury that results in great loss of blood. Other body fluids seep into the blood to make up the volume, the blood is diluted, and the result may be anemia.

Another type of anemia is caused by an increased destruction of red blood cells, which can be the result of several conditions in the body. In some cases it may be inherited, or it may come from a transfusion of blood of the improper type, severe burns, allergies, or leukemia.

One kind of anemia many of us know about is nutritional anemia. The most common and least severe anemia of this kind develops when there is not enough iron for the formation of red cells. Iron is necessary for the body to manufacture hemoglobin.

Many of the common foods we eat contain only small amounts of iron. Also, many people cannot afford foods that have a high iron content, such as meat and leafy vegetables. So iron deficiency is not a rare condition.

The symptoms of this anemia are generally a paleness, weakness, a tendency to tire easily, faintness, and difficulty in breathing. If the patient is able to get enough rest and a good diet, he is usually able to recover quite rapidly.

In an adult human body there are about seven quarts of blood. These seven quarts form the most amazing transportation system imaginable.

The blood circulates through the body so that it reaches every one

HOW MUCH BLOOD IS IN OUR BODY?

of the billions of cells that make up the body tissues. It brings food and oxygen to each cell, carries away waste products, carries hormones and other chemical substances, helps the body fight infection, and helps regulate body heat.

The blood is made up largely of a colorless liquid called "plasma," and it is the red corpuscles floating in this liquid that give blood its red color.

It is when we consider how many of these blood cells there are in the seven quarts of blood that our imagination is staggered. There are about 25 billion of them! In a single drop of blood there are some 300,000,000 red corpuscles. If the cells were joined together in a chain, keeping their actual size, the chain would go four times around the earth.

Even though the cells are tiny, they have a tremendous surface area. For instance, if you could weave them into a carpet, the total surface area of this carpet would be 4,900 square yards. Since at any one given moment one-quarter of the blood is to be found in the lungs, about 1,200 square yards of blood-cell surface are constantly being exposed to the air. Every second, 2 billion blood cells pass by the air chambers of the lungs!

Because the air in lowland regions is under greater pressure, it contains more oxygen than at high altitudes. So the higher up a person lives, the higher is the number of blood cells he has. A person living in the mountain regions of Switzerland may have 50 per cent more blood cells than one living in New York.

What people call "heart attack" is one of the chief causes of death in the United States. In three out of four cases, the victim is a man, and the age is usually between fifty and seventy years.

WHAT IS A HEART ATTACK?

A typical heart attack is often caused by "coronary thrombosis." In fact, many people simply call it a "coronary." This is because it starts with the coronary arteries, the two blood vessels that supply the heart with blood.

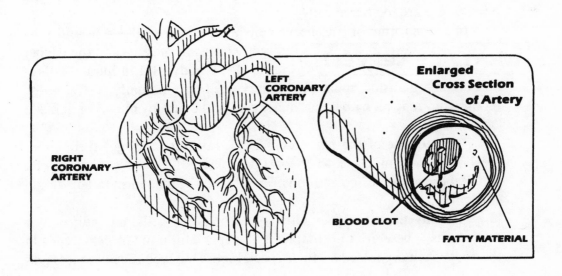

RIGHT CORONARY ARTERY

LEFT CORONARY ARTERY

Enlarged Cross Section of Artery

BLOOD CLOT

FATTY MATERIAL

When one of these arteries becomes clogged, the blood supply of part of the heart is shut off. The tissue in this part of the heart begins at once to degenerate and die, just the same as if it had been wounded.

When one coronary artery becomes clogged, the smaller branches of the other artery take up the work over a period of time. After a while, most of the areas of the heart that have been cut off receive the blood they need.

If the second artery can carry on the work for both, the person lives. Fortunately, in most cases the second artery can do the job, providing the heart is spared from all strain during this period.

In many patients, a heart attack occurs after some unusual physical exertion, emotional upset, exposure to extreme cold, eating a heavy meal —or any situation where the heart is called upon to do a bigger job than usual. These things do not actually cause the heart attack, but there is some relationship. In many cases, however, an attack can occur while a person is at rest.

The symptoms of a heart attack usually include pain beneath the breastbone. But the pain may also first be felt in the arms, neck, or left shoulder. There is sweating and shortness of breath. The person may become pale and be in a state of shock, and the pulse may become weak. A person should immediately call a doctor if such symptoms appear.

The cells whose job it is to keep our body informed of conditions in the outer world are the nerve cells.

In lower forms of life, nerve cells are located in the skin and they

WHAT ARE NERVES?

directly transmit messages to the deeper parts of the body. But in human beings and other organisms, most of the nerve cells are actually in the body, though they may pick up their "messages" in the skin by means of delicate "antennae."

The purpose of the nerve cells is to transmit messages throughout the body, each message to the proper place. The nerve fibers along which these messages go are constructed like a cable, and are amazingly efficient.

Actually there are four chief types of nerve cells, or "nerves," or nerve units. These are the completely independent units of nerve cells in the body, each organized to do its special job. One type receives messages such as heat, cold, light, and pain from the outer world, and conducts them to the interior of the body. These might be called "the sensory units."

Another type might be called "the motor unit." It receives impulses from the sensory units and responds to them by sending a nerve current to various structures in the body, such as the muscles and the glands. The reaction that results is called a "reflex." A "heat message," for example, would make certain muscles react and pull a hand away from a hot surface.

A third type of nerve unit does a connecting job. It transmits messages over longer distances in the body. It connects motor cells in one part of the body with sensory cells in another part.

A fourth type of nerve unit has the job of carrying messages from the outer world, such as cold, heat, and pain, to the brain where we "translate" the message into feeling.

There are very few cases of people walking in their sleep. But while sleepwalking is a peculiar form of behavior, there is nothing mysterious about it.

WHY DO PEOPLE WALK IN THEIR SLEEP?

To understand it let us start with sleep itself. We need to sleep so that our tired organs and tissues of the body will rest and be restored. We still do not have an exact scientific explanation of how and why we sleep, but it is believed that there is a "sleep center" in the brain which regulates the sleeping and waking of the body.

What regulates this sleep center? The blood. The activity of our body all day releases certain substances into the blood. One of these is calcium. It passes into the blood and stimulates the sleep center. And the sleep center has been "sensitized" before by special substances so that it will react to the calcium.

When the sleep center goes to work, it does two things. The first is it blocks off part of the brain so that we no longer have the will to do anything, and we no longer have consciousness. We might call this "brain sleep."

The second thing it does is block off certain nerves in the brain stem so that internal organs and our limbs fall asleep. Let us call this "body sleep." And normally these two reactions, or kinds of sleep, are connected. But under certain conditions they may be separated! The brain may sleep while the body is awake. This might happen to a person whose nervous system does not react normally. So such people might get out of bed while their brain is asleep and walk about! The brain and body sleep have become disassociated, and they are sleep walkers.

Did you know that you really cry all day long? Every time you blink your eye you are "crying"! You see, there is a tear gland that is situated over the outer corner of each eye. Every time your eyelid closes, it creates a

WHY DO ONIONS MAKE US CRY?

suction which takes out some fluid from the tear gland. This fluid we call "tears."

Normally, this fluid has only one purpose. This is to irrigate the cornea of the eye and so prevent it from drying out. But suppose some irritating substance reaches the eye? The eye automatically blinks and tears appear to wash the eye and protect it against the irritant.

We are all familiar with the experience of having smoke get in our eyes. It makes us cry. Well, the onion sends out an irritating substance too. The onion has an oil containing sulphur which not only gives it its sharp odor, but which irritates the eye. The eye reacts by blinking and by producing tears to wash away the irritant! It is as simple as that.

The onion is an interesting vegetable. It is a member of the lily family, and it is a native of Asia. The onion has been used as food for thousands of years, going back to the early history of man.

The three best known types of onion are the Spanish, the Bermuda, and the Egyptian. We actually import quite a lot of onions from Spain and Egypt, though we grow all kinds of onions right here in the United States. The Spanish and Bermuda onions are both mild in flavor, so they are usually the kind we try to eat raw. When you boil an onion you drive off its strong oil.

The simplest way to describe an optical illusion is that it is a "trick" that our eyes play on us. We seem to see something that isn't really so. Or we may be able to see the same object in two completely different ways.

WHAT IS AN OPTICAL ILLUSION?

If our eyes are functioning properly, and they are instruments for seeing exactly what is before us, how can they play "tricks" on us? Here is what makes it possible. Vision is not a physical

In drawing below, the eye wants to see a 3-D figure, but each end of the figure presents two separate sets of information. The figure makes no sense at all. Place finger across middle of drawing to separate the sets of information.

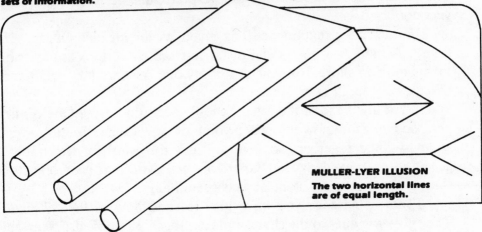

MULLER-LYER ILLUSION
The two horizontal lines
are of equal length.

process. It is not like photography, for instance, which works mechanically. Vision is really a psychological experience, because it is not the eyes that see, but the brain!

The eyes are mechanical instruments for receiving impressions. But when those images reach the brain, a judgment takes place. The cells of the brain have to decide what they think this image is.

What helps the brain make that decision? One of the important things is the work that the eye muscles have to do in order to see a thing. In judging distances, angles, and the relationship of things in space, our eyes have to move back and forth. Our brain says that our eyes have traveled a certain distance because the brain has an idea of the amount of energy and the time it took for our eyes to move back and forth.

So now we have the possibility of one kind of optical illusion. Suppose there are two lines of equal length, but one is vertical and one is horizontal. The horizontal line will seem shorter to us because it is easier for the eyeballs to move from side to side than up and down. So the brain decides the horizontal line must be shorter!

When we look out across a field, how do we know one distant object is bigger than another, or that one is behind another? Why don't we see everything "flat," instead of in three dimensions, in proper relation to each other?

HOW DO WE SEE IN THREE DIMENSIONS?

The fact is that we "see" things not only with our eyes but with our minds

129

as well. We see things in the light of experience. And unless our mind can use the cues it has learned to interpret what we see, we can become very confused.

For instance, experience has given us an idea about the size of things. A man in a boat some distance from shore looks much smaller than a man on shore. But you do not say one is a very large man and the other a very small man.

What are some of the other "cues" your mind uses? One of them is perspective. You know that when you look down the railroad tracks they seem to come together. So you consider the width of the tracks and get an idea about distance. Experience tells you that near objects look sharply defined and distant objects seem hazy.

From experience you have also learned how to "read" shadows. They give you cues to the shape and relationship of objects. Near objects often cover up parts of things that are farther away.

Moving the head will help you decide whether a tree or pole is farther away. Close one eye and move your head. The object farther away will seem to move with you, while nearer objects go the other way.

The combined action of both eyes working together also gives you important cues. As objects move nearer to you and you try to keep them in focus, your eyes converge and there is a strain on the eye muscles. This strain becomes a cue to distance.

Most people think we just have two tonsils, located on either side of the throat just behind the tongue. But this isn't true.

There are several pairs of tonsils of different sizes. Tonsils are small

WHAT DO OUR TONSILS DO?

bundles of a special kind of tissue called "lymphoid." Because of their location in the throat, they have a special job. They are the first line of defense against infections entering through the nose and mouth.

The largest pair near the palate are "the palatine" tonsils. High in the back of the throat are some smaller ones. These are called "the adenoids." Other small tonsils are found just below the surface in the back of the tongue, and there are still others in the back of the pharynx.

The tonsils are covered by the same smooth membrane that lines the mouth. In the tonsils, this membrane dips down to form deep, thin pockets called "crypts." The crypts trap germs and other harmful material from the mouth. The white blood cells surround the germs and help to destroy them. So fighting infection is the normal work of the tonsils.

Sometimes germs become active inside the tissue of the tonsils, and this may cause inflammation of the whole tonsil. This inflammation is called "tonsillitis." One or usually both palatine tonsils become enlarged, red, and sore. The crypts are swollen and sometimes discharge thick pus. This is acute tonsillitis. It is an infection that happens suddenly and usually goes away in four or five days.

Acute tonsillitis develops more often in childhood than in infancy or adulthood. It also happens more often during the winter months, when colds are common.

It seems like such a simple thing to us to sniff something and smell it. But the process of smelling, and the whole subject of odor, is quite a complicated thing.

WHAT IS SMELL?

Man's sense of smell is poorly developed compared to that of other creatures. Man's organ of smell is located in the nose, at least this is the place where the "messages" of smelling are received. This organ is quite small. Each side of the nose is only as large as a fingernail!

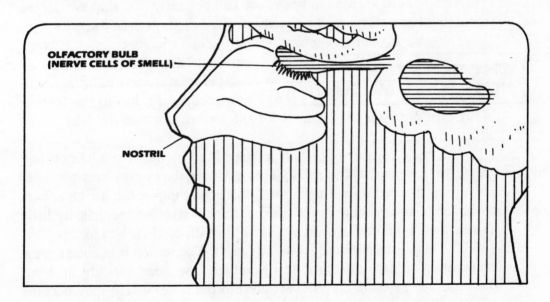

OLFACTORY BULB
(NERVE CELLS OF SMELL)

NOSTRIL

This organ is really a mucous membrane containing nerve cells which are surrounded by nerve fibers, kept moist by mucous glands. Through the cells, delicate hairs stick out into the nasal cavity.

But the tips of these hairs are covered by a fatty layer of cells. If they become uncovered and dry, our ability to smell disappears. In ordinary breathing, the stream of air does not come in contact with the smelling area, so if we want to smell, we have to sniff. This sends the air to the right place.

The substance that we smell must actually be dissolved in the fatty layer that covers the hairs before we can smell it! This is why it takes us a bit of time to "get" a smell. It is also why substances that have an odor have to be both volatile, or able to move, and part of an oily substance that can dissolve in that layer that covers the "smelling" hairs.

The way a thing smells depends on certain groups of atoms that carry odors. So that odor depends on a chemical formula, and each type of odor has a different chemical formula. And it takes only a very tiny amount of an odorous substance to excite our sense of smell.

There is a small smell center in the brain which receives the "messages" from the nerves in the nose and tells us what we are smelling.

When it comes to the human body, you can be pretty sure that everything found in it has a purpose. This is also true of the mucus in the nose.

The nose is the passageway through which the air enters our body.

WHY DOES THE NOSE HAVE MUCUS?

A great deal has to be done to that air however before it enters our lungs. It has to be warmed, and it has to be cleaned. Many dust particles that enter with the air are removed by way of the nose.

The first cleansing of this air is carried out by the bristle hairs which are at the entrance to the noise. This is where the coarse dust particles are removed. Starting with the nose and extending to the air chambers of the lungs, the passageway is lined with cells which have delicate little hairs growing out of them. These hairs are called "cilia."

The mucus in our nose is clear as glass. The reason it becomes greyish green in color is that tiny dust granules have been brought up from the windpipe by the cilia and carried into the nose, where they became mixed with the mucus.

Does "thought" take place at the fastest speed possible? In times past, this was held to be true, which explains the expression "quick as thought."

Today we know that thought is an impulse which must travel along a

WHAT IS THE SPEED OF THOUGHT?

nerve fiber in our body, and this speed can be measured accurately. The surprising thing is that thought turns out to be a very slow process.

A nerve impulse moves at a speed of only about 155 miles an hour! This means that a message can be sent quicker outside of our body than from one part of our body to another! Television, radio, and the telephone all convey messages more swiftly than our nerves do. A thought traveling by nerve from New York to Chicago would arrive hours later than the same thought sent by telegraph, radio, telephone, or TV.

When something happens to our toe, for instance, it actually takes a while for that impulse to be received by our brain. Suppose you were a giant with your head in Alaska and your feet at the tip of South Africa. If a shark bit your toe on Monday morning, your brain would not know it until Wednesday night. And if you decided to pull your toe out of the water, it would take the rest of the week to send that thought back down to your foot!

Different kinds of "signals" make us react at different speeds. We react more quickly to sound than to light, to bright light than to dull light, to red than to white, and to something unpleasant than to something pleasant.

Everybody's nervous system sends thoughts at a slightly different speed. That is why certain people can react more quickly to signals than others.

How do we know what is going on in the world around us? We use our senses. Through them we can see, hear, feel, and taste.

But there are some scientists who believe that man can gain informa-

WHAT IS THE THEORY BEHIND ESP?

tion without the use of senses. They believe the human mind has certain powers that have not yet been understood, and so it is possible to take in information that has not passed through the senses.

This process is called "extrasensory perception," or ESP. "Extrasensory" means "outside the senses." Many of the scientists who have studied this subject are psychologists. Their field of work is called "parapsychology." It is concerned with things that happen for which no physical cause can be found.

There are supposed to be three kinds of ESP. An example of one would be when someone seems able to read the thoughts in the mind of another person. A second kind of ESP is illustrated by this case: A woman living in one town dreams that her daughter, who lives in another town, had been hurt in an accident. The next day she learns that her daughter was hit by an automobile the night before.

A third kind of ESP would be the case of people who seem able to look into the future and know what will happen.

We know that some such cases really seem to happen, but many times it is difficult to really check the reports to see if they are true. Also, many people want to believe it and do not record very accurately what actually happened.

A great many experiments have been done by certain scientists to prove ESP exists, but the existence of ESP is still an open question for most scientists.

Sleep, as we know, is important to us because it helps restore tired organs and tissues in our body. But how much sleep do we actually need?

For most of us, eight hours seems to be about the right amount. Yet

HOW MUCH SLEEP DO WE NEED?

we know that there are a great many people who get along perfectly with less sleep, and some who may even need more. A great deal depends on the way we live. But a good general rule to follow is to sleep as long as we have to in order to feel happy and be able to work at our best when we awaken.

There are actually different kinds of sleep. There is a deep sleep and a shallow sleep. In a shallow sleep, our body does not get the same kind of rest it gets in a deep sleep, so that after eight hours of a shallow sleep we may still feel tired. But a short, deep sleep can be very restful.

Alexander the Great was able to get a deep sleep whenever he needed it. Once, during the night before an important battle, he remained awake longer than anyone else. Then he wrapped himself in a cloak and lay down on the earth. He slept so deeply that he did not hear the noise of the army preparing for battle. His general had to wake him three times to give the command to attack!

Normally when we go to sleep, our "sleep center" blocks off nerves so that both our brain and our body go to sleep. One prevents us from wanting to do anything, and the other makes our internal organs and limbs go to sleep. But sometimes only one goes to sleep and the other does not. A very tired soldier can sometimes fall asleep (brain sleep) and keep on marching, because his body is not asleep!

Just being able to stand up or to walk, is one of the most amazing tricks it is possible to learn! It is a trick, and it must learned.

If a four-legged visitor from another planet came to see us, he would

WHY CAN WE BALANCE OURSELVES ON TWO LEGS?

marvel at the ability we have to do this. If he tried to do it, it would take him a considerable time to learn the trick, just as it took time for you to learn it when you were a baby.

When you stand still, you are performing a constant act of balancing. You change from one leg to the other, you use pressure on your joints, and your muscles tell your body to go this way and that way.

Just to keep our balance as we stand still takes the work of about 300 muscles in our body! That is why we get tired when we stand. Our muscles are constantly at work. In fact, standing is work!

In walking, we not only use our balancing trick, but we also make use of two natural forces to help us. The first is air pressure. Our thigh bone fits into the socket of the hip joint so snugly that it forms a kind of vacuum. The air pressure on our legs helps keep it there securely. This air pressure also makes the leg hang from the body as if it had very little weight.

The second natural force we use in walking is the pull of the earth's gravity. After our muscles have raised our leg, the earth pulls it downward again, and keeps it swinging like a pendulum.

When you see an acrobat walking across a tightrope and balancing himself, remember he is only doing a more difficult trick of balancing than you do every day. And like you, he had to learn and practice it for a long, long time!

CHAPTER 4
HOW
THINGS BEGAN

"Zoo" is short for "zoological garden." And a zoological garden is a place where living animals are kept and exhibited.

Why do we keep wild animals in zoos? The most important reason is that everyone is interested in animals. Another reason is that scientists are able to learn many important things by studying living animals.

WHO STARTED THE FIRST ZOO?

The first zoo we know anything about was started as long ago as 1150 B.C. by a Chinese emperor, and it had many kinds of deer, birds, and fish in it. Even though it was somewhat like our modern zoos, there was one big catch to it. It probably was not open to the public but was kept for the amusement of the emperor and his court.

Since it costs a great deal of money to put together a zoo and maintain it, zoos in ancient times were assembled and owned by kings and rich lords. Many of them had collections of rare birds, fish, and animals of all kinds.

The first real public zoological garden in the world was opened in Paris in 1793. This was the famous Jardin des Plantes. In it were animals, a museum, and a botanical garden.

The next big zoological garden to be opened was in 1829 in Regent's Park in London. Then came the Zoological Garden of Berlin, which was begun in 1844 and became one of the finest and best in the world.

In the United States, the first zoo to be opened was in Philadelphia in 1874, and in the next year the Zoological Garden opened in Cincinnati. Today there are public zoos in most of the large cities in the United States and even in many of the smaller cities.

A duel, as we think of it today, is a prearranged encounter in accordance with certain rules between two persons with deadly weapons, for the purpose of deciding a point of honor. According to this definition, certain famous battles between two men were

HOW DID DUELING ORIGINATE?

not really duels. For example, Hector and Achilles were supposed to have fought each other, but this was not a duel.

The reason for this is that in ancient times there was something called a "judicial duel." This was a legalized form of combat and it decided questions of justice rather than of personal honor. For instance, sometimes when a war was impending, a captive from the hostile tribe was armed and he fought with the national champion. The outcome of the duel was supposed to be an omen, since it was believed that the one who won deserved to win. At other times, such "duels" were a substitute for a trial in court.

In time, this form of dueling was abolished, and the duel of honor came into being. These began about the sixteenth century.

The custom of dueling became so popular that between 1601 and 1609, more than 2,000 Frenchmen of noble birth were killed in duels! The church and other officials protested against this custom, and in 1602 the French king issued an edict condemning to death whoever should give or accept a challenge to a duel or act as a second. This proved to be too strict, and in 1609 it was changed so that permission to engage in a duel could be obtained from the king.

Duels also became popular in England, and there too protests finally made them illegal. In Germany, however, student duels were a part of German student life until fairly recent times. It was considered an honor for a student to have participated in these duels.

Golf, as we know it today, probably originated in Scotland. But in tracing the beginnings of golf we have to go back hundreds of years before that.

In the early days of the Roman Empire, there was a game known as

WHERE DID GOLF ORIGINATE?

"paganica." It was played with a leather ball stuffed with feathers and a bent stick for a club. In England, there is evidence that a game like golf was played as far back as the middle of the fourteenth century. And in the British Museum there is a picture in a book from the sixteenth century which shows three players, each with a ball and club, putting at a hole in the ground.

During the fifteenth century, golf was becoming so popular in Scotland that laws were passed forbidding people to play because it was taking up too much of their time! Among other things, the interest in golf was causing people to neglect archery, and it was also interfering with attendance at church on Sundays.

Golf has been known since old times as the "royal and ancient" game. This is because royalty seemed to be very fond of it. James IV, James V, and Mary Stuart all enjoyed the game.

Golf clubs began to be founded in the eighteenth century. The first one was probably founded in 1744, The Honourable Company of Edinburgh Golfers. The Royal and Ancient Golf Club of St. Andrews, founded in 1754, frames and revises the rules of golf. Its decisions are accepted by clubs everywhere, except in the United States. In 1951, the Royal and Ancient and the U.S. Golf Association agreed upon a uniform code.

In the United States, golf was played as long ago as 1799. But another hundred years passed before golf began to be played in a regular and continuous way in the United States. The first golf club in the United States was founded in 1888 in Yonkers, New York.

WHO FIRST WROTE MUSIC?

All primitive people seem to have made music of some sort. But the sounds they made were very different from those of modern music. This music often consisted of long and loud exclamations, sighs, moans, and shouts. Dancing, clapping, and drumming went along with the singing.

Folk music has existed for centuries, passed from generation to generation by being heard, not by being written down.

Composed music is many centuries old. Ancient civilizations such as the Chinese, Hindu, Egyptian, Assyrian, and Hebrew all had music. Most of it was unlike ours. The Greeks made complicated music by putting tones together similar to present-day scales. For notation they used the letters of the alphabet written above the syllables of the words.

After the Greeks and Romans (who copied Greek music), the early Christian church was important in the growth of the art of music. Saint Ambrose and Saint Gregory began a style of music known as "plain song."

This was a type of chant sung in unison. Tones followed one another in a way similar to the method developed by the Greeks. Churchmen also learned to write music down. The modern method of writing music developed from their system.

In 1600, the first opera, *Eurydice*, was produced by Jacopo Peri. Later on, men like Monteverde wrote not only operas but music for instruments, such as the violin. Music began to be written for court dances, pageants, and miracle plays. And in time much of the great music we enjoy today was composed by such men as Bach, Handel, Haydn, Mozart, and Beethoven.

The first recording was made by Thomas Edison in 1877. His first machine had a cylinder turned by a hand crank. There was also a horn and a blunted needle, or "stylus." At the small end of the horn there was a flexible cover.

HOW WAS THE FIRST RECORDING MADE?

Sound waves that entered the large end of the horn moved this cover one way or another. To this the stylus was attached. It moved up and down with the sound waves too.

The cylinder was covered by a layer of tin foil. The stylus pressed against this foil. Gears moved the horn with its attached stylus slowly along the cylinder, as the crank was turned. In this way, as the stylus went around the cylinder many times, it made a crease in the tin foil.

When someone sang or talked into the horn, it made the stylus move up and down. The stylus made a deeper groove in the tin foil when it was down, a lighter crease when it was in an upward position. The changing depth of the groove was the pattern of the sound waves made by a person singing of talking. It was the record of the sound.

To play the record, the stylus and horn were moved back to the beginning of the groove. As the stylus followed the groove, it caused the flexible cover in the horn to vibrate in the same pattern. This made the air in the horn move to-and-fro, and this made a sound like the original sound recorded!

Man's desire to be able to take photographs goes back hundreds of years.

From the eleventh to the sixteenth century, there was a device called "the camera obscura," which was a forerunner of the photographic camera. Its purpose was to show on paper an image which could be traced by hand to give accurate drawings of natural scenes.

WHO MADE THE FIRST PHOTOGRAPH?

In 1802, two men, Wedgwood and Humphry, took an important step forward. They recorded by contact printing, on paper coated with silver nitrate or silver chloride, silhouettes and images of paintings made upon glass. But they could not make these prints permanent.

In 1816, Joseph Niepce made a photographic camera with which he could get a negative image. And in 1835, William Talbot was able to obtain permanent images. Talbot was the first to make positives from negatives, the first to make enlargements by photography, and the first to publish (in 1844) a book illustrated with photographs.

From then on, a whole series of improvements and developments came one after the other. The popular Kodak box camera was placed on the market in 1888, and photography as we know it was on its way.

Most photographic processes depend on the fact that the chemical silver nitrate reacts to light by turning black. And this was discovered way back in the seventeenth century by alchemists who were trying to find a way to turn common metals to gold.

The first printing of any kind was done by the Chinese and Japanese in the fifth century. At that time and for hundreds of years afterward, books were so scarce and so hard to make, that few people could read or had books from which to learn.

WHO MADE THE FIRST PRINTING PRESS?

The first printers used blocks of wood as the printing forms. Pictures were carved into their faces. The blocks were then inked and printed on the crude presses of the day. Later, words were added to the pictures, but these too had to be carefully carved into the wood.

A method was needed to shorten the long labor of hand carving each page. It took nearly a thousand years before any real change was made in the method used to reproduce the written word.

Many men were at work on the problem. Johann Gutenberg, a German printer living in Mainz, is generally believed to be the man who first

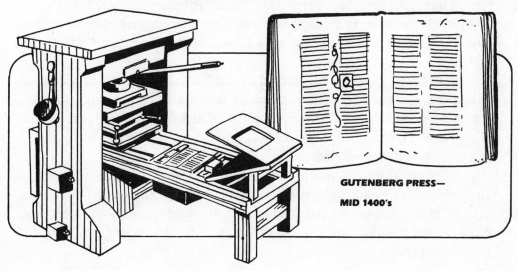

GUTENBERG PRESS—

MID 1400's

solved the problem. Gutenberg hit upon the idea of using movable metal type. He printed his first book, the famous Gutenberg Bible, by this method between 1453 and 1456.

Gutenberg's type was cast in a mold, each letter separately. When taken out of the mold, the type could be easily assembled, or "set," in words, lines, and pages. Once set and printed, the pages were broken up, and the letters reset and used again to print other pages.

This system is still in use today, though later inventors have greatly speeded up the ways in which the type is cast and set.

WHO MADE THE FIRST PAINTINGS?

Many artists today paint pictures in which they make no effort to show the world around them. But when man began to paint pictures, that is exactly what he wanted to do. In caves, where early man lived thousands of years ago, paintings have been found that show animals as lifelike as can be.

These were made by the people of the Old Stone Age of Europe. Many thousands of years later, when the Egyptians had created one of man's first civilizations, paintings were also lifelike. The Egyptians believed there was a life after death, so they painted on the walls of their tombs everything that went on in their lives. There were figures of men, women, and children with animals, boats, and other objects.

The most artistic people of any age, except perhaps the Chinese, were the Greeks, who were at the height of their glory about 500 B.C. Their aim in painting was the imitation of life, but life in its perfect or ideal form.

Christianity, which originated in the Near East, brought an important change in art. The naturalism of ancient art was replaced by Oriental styles with flat designs and symbolism. During the Medieval period, which lasted from about 500 to 1500, the arts of fresco and of illuminating manuscripts were perfected.

Fresco is done by painting with a brush directly into fresh plaster, so that when it is dry the picture is a permanent part of the wall. The illustration of manuscripts or books, which is called "illumination," was practiced by the monks. They made exquisite letters and pictures and full-page illustrations.

A coin is a piece of metal of a given weight and alloy with the mark or stamp of those who issued it.

The first coins were made in the seventh century B.C. by the Lydians.

WHEN WERE THE FIRST COINS MADE?

They were a wealthy and powerful people living in Asia Minor. These primitive coins were made of "electrum," which is a natural composition of 75 per cent gold and 25 per cent silver. They were about the size and shape of a bean and were known as "staters" or "standards."

The Greeks saw these coins and appreciated the usefulness of a standard metal money, so they began to make coins too. About 100 years later, many cities on the mainland of Greece and Asia Minor, on the islands of the Aegean Sea and Sicily, and in southern Italy had coinages of their own. Gold coins were the most valuable. Next came silver and finally copper.

Greek coinage lasted for about 500 years. The Romans adopted the idea and carried it on for about another 500 years. Then the art of coinage declined. From the year 500 to about 1400, coins were thin and unattractive. But in the fifteenth century, the art of coinage was revived. Metal became more plentiful. Skilled artists were employed to engrave the dies.

The first coins in America were struck by the English in 1652. They were the New England shillings, and were crude coins about the size of a quarter.

Coins are issued by a mint, which is an institution established just for this purpose. It wasn't until 300 years after the discovery of America by Columbus that the United States Mint was founded.

WHAT WERE THE FIRST AMERICAN COINS?

Before that, coins were quite a problem in this country. During the long colonial period, there was a constant shortage of them, and those that were in circulation kept losing their value. There were a small number of English coins available, but they had to be used chiefly to pay for imports.

Some of the colonies tried to start their own mints, but the British government suppressed these movements. So most business was carried on by barter, which means the exchange of one product for another, or by the use of foreign coins that found their way into the colonies. The most popular of the foreign coins were the Spanish dollars.

After the signing of the Declaration of Independence, several of the states gave contracts to private mints to coin copper cents. Finally, in 1792, the United States Congress, using the right given to it under the Constitution, established the first mint at Philadelphia.

The act which established the mint provided for the coinage of the gold eagle ($10), half-eagle, and a quarter-eagle; the silver dollar, half-dollar, quarter-dollar, disme (later spelled dime), and half-disme; the copper cent and half-cent. The first coins struck in the new mint were silver half-dismes, made in October, 1792. According to tradition, these coins were made from George Washington's table silver, brought to the mint for melting from his home just two doors away! The first coins made for general circulation were cents and half-cents, issued early in 1793.

If you have never seen a goldfish before and had to think up a name for it, what do you think it would be? Perhaps you would look at its bright color in the sun and say it looks golden, so let's call it "goldfish"? Well,

HOW DID SOME FISH GET THEIR NAMES?

many fish got their names because of their appearance or some special quality about them.

For example, "shark" comes from the Greek *Karckarios* and the Latin *carcharus*, which mean "sharp teeth"! Does the porpoise resemble

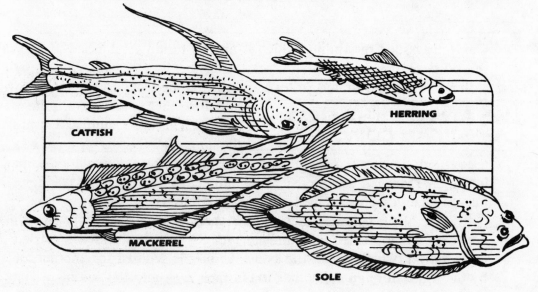

a hog a little bit? It gets its name from the Latin words *porcus pisces,* which means "hog-fish." The swordfish is an easy one. The upper jaw of this fish really looks like a sword.

The whale is simply the modern spelling of an Anglo-Saxon word *hwal.* The sunfish is so named because it has a round shape like the sun. That catfish got its name because of its large, glaring eyes. Is there any question as to how the flying fish got its name?

The "sole" comes from the Latin word *solea,* which means "the bottom." Herring comes from an Anglo-Saxon word *haring,* which means "a multitude," or "many," and of course the herring is always found in multitudes.

Have you ever examined a mackerel? Then you probably noticed the spots on it. The word "mackerel" comes from the Danish word *mackreel* which means "spots"! A "smelt" got its name because it has a peculiar smell.

What's interesting about the salmon? The way it jumps over obstacles on its way upstream. So the word "salmon" comes from the Latin *salmo* which means a "leaping fish"! The trout loves to go after bait. And "trout" comes from the Latin *trocta,* which means "the greedy fish."

Nicknames often give a better description of the person or place we are talking about. This is also true of the states that make up the United States. The actual name of the state may have some historical basis, but the nickname gives us an idea of what the state and its people are like.

HOW DID THE STATES GET THEIR NICKNAMES?

Let's consider some of the most interesting ones and see how they started. Pennsylvania is called "The Keystone State" because it was the central state of the original thirteen and the seventh in order at the time of the formation of the Constitution.

Texas is called "The Lone Star State" on account of the single star in the center of its flag. Ohio is "The Buckeye State" from the number of buckeye trees that used to grow there.

Indiana is called "The Hoosier State" for a curious reason. In the early days, the boatmen of Indiana were quite tough and rude and they were able to silence anyone in an argument. So they were called "hushers," and in time this became "hoosier" and the name was applied to the whole state and its people.

Delaware is sometimes called "The Diamond State" because of its great value in proportion to its size. Michigan is called "The Wolverine State" because of the many prairie wolves that used to be found there.

Wisconsin is called "The Badger State," but not because badgers used to be plentiful there. The reason is that the first workers who came to the Wisconsin mines made homes for themselves in the earth as best they could, somewhat like the badger does, and these people came to be called "badgers." New York is called "The Empire State" because of its wealth and resources.

Honey is one of the most amazing products found in nature. It has been used since very ancient times, since it was practically the only way early man could get sugar.

WHEN WAS HONEY FIRST USED?

It was used by the ancients as a medicine, to make a beverage called "mead," and in a mixture with wine and other alcoholic drinks. In Egypt, it was used as an embalming material for their mummies. In ancient India, it was used to preserve fruit and in the making of cakes and other foods. Honey is mentioned in the Bible, in the Koran, and in the writings of many ancient Greeks. So you see its use goes far back in history.

There are hundreds of ways in which honey is used today. It gives flavor to foods, fruits, candies, and baked goods. It is used in ice cream. It is used in medicines and in feeding babies. It is given to athletes as a source of energy. Honey has antiseptic properties and has been used in healing wounds and cuts. It has been used in hand lotions, in cigarettes, in antifreeze, and even as the center for golf balls!

The cabbage is a very ancient plant, and the food plants that have descended from it include many that you would never imagine have anything to do with the cabbage!

WHERE DID THE CABBAGE COME FROM?

Thousands of years ago, the cabbage was a useless plant which grew along the seacoast in different parts of Europe. It had showy yellow flowers and frilled leaves. From this wild parent plant, more than 150 varieties of cultivated plants have been developed. The best known kinds are the common cabbage, kale, Brussels sprouts, cauliflower, broccoli, and kohlrabi.

In the common cabbage there is one central bud and the leaves grow close together about it, fold over it, and form a large, solid head. Red and white cabbages have smooth leaves. Fresh white cabbage is eaten raw in salads or cooked as a vegetable.

Kale resembles the wild cabbage, since all the leaves grow to full size and remain separate from one another. Brussels sprouts combine features of both cabbage and kale. Tiny cabbage-like heads form on the stalk at the bases of the larger leaves, which are full and open.

In the cauliflower, it is the delicately flavored flower buds and not the leaves which are eaten. These buds have developed into a solid mass with a few loose leaves around it. Because cauliflower was difficult to raise, the Italians developed a hardier variety called broccoli. Kohlrabi has a ball-shaped enlargement of the stem just above the ground, and these enlargements are eaten when young and tender.

Tradition gives the credit for designing the American flag to Betsy Ross. But historians doubt that this is quite accurate. We do know that in May, 1776, Congress appointed George Washington, Robert Morris,

WHY IS THE UNITED STATES FLAG RED, WHITE, AND BLUE?

and Col. George Ross to plan a flag. On June 14, 1777, Congress approved a design. But who actually suggested the design is not really known!

The idea of representing the 13 colonies by 13 stripes was used in the old flag of the Philadelphia Light Horse Troop, and this may be the origin of the stripes in our national flag. At one time, it was proposed that the Union Jack of England be kept in the upper canton, or corner. But then it was decided to substitute 13 stars for the Union Jack, and this is the resolution Congress approved on June 14, 1777: "Resolved, that the Flag of the United States be 13 stripes, alternate red and white; that the union be 13 stars, white on a blue field, representing a new constellation."

As new states joined the union, not only were new stars added to the flag, but new stripes as well! When the number of stripes had increased to 18, the shape was so bad that the original design had to be restored. Today, of course, we have 50 stars and 13 stripes on our flag.

While we cannot know how our flag happened to be red, white, and blue, we can take George Washington's interpretation of it as a noble one: "We take the stars from heaven, the red from our mother country, separating it by white stripes, thus showing that we have separated from her; and the white stripes shall go down to posterity representing liberty."

Piracy, which is robbery on the high seas, has been going on for thousands of years.

Even ancient Greek and Roman ships were often attacked by

WHO WERE THE FIRST PIRATES?

pirates in the Aegean and Mediterranean seas. In fact, the pirates became so powerful that they set up their own kingdom in part of what is now Turkey. The Romans had to send an expedition to destroy them in the year 67 B.C.

A great period of piracy lasted from the 1300's to 1830. Pirates established themselves in ports of northern Africa in what were called the Barbary States: Morocco, Algiers, Tunis, and Tripoli. They would capture and loot European ships that sailed the Mediterranean and sell their passengers and crews into slavery or hold them for ransom. This piracy did not stop until the French conquered Algiers in 1830.

One of the names we have for pirates is "buccaneers." These were the pirates who operated during the late 1500's and 1600's in the Spanish Main. Originally the term "Spanish Main" meant the Caribbean coast of Central and South America. In buccaneering days it usually meant the Caribbean Sea itself.

The buccaneers were mostly sailors and runaway servants from different countries who had gathered on the islands and in the harbors of the West Indies. They hunted wild cattle and dried the meat over grills called "boucans," and that's how the buccaneers got their name.

Pirates often buried their gold, silver, and jewels in the ground. They wanted to keep their hiding places secret. There are many people who believe that a great deal of buried pirate treasure is still to be found along the Gulf Coast from Florida to Texas.

One of the oldest customs of mankind is the celebration of the New Year. How did it begin? Some people say the Chinese were the first to start it, others believe it was the ancient Germans, and still others claim

WHY DO WE CELEBRATE THE NEW YEAR?

it was the Romans.

We know that the Chinese have always had a great festival at the time of their New Year which comes later than ours. The Chinese New Year festivals last several days.

The ancient Germans established a New Year festival because of the changing seasons. The German winter began about the middle of November. This was the time when they gathered the harvest. Because everybody came together at this time for the happy occasion, and because it meant they would have a period of rest from work afterwards, they would make merry and have a great holiday. Even though it was November, they considered it the beginning of a new year!

When the Romans conquered Europe, they changed this time of celebration to the first of January. For them, the coming of the New Year was a symbol of starting up a new life with new hope for the future. This custom and this meaning has lasted to this day. We greet the New Year happily, hoping it will bring us a good, new life!

The origin of many customs is hard to trace, but this one has a definite beginning . . . and it reads like a fairy tale!

Many years ago, a beautiful girl in Holland wanted to marry a

WHERE DID THE BRIDAL SHOWER GET ITS NAME?

miller. He did not have much money, but he was loved by everyone because he used to give his flour and bread to the poor.

The father of the girl objected to the marriage and said that he would not give his daughter her dowry if she married the miller. The people whom the miller had befriended heard about this and decided to do something. None of them had much money, but they thought that if each one contributed some gift, the beautiful girl and the poor miller could marry after all.

So they got together and went to the girl's house with their gifts. Some brought utensils for the kitchen, and others brought useful articles for the house such as linens and lamps. They "showered" her with gifts, and she was able to marry the man she loved after all!

This was the first bridal "shower," and the custom has remained ever since.

The wedding cake goes back to Roman times. In those days, among the highest members of the rich families, a special kind of cake was used in wedding ceremonies. The bride and groom not only ate this cake to-

WHEN DID THE WEDDING CAKE ORIGINATE?

gether, but treated the guests It is even said that the cake was broken over the bride's head as a symbol of plentifulness! Each of the guests took a piece of cake so they too could have plentifulness in their lives.

Many peoples all over the world have used bridal cakes in their marriage ceremonies. Several of the American Indian tribes had special kinds of cakes made, which the bride would present to the groom.

In Europe, it became the custom for guests to bring to the wedding spiced buns which were piled up in a big heap on a table. The bride and groom were supposed to try to kiss each other over this mound of cake for good luck. The story is told that a French cook, traveling through England, thought it would be a good idea to make one mass out of this mound of little cakes . . . and that is how our present kind of wedding cake was born!

Furniture is anything on which people sit, sleep, or eat. So when the early cave man slept on a wolf skin on the floor, that was his furniture. When he made a crude box in which to keep his bone tools, he made the

WHEN WAS FURNITURE FIRST USED?

first chest.

The first records we have of furniture as we think of it today comes from the Egyptians. At least 4,000 years ago, they were using chairs, tables, stools, and chests. Some of the chairs had high backs and arms, decorated with carved animals' heads. Others were simple square stools with crossed legs which folded together like camp chairs. Egyptian beds were only a framework, often very low. The Egyptians did not use pillows. They used headrests of wood and ivory.

The Babylonians and Assyrians also had elaborate furniture. Kings and queens rested on high couches with footstools, or sat in high-backed chairs while they ate from high stands and tables.

Greek home life was very simple. The Greeks used only beds, chairs, and light tables for serving food. During meals the men rested on low beds and the women sat in chairs. The beds were like the Egyptian beds.

The Romans copied Greek styles. But they liked to fill their houses with objects for decorations, so they needed more kinds of furniture. They developed the cupboard, which they used for storing extra objects. They also used carved and painted wooden chests. The Romans made tables with metal, ivory, and stone decorations.

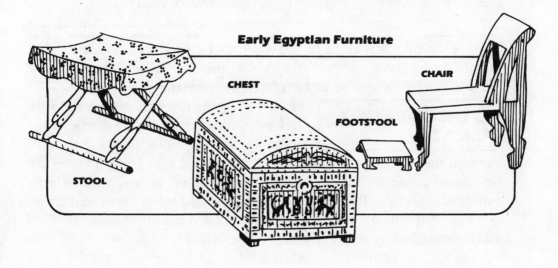

Early Egyptian Furniture

CHEST

CHAIR

FOOTSTOOL

STOOL

What we call a "world's fair" is really an exposition. The fair is one of the oldest and most popular means of selling and trading goods. Fairs are really large markets held in most parts of the world in important agricultural and industrial centers.

WHEN WAS THE FIRST WORLD'S FAIR?

Expositions, which are often called world's fairs, are for a different purpose. These large displays are set up mainly to show the industrial and artistic development of a particular country or a particular period.

The first exposition, or "world's fair," was The Great Exhibition of the Works of Industry of all Nations. It was held in Hyde Park, London, in 1851. The exhibition was housed in one building, the Crystal Palace. This permanent building was made entirely of iron and glass, like a huge greenhouse. It was destroyed by fire in 1936.

The first United States international exposition was in New York City in 1853. Although nearly 5,000 exhibitors took part, about half of them from 23 foreign nations, it was not a success.

The United States' first great exposition was the Centennial in Philadelphia, Pennsylvania, in 1876. It commemorated the 100th anniversary of the signing of the Declaration of Independence. There, for the first time, thousands of people saw the products and manufactures of the entire nation brought together. Alexander Graham Bell exhibited his telephone publicly for the first time at the Centennial.

After the success of this exposition, many others followed. Among them was the Columbia Exposition held in Chicago, Illinois, in 1893 to celebrate the 400th anniversary of the discovery of America.

When white men first came to Alaska, they found Eskimos, Aleuts, and Indians living there. In fact, Alaska was one of the last large areas of the world to be discovered and explored by white men.

WHO DISCOVERED ALASKA?

In the early eighteenth century, the Russians were moving through Siberia to the Pacific Ocean. In 1728, Vitus Bering, a Dane in the service of the Russian navy, sailed east from Kanchatka. He drifted along St. Lawrence Island, but failed to reach the Alaska mainland. In 1741, Bering led a second expedition in two small ships.

One ship, the *St. Peter,* was under his command, and the *St. Paul* was commanded by Alexei Chrikov. The two ships were separated during a storm, but both reached Alaska.

For the next 200 years, Russian fur traders hunted fur-bearing animals throughout Alaskan waters. They established many settlements, and in some of these places the quaint churches built by Aleuts and Indians under the guidance of Russian missionary priests can still be seen.

Later on, sea captains from Spain, France, and Great Britain explored the Alaska coast. But it was the Russians who used Alaska as a source of fur, and millions of these furs were sent by the Russians to European capitals. Then some of the fur-bearing animals began to be wiped out, and by the 1820's the Russians began to leave the Alaskan coast.

The Russian tsar, Alexander II, was not very interested in Alaska. William H. Seward, secretary of state under Abraham Lincoln, urged that we buy Alaska from the Russians. On March 30, 1867, the Alaskan territory was sold to the United States for $7,200,000. We bought it at less than two cents an acre! Today, Alaska is not only the 49th state in the United States, but its value to this country could hardly be measured in dollars!

If there is one sight in London that every visitor wants to see it is the Tower. The history and grandeur of England seems to be present wherever you turn.

WHEN WAS THE TOWER OF LONDON BUILT?

On the spot where the Tower now stands there was probably first a British fort, then a Roman one, and perhaps a Saxon one. William the Conqueror may have started building the White Tower, which is the oldest part of the present fortress. Most of the other buildings were put up during the reign of Henry III (1216-72).

William the Conquerer built the Tower in order to make the citizens of London afraid of him, but it has been used more as a prison than a fortress.

The Tower of London is still maintained as an arsenal. During the two World Wars, it was again used as a prison. It occupies a site on the old city wall of London and covers an area of nearly 13 acres. The outer wall is surrounded by a deep moat which was drained in 1843.

While there is a garrison of soldiers assigned to the Tower, the most interesting people tourists see there are the "Beefeaters." They are the "Yeomen Wardens," a body of about 40 men specially chosen for this job of defending the Tower. They wear a quaint costume which is said to date back to the time of Henry VIII or Edward VI. The reason they are known as "Beefeaters" is that in ancient times they were served beef every day as rations.

Tower of London

GUARD CALLED A "BEEFEATER"

Hawaii is the most recent state to become part of the United States. It is made up of a group of islands in the Pacific Ocean, some 2,400 miles southwest of California. The state includes eight large and many small islands, and has a total area of about 6,420 square miles.

HOW WAS HAWAII FORMED?

According to Hawaiian legends, there was a volcano goddess called Pele who formed the islands. From time to time Pele returns to the island's craters and kindles her fires into eruptions.

The strange fact is that the Hawaiian Islands are actually the tops of great volcanoes which have been thrust up from the bottom of the ocean. For example, the island of Hawaii ("the Big Island"), which is twice as large as all the other islands together, was piled up by five volcanoes whose eruptions overlapped one another. Two of these are still active and they are still continuing the process of island building.

One of these volcanoes, Mauna Loa, erupts every few years. In 1950, it erupted for 23 days and lava flowed down into the sea. It turned the water into steam, killing many fish.

Another volcano, Mauna Kea, is dormant. It is the highest mountain in the Pacific. It rises over 13,780 feet above sea level, but its base goes down to about 18,000 feet under the ocean. If measured from its underwater base, it is the world's tallest mountain.

On the island of Maui there is a volcano called Haleakala which rises to a height of about 10,025 feet. It is the world's largest inactive volcano. Its crater is about 20 miles around and some 2,720 feet deep.

The word "college" originally meant any society or union of persons engaged in some common activity. For example, there is a college of cardinals which elects the pope at Rome, and the United States has an

WHEN WAS THE FIRST UNIVERSITY STARTED?

electoral college to choose the president and vice president.

In medieval times, any corporation or society organized for a common interest was called a "university." So the earliest educational universities were merely societies of scholars or teachers formed for mutual protection. There were no permanent buildings. Instructors and students simply rented a hall or a large room.

In time, these institutions grew, buildings were built, certain legal rights and privileges were obtained, and the universities became permanent. The first such university was in Salerno, Italy. As far back as the ninth century it was well known as a school of medicine. It was formally made a university in 1231.

Toward the end of the twelfth century at Bologna, Italy, a many-sided university was established, The school at Bologna taught law, medicine, arts, and theology.

The most famous of the medieval schools of higher learning was the University of Paris, officially organized in the last half of the twelfth century. It became a model for all the later universities of Europe.

Two great English universities were modeled upon the University of Paris. Oxford and Cambridge were both legally recognized by the thirteenth century. A university, remember, usually includes a number of colleges. This means that degrees are given in many different fields at a university.

Many institutions start as colleges and later become universities. In the United States, the first college was Harvard, founded at Cambridge, Massachusetts, in 1636. Today it is a great university.

Men have lived together in groups since the very earliest times. Each group tried to keep together and to find ways that would keep the group going after its individual members were gone.

WHY WERE SCHOOLS STARTED?

In order for the group and its values to survive, it was necessary for the older members to teach children all that they had learned so that they could solve the problems they would face. Young people had to be trained to carry on the customs, knowledge, and skills of the group. So the idea of "education" existed long before there were actual schools.

But when letters were invented, schools became a necessity. Special learning was required to master the symbols. And the existence of these symbols made it possible to accumulate and transmit knowledge on a scale that had never been possible before.

Ordinary life in the group did not provide this type of education. So a special organization was needed to take over the job of providing it. And this was the school.

Nobody knows when the first schools appeared. We do know that they were in existence in Egypt and perhaps in China and in some other countries 5,000 to 6,000 years ago.

Actually, it was not until the eighteenth century that the idea of education for all as a way of improving man and his society began to spread. And it was only about 100 years ago that people began to consider an education as the right of every child.

The principal religions in the world today are the Hindu, Buddhist, Confucianist, Taoist, Shinto, Zoroastrian, Mohammedan, Jewish, and Christian.

HOW DID THE MAJOR RELIGIONS START?

The Hindu religion of India was formed about 3,000 years ago. Founders of this faith considered that Brahma was the first great god. Brahma created all forms of life and multiples of other gods.

Buddha was a great religious teacher who lived about 3,000 years ago. In its original form Buddhism does not depend upon a god or gods but teaches that man can purify himself of all desires and thus do away with evil and suffering. There are various sects and modifications of Buddhism.

Confucianism, based on the teachings of Confucius, a sixth century B.C. philosopher, is concerned almost wholly with man's right conduct toward his fellow man.

Taoism sprang from a little book called *Tao Te king,* which was written by Lâo-tse in the sixth century B.C. It calls upon its followers to find and follow the natural way of life.

Shinto is the primitive religion of Japan. It has been modified by many later contacts and teachers, mostly Chinese.

The Zoroastrian religion stems from the teachings of Zarathustra, or Zoroaster, prophet of Iran born probably in the seventh century B.C. This religion elevates Ahura Mazda (Wise Lord) as the great One God. The Mohammedan religion is based on the teachings of Mohammed, prophet of Arabia in the sixth century A.D.

Judaism is the oldest one-god (monotheistic) religion. Originating in Palestine, which was the early home of the Jews, it went with the Jewish people wherever they traveled. The Christian religion is based on the teachings of Jesus Christ. He was born in Palestine between 8 and 4 B.C.

To us, the right to a trial by jury is one of man's most sacred and natural rights. But it took man a long time to reach the point where this right was recognized.

HOW DID TRIAL BY JURY BEGIN?

When the Normans conquered England in 1066, they started a kind of jury. But the men on a jury were not there to listen as witnesses. They were supposed to decide a case on the basis of their own knowledge of the facts.

It was not until the reign of Henry II in the twelfth century that a big change was made. It was decided that the jury must decide a case solely on the evidence heard in court.

And this, of course, is the whole basis of the trial by jury system we have today. Twelve members of the trial jury listen to the evidence given by witnesses, to the arguments of the lawyers, and to the instructions of the judge. They then retire to a room to decide on their verdict. There seems to be no special reason why the number of jurors is 12, simply that Henry II in 1166 so decided and it has been that way since.

Before jury trials, trials were conducted in different ways. One method was "trial by compurgation." This meant that an accused person brought into court a number of neighbors who were willing to swear that he was innocent.

A second method was "trial by ordeal." The accused was subjected to all kinds of ordeals, like plunging his hands into burning oil, or carrying a piece of red-hot iron. If he survived the ordeal, he was declared innocent.

A third method was "trial by combat." Here a man had to do battle and defeat his enemy. If he won, he was innocent!

The Eskimos are just one more kind of North American Indian. They look Mongolian, but no more so than some other native peoples of North and South America.

WHERE DID ESKIMOS COME FROM?

Like the rest of the Indians, the Eskimos came from Asia. It is believed that the first Eskimos came to North America by way of the Bering Strait and Alaska 2,000 to 3,000 years ago.

Some then moved along the western coast of Alaska and then along the southern coast as far as the place where the city of Anchorage now is. Others moved out upon the Aleutian Islands. But most of them moved east along the northern coasts of Alaska and Canada.

The first known meeting of Eskimos and Europeans was around the

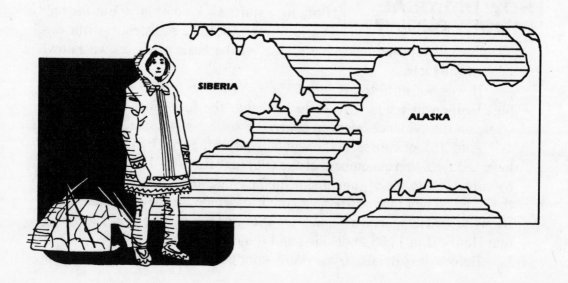

year A.D. 1000, when the Norse discoverers of America saw Eskimos, probably in Labrador or Newfoundland. The Eskimos later met the Northmen in Greenland.

During the twelfth and thirteenth centuries, there was a great deal of intermarriage between the Europeans and the Eskimos in Greenland. Many of the Eskimos there today are now practically European in appearance.

As a matter of fact, it is important to realize that Eskimos differ among themselves almost as much as Europeans do. Some of them look like blond Scandinavians or Germans. Others look like dark southern Italians.

The reason Eskimos live in the north is probably that they are a hunting people and their country is one of the best for hunting in all of North America.

The Canadian people are made up of different national stocks and races. The first known inhabitants of the country were the Indians.

It is believed the Indians crossed into this continent across the

WHEN DID PEOPLE SETTLE IN CANADA?

Bering Strait and Sea from eastern Asia at least 10,000 years ago. When Europeans first explored the country, Indian bands were living in most of the forested areas. There were only a few Indians in the provinces near the Atlantic Ocean.

The second group of people to enter Canada were the Eskimos. They crossed the Bering Strait from Asia less than 3,000 years ago. There are few records of their early movements.

The first white settlers in Canada were the French. They came in greatest numbers to Quebec, but also to Nova Scotia, where they cleared farms on the southern side of the Bay of Fundy.

The French built their citadel at Quebec City, where the St. Lawrence River narrows, and carved farms out of the forests in the territory. By the time of the British conquest in 1763, there were about 60,000 French in Canada, living chiefly between Quebec and Montreal.

There were not many British in Canada until the American Revolutionary War drove large numbers northward.

Throughout the nineteenth century, thousands of British immigrants came to Canada. The descendants of these peoples from England,

Scotland, and Ireland now make up about half the population.

Around the turn of the century, immigrants came in increasing numbers from Europe, and the largest numbers came from central and eastern Europe—Germans, Czechs, Poles, Rumanians, and Ukranians.

To us it seems so natural to put up an umbrella to keep the water off when it rains. But actually the umbrella was not invented as protection against rain. Its first use was as a shade against the sun!

WHEN WAS THE UMBRELLA INVENTED?

Nobody knows who first invented it, but the umbrella was used in very ancient times. Probably the first to use it were the Chinese, way back in the eleventh century B.C.!

We know that the umbrella was used in ancient Egypt and Babylon as a sunshade. And there was a strange thing connected with its use: it became a symbol of honor and authority. In the Far East in ancient times, the umbrella was allowed to be used only by royalty or by those in high office.

In Europe, the Greeks were the first to use the umbrella as a sunshade. And the umbrella was in common use in ancient Greece. But it is believed that the first persons in Europe to use umbrellas as protection against the rain were the ancient Romans.

During the Middle Ages, the use of the umbrella practically disappeared. Then it appeared again in Italy in the late sixteenth century. And again it was considered a symbol of power and authority. By 1680, the umbrella appeared in France, and later on in England.

By the eighteenth century, the umbrella was used against rain throughout most of Europe. Umbrellas have not changed much in style during all this time, though they have become much lighter in weight. It wasn't until the twentieth century that women's umbrellas began to be made in a whole variety of colors.

Today, of course, it is almost impossible for us to imagine living without electricity. But man has been able to use electricity only since 1800.

In 1800, Alessandro Volta invented the first battery, and so gave

WHEN DID MAN FIRST USE ELECTRICITY?

the world its first continuous, reliable source of electric current. Soon it was discovered that an electric current can be used to produce heat, light, chemical action, and magnetic effects.

Volta's discovery that there is a continuous "flow" of electricity was a great step forward. Various types of machines had been developed, but they would only provide a surge of electricity. Volta's discovery led to many developments in the use of electricity.

Sir Humphry Davy found that electric currents would decompose various substances in solution. From these experiments have come processes that led to the production of low-cost aluminum, pure copper, chlorine, various acids and fertilizers, and special steels.

Then it was discovered that magnetism could be produced by an electric current. A coil of wire through which an electric current is passing acts like a bar magnet. This discovery led to all kinds of electrical devices in which some kind of mechanical motion is produced.

Later on, Michael Faraday found a way to do the opposite—produce electric fields by magnets in motion. This eventually led to the development of electric dynamos and transformers.

So you see that man began to use electricity for practical purposes only recently in his history—and new discoveries and developments are still taking place.

There are several fascinating things about this famous symbol of America's history. One is that it was not called the Liberty Bell until it was about 100 years old. The other is that, in a sense, it has always been cracked!

HOW DID THE LIBERTY BELL BECOME CRACKED?

The bell was ordered to be made in England by the Pennsylvania Assembly to hang in the new State House (now Independence Hall). It was first called the State House Bell. It arrived in Philadelphia in 1752.

The very first time the bell was struck, the bell cracked! It had to be recast twice before it was repaired, and it was finally hung in the State House in 1753.

The bell rang on July 18, 1776, when Philadelphians celebrated the adoption of the Declaration of Independence. This caught the people's imagination and the bell became a symbol of the American Revolution.

The bell rang again in 1783 to announce that the United States had won independence. From then on, the bell rang on all important patri-

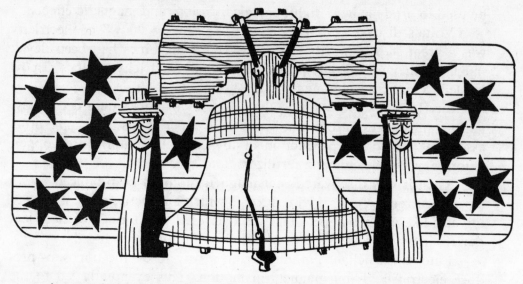

otic occasions. It rang on every July 4th, and to mark the birthdays or the deaths of great men.

In 1835, the bell cracked while tolling the death of Chief Justice John Marshall. After a while, it was repaired. Around this time, the abolitionists (people who wanted to free the Negro slaves) were becoming active in Philadelphia. The sentiment in Pennsylvania was so strong against slavery that the bell was given its present name—the Liberty Bell.

An attempt was made to fix the bell in 1845-1846, but it cracked again as it rang for George Washington's birthday in 1846. This time no one was able to fix it. So it was taken down from the belfry and was finally set upon a framework on the ground floor of Independence Hall tower in 1915.

We assume it is perfectly natural for the government to undertake the job of delivering our letters and packages. But this idea of government service was very slow in developing.

HOW DID THE POSTAL SYSTEM START?

In ancient times in Persia and Rome, the government did arrange for the sending of messages, but these were only concerned with government business. During most of the Middle Ages, merchant guilds and associations and certain universities maintained a limited messenger service for the use of their members.

It was in the sixteenth century that governments began to have regular postal services. They had three chief reasons for doing this. One was to enable them to inspect suspicious correspondence. The second was to produce revenue. And the third was to provide a service for the public. This last reason is practically the only purpose of the postal service today.

Henry VIII had a government postal service in England, and this was enlarged by later rulers. In 1609, no one was allowed to carry letters except messengers authorized by the government. But in 1680, a London merchant started his own penny post for the city and suburbs, and it became quite successful. So the government took it over and continued the service till 1801.

The whole system was finally changed in 1840. Stamps were introduced, and rates made uniform for all distances within the country, varying only according to the weight of the piece of mail. All other countries modeled their postal systems on that of Great Britain.

Just before the days of telegraphs and railways, the United States Government established a mail system that came to be known as the Pony Express. It started in 1860, and ran from St. Joseph, Missouri, to the Pacific coast.

WHAT WAS THE PONY EXPRESS?

To carry the mail, a fleet of horses was used. Each horse would be ridden for 10 to 15 miles, and then the rider would jump on a fresh horse for the next stage. A rider would travel three stages, or 30 miles, before passing on the mail pouch to the next rider.

These riders were tough men with a great deal of courage. They braved all kinds of weather and the danger of attack by Indians to get the mail through. But they actually rode horses, not ponies, so the name "Pony Express" is not accurate!

The dream of a flying machine that would rise straight up is an old one. Leonardo da Vinci made drawings for a gigantic screwlike helicopter about A.D. 1500. He never tried to build one because he had no motor to drive it.

WHO INVENTED THE HELICOPTER?

No one knows where it came from, but a toy helicopter known as "the Chinese top" was shown in France in 1783.

In 1796, Sir George Cayley made experimental forms of Chinese tops and also designed a steam-driven helicopter.

For the next 100 years, a number of people made designs for helicopters. Some were fantastic, others almost practical, and a few of them actually flew. But there were no powerful, lightweight engines. It was not until such engines were made during World War I that anyone made a helicopter that got off the ground with a man aboard.

Igor Sikorsky built two helicopters in 1909 and 1910. One of them actually lifted its own weight. Toward the end of 1917, two Austro-Hungarian officers built a helicopter to take the place of observation balloons. It made a number of flights to high altitudes but was never allowed to fly freely.

Work on helicopters continued in many countries, but none of the machines were what the inventors had hoped for. In 1936, an announcement came from Germany that the Focke-Wulf Company had built a successful helicopter. In 1937 it flew cross-country at speeds close to 70 miles an hour and went up more than 11,000 feet.

In 1940, Sikorsky showed his first practical helicopter and it was delivered to the United States Army in 1942.

A broom and a brush are somewhat alike. A broom, of course, is used for cleaning only, but many brushes serve this purpose too. However, the brush was invented many thousands of years before the broom.

WHO INVENTED THE BROOM?

The cave man used brushes made of a bunch of animal hairs attached to the end of a stick. The kitchen broom was originally a tuft of twigs, rushes, or fibers tied to a long handle. In colonial times in America, this was the kind of broom that was used. And in many parts of Europe today, you can still see streets and floors of homes being swept with such brooms.

The kitchen broom as we now know it is made from stalks of corn, and this kind of broom is an American invention. There is a story about the origin of it that may or may not be true. According to this story, a friend in India sent Benjamin Franklin one of the clothes brushes made and used in that country. It looked very much like a whisk broom.

A few seeds still clung to its straws, and Franklin planted them. They sprouted—and within a few years broom corn was being cultivated.

One day an old bachelor of Hadley, Massachusetts, needed a new broom. He cut a dozen stalks of broom corn, tied them together, and swept out his house. After that he never again used a birch broom.

In fact, he began to make corn brooms and sell them to his neighbors. When he died in 1843, broom making was an important industry, and the town of Hadley was growing nearly a thousand acres of broom corn a year! Today, much of the work of broom making is still done by hand.

Stockings were originally made of leather to cover the legs for protection. But even the idea of protecting the legs in this way was not a common practice until after the beginning of the Christian Era.

WHO INVENTED STOCKINGS?

The first people who tried to make a stocking of any kind like the ones we wear today were the French, and in the seventh century, French men wore leather stockings for protection and warmth.

Soon people began to want to make the stockings more attractive. So fabric stockings appeared, made of pieces of cloth, silk, or velvet sewn together. They were often decorated with gold embroidery, and were worn by fashionable people.

The first knitted worsted stockings appeared in London about the year 1565. Queen Elizabeth received a gift of silk knitted hose which pleased her so greatly that from that time on she wore silk stockings. These silk stockings were made in Italy, and only the very rich could afford them.

It wasn't until the beginning of the twentieth century that silk stockings really became available for the average person to wear.

Thousands and thousands of years ago, primitive man started the custom of using a headpiece of stone to mark the grave of the dead. If we observe what many primitive people do today, and believe it is done for

WHY DO WE HAVE GRAVESTONES?

the same reasons, then the custom seemed to have this purpose: to keep the evil spirits that are supposed to live in dead bodies from rising up!

The gravestone was also a way of warning people away from the spot where those evil spirits lived. Over the centuries, of course, the purpose of a gravestone changed. The Greeks ornamented their gravestones with sculpture. The Hebrews marked their graves with stone pillars. The Egyptians built great tombs and pyramids to mark the places where their dead were buried.

When Christianity appeared, the marking of graves became a common practice. Christianity took over the sign of the cross and ring, which to primitive people was a symbol of the sun. Later on, this was changed to a simple cross, and it is still used today.

There are many types of beards, of course, and each one has a different name for a special reason. A short, pointed beard is called a "Vandyke." This is because the Flemish painter Anthony Van Dyck used to paint

HOW WERE BEARDS NAMED?

men with this kind of beard. The English way of spelling his name was "Van Dyke," and this name soon came to be applied to the kind of beard he had painted!

A "goatee" is just a little bit of a beard on the chin, and the name comes from the fact that it resembles the beard of a he-goat. A tuft of beard under the lower lip is called an "imperial," because Emperor Napoleon III of France used to wear one.

When a man has hair along the cheeks past both ears, he is said to have "burnsides." This is named after a general of the Civil War, General Ambrose Burnside. Sometimes a type of this beard has the name twisted around and is called sideburns!

VANDYKE   BURNSIDE   IMPERIAL

If you had to name the most long-lasting material made by man, would you say it was brick? Well, it happens to be so, and brick will outlast granite, limestone, or even iron!

WHEN WAS BRICK FIRST USED?

Brick, of course, is a modern building material. It is being used today everywhere in the world. But actually, brick is as old as the history of civilization! The Babylonians and Egyptians made and used bricks at least 3,000 years before the birth of Christ. Some excavations suggest that it was used even earlier.

The making of brick in early times was very crude. Brick is made of clay or shale and baked or burned at a high temperature. In early times, raw clay was used to make brick, but no machinery to make it had been invented. The clay was crushed and mixed with water by workmen who trampled it with their bare feet. Straw was mixed with the wet clay to hold the bricks together. The mixture was then formed by hand into different sizes and shapes and placed in the sun to dry.

This crude method was followed for many years until it was discovered that burning the clay with fire made the bricks much harder and better able to withstand dampness. Straw was then no longer needed.

Bricks were first brought to the United States from England as ballast for boats. Soon after the settlement of Virginia and Massachusetts, small kilns were set up. Machines to make brick were invented about 1880 in England.

Almost everybody loves some sort of melon, whether it be muskmelon, honeydew melon, or watermelon. And when something is so popular today, it is hard to believe that it has actually been known and enjoyed for thousands and thousands of years!

WHERE DID MELON ORIGINATE?

The melon is a native of Asia, which means that it grows there without being planted by man. It is quite probable that many thousands of years ago the melon was introduced into other countries. The ancient Egyptians had the melon as one of their delicacies. The ancient Romans and probably the Greeks too enjoyed melons as much as we do! The first people to cultivate the melon in modern times were the French, and that was more than 300 years ago.

Today, melons are an important crop in the United States. Most melons are raised for the local markets, but in the states of California, Colorado, Texas, Georgia, and Florida they are grown by the carloads to be shipped to distant points.

All melons belong to the gourd family. Originally, muskmelons grew in southern Asia and watermelons in tropical Africa. But during centuries of cultivation, they have spread to many countries, and many varieties have been developed from these two types.

Muskmelons get their names from the faint, musky perfume that they have. Muskmelons are also called "cantaloupes." Casaba melons are large, with smooth, yellowish-green rinds. They ripen late in the season and pack and keep better than other melons.

Honeydew melons have a very smooth rind and their flesh is a deep green. Watermelons are much larger than muskmelons, and much juicier.

Man has been skating in one way or another for more than 500 years! Ice skating is much older than roller skating, since roller skating goes back only to the eighteenth century.

WHO INVENTED SKATING?

Wheeled skates were used on the roads of Holland about 200 years ago, and we cannot really know who was the first to make them or use them. A man in New York called J. L. Plimpton invented the four-wheeled skate in 1863. It worked on rubber pads and these were the skates that really made this sport popular.

The next development was roller skates with ball bearings. The wheels of roller skates were first made of turned boxwood, but the edges of the wooden wheels broke too easily. Soon wheels were made of hard composition or of steel. Roller skate races were popular in most United States cities until about 1910, when motorcycle and automobile races took their place. But, of course, roller skating has remained a favorite sport with young people.

Ice skating goes back beyond the sixteenth century. At that time the Norsemen bound runners made of bone to their feet and skimmed over the icy surfaces.

Iron runners were next used in skating, followed by the steel runners of today. In early days, the skate-runner was attached to the foot by leather thongs. Later, the skate was clamped and strapped to the shoe. In the modern skate the blade is permanently attached to the skating shoe.

You may think that skiing is a modern sport, but it is actually one of the oldest forms of travel known to man! The word itself comes from the Icelandic word *scidh,* which means "snowshoe" or "piece of wood."

HOW DID SKIING BEGIN?

Some historians claim that skiing goes back to the Stone Age, and they have found ancient carvings that show people on skis. Long before Christianity appeared, the ancient Lapps were known in Scandinavia as *Skrid-Finnen,* or "sliders." They even had a goddess of ski, and their winter god was shown on a pair of skis with curved toes!

The first skis of which there is any record were long, curved frames, often made of the bones of animals, and held to the foot by thongs. And there is a picture carved on stone that is 900 years old that shows a ski runner.

Skiing as a sport began in Norway, in the province of Telemark. In fact, the town of Morgedal in this Norwegian province is known as "the cradle of skiing." Because this region would be snowbound for long periods at a time, it was necessary to use skis to get about. In winter, when the natives went hunting or trapping in the mountains, or to neighboring villages to market or to visit, they had to depend on skis.

And if you think skiing meets are a modern development, it may surprise you to know that in Norway they were having skiing competitions for prizes way back in 1767!

Wrestling is one of the earliest sports known to man. Many hundreds of scenes of wrestling matches are sculptured on the walls of ancient Egyptian tombs. And they show practically all the holds and falls known to us

HOW OLD IS THE SPORT OF WRESTLING?

today. So wrestling was a highly developed sport at least 5,000 years ago!

Wrestling as an organized and scientific sport was probably introduced into Greece from Egypt or Asia. But there is a Greek legend that it was invented by the hero Theseus.

Wrestling was an important branch of athletics in ancient Greece. The Greek wrestlers used to rub oil on themselves and then rub fine sand on the oil, to afford a better hold. The champion wrestler of the ancient world was Milo of Croton, who scored 32 victories in the national games, and had six Olympic victories.

In Japan, where wrestling is very popular, the first recorded wrestling match took place in 23 B.C. The Japanese have a style of wrestling called "Sumo," in which weight is very important. Some Sumo champions have weighed as much as 300 pounds, and were tremendously strong—but still quite light on their feet.

In Britain, wrestling was cultivated even in earliest times. Did you know that King Henry VIII liked wrestling and was considered to be very good!

Some form of handkerchief has been used by man since the very earliest times. Probably the first form of handkerchief was the tail of a jackal which was mounted on a stick. Primitive people used this both as a handkerchief and a fan.

HOW LONG HAVE HANDKERCHIEFS BEEN USED?

We know that many savage races made little mats of straw which they wore on their heads and used to wipe away perspiration. This was probably the chief early use of the handkerchief.

In Greek and Roman times, there were not only handkerchiefs but napkins too. Napkins were used for drying the hands at the table. Handkerchiefs were made out of small linen squares which were put inside the clothes and taken along on trips.

In the seventeenth century in France, handkerchiefs became very elegant. They were made of lace and often decorated with gems. When snuff became popular in the eighteenth century, women began to use handkerchiefs of colored cloth.

Marie Antoinette persuaded Louis XVI of France to issue a law that handkerchiefs had to be square in shape, instead of round, or oval, or oblong!

CHAPTER 5
HOW THINGS ARE MADE

The planets in our solar system, as you know, move in orbits around the sun. A planetarium is a device for showing this motion of the planets in their orbits.

WHAT IS A PLANETARIUM?

In the sky, the planets look like stars, but they slowly change their positions among the stars from night to night. Mechanical devices to show these motions have been made for several centuries. The first machines had a number of small balls to represent the planets and the sun. Complicated gears controlled the motions of the balls representing the planets so that they moved around the ball representing the sun just as the real planets move around the real sun.

About 1920, a new kind of planetarium, the Zeiss, was invented in Germany. There are now planetariums of this type in many major cities.

The visitor to a modern planetarium sits in a circular theatre with several hundred chairs and sees overhead a wonderfully accurate and beautiful artificial sky. At the center of this room stands the planetarium instrument, which is a complicated machine made up of more than 100 "stereopticons," a special type of projector. These projectors are like those used in motion picture theatres, except that there is no motion in the separate pictures which each projector throws on the dome-shaped ceiling above the audience.

Some of the pictures show the stars, and these pictures are very carefully fitted together on the dome so that they form a single picture, a nearly perfect one of the night sky. Other projectors, like small searchlights, throw spots of light on the dome for the sun, moon, and planets.

171

There are electric motors and very complicated gears to move these projectors to show the motions of the sun, moon, and planets among the stars. The heavens can be shown as seen from any place on the earth at any time in the past, present, or future.

A telescope is used in looking at distant objects on earth and in studying the stars and other heavenly bodies.

A telescope works by gathering light sent from an object—more light

HOW DO TELESCOPES MAKE THINGS APPEAR CLOSER?

than the naked eye can gather—and focusing it to a tiny, sharp point. This point is then magnified to an image which seems very large and close to the observer.

There are two main types of telescopes, the "refracting" and "reflecting." The refractor uses a lens and the reflector uses a mirror to gather light. In a refractor, the observer looks directly at the object. In a reflector he looks at its reflection in a mirror. In both kinds of telescopes, objects are seen upside down. Another lens may be added to the eyepiece to turn the image right side up, but this is not necessary for studying stars.

The refracting telescope has a closed tube. In the top of the tube is the "object glass," made of two or more lenses, through which passes the light from the object. This light is "refracted" (bent) by the lenses to a bright, sharp focus at the lower end of the tube, where the eyepiece is located. The eyepiece then acts like an ordinary magnifying glass and enlarges this bright image.

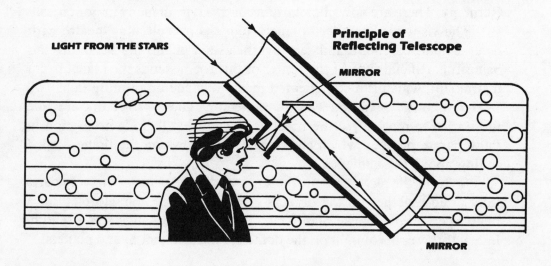

LIGHT FROM THE STARS

Principle of Reflecting Telescope

MIRROR

MIRROR

The reflecting telescope needs only one lens in the eyepiece. Its tube is usually a skeleton framework, open at the top. At the lower end of the tube is a mirror made of glass coated with silver or aluminum and shaped like a large, shallow dish.

Light from a star or other distant object is gathered by this mirror and "reflected" to a bright, sharp focus. A smaller mirror at this focal point sends the image to an eyepiece or camera located at the side of the tube.

What keeps a satellite going in orbit? To understand this we must go back to a certain principle formulated by Sir Isaac Newton back in the seventeenth century. It is known as Newton's First Law of Motion and it says

HOW DO SATELLITES STAY IN ORBIT?

that "every body persists in a state of rest, or of uniform motion in a straight line, unless compelled by external force to change its state."

Now let's see how this applies to a rocket shot into the air. According to Newton's law, it should continue in "uniform motion in a straight line" unless forced to change by some external force. What is that external force? It is the force of the earth's gravity, which pulls all things toward the center of the earth. So instead of flying off into space in a straight line, the rocket is pulled down toward the center of the earth.

Gravity pulls it down at the rate of 14 feet per second. The earth, however, is curved. So as the rocket falls, the earth curves away from it. Now if the rocket is traveling at a speed of 17,000 miles an hour (or 4.7 miles a second), its falling toward the earth will be balanced by the curving away of the earth's surface. In this way, even though it keeps falling, it will keep going around the earth in orbit.

But now something else comes into play—friction. Since the rocket has not gone high enough to escape from the atmosphere around the earth, the force of friction will be slowing it up and thus changing that "balance." As a result, the rocket-satellite will finally fall back to earth.

If a rocket does escape from the earth's atmosphere and from the pull of the earth's gravity, then it comes under the pull of the sun's gravity, and it then goes into orbit around the sun. But since there is no atmosphere there, and therefore no friction to slow it up, it can continue in orbit around the sun forever!

A spectroscope is simply a machine used to take pictures of a spectrum. These pictures are called spectrographs. By using a spectroscope, an astronomer can tell you what a star is made of that is billions of miles

WHAT IS A SPECTROSCOPE?

away. He can not only tell you the elements present in that star, but what its temperature is, how fast it is moving, and whether it is moving toward or away from the earth!

All of this is possible because of the fact that white light is really made up of many different colors. When you shine white light through a prism (a triangular piece of glass), it is split up into a band of colors like a rainbow. This is known as the spectrum.

In 1814, a man called Joseph von Fraunhofer looked at the spectrum through—of all things—a telescope! He noticed that all across the spectrum there were hundreds of parallel lines, and he carefully mapped the exact positions of many of these dark lines as they appeared on the spectrum. These are still known as "Fraunhofer lines."

What is the meaning of these lines? Each chemical element in a gaseous or vaporous state has its own pattern of lines occupying its own place in the spectrum. The lines stand for the colors taken up from the sunlight by the element when it is heated to the point that it glows.

This gave scientists a way to find out the materials present in any substance, no matter how far away. Each element always makes its own "dark line," different from those of any other element. By simply comparing the spectrum of a material being studied with the spectra of elements already known in the laboratory, a scientist can tell what it is.

Man has always recognized this need to measure. Problems arose, however: how can we measure heavier, taller, farther, and so on. Units of measurement were needed that everyone would recognize and that could

WHY IS A FOOT 12 INCHES LONG?

be used easily. If you wanted to measure the distance between two cities, for example, you would want a fairly large unit such as a mile.

In ancient times, the units of measure were not very exact. They were developed in most cases from familiar things or the human body, just as you might "step off" a distance or measure by means of your hand. In Rome and elsewhere, people used the length of a man's foot to measure length. But since every man's foot differs in size, at one time in the Roman Empire there were 200 different lengths for the foot!

Other units of measurement were just as inexact. The width of a finger or the length of the index finger to the first joint, was the origin of our inch. The yard was the length of a man's arm. The length of a thousand paces (a pace was a double step) was used for long distances and became our mile.

The measuring stick used to build the pyramids in Egypt was two cubits long. A cubit was the length of the arm from the elbow to the end of the middle finger.

Today, it is necessary to have very exact units of measurement. The Congress of the United States has the right to fix the standards of weights of measures for this country. At Washington, D. C., there is a National Bureau of Standards which keeps the standard units of measure to which all others must be compared.

Most of us never have an occasion to make very small measurements. But in building certain types of machines and in other work a difference of 1/1,000 of an inch can be quite important.

WHAT IS A MICROMETER?

To make these kinds of measurements, machinists use what is called a "micrometer." The name comes from the Greek words meaning "small measure." With the help of a micrometer, instruments can be constructed that will be accurate within 1/1,000,000 of an inch!

In measuring the thickness of an object, the object is placed between a fixed rest and one end of the spindle, or screw. The spindle is forced against the object by being turned. In this way, for example, the thickness of a piece of paper can be measured. There are scales that show how far the spindle is from the fixed rest, giving the thickness of the object.

The most common type of micrometer is operated by a screw which has 40 threads to the inch. So each turn of the screw moves the measuring spindle 1/40 of an inch.

A scale, which revolves with the screw, is divided into 25 parts. It therefore indicates the fractions of a turn in units of 1/1,000 of an inch. Such a micrometer might also have what is called a "vernier" scale. On this scale a movement of 1/10,000 of an inch can be read.

Micrometer readings are usually written as decimals or as "mils." The thickness of an ordinary sheet of newspaper, for example is about .0035 inch or 35 mils.

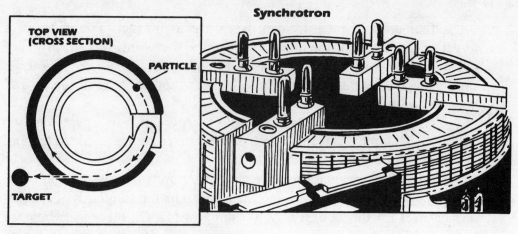

Synchrotron

TOP VIEW
(CROSS SECTION)

PARTICLE

TARGET

Particle goes round and round until it reaches
peak energy and whirls out toward the target.

First, what is an atom? Strangely enough, science still does not have the complete answer to this question. What is known about atoms is constantly changing. In fact, atom-smashing machines are providing new information about the atom all the time.

WHAT IS AN ATOM SMASHER?

At one time, an atom was thought to be the tiniest possible particle of matter. Now we know that an atom consists of even smaller particles—there are more than 20 different particles in the core of the atom! Basically, we might say that the atom consists of a heavy, central core (the nucleus) and its related electrons. The basic particles in the nucleus are known as protons and neutrons, and surrounding the nucleus are electrons.

When the structure of an atom is disturbed, some very curious things may happen. Energy may be given off, or the atoms may turn into other elements. When it was discovered that this could happen, the age of atom-smashing began. For example, when protons were speeded up and driven into certain atoms (like bullets being fired into an object) the atoms were broken up, or "smashed."

Soon the search was on for new atomic "bullets." When deutrons (the nucleus of an atom of a substance called deuterium) were fired into atoms, new kinds of changes took place in the elements. A particle of the original atom might be "knocked out," and the atom would become an atom of an entirely different element. Also, great amounts of energy might be released.

Machines were soon developed to shatter atoms. One machine developed is called a "cyclotron." It uses a powerful electromagnet to make

176

high speed protons or deutrons move round and round in a spiral path. Now there are even stronger machines for hurling particles into the nucleus of the atom, called "betatrons" and "synchrotrons." These machines enable particles to break into the nucleus of the atom with greater force and accuracy.

Men have developed certain fairly good methods to look for and find oil. But first, how does oil get into the ground to begin with?

Scientists think that petroleum was formed from plants and animals

HOW IS OIL LOCATED UNDERGROUND?

that lived ages ago in and around warm seas that covered much of the earth. As the plants and animals died, they piled up on the sea bottom. In time, millions of tons of sand and mud covered them. Under pressure, the mud and sand changed to rock. The plants and animals turned to a dark liquid trapped in the pores of the rock.

So when men go looking for oil, they know that it is most likely to be found in rocks that used to be the bottoms of old seas. However, oil does not collect in all these rocks. It collects in places called "traps." An oil trap consists of porous rock between layers of nonporous rock. The oil collects in tiny spaces in the rock.

The oil hunter searches for oil traps in several ways, using scientific instruments. These instruments do not actually show whether there is oil, they only help the oil hunter locate what may be an oil trap.

One of the instruments is a gravity meter. Heavy rocks pull harder,

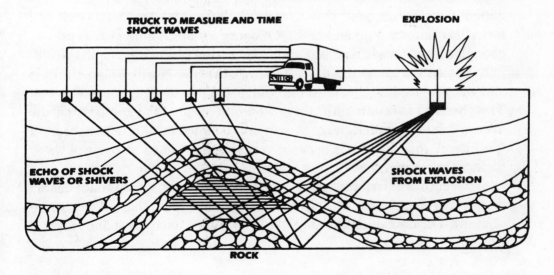

TRUCK TO MEASURE AND TIME SHOCK WAVES

EXPLOSION

ECHO OF SHOCK WAVES OR SHIVERS

SHOCK WAVES FROM EXPLOSION

ROCK

or have a greater force of gravity, than light rocks. The gravity meter gives clues to underground formations by measuring the "pull" of buried rocks.

A magnetometer, which measures variations in the earth's magnetic field, may also be used to gain information on underground rock formations. But the most widely used method for searching for oil is to make a small earthquake by setting off a charge of dynamite. Then the earth's shivers, which travel faster through some types of rock than they do through others, are timed and measured.

But there is still no guarantee after all these measurements that oil will actually be found in any particular spot!

Most people assume a compass needle points "north." And by this they really mean the geographical North Pole. Well, a compass obviously does point in a northerly direction, but not to the North Pole.

WHERE DOES A COMPASS REALLY POINT?

All compass needles in the Northern Hemisphere point to a place known as the North Magnetic Pole. This is located on a peninsula called the Boothia Peninsula, and it is at the northernmost point of the Arctic Coast of North America. It was discovered by Sir James Clark Ross in 1831.

In the Southern Hemisphere, all compass needles point to the South Magnetic Pole, which is located in Antarctica, south of Australia. By the way, a curious thing about the North Magnetic Pole is that it is impossible to point to a particular spot and say it is located here. The North Magnetic Pole travels around in a 20-mile circle, and it even shifts back and forth between morning and night. Of course, that 20-mile area is precise enough a location when considered from distant places around the world.

Today, we know the difference between the North Magnetic Pole and the geographical North Pole, but people in ancient times did not. They lived so far from both, that to them it seemed the compass needle always pointed north. Later on, when sailors sailed the Arctic seas around Greenland, that difference became very puzzling. In some parts of those regions the compass needle points almost west!

Because of this difference between the two poles, which is noticeable in most parts of the world, ship captains sail by charts that take this into account. The captain of the ship may make allowance for it and sail in a true direction.

Sand is really a collection of tiny rocks. Sand is the result of the breakup of the solid rock surfaces of the earth during a period of millions of years. Some rock fragments undergo a chemical action or become dissolved into

WHAT IS SAND?

a fine powdery mass that becomes soil. The fragments that are too hard or could resist the chemical action remain gritty particles that we call sand. Each particle may be from a tenth to a hundredth of an inch in diameter.

In the breakup of ancient rocks, pieces of gravel would be picked up by floods and rivers and they would be rolled along down into the valleys and river beds. As they rolled, many of the gravel pebbles were cracked and gradually they became worn down into grains of sands.

If you look at sand under a magnifying glass, you will notice that there can be quite a collection of different particles. Those that are smooth and well-rounded have either traveled a long distance or have been churned around by the surf on the shore of an ocean. The particles with sharper edges have splintered off more recently and have not traveled very far.

Usually, each grain of sand is composed of only one mineral. But if you pick up a handful of sand, there may be a variety of minerals in it. The most common mineral in sand is quartz.

If there are iron compounds in the sand, it may have interesting colors. Some sands contain rare minerals such as gold, zircon, and garnet. The "white sands" of New Mexico are nearly pure gypsum.

Some sand is so firm and hard-packed that it can be used as a track for auto racing. This firmness is caused by the presence of just enough water to fill the spaces between the grains.

Salt is one of the most common minerals. Chemically, salt (or sodium chloride), is a compound of sodium and chlorine. The common salt we use at home is produced in various ways: from sea water, or the water of

WHAT IS SALT?

salt lakes, from salt springs, and from deposits of rock salt.

A gallon of ordinary sea water contains about a quarter of a pound of salt. Some salt lakes, such as the Dead Sea or Great Salt Lake, contain even larger percentages of salt.

Beds of rock salt are found in various parts of the world and are sometimes hundreds of feet thick. They were probably formed by the evaporation of ancient seas, whose bottoms were later covered by layers of mud and sand. Salt springs may have been formed by the filtering of water through these beds of rock salt.

Most commercial salt is made from rock salt. Wells are drilled down to the salt beds. Pure water is pumped down to the rock salt through a pipe. The water dissolves the salt. The brine, or salt water, is forced up to the surface through another pipe.

After the salt has been brought up in the form of brine, it is evaporated by steam in open pans or in vacuum pans until it forms grains. These grains are dried and then graded. Table salt has a very fine grain. Salt today has many uses in industry, such as in the manufacture of glass, soap, and leather.

Pepper comes from the fruit or seeds of a shrub which originally grew on the western coast of India. Today, however, we get more than 80 per cent of our pepper from the East Indies, mainly Indonesia.

HOW IS PEPPER MADE?

While pepper can grow wild, most of it is cultivated on plantations. The pepper plants require quite a bit of care. They require constant trimming and fertilization, and underbrush must be cut away. The fruit is green at first, then yellow, and turns red when it is ripe. A pepper shrub will yield fruit in three years, and in seven years it will reach full production.

The pepper berries are picked when they turn red, but just before they are quite ripe. This is because they are more pungent in this condition. They are then spread out to dry in the sun. After they are dried, they turn black. Then it is a simple matter of grinding them to obtain ordinary black pepper.

White pepper is not as strong as the black. It is made of ripe berries from which the outer coat has been removed before grinding.

Other types of "pepper," such as Cayenne pepper, paprika, and tabasco pepper, are not related to ordinary black pepper except by taste. The red peppers belong to an entirely different plant. There are many varieties of these and they vary greatly in size. The small red types contain a substance which is very hot or burning to the taste. In the United States, we grow the large "bell" peppers, which are quite mild and are often stuffed to make a variety of tasteful dishes.

Strange as it may seem, nobody really knows what decides the taste of any given thing. We know what taste is produced by certain substances and combinations, but the "law" which determines what the taste of any

WHY IS SUGAR SWEET?

given substance should be is still not understood.

The effect a food has on our taste nerves is connected in some way with its chemical constitution. For instance, when hydrogen ions are present, there is likely to be a sour taste. Amino acids have a sweet taste. Sugar has the kind of acids, or chemical composition, that makes us feel it tastes sweet.

More than 2,000 years ago, Democritus, a Greek philosopher, said that the taste of foods depends on the kind of atoms they throw off. Surprisingly enough, his statement is considered correct today! Unless a substance is in solution, so that the atoms can move about freely, we cannot taste it. We cannot taste a glass marble!

Our taste buds are able to register four sensations: sweet, saline, bitter, and sour. But our tongue is not equally sensitive at all points to all four tastes. The tip of our tongue is sensitive to sweet tastes, the back is more sensitive to bitter, and the sides react to sour and salt tastes.

There is really no such thing as "pure" taste. Our tongue does not just react to sweetness or saltiness, it also is sensitive to weight, roughness or smoothness, temperature, mildness, and other factors. The combination of all these sensations results in what we call the taste of food.

Most of us think of milk simply as a food. And milk is about the most nearly perfect food known to man. But did you know that there are many uses for milk that have nothing to do with food?

WHAT PRODUCTS ARE MADE FROM MILK?

In each quart of milk there is about a quarter of a pound of food solids. One of these solids is casein, or curd. The casein in skim milk has recently begun to be used in many interesting ways.

The milk is treated with acids to remove the casein. The curd that forms is then dried and powdered. Powdered casein is used in medicines and for beauty preparations. It is used to coat paper and yarn, to waterproof paper and cloth, and to make glue, paint, and putty.

When the powder is moistened and mixed with certain chemicals, it forms a plastic. In this form it is used to make combs, knife and brush handles, buttons, and toys.

Today, milk undergoes many processes before it reaches our table. It is pasteurized (heated to a high temperature) to kill any harmful bacteria that may be in the milk. It is homogenized, which means it is forced through a small opening under high pressure. This breaks up the fat globules into very small particles and scatters them through the milk so the fat will not rise to the surface.

In many areas, milk is fortified with Vitamin D. And then, of course, there are many new ways of preserving milk, since milk cannot be kept fresh for long periods. One way is to remove the water from the milk and make it into powdered milk. Another way is to remove about half the water by evaporation and make evaporated milk. Still another way is to evaporate milk and add sugar to make sweetened condensed milk.

All cheeses are made basically the same way. A "starter" composed of certain bacteria is added to fresh milk. These bacteria cause the milk to develop a slight acidity, and this is known as "ripening."

HOW MANY KINDS OF CHEESE ARE MADE?

When the ripening has progressed to the proper stage, rennet is added. Rennet is part of the natural digestive juices from a sheep. This causes the formation of a curd, or solid portion. Then the whey (liquid portion) is drawn off, and the curd is salted and

cured. This is a very brief description of the making of cheddar cheese, which is typical.

Cheese is made in all parts of the world today and from many different kinds of milk. More than 400 varieties of cheese are manufactured in Europe, and about 300 in the United States.

Many countries have developed special kinds of cheese which have become popular all over the world. Some of the most famous world cheeses are Cheshire, Cheddar, and Stilton of England; Edam and Gouda of Holland; Roquefort, Camembert, and Brie of France; Parmesan, Gorgonzola, and Bel Paese of Italy; Gruyère and Swiss of Switzerland; Limburger of Belgium.

Today, many people believe that Canada and the United States make cheeses as fine as Europe's. A large part of the Canadian cheese is shipped to England. The United States produces more than 1,000,000,000 pounds of cheese annually, and almost half of it comes from Wisconsin. Other leading cheese-producing states are Illinois, Missouri, New York, Minnesota, and Indiana.

Chemistry is the science used to find out what things are made of and how they can be changed. By change, the chemist means a chemical change.

A chemist works carefully and makes many tests to be certain that

WHAT DOES A CHEMIST DO?

his experiments and discoveries are right. A chemist works on things that are part of the life of everyone in today's world. Chemistry is used in making paper, ink, preservatives for food, and poisons for insects. Chemistry studies the combinations of metals to make alloys. It teaches how to enrich soils and how to make paints.

Chemistry has developed to such an extent, that a chemist today usually specializes in one field of chemistry. Here are the various sections of chemistry in which a chemist can work.

"Organic chemistry" includes all substances that make up the bodies of plants and animals. "Inorganic chemistry" deals with all other compounds found in nature. "Qualitative analysis" shows what an unknown substance is, and what elements and compounds make it up. "Quantitative analysis" breaks up a substance into its simplest parts. It shows how much of each part the substance contains.

"Physical chemistry" deals with problems of both chemical and physical changes. From it is learned such things as why salt makes water more difficult to boil or freeze. "Physiological chemistry" (biochemistry) deals with the chemical changes that go on in living things. "Applied chemistry" finds out how discoveries made in other branches of chemistry can be used.

Being a chemist today means being something of a specialist, because the whole field of chemistry has become so big. One of the most exciting developments in chemistry is that today a chemist can become a creator of new materials. He can take molecules apart and put them together in different ways so that a new compound is produced in his laboratory.

Many people have strange ideas about hypnotism. They believe, for instance, that a hypnotized person might not be able to be awakened. This is not true. They think that a hypnotized person can be made to commit

IS HYPNOTISM DANGEROUS?

crimes or act in ways that are harmful. This is not true either.

There is a kind of danger involved with hypnotism—and that is to have it conducted by an untrained person, one who is not trained in psychology. This is because hypnotism can, in some cases, damage the personality of the subject.

But hypnotism is being used today in medical treatment of the body, in dentistry to prevent people from feeling pain, in surgery, and in psychological treatment of persons.

When a person is hypnotized, he is in a sort of trance that resembles sleep. But there are many degrees of depth in hypnosis. A hypnotized person may be wide awake and know everything that is going on about him. Or he may be in such a deep trance that he knows nothing of what is taking place about him, except the ideas, commands, or suggestions given him by the hypnotist.

These commands and suggestions which the subject will follow can range from standing, walking, shivering, or perspiring. The hypnotist can also make the subject's heart beat faster or slower, and make his face turn white or blush a bright red.

The fascinating thing is that the hypnotist can also control the feelings of the subject. So he can make him hate his favorite food, or like a food he always hated. This change may only last as long as the person is hypnotized, or it may last for several months. In some cases, the change is permanent.

Archimedes was a mathematician and inventor who lived in the ancient Greek colony of Syracuse, Sicily. The king of Syracuse, Hiero, asked Archimedes if he could tell whether the royal golden crown con-

WHAT IS ARCHIMEDES' PRINCIPLE?

tained any silver. Archimedes was puzzled by this problem for a long time. One day as he stepped into his bath he noticed the rise of water. He rushed through the streets crying "Eureka!"

He now knew how to solve Hiero's problem. He first weighed the crown. He then found a lump of gold and a lump of silver, each weighing the same as the crown. Then he dropped the crown into a vessel of water and measured the rise of the liquid. He did the same with the lump of gold. If the crown had been pure gold, the rise would have been the same. But there was a difference, and by also measuring the rise in the water when the lump of silver was dropped into it, Archimedes found the exact proportions of the two metals in the crown.

The law of specific gravity, or Archimedes' Principle, states that any object immersed in a liquid is buoyed up by a force equal to the weight of the liquid displaced.

Archimedes was also the inventor of many scientific devices for use in ancient warfare. When the Romans attacked the city of Syracuse by land and sea in 214 B.C., they were held off for nearly three years by the inventions of Archimedes. He created catapults that were able to hurl huge stones at the Romans. He also wrote books on geometry and physics and knew much about the power of levers.

Archimedes was killed by a Roman soldier during the capture of Syracuse, supposedly while he was absorbed in drawing a mathematical figure.

A boat is a pretty big object, yet it floats easily on the surface of a lake or ocean. Why? Well, something floats in a liquid, or fluid, because the fluid holds it up. The fluid actually offsets the force of gravity, which

WHAT MAKES A BOAT FLOAT?

pulls everything to the center of the earth.

That upward push on a floating object is called "buoyant force," or simply "buoyancy." This force acts on every object that is in a fluid. If you want to feel this force, just take a blown-up beach ball into the water. The water seems to push up on the ball.

The buoyant force of a liquid acts on objects that cannot float too. For example, a stone feels lighter in your hand underwater than when you hold it in the air.

The buoyant force of a fluid is not always strong enough to lift a solid body. And it is not the weight of the body that decides this. For example, a small stone sinks, but a 100-pound piece of balsa wood floats. Whether a body will sink or float depends on its density. If you compare two blocks of the same size, one made of steel and one made of cork, the block of steel will weigh more, even though it occupies the same amount of space. So the density of steel is greater than that of cork.

Density depends on weight and on size. If two bodies have the same weight, the smaller one is the denser body. Fluids also have density.

When a solid body is placed in a liquid, it pushes some of the fluid aside. If the solid is more dense than the fluid, it weighs more than the fluid it pushes aside, and it will sink. If the solid is less dense than the fluid, it will float.

A ship is a metal shell and contains large quantities of air. The ship as a whole, with air inside, is less dense than water. It weighs less than the water it pushes aside. That is why it floats.

Why can a needle or a thin razor blade be made to float on water? Why can some insects walk on water? Why do soap bubbles act as if they were surrounded by a rubber film?

WHAT IS SURFACE TENSION?

The explanation for all of these is the existence of surface tension. It is called that because the surface of every liquid seems to be under tension, like the tension of a stretched sheet of rubber. The surface tends to shrink to the least possible area.

Surface tension is believed to be caused by the attraction of molecules for one another. Molecules in the surface of a liquid are attracted inward, toward the liquid, more strongly than outward. This is because there are more molecules just beneath the surface than above it.

Molecules in the midst of the liquid are attracted equally in all directions. So the effect does not take place in the midst of a liquid.

If you watch a slowly dripping water faucet, you will see the water gradually extend downward. Surface tension is holding it together. Finally, the weight of the water is too great for the surface tension to support, and a drop separates and falls. The falling drop draws itself into a tiny sphere by surface tension, because a sphere has the smallest possible area for the enclosed volume of water.

Another example of surface tension can be seen when you fill a teaspoon with water right to the very top. Surface tension keeps it from overflowing.

If you rub a glass rod with silk, you will find that small pieces of dry paper jump to the rod and cling to it. The same things happens if you rub a piece of plastic with fur.

WHAT IS STATIC ELECTRICITY?

What has happened to the glass and plastic? Scientists say they acquired an electric charge, that is, they became charged with electricity. And the charges produced by rubbing one material with another are called "static electricity."

"Static" means "at rest," so static electricity is made up of electric charges that are ordinarily at rest. Electricity that travels along wires is electricity in motion. It is called "current electricity."

All matter is made up of tiny particles called "atoms." And each atom is made of even smaller particles. Some of these smaller particles are charged with electricity. There are two kinds of charges: positive (or plus) and negative (or minus). The particles with a positive charge are called "protons." Those with a negative charge are called "electrons."

Normally, a piece of glass has equal numbers of protons and electrons. The positive charges of the protons and the negative charges of the electrons cancel each other out. So there is no net charge on the glass.

But when the glass is rubbed with silk, some of its electrons are pulled away. The glass then has more protons than electrons. It has a net positive charge. This positive charge is equal to the combined charges of the extra protons.

Rubbing plastic with fur gives the plastic a negative charge. This is because electrons are pulled off the fur by the plastic. The plastic has more electrons than protons.

A Greek named Thales, who lived about 600 B.C., was the first to observe static electricity. He rubbed amber with a woolen cloth and found it attracted light objects. But he could not explain why this happened.

Certain fabrics have to be dry cleaned instead of washed with water, because water may shrink or discolor them. Wools, silks, satins, and velvets are examples of such fabrics.

HOW ARE CLOTHES DRY CLEANED?

In dry cleaning, a "solvent" replaces the water. Today, the solvents that are used are synthetics. They dissolve greases, oils, and other dirt in the fabric and then they evaporate.

In a dry-cleaning plant, the garments are placed in a cleaning machine that is very much like a washing machine. But instead of water, a solvent is used. As the machine revolves, the solvent goes through the clothes. Then it goes into a filter to be purified, and back into the machine again. Because solvents are expensive, they are used over and over again.

The solvent is mixed with a detergent that helps to loosen the dirt and float it away. The clothes tumble gently in the mixture until the dirt is washed out. Then they are rinsed in fresh solvent. Detergent is not used in the rinsing.

The machine then spins the clothes at high speed until most of the solvent is removed. A dryer tumbles the clothes loosely in warm air. The warm air helps evaporate the solvent.

After drying, the garments go to a "spotter." His job is to take out stains that are left. To do this he must first find out what the stain is and what chemicals will loosen it. He also tests the fabric to make sure the color will not run. The next step is pressing, and this is usually done by machines, though dresses may be "touched up" with a hand iron.

The first dry-cleaning plant in the world was opened in Paris in 1845. But long before that people were using solvents instead of water to clean certain fabrics. The first solvent to be used was probably turpentine, which is mentioned as a cleaner in a book written in 1690!

Many customs have arisen in the world concerning the bodies of the dead. Among some peoples it was and still is considered very important not to allow the body of the dead person to decay. The art of preserving dead bodies from decay is called "embalming."

WHAT IS EMBALMING?

It originated in ancient Egypt. The Egyptians preserved certain of their dead as mummies, and from there the custom spread to other parts of the world. From the time of the Middle Ages until about 1700, embalming was carried on in Europe by methods that were somewhat like the ancient Egyptian's. The organs were removed and herbs put in their place, the body was soaked in spirits of wine, cloths soaked in spirits were applied to the body, and there was a final wrapping in waxed or tarred sheets.

During the nineteenth century, embalmers in Europe developed various chemicals which they injected into the body to preserve it. Some of these embalming fluids were: aluminum salts and arsenic; a saturated solution of arsenic; zinc chlorida solution; and bichloride of mercury solution.

Modern embalming actually had its start in the Civil War. Certain experts in the process traveled about the country teaching and demonstrating how to preserve the bodies of the Civil War dead, and so the knowledge spread throughout the United States.

The basic thing that is done is that the embalming fluid replaces the blood of the body, and this helps preserve it. There are laws in all states that prohibit the use of certain chemicals for this purpose, and specify that certain others must be used.

A dam is a wall-like barrier built across a stream valley to block the flow of water. Man has been putting up dams for thousands of years because he finds them useful or necessary. What are some of these uses and needs?

WHY ARE DAMS BUILT?

Some dams direct the water they have blocked into canals, pipelines, or tunnels. These dams supply irrigation, water power, or water supply systems. Dams that raise the level of the water are used to produce water power, or to provide pools deep enough to float boats over obstructions in the stream bed. They may also form ponds or lakes for recreation, such as swimming, fishing, or boating. In some cases, they stop the rise and fall of water due to tides.

Dams are also used to store water for use during the growing season. They are used to meet year-round needs for city water supplies, or to add to low flows in the dry season to make water power more dependable.

Dams are used to improve water conditions in areas that have a great deal of water pollution, or to make streams more attractive for recreation. Dams that are used to store flood waters lessen damages from flooding downstream. But these dams must be emptied as fast as possible after the flood, in order to be ready for another flood.

So you see there are many purposes for building dams. Sometimes a dam is built for a combination of reasons. Many of the dams built in ancient times were simply to supply water for irrigation needs. Many of them were dikes of stone and brush across the stream which directed water into a ditch where it flowed to fields or orchards. Later on, dams were built to provide a fall of water to drive water wheels to grind grain or to operate all kinds of mills.

When light strikes a surface, it is either absorbed (taken in), or reflected (bounces back). A mirror is a smooth surface that reflects light.

What happens is quite simple: light is reflected from a mirror in

HOW DO WE SEE OURSELVES IN A MIRROR?

about the same way that a rubber ball bounces from a wall. If you throw the ball straight forward at the wall, it will come straight back. If you throw it at an angle, it will bounce off at the same angle in the other direction.

When light strikes a mirror at an angle, it bounces back at an equal angle in another direction. The first angle is called "the angle of incid-

ence"; the second is called "the angle of reflection." The two angles are always equal.

The mirror you usually use is called a "plane" mirror, which means it has a flat surface. Curved mirrors do not produce true images, but distort them. A mirror consists of a piece of glass with a coating on the back made of silver nitrate. The silver backing keeps the light from passing through the glass. It is the actual reflecting surface, while the glass is just to protect the soft silver from scratches and tarnish.

Now imagine you are standing before a mirror. Light rays strike your body and are reflected from it. (This is the way we see things. You are able to see objects because light rays are reflected from them.) These light rays strike the mirror and bounce back to your eyes. So you see a clear image of yourself!

But in a mirror you look as though you are really behind the mirror. The image you see is called a "virtual" image, because the light rays seem to come to a focus behind the mirror. You also see yourself reversed. Your right hand appears to be left, and everything else is reversed from one side to the other.

Did you ever wonder why a polar bear is white? Or certain caterpillars are green? Or why a field mouse has a brownish color? Nature is protecting these animals from being detected by their enemies by providing them

WHAT IS CAMOUFLAGE?

with "camouflage."

Men noticed long ago that many

animals, birds, and insects were concealed from their enemies or sometimes their prey by a coloring which resembled their surroundings. But no one thought of applying this principle to the benefit of man. With the coming of modern warfare, and the need to conceal a great many troops and targets, camouflage began to be applied to man.

Actually, a beginning in this direction was made in India about the middle of the nineteenth century. Instead of having soldiers wear the brilliant red and blue uniforms then in use, they were dressed in earth-colored uniforms and were thus harder to detect.

This idea was developed in many ways. Soldiers in most armies were given uniforms whose colors helped them remain concealed. When warships were painted gray all over, the idea was the same. It made the ship harder to see in the water.

The word "camouflage" comes from a French word meaning "to disguise." The art of camouflage did not make much progress until the days of World War I. During this war, camouflage became an important part of providing protection and it was applied to almost every branch of military and naval service.

During World War II, camouflage became more important than ever and was used to protect factories and bridges as well as men.

A share of stock in a company is a share in the ownership of the company. The company issues "stock certificates" in order to raise money for its needs and for growth. Stockholders share in the company's profits by receiving payments called "dividends."

HOW DOES THE STOCK MARKET WORK?

When a company continues to grow and issues more stock, it might ask to be "listed" on the New York Stock Exchange. This means that it will have the right to have its stock bought and sold, or "traded" at the Exchange. So the stock exchange is a market place for stocks and bonds.

The prices of stocks and bonds are not regulated by anyone. They are determined only by their value to the people who want to buy and sell. The prices depend on how much buyers are willing to pay for a stock, and how cheaply owners are willing to sell.

The actual buying and selling is done by a "broker," who acts as an agent or representative for the people who want to buy and sell stocks. The broker carries out his customers' orders for which he gets a small percentage of the sale or purchase price, which is known as a "commission." Commission rates are set by the Exchange, so all brokers charge the same rates.

Most stockholders give their orders to buy and sell to their brokers over the telephone. But some go directly to the "brokerage office." Here, on the "ticker tape," they can see every purchase and sale of every stock listed on the New York Stock Exchange in units of 100 shares.

The development of the match has a very long history. Even the cave man had a way of starting a fire. He would strike a spark from a flint.

The Egyptian twirled his bow drill on a piece of wood and by this

WHAT MAKES A MATCH LIGHT?

friction lighted his fire. The Greek rubbed pieces of bay and buckthorn together. The Roman struck two flinty stones together and caught the spark on a sulfured splint of wood. During the Middle Ages, sparks struck by flint and steel were caught on charred rags, dried moss, or fungus.

Modern matches were made possible by the discovery of phosphorus, an element that burns at a low temperature. Today, of course, we have two types of matches in common use. One is the friction match, which can be lighted on any rough surface. The second is the safety match, which can be lighted by rubbing it on a specially prepared surface.

The friction match is made by first dipping the match into a solution of ammonium phosphate. The chief reason for this is to prevent "afterglow." Then the match head is dipped into melted paraffin, and next into a paste containing glue, lead oxide, and a compound of phosphorus.

The match lights because friction causes the phosphorus and lead compounds to explode. This sets fire to the paraffin, and this then sets fire to the wood.

In the safety match, the tip contains two chemicals, antimony sulfide and potassium chlorate. The side of the box you rub it on contains red phosphorus. The material on the tip of the match will not ignite easily unless it is rubbed on this prepared surface. The friction produced by the rubbing vaporizes a little of the red phosphorus, which ignites and sets fire to the tip of the match.

Licorice is a product made from the long, sweet root of a plant that belongs to the pea family. The scientific name of this plant is *Glycyrrhiza glabra*. The word *glycyrrhiza* means "sweet root," and if you keep saying

WHAT IS LICORICE?

that word long enough you'll see how we came to get the word "licorice"!

The plant grows three to five feet tall, with pale blue, pealike flowers, and leaves of 9 to 17 leaflets. The licorice plant is a native of southern Europe and western Asia. Today, it is cultivated chiefly in Italy, Spain, and the Soviet Union.

The United States imports large quantities of licorice, although some is grown in Louisiana and California. The plants are raised from seed or from root divisions. Along the Mediterranean coast of Europe, the growing and production of licorice is quite an important industry.

Roots are dug when the plants are three years old. When they are harvested, they are full of water, so they must be dried out for six months to a year. The dried roots are then cut into pieces six inches to a foot long, sorted, and baled.

To prepare licorice, the roots are crushed and boiled. The liquid that remains is then evaporated. This leaves a paste or black stick licorice. These licorice sticks are made from the paste mixed with a little starch so they will not melt in warm weather.

Licorice is used in medicines as a cough remedy, as a laxative, and to make some medicines taste better. In France, Egypt, and some other countries, the root extract is used to make a cooling drink!

The economic system in the United States is sometimes called capitalism. It is more accurately described as a system of free enterprise. Under communism, all industry is taken over by the government. In the free enter-

WHAT IS CAPITALISM?

prise system the plant, machinery, and other equipment used by industry is the property of private citizens.

Business may be carried on by a single person, by two or more people in a partnership, or by corporations. Large-scale industries are usually operated by corporations in which many individuals have bought shares of stock or have invested their money.

Businesses are operated by their owners for the sake of profit, or a return, above cost of production, which may or may not be realized.

Capital and credit—the money funds needed to build plants, pay wages, and purchase machinery and raw materials—are supplied by such institutions as banks and insurance companies. Industry has to pay interest for the use of these funds. This interest is part of the cost of production.

Although the main necessities for living under the system of free enterprise are supplied by private business, some important needs are taken care of by government. Schools are maintained by local and state governments. In many cities and states, the streetcar lines and the gas, electricity, and water works are publicly owned. The federal government runs the postal system. Some of these services have to be paid for by taxes levied upon the general public, while others are supplied at a price to users.

Have you ever wished you could pick up a stone from the ground and change it into a diamond? Or hold a piece of metal in your hand and have it suddenly become pure gold?

WHAT IS ALCHEMY?

Men have had just such wishes since the earliest times. And they actually tried to do something about it! Alchemy is the so-called art or science of trying to change base (the less valuable) metals, such as mercury and lead, into gold and silver. It was practiced for many centuries.

An old myth says that alchemy was first taught to man by the fallen angels. The Greeks and Arabs were the first alchemists. From them the

interest in this imaginary art spread to western Europe, where it reached its peak in the Middle Ages. Since changing other metals to gold and silver held out the promise of limitless wealth, many people gave everything they had to the alchemists in the hope they would make them rich. And the false promises of the alchemists took many a fortune from such victims.

In castles and dungeons, strange men shouted weird words over boiling pots in the hope of finding the great secret. Some alchemists tried to produce gold from mercury alone, while others mixed mercury with sulphur, arsenic, or sal ammoniac.

Later on, alchemy included the search for a magic substance called "the philosophers' stone," which was believed to have the power of curing all diseases and of making life last forever, as well as of changing base metals into gold.

Although the study of alchemy was not scientific, it gave rise to much valuable information concerning various substances. It may be said that alchemy was the forerunner of chemistry. Many of the alchemists were nothing more than adventurers, but there were a few great men among them who honestly believed in the possibilities of alchemy.

In the first century in China, a method was invented for making paper from the stringy inner bark of the mulberry tree. The Chinese pounded the bark in water to separate the fibers, then poured the soupy mixture

HOW IS PAPER MADE?

onto a tray with a bottom of thin bamboo strips. The water drained away and the soft mat was laid on a smooth surface to dry.

In time, machinery was invented to "beat" the paper-making material to the condition of pulp. Other machinery was devised to squeeze the water out more efficiently. One of the most important events in the history of paper was the invention of a machine to make a continuous sheet, or "web" of paper. This was invented by a Frenchman named Louis Robert in 1798, but two Englishmen, Henry and Sealy Fourdrinier, bought the patent from him and improved the machine. Today the "Fourdrinier" is still the basic machine for making continuous sheets of paper.

Until about 1860, practically all paper was made from rags. Many kinds of paper today are still made from rags, old rope, and burlap. The material is cut into small pieces, boiled and cleaned, and raveled out into threads. A machine then beats them, and other materials are added to give the paper certain qualities. A filler, such as talc, gives the paper a smoother surface.

In making newsprint, book paper, and other papers from wood pulps, a mixture of pulp is prepared which goes to the Fourdrinier to be made into a continuous sheet. Presses squeeze out some of the water, but then it must go to huge, revolving steam-heated drying cylinders which reduce the moisture still more. Then the bare sheet passes through polished rolls which give the paper a smooth, level finish.

Lithography means "stone writing." Actually, it is a simple method of printing. The design to be printed is drawn upon the printing surface. It does not need to be cut or engraved into a plate or raised above the surface of the plate. The subject is

WHAT IS LITHOGRAPHY?

drawn right on a stone.

The best lithographer's stone is a gray, smooth-grained limestone. After the design is drawn on the stone, the stone is dampened with water so that all the surface is wet except the part covered by the greasy ink. Water will not stick to this part. An inking roller, carrying a thick, oily ink, is then rolled over the stone.

Because they are wet, the parts of the stone not covered with the design will not pick up any ink from the roller. The design itself, drawn in greasy crayon, picks up more ink. When the form is ready to print, a

STONE

sheet of paper is pressed against the stone. The sheet picks up the ink from the design, but that is all, for the damp stone around the pattern keeps the ink from spreading or smearing.

Lithography is not a difficult process. All that is needed are a stone, the grease crayons, a sponge to dampen the stone, and a roller to do the inking. If an error is made, the mistake can be wiped from the stone and redrawn.

There is a modern form of lithography that is called "offset printing." Instead of a stone, shiny sheets of zinc and aluminum are used. The subjects to be printed are laid down photographically on these flexible plates. Rotary presses automatically moisten, ink, and print hundreds of impressions per hour.

The Eiffel Tower was designed for the Paris Exposition of 1889. It was intended to be the symbol and main attraction of the exposition, just as most World Fairs have one structure to symbolize it. It is made of beau-

WHY WAS THE EIFFEL TOWER BUILT?

tiful columns of iron latticework, and rises 984 feet in the air.

There are platforms at 190 feet, at 381 feet, and at 906 feet, which can be reached by elevators. A circular staircase continues to a scientific laboratory at the top. In the laboratory, meteorologists study temperatures, air currents, clouds, winds, and rainfall. By international agreement, a wireless station sends time signals into space daily.

You can see the Eiffel Tower from any part of Paris, since most buildings in the city are quite low. As a tourist attraction, the Eiffel Tower is hard to beat. It stands in a beautiful setting and as you go up in the elevator one of the most beautiful cities in the world unfolds before you.

The tower was built by Alexandre Eiffel, who also built many outstanding bridges in various parts of the world. In the city of Nice, France, there is an observatory with a movable dome that he built, and he also built the framework for the Statue of Liberty. Eiffel also invented movable section bridges, and he was the first to study the effects of air currents on planes by using models in an air tunnel.

The Eiffel Tower cost more than $1,000,000 to build. It was paid for by Eiffel except for $292,000 contributed by the government. In payment, Eiffel was allowed to collect visitors' admission fees for 20 years.

In Shakespeare's play *Julius Caesar,* a soothsayer, a person who was supposed to foretell the future, tells Caesar to "beware the ides of March."

This phrase has become so well known that some people imagine it means something mysterious. But all it actually means is beware the 15th day of March! The "ides" was the name given in the Roman calendar to the 13th day of the month. There were four exceptions to this: the months of March, May, July, and October. In these months, the ides fell on the 15th day. The soothsayer in the play was predicting that something terrible would happen to Julius Caesar on the 15th day of March—and of course something did. He was assassinated on that day!

WHAT IS THE IDES OF MARCH?

The Roman calendar was an interesting combination of confusion and superstition. There were twelve months in this calendar: Martius, Aprilis, Maius, Junius, Quintilis, Sextilis, September, October, November, December, Januarius, and Februarius. March 1st was the official New Year's Day for the Romans until 153 B.C., when the year was declared to start with January 1st.

The Roman calendar was not the same every year, and there was a group of officials who decided how it should work. They were called "the pontifices." Every month they would watch for the new moon. When it was seen, they would proclaim how many days were to be counted before "the nones." This was a special day of the month. The "ides" was the day of the full moon. The first day of the month was called "the calends."

Because each year had a different length, there was great confusion in the calendar. In 46 B.C., Julius Caesar made changes to uniform the calendar. After that, a "Julian" calendar (named after him) was used by most of Europe for hundreds of years.

Man has been replacing missing natural teeth since very ancient times. These artificial teeth were made out of wood, or animal teeth, or even human teeth! Then, at the end of the eighteenth century, a one-piece set of porcelain artificial teeth was created for the first time.

WHAT ARE FALSE TEETH MADE OF?

At the beginning of the nineteenth century, another great step forward was made. A man called Fonzi, an Italian dentist practicing in Paris, made individual porcelain teeth mounted on gold or platinum bases. Porcelain teeth were introduced into the United States about 1817.

The next step was to improve the appearance of such teeth by making them harmonize with the shape of the face. Before that, false teeth would sometimes change the whole facial expression of the people who wore them and make them look quite peculiar.

Today, people who wear false teeth can look just as they did before. False teeth made out of porcelain, plastics, and glass can be made in such a variety of shapes, sizes, and colors, that they can match perfectly almost any natural teeth. They are usually fastened to plastic bases that look like the natural gums.

About one-fifth of all artificial teeth are made of plastic. They have an advantage over porcelain teeth in that they are less brittle, easier to grind and polish, are more solidly joined to the plastic base, and they make less noise when they are used.

But porcelain teeth wear better and are better for chewing. This is probably the reason that porcelain is still preferred in making false teeth.

Did you know that a thermostat automatically regulates temperature? Now you may not think this is important, but where a thermostat is used it makes a big difference in comfort and efficiency.

HOW DOES A THERMOSTAT WORK?

A thermostat controls the heating of homes and heating devices used in industry. Thermostats also regulate the temperature of such appliances as electric blankets, irons, toasters, clothes dryers, waffle irons, ovens, and water heaters. In an air-conditioning system, thermostats feel warmth and signal for more cold air from the cooling equipment.

How does a thermostat work? Like a thermometer, a thermostat also "feels" temperature changes. A thermometer just shows the changes on a scale, but a thermostat also operates some type of equipment, such as a heating furnace, to maintain temperature at a previously selected point.

For example, if the furnace is to keep your house at a certain temperature, the thermostat dial is set at that point. If the air becomes colder in the house, the thermostat senses, or feels, this and sends an electrical signal to the furnace. This signal causes the furnace to start.

When the room warms to the desired temperature, the thermostat

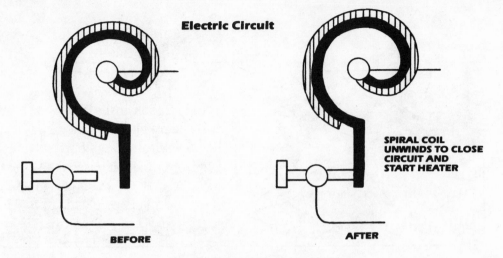

Electric Circuit

SPIRAL COIL
UNWINDS TO CLOSE
CIRCUIT AND
START HEATER

BEFORE

AFTER

automatically sends another signal that stops the furnace. When the room gets cold again, the furnace starts once more.

Instead of using mercury to feel temperature changes (as in a thermometer), thermostats commonly use a strip of specially built metals. These metals always bend at the same rate according to temperature. The bending of the metal strip causes an electrical contact to be broken or made, and the change in the electric current that is made causes a switch to go on or off.

A "fertilizer" is any substance that will increase the growth and yield of plants when added to the soil. If the soil has never been tilled before, it needs little or no fertilizing. But each new crop that grows in a soil draws

WHY ARE FERTILIZERS USED?

valuable chemicals out of it. In time, such soil will be almost worthless for crops unless it is made fertile again.

So the purpose of fertilizer is to return to the soil those valuable chemicals that have been drawn out of it. The most common of all fertilizers, and still the most important one on the average farm, is the manure of animals. It is called the complete fertilizer because it contains three basic elements: nitrogen, phosphorus, and potassium.

Sometimes the soil does not need a complete fertilizer. The soil may be exhausted of only a single element necessary to the growth of crops. Then an incomplete artificial fertilizer is used. It supplies the soil only with those elements in which it is deficient.

Artificial fertilizers are made in a variety of ways, and they work quite well. But they have one drawback. They will greatly enrich the soil during the first few years of their use. After that time, unless certain green crops are plowed under, the artificial fertilizers begin to lose their effectiveness. Plowing under the green crops supplies the soil with organic matter which it needs.

How does a farmer know what elements are lacking in his soil and what fertilizers to use? The individual states and the U. S. Department of Agriculture have laboratories that will test samples of the soil, and their analysis tells the farmer what his soil lacks and the kind of fertilizer that will do the most good.

Fertilizers have been used since very ancient times. The Hindus and Chinese used them, and the North American Indians used to put a dead fish in each hole in which they planted grains of corn.

There are many kinds of sugars in nature, and glucose is the most common of them. It is found in honey and in many fruits, particularly grapes. That is why glucose is often called "grape sugar." Another chemical name for it is "dextrose."

WHAT IS GLUCOSE?

Ordinary sugar, which is cane sugar or beet sugar, is called "sucrose" by chemists. It is a combination of glucose and fructose.

The starch which is so common in plants and which is found in flour, cereals, and potatoes, is all built of glucose. Chemists say that the very large starch molecule is made up of many smaller glucose molecules tied together.

Starch can be split in many ways, and it always finally gives glucose. That is what happens when starch is digested. The glucose then gets into the blood and is burned. Some of the glucose which is not burned gets into the liver, and there it builds "glycogen," which is also made of very large molecules and is very similar to plant starch.

Glucose is stored up in the animal body in the form of glycogen and is digested again when the body is starved.

Glucose is made from vegetable starches of all kinds. The chemical change through which starch is changed is called "hydrolysis." This word means dissolution with water. It can be done by heating with a dilute acid or with the help of natural enzymes.

Nearly all of the glucose so produced is directly changed into alcohol with other enzymes. Alcohol, which is necessary for many industries, is the goal of the process.

Glucose itself is not used very much. It is found chiefly in pastries and candy since it is cheaper than cane sugar. It comes mixed with water as a thick syrup. Glucose is also less sweet than cane sugar.

A language is not a lot of "rules and grammar." A language is the means by which one person expresses his thoughts and feelings to another person so that he understands them!

WHAT IS LANGUAGE?

A language could be made up of signs, or sounds, or facial expressions, or just gestures or bodily actions! Or it can be a combination of these things. When you have something to say you not only speak, you make gestures and facial expressions.

The test of whether we have a language is whether we are understood. If you invented a language of your own and nobody understood you, you would not have a true language.

As civilizations developed, people began to live in large groups, life became more complicated, more and more knowledge was acquired, and languages became more complicated and highly developed.

But surprisingly enough, we do not really know how languages began. Some think they began from the natural cries and exclamations that people made to express surprise, pleasure, or pain. Others think languages began by imitation of the sounds of nature. Still others believe that it began by imitating the sounds of animals. And it is possible that each of these methods had a part in the beginning of language, but how much we do not know.

We do know that practically all the languages spoken on earth today can be traced back to some common source; that is, an ancestor language which has many descendants. The ancestor language together with all the language which developed from it, is called a "family" of languages.

English is a member of the Indo-European family of languages. Other members of this family are French, Italian, German, Norwegian, and Greek.

INDEX

206

208